THE ROSIE PROJECT

THE ROSIE PROJECT

GRAEME SIMSION

ISIS

LARGE PRINT

Oxford

First published in Great Britain 2013
by
Michael Joseph an Imprint of Penguin Books Ltd.
First published in Australia 2013
by
The Text Publishing Company

Published in Large Print 2013 by ISIS Publishing Ltd.,
7 Centremead, Osney Mead, Oxford OX2 0ES
by arrangement with
Penguin Books Ltd. and The Text Publishing Company

CIP data is available for this title from the British Library

ISBN 978–0–7531–9246–7 (hb)
ISBN 978–0–7531–9247–4 (pb)

Printed and bound in Great Britain by
T. J. International Ltd., Padstow, Cornwall

To Rod and Lynette

CHAPTER
ONE

I may have found a solution to the Wife Problem. As with so many scientific breakthroughs, the answer was obvious in retrospect. But had it not been for a series of unscheduled events, it is unlikely I would have discovered it.

The sequence was initiated by Gene insisting I give a lecture on Asperger's syndrome that he had previously agreed to deliver himself. The timing was extremely annoying. The preparation could be time-shared with lunch consumption, but on the designated evening I had scheduled ninety-four minutes to clean my bathroom. I was faced with a choice of three options, none of them satisfactory.

1. Cleaning the bathroom after the lecture, resulting in loss of sleep with a consequent reduction in mental and physical performance.
2. Rescheduling the cleaning until the following Tuesday, resulting in an eight-day period of compromised bathroom hygiene and consequent risk of disease.

3. Refusing to deliver the lecture, resulting in damage to my friendship with Gene.

I presented the dilemma to Gene, who, as usual, had an alternative solution.

"Don, I'll pay for someone to clean your bathroom."

I explained to Gene — again — that all cleaners, with the possible exception of the Hungarian woman with the short skirt, made errors. Short-skirt Woman, who had been Gene's cleaner, had disappeared following some problem with Gene and Claudia.

"I'll give you Eva's mobile number. Just don't mention me."

"What if she asks? How can I answer without mentioning you?"

"Just say you're contacting her because she's the only cleaner who does it properly. And if she mentions me, say nothing."

This was an excellent outcome, and an illustration of Gene's ability to find solutions to social problems. Eva would enjoy having her competence recognised and might even be suitable for a permanent role, which would free up an average of three hundred and sixteen minutes per week in my schedule.

Gene's lecture problem had arisen because he had an opportunity to have sex with a Chilean academic who was visiting Melbourne for a conference. Gene has a project to have sex with women of as many different nationalities as possible. As a professor of psychology, he is extremely interested in human sexual attraction, which he believes is largely genetically determined.

This belief is consistent with Gene's background as a geneticist. Sixty-eight days after Gene hired me as a post-doctoral researcher, he was promoted to head of the Psychology Department, a highly controversial appointment that was intended to establish the university as the Australian leader in evolutionary psychology and increase its public profile.

During the time we worked concurrently in the Genetics Department, we had numerous interesting discussions which continued after his change of position. I would have been satisfied with our relationship for this reason alone, but Gene also invited me to dinner at his house and performed other friendship rituals, resulting in a social relationship. His wife Claudia, who is a clinical psychologist, is now also a friend. Making a total of two.

Gene and Claudia tried for a while to assist me with the Wife Problem. Unfortunately, their approach was based on the traditional dating paradigm, which I had previously abandoned on the basis that the probability of success did not justify the effort and negative experiences. I am thirty-nine years old, tall, fit and intelligent, with a relatively high status and above-average income as an associate professor. Logically, I should be attractive to a wide range of women. In the animal kingdom, I would succeed in reproducing.

However, there is something about me that women find unappealing. I have never found it easy to make friends, and it seems that the deficiencies that caused this problem have also affected my attempts at romantic relationships. The Apricot Ice-cream Disaster is a good example.

Claudia had introduced me to one of her many friends. Elizabeth was a highly intelligent computer scientist, with a vision problem that had been corrected with glasses. I mention the glasses because Claudia showed me a photograph, and asked me if I was okay with them. An incredible question! From a psychologist! In evaluating Elizabeth's suitability as a potential partner — someone to provide intellectual stimulation, to share activities with, perhaps even to breed with — Claudia's first concern was my reaction to her choice of glasses frames, which was probably not even her own but the result of advice from an optometrist. This is the world I have to live in. Then Claudia told me, as though it was a problem: "She has very firm ideas."

"Are they evidence-based?"

"I guess so," Claudia said.

Perfect. She could have been describing me.

We met at a Thai restaurant. Restaurants are minefields for the socially inept, and I was nervous as always in these situations. But we got off to an excellent start when we both arrived at exactly 7.00p.m. as arranged. Poor synchronisation is a huge waste of time.

We survived the meal without her criticising me for any social errors. It is difficult to conduct a conversation while wondering whether you are looking at the correct body part but I locked on to her bespectacled eyes, as recommended by Gene. This resulted in some inaccuracy in the eating process, which she did not seem to notice. On the contrary, we had a highly productive discussion about simulation algorithms. She was so interesting! I could already see the possibility of a permanent relationship.

The waiter brought the dessert menus and Elizabeth said, "I don't like Asian desserts."

This was almost certainly an unsound generalisation, based on limited experience, and perhaps I should have recognised it as a warning sign. But it provided me with an opportunity for a creative suggestion.

"We could get an ice-cream across the road."

"Great idea. As long as they've got apricot."

I assessed that I was progressing well at this point, and did not think the apricot preference would be a problem. I was wrong. The ice-cream parlour had a vast selection of flavours, but they had exhausted their supply of apricot. I ordered a chocolate chilli and liquorice double cone for myself and asked Elizabeth to nominate her second preference.

"If they haven't got apricot, I'll pass."

I couldn't believe it. All ice-cream tastes essentially the same, due to chilling of the tastebuds. This is especially true of fruit flavours. I suggested mango.

"No thanks, I'm fine."

I explained the physiology of tastebud chilling in some detail. I predicted that if I purchased a mango and a peach ice-cream she would be incapable of differentiating. And, by extension, either would be equivalent to apricot.

"They're completely different," she said. "If you can't tell mango from peach, that's your problem."

Now we had a simple objective disagreement that could readily be resolved experimentally. I ordered a minimum-size ice-cream in each of the two flavours. But by the time the serving person had prepared them, and I turned to ask Elizabeth to close her eyes for the experiment, she had gone. So much for "evidence-based". And for computer "scientist".

Afterwards, Claudia advised me that I should have abandoned the experiment prior to Elizabeth leaving. Obviously. But at what point? Where was the signal? These are the subtleties I fail to see. But I also fail to see why heightened sensitivity to obscure cues about ice-cream flavours should be a prerequisite for being someone's partner. It seems reasonable to assume that some women do not require this. Unfortunately, the process of finding them is impossibly inefficient. The Apricot Ice-cream Disaster had cost a whole evening of my life, compensated for only by the information about simulation algorithms.

Two lunchtimes were sufficient to research and prepare my lecture on Asperger's syndrome, without sacrificing nourishment, thanks to the provision of Wi-Fi in the medical library café. I had no previous knowledge of autism spectrum disorders, as they were outside my specialty. The subject was fascinating. It seemed appropriate to focus on the genetic aspects of the syndrome, which might be unfamiliar to my audience. Most diseases have some basis in our DNA, though in many cases we have yet to discover it. My own work focuses on genetic predisposition to cirrhosis of the liver. Much of my working time is devoted to getting mice drunk.

Naturally, the books and research papers described the symptoms of Asperger's syndrome, and I formed a provisional conclusion that most of these were simply variations in human brain function that had been inappropriately medicalised because they did not fit social norms — *constructed* social norms — that reflected the most common human configurations rather than the full range.

The lecture was scheduled for 7.00p.m. at an inner-suburban school. I estimated the cycle ride at twelve minutes, and allowed three minutes to boot my computer and connect it to the projector.

I arrived on schedule at 6.57p.m., having let Eva, the short-skirted cleaner, into my apartment twenty-seven minutes earlier. There were approximately twenty-five people milling around the door and the front of the classroom, but I immediately recognised Julie, the convenor, from Gene's description: "blonde with big tits". In fact, her breasts were probably no more than one and a half standard deviations from the mean size for her body weight, and hardly a remarkable identifying feature. It was more a question of elevation and exposure, as a result of her choice of costume, which seemed perfectly practical for a hot January evening.

I may have spent too long verifying her identity, as she looked at me strangely.

"You must be Julie," I said.

"Can I help you?"

Good. A practical person. "Yes, direct me to the VGA cable. Please."

"Oh," she said. "You must be Professor Tillman. I'm so glad you could make it."

She extended her hand but I waved it away. "The VGA cable, please. It's 6.58."

"Relax," she said. "We never start before 7.15. Would you like a coffee?"

Why do people value others' time so little? Now we would have the inevitable small talk. I could have spent fifteen minutes at home practising aikido.

I had been focusing on Julie and the screen at the front of the room. Now I looked around and realised that I had failed to observe nineteen people. They were children, predominantly male, sitting at desks. Presumably these were the victims of Asperger's syndrome. Almost all of the literature focuses on children.

Despite their affliction, they were making better use of their time than their parents, who were chattering aimlessly. Most were operating portable computing devices. I guessed their ages as between eight and thirteen. I hoped they had been paying attention in their science classes, as my material assumed a working knowledge of organic chemistry and the structure of DNA.

I realised that I had failed to reply to the coffee question.

"No."

Unfortunately, because of the delay, Julie had forgotten the question. "No coffee," I explained. "I never drink coffee after 3.48p.m. It interferes with

8

sleep. Caffeine has a half-life of three to four hours, so it's irresponsible serving coffee at 7.00p.m. unless people are planning to stay awake until after midnight. Which doesn't allow adequate sleep if they have a conventional job." I was trying to make use of the waiting time by offering practical advice, but it seemed that she preferred to discuss trivia.

"Is Gene all right?" she asked. It was obviously a variant on that most common of formulaic interactions, "How are you?"

"He's fine, thank you," I said, adapting the conventional reply to the third-person form.

"Oh. I thought he was ill."

"Gene is in excellent health except for being six kilograms overweight. We went for a run this morning. He has a date tonight, and he wouldn't be able to go out if he was ill."

Julie seemed unimpressed and, in reviewing the interaction later, I realised that Gene must have lied to her about his reason for not being present. This was presumably to protect Julie from feeling that her lecture was unimportant to Gene and to provide a justification for a less prestigious speaker being sent as a substitute. It seems hardly possible to analyse such a complex situation involving deceit and supposition of another person's emotional response, and then prepare your own plausible lie, all while someone is waiting for you to reply to a question. Yet that is exactly what people expect you to be able to do.

Eventually, I set up my computer and we got started, *eighteen minutes late.* I would need to speak

forty-three per cent faster to finish on schedule at
8.00p.m. — a virtually impossible performance goal.
We were going to finish late, and my schedule for the
rest of the night would be thrown out.

CHAPTER
TWO

I had titled my talk *Genetic Precursors to Autism Spectrum Disorders* and sourced some excellent diagrams of DNA structures. I had only been speaking for nine minutes, a little faster than usual to recover time, when Julie interrupted.

"Professor Tillman. Most of us here are not scientists, so you may need to be a little less technical." This sort of thing is incredibly annoying. People can tell you the supposed characteristics of a Gemini or a Taurus and will spend five days watching a cricket match, but cannot find the interest or the time to learn the basics of what they, as humans, are made up of.

I continued with my presentation as I had prepared it. It was too late to change and surely some of the audience were informed enough to understand.

I was right. A hand went up, a male of about twelve.

"You are saying that it is unlikely that there is a single genetic marker, but rather that several genes are implicated and the aggregate expression depends on the specific combination. Affirmative?"

Exactly! "Plus environmental factors. The situation is analogous to bipolar disorder, which —"

Julie interrupted again. "So, for us non-geniuses, I think Professor Tillman is reminding us that Asperger's is something you're born with. It's nobody's fault."

I was horrified by the use of the word "fault", with its negative connotations, especially as it was being employed by someone in authority. I abandoned my decision not to deviate from the genetic issues. The matter had doubtless been brewing in my subconscious, and the volume of my voice may have increased as a result.

"Fault! Asperger's isn't a fault. It's a variant. It's potentially a major advantage. Asperger's syndrome is associated with organisation, focus, innovative thinking and rational detachment."

A woman at the rear of the room raised her hand. I was focused on the argument now, and made a minor social error, which I quickly corrected.

"The fat woman — *overweight* woman — at the back?"

She paused and looked around the room, but then continued, "Rational detachment: is that a euphemism for lack of emotion?"

"Synonym," I replied. "Emotions can cause major problems."

I decided it would be helpful to provide an example, drawing on a story in which emotional behaviour would have led to disastrous consequences.

"Imagine," I said. "You're hiding in a basement. The enemy is searching for you and your friends. Everyone has to keep totally quiet, but your baby is crying." I did an impression, as Gene would, to make the story more convincing: "Waaaaa." I paused dramatically. "You have a gun."

Hands went up everywhere.

Julie jumped to her feet as I continued. "With a silencer. They're coming closer. They're going to kill you all. What do you do? The baby's screaming —"

The kids couldn't wait to share their answer. One called out, "Shoot the baby," and soon they were all shouting, "Shoot the baby, shoot the baby."

The boy who had asked the genetics question called out, "Shoot the enemy," and then another said, "Ambush them."

The suggestions were coming rapidly.

"Use the baby as bait."

"How many guns do we have?"

"Cover its mouth."

"How long can it live without air?"

As I had expected, all the ideas came from the Asperger's "sufferers". The parents made no constructive suggestions; some even tried to suppress their children's creativity.

I raised my hands. "Time's up. Excellent work. All the rational solutions came from the aspies. Everyone else was incapacitated by emotion."

One boy called out, "Aspies rule!" I had noted this abbreviation in the literature, but it appeared to be new to the children. They seemed to like it, and soon were standing on the chairs and then the desks, punching the air and chanting "Aspies rule!" in chorus. According to my reading, children with Asperger's syndrome frequently lack self-confidence in social situations.

Their success in problem-solving seemed to have provided a temporary cure for this, but again their parents were failing to provide positive feedback, shouting at them and in some cases attempting to pull them down from the desks. Apparently they were more concerned with adherence to social convention than the progress their children were making.

I felt I had made my point effectively, and Julie did not think we needed to continue with the genetics. The parents appeared to be reflecting on what their children had learned and left without interacting with me further. It was only 7.43p.m. An excellent outcome.

As I packed up my laptop, Julie burst out laughing.

"Oh my God," she said. "I need a drink."

I was not sure why she was sharing this information with someone she had known for only forty-six minutes. I planned to consume some alcohol myself when I arrived home but saw no reason to inform Julie.

She continued, "You know, we never use that word. Aspies. We don't want them thinking it's some sort of club." More negative implications from someone who was presumably paid to assist and encourage.

"Like homosexuality?" I said.

"Touché," said Julie. "But it's different. If they don't change, they're not going to have real relationships — they'll never have partners." This was a reasonable argument, and one that I could understand, given my own difficulties in that sphere. But Julie changed the subject. "But you're saying there are things — useful things — they can do better than . . . non-aspies? Besides killing babies."

14

"Of course." I wondered why someone involved in the education of people with uncommon attributes was not aware of the value of and market for such attributes. "There's a company in Denmark that recruits aspies for computer applications testing."

"I didn't know that," said Julie. "You're really giving me a different perspective." She looked at me for a few moments. "Do you have time for a drink?" And then she put her hand on my shoulder.

I flinched automatically. Definitely inappropriate contact. If I had done that to a woman there would almost certainly have been a problem, possibly a sexual harassment complaint to the Dean, which could have consequences for my career. Of course, no one was going to criticise *her* for it.

"Unfortunately, I have other activities scheduled."

"No flexibility?"

"Definitely not." Having succeeded in recovering lost time, I was not about to throw my life into chaos again.

Before I met Gene and Claudia I had two other friends. The first was my older sister. Although she was a mathematics teacher, she had little interest in advances in the field. However, she lived nearby and would visit twice weekly and sometimes randomly. We would eat together and discuss trivia, such as events in the lives of our relatives and social interactions with our colleagues. Once a month, we drove to Shepparton for Sunday dinner with our parents and brother. She was single, probably as a result of being shy and not conventionally attractive. Due to gross and inexcusable medical incompetence, she is now dead.

The second friend was Daphne, whose friendship period also overlapped with Gene and Claudia's. She moved into the apartment above mine after her husband entered a nursing home, as a result of dementia. Due to knee failure, exacerbated by obesity, she was unable to walk more than a few steps, but she was highly intelligent and I began to visit her regularly. She had no formal qualifications, having performed a traditional female homemaker role. I considered this to be an extreme waste of talent — particularly as her descendants did not return the care. She was curious about my work, and we initiated the Teach Daphne Genetics Project, which was fascinating for both of us.

She began eating her dinner in my apartment on a regular basis, as there are massive economies of scale in cooking one meal for two people, rather than two separate meals. Each Sunday at 3.00p.m. we would visit her husband at the nursing home, which was 7.3 kilometres away. I was able to combine a 14.6-kilometre walk pushing a wheelchair with interesting conversation about genetics. I would read while she spoke to her husband, whose level of comprehension was difficult to determine but definitely low.

Daphne had been named after the plant that was flowering at the time of her birth, on the twenty-eighth of August. On each birthday, her husband would give her daphne flowers, and she considered this a highly romantic action. She complained that her approaching birthday would be the first occasion in fifty-six years on which this symbolic act would not be performed. The solution was obvious, and when I wheeled her to my apartment for dinner on her seventy-eighth birthday, I had purchased a quantity of the flowers to give her.

She recognised the smell immediately and began crying. I thought I had made a terrible error, but she explained that her tears were a symptom of happiness. She was also impressed by the chocolate cake that I had made, but not to the same extent.

During the meal, she made an incredible statement: "Don, you would make someone a wonderful husband."

This was so contrary to my experiences of being rejected by women that I was temporarily stunned. Then I presented her with the facts — the history of my attempts to find a partner, beginning with my assumption as a child that I would grow up and get married and finishing with my abandonment of the idea as the evidence grew that I was unsuitable.

Her argument was simple: there's someone for everyone. Statistically, she was almost certainly correct. Unfortunately, the probability that I would find such a person was vanishingly small. But it created a disturbance in my brain, like a mathematical problem that we know must have a solution.

For her next two birthdays, we repeated the flower ritual. The results were not as dramatic as the first time, but I also purchased gifts for her — books on genetics — and she seemed very happy. She told me that her birthday had always been her favourite day of the year. I understood that this view was common in children, due to the gifts, but had not expected it in an adult.

Ninety-three days after the third birthday dinner, we were travelling to the nursing home, discussing a genetics paper that Daphne had read the previous day, when it became apparent that she had forgotten some significant points. It was not the first time in recent weeks that her memory had been faulty, and I immediately organised an assessment of her cognitive functioning. The diagnosis was Alzheimer's disease.

Daphne's intellectual capability deteriorated rapidly, and we were soon unable to have our discussions about genetics. But we continued our meals and walks to the nursing home. Daphne now spoke primarily about her past, focusing on her husband and family, and I was able to form a generalised view of what married life could be like. She continued to insist that I could find a compatible partner and enjoy the high level of happiness that she had experienced in her own life. Supplementary research confirmed that Daphne's arguments were supported by evidence: married men are happier and live longer.

One day Daphne asked, "When will it be my birthday again?" and I realised that she had lost track of dates. I decided that it would be acceptable to lie in order to maximise her happiness. The problem was to source some daphne out of season, but I had unexpected success. I was aware of a geneticist who was working on altering and extending the flowering of plants for commercial reasons. He was able to supply my flower vendor with some daphne, and we had a simulated birthday dinner. I repeated the procedure each time Daphne asked about her birthday.

Eventually, it was necessary for Daphne to join her husband at the nursing home, and, as her memory failed, we celebrated her birthdays more often, until I was visiting her daily. The flower vendor gave me a special loyalty card. I calculated that Daphne had reached the age of two hundred and seven, according to the number of birthdays, when she stopped recognising me, and three hundred and nineteen when she no longer responded to the daphne and I abandoned the visits.

I did not expect to hear from Julie again. As usual, my assumptions about human behaviour were wrong. Two days after the lecture, at 3.37p.m., my phone rang with an unfamiliar number. Julie left a message asking me to call back, and I deduced that I must have left something behind.

I was wrong again. She wanted to continue our discussion of Asperger's syndrome. I was pleased that my input had been so influential. She suggested we meet over dinner, which was not the ideal location for productive discussion, but, as I usually eat dinner alone, it would be easy to schedule. Background research was another matter.

"What specific topics are you interested in?"

"Oh," she said, "I thought we could just talk generally . . . get to know each other a bit."

This sounded unfocused. "I need at least a broad indication of the subject domain. What did I say that particularly interested you?"

"Oh . . . I guess the stuff about the computer testers in Denmark."

"Computer *applications* testers." I would definitely need to do some research. "What would you like to know?"

"I was wondering how they found them. Most adults with Asperger's syndrome don't know they have it."

It was a good point. Interviewing random applicants would be a highly inefficient way to detect a syndrome that has an estimated prevalence of less than 0.3 per cent.

I ventured a guess. "I presume they use a questionnaire as a preliminary filter." I had not even finished the sentence when a light went on in my head — not literally, of course.

A questionnaire! Such an obvious solution. A purpose-built, scientifically valid instrument incorporating current best practice to filter out the time wasters, the disorganised, the ice-cream discriminators, the visual-harassment complainers, the crystal gazers, the horoscope readers, the fashion obsessives, the religious fanatics, the vegans, the sports watchers, the creationists, the smokers, the scientifically illiterate, the homeopaths, leaving, ideally, the perfect partner, or, realistically, a manageable shortlist of candidates.

"Don?" It was Julie, still on the line. "When do you want to get together?"

Things had changed. Priorities had shifted.

"It's not possible," I said. "My schedule is full."

I was going to need all available time for the new project.

The Wife Project.

20

CHAPTER
THREE

After speaking with Julie, I went immediately to Gene's office in the Psychology building, but he was not there. Fortunately his personal assistant, The Beautiful Helena, who should be called The Obstructive Helena, was not there either and I was able to access Gene's diary. I discovered that he was giving a public lecture, due to finish at 5.00p.m., with a gap before a meeting at 5.30p.m. Perfect. I would merely have to reduce the length of my scheduled gym session. I booked the vacant slot.

After an accelerated workout at the gym, achieved by deleting the shower and change tasks, I jogged to the lecture theatre, where I waited outside the staff entrance. Although I was perspiring heavily from the heat and exercise, I was energised, both physically and mentally. As soon as my watch showed 5.00p.m., I walked in. Gene was at the lectern of the darkened theatre, still talking, apparently oblivious to time, responding to a question about funding. My entrance had allowed a shaft of light into the room, and I realised that the audience's eyes were now on me, as if expecting me to say something.

"Time's up," I said. "I have a meeting with Gene."

People immediately started getting up, and I observed the Dean in the front row with three people in corporate costumes. I guessed that they were there as potential providers of finance and not because of an intellectual interest in primate sexual attraction. Gene is always trying to solicit money for research, and the Dean is constantly threatening to downsize the Genetics and Psychology departments because of insufficient funding. It is not an area I involve myself in.

Gene spoke over the chatter. "I think my colleague Professor Tillman has given us a signal that we should discuss the finances, critical as they are to our ongoing work, at another time." He looked towards the Dean and her companions. "Thank you again for your interest in my work — and of course that of my colleagues in the Department of Psychology." There was applause. It seemed that my intervention had been timely.

The Dean and her corporate friends swept past me. She said, just to me, "Sorry to hold up your meeting, Professor Tillman. I'm sure we can find the money elsewhere." This was good to hear, but now, annoyingly, there was a throng around Gene. A woman with red hair and several metal objects in her ears was talking to him. She was speaking quite loudly.

"I can't believe you used a public lecture to push your own agenda."

"Lucky you came then. You've changed one of your beliefs. That'd be a first."

It was obvious that there was some animosity on the woman's part even though Gene was smiling.

"Even if you were right, which you're not, what about the social impact?"

I was amazed by Gene's next reply, not by its intent, which I am familiar with, but by its subtle shift in topic. Gene has social skills at a level that I will never have.

"This is sounding like a café discussion. Why don't we pick it up over coffee sometime?"

"Sorry," she said. "I've got research to do. You know, evidence."

I moved to push in but a tall blonde woman was ahead of me, and I did not want to risk body contact. She spoke with a Norwegian accent.

"Professor Barrow?" she said, meaning Gene. "With respect, I think you are oversimplifying the feminist position."

"If we're going to talk philosophy, we should do it in a coffee shop," Gene replied. "I'll catch you at Barista's in five."

The woman nodded and walked towards the door.

Finally, we had time to talk.

"What's her accent?" Gene asked me. "Swedish?"

"Norwegian," I said. "I thought you had a Norwegian already."

I told him that we had a discussion scheduled, but Gene was now focused on having coffee with the woman. Most male animals are programmed to give higher priority to sex than to assisting an unrelated individual, and Gene had the additional motivation of his research project. Arguing would be hopeless.

"Book the next slot in my diary," he said.

The Beautiful Helena had presumably departed for the day, and I was again able to access Gene's diary. I amended my own schedule to accommodate the appointment. From now on, the Wife Project would have maximum priority.

I waited until exactly 7.30 a.m. the next day before knocking on Gene and Claudia's door. It had been necessary to shift my jog to the market for dinner purchases back to 5.45 a.m., which in turn had meant going to bed earlier the previous night, with a flow-on effect to a number of scheduled tasks.

I heard sounds of surprise through the door before their daughter Eugenie opened it. Eugenie was, as always, pleased to see me, and requested that I hoist her onto my shoulders and jump all the way to the kitchen. It was great fun. It occurred to me that I might be able to include Eugenie and her half-brother Carl as my friends, making a total of four.

Gene and Claudia were eating breakfast, and told me that they had not been expecting me. I advised Gene to put his diary online — he could remain up to date and I would avoid unpleasant encounters with The Beautiful Helena. He was not enthusiastic.

I had missed breakfast, so I took a tub of yoghurt from the refrigerator. Sweetened! No wonder Gene is overweight. Claudia is not yet overweight, but I had noticed some increase. I pointed out the problem, and identified the yoghurt as the possible culprit.

Claudia asked whether I had enjoyed the Asperger's lecture. She was under the impression that Gene had delivered the lecture and I had merely attended. I corrected her mistake and told her I had found the subject fascinating.

"Did the symptoms remind you of anyone?" she asked.

They certainly did. They were an almost perfect description of Laszlo Hevesi in the Physics Department. I was about to relate the famous story of Laszlo and the pyjamas when Gene's son Carl, who is sixteen, arrived in his school uniform. He walked towards the refrigerator, as if to open it, then suddenly spun around and threw a full-blooded punch at my head. I caught the punch and pushed him gently but firmly to the floor, so he could see that I was achieving the result with leverage rather than strength. This is a game we always play, but he had not noticed the yoghurt, which was now on our clothes.

"Stay still," said Claudia. "I'll get a cloth."

A cloth was not going to clean my shirt properly. Laundering a shirt requires a machine, detergent, fabric softener and considerable time.

"I'll borrow one of Gene's," I said, and headed to their bedroom.

When I returned, wearing an uncomfortably large white shirt, with a decorative frill in the front, I tried to introduce the Wife Project, but Claudia was engaged in child-related activities. This was becoming frustrating. I booked dinner for Saturday night and asked them not to schedule any other conversation topics.

The delay was actually opportune, as it enabled me to undertake some research on questionnaire design, draw up a list of desirable attributes, and produce a draft proforma survey. All this, of course, had to be arranged around my teaching and research commitments and an appointment with the Dean.

On Friday morning we had yet another unpleasant interaction as a result of me reporting an honours-year student for academic dishonesty. I had already caught Kevin Yu cheating once. Then, marking his most recent assignment, I had recognised a sentence from another student's work of three years earlier.

Some investigation established that the past student was now Kevin's private tutor, and had written at least part of his essay for him. This had all happened some weeks ago. I had reported the matter and expected the disciplinary process to take its course. Apparently it was more complicated than this.

"The situation with Kevin is a little awkward," said the Dean. We were in her corporate-style office and she was wearing her corporate-style costume of matching dark-blue skirt and jacket, which, according to Gene, is intended to make her appear more powerful. She is a short, slim person, aged approximately fifty, and it is possible that the costume makes her appear bigger, but I cannot see the relevance of physical dominance in an academic environment.

"This is Kevin's third offence, and university policy requires that he be expelled," she said.

The facts seemed to be clear and the necessary action straightforward. I tried to identify the awkwardness that the Dean referred to. "Is the evidence insufficient? Is he making a legal challenge?"

"No, that's all perfectly clear. But the first offence was very naive. He cut and pasted from the internet, and was picked up by the plagiarism software. He was in his first year and his English wasn't very good. And there are cultural differences."

I had not known about this first offence.

"The second time, you reported him because he'd borrowed from an obscure paper that you were somehow familiar with."

"Correct."

"Don, none of the other lecturers are as . . . vigilant . . . as you."

It was unusual for the Dean to compliment me on my wide reading and dedication.

"These kids pay a lot of money to study here. We rely on their fees. We don't want them stealing blatantly from the internet. But we have to recognise that they need assistance, and . . . Kevin has only a semester to go. We can't send him home after three and a half years without a qualification. It's not a good look."

"What if he was a medical student? What if you went to the hospital and the doctor who operated on you had cheated in their exams?"

"Kevin's not a medical student. And he didn't cheat on his exams, he just got some help with an assignment."

It seemed that the Dean had been flattering me only in order to procure unethical behaviour. But the solution to her dilemma was obvious. If she did not want to break the rules, then she should change the rules. I pointed this out.

I am not good at interpreting expressions, and was not familiar with the one that appeared on the Dean's face. "We can't be seen to allow cheating."

"Even though we do?"

The meeting left me confused and angry. There were serious matters at stake. What if our research was not accepted because we had a reputation for low academic standards? People could die while cures for diseases were delayed. What if a genetics laboratory hired a person whose qualification had been achieved through cheating, and that person made major errors? The Dean seemed more concerned with perceptions than with these crucial matters.

I reflected on what it would be like to spend my life living with the Dean. It was a truly terrible thought. The underlying problem was the preoccupation with image. My questionnaire would be ruthless in filtering out women who were concerned with appearance.

CHAPTER
FOUR

Gene opened the door with a glass of red wine in his hand. I parked my bicycle in their hallway, took off my backpack and retrieved the Wife Project folder, pulling out Gene's copy of the draft. I had pruned it to sixteen double-sided pages.

"Relax, Don, plenty of time," he said. "We're going to have a civilised dinner, and then we'll do the questionnaire. If you're going to be dating, you need dinner practice."

He was, of course, right. Claudia is an excellent cook and Gene has a vast collection of wines, organised by region, vintage and producer. We went to his "cellar", which is not actually below ground, where he showed me his recent purchases and we selected a second bottle. We ate with Carl and Eugenie, and I was able to avoid small talk by playing a memory game with Eugenie. She noticed my folder marked "Wife Project", which I put on the table as soon as I finished dessert.

"Are you getting married, Don?" she asked.

"Correct."

"Who to?"

I was about to explain, but Claudia sent Eugenie and Carl to their rooms — a good decision, as they did not have the expertise to contribute.

I handed questionnaires to Claudia and Gene. Gene poured port for all of us. I explained that I had followed best practice in questionnaire design, including multiple-choice questions, Likert scales, cross-validation, dummy questions and surrogates. Claudia asked for an example of the last of these.

"Question 35: *Do you eat kidneys?* Correct answer is *(c) occasionally*. Testing for food problems. If you ask directly about food preferences, they say 'I eat anything' and then you discover they're vegetarian."

I am aware that there are many arguments in favour of vegetarianism. However, as I eat meat I considered it would be more convenient if my partner did so also. At this early stage, it seemed logical to specify the ideal solution and review the questionnaire later if necessary.

Claudia and Gene were reading.

Claudia said, "For an appointment, I'm guessing *(b) a little early*."

This was patently incorrect, demonstrating that even Claudia, who was a good friend, would be unsuitable as a partner.

"The correct answer is *(c) on time*," I said. "Habitual earliness is cumulatively a major waste of time."

"I'd allow *a little early*," said Claudia. "She might be trying hard. That's not a bad thing."

An interesting point. I made a note to consider it, but pointed out that *(d) a little late* and *(e) very late* were definitely unacceptable.

"I think if a woman describes herself as a brilliant cook she's a bit up herself," said Claudia. "Just ask her if she enjoys cooking. Mention that you do too."

This was exactly the sort of input I was looking for — subtle nuances of language that I am not conscious of. It struck me that if the respondent was someone like me she would not notice the difference, but it was unreasonable to require that my potential partner share my lack of subtlety.

"No jewellery, no make-up?" said Claudia, correctly predicting the answers to two questions that had been prompted by my recent interaction with the Dean.

"Jewellery isn't always about appearance," she said. "If you have to have a question, drop the jewellery one and keep the make-up. But just ask if she wears it daily."

"Height, weight *and* body mass index." Gene was skimming ahead. "Can't you do the calculation yourself?"

"That's the purpose of the question," I said. "Checking they can do basic arithmetic. I don't want a partner who's mathematically illiterate."

"I thought you might have wanted to get an idea of what they look like," said Gene.

"There's a question on fitness," I said.

"I was thinking about sex," said Gene.

"Just for a change," said Claudia, an odd statement as Gene talks constantly about sex. But he had made a good point.

"I'll add a question on HIV and herpes."

"Stop," said Claudia. "You're being way too picky."

I began to explain that an incurable sexually transmitted disease was a severe negative but Claudia interrupted.

"About everything."

It was an understandable response. But my strategy was to minimise the chance of making a type-one error — wasting time on an unsuitable choice. Inevitably, that increased the risk of a type-two error — rejecting a suitable person. But this was an acceptable risk as I was dealing with a very large population.

Gene's turn: "Non-smoking, fair enough. But what's the right answer on drinking?"

"Zero."

"Hang on. You drink." He pointed to my port glass, which he had topped up a few moments earlier. "You drink quite a bit."

I explained that I was expecting some improvement for myself from the project.

We continued in this manner and I received some excellent feedback. I did feel that the questionnaire was now less discriminating, but was still confident it would eliminate most if not all of the women who had given me problems in the past. Apricot Ice-cream Woman would have failed at least five questions.

My plan was to advertise on traditional dating sites, but to provide a link to the questionnaire in addition to posting the usual insufficiently discriminating information about height, profession and whether I enjoyed long walks on the beach.

Gene and Claudia suggested that I also undertake some face-to-face dating to practise my social skills. I could see the value of validating the questionnaires in the field, so, while I waited for online responses to arrive, I printed some questionnaires and returned to the dating process that I thought I had abandoned forever.

I began by registering with Table for Eight, run by a commercial matchmaking organisation. After an undoubtedly unsound preliminary matching process, based on manifestly inadequate data, four men and four women, including me, were provided with details of a city restaurant at which a booking had been made. I packed four questionnaires and arrived precisely at 8.00p.m. *Only one woman was there!* The other three were late. It was a stunning validation of the advantages of field work. These women may well have answered *(b) a little early* or *(c) on time*, but their actual behaviour demonstrated otherwise. I decided to temporarily allow *(d) a little late*, on the basis that a single occasion might not be representative of their overall performance. I could hear Claudia saying, "Don, everyone's late occasionally."

There were also two men seated at the table. We shook hands. It struck me that this was equivalent to bowing prior to a martial-arts bout.

I assessed my competition. The man who had introduced himself as Craig was about my own age, but overweight, in a white business shirt that was too tight for him. He had a moustache, and his teeth were poorly maintained. The second, Danny, was probably a few years younger than me, and appeared to be in good health. He wore a white t-shirt. He had tattoos on his arms and his black hair contained some form of cosmetic additive.

The on-time woman's name was Olivia, and she initially (and logically) divided her attention among the three men. She told us she was an anthropologist. Danny confused it with an archaeologist and then Craig made a racist joke about pygmies. It was obvious, even to me, that Olivia was unimpressed by these responses, and I enjoyed a rare moment of not feeling like the least socially competent person in the room. Olivia turned to me, and I had just responded to her question about my job when we were interrupted by the arrival of the fourth man, who introduced himself as Gerry, a lawyer, and two women, Sharon and Maria, who were, respectively, an accountant and a nurse. It was a hot night, and Maria had chosen a dress with the twin advantages of coolness and overt sexual display. Sharon was wearing the conventional corporate uniform of trousers and jacket. I guessed that they were both about my age.

Olivia resumed talking to me while the others engaged in small talk — an extraordinary waste of time when a major life decision was at stake. On Claudia's advice, I had memorised the questionnaire. She thought that asking questions directly from the forms could create the wrong "dynamic" and that I should attempt to incorporate them subtly into conversation. Subtlety, I had reminded her, is not my strength. She suggested that I not ask about sexually transmitted diseases and that I make my own estimates of weight, height and body mass index. I estimated Olivia's BMI at nineteen: slim, but no signs of anorexia. I estimated Sharon the Accountant's at twenty-three, and Maria the Nurse's at twenty-eight. The recommended healthy maximum is twenty-five.

Rather than ask about IQ, I decided to make an estimate based on Olivia's responses to questions about the historical impact of variations in susceptibility to syphilis across native South American populations. We had a fascinating conversation, and I felt that the topic might even allow me to slip in the sexually-transmitted-diseases question. Her IQ was definitely above the required minimum. Gerry the Lawyer offered a few comments that I think were meant to be jokes, but eventually left us to continue uninterrupted.

At this point, the missing woman arrived, *twenty-eight minutes late*. While Olivia was distracted, I took the opportunity to record the data I had acquired so far on three of the four questionnaires in my lap. I did not waste paper on the most recent arrival, as she announced that she was "always late". This did not seem to concern Gerry the Lawyer, who presumably billed by the six-minute interval, and should consequently have considered time to be of great value. He obviously valued sex more highly as his conversation began to resemble that of Gene.

With the arrival of Late Woman, the waiter appeared with menus. Olivia scanned hers then asked, "The pumpkin soup, is it made with vegetable stock?"

I did not hear the answer. The question provided the critical information. Vegetarian.

She may have noted my expression of disappointment. "I'm Hindu."

I had previously deduced that Olivia was probably Indian from her sari and physical attributes. I was not sure whether the term "Hindu" was being used as a genuine statement of religious belief or as an indicator of cultural heritage. I had been reprimanded for failing to make this distinction in the past.

"Do you eat ice-cream?" I asked. The question seemed appropriate after the vegetarian statement. Very neat.

"Oh yes, I am not vegan. As long as it is not made with eggs."

This was not getting any better.

"Do you have a favourite flavour?"

"Pistachio. Very definitely pistachio." She smiled.

Maria and Danny had stepped outside for a cigarette. With three women eliminated, including Late Woman, my task was almost complete.

My lambs' brains arrived, and I cut one in half, exposing the internal structure. I tapped Sharon, who was engaged in conversation with Craig the Racist, and pointed it out to her. "Do you like brains?"

Four down, job complete. I continued my conversation with Olivia, who was excellent company, and even ordered an additional drink after the others had departed in the pairs that they had formed. We stayed, talking, until we were the last people in the restaurant. As I put the questionnaires in my backpack, Olivia gave me her contact information, which I wrote down in order not to be rude. Then we went our separate ways.

Cycling home, I reflected on the dinner. It had been a grossly inefficient method of selection, but the questionnaire had been of significant value. Without the questions it prompted, I would undoubtedly have attempted a second date with Olivia, who was an interesting and nice person. Perhaps we would have gone on a third and fourth and fifth date, then one day, when all of the desserts at the restaurant contained egg, we would have crossed the road to the ice-cream parlour, and discovered they had no egg-free pistachio. It was better to find out before we made an investment in the relationship.

CHAPTER
FIVE

I stood inside the entrance of a suburban house that reminded me of my parents' brick veneer residence in Shepparton. I had resolved never to attend another singles party, but the questionnaire allowed me to avoid the agony of unstructured social interaction with strangers.

As the female guests arrived, I gave each a questionnaire to complete at their convenience and return to me either at the party or by mail. The host, a woman, initially invited me to join the crowd in the living room, but I explained my strategy and she left me alone. After two hours, a woman of about thirty-five, estimated BMI twenty-one, returned from the living room, holding two glasses of sparkling wine. In her other hand was a questionnaire.

She passed me a glass. "I thought you might be thirsty," she said in an attractive French accent.

I was not thirsty, but I was pleased to be offered alcohol. I had decided that I would not give up drinking unless I found a non-drinking partner. And, after some self-analysis, I had concluded that *(c) moderately* was an acceptable answer to the drinking question and made a note to update the questionnaire.

"Thank you." I hoped she would give me the questionnaire and that it might, improbably, signal the end of my quest. She was extremely attractive, and her gesture with the wine indicated a high level of consideration not exhibited by any of the other guests or the host.

"You are a researcher, am I right?" She tapped the questionnaire.

"Correct."

"Me, also," she said. "There are not many academics here tonight." Although it is dangerous to draw conclusions based on manner and conversation topics, my assessment of the guests was consistent with this observation.

"I'm Fabienne," she said, and extended her free hand, which I shook, careful to apply the recommended level of firmness. "This is terrible wine, no?"

I agreed. It was a carbonated sweet wine, acceptable only because of its alcohol content.

"You think we should go to a wine bar and get something better?" she asked.

I shook my head. The poor wine quality was annoying but not critical.

Fabienne took a deep breath. "Listen. I have drunk two glasses of wine, I have not had sex for six weeks, and I would rather wait six more than try anyone else here. Now, can I buy you a drink?"

It was a very kind offer. But it was still early in the evening. I said, "More guests are expected. You may find someone suitable if you wait."

Fabienne gave me her questionnaire and said, "I presume you will be notifying the winners in due course." I told her that I would. When she had gone, I quickly checked her questionnaire. Predictably, she failed in a number of dimensions. It was disappointing.

My final non-internet option was speed dating, an approach I had not previously tried.

The venue was a function room in a hotel. At my insistence, the convenor disclosed the *actual* start time, and I waited in the bar to avoid aimless interaction until then. When I returned, I took the last remaining seat at a long table, opposite a person labelled Frances, aged approximately fifty, BMI approximately twenty-eight, not conventionally attractive.

The convenor rang a bell and my three minutes with Frances commenced.

I pulled out my questionnaire and scribbled her name on it — there was no time for subtlety under these circumstances.

"I've sequenced the questions for maximum speed of elimination," I explained. "I believe I can eliminate most women in less than forty seconds. Then you can choose the topic of discussion for the remaining time."

"But then it won't matter," said Frances. "I'll have been eliminated."

"Only as a potential partner. We may still be able to have an interesting discussion."

"But I'll have been eliminated."

I nodded. "Do you smoke?"

"Occasionally," she said.

I put the questionnaire away.

"Excellent." I was pleased that my question sequencing was working so well. We could have wasted time talking about ice-cream flavours and make-up only to find that she smoked. Needless to say, smoking was not negotiable. "No more questions. What would you like to discuss?"

Disappointingly, Frances was not interested in further conversation after I had determined that we were not compatible. This turned out to be the pattern for the remainder of the event.

These personal interactions were, of course, secondary. I was relying on the internet, and completed questionnaires began to flow in shortly after my initial postings. I scheduled a review meeting in my office with Gene.

"How many responses?" he asked.

"Two hundred and seventy-nine."

He was clearly impressed. I did not tell him that the quality of responses varied widely, with many questionnaires only partially completed.

"No photos?"

Many women had included photos, but I had suppressed them in the database display to allow space for more important data.

"Let's see the photos," Gene said.

I modified the settings to show photos, and Gene scanned a few before double-clicking on one. The resolution was impressive. It seemed that he approved, but a quick check of the data showed that the candidate was totally unsuitable. I took the mouse back and deleted her. Gene protested.

"Wha wha wha? What're you doing?"

"She believes in astrology and homeopathy. And she calculated her BMI incorrectly."

"What was it?"

"Twenty-three point five."

"Nice. Can you undelete her?"

"She's totally unsuitable."

"How many *are* suitable?" asked Gene, finally getting to the point.

"So far, zero. The questionnaire is an excellent filter."

"You don't drink you're setting the bar just a tiny bit high?"

I pointed out that I was collecting data to support life's most critical decision. Compromise would be totally inappropriate.

"You always have to compromise," Gene said. An incredible statement and totally untrue in his case.

"You found the perfect wife. Highly intelligent, extremely beautiful and she lets you have sex with other women."

Gene suggested that I not congratulate Claudia in person for her tolerance, and asked me to repeat the number of questionnaires that had been completed. The actual total was greater than the number I had told him, as I had not included the paper questionnaires. Three hundred and four.

"Give me your list," said Gene. "I'll pick out a few for you."

"None of them meet the criteria. They all have some fault."

"Treat it as practice."

He did have a point. I had thought a few times about Olivia the Indian Anthropologist, and considered the implications of living with a Hindu vegetarian with a strong ice-cream preference. Only reminding myself that I should wait until an exact match turned up had stopped me from contacting her. I had even rechecked the questionnaire from Fabienne the Sex-Deprived Researcher.

I emailed the spreadsheet to Gene.

"No smokers."

"Okay," said Gene, "but you have to ask them out. To dinner. At a proper restaurant."

Gene could probably tell that I was not excited by the prospect. He cleverly addressed the problem by proposing an even less acceptable alternative.

"There's always the faculty ball."

"Restaurant."

Gene smiled as if to compensate for my lack of enthusiasm. "It's easy. 'How about we do dinner tonight?' Say it after me."

"How about we do dinner tonight?" I repeated.

"See, that wasn't so hard. Make only positive comments about their appearance. Pay for the meal. Do not mention sex." Gene walked to the door, then turned back. "What about the paper ones?"

I gave him my questionnaires from Table for Eight, the singles party and, at his insistence, even the partially completed ones from the speed dating. Now it was out of my hands.

CHAPTER
SIX

Approximately two hours after Gene left my office with the completed Wife Project questionnaires, there was a knock on the door. I was weighing student essays, an activity that is not forbidden, but I suspect only because nobody is aware that I am doing it. It was part of a project to reduce the effort of assessment, by looking for easily measured parameters such as the inclusion of a table of contents, or a typed versus handwritten cover sheet, factors which might provide as good an indication of quality as the tedious process of reading the entire assignment.

I slipped the scales under my desk as the door opened and looked up to see a woman I did not recognise standing in the doorway. I estimated her age as thirty and her body mass index at twenty.

"Professor Tillman?"

As my name is on the door, this was not a particularly astute question.

"Correct."

"Professor Barrow suggested I see you."

I was amazed at Gene's efficiency, and looked at the woman more carefully as she approached my desk. There were no obvious signs of unsuitability. I did not detect any make-up. Her body shape and skin tone were consistent with health and fitness. She wore glasses with heavy frames that revived bad memories of Apricot Ice-cream Woman, a long black t-shirt that was torn in several places, and a black belt with metal chains. It was lucky that the jewellery question had been deleted because she was wearing big metal earrings and an interesting pendant round her neck.

Although I am usually oblivious to dress, hers seemed incompatible with my expectation of a highly qualified academic or professional and with the summer weather. I could only guess that she was self-employed or on holiday and, freed from workplace rules, had chosen her clothes randomly. I could relate to this.

There had been quite a long gap since either of us had spoken and I realised it must be my turn. I looked up from the pendant and remembered Gene's instructions.

"How about we do dinner tonight?"

She seemed surprised at my question then replied, "Yeah, right. How about we do dinner? How about Le Gavroche and you're paying?"

"Excellent. I'll make a reservation for 8.00p.m."

"You're kidding."

It was an odd response. Why would I make a confusing joke with someone I barely knew?

"No. Is 8.00p.m. tonight acceptable?"

"Let me get this straight. You're offering to buy me dinner at Le Gavroche tonight?"

Coming on top of the question about my name, I was beginning to think that this woman was what Gene would call "not the sharpest tool in the shed". I considered backing out, or at least employing some delaying tactic until I could check her questionnaire, but could not think of any socially acceptable way to do this, so I just confirmed that she had interpreted my offer correctly. She turned and left and I realised that I did not even know her name.

I called Gene immediately. There seemed to be some confusion on his part at first, followed by mirth. Perhaps he had not expected me to handle the candidate so effectively.

"Her name's Rosie," he said. "And that's all I'm telling you. Have fun. And remember what I said about sex."

Gene's failure to provide me with more details was unfortunate, because a problem arose. Le Gavroche did not have a table available at the agreed time. I tried to locate Rosie's profile on my computer, and for once the photos were useful. The woman who had come to my office did not look like any candidate whose name began with "R". She must have been one of the paper responses. Gene had left and his phone was off.

I was forced to take action that was not strictly illegal, but doubtless immoral. I justified it on the basis that it would be more immoral to fail to meet my commitment to Rosie. Le Gavroche's online reservation system had a facility for VIPs and I made a reservation under the name of the Dean after logging on using relatively unsophisticated hacking software.

I arrived at 7.59p.m. The restaurant was located in a major hotel. I chained my bike in the foyer, as it was raining heavily outside. Fortunately it was not cold and my Gore-Tex jacket had done an excellent job of protecting me. My t-shirt was not even damp underneath.

A man in uniform approached me. He pointed towards the bike, but I spoke before he had a chance to complain.

"My name is Professor Lawrence and I interacted with your reservation system at 5.11 p.m."

It appeared that the official did not know the Dean, or assumed that I was another Professor Lawrence, because he just checked a clipboard and nodded. I was impressed with the efficiency, though it was now 8.01 p.m. and Rosie was not there. Perhaps she was *(b) a little early* and already seated.

But then a problem arose.

"I'm sorry, sir, but we have a dress code," said the official.

I knew about this. It was in bold type on the website: Gentlemen are required to wear a jacket.

"No jacket, no food, correct?"

"More or less, sir."

What can I say about this sort of rule? I was prepared to keep my jacket on throughout the meal. The restaurant would presumably be air-conditioned to a temperature compatible with the requirement.

I continued towards the restaurant entrance, but the official blocked my path. "I'm sorry. Perhaps I wasn't clear. You need to wear a jacket."

"I'm wearing a jacket."

"I'm afraid we require something a little more formal, sir."

The hotel employee indicated his own jacket as an example. In defence of what followed, I submit the Oxford English Dictionary (Compact, 2nd Edition) definition of "jacket": *1(a) An outer garment for the upper part of the body.*

I also note that the word "jacket" appears on the care instructions for my relatively new and perfectly clean Gore-Tex "jacket". But it seemed his definition of jacket was limited to "conventional suit jacket".

"We would be happy to lend you one, sir. In this style."

"You have a supply of jackets? In every possible size?" I did not add that the need to maintain such an inventory was surely evidence of their failure to communicate the rule clearly, and that it would be more efficient to improve their wording or abandon the rule altogether. Nor did I mention that the cost of jacket purchase and cleaning must add to the price of their meals. Did their customers know that they were subsidising a jacket warehouse?

"I wouldn't know about that, sir," he said. "Let me organise a jacket."

Needless to say I was uncomfortable at the idea of being re-dressed in an item of public clothing of dubious cleanliness. For a few moments, I was overwhelmed by the sheer unreasonableness of the situation. I was already under stress, preparing for the second encounter with a woman who might become my life partner. And now the institution that I was paying to supply us with a meal — the *service provider* who should surely be doing everything possible to make me comfortable — was putting arbitrary obstacles in my way. My Gore-Tex jacket, the high-technology garment that had protected me in rain and snowstorms, was being irrationally, unfairly and obstructively contrasted with the official's essentially decorative woollen equivalent. I had paid $1,015 for it, including $120 extra for the customised reflective yellow. I outlined my argument.

"My jacket is superior to yours by all reasonable criteria: impermeability to water, visibility in low light, storage capacity." I unzipped the jacket to display the internal pockets and continued, "Speed of drying, resistance to food stains, hood . . ."

The official was still showing no interpretable reaction, although I had almost certainly raised my voice.

"Vastly superior tensile strength . . ."

To illustrate this last point, I took the lapel of the employee's jacket in my hands. I obviously had no intention of tearing it but I was suddenly grabbed from behind by an unknown person who attempted to throw me to the ground. I automatically responded with a safe, low-impact throw to disable him without dislodging my glasses. The term "low impact" applies to a martial-arts practitioner who knows how to fall. This person did not, and landed heavily.

I turned to see him — he was large and angry. In order to prevent further violence, I was forced to sit on him.

"Get the fuck off me. I'll fucking kill you," he said.

On that basis, it seemed illogical to grant his request. At that point another man arrived and tried to drag me off. Concerned that Thug Number One would carry out his threat, I had no choice but to disable Thug Number Two as well. No one was seriously hurt, but it was a very awkward social situation, and I could feel my mind shutting down.

Fortunately, Rosie arrived.

Jacket Man said, apparently in surprise, "Rosie!"

Obviously he knew her. She looked from him to me and said, "Professor Tillman — Don — what's going on?"

"You're late," I said. "We have a social problem."

"You know this man?" said Jacket Man to Rosie.

"What do you think, I guessed his name?" Rosie sounded belligerent and I thought this might not be the best approach. Surely we should seek to apologise and leave. I was assuming we would not now be eating in the restaurant.

A small crowd had gathered and it occurred to me that another thug might arrive, so I needed to work out a way of freeing up a hand without releasing the original two thugs. In the process one poked the other in the eye, and their anger levels increased noticeably. Jacket Man added, "He assaulted Jason."

Rosie replied, "Right. Poor Jason. Always the victim." I could now see her. She was wearing a black dress without decoration, thick-soled black boots and vast amounts of silver jewellery on her arms. Her red hair was spiky like some new species of cactus. I have heard the word "stunning" used to describe women, but this was the first time I had actually been stunned by one. It was not just the costume or the jewellery or any individual characteristic of Rosie herself: it was their combined effect. I was not sure if her appearance would be regarded as conventionally beautiful or even acceptable to the restaurant that had rejected my jacket. "Stunning" was the perfect word for it. But what she did was even more stunning. She took her phone from her bag and pointed it at us. It flashed twice. Jacket Man moved to take it from her.

"Don't you fucking think about it," Rosie said. "I'm going to have so much fun with these photos that these guys will never stand on a door again. *Professor teaches bouncers a lesson.*"

As Rosie was speaking, a man in a chef's hat arrived. He spoke briefly to Jacket Man and Rosie and, on the basis that we would be permitted to leave without further harassment, Rosie asked me to release my assailants. We all got to our feet, and, in keeping with tradition, I bowed, then extended my hand to the two men, who I had concluded must be security personnel. They had only been doing what they were paid for, and had risked injury in the course of their duties. It seemed that they were not expecting the formalities, but then one of them laughed and shook my hand, and the other followed his example. It was a good resolution, but I no longer felt like eating at the restaurant.

I collected my bike and we walked into the street. I expected Rosie to be angry about the incident, but she was smiling. I asked her how she knew Jacket Man.

"I used to work there."

"You selected the restaurant because you were familiar with it?"

"You could say that. I wanted to stick it up them." She began to laugh. "Maybe not quite that much."

I told her that her solution was brilliant.

"I work in a bar," she said. "Not just a bar — the Marquess of Queensbury. I deal with jerks for a living."

I pointed out that if she had arrived on schedule she could have used her social skills and the violence would have been unnecessary.

"Glad I was late then. That was judo, right?"

"Aikido." As we crossed the road, I switched my bike to my other side, between Rosie and me. "I'm also proficient in karate, but aikido was more appropriate."

"No way. It takes forever to learn that stuff, doesn't it?"

"I commenced at seven."

"How often do you train?"

"Three times per week, except in the case of illness, public holidays and travel to overseas conferences."

"What got you into it?" asked Rosie.

I pointed to my glasses.

"Revenge of the nerds," she said.

"This is the first time I've required it for self-defence since I was at school. It's primarily for fitness." I had relaxed a little, and Rosie had provided an opportunity to slip in a question from the Wife Project questionnaire. "Do you exercise regularly?"

"Depends what you call regularly." She laughed. "I'm the unfittest person on the planet."

"Exercise is extremely important for maintaining health."

"So my dad tells me. He's a personal trainer. Constantly on my case. He gave me a gym membership for my birthday. At his gym. He has this idea we should train for a triathlon together."

"Surely you should follow his advice," I said.

"Fuck, I'm almost thirty. I don't need my dad telling me what to do." She changed the subject. "Listen, I'm starving. Let's get a pizza."

I was not prepared to consider a restaurant after the preceding trauma. I told her that I intended to revert to my original plan for the evening, which was cooking at home.

"Got enough for two?" she asked. "You still owe me dinner."

This was true but there had been too many unscheduled events already in my day.

"Come on. I won't criticise your cooking. I can't cook to save my life."

I was not concerned about my cooking being criticised. But the lack of cooking skills on her part was the third fault *so far* in terms of the Wife Project questionnaire, after the late arrival and the lack of fitness. There was almost certainly a fourth: it was unlikely that her profession as waitress and barmaid was consistent with the specified intellectual level. There was no point in continuing.

Before I could protest, Rosie had flagged down a minivan taxi with sufficient capacity for my bike.

"Where do you live?" she asked.

CHAPTER
SEVEN

"Wow, Mr Neat. How come there are no pictures on the walls?"

I had not had visitors since Daphne moved out of the building. I knew that I only needed to put out an extra plate and cutlery. But it had already been a stressful evening, and the adrenaline-induced euphoria that had immediately followed the Jacket Incident had evaporated, at least on my part. Rosie seemed to be in a permanently manic state.

We were in the living area, which adjoins the kitchen.

"Because after a while I would stop noticing them. The human brain is wired to focus on differences in its environment — so it can rapidly discern a predator. If I installed pictures or other decorative objects, I would notice them for a few days and then my brain would ignore them. If I want to see art, I go to the gallery. The paintings there are of higher quality, and the total expenditure over time is less than the purchase price of cheap posters." In fact, I had not been to an art gallery since the tenth of May, three years before. But this information would weaken my argument and I saw no reason to share it with Rosie and open up other aspects of my personal life to interrogation.

Rosie had moved on and was now examining my CD collection. The investigation was becoming annoying. Dinner was already late.

"You really love Bach," she said. This was a reasonable deduction, as my CD collection consists only of the works of that composer. But it was not correct.

"I decided to focus on Bach after reading *Gödel, Escher, Bach* by Douglas Hofstadter. Unfortunately I haven't made much progress. I don't think my brain works fast enough to decode the patterns in the music."

"You don't listen to it for fun?"

This was beginning to sound like the initial dinner conversations with Daphne and I didn't answer.

"You've got an iPhone?" she said.

"Of course, but I don't use it for music. I download podcasts."

"Let me guess — on genetics."

"Science in general."

I moved to the kitchen to begin dinner preparation and Rosie followed me, stopping to look at my whiteboard schedule.

"Wow," she said, again. This reaction was becoming predictable. I wondered what her response to DNA or evolution would be.

I commenced retrieval of vegetables and herbs from the refrigerator. "Let me help," she said. "I can chop or something." The implication was that chopping could be done by an inexperienced person unfamiliar with the recipe. After her comment that she was unable to cook even in a life-threatening situation, I had visions of huge chunks of leek and fragments of herbs too fine to sieve out.

"No assistance is required," I said. "I recommend reading a book."

I watched Rosie walk to the bookshelf, briefly peruse the contents, then walk away. Perhaps she used IBM rather than Mac software, although many of the manuals applied to both.

The sound system has an iPod port that I use to play podcasts while I cook. Rosie plugged in her phone, and music emanated from the speakers. It was not loud, but I was certain that if I had put on a podcast without asking permission when visiting someone's house, I would have been accused of a social error. *Very* certain, as I had made this exact mistake at a dinner party four years and sixty-seven days ago.

Rosie continued her exploration, like an animal in a new environment, which of course was what she was. She opened the blinds and raised them, creating some dust. I consider myself fastidious in my cleaning, but I do not need to open the blinds and there must have been dust in places not reachable without doing so. Behind the blinds are doors, and Rosie released the bolts and opened them.

I was feeling very uncomfortable at this violation of my personal environment. I tried to concentrate on food preparation as Rosie stepped out of sight onto the balcony. I could hear her dragging the two big pot plants, which presumably were dead after all these years. I put the herb and vegetable mixture in the large saucepan with the water, salt, rice wine vinegar, mirin, orange peel and coriander seeds.

"I don't know what you're cooking," Rosie called out, "but I'm basically vegetarian."

Vegetarian! I had already commenced cooking! Based on ingredients purchased on the assumption that I would be eating alone. And what did "basically" mean — did it imply some limited level of flexibility, like my colleague Esther, who admitted, only under rigorous questioning, that she would eat pork if necessary to survive?

Vegetarians and vegans can be incredibly annoying. Gene has a joke: "How can you tell if someone is a vegan? Just wait ten minutes and they'll tell you." If this were so, it would not be so much of a problem. No! Vegetarians arrive for dinner and then say, "I don't eat meat." *This was the second time.* The Pig's Trotter Disaster happened six years ago, when Gene suggested that I invite a woman to dinner at my apartment. He argued that my cooking expertise would make me more desirable and I would not have to deal with the pressure of a restaurant environment. "And you can drink as much as you like and stagger to the bedroom."

The woman's name was Bethany, and her internet profile did *not* mention vegetarianism. Realising that the quality of the meal would be critical, I borrowed a recently published book of "nose to tail" recipes from the library, and planned a multi-course meal featuring various parts of the animal: brains, tongue, mesentery, pancreas, kidneys, etc.

57

Bethany arrived on time and seemed very pleasant. We had a glass of wine, and then things went downhill. We started with fried pig's trotter, which had been quite complex to prepare, and Bethany ate very little of hers.

"I'm not big on pig's trotters," she said. This was not entirely unreasonable: we all have preferences and perhaps she was concerned about fat and cholesterol. But when I outlined the courses to follow, she declared herself to be a vegetarian. Unbelievable!

She offered to buy dinner at a restaurant but, having spent so much time in preparation, I did not want to abandon the food. I ate alone and did not see Bethany again.

Now Rosie. In this case it might be a good thing. Rosie could leave and life would return to normal. She had obviously not filled in the questionnaire honestly, or Gene had made an error. Or possibly he had selected her for her high level of sexual attractiveness, imposing his own preferences on me.

Rosie came back inside, looking at me, as if expecting a response. "Seafood is okay," she said. "If it's sustainable."

I had mixed feelings. It is always satisfying to have the solution to a problem, but now Rosie would be staying for dinner. I walked to the bathroom, and Rosie followed. I picked up the lobster from the bath, where it had been crawling around.

"Oh shit," said Rosie.

"You don't like lobster?" I carried it back to the kitchen.

"I love lobster but . . ."

The problem was now obvious and I could sympathise.

"You find the killing process unpleasant. Agreed."

I put the lobster in the freezer, and explained to Rosie that I had researched lobster-execution methods, and the freezer method was considered the most humane. I gave her a website reference.

While the lobster died, Rosie continued her sniffing around. She opened the pantry and seemed impressed with its level of organisation: one shelf for each day of the week, plus storage spaces for common resources, alcohol, breakfast, etc., and stock data on the back of the door.

"You want to come and sort out my place?"

"You want to implement the Standardised Meal System?" Despite its substantial advantages, most people consider it odd.

"Just cleaning out the refrigerator would do," she said. "I'm guessing you want Tuesday ingredients?"

I informed her that, as today was Tuesday, no guessing was required.

She handed me the nori sheets and bonito flakes. I requested macadamia nut oil, sea salt and the pepper grinder from the common resources area.

"Chinese rice wine," I added. "Filed under alcohol."

"Naturally," said Rosie.

She passed me the wine, then began looking at the other bottles in the alcohol section. I purchase my wine in half-bottles.

"So, you cook this same meal every Tuesday, right?"

"Correct." I listed the eight major advantages of the Standardised Meal System.

1. No need to accumulate recipe books.
2. Standard shopping list — hence very efficient shopping.
3. Almost zero waste — nothing in the refrigerator or pantry unless required for one of the recipes.
4. Diet planned and nutritionally balanced in advance.
5. No time wasted wondering what to cook.
6. No mistakes, no unpleasant surprises.
7. Excellent food, superior to most restaurants at a much lower price (see point 3).
8. Minimal cognitive load required.

"Cognitive load?"

"The cooking procedures are in my cerebellum — virtually no conscious effort is required."

"Like riding a bike."

"Correct."

"You can make lobster whatever without thinking?"

"Lobster, mango and avocado salad with wasabi-coated flying fish roe and crispy seaweed and deep-fried leek garnish. Correct. My current project is quail-boning. It still requires conscious effort."

Rosie was laughing. It brought back memories of school days. Good ones.

As I retrieved additional ingredients for the dressing from the refrigerator, Rosie brushed past me with two half-bottles of chablis and put them in the freezer with the lobster.

"Our dinner seems to have stopped moving."

"Further time is required to be certain of death," I said. "Unfortunately, the Jacket Incident has disrupted the preparation schedule. All times will need to be recalculated." I realised at this point that I should have put the lobster in the freezer as soon as we arrived home, but my brain had been overloaded by the problems created by Rosie's presence. I went to the whiteboard and started writing up revised preparation times. Rosie was examining the ingredients.

"You were going to eat all this by yourself?"

I had not revised the Standardised Meal System since Daphne's departure, and now ate the lobster salad by myself on Tuesdays, deleting the wine to compensate for the additional calorie intake.

"The quantity is sufficient for two," I said. "The recipe can't be scaled down. It's infeasible to purchase a fraction of a live lobster." I had intended the last part as a mild joke, and Rosie reacted by laughing. I had another unexpected moment of feeling good as I continued recalculating times.

Rosie interrupted again. "If you were on your usual schedule, what time would it be now?"

"6.38p.m."

The clock on the oven showed 9.09p.m. Rosie located the controls and started adjusting the time. I realised what she was doing. A perfect solution. When she was finished, it showed 6.38p.m. No recalculations required. I congratulated her on her thinking. "You've created a new time zone. Dinner will be ready at 8.55p.m. — Rosie time."

"Beats doing the maths," she said.

Her observation gave me an opportunity for another Wife Project question. "Do you find mathematics difficult?"

She laughed. "It's only the single hardest part of what I do. Drives me nuts."

If the simple arithmetic of bar and restaurant bills was beyond her, it was hard to imagine how we could have meaningful discussions.

"Where do you hide the corkscrew?" she asked.

"Wine is not scheduled for Tuesdays."

"Fuck that," said Rosie.

There was a certain logic underlying Rosie's response. I would only be eating a single serve of dinner. It was the final step in the abandonment of the evening's schedule.

I announced the change. "Time has been redefined. Previous rules no longer apply. Alcohol is hereby declared mandatory in the Rosie Time Zone."

CHAPTER
EIGHT

As I completed dinner preparation, Rosie set the table — not the conventional dining table in the living room, but a makeshift table on the balcony, created by taking a whiteboard from the kitchen wall and placing it on top of the two big plant pots, from which the dead plants had been removed. A white sheet from the linen cupboard had been added in the role of tablecloth. Silver cutlery — a housewarming gift from my parents that had never been used — and the decorative wine glasses were on the table. She was destroying my apartment!

It had never occurred to me to eat on the balcony. The rain from early in the evening had cleared when I came outside with the food, and I estimated the temperature at twenty-two degrees.

"Do we have to eat right away?" asked Rosie, an odd question, since she had claimed that she was starving some hours ago.

"No, it won't get cold. It's already cold." I was conscious of sounding awkward. "Is there some reason to delay?"

"The city lights. The view's amazing."

"Unfortunately it's static. Once you've examined it, there's no reason to look again. Like paintings."

"But it changes all the time. What about in the early morning? Or when it rains? What about coming up here just to sit?"

I had no answer that was likely to satisfy her. I had seen the view when I bought the apartment. It did not change much in different conditions. And the only times I just sat were when I was waiting for an appointment or if I was reflecting on a problem, in which case interesting surroundings would be a distraction.

I moved into the space beside Rosie and refilled her glass. She smiled. She was almost certainly wearing lipstick.

I attempt to produce a standard, repeatable meal, but obviously ingredients vary in their quality from week to week. Today's seemed to be of unusually high standard. The lobster salad had never tasted so good.

I remembered the basic rule of asking a woman to talk about herself. Rosie had already raised the topic of dealing with difficult customers in a bar, so I asked her to elaborate. This was an excellent move. She had a number of hilarious stories, and I noted some interpersonal techniques for possible future use.

We finished the lobster. Then Rosie opened her bag and pulled out a pack of cigarettes! How can I convey my horror? Smoking is not only unhealthy in itself, and dangerous to others in the vicinity. It is a clear indication of an irrational approach to life. There was a good reason for it being the first item on my questionnaire.

Rosie must have noticed my shock. "Relax. We're outside."

There was no point in arguing. I would not be seeing her again after tonight. The lighter flamed and she held it to the cigarette between her artificially red lips.

"Anyhow, I've got a genetics question," she said.

"Proceed." I was back in the world I knew.

"Someone told me you can tell if a person's monogamous by the size of their testicles."

The sexual aspects of biology regularly feature in the popular press, so this was not as stupid a statement as it might appear, although it embodied a typical misconception. It occurred to me that it could be some sort of code for a sexual advance, but I decided to play safe and respond to the question literally.

"Ridiculous," I said.

Rosie seemed very pleased with my answer.

"You're a star," she said. "I've just won a bet."

I proceeded to elaborate and noted that Rosie's expression of satisfaction faded. I guessed that she had oversimplified her question and that my more detailed explanation was in fact what she had been told.

"There may be some correlation at the individual level, but the rule applies to species. Homo sapiens are basically monogamous, but tactically unfaithful. Males benefit from impregnating as many females as possible, but are able to support only one set of offspring. Females seek maximum-quality genes for their children plus a male to support them."

I was just settling into the familiar role of lecturer when Rosie interrupted.

"What about the testicles?"

"Bigger testicles produce more semen. Monogamous species require only sufficient for their mate. Humans need extra to take advantage of random opportunities and to attack the sperm of recent intruders."

"Nice," said Rosie.

"Not really. The behaviour evolved in the ancestral environment. The modern world requires additional rules."

"Yeah," said Rosie. "Like being there for your kids."

"Correct. But instincts are incredibly powerful."

"Tell me about it," said Rosie.

I began to explain. "Instinct is an expression of —"

"Rhetorical question," said Rosie. "I've lived it. My mother went gene shopping at her medical graduation party."

"These behaviours are unconscious. People don't deliberately —"

"I get that."

I doubted it. Non-professionals frequently misinterpret the findings of evolutionary psychology. But the story was interesting.

"You're saying your mother engaged in unprotected sex outside her primary relationship?"

"With some other student," replied Rosie. "While she was dating my" — at this point Rosie raised her hands and made a downwards movement, twice, with the index and middle fingers of both hands — "father.

My real dad's a doctor. I just don't know which one. Really, really pisses me off."

I was fascinated by the hand movements and silent for a while as I tried to work them out. Were they a sign of distress at not knowing who her father was? If so, it was not one I was familiar with. And why had she chosen to punctuate her speech at that point . . . of course! Punctuation!

"Quotation marks," I said aloud as the idea hit me.

"What?"

"You made quotation marks around 'father' to draw attention to the fact that the word should not be interpreted in the usual way. Very clever."

"Well, there you go," she said. "And there I was thinking you were reflecting on my minor problem with my whole fucking life. And might have something intelligent to say."

I corrected her. "It's not a minor problem at all!" I pointed my finger in the air to indicate an exclamation mark. "You should insist on being informed." I stabbed the same finger to indicate a full stop. This was quite fun.

"My mother's dead. She died in a car accident when I was ten. She never told anyone who my father was — not even Phil."

"Phil?" I couldn't think of how to indicate a question mark, and decided to drop the game temporarily. This was no time for experimentation.

"My" — hands up, fingers wiggled — "father. Who'd go apeshit if I told him I wanted to know."

Rosie drank the remaining wine in her glass and refilled it. The second half-bottle was now empty. Her story was sad, but not uncommon. Although my parents continued to make routine, ritual contact, it was my assessment that they had lost interest in me some years ago. Their duty had been completed when I was able to support myself. Her situation was somewhat different, however, as it involved a stepfather. I offered a genetic interpretation.

"His behaviour is completely predictable. You don't have his genes. Male lions kill the cubs from previous matings when they take over a pride."

"Thanks for that information."

"I can recommend some further reading if you are interested. You seem quite intelligent for a barmaid."

"The compliments just keep on coming."

It seemed I was doing well, and I allowed myself a moment of satisfaction, which I shared with Rosie.

"Excellent. I'm not proficient at dating. There are so many rules to remember."

"You're doing okay," she said. "Except for staring at my boobs."

This was disappointing feedback. Rosie's dress was quite revealing, but I had been working hard to maintain eye contact.

"I was just examining your pendant," I said. "It's extremely interesting."

Rosie immediately covered it with her hand. "What's on it?"

"An image of Isis with an inscription: *Sum omnia quae fuerunt suntque eruntque ego.* 'I am all that has been, is and will be.'" I hoped I had read the Latin correctly; the writing was very small.

Rosie seemed impressed. "What about the pendant I had on this morning?"

"Dagger with three small red stones and four white ones."

Rosie finished her wine. She seemed to be thinking about something. It turned out not to be anything profound.

"Want to get another bottle?"

I was a little stunned. We had already drunk the recommended maximum amount. On the other hand, she smoked, so obviously she had a careless attitude to health.

"You want more alcohol?"

"Correct," she said, in an odd voice. She may have been mimicking me.

I went to the kitchen to select another bottle, deciding to reduce the next day's alcohol intake to compensate. Then I saw the clock: 11.40p.m. I picked up the phone and ordered a taxi. With any luck it would arrive before the after-midnight tariff commenced. I opened a half-bottle of shiraz to drink while we waited.

Rosie wanted to continue the conversation about her biological father.

"Do you think there might be some sort of genetic motivation? That it's built into us to want to know who our parents are?"

"It's critical for parents to be able to recognise their own children. So they can protect the carriers of their genes. Small children need to be able to locate their parents to get that protection."

"Maybe it's some sort of carry-over from that."

"It seems unlikely. But possible. Our behaviour is strongly affected by instinct."

"So you said. Whatever it is, it eats me up. Messes with my head."

"Why don't you ask the candidates?"

"'Dear Doctor. Are you my father?' I don't think so."

An obvious thought occurred to me, obvious because I am a geneticist.

"Your hair is a very unusual colour. Possibly —"

She laughed. "There aren't any genes for this shade of red."

She must have seen that I was confused.

"This colour only comes out of a bottle."

I realised what she was saying. She had deliberately dyed her hair an unnaturally bright colour. Incredible. It hadn't even occurred to me to include hair dyeing on the questionnaire. I made a mental note to do so.

The doorbell buzzed. I had not mentioned the taxi to her, so brought her up to date with my plan. She quickly finished her wine, then stuck her hand out and it seemed to me that I was not the only one feeling awkward.

"Well," she said, "it's been an evening. Have a good life."

It was a non-standard way of saying goodnight. I thought it safer to stick with convention.

"Goodnight. I've really enjoyed this evening." I added, "Good luck finding your father" to the formula.

"Thanks."

Then she left.

I was agitated, but not in a bad way. It was more a case of sensory overload. I was pleased to find some wine left in the bottle. I poured it into my glass and phoned Gene. Claudia answered and I dispensed with pleasantries.

"I need to speak with Gene."

"He's not home," said Claudia. She sounded disoriented. Perhaps she had been drinking. "I thought he was having lobster with you."

"Gene sent me the world's most incompatible woman. A barmaid. Late, vegetarian, disorganised, irrational, unhealthy, smoker — smoker! — psychological problems, can't cook, mathematically incompetent, unnatural hair colour. I presume he was making a joke."

Claudia must have interpreted this as a statement of distress because she said, "Are you all right, Don?"

"Of course," I said. "She was highly entertaining. But totally unsuitable for the Wife Project." As I said these words, indisputably factual, I felt a twinge of regret at odds with my intellectual assessment. Claudia interrupted my attempt to reconcile the conflicting brain states.

"Don, do you know what time it is?"

I wasn't wearing a watch. And then I realised my error. I had used the kitchen clock as my reference when phoning the taxi. The clock that Rosie had reset. It must have been almost 2.30a.m. How could I have lost track of time like that? It was a severe lesson in the dangers of messing with the schedule. Rosie would be paying the after-midnight tariff in the taxi.

I let Claudia return to sleep. As I picked up the two plates and two glasses to bring them inside, I looked again at the night-time view of the city — the view I had never seen before even though it had been there all the time.

I decided to skip my pre-bed aikido routine. And to leave the makeshift table in place.

CHAPTER
NINE

"I threw her in as a wild card," said Gene when I woke him up from the unscheduled sleep he was taking under his desk the next day.

Gene looked terrible and I told him he should refrain from staying up so late — although for once I had been guilty of the same error. It was important that he eat lunch at the correct time to get his circadian rhythm back on schedule. He had a packed lunch from home, and we headed for a grassy area in the university grounds. I collected seaweed salad, miso soup and an apple from the Japanese café on the way.

It was a fine day. Unfortunately this meant that there were a number of females in brief clothing sitting on the grass and walking by to distract Gene. Gene is fifty-six years old, although that information is not supposed to be disclosed. At that age, his testosterone should have fallen to a level where his sex drive was significantly reduced. It is my theory that his unusually high focus on sex is due to mental habit. But human physiology varies, and he may be an exception.

Conversely, I think Gene believes I have an abnormally low sex drive. This is not true — rather I am not as skilled as Gene in expressing it in a socially appropriate way. My occasional attempts to imitate Gene have been unsuccessful in the extreme.

We found a bench to sit on and Gene commenced his explanation.

"She's someone I know," he said.

"No questionnaire?"

"No questionnaire."

This explained the smoking. In fact, it explained everything. Gene had reverted to the inefficient practice of recommending acquaintances for dates. My expression must have conveyed my annoyance.

"You're wasting your time with the questionnaire. You'd be better off measuring the length of their earlobes."

Sexual attraction is Gene's area of expertise. "There's a correlation?" I asked.

"People with long earlobes are more likely to choose partners with long earlobes. It's a better predictor than IQ."

This was incredible, but much behaviour that developed in the ancestral environment seems incredible when considered in the context of the current world. Evolution has not kept up. But earlobes! Could there be a more irrational basis for a relationship? No wonder marriages fail.

"So, did you have fun?" asked Gene.

I informed him that his question was irrelevant: my goal was to find a partner and Rosie was patently unsuitable. Gene had caused me to waste an evening.

"But did you have fun?" he repeated.

Did he expect a different answer to the same question? To be fair, I had not given him a proper answer, but for a good reason. I had not had time to reflect on the evening and determine a proper response. I guessed that "fun" was going to be an over-simplification of a very complex experience.

I provided Gene with a summary of events. As I related the story of the dinner on the balcony, Gene interrupted. "If you see her again —"

"There is zero reason for me to see her again."

"If you see her again," Gene continued, "it's probably not a good idea to mention the Wife Project. Since she didn't measure up."

Ignoring the incorrect assumption about seeing Rosie again, this seemed like good advice.

At that point, the conversation changed direction dramatically, and I did not have an opportunity to find out how Gene had met Rosie. The reason for the change was Gene's sandwich. He took a bite, then called out in pain and snatched my water bottle.

"Oh shit. Oh shit. Claudia put chillies in my sandwich."

It was difficult to see how Claudia could make an error of this kind. But the priority was to reduce the pain. Chilli is insoluble in water, so drinking from my bottle would not be effective. I advised him to find some oil. We headed back to the Japanese café, and were not able to have any further conversation about Rosie. However, I had the basic information I needed. Gene had selected a woman without reference to the questionnaire. To see her again would be in total contradiction to the rationale for the Wife Project.

Riding home, I reconsidered. I could see three reasons that it might be necessary to see Rosie again.

1. Good experimental design requires the use of a control group. It would be interesting to use Rosie as a benchmark to compare with women selected by the questionnaire.
2. The questionnaire had not produced any matches to date. I could interact with Rosie in the meantime.
3. As a geneticist with access to DNA analysis, and the knowledge to interpret it, I was in a position to help Rosie find her biological father.

Reasons 1 and 2 were invalid. Rosie was clearly not a suitable life partner. There was no point in interaction with someone so patently inappropriate. But Reason 3 deserved consideration. Using my skills to assist her in a search for important knowledge aligned with my life purpose. I could do it in the time set aside for the Wife Project until a suitable candidate emerged.

In order to proceed, I needed to re-establish contact with Rosie. I did not want to tell Gene that I planned to see her again so soon after telling him that the probability of my doing so was zero. Fortunately, I recalled the name of the bar she worked at: the Marquess of Queensbury.

There was only one bar of that name, in a back street of an inner suburb. I had already modified the day's schedule, cancelling my market trip to catch up on the lost sleep. I would purchase a ready-made dinner instead. I am sometimes accused of being inflexible, but I think this demonstrates an ability to adapt to even the strangest of circumstances.

I arrived at 7.04p.m. only to find that the bar did not open until 9.00p.m. *Incredible*. No wonder people make mistakes at work. Would it be full of surgeons and flight controllers, drinking until after midnight then working the next day?

I ate dinner at a nearby Indian restaurant. By the time I had worked my way through the banquet, and returned to the bar, it was 9.27p.m. There was a security official at the door, and I prepared myself for a repeat of the previous night. He examined me carefully, then asked, "Do you know what sort of place this is?"

I am quite familiar with bars, perhaps even more familiar than most people. When I travel to conferences, I generally find a pleasant bar near my hotel and eat and drink there every evening. I replied in the affirmative and entered.

I wondered if I had come to the right location. The most obvious characteristic of Rosie was that she was female, and the patrons at the Marquess of Queensbury were without exception male. Many were wearing unusual costumes, and I took a few minutes to examine the range. Two men noted me looking at them and one smiled broadly and nodded. I smiled back. It seemed to be a friendly place.

77

But I was there to find Rosie. I walked to the bar. The two men followed and sat on either side of me. The clean-shaven one was wearing a cut-off t-shirt and clearly spent time at the gym. Steroids could also have been involved. The one with the moustache wore a leather costume and a black cap.

"I haven't seen you here before," said Black Cap.

I gave him the simple explanation. "I haven't been here before."

"Can I buy you a drink?"

"You're offering to buy my drink?" It was an unusual proposition from a stranger, and I guessed that I would be expected to reciprocate in some way.

"I think that's what I said," said Black Cap. "What can we tempt you with?"

I told him that the flavour didn't matter, as long as it contained alcohol. As in most social situations, I was nervous.

Then Rosie appeared from the other side of the bar, dressed conventionally for her role in a collared black shirt. I was hugely relieved. I had come to the correct place and she was on duty. Black Cap waved to her. He ordered three Budweisers. Then Rosie saw me.

"Don."

"Greetings."

Rosie looked at us and asked, "Are you guys together?"

"Give us a few minutes," said Steroid Man.

Rosie said, "I think Don's here to see me."

"Correct."

"Well, pardon us interrupting your social life with drinks orders," Black Cap said to Rosie.

"You could use DNA," I said.

Rosie clearly didn't follow, due to lack of context. "What?"

"To identify your father. DNA is the obvious approach."

"Sure," said Rosie. "Obvious. 'Please send me your DNA so I can see if you're my father.' Forget it, I was just mouthing off."

"You could collect it." I wasn't sure how Rosie would respond to the next part of my suggestion. "Surreptitiously."

Rosie went silent. She was at least considering the idea. Or perhaps wondering whether to report me. Her response supported the first possibility. "And who's going to analyse it?"

"I'm a geneticist."

"You're saying if I got a sample, you could analyse it for me?"

"Trivial," I said. "How many samples do we need to test?"

"Probably only one. I've got a pretty good idea. He's a family friend."

Steroid Man coughed loudly, and Rosie fetched two beers from the refrigerator. Black Cap put a twenty-dollar note on the counter, but Rosie pushed it back and waved them away.

I tried the cough trick myself. Rosie took a moment to interpret the message this time, but then got me a beer.

"What do you need?" she asked. "To test the DNA?"

I explained that normally we would use scrapings from the inner cheek, but that it would be impractical to obtain these without the subject's knowledge. "Blood is excellent, but skin scrapings, mucus, urine —"

"Pass," said Rosie.

"— faecal material, semen —"

"It keeps getting better," said Rosie. "I can screw a sixty-year-old family friend in the hope that he turns out to be my father."

I was shocked. "You'd have sex —"

Rosie explained that she was making a joke. On such a serious matter! It was getting busy around the bar, and there were a lot of cough signals happening. An effective way to spread disease. Rosie wrote a telephone number on a piece of paper.

"Call me."

CHAPTER
TEN

The next morning, I returned with some relief to the routine that had been so severely disrupted over the past two days. My Tuesday, Thursday and Saturday runs to the market are a feature of my schedule, combining exercise, meal-ingredients purchase and an opportunity for reflection. I was in great need of the last of these.

A woman had given me her phone number and told me to call her. More than the Jacket Incident, the Balcony Meal and even the excitement of the potential Father Project, this had disrupted my world. I knew that it happened regularly: people in books, films and TV shows do exactly what Rosie had done. But it had never happened to me. No woman had ever casually, unthinkingly, automatically, written down her phone number, given it to me and said, "Call me." I had temporarily been included in a culture that I considered closed to me. Although it was entirely logical that Rosie should provide me with a means of contacting her, I had an irrational feeling that, when I called, Rosie would realise she had made some kind of error.

I arrived at the market and commenced purchasing. Because each day's ingredients are standard, I know which stalls to visit, and the vendors generally have my items pre-packaged in advance. I need only pay. The vendors know me well and are consistently friendly.

However, it is not possible to time-share major intellectual activity with the purchasing process, due to the quantity of human and inanimate obstacles: vegetable pieces on the ground, old ladies with shopping buggies, vendors still setting up stalls, Asian women comparing prices, goods being delivered and tourists taking photos of each other in front of the produce. Fortunately I am usually the only jogger.

On the way home, I resumed my analysis of the Rosie situation. I realised that my actions had been driven more by instinct than logic. There were plenty of people in need of help, many in more distress than Rosie, and numerous worthy scientific projects that would represent better use of my time than a quest to find one individual's father. And, of course, I should be giving priority to the Wife Project. Better to push Gene to select more suitable women from the list, or to relax some of the less important selection criteria, as I had already done with the no-drinking rule.

The logical decision was to contact Rosie and explain that the Father Project was not a good idea. I phoned at 6.43 a.m. on returning from the run and left a message for her to call back. When I hung up, I was sweating despite the fact that the morning was still cool. I hoped I wasn't developing a fever.

Rosie called back while I was delivering a lecture. Normally, I turn my phone off at such times, but I was anxious to put this problem to bed. I was feeling stressed at the prospect of an interaction in which it was necessary for me to retract an offer. Speaking on the phone in front of a lecture theatre full of students was awkward, especially as I was wearing a lapel microphone.

They could hear my side of the conversation.

"Hi, Rosie."

"Don, I just want to say thanks for doing this thing for me. I didn't realise how much it had been eating me up. Do you know that little coffee shop across from the Commerce Building — Barista's? How about two o'clock tomorrow?"

Now that Rosie had accepted my offer of help, it would have been immoral, and technically a breach of contract, to withdraw it.

"Barista's 2.00p.m. tomorrow," I confirmed, though I was temporarily unable to access the schedule in my brain due to overload.

"You're a star," she said.

Her tone indicated that this was the end of her contribution to the conversation. It was my turn to use a standard platitude to reciprocate, and the obvious one was the simple reflection of "You're a star". But even I realised that made no sense. She was the beneficiary of my star-ness in the form of my genetics expertise. On reflection, I could have just said "Goodbye" or "See you", but I had no time for reflection. There was considerable pressure to make a timely response.

"I like you too."

The entire lecture theatre exploded in applause.

A female student in the front row said, "Smooth." She was smiling.

Fortunately I am accustomed to creating amusement inadvertently.

I did not feel too unhappy at failing to terminate the Father Project. The amount of work involved in one DNA test was trivial.

We met at Barista's the next day at 2.07p.m. Needless to say, the delay was Rosie's fault. My students would be sitting in their 2.15p.m. lecture waiting for my arrival. My intention had been only to advise her on the collection of a DNA sample, but she seemed unable to process the instructions. In retrospect, I was probably offering too many options and too much technical detail too rapidly. With only seven minutes to discuss the problem (allowing one minute for running to the lecture), we agreed that the simplest solution was to collect the sample together.

We arrived at the residence of Dr Eamonn Hughes, the suspected father, on the Saturday afternoon. Rosie had telephoned in advance.

Eamonn looked older than I had expected. I guessed sixty, BMI twenty-three. Eamonn's wife, whose name was Belinda (approximately fifty-five, BMI twenty-eight), made us coffee, as predicted by Rosie. This was critical, as we had decided that the coffee-cup rim would be an ideal source of saliva. I sat beside Rosie, pretending to be her friend. Eamonn and Belinda were

84

opposite, and I was finding it hard to keep my eyes away from Eamonn's cup.

Fortunately, I was not required to make small talk. Eamonn was a cardiologist and we had a fascinating discussion about genetic markers for cardiac disease. Eamonn finally finished his coffee and Rosie stood up to take the cups to the kitchen. There, she would be able to swab the lip of the cup and we would have an excellent sample. When we discussed the plan, I suggested that this would be a breach of social convention, but Rosie assured me that she knew Eamonn and Belinda well as family friends, and, as a younger person, she would be allowed to perform this chore. For once, my understanding of social convention proved more accurate. Unfortunately.

As Rosie picked up Belinda's cup, Belinda said, "Leave it, I'll do it later."

Rosie responded, "No, please," and took Eamonn's cup.

Belinda picked up my cup and Rosie's and said, "Okay, give me a hand." They walked out to the kitchen together. It was obviously going to be difficult for Rosie to swab Eamonn's cup with Belinda present, but I could not think of a way of getting Belinda out of the kitchen.

"Did Rosie tell you I studied medicine with her mother?" asked Eamonn.

I nodded. Had I been a psychologist, I might have been able to infer from Eamonn's conversation and body language whether he was hiding the fact that he was Rosie's father. I might even have been able to lead the conversation in a direction to trap him. Fortunately we were not relying on my skills in this arena. If Rosie succeeded in collecting the sample, I would be able to provide a far more reliable answer than one derived from observations of behaviour.

"If I can offer you a little encouragement," Eamonn said, "Rosie's mother was a bit wild in her younger days. Very smart, good-looking, she could have had anyone. All the other women in medicine were going to marry doctors." He smiled. "But she surprised us all and picked the guy from left field who persisted and stuck around."

It was lucky I wasn't looking for clues. My expression must have conveyed my total lack of comprehension.

"I suspect Rosie may follow in her mother's footsteps," he said.

"In what component of her life?" It seemed safer to seek clarification than assume that he meant getting pregnant to an unknown fellow student or dying. These were the only facts I knew about Rosie's mother.

"I'm just saying I think you're probably good for her. And she's had a rough time. Tell me to mind my own business if you like. But she's a great kid."

Now the intent of the conversation was clear, although Rosie was surely too old to be referred to as a kid. Eamonn thought I was Rosie's boyfriend. It was an understandable error. Correcting it would necessarily involve telling a lie, so I decided to remain silent. Then we heard the sound of breaking crockery.

Eamonn called out, "Everything okay?"

"Just broke a cup," said Belinda.

Breaking the cup was not part of the plan. Presumably, Rosie had dropped it in her nervousness or in trying to keep it from Belinda. I was annoyed at myself for not having a back-up plan. I had not treated this project as serious field work. It was embarrassingly unprofessional, and it was now my responsibility to find a solution. It would surely involve deception, and I am not skilled at deception.

My best approach was to source the DNA for a legitimate reason.

"Have you heard about the Genographic Project?"

"No," said Eamonn.

I explained that with a sample of his DNA we could trace his distant ancestry. He was fascinated. I offered to have his DNA processed if he organised a cheek scraping and sent it to me.

"Let's do it now, before I forget," he said. "Will blood do?"

"Blood is ideal for DNA testing, but —"

"I'm a doctor," he said. "Give me a minute."

Eamonn left the room, and I could hear Belinda and Rosie speaking in the kitchen.

Belinda said, "Seen your father at all?"

"Next question," said Rosie.

Belinda instead responded with a statement. "Don seems nice."

Excellent. I was doing well.

"Just a friend," said Rosie.

If she knew how many friends I had, she might have realised what a great compliment she had paid me.

"Oh well," said Belinda.

Rosie and Belinda returned to the living room at the same time as Eamonn with his doctor's bag. Belinda reasonably deduced that there was some medical problem, but Eamonn explained about the Genographic Project. Belinda was a nurse and she took the blood with professional expertise.

As I handed the filled tube to Rosie to put in her handbag, I noticed her hands were shaking. I diagnosed anxiety, presumably related to the imminent confirmation of her paternity. I was not surprised when she asked, only seconds after leaving the Hughes's residence, if we could process the DNA sample immediately. It would require opening the lab on a Saturday evening but at least the project would be completed.

The laboratory was empty: throughout the university, the archaic idea of working Monday to Friday results in an incredible under-utilisation of expensive facilities. The university was trialling analysis equipment that could test for parent-child relationships very quickly. And we had an ideal DNA sample. It is possible to extract DNA from a wide variety of sources and only a few cells are needed for an analysis, but the preparatory work can be time consuming and complex. Blood was easy.

The new machine was located in a small room that had once been a tea-room with sink and refrigerator. For a moment I wished it had been more impressive — an unusual intrusion of ego into my thoughts. I unlocked the refrigerator and opened a beer. Rosie coughed loudly. I recognised the code and opened one for her also.

I tried to explain the process to Rosie as I set up, but she seemed unable to stop talking, even as she used the scraper on her inner cheek to provide me with her DNA sample.

"I can't believe it's this easy. This quick. I think I've always known at some level. He used to bring me stuff when I was a kid."

"It's a vastly over-specified machine for such a trivial task."

"One time he brought me a chess set. Phil gave me girly stuff — jewellery boxes and shit. Pretty weird for a personal trainer when you think about it."

"You play chess?" I asked.

"Not really. That's not the point. He respected that I have a brain. He and Belinda never had any kids of their own. I have a sense that he was always around. He might even have been my mum's best friend. But I've never consciously thought of him as my father."

"He's not," I said.

The result had come up on the computer screen. Job complete. I began packing up.

"Wow," said Rosie. "Ever thought of being a grief counsellor?"

"No. I considered a number of careers, but all in the sciences. My interpersonal skills are not strong."

Rosie burst out laughing. "You're about to get a crash course in advanced grief counselling."

It turned out that Rosie was making a sort of joke, as her approach to grief counselling was based entirely on the administration of alcohol. We went to Jimmy Watson's on Lygon Street, a short walk away, and as usual, even on a weekend, it was full of academics. We sat at the bar, and I was surprised to find that Rosie, a professional server of drinks, had a very poor knowledge of wine. A few years ago Gene suggested that wine was the perfect topic for safe conversation and I did some research. I was familiar with the backgrounds of the wines offered regularly at this bar. We drank quite a lot.

Rosie had to go outside for a few minutes due to her nicotine addiction. The timing was fortunate, as a couple emerged from the courtyard and passed the bar. The man was Gene! The woman was not Claudia, but I recognised her. It was Olivia, the Indian Vegetarian from Table for Eight. Neither saw me, and they went past too quickly for me to say anything.

My confusion at seeing them together must have contributed to my next decision. A waiter came up to me and said, "There's a table for two that's just come free in the courtyard. Are you eating with us?"

I nodded. I would have to freeze the day's market purchases for the following Saturday, with the resulting loss of nutrients. Instinct had again displaced logic.

Rosie's reaction to finding a table being set for us on her return appeared to be positive. Doubtless she was hungry but it was reassuring to know that I had not committed a faux pas, always more likely when different genders are involved.

The food was excellent. We had freshly shucked oysters (sustainable), tuna sashimi (selected by Rosie and probably not sustainable), eggplant and mozzarella stack (Rosie), veal sweetbreads (me), cheese (shared) and a single serving of passionfruit mousse (divided and shared). I ordered a bottle of Marsanne and it was an excellent accompaniment.

Rosie spent much of the meal trying to explain why she wanted to locate her biological father. I could see little reason for it. In the past, the knowledge might have been useful to determine the risk of genetically influenced diseases, but today Rosie could have her own DNA analysed directly. Practically, her stepfather Phil seemed to have executed the father role, although Rosie had numerous complaints about his performance. He was an egotist; he was inconsistent in his attitude towards her; he was subject to mood swings. He was also strongly opposed to alcohol. I considered this to be a thoroughly defensible position, but it was a cause of friction between them.

Rosie's motivation seemed to be emotional, and, while I could not understand the psychology, it was clearly very important to her happiness.

After Rosie had finished her mousse, she left the table to "go to the bathroom". It gave me time to reflect and I realised that I was in the process of completing a non-eventful and in fact highly enjoyable dinner with a woman, a significant achievement that I was looking forward to sharing with Gene and Claudia.

I concluded that the lack of problems was due to three factors.

1. I was in a familiar restaurant. It had never occurred to me to take a woman — or indeed anyone — to Jimmy Watson's, which I had only previously used as a source of wine.

2. Rosie was not a date. I had rejected her, comprehensively, as a potential partner, and we were together because of a joint project. It was like a meeting.

3. I was somewhat intoxicated — hence relaxed. As a result, I may also have been unaware of any social errors.

At the end of the meal, I ordered two glasses of sambuca and said, "Who do we test next?"

CHAPTER
ELEVEN

Besides Eamonn Hughes, Rosie knew of only two other "family friends" from her mother's medical graduation class. It struck me as unlikely that someone who had illicit sex with her mother would remain in contact, given the presence of Phil. But there was an evolutionary argument that he would wish to ensure that the carrier of his genes was receiving proper care. Essentially this was Rosie's argument also.

The first candidate was Dr Peter Enticott, who lived locally. The other, Alan McPhee, had died from prostate cancer, which was good news for Rosie, as, lacking a prostate gland, she could not inherit it. Apparently he had been an oncologist, but had not detected the cancer in himself, a not-uncommon scenario. Humans often fail to see what is close to them and obvious to others.

Fortunately, he had a daughter, with whom Rosie had socialised when she was younger. Rosie arranged a meeting with Natalie in three days' time, ostensibly to view Natalie's newborn baby.

I reverted to the normal schedule, but the Father Project kept intruding into my thoughts. I prepared for the DNA collection — I did not want a repeat of the broken cup problem. I also had another altercation with the Dean, as a result of the Flounder Incident.

One of my tasks is to teach genetics to medical students. In the first class of the previous semester, a student, who did not identify himself, had raised his hand shortly after I showed my first slide. The slide is a brilliant and beautiful diagrammatic summary of evolution from single-cell organisms to today's incredible variety of life. Only my colleagues in the Physics Department can match the extraordinary story that it tells. I cannot comprehend why some people are more interested in the outcome of a football match or the weight of an actress.

This student belonged to another category.

"Professor Tillman, you used the word 'evolved'."

"Correct."

"I think you should point out that evolution is just a theory."

This was not the first time I had received a question — or statement — of this kind. I knew from experience that I would not sway the student's views, which would inevitably be based on religious dogma. I could only ensure that the student was not taken seriously by other trainee doctors.

"Correct," I replied, "but your use of the word 'just' is misleading. Evolution is a theory supported by overwhelming evidence. Like the germ theory of disease, for example. As a doctor, you will be expected to rely on science. Unless you want to be a faith healer. In which case you are on the wrong course."

There was some laughter. Faith Healer objected.

"I'm not talking about faith. I'm talking about creation *science*."

There were only a few moans from the class. No doubt many of the students were from cultures where criticism of religion is not well tolerated. Such as ours. I had been forbidden to comment on religion after an earlier incident. But we were discussing science. I could have continued the argument, but I knew better than to be sidetracked by a student. My lectures are precisely timed to fit within fifty minutes.

"Evolution is a theory," I said. "There is no other theory of the origins of life with wide acceptance by scientists, or of any utility to medicine. Hence we will assume it in this class." I believed I had handled the situation well, but I was annoyed that time had been insufficient to argue the case against the pseudo-science of creationism.

Some weeks later, eating in the University Club, I found a means of making the point succinctly. As I walked to the bar, I noticed one of the members eating a flounder, with its head still in place. After a slightly awkward conversation, I obtained the head and skeleton, which I wrapped and stored in my backpack.

Four days later, I had the class. I located Faith Healer, and asked him a preliminary question. "Do you believe that fish were created in their current forms by an intelligent designer?"

He seemed surprised at the question, perhaps because it had been seven weeks since we had suspended the discussion. But he nodded in agreement.

I unwrapped the flounder. It had acquired a strong smell, but medical students should be prepared to deal with unpleasant organic objects in the interests of learning. I indicated the head: "Observe that the eyes are not symmetrical." In fact the eyes had decomposed, but the location of the eye sockets was quite clear. "This is because the flounder evolved from a conventional fish with eyes on opposite sides of the head. One eye slowly migrated around, but just far enough to function effectively. Evolution did not bother to tidy up. But surely an intelligent designer would not have created a fish with this imperfection." I gave Faith Healer the fish to enable him to examine it and continued the lecture.

He waited until the beginning of the new teaching year to lodge his complaint.

In my discussion with the Dean, she implied that I had tried to humiliate Faith Healer, whereas my intent had been to advance an argument. Since he had used the term "creation *science*", with no mention of religion, I made the case that I was not guilty of denigrating religion. I was merely contrasting one theory with another. He was welcome to bring counter-examples to class.

"Don," she said, "as usual you haven't technically broken any rules. But — how can I put it? — if someone told me that a lecturer had brought a dead fish to class and given it to a student who had made a statement of religious faith, I would guess that the lecturer was you. Do you understand where I'm coming from?"

"You're saying that I am the person in the faculty most likely to act unconventionally. And you want me to act more conventionally. That seems an unreasonable request to make of a scientist."

"I just don't want you to upset people."

"Being upset and complaining because your theory is disproven is unscientific."

The argument ended, once again, with the Dean being unhappy with me, though I had not broken any rules, and me being reminded that I needed to try harder to "fit in". As I left her office, her personal assistant, Regina, stopped me.

"I don't think I have you down for the faculty ball yet, Professor Tillman. I think you're the only professor who hasn't bought tickets."

Riding home, I was aware of a tightness in my chest and realised it was a physical response to the Dean's advice. I knew that, if I could not "fit in" in a science department of a university, I could not fit in anywhere.

Natalie McPhee, daughter of the late Dr Alan McPhee, potential biological father of Rosie, lived eighteen kilometres from the city, within riding distance, but Rosie decided we should travel by car. I was amazed to find that she drove a red Porsche convertible.

"It's Phil's."

"Your 'father's'?" I did the air quotes.

"Yeah, he's in Thailand."

"I thought he didn't like you. But he lent you his car?"

"That's the sort of thing he does. No love, just stuff."

The Porsche would be the perfect vehicle to lend to someone you did not like. It was seventeen years old (thus using old emissions technology), had appalling fuel economy, little leg room, high wind noise and a non-functioning air-conditioning system. Rosie confirmed my guess that it was unreliable and expensive to maintain.

As we arrived at Natalie's, I realised I had spent the entire journey listing and elaborating on the deficiencies of the vehicle. I had avoided small talk, but had not briefed Rosie on the DNA collection method.

"Your task is to occupy her in conversation while I collect DNA." This would make best use of our respective skills.

It soon became clear that my back-up plan would be necessary. Natalie did not want to drink: she was abstaining from alcohol while breastfeeding her baby, and it was too late for coffee. These were responsible choices, but we would not be able to swab a cup or glass.

I deployed Plan B.

"Can I see the baby?"

"He's asleep," she said, "so you'll have to be quiet."

I stood up and so did she.

"Just tell me where to go," I said.

"I'll come with you."

The more I insisted that I wanted to see the baby alone, the more she objected. We went to its room and, as she had predicted, it was sleeping. This was very annoying, as I had a number of plans that involved collecting DNA in a totally non-invasive way from the baby, who was, of course, also related to Alan McPhee. Unfortunately I had not factored in the mother's protective instinct. Every time I found a reason to leave the room, Natalie followed me. It was very awkward.

Finally, Rosie excused herself to go to the bathroom. Even if she had known what to do, she could not have visited the baby, as Natalie had positioned herself so that she could see the bedroom door and was checking frequently.

"Have you heard about the Genographic Project?" I asked.

She hadn't and was not interested. She changed the topic.

"You seem very interested in babies."

There was surely an opportunity here if I could find a way to exploit it. "I'm interested in their behaviour. Without the corrupting influence of a parent present."

She looked at me strangely. "Do you do any stuff with kids? I mean Scouts, church groups . . ."

"No," I said. "It's unlikely that I'd be suitable."

Rosie returned and the baby started crying.

"Feeding time," said Natalie.

"We should be going," said Rosie.

Failure! Social skills had been the problem. With good social skills I could surely have got to the baby.

"I'm sorry," I said as we walked to Phil's ridiculous vehicle.

"Don't be." Rosie reached into her handbag and pulled out a wad of hair. "I cleaned her hairbrush for her."

"We need roots," I said. But there was a lot of hair, so it was likely we would find a strand with its root attached.

She reached into her bag again and retrieved a toothbrush. It took me a few moments to realise what this meant.

"You stole her toothbrush!"

"There was a spare in the cupboard. It was time for a new one."

I was shocked at the theft, but we would now almost certainly have a usable sample of DNA. It was difficult not to be impressed by Rosie's resourcefulness. And if Natalie was not replacing her toothbrush at regular intervals Rosie had done her a favour.

Rosie did not want to analyse the hair or toothbrush immediately. She wanted to collect DNA from the final candidate and test the two samples together. This struck me as illogical. If Natalie's sample were a match, we would not need to collect further DNA. However, Rosie did not seem to grasp the concept of sequencing tasks to minimise cost and risk.

After the problem with the baby access, we decided to collaborate on the most appropriate approach for Dr Peter Enticott.

"I'll tell him I'm thinking about studying medicine," she said. Dr Enticott was now in the Medical Faculty at Deakin University.

She would arrange to meet him over coffee, which would provide an opportunity to use the coffee-cup swab procedure that currently had a one hundred per cent failure rate. I thought it unlikely that a barmaid could convince a professor that she had the credentials to study medicine. Rosie seemed insulted by this, and argued that it did not matter in any case. We only had to persuade him to have a drink with us.

A bigger problem was how to present me, as Rosie did not think she could do the job alone. "You're my boyfriend," she said. "You'll be financing my studies, so you're a stakeholder." She looked at me hard. "You don't need to overplay it."

On a Wednesday afternoon, with Gene covering a lecture for me in return for the Asperger's night, we travelled in Phil's toy car to Deakin University. I had been there many times before for guest lectures and collaborative research. I even knew some researchers in the Medical Faculty, though not Peter Enticott.

We met him at an outdoor café crowded with medical students back early from the summer break. Rosie was amazing! She spoke intelligently about medicine, and even psychiatry, in which she said she hoped to specialise. She claimed to have an honours degree in behavioural science and postgraduate research experience.

Peter seemed obsessed with the resemblance between Rosie and her mother, which was irrelevant for our purposes. Three times he interrupted Rosie to remind her of their physical similarity, and I wondered if this might indicate some particular bond between him and Rosie's mother — and hence be a predictor of paternity. I looked, as I had done in Eamonn Hughes's living room, for any physical similarities between Rosie and her potential father, but could see nothing obvious.

"That all sounds very positive, Rosie," said Peter. "I don't have anything to do with the selection process — at least officially." His wording appeared to imply the possibility of unofficial, and hence unethical, assistance. Was this a sign of nepotism and thus a clue that he was Rosie's father?

"Your academic background is fine, but you'll have to do the GAMSAT." Peter turned to me. "The standard admission test for the MD programme."

"I did it last year," said Rosie. "I got seventy-four."

Peter looked hugely impressed. "You can walk into Harvard with that score. But we take other factors into account here, so, if you do decide to apply, make sure you let me know."

I hoped he never went for a drink at the Marquess of Queensbury.

A waiter brought the bill. As he went to take Peter's cup, I automatically put my hand on it to stop him. The waiter looked at me extremely unpleasantly and snatched it away. I watched as he took it to a cart and added it to a tray of crockery.

Peter looked at his phone. "I have to go," he said. "But now that you've made contact, stay in touch."

As Peter left, I could see the waiter looking towards the cart.

"You need to distract him," I said.

"Just get the cup," said Rosie.

I walked towards the cart. The waiter was watching me but, just as I reached the tray, he snapped his head in Rosie's direction and began walking quickly towards her. I grabbed the cup.

We met at the car, which was parked some distance away. The walk gave me time to process the fact that I had, under pressure to achieve a goal, been guilty of theft. Should I send a cheque to the café? What was a cup worth? Cups were broken all the time, but by random events. If everyone stole cups, the café would probably become financially non-viable.

"Did you get the cup?"

I held it up.

"Is it the right one?" she said.

I am not good at non-verbal communication, but I believe I managed to convey the fact that while I might be a petty thief I do not make errors of observation.

"Did you pay the bill?" I asked.

"That's how I distracted him."

"By paying the bill?"

"No, you pay at the counter. I just took off."

"We have to go back."

"Fuck 'em," said Rosie, as we climbed into the Porsche and sped off.

What was happening to me?

CHAPTER
TWELVE

We drove towards the university and the lab. The Father Project would soon be over. The weather was warm, though there were dark clouds on the horizon, and Rosie lowered the convertible roof. I was mulling over the theft.

"You still obsessing about the bill, Don?" Rosie shouted over the wind noise. "You're hilarious. We're stealing DNA, and you're worried about a cup of coffee."

"It's not illegal to take DNA samples," I shouted back. This was true, although in the UK we would have been in violation of the Human Tissue Act of 2004. "We should go back."

"Highly inefficient use of time," said Rosie in a strange voice, as we pulled up at traffic lights and were briefly able to communicate properly. She laughed and I realised she had been imitating me. Her statement was correct, but there was a moral question involved, and acting morally should override other issues.

"Relax," she said. "It's a beautiful day, we're going to find out who my father is and I'll put a cheque in the mail for the coffee. *Promise.*" She looked at me. "Do you know how to relax? How to just have fun?"

It was too complex a question to answer over the wind noise as we pulled away from the lights. And the pursuit of fun does not lead to overall contentment. Studies have shown this consistently.

"You missed the exit," I said.

"Correct," she replied, in the joke voice. "We're going to the beach." She spoke right over the top of my protests. "Can't hear you, can't hear you."

Then she put on some music — very loud rock music. Now she really couldn't hear me. I was being kidnapped! We drove for ninety-four minutes. I could not see the speedometer, and was not accustomed to travelling in an open vehicle, but I estimated that we were consistently exceeding the speed limit.

Discordant sound, wind, risk of death — I tried to assume the mental state that I used at the dentist.

Finally, we stopped in a beachside car park. It was almost empty on a weekday afternoon.

Rosie looked at me. "Smile. We're going for a walk, then we're going to the lab, and then I'm going to take you home. And you'll never see me again."

"Can't we just go home now?" I said, and realised that I sounded like a child. I reminded myself that I was an adult male, ten years older and more experienced than the person with me, and that there must be a purpose for what she was doing. I asked what it was.

"I'm about to find out who my dad is. I need to clear my head. So can we walk for half an hour or so, and can you just pretend to be a regular human being and listen to me?"

I was not sure how well I could imitate a regular human being, but I agreed to the walk. It was obvious that Rosie was confused by emotions, and I respected her attempt to overcome them. As it turned out, she hardly spoke at all. This made the walk quite pleasant — it was virtually the same as walking alone.

As we approached the car on our return, Rosie asked, "What music *do* you like?"

"Why?"

"You didn't like what I was playing on the drive down, did you?"

"Correct."

"So, your turn going back. But I don't have any Bach."

"I don't really listen to music," I said. "The Bach was an experiment that didn't work."

"You can't go through life not listening to music."

"I just don't pay it any attention. I prefer to listen to information."

There was a long silence. We had reached the car.

"Did your parents listen to music? Brothers and sisters?"

"My parents listened to rock music. Primarily my father. From the era in which he was young."

We got in the car and Rosie lowered the roof again. She played with her iPhone, which she was using as the music source.

"Blast from the past," she said, and activated the music.

I was just settling into the dentist's chair again when I realised the accuracy of Rosie's words. I knew this music. It had been in the background when I was growing up. I was suddenly taken back to my room, door closed, writing in BASIC on my early-generation computer, the song in the background.

"I know this song!"

Rosie laughed. "If you didn't, that'd be the final proof that you're from Mars."

Hurtling back to town, in a red Porsche driven by a beautiful woman, with the song playing, I had the sense of standing on the brink of another world. I recognised the feeling, which, if anything, became stronger as the rain started falling and the convertible roof malfunctioned so we were unable to raise it. It was the same feeling that I had experienced looking over the city after the Balcony Meal, and again after Rosie had written down her phone number. Another world, another life, proximate but inaccessible.

The elusive . . . *Sat-is-fac-tion*.

It was dark when we arrived back at the university. We were both wet. With the aid of the instruction manual, I was able to close the car roof manually.

In the lab, I opened two beers (no cough-signal required) and Rosie tapped her bottle against mine.

"Cheers," she said. "Well done."

"You promise to send a cheque to the café?"

"Whatever. Promise." Good.

"You were brilliant," I said. I had been meaning to convey this for some time. Rosie's performance as an aspiring medical student had been very impressive.

"But why did you claim such a high score on the medical admission test?"

"Why do you think?"

I explained that if I could have deduced the answer, I would not have asked.

"Because I didn't want to look stupid."

"To your potential father?"

"Yeah. To him. To anybody. I'm getting a bit sick of certain people thinking I'm stupid."

"I consider you remarkably intelligent —"

"Don't say it."

"Say what?"

"For a barmaid. You were going to say that, weren't you?"

Rosie had predicted correctly.

"My mother was a doctor. So is my father, if you're talking about genes. And you don't have to be a professor to be smart. I saw your face when I said I got seventy-four on the GAMSAT. You were thinking, 'He won't believe this woman is that smart.' But he did. So, put your prejudices away."

It was a reasonable criticism. I had little contact with people outside academia, and had formed my assumptions about the rest of the world primarily from watching films and television as a child. I recognised that the characters in *Lost in Space* and *Star Trek* were probably not representative of humans in general. Certainly, Rosie did not conform to my barmaid stereotype. It was quite likely that many of my other assumptions about people were wrong. This was no surprise.

108

The DNA analyser was ready.

"Do you have a preference?" I asked.

"Whichever. I don't want to make any decisions."

I realised that she was referring to the sequence of testing rather than the choice of father. I clarified the question.

"I don't know," she said. "I've been thinking about it all afternoon. Alan's dead, which would suck. And Natalie would be my sister, which I've got to tell you is pretty weird. But it's a sort of closure if that makes sense. I like Peter, but I don't really know anything about him. He's probably got a family."

It struck me once again that this Father Project had not been well thought through. Rosie had spent the afternoon trying to subdue unwanted emotions, yet the motivation for the project seemed to be entirely emotional.

I tested Peter Enticott first, as the hair from Natalie's brush required more time for pre-processing. No match.

I had found several roots in the wad of hair, so there was no need to have stolen the toothbrush. As I processed them, I reflected that Rosie's first two candidates, including the one she had felt was a high probability, Eamonn Hughes, had not matched. It was my prediction that Alan's daughter would not match either.

I was right. I remembered to look at Rosie for her reaction. She looked very sad. It seemed we would have to get drunk again.

"Remember," she said, "the sample's not from him; it's his daughter's."

"I've already factored it in."

"Naturally. So that's it."

"But we haven't solved the problem." As a scientist I am not accustomed to abandoning difficult problems.

"We're not going to," said Rosie. "We've tested everyone I ever heard of."

"Difficulties are inevitable," I said. "Major projects require persistence."

"Save it for something that matters to you."

Why do we focus on certain things at the expense of others? We will risk our lives to save a person from drowning, yet not make a donation that could save dozens of children from starvation. We install solar panels when their impact on CO_2 emissions is minimal — and indeed may have a net negative effect if manufacturing and installation are taken into account — rather than contributing to more efficient infrastructure projects.

I consider my own decision-making in these areas to be more rational than that of most people but I also make errors of the same kind. We are genetically programmed to react to stimuli in our immediate vicinity. Responding to complex issues that we cannot perceive directly requires the application of reasoning, which is less powerful than instinct.

This seemed to be the most likely explanation for my continued interest in the Father Project. Rationally, there were more important uses for my research capabilities, but instinctively I was driven to assist Rosie with her more immediate problem. As we drank a glass of Muddy Water Pinot Noir at Jimmy Watson's before Rosie had to go to work, I tried to persuade her to continue with the project but she argued, rationally enough, that there was now no reason to consider any member of her mother's graduation class more likely than any other. She guessed that there would be a hundred or more students, and pointed out that thirty years ago, as a result of entrenched gender bias, the majority would be male. The logistics of finding and testing fifty doctors, many of whom would be living in other cities or countries, would be prohibitive. Rosie said she didn't care *that* much.

Rosie offered me a lift home, but I decided to stay and drink.

CHAPTER
THIRTEEN

Before abandoning the Father Project, I decided to check Rosie's estimate of the number of father candidates. It occurred to me that some possibilities could be easily eliminated. The medical classes I teach contain numerous foreign students. Given Rosie's distinctly pale skin, I considered it unlikely that her father was Chinese, Vietnamese, black or Indian.

I began with some basic research — an internet search for information about the medical graduation class, based on the three names I knew.

The results exceeded my expectations, but problem-solving often requires an element of luck. It was no surprise that Rosie's mother had graduated from my current university. At the time, there were only two medical courses in Melbourne.

I found two relevant photos. One was a formal photo of the entire graduation class, with the names of the one hundred and forty-six students. The other was taken at the graduation party, also with names. There were only one hundred and twenty-four faces, presumably because some students did not attend. Since the gene-shopping had occurred at the party, or after, we would not have to worry about the non-attendees. I verified that the one hundred and twenty-four were a subset of the one hundred and forty-six.

I had expected that my search would produce a list of graduates and probably a photo. An unexpected bonus was a "Where are they now?" discussion board. But the major stroke of luck was the information that a thirtieth anniversary reunion had been scheduled. The date was only three weeks away. We would need to act quickly.

I ate dinner at home and rode to the Marquess of Queensbury. Disaster! Rosie wasn't working. The barman informed me that Rosie worked only three nights per week, which struck me as insufficient to provide an adequate income. Perhaps she had a day job as well. I knew very little about her, beyond her job, her interest in finding her father and her age, which, based on her mother's graduation party being thirty years earlier, must be twenty-nine. I had not asked Gene how he had met her. I did not even know her mother's name to identify her in the photo.

The barman was friendly, so I ordered a beer and some nuts and reviewed the notes I had brought.

There were sixty-three males in the graduation party photo, a margin of only two over the females, insufficient to support Rosie's claim of discrimination. Some were unambiguously non-Caucasian, though not as many as I expected. It was thirty years ago, and the influx of Chinese students had not yet commenced. There was still a large number of candidates, but the reunion offered an opportunity for batch processing.

I had by now deduced that the Marquess of Queensbury was a gay bar. On the first visit, I had not observed the social interactions, as I was too focused on finding Rosie and initiating the Father Project, but this time I was able to analyse my surroundings in more detail. I was reminded of the chess club to which I belonged when I was at school. People drawn together by a common interest. It was the only club I had ever joined, excluding the University Club, which was more of a dining facility.

I did not have any gay friends, but this was related to my overall small number of friends rather than to any prejudice. Perhaps Rosie was gay? She worked in a gay bar, although the clients were all males. I asked the barman. He laughed.

"Good luck with that one," he said. It didn't answer the question, but he had moved on to serve another customer.

As I finished lunch at the University Club the following day, Gene walked in, accompanied by a woman I recognised from the singles party — Fabienne the Sex-Deprived Researcher. It appeared that she had found a solution to her problem. We passed each other at the dining-room entrance.

Gene winked at me, and said, "Don, this is Fabienne. She's visiting from Belgium and we're going to discuss some options for collaboration." He winked again, and quickly moved past.

Belgium. I had assumed Fabienne was French. Belgian explained it. Gene already had France.

I was waiting outside the Marquess of Queensbury when Rosie opened the doors at 9.00p.m.

"Don." Rosie looked surprised. "Is everything okay?"

"I have some information."

"Better be quick."

"It's not quick, there's quite a lot of detail."

"I'm sorry, Don, my boss is here. I'll get into trouble. I need this job."

"What time do you finish?"

"3 a.m."

I couldn't believe it! What sort of jobs did Rosie's patrons have? Maybe they all worked in bars that opened at 9.00p.m. and had four nights a week off. A whole invisible nocturnal subculture, using resources that would otherwise stand idle. I took a huge breath and a huge decision.

"I'll meet you then."

I rode home, went to bed, and set the alarm for 2.30a.m. I cancelled the run I had scheduled with Gene for the following morning to retrieve an hour. I would also skip karate.

At 2.50a.m. I was riding through the inner suburbs. It was not a totally unpleasant experience. In fact, I could see major advantages for myself in working at night. Empty laboratories. No students. Faster response times on the network. No contact with the Dean. If I could find a pure research position, with no teaching, it would be entirely feasible. Perhaps I could teach via video-link at a university in another time zone.

I arrived at Rosie's workplace at exactly 3.00 a.m. The door was locked and a "Closed" sign was up. I knocked hard. Rosie came to the door.

"I'm stuffed," she said. This was hardly surprising. "Come in — I'm almost done."

Apparently the bar closed at 2.30 a.m. but Rosie had to clean up.

"You want a beer?" she said. A beer! At 3 a.m. Ridiculous.

"Yes, please."

I sat at the bar watching her clean up. The question I had asked sitting in the same place the previous day popped into my mind.

"Are you gay?" I asked.

"You came here to ask me that?"

"No, the question is unrelated to the main purpose of my visit."

"Pleased to hear it, alone at three in the morning in a bar with a strange man."

"I'm not strange."

"Not much," she said, but she was laughing, presumably making a joke to herself based on the two meanings of *strange*. I still didn't have an answer to the gay question. She opened a beer for herself. I pulled out my folder and extracted the party photo.

"Is this the party where your mother was impregnated?"

"Shit. Where did this come from?"

I explained about my research and showed her my spreadsheet. "All names are listed. Sixty-three males, nineteen obviously non-Caucasian, as determined by visual assessment and supported by names, three already eliminated."

"You've got to be kidding. We're not testing . . . thirty-one people."

"Forty-one."

"Whatever. I don't have an excuse to meet any of them."

I told her about the reunion.

"Minor problem," said Rosie. "We're not invited."

"Correct," I said. "The problem is minor and already solved. There will be alcohol."

"So?"

I indicated the bar, and the collection of bottles on shelves behind it. "Your skills will be required."

"You're kidding me."

"Can you secure employment at the event?"

"Hang on, hang on. This is getting seriously crazy. You think we're going to turn up at this party and start swabbing people's glasses. Oh man."

"Not us. You. I don't have the skills. But, otherwise, correct."

"Forget it."

"I thought you wanted to know who your father was."

"I told you," she said. "Not that much."

Two days later, Rosie appeared at my apartment. It was 8.47p.m., and I was cleaning the bathroom, as Eva the short-skirted cleaner had cancelled due to illness. I buzzed her upstairs. I was wearing my bathroom-cleaning costume of shorts, surgical boots and gloves but no shirt.

"Wow." She stared at me for a few moments. "This is what martial-arts training does, is it?" She appeared to be referring to my pectoral muscles. Then suddenly she jumped up and down like a child.

"We got the gig! I found the agency and I offered them shit rates and they went yeah, yeah, yeah, don't tell anyone. I'll report them to the union when it's over."

"I thought you didn't want to do this."

"Changed my mind." She gave me a stained paperback. "Memorise this. I've got to get to work." She turned and left.

I looked at the book — *The Bartender's Companion: A Complete Guide to Making and Serving Drinks*. It appeared to specify the duties of the role I was to perform. I memorised the first few recipes before finishing the bathroom. As I prepared for sleep, having skipped the aikido routine to spend further time studying the book, it occurred to me that things *were* getting crazy. It was not the first time that my life had become chaotic and I had established a protocol for dealing with the problem and the consequent disturbance to rational thinking. I called Claudia.

She was able to see me the next day. Because I am not officially one of her clients, we have to have our discussions over coffee rather than in her office. And I am the one accused of rigidity!

I outlined the situation, omitting the Father Project component, as I did not want to admit to the surreptitious collection of DNA, which Claudia was likely to consider unethical. Instead I suggested that Rosie and I had a common interest in movies.

"Have you talked to Gene about her?" asked Claudia.

I told her that Gene had introduced Rosie as a candidate for the Wife Project, and that he would only encourage me to have sex with her. I explained that Rosie was totally unsuitable as a partner, but was presumably under the illusion that I was interested in her on that basis. Perhaps she thought that our common interest was an excuse for pursuing her. I had made a major social error in asking her about her sexual orientation — it would only reinforce that impression.

Yet Rosie had never mentioned the Wife Project. We had been sidetracked so quickly by the Jacket Incident, and after that things had unfolded in a totally unplanned way. But I saw a risk that at some point I would hurt her feelings by telling her that she had been eliminated from consideration for the Wife Project after the first date.

"So that's what you're worried about," said Claudia. "Hurting her feelings?"

"Correct."

"That's excellent, Don."

"Incorrect. It's a major problem."

"I mean that you're concerned about her feelings. And you're enjoying time together?"

"Immensely," I said, realising it for the first time.

"And is she enjoying herself?"

"Presumably. But she applied for the Wife Project."

"Don't worry about it," said Claudia. "She sounds pretty resilient. Just have some fun."

A strange thing happened the next day. For the first time ever, Gene made an appointment to see me in his office. I had always been the one to organise conversations, but there had been an unusually long gap as a result of the Father Project.

Gene's office is larger than mine, due to his higher status rather than any actual requirement for space. The Beautiful Helena let me in, as Gene was late in returning from a meeting. I took the opportunity to check his world map for pins in India and Belgium. I was fairly certain that the Indian one had been there before, but it was possible that Olivia was not actually Indian. She had said she was Hindu, so she could have been Balinese or Fijian or indeed from any country with a Hindu population. Gene worked on nationalities rather than ethnicities, in the same way that travellers count the countries they have visited. North Korea predictably remained without a pin.

Gene arrived, and commanded The Beautiful Helena to fetch us coffees. We sat at his table, as if in a meeting.

"So," said Gene, "you've been talking to Claudia." This was one of the negatives of not being an official client of Claudia: I did not have the protection of confidentiality. "I gather you've been seeing Rosie. As the expert predicted."

120

"Yes," I said, "but not for the Wife Project." Gene is my best friend, but I still felt uncomfortable about sharing information about the Father Project. Fortunately he did not pursue it, probably because he assumed I had sexual intentions towards Rosie. In fact I was amazed that he didn't immediately raise the topic.

"What do you know about Rosie?" he asked.

"Not very much," I said honestly. "We haven't talked much about her. Our discussion has focused on external issues."

"Give me a break," he said. "You know what she does, where she spends her time."

"She's a barmaid."

"Okay," said Gene. "That's all you know?"

"And she doesn't like her father."

Gene laughed for no obvious reason. "I don't think he's Robinson Crusoe." This seemed a ludicrous statement about Rosie's paternity until I recalled that the reference to the fictional shipwreck survivor could be used as a metaphorical phrase meaning "not alone" or in this context "not alone in not being liked by Rosie". Gene must have noticed my puzzled expression as I worked it out, and elaborated: "The list of men that Rosie likes is not a long one."

"She's gay?"

"Might as well be," said Gene. "Look at the way she dresses."

Gene's comment seemed to refer to the type of costume she was wearing when she first appeared in my office. But she dressed conventionally for her bar work and on our visits to collect DNA had worn unexceptional jeans and tops. On the night of the Jacket Incident she had been unconventional but extremely attractive.

Perhaps she did not want to send out mating signals in the environment in which Gene had encountered her, presumably a bar or restaurant. Much of women's clothing is designed to enhance their sexual attraction in order to secure a mate. If Rosie was not looking for a mate, it seemed perfectly rational for her to dress otherwise. There were many things that I wanted to ask Gene about Rosie, but I suspected that asking would imply a level of interest that Gene would misinterpret. But there was one critical question.

"Why was she prepared to participate in the Wife Project?"

Gene hesitated a while. "Who knows?" he said. "I don't think she's a lost cause, but just don't expect too much. She's got a lot of issues. Don't forget the rest of your life."

Gene's advice was surprisingly perceptive. Did he know how much time I was spending with the cocktail book?

CHAPTER
FOURTEEN

My name is Don Tillman and I am an alcoholic. I formed these words in my head but I did not say them out loud, not because I was drunk (which I was) but because it seemed that if I said them they would be true, and I would have no choice but to follow the rational path which was to stop drinking permanently.

My intoxication was a result of the Father Project — specifically the need to gain competence as a drinks waiter. I had purchased a cocktail shaker, glasses, olives, lemons, a zester and a substantial stock of liquor as recommended in *The Bartender's Companion* in order to master the mechanical component of cocktail making. It was surprisingly complex, and I am not naturally a dextrous person. In fact, with the exception of rock climbing, which I have not practised since I was a student, and martial arts, I am clumsy and incompetent at most forms of sport. The expertise in karate and aikido is the result of considerable practice over a long period.

I practised first for accuracy, then speed. At 11.07p.m., I was exhausted, and decided that it would be interesting to test the cocktails for quality. I made a classic martini, a vodka martini, a margarita and a cock-sucking cowboy — cocktails noted by the book as being among the most popular. They were all excellent, and tasted far more different from one another than ice-cream varieties. I had squeezed more lime juice than was requited for the margarita, and made a second so as not to waste it.

Research consistently shows that the risks to health outweigh the benefits of drinking alcohol. My argument is that the benefits to my *mental* health justify the risks. Alcohol seems to both calm me down and elevate my mood, a paradoxical but pleasant combination. And it reduces my discomfort in social situations.

I generally manage my consumption carefully, scheduling two days abstinence per week, although the Father Project had caused this rule to be broken a number of times. My level of consumption does not of itself qualify me as an alcoholic. However, I suspect that my strong antipathy towards discontinuing it might do so.

The Mass DNA Collection Subproject was proceeding satisfactorily, and I was working my way through the cocktail book at the required rate. Contrary to popular belief, alcohol does not destroy brain cells.

As I prepared for bed, I felt a strong desire to telephone Rosie and report on progress. Logically it was not necessary, and it is a waste of effort to report that a project is proceeding to plan, which should be the default assumption. Rationality prevailed. Just.

Rosie and I met for coffee twenty-eight minutes before the reunion function. To my first-class honours degree

124

and PhD, I could now add a Responsible Service of Alcohol certificate. The exam had not been difficult.

Rosie was already in server uniform, and had brought a male equivalent for me.

"I picked it up early and washed it," she said. "I didn't want a karate exhibition."

She was obviously referring to the Jacket Incident, even though the martial art I had employed was aikido.

I had prepared carefully for the DNA collection — zip-lock bags, tissues, and pre-printed adhesive labels with the names from the graduation photo. Rosie insisted that we did not need to collect samples from those who had not attended the graduation party, so I crossed out their names. She seemed surprised that I had memorised them, but I was determined not to cause errors due to lack of knowledge.

The reunion was held at a golf club, which seemed odd to me, but I discovered that the facilities were largely for eating and drinking rather than supporting the playing of golf. I also discovered that we were vastly overqualified. There were regular bar personnel who were responsible for preparing the drinks. Our job was merely to take orders, deliver drinks and, most importantly, collect the empty glasses. The hours spent in developing my drink-making skills had apparently been wasted.

The guests began arriving, and I was given a tray of drinks to distribute. I immediately perceived a problem. No name tags! How would we identify the DNA sources? I managed to find Rosie, who had also realised the problem but had a solution, based on her knowledge of social behaviour.

"Say to them, 'Hi, I'm Don and I'll be looking after you this evening, Doctor —'" She demonstrated how to give the impression that the sentence was incomplete, encouraging them to contribute their name. Extraordinarily, it turned out to work 72.5 per cent of the time. I realised that I needed to do this with the women as well, to avoid appearing sexist.

Eamonn Hughes and Peter Enticott, the candidates we had eliminated, arrived. As a family friend, Eamonn must have known Rosie's profession, and she explained to him that I worked evenings to supplement my academic income. Rosie told Peter Enticott that she did bar work part-time to finance her PhD. Perhaps they both assumed that we had met through working together.

Actually swabbing the glasses discreetly proved the most difficult problem and I was able to get at most one sample from each tray that I returned to the bar. Rosie was having even more problems.

"I can't keep track of all the names," she said, frantically, as we passed each other with drinks trays in our hands. It was getting busy and she seemed a little emotional. I sometimes forget that many people are not familiar with basic techniques for remembering data. The success of the subproject would be in my hands.

"There will be adequate opportunity when they sit down," I said. "There is no reason for concern."

I surveyed the tables set for dinner, ten seats per table, plus two with eleven seats, and calculated the attendance at ninety-two. This of course included female doctors. Partners had not been invited. There was a small risk that Rosie's father was a transsexual. I made a mental note to check the women for signs of male features, and test any that appeared doubtful. Overall, however, the numbers looked promising.

When the guests sat down, the mode of service moved from provision of a limited selection of drinks to taking orders. Apparently, this arrangement was unusual. Normally, we would just bring bottles of wine, beer and water to the table, but, as this was an upmarket function, the club was taking orders and we had been told to "push the top shelf stuff", apparently to increase the club's profits. It occurred to me that if I did this well I might be forgiven for any other errors.

I approached one of the tables of eleven. I had already introduced myself to seven of the guests, and obtained six names.

I commenced with a woman whose name I already knew.

"Greetings, Dr Collie. What can I get you to drink?"

She looked at me strangely and for a moment I thought I had made an error with the word-association method I was using and that her name was perhaps Doberman or Poodle. But she did not correct me.

"Just a white wine, thanks."

"I recommend a margarita. World's most popular cocktail."

"You're doing cocktails?"

"Correct."

"In that case," she said, "I'll have a martini."

"Standard?"

"Yes, thanks." Easy.

I turned to the unidentified man beside her and tried the Rosie name-extraction trick. "Greetings, my name is Don and I'll be looking after you this evening, Doctor —"

"You said you're doing cocktails?"

"Correct."

"Have you heard of a Rob Roy?"

"Of course."

"Well, put me down for one."

"Sweet, dry or perfect?" I asked.

One of the men opposite my customer laughed. "Cop that, Brian."

"Perfect," said the man I now knew as Dr Brian Joyce. There were two Brians but I had already identified the first.

Dr Walsh (female, no transsexual characteristics) ordered a margarita.

"Standard, premium, strawberry, mango, melon or sage and pineapple?" I asked.

"Sage and pineapple? Why not?"

My next customer was the only remaining unidentified man, the one who had laughed at Brian's order. He had previously failed to respond to the name-extraction trick. I decided not to repeat it.

"What would you like?" I asked.

"I'll have a double-coddled Kurdistani sailmaker with a reverse twist," he said. "Shaken, not stirred."

I was unfamiliar with this drink, but assumed the professionals behind the bar would know it.

"Your name, please?"

"Sorry?"

"I require your name. To avoid errors."

There was a silence. Dr Jenny Broadhurst, beside him, said, "His name's Rod."

"Dr Roderick Broadhurst, correct?" I said by way of confirmation. The rule against partners did not apply, of course, to people who were in a relationship with someone from the same class. There were seven such couples and Jenny was predictably sitting beside her husband.

"What —" started Rod, but Jenny interrupted.

"Quite correct. I'm Jenny and I'll have a sage and pineapple margarita too, please." She turned to Rod. "Are you being a jerk? About the sailmaker? Pick on someone with your own complement of synapses."

Rod looked at her, then at me. "Sorry, mate, just taking the piss. I'll have a martini. Standard."

I collected the remainder of the names and orders without difficulty. I understood that Jenny had been trying to tell Rod discreetly that I was unintelligent, presumably because of my waiter role. She had used a neat social trick, which I noted for future use, but had made a factual error which Rod had not corrected. Perhaps one day he or she would make a clinical or research mistake as a result of this misunderstanding.

Before I returned to the bar, I spoke to them again.

"There is no experimental evidence of a correlation between synapse numbers and intelligence level within primate populations. I recommend reading Williams and Herrup, *Annual Review of Neuroscience*." I hoped this would be helpful.

Back at the bar, the cocktail orders caused some confusion. Only one of the three bar persons knew how to make a Rob Roy, and then only a conventional one. I gave her the instructions for the perfect version. Then there was an ingredient problem with the sage and pineapple margarita. The bar had pineapple (tinned — the book had said "fresh if possible" so I decided that this would be acceptable) but no sage. I headed for the kitchen where they could not even offer me dried sage. Obviously this was not what *The Bartender's Companion* had called a "well-stocked bar, ready for any occasion". The kitchen staff were also busy, but we settled on coriander leaves and I took a quick mental inventory of the bar's ingredients to avoid further problems of this kind.

Rosie was also taking orders. We had not yet progressed to the stage of collecting glasses, and some people seemed to be drinking quite slowly. I realised that our chances would be improved if there was a high turnover of drinks. Unfortunately, I was unable to encourage faster consumption, as I would be violating my duty as the holder of a Responsible Service of Alcohol certificate. I decided to take a middle ground by reminding them of some of the delicious cocktails available.

As I took orders, I observed a change in the dynamic of the ecosystem, evidenced by Rosie looking annoyed as she came past me.

"Table Five won't let me take their order. They want to wait for you." It appeared that almost everyone wanted cocktails rather than wine. No doubt the proprietors would be pleased with the profit results. Unfortunately it appeared that staff numbers had been calculated on the basis that most orders would be for beer or wine, and the bar personnel were having trouble keeping up. Their knowledge of cocktails was surprisingly poor, and I was having to dictate recipes along with the orders.

The solution to both problems was simple. Rosie went behind the bar to assist while I took all the orders myself. A good memory was a huge asset, as I did not need to write anything down, or process just one table at a time. I took orders for the whole room, then relayed them back to the bar at consistent intervals. If people needed "time to think", I left them and returned rather than waiting. I was actually running rather than walking, and increased my word rate to the maximum that I considered comprehensible. The process was very efficient, and seemed to be appreciated by the diners, who would occasionally applaud when I was able to propose a drink to meet a particular requirement or replayed a table's orders when they were concerned that I might have misheard.

People were finishing their drinks, and I found that I could swab three glasses between the dining room and the bar. The remainder I grouped together and indicated to Rosie as I left the tray on the bar, rapidly advising her of the owners' names.

She seemed a little pressured. I was enjoying myself immensely. I had the presence of mind to check the cream supplies before dessert was served. Predictably the quantity was insufficient for the number of cocktails I expected to sell to complement the mango mousse and sticky date pudding. Rosie headed for the kitchen to find more. When I returned to the bar, one of the barmen called out to me, "I've got the boss on the phone. He's bringing cream. Do you need anything else?" I surveyed the shelves and made some predictions based on the "ten most popular dessert cocktails".

"Brandy, Galliano, crème de menthe, Cointreau, advocaat, dark rum, light rum."

"Slow down, slow down," he said.

I wasn't slowing down now. I was, as they say, on a roll.

CHAPTER
FIFTEEN

The boss, a middle-aged man (estimated BMI twenty-seven), arrived with the additional supplies just in time for dessert, and did some reorganisation of the process behind the bar. Dessert was great fun, although it was hard to hear orders over the volume of conversation. I sold primarily the cream-based cocktails, with which most of the diners were unfamiliar, but responded to enthusiastically.

As the food waiters cleared the dessert dishes, I made a rough mental calculation of our coverage. It depended a great deal on Rosie, but I believed we had samples from at least eighty-five per cent of the males. Good, but not optimum use of our opportunity. Having ascertained the names of the guests, I had determined that all but twelve of the Caucasian males from the graduation party were present. The missing twelve included Alan McPhee, unable to attend due to death, but already eliminated by means of his daughter's hairbrush.

I headed for the bar, and Dr Ralph Browning followed me. "Can I bother you for another Cadillac? That was maybe the best drink I've ever had."

The bar staff were packing up, but the boss said to Rosie, "Make the man a Cadillac."

Jenny and Rod Broadhurst appeared from the dining room. "Make that three," said Rod.

The other bar personnel surrounded the owner, and there was a conversation.

"These guys have to go," said the boss to me, shrugging his shoulders. He turned to Rosie. "Double time?"

Meanwhile, the diners were forming a throng around the bar, raising their hands for attention.

Rosie handed a Cadillac to Dr Browning then turned to the boss. "Sorry, I need at least two to stay. I can't run a bar for a hundred people by myself."

"Me and him," said the boss, pointing to me.

Finally, I had a chance to use my expertise. Rosie lifted the hinged part of the bar and let me through.

Dr Miranda Ball raised her hand. "Same again, please."

I called to Rosie, loudly, as the bar area was now very noisy. "Miranda Ball. Alabama Slammer. One part each sloe gin, whisky, Galliano, triple sec, orange juice, orange slice and a cherry."

"We're out of triple sec," yelled Rosie.

"Substitute Cointreau. Reduce the quantity by twenty per cent."

Dr Lucas put his finished drink on the bar, and raised his finger. One more.

"Gerry Lucas. Empty glass," I called.

Rosie took the glass: I hoped she realised that we didn't have a sample for him yet.

"Another Anal Probe for Dr Lucas."

134

"Got that," she called from the kitchen. Excellent, she had remembered to swab.

Dr Martin van Krieger called out, loudly, "Is there a cocktail with Galliano and tequila?"

The crowd quietened. This sort of question had become common during dinner, and the guests had seemed impressed with my responses. I took a few moments to think.

Martin called out again, "Don't worry if there isn't."

"I'm re-indexing my internal database," I said to explain the delay. It took a few moments. "Mexican Gold or Freddy Fudpucker." The crowd applauded.

"One of each," he said.

Rosie knew how to make a Freddy Fudpucker. I gave the boss the Mexican Gold recipe.

We continued in this mode, with great success. I decided to take advantage of the opportunity to test all male doctors present, including those I had previously filtered out because of incompatible ethnic appearance. At 1.22 a.m. I was confident that we had tested all but one person. It was time to be proactive.

"Dr Anwar Khan. Approach the bar please." It was an expression I had heard used on television. I hoped it carried the required authority.

Dr Khan had drunk only from his water glass, and carried it with him to the bar. "You haven't ordered a drink all night," I said.

"Is that a problem? I don't drink alcohol."

"Very wise," I said, although I was providing a bad example, with a beer open beside me. "I recommend a Virgin Colada. Virgin Mary. Virgin —"

At this moment, Dr Eva Gold put her arm around Dr Khan. She was obviously affected by alcohol. "Loosen up, Anwar."

Dr Khan looked back at her, and then at the crowd, who were, in my assessment, also exhibiting the effects of intoxication.

"What the hell," he said. "Line up the virgins."

He put his empty glass on the bar.

I did not leave the golf club until very late. The last guests departed at 2.32a.m., two hours and two minutes after the scheduled completion time. Rosie, the boss and I had made one hundred and forty-three cocktails. Rosie and the boss also sold some beer of which I did not keep track.

"You guys can go," said the boss. "We'll clean up in the morning." He extended his hand to me and I shook it according to custom, although it seemed very late for introductions. "Amghad," he said. "Nice work, guys."

He didn't shake Rosie's hand but looked at her and smiled. I noticed that she was looking a little tired. I was still full of energy.

"Got time for a drink?" said Amghad.

"Excellent idea."

"You've got to be kidding," said Rosie. "I'm going. All the stuffs in your bag. You don't want a lift, Don?"

I had my cycle, and had only drunk three beers over the course of a long evening. I estimated that my blood alcohol would be well below the legal limit, even after a drink with Amghad. Rosie departed.

"What's your poison?" said Amghad.

"Poison?"

"What do you want to drink?"

Of course. But why, why, why can't people just say what they mean?

"Beer, please."

Amghad opened two pale ales and we clicked bottles.

"How long have you been doing this?" he asked.

Though some deception had been necessary for the purposes of the Father Project, I was not comfortable with it.

"This is my first work in the field," I said. "Did I make some error?"

Amghad laughed. "Funny guy. Listen," he said. "This place here is okay, but it's mostly steak and beer and mid-range wine. Tonight was a one-off, and mainly because of you." He drank some beer, and looked at me without speaking for a while. "I've been thinking of opening in the inner west — a little cocktail bar with a bit of flair. New York feel, but something a bit extra behind the bar, if you know what I mean. If you're interested —"

He was offering me a job! This was flattering, considering my limited experience, and my immediate irrational thought was that I wished Rosie had been present to witness it.

"I already have a job. Thank you."

"I'm not talking about a job. I'm talking about a share in a business."

"No, thank you," I said. "I'm sorry. But I think you would find me unsatisfactory."

"Maybe, but I'm a pretty good judge. Give me a call if you change your mind. I'm in no hurry."

The following day was Sunday.

Rosie and I arranged to meet at the lab at 3.00p.m. She was predictably late, and I was already at work. I confirmed that we had obtained samples from all attendees at the reunion, meaning we had now tested all but eleven of the Caucasian males in the class.

Rosie arrived in tight blue jeans and a white shirt and headed for the refrigerator. "No beer until all samples are tested," I said.

The work took some time, and I needed to source additional chemicals from the main laboratory.

At 7.06p.m. Rosie went out for pizza, an unhealthy choice, but I had missed dinner the previous night and calculated that my body would be able to process the extra kilojoules. When she returned, I was testing the fourth-to-last candidate. As we were opening the pizza, my mobile phone rang. I realised immediately who it was.

"You didn't answer at home," said my mother. "I was worried." This was a reasonable reaction on her part, as her Sunday phone call is part of my weekly schedule. "Where are you?"

"At work."

"Are you all right?"

"I'm fine."

It was embarrassing to have Rosie listen to a personal conversation, and I did everything I could to terminate it quickly, keeping my responses as brief as possible.

Rosie started laughing — fortunately not loudly enough for my mother to hear — and making funny faces.

"Your mother?" she said when I was finally able to hang up.

"Correct. How did you guess?"

"You sound like any sixteen-year-old boy talking to his mum in front of —" She stopped. My annoyance must have been obvious. "Or me talking to Phil."

It was interesting that Rosie also found conversation with a parent difficult. My mother is a good person, but very focused on sharing personal information. Rosie picked up a slice of pizza and looked at the computer screen.

"I'm guessing no news."

"Plenty of news. Five more eliminated, only four to go. Including this one." The result had come up while I was on the phone. "Delete Anwar Khan."

Rosie updated the spreadsheet. "Allah be praised."

"World's most complicated drink order," I reminded her. Dr Khan had ordered five different drinks, compensating for his abstinence earlier in the evening. At the end of the night, he had left with his arm around Dr Gold.

"Yeah and I messed it up too. Put rum in the Virgin Colada."

"You gave him alcohol?" I presumed this was in violation of his personal or religious standards.

"Maybe he'll miss out on his seventy-two virgins."

I was familiar with this religious theory. My public position, as negotiated with the Dean, is that I regard

139

all non-science based beliefs as having equal merit. But I found this one curious.

"Seems irrational," I said. "Wanting virgins. Surely a woman with sexual experience would be preferable to a novice."

Rosie laughed and opened two beers. Then she stared at me, in the way that I am not supposed to do to others. "Amazing. You. You're the most amazing person I've ever met. I don't know why you're doing this, but thanks." She tapped her bottle against mine and drank.

It was enjoyable to be appreciated, but this was exactly what I had been worried about when I spoke to Claudia. Now Rosie was asking about my motives. She had applied for the Wife Project and presumably had expectations on that basis. It was time to be honest.

"Presumably you think it's in order to initiate a romantic relationship."

"The thought had crossed my mind," said Rosie.

Assumption confirmed.

"I'm extremely sorry if I've created an incorrect impression."

"What do you mean?" said Rosie.

"I'm not interested in you as a partner. I should have told you earlier, but you're totally unsuitable." I tried to gauge Rosie's reaction, but the interpretation of facial expressions is not one of my strengths.

"Well, you'll be pleased to know I can cope. I think you're pretty unsuitable too," she said.

This was a relief. I hadn't hurt her feelings. But it did leave a question unanswered.

"Then why did you apply for the Wife Project?" I was using the word "apply" loosely, as Gene had not required Rosie to complete the questionnaire. But her answer suggested a more serious level of miscommunication.

"Wife Project?" she said, as if she had never heard of it.

"Gene sent you to me as a candidate for the Wife Project. A wild card."

"He did what?"

"You haven't heard of the Wife Project?" I asked, trying to establish the correct starting point.

"No," she said, speaking in the tone that is traditionally used for giving instructions to a child. "I have never heard of the Wife Project. But I'm about to. In detail."

"Of course," I said. "But we should time-share it with pizza-consumption and beer-drinking."

"Of course," said Rosie.

I explained in some detail about the Wife Project, including the review with Gene and field visits to dating establishments. I finished as we consumed the final slices of pizza. Rosie had not really asked any questions except to make exclamations such as "Jesus" and "Fuck".

"So," said Rosie. "Are you still doing it? The Wife Project?"

I explained that the project was still technically active, but in the absence of any qualified candidates there had been no progress.

141

"What a shame," said Rosie. "The perfect woman hasn't checked in yet."

"I would assume that there is more than one candidate who meets the criteria," I said, "but it's like finding a bone-marrow donor. Not enough registrations."

"I can only hope that enough women realise their civic duty and take the test."

It was an interesting comment. I didn't really feel it was a duty. In the last few weeks, reflecting on the Wife Project and its lack of success, I had felt sad that there were so many women who were looking for partners, and desperate enough to register, even though there was only a low probability that they would meet the criteria.

"It's entirely optional," I said.

"How nice for them. Here's a thought for you. Any woman who takes that test is happy to be treated as an object. You can say that's their choice. But, if you spent two minutes looking at how much society forces women to think of themselves as objects, you might not think so. What I want to know is, do you want a woman who thinks like that? Is that the sort of wife you want?" Rosie was sounding angry. "You know why I dress the way I do? Why these glasses? Because I *don't* want to be treated as an object. If you knew how insulted I am that you think I was an applicant, a *candidate* —"

"Then why did you come to see me that day?" I asked. "The day of the Jacket Incident?"

She shook her head. "Remember at your apartment, on your balcony, I asked you a question about the size of testicles?"

142

I nodded.

"It didn't strike you as odd that here I was, on a first date, asking about testicles?"

"Not really. On a date I'm too focused on not saying odd things myself."

"Okay, strike that." She seemed a little calmer. "The reason I asked the question was that I had a bet with Gene. Gene, who is a sexist pig, bet me that humans were naturally non-monogamous, and that the evidence was the size of their testicles. He sent me to a genetics expert to settle the bet."

It took me a few moments to process fully the implications of what Rosie was saying. Gene had not prepared her for the dinner invitation. A woman — Rosie — had accepted an offer of a date with me without being pre-warned, set up. I was suffused with an irrationally disproportionate sense of satisfaction. But Gene had misled me. And it seemed he had taken advantage of Rosie financially.

"Did you lose much money?" I asked. "It seems exploitative for a professor of psychology to make a bet with a barmaid."

"I'm not a fucking barmaid."

I could tell by the use of the obscenity that Rosie was getting angry again. But she could hardly contradict the evidence. I realised my error — one that would have caused trouble if I had made it in front of a class.

"Bar-*person*."

"*Bartender* is the established non-sexist term," she said. "That's not the point. It's my part-time job. I'm

143

doing my PhD in psychology, okay? In Gene's department. Does that make sense now?"

Of course! I suddenly remembered where I had seen her before — arguing with Gene after his public lecture. I recalled that Gene had asked her to have coffee with him — as he habitually did with attractive women — but that she had refused. For some reason I felt pleased about this. But if I had recognised her when she first came to my office, the whole misunderstanding could have been avoided. Everything now made sense, including the performance she had given in her medical-school enquiry. Except for two things.

"Why didn't you tell me?"

"Because I *am* a barmaid, and I'm not ashamed of it. You can take me or leave me as a barmaid." I assumed she was speaking metaphorically.

"Excellent," I said. "That explains almost everything."

"Oh, that's fine then. Why the 'almost'? Don't feel you have to leave anything hanging."

"Why Gene didn't tell me."

"Because he's an arsehole."

"Gene is my best friend."

"God help you," she said.

With matters clarified, it was time to finish the project, although our chances of finding the father tonight were looking poor. Fourteen candidates remained and we had only three samples left. I got up and walked to the machine.

"Listen," said Rosie. "I'm going to ask you again. Why are you doing this?"

I remembered my reflection on this question, and the answer I had reached involving scientific challenge and altruism to adjacent humans. But as I began my explanation I realised that it was not true. Tonight we had corrected numerous invalid assumptions and errors in communication. I should not create a new one.

"I don't know," I said.

I turned back to the machine and began to load the sample. My work was interrupted by a sudden smashing of glass. Rosie had thrown a beaker, fortunately not one containing an untested sample, against the wall.

"I am so *so* over this." She walked out.

The next morning there was a knock at my office door. Rosie.

"Enter," I said. "I assume you want to know the final three results."

Rosie walked unnaturally slowly to my desk where I was reviewing some potentially life-changing data. "No," she said. "I figured they were negative. Even you would have phoned if you'd got a match."

"Correct."

She stood and looked at me without saying anything. I am aware that such silences are provided as opportunities for me to speak further, but I could think of nothing useful to say. Finally, she filled the gap.

"Hey — sorry I blew up last night."

"Totally understandable. It's incredibly frustrating to work so hard for no result. But very common in science." I remembered that she was a science graduate, as well as a barmaid. "As you know."

"I meant your Wife Project. I think it's wrong, but you're no different from every other man I know in objectifying women — just more honest about it. Anyway, you've done so much for me —"

"A communication error. Fortunately now rectified. We can proceed with the Father Project without the personal aspect."

"Not till I understand why you're doing it."

That difficult question again. But she had been happy to proceed when she thought that my motivation was romantic interest even though she did not reciprocate that interest.

"There has been no change in my motivation," I said, truthfully. "It was your motivation that was a concern. I thought you were interested in me as a partner. Fortunately, that assumption was based on false information."

"Shouldn't you be spending the time on your objectification project?"

The question was perfectly timed. The data I was looking at on my screen indicated a major breakthrough.

"Good news. I have an applicant who satisfies all requirements."

"Well," said Rosie, "you won't be needing me."

This was a truly strange response. I hadn't needed Rosie for anything other than her own project.

CHAPTER
SIXTEEN

The candidate's name was Bianca Rivera and she met all criteria. There was one obstacle, to which I would need to devote time. She noted that she had twice won the state ballroom dancing championship, and required her partner to be an accomplished dancer. It seemed perfectly reasonable for her to have some criteria of her own, and this one was easy to satisfy. And I had the perfect place to take her.

I called Regina, the Dean's assistant, and confirmed that she was still selling tickets for the faculty ball. Then I emailed Bianca and invited her as my partner. She accepted! I had a date — the perfect date. Now I had ten days to learn to dance.

Gene entered my office as I was practising my dance steps.

"I think the longevity statistics were based on marriages to live women, Don."

He was referring to the skeleton I was using for practice. I had obtained it on loan from the Anatomy Department, and no one had asked what I required it for. Judging from the pelvis size, it was almost certainly a male skeleton, but this was irrelevant for dancing practice. I explained its purpose to Gene, pointing out the scene from the film *Grease* that was showing on the wall of my office.

"So," said Gene, "Ms Right — sorry, Dr Right, PhD, just popped into your inbox."

"Her name's not Wright," I said, "it's Rivera."

"Photo?"

"Not necessary. The meeting arrangements are quite precise. She's coming to the faculty ball."

"Oh shit." Gene went silent for a while and I resumed dancing practice. "Don, the faculty ball is Friday after next."

"Correct."

"You can't learn to dance in nine days."

"Ten. I started yesterday. The steps are trivial to remember. I just need to practise the mechanics. They're considerably less demanding than martial arts."

I demonstrated a sequence.

"Very impressive," said Gene. "Sit down, Don."

I sat.

"I hope you're not too pissed off at me about Rosie," he said.

I had almost forgotten. "Why didn't you tell me she was a psychology student? And about the bet?"

"From what Claudia said, you guys seemed to be having a good time. I thought if she wasn't telling you it was for a reason. She may be a bit twisted but she's not stupid."

"Perfectly reasonable," I said. On matters of human interaction, why argue with a professor of psychology?

"I'm glad one of you is all right with it," said Gene. "I have to tell you, Rosie was a little unhappy with me. A little unhappy with life. Listen, Don, I persuaded her to go to the ball. Alone. If you knew how often Rosie takes my advice, you'd realise what a big deal that was. I was going to suggest you do the same."

"Take your advice?"

"No, go to the ball — alone. Or invite Rosie as your partner."

I now saw what Gene was suggesting. Gene is so focused on attraction and sex that he sees it everywhere. This time he was totally in error.

"Rosie and I discussed the question of a relationship explicitly. Neither of us is interested."

"Since when do women discuss anything explicitly?" said Gene.

I visited Claudia for some advice on my crucial date with Bianca. I assumed that she would be there in her role as Gene's wife, and I advised her that I might require assistance on the night. It turned out she wasn't even aware of the ball.

"Just be yourself, Don. If she doesn't want you for yourself, then she's not the right person for you."

"I think it's unlikely that any woman would accept me for myself."

"What about Daphne?" asked Claudia.

It was true — Daphne was unlike the women I had dated. This was excellent therapy; refutation by counter-example. Perhaps Bianca would be a younger, dancing, version of Daphne.

"And what about Rosie?" asked Claudia.

"Rosie is totally unsuitable."

"I wasn't asking that," said Claudia. "Just whether she accepts you for yourself."

I thought about it for a few moments. It was a difficult question.

"I think so. Because she isn't evaluating me as a partner."

"It's probably good that you feel like that," said Claudia.

Feel! Feel, feel, feel! Feelings were disrupting my sense of well-being. In addition to a nagging desire to be working on the Father Project rather than the Wife Project, I now had a high level of anxiety related to Bianca.

Throughout my life I have been criticised for a perceived lack of emotion, as if this were some absolute fault. Interactions with psychiatrists and psychologists — even including Claudia — start from the premise that I should be more "in touch" with my emotions. What they really mean is that I should give in to them. I am perfectly happy to detect, recognise and analyse emotions. This is a useful skill and I would like to be better at it. Occasionally an emotion can be enjoyed — the gratitude I felt for my sister who visited me even during the bad times, the primitive feeling of well-being after a glass of wine — but we need to be vigilant that emotions do not cripple us.

I diagnosed brain overload and set up a spreadsheet to analyse the situation.

I began by listing the recent disturbances to my schedule. Two were unquestionably positive. Eva, the short-skirted cleaner, was doing an excellent job and had freed up considerable time. Without her, most of the recent additional activities would not have been possible. And, anxiety notwithstanding, I had my first fully qualified applicant for the Wife Project. I had made a decision that I wanted a partner and for the first time I had a viable candidate. Logic dictated that the Wife Project, to which I had planned to allocate most of my free time, should now receive maximum attention. Here, I identified Problem Number One. My emotions were not aligned with logic. I was reluctant to pursue the opportunity.

I did not know whether to list the Father Project as positive or negative but it had consumed enormous time for zero outcome. My arguments for pursuing it had always been weak, and I had done far more than could reasonably be expected of me. If Rosie wanted to locate and obtain DNA from the remaining candidates, she could do so herself. She now had substantial practical experience with the collection procedure. I could offer to perform the actual tests. Once again, logic and emotion were not in step. I wanted to continue the Father Project. Why?

It is virtually impossible to make useful comparisons of levels of happiness, especially across long periods of time. But if I had been asked to choose the happiest day of my life, I would have nominated, without hesitation, the first day I spent at the American Museum of Natural History in New York when I travelled there for a conference during my PhD studies. The second-best day was the second day there, and the third-best the third day there. But after recent events, it was not so clear. It was difficult to choose between the Natural History Museum and the night of cocktail-making at the golf club. Should I therefore consider resigning my job and accepting Amghad's offer of a partnership in a cocktail bar? Would I be permanently happier? The idea seemed ludicrous.

The cause of my confusion was that I was dealing with an equation which contained large negative values — most seriously the disruption to my schedule — and large positive values — the consequential enjoyable experiences. My inability to quantify these factors accurately meant that I could not determine the net result — negative or positive. And the margin of error was huge. I marked the Father Project as being of undetermined net value, and ranked it the most serious disturbance.

The last item on my spreadsheet was the immediate risk that my nervousness and ambivalence about the Wife Project would impede my social interaction with Bianca. I was not concerned about the dancing — I was confident that I could draw on my experience of preparing for martial-arts competitions, with the supplementary advantage of an optimum intake of alcohol, which for martial arts is not permitted. My concern was more with social faux pas. It would be terrible to lose the perfect relationship because I failed to detect sarcasm or looked into her eyes for greater or less than the conventional period of time. I reassured myself that Claudia was essentially correct: if these things concerned Bianca excessively, she was not the perfect match, and I would at least be in a position to refine the questionnaire for future use.

I visited a formal costume hire establishment as recommended by Gene and specified maximum formality. I did not want a repeat of the Jacket Incident.

CHAPTER
SEVENTEEN

The ball was on a Friday evening at a reception centre on the river. For efficiency, I had brought my costume to work, and practised the cha-cha and rhumba with my skeleton while I waited to leave. When I went to the lab to get a beer, I felt a strong twinge of emotion. I was missing the stimulation of the Father Project.

The morning suit, with its tails and tall hat, was totally impractical for cycling, so I took a taxi and arrived at exactly 7.55p.m., as planned. Behind me, another taxi pulled up and a tall, dark-haired woman stepped out. She was wearing the world's most amazing dress: multiple bright colours — red, blue, yellow, green — with a complex structure including a split up one side. I had never seen anyone so spectacular. Estimated age thirty-five, BMI twenty-two, consistent with the questionnaire responses. Neither a little early nor a little late. Was I looking at my future wife? It was almost unbelievable.

As I stepped out of the taxi, she looked at me for a moment then turned and walked towards the door. I took a deep breath and followed. She stepped inside and looked around. She saw me again, and looked more carefully this time. I approached her, close enough to speak, being careful not to invade her personal space. I looked into her eyes. I counted one, two. Then I lowered my eyes a little, downwards, but only a tiny distance.

"Hi," I said. "I'm Don."

She looked at me for a while before extending her hand to shake with low pressure.

"I'm Bianca. You've . . . really dressed up."

"Of course, the invitation specified formal."

After approximately two seconds she burst into laughter. "You had me for a minute there. So deadpan. You know, you write 'good sense of humour' on the list of things you're looking for, but you never expect to get a real comedian. I think you and I are going to have fun."

Things were going extremely well.

The ballroom was huge — dozens of tables with formally dressed academics. *Everyone* turned to look at us, and it was obvious that we had made an impression. At first I thought it must be Bianca's spectacular dress, but there were numerous other interestingly dressed women. Then I noticed that the men were almost without exception dressed in black suits with white shirts and bowties. None wore tails or a hat. It accounted for Bianca's initial reaction. It was annoying, but not a situation I was unfamiliar with. I doffed my hat to the crowd and they shouted greetings. Bianca seemed to enjoy the attention.

We were at table twelve, according to the seating index, right on the edge of the dance floor. A band was tuning up. Observing their instruments, it seemed that my skills at cha-cha, samba, rhumba, foxtrot, waltz, tango and lambada would not be required. I would need to draw on the work of the second day of the dancing project — rock 'n' roll.

Gene's recommendation to arrive thirty minutes after the official start time meant that all but three of the seats at the table were already occupied. One of these belonged to Gene, who was walking around, pouring Champagne. Claudia was not present.

I identified Laszlo Hevesi from Physics, who was dressed totally inappropriately in combat trousers and a hiking shirt, sitting next to a woman whom I recognised with surprise as Frances from the speed-dating night. On Laszlo's other side was The Beautiful Helena. There was also a dark-haired man of about thirty (BMI approximately twenty) who appeared not to have shaved for several days, and, beside him, the most beautiful woman I had ever seen. In contrast to the complexity of Bianca's costume, she was wearing a green dress with zero decoration, so minimal that it did not even have straps to hold it in place. It took me a moment to realise that its wearer was Rosie.

Bianca and I took the two vacant seats between Stubble Man and Frances, following the alternating male-female pattern that had been established. Rosie began the introductions, and I recognised the protocol that I had learned for conferences and never actually used.

"Don, this is Stefan." She was referring to Stubble Man. I extended my hand, and shook, matching his pressure, which I judged as excessive. I had an

156

immediate negative reaction to him. I am generally not competent at assessing other humans, except through the content of their conversation or written communication. But I am reasonably astute at identifying students who are likely to be disruptive.

"Your reputation precedes you," Stefan said.

Perhaps my assessment was too hasty.

"You're familiar with my work?"

"You might say that." He laughed.

I realised that I could not pursue the conversation until I introduced Bianca.

"Rosie, Stefan, allow me to present Bianca Rivera."

Rosie extended her hand and said, "Delighted to meet you."

They smiled hard at each other and Stefan shook Bianca's hand also.

My duty done, I turned to Laszlo, whom I had not spoken to for some time. Laszlo is the only person I know with poorer social skills than mine, and it was reassuring to have him nearby for contrast.

"Greetings, Laszlo," I said, assessing that formality would not be appropriate in his case. "Greetings, Frances. You found a partner. How many encounters were required?"

"Gene introduced us," said Laszlo. He was staring inappropriately at Rosie. Gene gave a "thumbs up" signal to Laszlo, then moved between Bianca and me with the Champagne bottle. Bianca immediately upended her glass. "Don and I don't drink," she said, turning mine down as well. Gene gave me a huge smile. It was an odd response to an annoying version-control oversight on my part — Bianca had apparently responded to the original questionnaire.

Rosie asked Bianca, "How do you and Don know each other?"

"We share an interest in dancing," Bianca said.

I thought this was an excellent reply, not referring to the Wife Project, but Rosie gave me a strange look.

"How nice," she said. "I'm a bit too busy with my PhD to have time for dancing."

"You have to be organised," said Bianca. "I believe in being *very* organised."

"Yes," said Rosie, "I —"

"The first time I made the final of the nationals was in the middle of my PhD. I thought about dropping the triathlon or the Japanese cookery course, but . . ."

Rosie smiled, but not in the way she usually did. "No, that would have been silly. Men love a woman who can cook."

"I like to think we've moved beyond that sort of stereotyping," said Bianca. "Don's quite a cook himself."

Claudia's suggestion that I mention my competence in cooking on the questionnaire had obviously been effective. Rosie provided some evidence.

"He's fabulous. We had the most amazing lobster on his balcony."

"Oh, really?"

It was helpful that Rosie was recommending me to Bianca, but Stefan was displaying the disruptive-student expression again. I applied my lecture technique of asking him a question first.

"Are you Rosie's boyfriend?"

Stefan did not have a ready answer, and in a lecture that would have been my cue to continue, with the student now healthily wary of me. But Rosie answered for him.

"Stefan is doing his PhD with me."

"I believe the term is *partner*," said Stefan.

"For this evening," said Rosie.

Stefan smiled. "First date."

It was odd that they did not seem to have agreed on the nature of their relationship. Rosie turned back to Bianca.

"And yours and Don's first date too?"

"That's right, Rosie."

"How did you find the questionnaire?"

Bianca looked quickly at me, then turned back to Rosie.

"Wonderful. Most men only want to talk about themselves. It was so nice to have someone focusing on me."

"I can see how that would work for you," said Rosie.

"And a dancer," Bianca said. "I couldn't believe my luck. But you know what they say: the harder I work, the luckier I get."

Rosie picked up her Champagne glass, and Stefan said, "How long have *you* been dancing, Don? Won any prizes?"

I was saved from answering by the arrival of the Dean.

She was wearing a complex pink dress, the lower part of which spread out widely, and was accompanied by a woman of approximately the same age dressed in the standard male ball costume of black suit and bowtie. The reaction of the ball-goers was similar to that at my entrance, without the friendly greetings at the end.

"Oh dear," said Bianca. I had a low opinion of the Dean, but the comment made me uncomfortable.

"You have a problem with gay women?" said Rosie, slightly aggressively.

"Not at all," said Bianca. "My problem's with her dress sense."

"You'll have fun with Don, then," said Rosie.

"I think Don looks *fabulous*," said Bianca. "It takes flair to pull off something a little different. Anyone can wear a dinner suit or a plain frock. Don't you think so, Don?"

I nodded in polite agreement. Bianca was exhibiting exactly the characteristics I was looking for. There was every chance she would be perfect. But for some reason my instincts were rebelling. Perhaps it was the no-drinking rule. My underlying addiction to alcohol was causing my subconscious to send a signal to reject someone who stopped me drinking. I needed to overcome it.

We finished our entreés and the band played a few loud chords. Stefan walked over to them and took the microphone from the singer.

"Good evening, everyone," he said. "I thought you should know that we have a former finalist in the national dancing championships with us this evening. You may have seen her on television. Bianca Rivera.

160

Let's give Bianca and her partner Don a few minutes to entertain us."

I had not expected my first performance to be so public, but there was the advantage of an unobstructed dance floor. I have given lectures to larger audiences, and participated in martial-arts bouts in front of crowds. There was no reason to be nervous. Bianca and I stepped onto the dance floor.

I took her in the standard jive hold that I had practised on the skeleton, and immediately felt the awkwardness, approaching revulsion, that I feel when forced into intimate contact with another human. I had mentally prepared for this, but not for a more serious problem. I had not practised with music. I am sure I executed the steps accurately, but not at precisely the correct speed, and not at the same time as the beat. We were immediately tripping over each other and the net effect was a *disaster*. Bianca tried to lead, but I had no experience with a living partner, let alone one who was trying to be in control.

People began laughing. I am an expert at being laughed at and, as Bianca pulled away from me, I scanned the audience to see who was not laughing, an excellent means of identifying friends. Gene and Rosie and, surprisingly, the Dean and her partner were my friends tonight. Stefan was definitely not.

Something major was required to save the situation. In my dancing research, I had noted some specialised moves that I had not intended to use but remembered because they were so interesting. They had the advantage of not being highly dependent on synchronised timing or body contact. Now was the time to deploy them.

I performed the running man, milking the cow, and the fishing imitation, reeling Bianca in, though she did not actually move as required. In fact she was standing totally still. Finally, I attempted a body-contact manoeuvre, traditionally used for a spectacular finish, in which the male swings the female on either side, over his back and between his legs. Unfortunately this requires cooperation on the part of the partner, particularly if she is heavier than a skeleton. Bianca offered no such cooperation and the effect was as if I had attacked her. Unlike aikido, dancing training apparently does not include practice in falling safely.

I offered to help her up, but she ignored my hand and walked towards the bathroom, apparently uninjured.

I went back to the table and sat down. Stefan was still laughing.

"You bastard," Rosie said to him.

Gene said something to Rosie, presumably to prevent inappropriate public anger, and she seemed to calm down.

Bianca returned to her seat, but only to collect her bag.

"The problem was synchronisation," I tried to tell her. "The metronome in my head is not set to the same frequency as the band."

Bianca turned away, but Rosie seemed prepared to listen to my explanation. "I turned off the sound during practice so I could focus on learning the steps."

Rosie did not reply and I heard Bianca speaking to Stefan. "It happens. This isn't the first time, just the worst. Men say they can dance . . ." She walked towards the exit without saying goodnight to me, but Gene followed and intercepted her.

This gave me an opportunity. I righted my glass, and filled it with wine. It was a poorly made gordo blanco with excessive residual sugar. I drank it and poured another. Rosie got up from her seat and walked over to the band. She spoke to the singer, then the drummer.

She returned and pointed at me in a stylised manner. I recognised the action — I had seen it twelve times. It was the signal that Olivia Newton-John gave to John Travolta in *Grease* to commence the dance sequence that I had been practising when Gene interrupted me nine days earlier. Rosie pulled me towards the dance floor.

"Dance," she said. "Just fucking dance."

I started dancing without music. This was what I had practised. Rosie followed according to my tempo. Then she raised her arm and started waving it in time with our movements. I heard the drummer start playing and could tell in my body that he was in time with us. I barely noticed the rest of the band start up.

Rosie was a good dancer and considerably easier to manipulate than the skeleton. I led her through the more difficult moves, totally focused on the mechanics and on not making errors. The *Grease* song finished and everyone clapped. But before we could return to the table, the band started again and the audience clapped in time: *Satisfaction*. It may have been due to the effect of the gordo blanco on my cognitive functions, but I was suddenly overwhelmed by an extraordinary feeling — not of satisfaction but of absolute joy. It was the feeling I had in the Museum of Natural History and when I was making cocktails. We started dancing again, and this time I allowed myself to focus on the sensations of my body moving to the beat of the song from my childhood and of Rosie moving to the same rhythm.

The music finished and everyone clapped again.

I looked for Bianca, my date, and located her near the exit with Gene. I had presumed she would be impressed that the problem was solved, but even from a distance and with my limited ability to interpret expressions, I could see that she was furious. She turned and left.

The rest of the evening was incredible, changed totally by one dance. *Everyone* came up to Rosie and me to offer compliments. The photographer gave us each a photo without charging us. Stefan left early. Gene obtained some high-quality Champagne from the bar, and we drank several glasses with him and a Hungarian postdoc named Klara from Physics. Rosie and I danced again, and then I danced with almost every woman at the ball. I asked Gene if I should invite the Dean or her partner, but he considered this to be a question beyond even his social expertise. In the end I did not, as the Dean was visibly in a bad mood. The crowd had made it clear that they would rather dance than listen to her scheduled speech.

At the end of the night, the band played a waltz, and when it was finished I looked around and it was just Rosie and me on the dance floor. And everyone applauded again. It was only later that I realised that I had experienced extended close contact with another human without feeling uncomfortable. I attributed it to my concentration on correctly executing the dance steps.

"You want to share a taxi?" asked Rosie.

It seemed a sensible use of fossil fuel.

In the taxi, Rosie said to me, "You should have practised with different beats. You're not as smart as I thought you were."

I just looked out the window of the taxi.

Then she said, "No way. No *fucking* way. You did, didn't you? That's worse. You'd rather make a fool of yourself in front of everyone than tell her she didn't float your boat."

"It would have been extremely awkward. I had no reason to reject her."

"Besides not wanting to marry a parakeet," said Rosie.

I found this incredibly funny, no doubt as a result of alcohol and decompensation after the stress. We both laughed for several minutes, and Rosie even touched me a few times on the shoulder. I didn't mind, but when we stopped laughing I felt awkward again and averted my gaze.

"You're unbelievable," said Rosie. "Look at me when I'm talking."

I kept looking out the window. I was already overstimulated. "I know what you look like."

"What colour eyes do I have?"

"Brown."

"When I was born, I had blue eyes," she said. "Baby blues. Like my mother. She was Irish but she had blue eyes. Then they turned brown."

I looked at Rosie. This was incredible.

"Your mother's eyes changed colour?"

"*My* eyes. It happens with babies. That was when my mother realised that Phil wasn't my father. She had blue eyes and so does Phil. And she decided to tell him. I suppose I should be grateful he wasn't a lion."

I was having trouble making sense of all that Rosie was saying, doubtless due to the effects of the alcohol and her perfume. However, she had given me an opportunity to keep the conversation on safe ground. The inheritance of common genetically influenced traits such as eye colour is more complex than is generally understood, and I was confident that I could speak on the topic for long enough to occupy the remainder of our journey. But I realised that this was a defensive action and impolite to Rosie who had risked considerable embarrassment and damage to her relationship with Stefan for my benefit.

I rolled back my thoughts and re-parsed her statement: "I suppose I should be grateful he wasn't a lion." I assumed she was referring to our conversation on the night of the Balcony Meal when I informed her that lions kill the offspring of previous matings. Perhaps she wanted to talk about Phil. This was interesting to me too. The entire motivation for the Father Project was Phil's failure in that role. But Rosie had offered no real evidence beyond his opposition to alcohol, ownership of an impractical vehicle and selection of a jewellery box as a gift.

"Was he violent?" I asked.

"No." She paused for a while. "He was just — all over the place. One day I'd be the most special kid in the world, next day he didn't want me there."

This seemed very general, and hardly a justification for a major DNA-investigation project. "Can you provide an example?"

"Where do I start? Okay, the first time was when I was ten. He promised to take me to Disneyland. I told everyone at school. And I waited and waited and waited and it never happened."

The taxi stopped outside a block of flats. Rosie kept talking, looking at the back of the driver's seat. "So I have this whole thing about rejection." She turned to me. "How do *you* deal with it?"

"The problem has never occurred," I told her. It was not the time to begin a new conversation.

"Bullshit," said Rosie. It appeared that I would need to answer honestly. I was in the presence of a psychology graduate.

"There were some problems at school," I said. "Hence the martial arts. But I developed some non-violent techniques for dealing with difficult social situations."

"Like tonight."

"I emphasised the things that people found amusing."

Rosie didn't respond. I recognised the therapy technique, but could not think of anything to do but elaborate.

"I didn't have many friends. Basically zero, except my sister. Unfortunately she died two years ago due to medical incompetence."

"What happened?" said Rosie, quietly.

"An undiagnosed ectopic pregnancy."

"Oh, Don," said Rosie, very sympathetically. I sensed that I had chosen an appropriate person to confide in.

"Was she . . . in a relationship?"

"No." I anticipated her next question. "We never found out the source."

"What was her name?"

This was, on the surface, an innocuous question, though I could see no purpose in Rosie knowing my sister's name. The indirect reference was unambiguous, as I had only one sister. But I felt very uncomfortable. It took me a few moments to realise why. Although there had been no deliberate decision on my part, I had not said her name since her death.

"Michelle," I said to Rosie. After that, neither of us spoke for a while.

The taxi driver coughed artificially. I presumed he wasn't asking for a beer.

"You want to come up?" said Rosie.

I was feeling overwhelmed. Meeting Bianca, dancing, rejection by Bianca, social overload, discussion of personal matters — now, just when I thought the ordeal was over, Rosie seemed to be proposing more conversation. I was not sure I could cope.

"It's extremely late," I said. I was sure this was a socially acceptable way of saying that I wanted to go home.

"The taxi fares go down again in the morning."

If I understood correctly, I was now definitely far out of my depth. I needed to be sure that I wasn't misinterpreting her.

"Are you suggesting I stay the night?"

"Maybe. First you have to listen to the story of my life."

Warning! Danger, Will Robinson. Unidentified alien approaching! I could feel myself slipping into the emotional abyss. I managed to stay calm enough to respond.

"Unfortunately I have a number of activities scheduled for the morning." Routine, normality.

Rosie opened the taxi door. I willed her to go. But she had more to say.

"Don, can I ask you something?"

"One question."

"Do you find me attractive?"

Gene told me the next day that I got it wrong. But he was not in a taxi, after an evening of total sensory overload, with the most beautiful woman in the world. I believed I did well. I detected the trick question. I wanted Rosie to like me, and I remembered her passionate statement about men treating women as objects. She was testing to see if I saw her as an object

169

or as a person. Obviously the correct answer was the latter.

"I haven't really noticed," I told the most beautiful woman in the world.

CHAPTER
EIGHTEEN

I texted Gene from the taxi. It was 1.08a.m. but he had left the ball at the same time as I did, and had further to travel. *Urgent. Run tomorrow 6a.m.* Gene texted back: *Sunday at 8: Bring Bianca's contact info.* I was about to insist on the earlier date when I realised that I could profitably use the time to organise my thoughts.

It seemed obvious that Rosie had invited me to have sex with her. I was right to have avoided the situation. We had both drunk a substantial quantity of Champagne, and alcohol is notorious for encouraging unwise decisions about sex. Rosie had the perfect example. Her mother's decision, doubtless prompted by alcohol, was still causing Rosie significant distress.

My own sexual experience was limited. Gene had advised that it was conventional to wait until the third date, and my relationships had never progressed beyond the first. In fact, Rosie and I had technically had only one date — the night of the Jacket Incident and the Balcony Meal.

I did not use the services of brothels, not for any moral reason, but because I found the idea distasteful. This was not a rational reason, but, since the benefits I was seeking were only primitive, a primitive reason was sufficient.

But I now seemed to have an opportunity for what Gene would call "no-strings-attached sex". The required conditions were in place: Rosie and I had clearly agreed that neither of us had an interest in a romantic relationship, then Rosie had indicated that she wanted to have sex with me. Did I want to have sex with Rosie? There seemed no logical reason not to, leaving me free to obey the dictates of my primitive desires. The answer was an extremely clear yes. Having made this completely rational decision, I could think of nothing else.

On Sunday morning, Gene met me outside his house. I had brought Bianca's contact details and checked her nationality — Panamanian. Gene was very pleased about the latter.

Gene wanted full details of my encounter with Rosie, but I had decided it was a waste of effort to explain it twice: I would tell him and Claudia together. As I had no other subject to discuss and Gene had difficulty in running and speaking concurrently, we spent the next forty-seven minutes in silence.

When we returned to Gene's house, Claudia and Eugenie were having breakfast.

I sat down and said, "I require some advice."

"Can it wait?" said Claudia. "We have to take Eugenie to horseriding and then we're meeting people for brunch."

172

"No. I may have made a social error. I broke one of Gene's rules."

Gene said, "Don, I think the Panamanian bird has flown. Put that one down to experience."

"The rule applies to Rosie, not Bianca. Never pass up a chance to have sex with a woman under thirty."

"Gene told you that?" said Claudia.

Carl had entered the room and I prepared to defend myself against his ritual attack, but he stopped to look at his father.

"I thought I should consult with you because you're a psychologist and with Gene because of his extensive practical experience," I said.

Gene looked at Claudia, then at Carl.

"In my misspent youth," he said. "*Not* my teens." He turned back to me. "I think this can wait till lunch tomorrow."

"What about Claudia?" I asked.

Claudia got up from the table. "I'm sure there's nothing Gene doesn't know."

This was encouraging, especially coming from his wife.

"You said what?" said Gene. We were having lunch in the University Club as scheduled.

"I said that I hadn't noticed her appearance. I didn't want her to think I saw her as a sexual object."

"Jesus," said Gene. "The one time you think before you speak is the one time you shouldn't have."

"I should have said she was beautiful?" I was incredulous.

"Got it in one," said Gene, incorrectly, as the problem was that I hadn't got it right the first time. "That'll explain the cake."

I must have looked blank. For obvious reasons.

"She's been eating chocolate cake. At her desk. For breakfast."

This seemed to me to be an unhealthy choice, consistent with smoking, but not an indicator of distress. But Gene assured me that it was to make herself feel better.

Having supplied Gene with the necessary background information, I presented my problem.

"You're saying she's not The One," said Gene. "Not a life partner."

"Totally unsuitable. But she's extremely attractive. If I'm going to have uncommitted sex with anyone, she's the perfect candidate. She has no emotional attachment to me either."

"So why the stress?" said Gene. "You have had sex before?"

"Of course," I said. "My doctor is strongly in favour."

"Frontiers of medical science," said Gene.

He was probably making a joke. I think the value of regular sex has been known for some time.

I explained further. "It's just that adding a second person makes it more complicated."

"Naturally," said Gene. "I should have thought of that. Why not get a book?"

The information was available on the internet, but a few minutes of examining the search results on "sexual

174

positions" convinced me that the book option would provide a more relevant tutorial with less extraneous information.

I had no difficulty finding a suitable book and, back in my office, selected a random position. It was called the Reverse Cowboy Position (Variant 2). I tried it — simple. But, as I had pointed out to Gene, the problem was the involvement of the second person. I got the skeleton from the closet and arranged it on top of me, following the diagram in the book.

There is a rule at the university that no one opens a door without knocking first. Gene violates it in my case but we are good friends. I do not consider the Dean my friend. It was an embarrassing moment, especially as the Dean was accompanied by another person, but entirely her fault. It was fortunate that I had kept my clothes on.

"Don," she said, "if you can leave off repairing that skeleton for a moment, I'd like you to meet Dr Peter Enticott from the Medical Research Council. I mentioned your work in cirrhosis and he was keen to meet you. To consider a *funding package*." She emphasised the last two words as though I was so unconnected with university politics that I might forget that funding was the centre of her world. She was right to do so.

I recognised Peter instantly. He was the former father candidate who worked at Deakin University, and who had prompted the cup-stealing incident. He also recognised me.

"Don and I have met," he said. "His partner is considering applying for the MD programme. And we met recently at a social occasion." He winked at me. "I don't think you're paying your academic staff enough."

We had an excellent discussion about my work with alcoholic mice. Peter seemed highly interested and I had to reassure him repeatedly that I had designed the research so there was no need for external grants. The Dean was making hand signals and contorting her face, and I guessed that she wanted me to misrepresent my study as requiring funding, so that she could divert the money to some project that would not be funded on its merits. I chose to feign a lack of comprehension, but this had the effect of increasing the intensity of the Dean's signalling. It was only afterwards that I realised that I should not have left the sexual positions book open on the floor.

I decided that ten positions would be sufficient initially. More could be learned if the initial encounter was successful. It did not take long — less time than learning the cha-cha. In terms of reward for effort, it seemed strongly preferable to dancing and I was greatly looking forward to it.

I went to visit Rosie in her workplace. The PhD students' area was a windowless space with desks along the walls. I counted eight students, including Rosie and Stefan, whose desk was beside Rosie's.

Stefan gave me an odd smile. I was still suspicious of him.

"You're all over Facebook, Don." He turned to Rosie. "You'll have to update your relationship status."

On his screen was a spectacular photo of Rosie and me dancing, similar to the one that the photographer had given me and which now sat by my computer at home. I was spinning Rosie, and her facial expression indicated extreme happiness. I had not technically been "tagged" as I was not registered on Facebook (social networking not being an interest of mine) but our names had been added to the photo: *A/Prof Don Tillman of Genetics and Rosie Jarman, PhD Candidate, Psychology.*

"Don't talk to me about it," said Rosie.

"You don't like the photo?" This seemed a bad sign.

"It's Phil. I don't want him seeing this."

Stefan said, "You think your father spends his life looking at Facebook?"

"Wait till he calls," said Rosie. " 'How much does he earn?' 'Are you screwing him?' 'What can he bench press?' "

"Hardly unusual questions for a father to ask about a man who's dating his daughter," said Stefan.

"I'm not dating Don. We shared a taxi. That's all. Right, Don?"

"Correct."

Rosie turned back to Stefan. "So you can stick your little theory where it fits. Permanently."

"I need to talk to you in private," I said to Rosie.

She looked at me very directly. "I don't think there's anything we need to say in private."

This seemed odd. But presumably she and Stefan shared information in the same way that Gene and I did. He had accompanied her to the ball.

"I was reconsidering your offer of sex," I said.

Stefan put his hand over his mouth. There was quite a long silence — I would estimate six seconds.

Then Rosie said, "Don, it was a joke. A joke."

I could make no sense of this. I could understand that she might have changed her mind. Perhaps the problem around the sexual objectification response had been fatal. But a joke? Surely I could not be so insensitive to social cues to have missed the fact that she was joking. Yes, I could be. I had failed to detect jokes in the past. Frequently. A joke. I had been obsessing about a joke.

"Oh. When should we meet about the other project?"

Rosie looked down at her desk. "There is no other project."

CHAPTER
NINETEEN

For a week, I did my best to return to my regular schedule, using the time freed up by Eva's cleaning and the cancellation of the Father Project to catch up on the karate and aikido training that I had been missing.

Sensei, fifth dan, a man who says very little, especially to the black belts, pulled me aside as I was working the punching bag in the dojo.

"Something has made you very angry," he said. That was all.

He knew me well enough to know that once an emotion was identified I would not let it defeat me. But he was right to speak to me, because I had not realised that I was angry.

I was briefly angry with Rosie because she unexpectedly refused me something I wanted. But then I became angry with myself over the social incompetence that had doubtless caused Rosie embarrassment.

I made several attempts to contact Rosie and got her answering service. Finally I left a message: "What if you get leukaemia and don't know where to source a bone-marrow transplant? Your biological father would be an excellent candidate with a strong motivation to assist. Failure to complete the project could result in death. There are only eleven candidates remaining."

She did not return my call.

"These things happen," said Claudia over the third coffee meeting in four weeks. "You get involved with a woman, it doesn't work out . . ."

So that was it. I had, in my own way, become "involved" with Rosie.

"What should I do?"

"It's not easy," said Claudia, "but anyone will give you the same advice. Move on. Something else will turn up."

Claudia's logic, built on sound theoretical foundations and drawing on substantial professional experience, was obviously superior to my own irrational feelings. But as I reflected on it, I realised that her advice, and indeed the discipline of psychology itself, embodied the results of research on normal humans. I am well aware that I have some unusual characteristics. Was it possible that Claudia's advice was not appropriate for me?

I decided on a compromise course of action. I would continue the Wife Project. If (and *only* if) there was further time available, I would use it for the Father Project, proceeding alone. If I could present Rosie with the solution, perhaps we could become friends again.

Based on the Bianca Disaster I revised the questionnaire, adding more stringent criteria. I included questions on dancing, racquet sports and bridge to eliminate candidates who would require me to gain competence in useless activities, and increased the difficulty of the mathematics, physics and genetics

180

problems. Option *(c) moderately* would be the *only* acceptable answer to the alcohol question. I organised for the responses to go directly to Gene, who was obviously engaging in the well-established research practice of making secondary use of the data. He could advise me if anyone met my criteria. Exactly.

In the absence of Wife Project candidates, I thought hard about the best way to get DNA samples for the Father Project.

The answer came to me as I was boning a quail. The candidates were doctors who would presumably be willing to contribute to genetics research. I just needed a plausible excuse to ask for their DNA. Thanks to the preparation I had done for the Asperger's lecture, I had one.

I pulled out my list of eleven names. Two were confirmed dead, leaving nine, seven of whom were living overseas, which explained their absence at the reunion. But two had local phone numbers. One was the head of the Medical Research Institute at my own university. I rang it first.

"Professor Lefebvre's office," said a woman's voice.

"It's Professor Tillman from the Department of Genetics. I'd like to invite Professor Lefebvre to participate in a research project."

"Professor Lefebvre is on sabbatical in the US. He'll be back in two weeks."

"Excellent. The project is *Presence of Genetic Markers for Autism in High-Achieving Individuals*. I require him to complete a questionnaire and provide a DNA sample."

Two days later, I had succeeded in locating all nine living candidates and posted them questionnaires, created from the Asperger's research papers, and cheek scrapers. The questionnaires were irrelevant, but were needed to make the research appear legitimate. My covering letter made clear my credentials as a professor of genetics at a prestigious university. In the meantime, I needed to find relatives of the two dead doctors.

I found an obituary for Dr Gerhard von Deyn, a victim of a heart attack, on the internet. It mentioned his daughter, a medical student at the time of his death. I had no trouble tracking down Dr Brigitte von Deyn and she was happy to participate in the survey. Simple.

Geoffrey Case was a much more difficult challenge. He had died a year after graduating. I had long ago noted his basic details from the reunion website. He had not married and had no (known) children.

Meanwhile the DNA samples trickled back. Two doctors, both in New York, declined to participate. Why would medical practitioners not participate in an important study? Did they have something to hide? Such as an illegitimate daughter in the same city that the request came from? It occurred to me that, if they suspected my motives, they could send a friend's DNA. At least refusal was better than cheating.

Seven candidates, including Dr von Deyn, Jr, returned samples. None of them was Rosie's father or half-sister. Professor Simon Lefebvre returned from his sabbatical and wanted to meet me in person.

"I'm here to collect a package from Professor Lefebvre," I said to the receptionist at the city hospital where he was based, hoping to avoid an actual meeting and interrogation. I was unsuccessful. She buzzed the phone, announced my name, and Professor Lefebvre appeared. He was, I assumed, approximately fifty-four years old. I had met many fifty-four-year-olds in the past thirteen weeks. He was carrying a large envelope, presumably containing the questionnaire, which was destined for the recycling bin, and his DNA.

As he reached me, I tried to take the envelope, but he extended his other hand to shake mine. It was awkward, but the net result was that we shook hands and he retained the envelope.

"Simon Lefebvre," he said. "So, what are you really after?"

This was totally unexpected. Why should he question my motives?

"Your DNA," I said. "And the questionnaire. For a major research study. Critical." I was feeling stressed and my voice doubtless reflected it.

"I'm sure it is." Simon laughed. "And you randomly select the head of medical research as a subject?"

"We were looking for high achievers."

"What's Charlie after this time?"

"Charlie?" I didn't know anyone called Charlie.

"All right," he said. "Dumb question. How much do you want me to put in?"

"No putting in is required. There is no Charlie involved. I just require the DNA . . . and the questionnaire."

Simon laughed, again. "You've got my attention. You can tell Charlie that. Shoot me through the project description. And the ethics approval. The whole catastrophe."

"Then I can have my sample?" I said. "A high response rate is critical for the statistical analysis."

"Just send me the paperwork."

Simon Lefebvre's request was entirely reasonable. Unfortunately I did not have the required paperwork, because the project was fictitious. To develop a plausible project proposal would potentially require hundreds of hours of work.

I attempted an estimate of the probability that Simon Lefebvre was Rosie's father. There were now four untested candidates: Lefebvre, Geoffrey Case (dead), and the two New Yorkers, Isaac Esler and Solomon Freyberg. On the basis of Rosie's information, any one of them had a twenty-five per cent probability of being her father. But having proceeded so far without a positive result, I had to consider other possibilities. Two of our results relied on relatives rather than direct testing. It was possible that one or both of these daughters were, like Rosie, the result of extra-relationship sex, which, as Gene points out, is a more common phenomenon than popularly believed. And there was the possibility that one or more of my respondents to the fictitious research project might have deliberately sent a false sample.

I also had to consider that Rosie's mother might not have told the truth. It took me a long time to think of this, as my default assumption is that people will be honest. But perhaps Rosie's mother wanted Rosie to believe that her father was a doctor, as she was, rather than a less prestigious person. On balance, I estimated the chance that Simon Lefebvre was Rosie's father was sixteen per cent. In developing documentation for the Asperger's research project I would be doing an enormous amount of work with a low probability that it would provide the answer.

I chose to proceed. The decision was barely rational.

In the midst of this work, I received a phone call from a solicitor to advise me that Daphne had died. Despite the fact that she had been effectively dead for some time, I detected in myself an unexpected feeling of loneliness. Our friendship had been simple. Everything was so much more complicated now.

The reason for the call was that Daphne had left me what the solicitor referred to as a "small sum" in her will. Ten thousand dollars. And she had also left a letter, written before she had gone to live in the nursing home. It was handwritten on decorative paper.

Dear Don,

Thank you for making the final years of my life so stimulating. After Edward was admitted to the nursing home, I did not believe that there was much left for me. I'm sure you know how much you have taught me, and how interesting our conversations have been, but you may not realise what a wonderful companion and support you have been to me.

I once told you that you would make someone a wonderful husband, and, in case you have forgotten, I am telling you again. I'm sure if you look hard enough, you will find the right person. Do not give up, Don.

I know you don't need my money, and my children do, but I have left you a small sum. I would be pleased if you would use it for something irrational.

Much love,
Your friend,
Daphne Speldewind

It took me less than ten seconds to think of an irrational purchase: in fact I allowed myself only that amount of time to ensure that the decision was not affected by any logical thought process.

The Asperger's research project was fascinating but very time-consuming. The final proposal was impressive and I was confident it would have passed the peer-review process if it had been submitted to a funding organisation. I was implying it had been, though I stopped short of forging an approval letter. I called Lefebvre's personal assistant and explained that I had forgotten to send him the documents, but would now bring them personally. I was becoming more competent at deception.

I arrived at reception, and the process of summoning Lefebvre was repeated. This time he was not holding an envelope. I tried to give him the documents and he tried to shake my hand, and we had a repeat of the confusion that had occurred the previous time. Lefebvre seemed to find this funny. I was conscious of being tense. After all this work, I wanted the DNA.

"Greetings," I said. "Documentation as requested. All requirements have been fulfilled. I now need the DNA sample and questionnaire."

Lefebvre laughed again, and looked me up and down. Was there something odd about my appearance? My t-shirt was the one I wear on alternate days, featuring the periodic table, a birthday gift from the year after my graduation, and my trousers were the serviceable pair that are equally suitable for walking, lecturing, research and physical tasks. Plus high-quality running shoes. The only error was that my socks, which would have been visible below my trousers, were of slightly different colours, a common error when dressing in poor light. But Simon Lefebvre seemed to find everything amusing.

"Beautiful," he said. Then he repeated my words in what seemed to be an attempt to imitate my intonation: "All requirements have been fulfilled." He added, in his normal voice, "Tell Charlie I promise I'll read the proposal."

Charlie again! This was ridiculous.

"The DNA," I said, forcefully. "I need the sample."

Lefebvre laughed as though I had made the biggest joke of all time. There were tears running down his face. Actual tears.

"You've made my day."

He grabbed a tissue from a box on the reception desk, wiped his face, blew his nose and tossed the used tissue in the bin as he left with my proposal.

I walked to the bin and retrieved the tissue.

CHAPTER
TWENTY

I sat with a newspaper in the University Club reading room for the third day in succession. I wanted this to look accidental. From my position, I could observe the queue at the counter where Rosie sometimes purchased her lunch, even though she was not qualified to be a member. Gene had given me this information, reluctantly.

"Don, I think it's time to leave this one alone. You're going to get hurt."

I disagreed. I am very good at dealing with emotions. I was prepared for rejection.

Rosie walked in and joined the queue. I got up and slipped in behind her.

"Don," she said. "What a coincidence."

"I have news on the project."

"There's no project. I'm sorry about . . . last time you saw me. Shit! You embarrass me and I say sorry."

"Apology accepted," I said. "I need you to come to New York with me."

"What? No. No, Don. Absolutely not."

We had reached the cash register and failed to select any food and had to return to the tail of the queue. By the time we sat down, I had explained the Asperger's

189

research project. "I had to invent an entire proposal — three hundred and seventy-one pages — for this one professor. I'm now an expert on the Savant phenomenon."

It was difficult to decode Rosie's reaction but she appeared to be more amazed than impressed.

"An unemployed expert if you get caught," she said. "I gather he's not my father."

"Correct." I had been relieved when Lefebvre's sample had tested negative, even after the considerable effort that had been required to obtain it. I had already made plans, and a positive test would have disrupted them.

"There are now only three possibilities left. Two are in New York, and both refused to participate in the study. Hence, I have categorised them as difficult, and hence I need you to come to New York with me."

"New York! Don, no. No, no, no, no. You're not going to New York and neither am I."

I had considered the possibility that Rosie would refuse. But Daphne's legacy had been sufficient to purchase two tickets.

"If necessary I will go alone. But I'm not confident I can handle the social aspects of the collection."

Rosie shook her head. "This is seriously crazy."

"You don't want to know who they are?" I said. "Two of the three men who may be your father?"

"Go on."

"Isaac Esler. Psychiatrist."

I could see Rosie digging deep into her memory.

"Maybe. Isaac. I think so. Maybe a friend of someone. Shit, it's so long ago." She paused. "And?"

"Solomon Freyberg. Surgeon."

"No relation to Max Freyberg?"

"Maxwell is his middle name."

"Shit. Max Freyberg. He's gone to New York now? No way. You're saying I've got one chance in three of being his daughter. And two chances in three of being Jewish."

"Assuming your mother told the truth."

"My mother wouldn't have lied."

"How old were you when she died?"

"Ten. I know what you're thinking. But I know I'm right."

It was obviously not possible to discuss this issue rationally. I moved to her other statement.

"Is there a problem with being Jewish?"

"Jewish is fine. Freyberg is not fine. But if it's Freyberg it would explain why my mother kept mum. No pun intended. You've never heard of him?"

"Only as a result of this project."

"If you followed football you would have."

"He was a footballer?"

"A club president. And well-known jerk. What about the third person?"

"Geoffrey Case."

"Oh my God." Rosie went white. "He died."

"Correct."

"Mum talked about him a lot. He had an accident. Or some illness — maybe cancer. Something bad, obviously. But I didn't think he was in her year."

It struck me now that we had been extremely careless in the way we had addressed the project, primarily because of the misunderstandings that had led to temporary abandonments followed by restarts. If we had worked through the names at the outset, such obvious possibilities would not have been overlooked.

"Do you know any more about him?"

"No. Mum was really sad about what happened to him. Shit. It makes total sense, doesn't it? Why she wouldn't tell me."

It made no sense to me.

"He was from the country," Rosie said. "I think his father had a practice out in the sticks."

The website had provided the information that Geoffrey Case was from Moree in northern New South Wales, but this hardly explained why Rosie's mother would have hidden his identity if he was the father. His only other distinguishing feature was that he was dead, so perhaps it was this to which Rosie was referring — her mother not wanting to tell her that her father had died. But surely Phil could have been given this information to pass on when Rosie was old enough to deal with it.

While we were talking, Gene entered. With Bianca! They waved to us then went upstairs to the private dining section. Incredible.

"Gross," said Rosie.

"He's researching attraction to different nationalities."

"Right. I just pity his wife."

I told Rosie that Gene and Claudia had an open marriage.

"Lucky her," said Rosie. "Are you planning to offer the same deal to the winner of the Wife Project?"

"Of course," I said.

"Of course," said Rosie.

"If that was what she wanted," I added in case Rosie had misinterpreted.

"You think that's likely?"

"If I find a partner, which seems increasingly *unlikely*, I wouldn't want a sexual relationship with anyone else. But I'm not good at understanding what other people want."

"Tell me something I don't know," said Rosie for no obvious reason.

I quickly searched my mind for an interesting fact. "Ahhh . . . The testicles of drone bees and wasp spiders explode during sex."

It was annoying that the first thing that occurred to me was related to sex. As a psychology graduate, Rosie may have made some sort of Freudian interpretation. But she looked at me and shook her head. Then she laughed. "I can't afford to go to New York. But you're not safe by yourself."

There was a phone number listed for an M. Case in Moree. The woman who answered told me that Dr Case, Sr, whose name was confusingly also Geoffrey, had passed away some years ago and that his widow Margaret had been in the local nursing home with Alzheimer's disease for the past two years. This was good news. Better that the mother was alive than the father — there is seldom any doubt about the identity of the biological mother.

I could have asked Rosie to come with me, but she had already agreed to the New York visit and I did not want to create an opportunity for a social error that might jeopardise the trip. I knew from my experience with Daphne that it would be easy to collect a DNA sample from a person with Alzheimer's disease. I hired a car and packed swabs, cheek-scraper, zip-lock bags and tweezers. I also took a university business card from before I was promoted to associate professor. *Doctor* Don Tillman receives superior service in medical facilities.

Moree is one thousand two hundred and thirty kilometres from Melbourne. I collected the hire car at 3.43p.m. after my last lecture on the Friday. The internet route-planner estimated fourteen hours and thirty-four minutes of driving each way.

When I was a university student, I had regularly driven to and from my parents' home in Shepparton, and found that the long journeys had a similar effect to my market jogs. Research has shown that creativity is enhanced when performing straightforward mechanical tasks such as jogging, cooking and driving. Unobstructed thinking time is always useful.

I took the Hume Highway north, and used the precise speed indication on the GPS to set the cruise control to the exact speed limit, rather than relying on the artificially inflated figure provided by the speedometer. This would save me some minutes without the risk of law-breaking. Alone in the car, I had the feeling that my whole life had been transformed into an adventure, which would culminate in the trip to New York.

I had decided not to play podcasts on the journey in order to reduce cognitive load and encourage my subconscious to process its recent inputs. But after three hours I found myself becoming bored. I take little notice of my surroundings beyond the need to avoid accidents, and in any case the freeway was largely devoid of interest. The radio would be as distracting as podcasts, so I decided to purchase my first CD since the Bach experiment. The service station just short of the New South Wales border had a limited selection but I recognised a few albums from my father's collection. I settled on Jackson Browne's *Running on Empty*. With the repeat button on, it became the soundtrack to my driving and reflections over three days. Unlike many people, I am very comfortable with repetition. It was probably fortunate that I was driving alone.

With my unconscious failing to deliver anything, I attempted an objective analysis of the state of the Father Project.

What did I know?

1. I had tested forty-one of forty-four candidates. (And also several of those of incompatible ethnic appearance.) None had matched. There was the possibility that one of the seven Asperger's survey respondents who had returned samples had sent

someone else's cheek scraping. I considered it unlikely. It would be easier simply not to participate, as Isaac Esler and Max Freyberg had done.

2. Rosie had identified four candidates as being known to her mother — Eamonn Hughes, Peter Enticott, Alan McPhee and, recently, Geoffrey Case. She had considered the first three as high probability, and this would also apply to Geoffrey Case. He was now clearly the most likely candidate.

3. The entire project was reliant on Rosie's mother's testimony that she had performed the critical sexual act at the graduation party. It was possible that she had lied because the biological father was someone less prestigious. This would explain her failure to reveal his identity.

4. Rosie's mother had chosen to remain with Phil. This was my first new thought. It supported the idea that the biological father was less appealing or perhaps unavailable for marriage. It would be interesting to know whether Esler or Freyberg were already married or with partners at that time.

5. Geoffrey Case's death occurred within months of Rosie's birth and presumably the realisation that Phil was not the father. It might have taken some time for Rosie's mother to organise a confirmatory DNA test, by which time Geoffrey Case might

have been dead and hence unavailable as an alternative partner.

This was a useful exercise. The project status was clearer in my mind, I had added some minor insights and I was certain that my journey was justified by the probability that Geoffrey Case was Rosie's father,

I decided to drive until I was tired — a radical decision, as I would normally have scheduled my driving time according to published studies on fatigue and booked accommodation accordingly. But I had been too busy to plan. Nevertheless, I stopped for rest breaks every two hours and found myself able to maintain concentration. At 11.43p.m., I detected tiredness, but rather than sleep I stopped at a service station, refuelled and ordered four double espressos. I opened the sunroof and turned up the CD player volume to combat fatigue, and at 7.19a.m. on Saturday, with the caffeine still running all around my brain, Jackson Browne and I pulled into Moree.

CHAPTER
TWENTY-ONE

I had set the GPS to take me to the nursing home, where I introduced myself as a family friend.

"I'm afraid she won't know you," said the nurse. This was the assumption I had made, although I was prepared with a plausible story if necessary. The nurse took me to a single room with its own bathroom. Mrs Case was asleep.

"Shall I wake her?" asked the nurse.

"No, I'll just sit here."

"I'll leave you to it. Call if you need anything."

I thought it would look odd if I left too quickly so I sat beside the bed for a while. I guessed Margaret Case was about eighty, much the same age as Daphne had been when she moved to the nursing home. Given the story Rosie had told me, it was very possible that I was looking at her grandmother.

As Margaret Case remained still and silent in her single bed, I thought about the Father Project. It was only possible because of technology. For all but the last few years of human existence, the secret would have died with Rosie's mother.

I believe it is the duty of science, of humanity, to discover as much as we can. But I am a physical scientist, not a psychologist.

The woman in front of me was not a fifty-four-year-old male medical practitioner who might have run from his parental responsibilities. She was totally helpless. It would be easy to take a hair sample, or to swab her toothbrush, but it felt wrong.

For these reasons, and for others that I did not fully grasp at the time, I decided not to collect a sample.

Then Margaret Case woke up. She opened her eyes and looked directly at me.

"Geoffrey?" she said, quietly but very clearly. Was she asking for her husband or for her long-dead son? There was a time when I would have replied without thinking, "They're dead," not out of malice but because I am wired to respond to the facts before others' feelings. But something had changed in me, and I managed to suppress the statement.

She must have realised that I was not the person she had hoped to see, and began crying. She was not making any noise, but there were tears on her cheeks. Automatically, because I had experienced this situation with Daphne, I pulled out my handkerchief and wiped away the tears. She closed her eyes again. But fate had delivered me my sample.

I was exhausted, and by the time I walked out of the nursing home there were tears in my own eyes from lack of sleep. It was early autumn, and this far north the day was already warm. I lay under a tree and fell asleep.

I woke to see a male doctor in a white coat standing over me and for a frightening moment I was taken back to the bad times of twenty years ago. It was only momentary; I quickly remembered where I was and he was only checking to see that I was not ill or dead. I was not breaking any rules. It was four hours and eight minutes since I had left Margaret Case's room.

The incident was a timely reminder of the dangers of fatigue and I planned the return trip more carefully. I scheduled a five-minute break every hour and at 7.06p.m. I stopped at a motel, ate an overcooked steak and went to bed. The early night enabled a 5.00a.m. start on the Sunday.

The highway bypasses Shepparton, but I took the turnoff and went to the city centre. I decided not to visit my parents. The extra sixteen kilometres involved in driving the full distance to their house and back to the highway would add a dangerous unplanned increment to what was already a demanding journey, but I did want to see the town.

I drove past Tillman Hardware. It was closed on Sunday, and my father and brother would be at home with my mother. My father was probably straightening pictures, and my mother asking my brother to clear his construction project from the dining table so she could set it for Sunday dinner. I had not been back since my sister's funeral.

The service station was open and I filled the tank. A man of about forty-five, BMI about thirty, was behind the counter. As I approached, I recognised him, and revised his age to thirty-nine. He had lost hair, grown a beard and gained weight, but he was obviously Gary Parkinson, who had been at high school with me. He had wanted to join the army and travel. He had apparently not realised this ambition. I was reminded how lucky I was to have been able to leave and reinvent my life.

"Hey, Don," he said, obviously also recognising me.

"Greetings, GP."

He laughed. "You haven't changed."

It was getting dark on Sunday evening when I arrived back in Melbourne and returned the rental car. I left the Jackson Browne CD in the player.

Two thousand four hundred and seventy-two kilometres according to the GPS. The handkerchief was safe in a zip-lock bag, but its existence did not change my decision not to test Margaret Case.

We would still have to go to New York.

I met Rosie at the airport. She remained uncomfortable about me purchasing her ticket, so I told her she could pay me back by selecting some Wife Project applicants for me to date.

"Fuck you," she said.

It seemed we were friends again.

I could not believe how much baggage Rosie had brought. I had told her to pack as lightly as possible but she exceeded the seven kilogram limit for carry-on luggage. Fortunately I was able to transfer some of her excess equipment to my bag. I had packed my ultra-light PC, toothbrush, razor, spare shirt, gym shorts, change of underwear and (annoyingly) bulky parting gifts from Gene and Claudia. I had only been allowed a week's leave and, even then, the Dean had made it difficult. It was increasingly obvious that she was looking for a reason to get rid of me.

Rosie had never been to the United States, but was familiar with international airport procedures. She was highly impressed by the special treatment that I received. We checked in at the service desk, where there was no queue, and were accompanied through security to the business-class lounge, despite travelling in economy class.

As we drank Champagne in the lounge, I explained that I had earned special privileges by being particularly vigilant and observant of rules and procedures on previous flights, and by making a substantial number of helpful suggestions regarding check-in procedures, flight scheduling, pilot training and ways in which security systems might be subverted. I was no longer expected to offer advice, having contributed "enough for a lifetime of flying".

"Here's to being special," said Rosie. "So, what's the plan?"

Organisation is obviously critical when travelling, and I had an hour-by-hour plan (with hours subdivided as necessary) replacing my usual weekly schedule. It incorporated the appointments that Rosie had made to meet the two father candidates — Esler the psychiatrist and Freyberg the cosmetic surgeon. Amazingly, she had made no other plans beyond arriving at the airport to meet me. At least it meant that there were no incompatible schedules to reconcile.

I opened the schedule on my laptop and began outlining it to Rosie. I had not even completed my list of activities for the flight when she interrupted.

"Fast forward, Don. What are we doing in New York? Between Saturday dinner at the Eslers and Freyberg on Wednesday — which is evening, right? We have four whole days of New York City in between."

"Saturday, after dinner, walk to the Marcy Avenue subway station and take the J, M or Z train to Delancey Street, change to the F train —"

"Overview, overview. Sunday to Wednesday. One sentence per day. Leave out eating, sleeping and travel."

That made it easy. "Sunday, Museum of Natural History; Monday, Museum of Natural History; Tuesday, Museum of Natural History; Wednesday —"

"Stop, wait! Don't tell me Wednesday. Keep it as a surprise."

"You'll probably guess."

"Probably," said Rosie. "How many times have you been to New York?"

"This is my third."

"And I'm guessing this is not going to be your first visit to the museum."

"No."

"What did you think I was going to do while you were at the museum?"

"I hadn't considered it. I presume you've made independent plans for your time in New York."

"You presume wrong," said Rosie. "We are going to see New York. Sunday and Monday, I'm in charge. Tuesday and Wednesday it's your turn. If you want me to spend two days at the museum, I'll spend two days at the museum. With you. But Sunday and Monday, I'm the tour guide."

"But you don't know New York."

"Nor do you." Rosie took our Champagne glasses to the bar to top them up. It was only 9.42a.m. in Melbourne, but I was already on New York time. While she was gone, I flipped open my computer again and connected to the Museum of Natural History site. I would have to replan my visits.

Rosie returned and immediately invaded my personal space. She shut the lid of the computer! Incredible. If I had done that to a *student* playing Angry Birds, I would have been in the Dean's office the next day. In the university hierarchy, I am an associate professor and Rosie is a PhD student. I was entitled to some respect.

"Talk to me," she said. "We've had no time to talk about anything except DNA. Now we've got a week, and I want to know who you are. And if you're going to be the guy who tells me who my father is, you should know who I am."

In less than fifteen minutes, my entire schedule had been torn apart, shattered, rendered redundant. Rosie had taken over.

An escort from the lounge took us to the plane for the fourteen-and-a-half-hour flight to Los Angeles. As a result of my special status, Rosie and I had two seats in a row of three. I am only placed next to other passengers when flights are full.

"Start with your childhood," said Rosie.

All it needed was for her to turn on the overhead light for the scenario of interrogation to be complete. I was a prisoner, so I negotiated — and made escape plans.

"We have to get some sleep. It's evening in New York."

"It's seven o'clock. Who goes to bed at seven? Anyway, I won't be able to sleep."

"I've brought sleeping pills."

Rosie was amazed that I would use sleeping pills. She thought I would have some objection to chemicals. She was right about not knowing much about me. We agreed that I would summarise my childhood experiences, which, given her background in psychology, she would doubtless consider hugely significant, eat dinner, take the sleeping pills and sleep. On the pretext of visiting the bathroom, I asked the cabin manager to bring our dinner as quickly as possible.

CHAPTER
TWENTY-TWO

Telling Rosie my life story was not difficult. Every psychologist and psychiatrist I have seen has asked for a summary, so I have the essential facts clear in my mind.

My father owns a hardware store in a regional city. He lives there with my mother and my younger brother, who will probably take over when my father retires or dies. My older sister died at the age of forty as a result of medical incompetence. When it happened, my mother did not get out of bed for two weeks, except to attend the funeral. I was very sad about my sister's death. Yes, I was angry too.

My father and I have an effective but not emotional relationship. This is satisfactory to both of us. My mother is very caring but I find her stifling. My brother does not like me. I believe this is because he saw me as a threat to his dream of inheriting the hardware store and now does not respect my alternative choice. The hardware store may well have been a metaphor for the affection of our father. If so, my brother won, but I am not unhappy about losing. I do not see my family very often. My mother calls me on Sundays.

I had an uneventful time at school. I enjoyed the science subjects. I did not have many friends and was briefly the object of bullying. I was the top student in the school in all subjects except English, where I was the top boy. At the end of my schooling I left home to attend university. I originally enrolled in computer science, but on my twenty-first birthday made a decision to change to genetics. This may have been the result of a subconscious desire to remain a student, but it was a logical choice. Genetics was a burgeoning field. There is no family history of mental illness.

I turned towards Rosie and smiled. I had already told her about my sister and the bullying. The statement about mental illness was correct, unless I included myself in the definition of "family". Somewhere in a medical archive is a twenty-year-old file with my name and the words "depression, bipolar disorder? OCD?" and "schizophrenia?" The question marks are important — beyond the obvious observation that I was depressed, no definitive diagnosis was ever made, despite attempts by the psychiatric profession to fit me into a simplistic category. I now believe that virtually all my problems could be attributed to my brain being configured differently from those of the majority of humans. All the psychiatric symptoms were a result of this, not of any underlying disease. Of course I was depressed: I lacked friends, sex and a social life, due to being incompatible with other people. My intensity and focus were misinterpreted as mania. And my concern with organisation was labelled as obsessive-compulsive disorder. Julie's Asperger's kids might well face similar problems in their lives. However, they had been labelled with an underlying syndrome, and perhaps the psychiatric profession would be intelligent enough to apply Occam's razor and see that the problems they might face would be largely due to their Asperger's brain configuration.

"What happened on your twenty-first birthday?" asked Rosie.

Had Rosie read my thoughts? What happened on my twenty-first birthday was that I decided that I needed to take a new direction in my life, because any change was better than staying in the pit of depression. I actually visualised it as a pit.

I told Rosie part of the truth. I don't generally celebrate birthdays, but my family had insisted in this case and had invited numerous friends and relatives to compensate for my own lack of friends.

My uncle made a speech. I understood that it was traditional to make fun of the guest of honour, but my uncle became so encouraged by his ability to provoke laughter that he kept going, telling story after story. I was shocked to discover that he knew some extremely personal facts, and realised that my mother must have shared them with him. She was pulling at his arm, trying to get him to stop, but he ignored her, and did not stop until he noticed that she was crying by which time he had completed a detailed exposition of my faults and of the embarrassment and pain that they had caused. The core of the problem, it seemed, was that I was a stereotypical computer geek. So I decided to change.

"To a genetics geek," said Rosie.

"That wasn't exactly my goal." But it was obviously the outcome. And I got out of the pit to work hard in a new discipline. Where was dinner?

"Tell me more about your father."

"Why?" I wasn't actually interested in why. I was doing the social equivalent of saying "over" to put the responsibility back on Rosie. It was a trick suggested by Claudia for dealing with difficult personal questions. I recalled her advice not to overuse it. But this was the first occasion.

"I guess because I want to see if your dad is the reason you're fucked-up."

"I'm not fucked-up."

"Okay, not fucked-up. Sorry, I didn't mean to be judgmental. But you're not exactly average," said Rosie, psychology PhD candidate.

"Agreed. Does 'fucked-up' mean 'not exactly average'?"

"Bad choice of words. Start again. I guess I'm asking because my father is the reason that *I'm* fucked-up."

An extraordinary statement. With the exception of her careless attitude to health, Rosie had never exhibited any sign of brain malfunction.

"What are the symptoms of being fucked-up?"

"I've got crap in my life that I wish I hadn't. And I'm not good at dealing with it. Am I making sense?"

"Of course," I said. "Unwanted events occur and you lack certain skills for minimising the personal impact. I thought when you said 'fucked-up' that there was some problem with your personality that you wanted to rectify."

"No, I'm okay with being me."

"So what is the nature of the damage caused by Phil?"

Rosie did not have an instant reply to this critical question. Perhaps this was a symptom of being fucked-up. Finally she spoke. "Jesus, what's taking them so long with dinner?"

Rosie went to the bathroom, and I took the opportunity to unwrap the presents that Gene and Claudia had given me. They had driven me to the airport, so it was impossible not to accept the packages. It was fortunate that Rosie was not watching when I opened them. Gene's present was a new book of sexual positions and he had inscribed it: "In case you run out of ideas." He had drawn the gene symbol that he uses as his signature underneath. Claudia's present was not embarrassing, but was irrelevant to the trip — a pair of jeans and a shirt. Clothes are always useful, but I had already packed a spare shirt, and did not see a need for additional trousers in only eight days.

Gene had again misconstrued the current nature of my relationship with Rosie, but this was understandable. I could not explain the real purpose for taking Rosie to New York and Gene had made an assumption consistent with his world view. On the way to the airport, I had asked Claudia for advice on dealing with so much time in the company of one person.

"Remember to listen," said Claudia. "If she asks you an awkward question, ask her why she's asking. Turn it back to her. If she's a psychology student, she'll love talking about herself. Take notice of your emotions as well as logic. Emotions have their own logic. And try to go with the flow."

In fact, Rosie spent most of the remainder of the flight to Los Angeles either sleeping or watching films, but confirmed — twice — that I had not offended her and she just needed time out.

I did not complain.

CHAPTER
TWENTY-THREE

We survived US Immigration. Previous experience had taught me not to offer observations or suggestions, and I did not need to use my letter of recommendation from David Borenstein at Columbia University characterising me as a sane and competent person. Rosie seemed extremely nervous, even to someone who is poor at judging emotional states, and I was worried that she would cause suspicion and that we would be refused entry *for no justifiable reason*, as had happened to me on a previous occasion.

The official asked, "What do you do?" and I said, "Genetics researcher," and he said, "Best in the world?" and I said, "Yes." We were through. Rosie almost ran towards Customs and then to the exit. I was several metres behind, carrying both bags. Something was obviously wrong.

I caught up to her outside the automatic doors, reaching into her handbag.

"Cigarette," she said. She lit a cigarette and took a long drag. "Just don't say anything, okay? If I ever needed a reason to give up, I've got one now. Eighteen and a half hours. Fuck."

It was fortunate that Rosie had told me not to say anything. I remained silent but shocked at the impact of addiction on her life.

She finished her cigarette and we headed to the bar. It was only 7.48a.m. in Los Angeles, but we could be on Melbourne time until our arrival in New York.

"What was the deal about 'best geneticist on the planet'?"

I explained that I had a special O-1 Visa for Aliens of Extraordinary Ability. I had needed a visa after the occasion when I was refused entry and this was deemed the safest choice. O-1 visas were quite rare and "yes" was the correct answer to any question about the extraordinariness of my abilities. Rosie found the word "alien" amusing. Correction, hilarious.

Since we did not have bags checked, and the immigration process had proceeded smoothly, I was able to implement my best-case alternative and we caught an earlier flight to New York. I had made plans for the time gained through this manoeuvre.

At JFK, I steered Rosie towards the Air Train. "We have two subway options."

"I supposed you've memorised the timetable," said Rosie.

"Not worth the effort. I just know the lines and stations we need for our journeys." I love New York. The layout is so logical, at least uptown from 14th Street.

When Rosie had telephoned Isaac Esler's wife she was very positive about some contact from Australia and news from the reunion. On the subway, Rosie said,

"You'll need an alias. In case Esler recognises your name from the Asperger's survey."

I had already considered this. "Austin," I said. "From *Austin Powers*. International Man of Mystery." Rosie thought this was hilarious. I had made a successful, deliberate joke that was not related to exhibiting some quirk in my personality. A memorable moment.

"Profession?" she asked.

"Hardware-store owner." The idea appeared in my brain spontaneously.

"Okaaaaaay," said Rosie. "Right."

We took the E train to Lexington Avenue and 53rd Street and headed uptown.

"Where's the hotel?" Rosie asked as I steered us towards Madison Avenue.

"Lower East Side. But we have to shop first."

"Fuck, Don, it's after 5.30. We're due at the Eslers' at 7.30. We don't have time for shopping. I need time to change."

I looked at Rosie. She was wearing jeans and shirt — conventional attire. I could not see the problem, but we had time. "I hadn't planned to go to the hotel before dinner, but since we arrived early —"

"Don, I've been flying for twenty-four hours. We are doing nothing more with your schedule until I've checked it for craziness."

"I've scheduled four minutes for the transaction," I said. We were already outside the Hermès store, which my research had identified as the world's best scarf shop. I walked in and Rosie followed.

The shop was empty except for us. Perfect.

"Don, you're not exactly dressed for this."

Dressed for shopping! I was dressed for travelling, eating, socialising, museum-visiting — and shopping: runners, cargo pants, t-shirt and the jumper knitted by my mother. This was not Le Gavroche. It seemed highly unlikely that they would refuse to participate in a commercial exchange on the basis of my costume. I was right.

Two women stood behind the counter, one (age approximately fifty-five, BMI approximately nineteen) wearing rings on all eight fingers, and the other (age approximately twenty, BMI approximately twenty-two) wearing huge purple glasses creating the impression of a human ant. They were very formally dressed. I initiated the transaction.

"I require a high-quality scarf."

Ring Woman smiled. "I can help you with that. It's for the lady?"

"No. For Claudia." I realised that this was not helpful but was not sure how to elaborate.

"And Claudia is" — she made circles with her hand — "what age?"

"Forty-one years, three hundred and fifty-six days."

"Ah," said Ring Woman, "so we have a birthday coming up."

"Just Claudia." My birthday was thirty-two days away, so it surely did not qualify as "coming up". "Claudia wears scarves, even in hot weather, to cover lines on her neck which she considers unattractive. So the scarf does not need to be functional, only decorative."

Ring Woman produced a scarf. "What do you think of this?"

It was remarkably light — and would offer almost zero protection against wind and cold. But it was certainly decorative, as specified.

"Excellent. How much?" We were running to schedule.

"This one is twelve hundred dollars."

I opened my wallet and extracted my credit card.

"Whoa whoa *whoa*," said Rosie. "I think we'd like to see what else you have before we rush into anything."

I turned to Rosie. "Our four minutes is almost up."

Ring Woman put three more scarves on the counter. Rosie looked at one. I copied her, looking at another. It seemed nice. They all seemed nice. I had no framework for discrimination.

It continued. Ring Woman kept throwing more scarves on the counter and Rosie and I looked at them. Ant Woman came to help. I finally identified one that I could comment intelligently on.

"This scarf has a fault! It's not symmetrical. Symmetry is a key component of human beauty."

Rosie had a brilliant response. "Maybe the scarf's lack of symmetry will highlight Claudia's symmetry."

Ant Woman produced a pink scarf with fluffy bits. Even I could see that Claudia would not approve and dropped it immediately on the reject pile.

"What's wrong with it?" said Rosie.

"I don't know. It's unsuitable."

"Come on," she said, "you can do better than that. Imagine who might wear it."

216

"Barbara Cartland," said Ring Woman.

I was not familiar with this name, but the answer suddenly came to me. "The Dean! At the ball."

Rosie burst out laughing. "Corrrrr-ect." She pulled another scarf from the pile. "What about this one?" It was virtually transparent.

"Julie," I said automatically, then explained to Rosie and the two women about the Asperger's counsellor and her revealing costume. Presumably she would not want a scarf to reduce its impact.

"This one?"

It was a scarf that I had quite liked because of its bright colours, but Rosie had rejected as too "loud".

"Bianca."

"Exactly." Rosie had not stopped laughing. "You know more about clothes than you think you do."

Ant Woman produced a scarf covered in pictures of birds.

I picked it up — the pictures were remarkably accurate. It was quite beautiful.

"Birds of the world," Ant Woman said.

"Oh my God, no!" said Rosie. "Not for Claudia."

"Why not? It's extremely interesting."

"Birds of the world! Think about it. Gene."

Scarves were being sourced from multiple locations, piling rapidly, being evaluated, tossed aside. It was happening so quickly that I was reminded of the Great Cocktail Night, except that we were the customers. I wondered if the women were enjoying their work as much as I had.

In the end I left the choice to Rosie. She chose the first scarf that they had shown us.

As we walked out of the store, Rosie said, "I think I just wasted an hour of your life."

"No, no, the outcome was irrelevant," I said. "It was so entertaining."

"Well," said Rosie, "any time you need entertaining, I could use a pair of Manolo Blahniks." From the word "pair", I guessed that she was referring to shoes.

"Do we have time?" We had already used the time that Rosie had intended for the hotel visit.

"I'm kidding, I'm kidding."

It was fortunate, as we had to move quickly to arrive at the Eslers' on schedule. But Rosie needed to change. There was a bathroom at Union Square station. Rosie dashed in and reappeared looking amazingly different.

"That was incredible," I said. "So quick."

Rosie looked at me. "You're going like that?" Her tone suggested dissatisfaction.

"These are my clothes," I said. "I have a spare shirt."

"Show it to me."

I reached into the bag to get the alternative shirt, which I doubted Rosie would prefer, and remembered Claudia's gift. I showed the shirt to Rosie.

"It was a gift from Claudia," I said. "I've got jeans as well, if that helps."

"All hail Claudia," said Rosie. "She earned the scarf."

"We'll be late."

"Politely late is fine."

Isaac and Judy Esler had an apartment in Williamsburg. My US cell-phone card was working to specification, and we were able to navigate by GPS to the location. I hoped that forty-six minutes met Rosie's definition of "politely late".

"Austin, remember," said Rosie as she rang the bell.

Judy answered the door. I estimated her age as fifty and her BMI as twenty-six. She spoke with a New York accent, and was concerned that we might have become lost. Her husband Isaac was a caricature of a psychiatrist: mid-fifties, short, receding hair, black goatee beard, BMI nineteen. He was not as friendly as his wife.

They offered us martinis. I remembered the effect this drink had had on me during the preparation for the Great Cocktail Night and resolved that I would have no more than three. Judy had made some fish-based canapés, and asked for details of our trip. She wanted to know whether we had been to New York before, what season it was in Australia (not a challenging question) and whether we planned to do any shopping and see any museums. Rosie handled all of these questions.

"Isaac's off to Chicago in the morning," said Judy. "Tell them what you'll be doing there."

"Just a conference," said Isaac. He and I did not need to do a great deal of talking to ensure the conversation continued.

He did ask me one thing before we moved to the dining room. "What do you do, Austin?"

"Austin runs a hardware store," said Rosie. "A very successful one."

219

Judy served a delicious meal based on farmed salmon, which she assured Rosie was sustainable. I had eaten very little of the poor-quality aeroplane food, and enjoyed Judy's meal immensely. Isaac opened some Pinot Gris from Oregon and was generous in refilling my glass. We talked about New York and the differences between Australian and American politics.

"Well," said Judy, "I'm so glad you could come. It makes up a little for missing the reunion. Isaac was so sorry not to be there."

"Not really," said Isaac. "Revisiting the past is not something to do lightly." He ate the last piece of fish from his plate and looked at Rosie. "You look a lot like your mother. She would have been a bit younger than you when I last saw her."

Judy said, "We got married the day after the graduation and moved here. Isaac had the biggest hangover at the wedding. He'd been a bad boy." She smiled.

"I think that's enough telling tales, Judy," said Isaac. "It was all a long time ago."

He stared at Rosie. Rosie stared at him.

Judy picked up Rosie's plate and mine, one in each hand. I decided that this was the moment to act, with everyone distracted. I stood and picked up Isaac's plate in one hand and then Judy's. Isaac was too busy playing the staring game with Rosie to object. I took the plates to the kitchen, swabbing Isaac's fork on the way.

"I imagine Austin and Rosie are exhausted," said Judy when we returned to the table.

"You said you're a hardware man, Austin?" Isaac stood up. "Can you spare five minutes to look at a tap for me? It's probably a job for a plumber, but maybe it's just a washer."

"He means faucet," said Judy, presumably forgetting we came from the same country as Isaac.

Isaac and I went down the stairs to the basement. I was confident I could help with the tap problem. My school holidays had been spent providing advice of exactly this kind. But as we reached the bottom of the stairs, the lights went out. I wasn't sure what had happened. A power failure?

"You okay, Don?" said Isaac, sounding concerned.

"I'm okay," I said. "What happened?"

"What happened is that you answered to Don, Austin."

We stood there in the dark. I doubted that there were social conventions for dealing with interrogation by a psychiatrist in a dark cellar.

"How did you know?" I asked.

"Two unsolicited communications from the same university in a month. An internet search. You make good dancing partners."

More silence and darkness.

"I know the answer to your question. But I made a promise that I would not reveal it. If I thought it was a matter of life or death, or a serious mental health issue, I would reconsider. But I see no reason to break the promise, which was made because the people involved had thought hard about what would be right. You came a long way for my DNA, and I'm guessing you got it

221

when you cleared the plates. You might want to think beyond your girlfriend's wishes before you proceed."

He turned on the light.

Something bothered me as we walked up the stairs. At the top, I stopped. "If you knew what I wanted, why did you let us come to your house?"

"Good question," he said. "Since you asked the question, I'm sure you can work out the answer. I wanted to see Rosie."

CHAPTER
TWENTY-FOUR

Thanks to carefully timed use of sleeping pills, I woke without any feeling of disorientation, at 7.06 a.m.

Rosie had fallen asleep in the train on the way to the hotel. I had decided not to tell her immediately about the basement encounter, nor mention what I had observed on the sideboard. It was a large photo of Judy and Isaac's wedding. Standing beside Isaac, dressed in the formal clothes required of a best man, was Geoffrey Case, who had only three hundred and seventy days to live. He was smiling.

I was still processing the implications myself, and Rosie would probably have an emotional response that could spoil the New York experience. She was impressed that I had collected the DNA, and even more impressed that I had acted so unobtrusively when I picked up the dishes to assist.

"You're in danger of learning some social skills."

The hotel was perfectly comfortable. After we checked in, Rosie said she had been worried that I would expect her to share a room in exchange for paying for her trip to New York. Like a prostitute! I was highly insulted. She seemed pleased with my reaction.

I had an excellent workout at the hotel gym, and returned to find the message light blinking. Rosie.

"Where were you?" she said.

"In the gym. Exercise is critical in reducing the effects of jet lag. Also sunlight. I've planned to walk twenty-nine blocks in sunlight."

"Aren't you forgetting something? Today is my day. And tomorrow. I own you until midnight Monday. Now get your butt down here. I'm hanging out for breakfast."

"In my gym clothes?"

"No, Don, not in your gym clothes. Shower, dress. You have ten minutes."

"I always have my breakfast before I shower."

"How old are you?" said Rosie, aggressively. She didn't wait for the answer. "You're like an old man — I always have my breakfast before I shower, don't sit in my chair, that's where I sit . . . *Do not fuck with me, Don Tillman*." She said the last words quite slowly. I decided it was best not to fuck with her. By midnight tomorrow it would be over. In the interim, I would adopt the dentist mindset.

It seemed I was in for a root-canal filling. I arrived downstairs and Rosie was immediately critical.

"How long have you had that shirt?"

"Fourteen years," I said. "It dries very quickly. Perfect for travelling." In fact it was a specialised walking shirt, though fabric technology had progressed significantly since it was made.

"Good," said Rosie. "It doesn't owe you anything. Upstairs. Other shirt."

224

"It's wet."

"I mean Claudia's shirt. And the jeans while you're at it. I'm not walking around New York with a bum."

When I came down for the second attempt at breakfast, Rosie smiled. "You know, you're not such a bad-looking guy underneath." She stopped and looked at me. "Don, you're not enjoying this, are you? You'd rather be by yourself in the museum, right?" She was extremely perceptive. "I get that. But you've done all these things for me, you've brought me to New York, and, by the way, I haven't finished spending your money yet. So I want to do something for you."

I could have argued that her *wanting* to do something for me meant she was ultimately acting in her own interests, but it might provoke more of the "don't fuck with me" behaviour.

"You're in a different place, you're in different clothes. When the medieval pilgrims used to arrive at Santiago after walking hundreds of kilometres they burned their clothes to symbolise that they'd changed. I'm not asking you to burn your clothes — yet. Put them on again on Tuesday. Just be open to something different. Let me show you my world for a couple of days. Starting with breakfast. We're in the city with the best breakfasts in the world."

She must have seen that I was resisting.

"Hey, you schedule your time so you don't waste it, right?"

"Correct."

"So, you've committed to two days with me. If you shut yourself down, you're wasting two days of your life that someone is trying to make exciting and productive and fun for you. I'm going to —" She stopped. "I left the guidebook in my room. When I come down, we're going to breakfast." She turned and walked to the elevators.

I was disturbed by Rosie's logic. I had always justified my schedule in terms of efficiency. But was my allegiance to efficiency or was it to the schedule itself? Was I really like my father, who had insisted on sitting in the same chair every night? I had never mentioned this to Rosie. I had my own special chair too.

There was another argument that she had not presented, because she could not have known it. In the last eight weeks I had experienced two of the three best times of my adult life, assuming all visits to the Museum of Natural History were treated as one event. They had both been with Rosie. Was there a correlation? It was critical to find out.

By the time Rosie came back I had performed a brain reboot, an exercise requiring a considerable effort of will. But I was now configured for adaptability.

"So?" she said.

"So, how do we find the world's best breakfast?"

We found the World's Best Breakfast round the corner. It may have been the unhealthiest breakfast I had ever eaten, but I would not put on significant weight, nor lose fitness, brain acuity or martial-arts skills if I neglected them for two days. This was the mode in which my brain was now operating.

"I can't believe you ate all that," said Rosie.

"It tasted so good."

"No lunch. Late dinner," she said.

"We can eat any time."

Our server approached the table. Rosie indicated the empty coffee cups. "They were great. I think we could both manage another."

"Huh?" said the server. It was obvious that she hadn't understood Rosie. It was also obvious that Rosie had very poor taste in coffee — or she had done as I had and ignored the label "coffee" and was enjoying it as an entirely new beverage. The technique was working brilliantly.

"One regular coffee with cream and one regular coffee without cream . . . please," I said.

"Sure."

This was a town where people talked straight. My kind of town. I was enjoying speaking American: cream instead of milk, elevator instead of lift, check instead of bill. I had memorised a list of differences between American and Australian usage prior to my first trip to the US, and had been surprised at how quickly my brain was able to switch into using them automatically.

We walked uptown. Rosie was looking at a guidebook called *Not for Tourists*, which seemed a very poor choice.

"Where are we going?" I asked.

"We're not going anywhere. We're there."

We were outside a clothing store. Rosie asked if it was okay to go inside.

"You don't have to ask," I said. "You're in control."

"I do about shops. It's a girl thing. I was going to say, 'I suppose you've been on Fifth Avenue before', but I don't suppose anything with you."

The situation was symmetrical. I knew not to suppose anything about Rosie, or I would have been surprised by her describing herself as a "girl", a term that I understood to be unacceptable to feminists when referring to adult women.

Rosie was becoming remarkably perceptive about me. I had never been beyond the conference centres and the museum, but with my new mind configuration, I was finding everything fascinating. A whole shop for cigars. The prices of jewellery. The Flatiron Building. The sex museum. Rosie looked at the last of these, and chose not to go in. This was probably a good decision — it might be fascinating, but the risk of a faux pas would be very high.

"Do you want to buy anything?" said Rosie.

"No."

A few minutes later, a thought occurred to me. "Is there somewhere that sells men's shirts?"

Rosie laughed. "On Fifth Avenue, New York City. Maybe we'll get lucky." I detected sarcasm, but in a friendly way. We found a new shirt of the same genre as the Claudia shirt at a huge store called Bloomingdale's, which was not, in fact, on Fifth Avenue. We could not choose between two candidate shirts and bought both. My wardrobe would be overflowing!

We arrived at Central Park.

"We're skipping lunch, but I could handle an ice-cream," said Rosie. There was a vendor in the park, and he was serving both cones and prefabricated confections.

I was filled with an irrational sense of dread. I identified it immediately. But I had to know. "Is the flavour important?"

"Something with peanuts. We're in the States."

"All ice-creams taste the same."

"Bullshit."

I explained about tastebuds.

"Wanna bet?" said Rosie. "If I can tell the difference between peanut and vanilla, two tickets to *Spiderman*. On Broadway. Tonight."

"The textures will be different. Because of the peanuts."

"Any two. Your choice."

I ordered an apricot and a mango. "Close your eyes," I said. It wasn't really necessary: the colours were almost identical, but I didn't want her to see me tossing a coin to decide which one to show her. I was concerned that with her psychological skills she might guess my sequence.

I tossed the coin and gave her an ice-cream.

"Mango," guessed Rosie, correctly. Toss, heads again. "Mango again." She picked the mango correctly three times, then the apricot, then the apricot again. The chances of her achieving this result randomly were one in thirty-two. I could be ninety-seven per cent confident she was able to differentiate. Incredible.

"So, *Spiderman* tonight?"

"No. You got one wrong."

Rosie looked at me, very carefully, then burst out laughing. "You're bullshitting me, aren't you? I can't believe it, you're making jokes."

She gave me an ice-cream. "Since you don't care, you can have the apricot."

I looked at it. What to say? She had been licking it.

Once again she read my mind. "How are you going to kiss a girl if you won't share her ice-cream?"

For several minutes, I was suffused with an irrational feeling of enormous pleasure, basking in the success of my joke, and parsing the sentence about the kiss: Kiss *a* girl, share *her* ice-cream — it was third-person, but surely not unrelated to the girl who was sharing her ice-cream right now with Don Tillman in his new shirt and jeans as we walked among the trees in Central Park, New York City, on a sunny Sunday afternoon.

I needed the hundred and fourteen minutes of time-out back at the hotel, although I had enjoyed the day immensely. Shower, email, relaxation exercises combined with stretches. I emailed Gene, copying in Claudia, with a summary of our activities.

Rosie was three minutes late for our 7.00p.m. foyer meeting. I was about to call her room when she arrived wearing clothes purchased that day — white jeans and a blue t-shirt thing — and the jacket she had worn the previous evening. I remembered a Gene-ism, something I had heard him say to Claudia. "You're looking very elegant," I said. It was a risky statement, but her reaction appeared to be positive. She did look very elegant.

230

We had cocktails at a bar with the World's Longest Cocktail List, including many I did not know, and we saw *Spiderman*. Afterwards, Rosie felt the story was a bit predictable but I was overwhelmed by everything, in a hugely positive way. I had not been to the theatre since I was a child. I could have ignored the story and focused entirely on the mechanics of the flying. It was just incredible.

We caught the subway back to the Lower East Side. I was hungry, but did not want to break the rules by suggesting that we eat. But Rosie had this planned too. A 10.00p.m. booking at a restaurant called Momofuku Ko. We were on Rosie time again.

"This is my present to you for bringing me here," she said.

We sat at a counter for twelve where we could watch the chefs at work. There were few of the annoying formalities that make restaurants so stressful.

"Any preferences, allergies, dislikes?" asked the chef.

"I'm vegetarian, but I eat sustainable seafood," said Rosie. "He eats everything — and I mean everything."

I lost count of the courses. I had sweetbreads and foie gras (first time!) and sea urchin roe. We drank a bottle of rosé Champagne. I talked to the chefs and they told me what they were doing. I ate the best food I had ever eaten. And I did not need to wear a jacket in order to eat. In fact, the man sitting beside me was wearing a costume that would have been extreme at the Marquess of Queensbury, including multiple facial piercings. He heard me speaking to the chef and asked me where I was from. I told him.

"How are you finding New York?"

I told him I was finding it highly interesting, and explained how we had spent our day. But I was conscious that, under the stress of talking to a stranger, my manner had changed — or, to be more precise, *reverted* — to my usual style. During the day, with Rosie, I had felt relaxed, and had spoken and acted differently, and this continued in my conversation with the chef, which was essentially a professional exchange of information. But informal social interaction with another person had triggered my regular behaviour. And my regular behaviour and speaking style is, I am well aware, considered odd by others. The man with the piercings must have noticed.

"You know what I like about New York?" he said. "There are so many weird people that nobody takes any notice. We all just fit right in."

"How was it?" said Rosie as we walked back to the hotel.

"The best day of my adult life," I said. Rosie seemed so happy with my response that I decided not to finish the sentence: "excluding the Museum of Natural History."

"Sleep in," she said. "9.30 here and we'll do the brunch thing again. Okay?"

It would have been totally irrational to argue.

CHAPTER
TWENTY-FIVE

"Did I cause any embarrassment?"

Rosie had been concerned that I might make inappropriate comments during our tour of the World Trade Center site. Our guide, a former firefighter named Frank, who had lost many of his colleagues in the attack, was incredibly interesting and I asked a number of technical questions that he answered intelligently and, it seemed to me, enthusiastically.

"You may have changed the tone a bit," she said. "You sort of moved the attention away from the emotional impact." So, I had reduced the sadness. Good.

Monday was allocated to visiting popular tourist sights. We had breakfast at Katz's Deli, where a scene for a film called *When Harry Met Sally* was shot. We went to the top of the Empire State Building, famous as a location for *An Affair to Remember*. We visited MOMA and the Met, which were excellent.

We were back at the hotel early — 4.32p.m.

"Back here at 6.30," said Rosie.

"What are we having for dinner?"

"Hot dogs. We're going to the baseball."

I *never* watch sport. Ever. The reasons are obvious — or should be to anyone who values their time. But my reconfigured mind, sustained by huge doses of positive reinforcement, accepted the proposition. I spent the next hundred and eighteen minutes on the internet, learning about the rules and the players.

On the subway, Rosie had some news for me. Before she left Melbourne, she had sent an email to Mary Keneally, a researcher working in her field at Columbia University. She had just received a reply and Mary could see her tomorrow. But she wouldn't be able to make it to the Museum of Natural History. She could come Wednesday, but would I be okay by myself tomorrow? Of course I would.

At Yankee Stadium we got beer and hot dogs. A man in a cap, estimated age thirty-five, estimated BMI forty (i.e. dangerously fat), sat beside me. He had three hot dogs! The source of the obesity was obvious.

The game started, and I had to explain to Rosie what was happening. It was fascinating to see how the rules worked in a real game. Every time there was an event on the field, Fat Baseball Fan would make an annotation in his book. There were runners on second and third when Curtis Granderson came to the plate and Fat Baseball Fan spoke to me. "If he bats in both of these guys he'll be heading the league on RBI. What are the odds?"

I didn't know what the odds were. All I could tell him was that they were somewhere between 9.9 and 27.2 per cent based on the batting average and percentage of home runs listed in the profile I had read.

I had not had time to memorise the statistics for doubles and triples. Fat Baseball Fan nevertheless seemed impressed and we began a very interesting conversation. He showed me how to mark the programme with symbols to represent the various events, and how the more sophisticated statistics worked. I had no idea sport could be so intellectually stimulating.

Rosie got more beer and hot dogs and Fat Baseball Fan started to tell me about Joe DiMaggio's "streak" in 1941 which he claimed was a uniquely odds-defying achievement. I was doubtful, and the conversation was just getting interesting when the game ended, so he suggested we take the subway to a bar in Midtown. As Rosie was in charge of the schedule, I asked for her opinion, and she agreed.

The bar was noisy and there was more baseball playing on a large television screen. Some other men, who did not appear to have previously met Fat Baseball Fan, joined our discussion. We drank a lot of beer, and talked about baseball statistics. Rosie sat on a stool with her drink and observed. It was late when Fat Baseball Fan, whose actual name was Dave, said he had to go home. We exchanged email addresses and I considered that I had made a new friend.

Walking back to the hotel, I realised that I had behaved in stereotypical male fashion, drinking beer in a bar, watching television and talking about sport. It is generally known that women have a negative attitude to such behaviour. I asked Rosie if I had offended her.

"Not at all. I had fun watching you being a guy — fitting in."

I told her that this was a highly unusual response from a feminist, but that it would make her a very attractive partner to conventional men.

"If I was interested in conventional men."

It seemed a good opportunity to ask a question about Rosie's personal life.

"Do you have a boyfriend?" I hoped I had used an appropriate term.

"Sure, I just haven't unpacked him from my suitcase," she said, obviously making a joke. I laughed, then pointed out that she hadn't actually answered my question.

"Don," she said, "don't you think that if I had a boyfriend you might have heard about him by now?"

It seemed to me entirely possible that I would not have heard about him. I had asked Rosie very few personal questions outside the Father Project. I did not know any of her friends, except perhaps Stefan who I had concluded was not her boyfriend. Of course, it would have been traditional to bring any partner to the faculty ball, and not to offer me sex afterwards, but not everyone was bound by such conventions. Gene was the perfect example. It seemed entirely possible that Rosie had a boyfriend who did not like dancing or socialising with academics, was out of town at the time, or was in an open relationship with her. She had no reason to tell me. In my own life, I had rarely mentioned Daphne or my sister to Gene and Claudia or vice versa. They belonged to different parts of my life. I explained this to Rosie.

"Short answer, no," she said. We walked a bit further. "Long answer: you asked what I meant about being fucked-up by my father. Psychology 101 — our first relationship with a male is with our fathers. It affects how we relate to men forever. So, lucky me, I get a choice of two. Phil, who's fucked in the head, or my real father who walked away from me and my mother. And I get this choice when I'm twelve years old and Phil sits me down and has this 'I wish your mother could be here to tell you' talk with me. You know, just the standard stuff your dad tells you at twelve — I'm not your dad, your mum who died before you could know her properly isn't the perfect person you thought she was, and you're only here because of your mother being easy and I wish you weren't so I could go off and have a life."

"He said that to you?"

"Not in those words. But that's what he meant."

I thought it highly unlikely that a twelve-year-old — even a female future psychology student — could correctly deduce an adult male's unspoken thoughts. Sometimes it is better to be aware of one's incompetence in these matters, as I am, than to have a false sense of expertise.

"So, I don't trust men. I don't believe they're what they say they are. I'm afraid they're going to let me down. That's my summary from seven years of studying psychology."

This seemed a very poor result for seven years of effort, but I assumed she was omitting the more general knowledge provided by the course.

"You want to meet tomorrow evening?" said Rosie. "We can do whatever you want to do."

I had been thinking about my plans for the next day.

"I know someone at Columbia," I said. "Maybe we could go there together."

"What about the museum?"

"I've already compressed four visits into two. I can compress two into one." There was no logic in this, but I had drunk a lot of beer, and I just felt like going to Columbia. *Go with the flow*.

"See you at eight — and don't be late," said Rosie. Then she kissed me. It was not a passionate kiss; it was on the cheek, but it was disturbing. Neither positive nor negative, just disturbing.

I emailed David Borenstein at Columbia then Skyped Claudia and told her about the day, omitting the kiss.

"Sounds like she's made a big effort," said Claudia.

This was obviously true. Rosie had managed to select activities that I would normally have avoided, but enjoyed immensely. "And you're giving her the guided tour of the Museum of Natural History on Wednesday?"

"No, I'm going to look at the crustaceans and the Antarctic flora and fauna."

"Try again," said Claudia.

CHAPTER
TWENTY-SIX

We took the subway to Columbia. David Borenstein had not replied to my email. I did not mention this to Rosie who invited me to her meeting, if it did not clash with mine.

"I'll say you're a fellow researcher," she said. "I'd like you to see what I do when I'm not mixing drinks."

Mary Keneally was an associate professor of psychiatry in the Medical Faculty. I had never asked Rosie the topic of her PhD. It turned out to be *Environmental Risks for Early Onset Bipolar Disorder*, a serious scientific topic. Rosie's approach appeared sound and well considered. She and Mary talked for fifty-three minutes, and then we all went for coffee.

"At heart," Mary said to Rosie, "you're a psychiatrist rather than a psychologist. You've never thought of transferring to Medicine?"

"I came from a medical family," said Rosie. "I sort of rebelled."

"Well, when you've finished rebelling, we've got a great MD programme here."

"Right," said Rosie. "Me at Columbia."

"Why not? In fact, since you've come all this way . . ." She made a quick phone call, then smiled. "Come and meet the Dean."

As we walked back to the Medical building, Rosie said to me, "I hope you're suitably impressed." We arrived at the Dean's office and he stepped out to meet us.

"Don," he said. "I just got your email. I haven't had a chance to reply." He turned to Rosie. "I'm David Borenstein. And you're with Don?"

We all had lunch at the faculty club. David told Rosie that he had supported my O-1 visa application. "I didn't lie," he said. "Any time Don feels like joining the main game, there's a job for him here."

Coal-oven pizza is supposedly environmentally unsound, but I treat statements of this kind with great suspicion. They are frequently emotionally based rather than scientific and ignore full life-cycle costs. Electricity good, coal bad. But where does the electricity come from? Our pizza at Arturo's was excellent. World's Best Pizza.

I was interested in one of the statements Rosie had made at Columbia.

"I thought you admired your mother. Why wouldn't you want to be a doctor?"

"It wasn't my mother. My father's a doctor too. Remember? That's what we're here for." She poured the rest of the red wine into her glass. "I thought about it. I did the GAMSAT, like I told Peter Enticott. And I did get seventy-four. Suck on that." Despite the aggressive words, her expression remained friendly. "I thought that doing Medicine would be a sign of some sort of obsession with my real father. Like I was following him rather than Phil. Even I could see that was a bit fucked-up."

Gene frequently states that psychologists are incompetent at understanding themselves. Rosie seemed to have provided good evidence for that proposition. Why avoid something that she would enjoy and be good at? And surely three years of undergraduate education in psychology plus several years of postgraduate research should have provided a more precise classification of her behavioural, personality and emotional problems than "fucked-up". Naturally I did not share these thoughts.

We were first in line when the museum opened at 10.30a.m. I had planned the visit according to the history of the universe, the planet and life. Thirteen billion years of history in six hours. At noon, Rosie suggested we delete lunch from the schedule to allow more time with the exhibits. Later, she stopped at the reconstruction of the famous Laetoli footprints made by hominids approximately 3.6 million years ago.

"I read an article about this. It was a mother and child, holding hands, right?"

It was a romantic interpretation, but not impossible.

"Have you ever thought of having children, Don?"

"Yes," I said, forgetting to deflect this personal question. "But it seems both unlikely and inadvisable."

"Why?"

"Unlikely, because I have lost confidence in the Wife Project. And inadvisable because I would be an unsuitable father."

"Why?"

"Because I'd be an embarrassment to my children."

Rosie laughed. I thought this was very insensitive, but she explained, "All parents are an embarrassment to their kids."

"Including Phil?"

She laughed again. "Especially Phil."

At 4.28p.m. we had finished the primates. "Oh no, we're done?" said Rosie. "Is there something else we can see?"

"We have two more things to see," I said. "You may find them dull."

I took her to the room of balls — spheres of different sizes showing the scale of the universe. The display is not dramatic, but the information is. Non-scientists, non-*physical*-scientists, frequently have no idea of scale — how small we are compared to the size of the universe, how big compared to the size of a neutrino. I did my best to make it interesting.

Then we went up in the elevator and joined the Heilbrunn Cosmic Pathway, a one-hundred-and-ten-metre spiral ramp representing a timeline from the big bang to the present. It is just pictures and photos and occasional rocks and fossils on the wall, and I didn't even need to look at them, because I know the story, which I related as accurately and dramatically as I could, putting all that we had seen during the day into context, as we walked down and round until we

242

reached the ground level and the tiny vertical hairline representing all of recorded human history. It was almost closing time now, and we were the only people standing there. On other occasions, I have listened to people's reactions as they reach the end. "Makes you feel a bit unimportant, doesn't it?" they say. I suppose that is one way of looking at it — how the age of the universe somehow diminishes our lives or the events of history or Joe DiMaggio's streak.

But Rosie's response was a verbal version of mine. "Wow," she said, very quietly, looking back at the vastness of it all. Then, in this vanishingly small moment in the history of the universe, she took my hand, and held it all the way to the subway.

CHAPTER
TWENTY-SEVEN

We had one critical task to perform before leaving New York the following morning. Max Freyberg, the cosmetic surgeon and potential biological father of Rosie, who was "booked solid", had agreed to see us for fifteen minutes at 6.45p.m. Rosie had told his secretary she was writing a series of articles for a publication about successful alumni of the university. I was carrying Rosie's camera and would be identified as a photographer.

Getting the appointment had been difficult enough, but it had become apparent that collecting the DNA would be far more difficult in a working environment than in a social or domestic location. I had set my brain the task of solving the problem before we departed for New York, and had expected it to have found a solution through background processing, but it had apparently been too occupied with other matters. The best I could think of was a spiked ring that would draw blood when we shook hands, but Rosie considered this socially infeasible.

She suggested clipping a hair, either surreptitiously or after identifying it as a stray that would mar the photo. Surely a cosmetic surgeon would care about his appearance. Unfortunately a clipped hair was unlikely to yield an adequate sample — it needed to be plucked to obtain a follicle. Rosie packed a pair of tweezers. For once I hoped I might have to spend fifteen minutes in a smoke-filled room. A cigarette butt would solve our problem. We would have to be alert to opportunities.

Dr Freyberg's rooms were in an older-style building on the Upper West Side. Rosie pushed the buzzer and a security guard appeared and took us up to a waiting area where the walls were totally covered with framed certificates and letters from patients praising Dr Freyberg's work.

Dr Freyberg's secretary, a very thin woman (BMI estimate sixteen) of about fifty-five with disproportionately thick lips, led us into his office. More certificates! Freyberg himself had a major fault: he was completely bald. The hair-plucking approach would not be viable. Nor was there any evidence that he was a smoker.

Rosie conducted the interview very impressively. Freyberg described some procedures that seemed to have minimal clinical justification, and talked about their importance to self-esteem. It was fortunate that I had been allocated the silent role, as I would have been strongly tempted to argue. I was also struggling to focus. My mind was still processing the hand-holding incident.

"I'm sorry," said Rosie, "but could I bother you for something to drink?"

Of course! The coffee swab solution.

"Sure," said Freyberg. "Tea, coffee?"

"Coffee would be great," said Rosie. "Just black. Will you have one yourself?"

"I'm good. Let's keep going." He pushed a button on his intercom. "Rachel. One black coffee."

"You should have a coffee," I said to him.

"Never touch it," said Freyberg.

"Unless you have a genetic intolerance of caffeine, there are no proven harmful effects. On the contrary —"

"What magazine is this for again?"

The question was straightforward and totally predictable. We had agreed the name of the fictitious university publication in advance, and Rosie had already used it in her introduction.

But my brain malfunctioned. Rosie and I spoke simultaneously. Rosie said, *"Faces of Change."* I said, *"Hands of Change."*

It was a minor inconsistency that any rational person would have interpreted as a simple, innocent error, which in fact it was. But Freyberg's expression indicated disbelief and he immediately scribbled on a notepad. When Rachel brought the coffee, he gave her the note. I diagnosed paranoia and started to think about escape plans.

"I need to use the bathroom," I said. I planned to phone Freyberg from the bathroom, so Rosie could escape while he took the call.

I walked towards the exit, but Freyberg blocked my path.

"Use my private one," he said. "I insist."

246

He led me through the back of his office, past Rachel to a door marked "Private" and left me there. There was no way to exit without returning the way we had come. I took out my phone, called 411 — directory assistance — and they connected me to Rachel. I could hear the phone ring and Rachel answer. I kept my voice low.

"I need to speak to Dr Freyberg," I said. "It's an emergency." I explained that my wife was a patient of Dr Freyberg and that her lips had exploded. I hung up and texted Rosie: *Exit now.*

The bathroom was in need of Eva's services. I managed to open the window, which had obviously not been used for a long time. We were four floors up, but there seemed to be plenty of handholds on the wall. I eased myself through the window and started climbing down, slowly, focusing on the task, hoping Rosie had escaped successfully. It had been a long time since I had practised rock climbing and the descent was not as simple as it first seemed. The wall was slippery from rain earlier in the day and my running shoes were not ideal for the task. At one point I slipped and only just managed to grasp a rough brick. I heard shouts from below.

When I finally reached the ground, I discovered that a small crowd had formed. Rosie was among them. She flung her arms around me. "Oh my God, Don, you could have killed yourself. It didn't matter that much."

"The risk was minor. It was just important to ignore the height issue."

We headed for the subway. Rosie was quite agitated. Freyberg had thought that she was some sort of private investigator, working on behalf of a dissatisfied patient. He was trying to have the security personnel detain her. Whether his position was legally defensible or not, we would have been in a difficult position.

"I'm going to get changed," said Rosie. "Our last night in New York City. What do you want to do?"

My original schedule specified a steakhouse, but now that we were in the pattern of eating together, I would need to select a restaurant suitable for a sustainable-seafood-eating "vegetarian".

"We'll work it out," she said. "Lots of options."

It took me three minutes to change my shirt. I waited downstairs for Rosie for another six. Finally I went up to her room and knocked. There was a long wait. Then I heard her voice.

"How long do you think it takes to have a shower?"

"Three minutes, twenty seconds," I said, "unless I wash my hair, in which case it takes an extra minute and twelve seconds." The additional time was due primarily to the requirement that the conditioner remain in place for sixty seconds.

"Hold on."

Rosie opened the door wearing only a towel. Her hair was wet, and she looked extremely attractive. I forgot to keep my eyes directed towards her face.

"Hey," she said. "No pendant." She was right. I couldn't use the pendant excuse. But she didn't give me a lecture on inappropriate behaviour. Instead, she smiled and stepped towards me. I wasn't sure if she was going to take another step, or if I should. In the end, neither of us did. It was an awkward moment but I suspected we had both contributed to the problem.

"You should have brought the ring," said Rosie.

For a moment, my brain interpreted "ring" as "wedding ring", and began constructing a completely incorrect scenario. Then I realised that she was referring to the spiked ring I had proposed as a means of obtaining Freyberg's blood.

"To come all this way and not get a sample."

"Fortunately, we have one."

"You got a sample? How?"

"His bathroom. What a slob. He should get his prostate checked. The floor —"

"Stop," said Rosie. "Too much information. But nice work."

"Very poor hygiene," I told her. "For a surgeon. A pseudo-surgeon. Incredible waste of surgical skill — inserting synthetic materials purely to alter appearance."

"Wait till you're fifty-five and your partner's forty-five and see if you say the same thing."

"You're supposed to be a feminist," I said, though I was beginning to doubt it.

"It doesn't mean I want to be unattractive."

"Your appearance should be irrelevant to your partner's assessment of you."

"Life is full of should-be's," said Rosie. "You're the geneticist. Everyone notices how people look. Even you."

"True. But I don't allow it to affect my evaluation of them."

I was on dangerous territory: the issue of Rosie's attractiveness had got me into serious trouble on the night of the faculty ball. The statement was consistent with my beliefs about judging people and with how I would wish to be judged myself. But I had never had to apply these beliefs to someone standing opposite me in a hotel bedroom wearing only a towel. It dawned on me that I had not told the full truth.

"Ignoring the testosterone factor," I added.

"Is there a compliment buried in there somewhere?"

The conversation was getting complicated. I tried to clarify my position. "It would be unreasonable to give you credit for being incredibly beautiful."

What I did next was undoubtedly a result of my thoughts being scrambled by a sequence of extraordinary and traumatic incidents in the preceding few hours: the hand-holding, the escape from the cosmetic surgery and the extreme impact of the world's most beautiful woman standing naked under a towel in front of me.

Gene should also take some blame for suggesting that earlobe size was a predictor of sexual attraction. Since I had never been so sexually attracted to a woman before, I was suddenly compelled to examine her ears. In a moment that was, in retrospect, similar to a critical incident in Albert Camus' *The Outsider*, I reached out and brushed her hair aside. But in this case, amazingly, the response was different from that documented in the novel we had studied in high school. Rosie put her arms round me and kissed me.

250

I think it is likely that my brain is wired in a non-standard configuration, but my ancestors would not have succeeded in breeding without understanding and responding to basic sexual signals. That aptitude was hardwired in. I kissed Rosie back. She responded.

We pulled apart for a moment. It was obvious that dinner would be delayed. Rosie studied me and said, "You know, if you changed your glasses and your haircut, you could be Gregory Peck in *To Kill a Mockingbird*."

"Is that good?" I assumed, given the circumstances, that it was, but wanted to hear her confirm it.

"He was only the sexiest man that ever lived."

We looked at each other some more, and I moved to kiss her again. She stopped me.

"Don, this is New York. It's like a holiday. I don't want you to assume it means anything more."

"What happens in New York stays in New York, right?" It was a line Gene had taught me for conference use. I had never needed to employ it before. It felt a little odd, but appropriate for the circumstances. It was obviously important that we both agreed there was no emotional continuation. Although I did not have a wife at home like Gene, I had a concept of a wife that was very different from Rosie, who would presumably step out on the balcony for a cigarette after sex. Oddly, the prospect didn't repel me as much as it should have.

"I have to get something from my room," I said.

"Good thinking. Don't take too long."

My room was only eleven floors above Rosie's, so I walked up the stairs. Back in my room, I showered, then thumbed through the book Gene had given me. He had been right after all. Incredible.

I descended the stairs to Rosie's room. Forty-three minutes had passed. I knocked on the door, and Rosie answered, now wearing a sleeping costume that was, in fact, more revealing than the towel. She was holding two glasses of Champagne.

"Sorry, it's gone a bit flat."

I looked around the room. The bed cover was turned down, the curtains were closed and there was just one bedside lamp on. I gave her Gene's book.

"Since this is our first — and probably only — time, and you are doubtless more experienced, I recommend that you select the position."

Rosie thumbed through the book, then started again. She stopped at the first page where Gene had written his symbol.

"Gene gave you this?"

"It was a present for the trip."

I tried to read Rosie's expression, and guessed anger, but that disappeared and she said, in a non-angry tone, "Don, I'm sorry, I can't do this. I'm really sorry."

"Did I say something wrong?"

"No, it's me. I'm really sorry."

"You changed your mind while I was gone?"

"Yeah," said Rosie. "That's what happened. I'm sorry."

"Are you sure I didn't do something wrong?" Rosie was my friend and the risk to our friendship was now at the forefront of my mind. The sex issue had evaporated.

"No, no, it's me," she said. "You were incredibly considerate."

It was a compliment I was unaccustomed to receiving. A very satisfying compliment. The night had not been a total disaster.

I could not sleep. I had not eaten and it was only 8.55p.m. Claudia and Gene would be at work now, back in Melbourne, and I did not feel like talking to either of them. I considered it inadvisable to contact Rosie again, so I rang my remaining friend. Dave had eaten already, but we walked to a pizza restaurant and he ate a second dinner. Then we went to a bar and watched baseball and talked about women. I do not recall much of what either of us said, but I suspect that little of it would have been useful in making rational plans for the future.

CHAPTER
TWENTY-EIGHT

My mind had gone blank. That is a standard phrase, and an exaggeration of the situation. My brain stem continued to function, my heart still beat, I did not forget to breathe. I was able to pack my bag, consume breakfast in my room, navigate to JFK, negotiate check-in and board the plane to Los Angeles. I managed to communicate with Rosie to the extent that it was necessary to coordinate these activities.

But reflective functioning was suspended. The reason was obvious — *emotional overload!* My normally well-managed emotions had been allowed out in New York — on the advice of Claudia, *a qualified clinical psychologist* — and had been dangerously overstimulated. Now they were running amok in my brain, crippling my ability to think. And I needed all my thinking ability to analyse the problem.

Rosie had the window seat and I was by the aisle. I followed the pre-take-off safety procedures, for once not dwelling on their unjustified assumptions and irrational priorities. In the event of impending disaster, we would all have something to do. I was in the opposite position. Incapacitated.

Rosie put her hand on my arm. "How are you feeling, Don?"

I tried to focus on analysing one aspect of the experience and the corresponding emotional reaction. I knew where to start. Logically, I did not need to go back to my room to get Gene's book. Showing a book to Rosie was not part of the original scenario I had planned back in Melbourne when I prepared for a sexual encounter. I may be socially inept, but with the kiss underway, and Rosie wearing only a towel, there should have been no difficulties in proceeding. My knowledge of positions was a bonus, but probably irrelevant the first time.

So why did my instincts drive me to a course of action that ultimately sabotaged the opportunity? The first-level answer was obvious. They were telling me not to proceed. But why? I identified three possibilities.

1. I was afraid that I would fail to perform sexually.

It did not take long to dismiss this possibility. I might well have been less competent than a more experienced person and could even have been rendered impotent by fear, though I considered this unlikely. But I was accustomed to being embarrassed, even in front of Rosie. The sexual drive was much stronger than any requirement to protect my image.

2. No condom.

I realised, on reflection, that Rosie had probably assumed that I had left her room to collect or purchase a condom. Obviously I should have obtained one, in line with all recommendations on safe sex, and presumably the concierge would have some for emergencies, along with spare toothbrushes and razors. The fact that I did not do so was further evidence that subconsciously I did not expect to proceed. Gene had once told me a story about racing around Cairo in a taxi trying to find a condom vendor. My motivation had clearly not been as strong.

3. I could not deal with the emotional consequences.

The third possibility only entered my mind after I eliminated the first and second. I immediately knew — instinctively! — that it was the correct one. My brain was already emotionally overloaded. It was not the death-defying climb from the surgeon's window or the memory of being interrogated in a dark cellar by a bearded psychiatrist who would stop at nothing to protect his secret. It was not even the experience of holding Rosie's hand from the museum to the subway, although that was a contributor. It was the total experience of hanging out with Rosie in New York.

My instincts were telling me that if I added any more to this experience — if I added the literally mind-blowing experience of having sex with her — my emotions would take over my brain. And they would drive me towards a relationship with Rosie. That would be a disaster for two reasons. The first was that she was totally unsuitable in the longer term. The second was that she had made it clear that such a relationship would not extend beyond our time in New York. These reasons were completely contradictory, mutually exclusive and based on entirely different premises. I had no idea which one was correct.

We were in the final stages of our descent into LAX. I turned to Rosie. It had been several hours since she asked her question, and I had now given it considerable thought. How was I feeling?

"Confused," I said to her.

I expected her to have forgotten the question, but perhaps the answer made sense in any case.

"Welcome to the real world."

I managed to stay awake for the first six hours of the fifteen-hour flight home from LA in order to reset my internal clock, but it was difficult.

Rosie had slept for a few hours then watched a movie. I looked over, and saw that she was crying. She removed her headphones and wiped her eyes.

"You're crying," I said. "Is there a problem?"

"Sprung," said Rosie. "It's just a sad story. *Bridges of Madison County*. I presume you don't cry at movies."

"Correct." I realised that this might be viewed as a negative, so added, in defence, "It seems to be a predominantly female behaviour."

"Thanks for that." Rosie went quiet again but seemed to have recovered from the sadness that the movie had stimulated.

"Tell me," she said, "do you feel anything when you watch a movie? You've seen *Casablanca?*"

I was familiar with this question. Gene and Claudia had asked it after we watched a DVD together. So my answer was the result of reflection.

"I've seen several romantic movies. The answer is no. Unlike Gene and Claudia, and apparently the majority of the human race, I am not emotionally affected by love stories. I don't appear to be wired for that response."

I visited Claudia and Gene for dinner on the Sunday night. I was feeling unusually jet-lagged, and as a result had some difficulty in providing a coherent account of the trip. I tried to talk about my meeting with David Borenstein at Columbia, what I saw at the museums and the meal at Momofuku Ko, but they were *obsessed* with grilling me about my interactions with Rosie. I could not reasonably be expected to remember every detail. And obviously I could not talk about the Father Project activities.

Claudia was very pleased with the scarf, but it provided another opportunity for interrogation. "Did Rosie help you choose this?"

Rosie, Rosie, Rosie.

"The sales assistant recommended it. It was very straightforward."

As I left, Claudia said, "So, Don, are you planning to see Rosie again?"

258

"Next Saturday," I said, truthfully, not bothering to tell her that it was not a social occasion — we had scheduled the afternoon to analyse the DNA.

She seemed satisfied.

I was eating lunch alone in the University Club, reviewing the Father Project file, when Gene arrived with his meal and a glass of wine and sat opposite me. I tried to put the file away, but succeeded only in giving him the correct impression that I was trying to hide something. Gene suddenly looked over at the service counter, behind me.

"Oh God!" he said.

I turned to look and Gene snatched the folder, laughing.

"That's private," I said, but Gene had opened it. The photo of the graduating class was on top.

Gene seemed genuinely surprised. "My God. Where did you get this?" He was studying the photo intently. "It must be thirty years old. What's all the scribble?"

"Organising a reunion," I said. "Helping a friend. Weeks ago." It was a good answer, considering the short time I had to formulate it, but it did have a major defect. Gene detected it.

"A friend? Right. One of your many friends. You should have invited me."

"Why?"

"Who do you think took the photo?"

Of course. Someone had been required to take the photo. I was too stunned to speak.

"I was the only outsider," said Gene. "The genetics tutor. Big night — everyone pumped, no partners. Hottest ticket in town."

Gene pointed to a face in the photo. I had always focused on the males, and never looked for Rosie's mother. But now that Gene was pointing to her, she was easy to identify. The resemblance was obvious, including the red hair, although the colour was less dramatic than Rosie's. She was standing between Isaac Esler and Geoffrey Case. As in Isaac Esler's wedding photo, Case was smiling broadly.

"Bernadette O'Connor." Gene sipped his wine. "Irish."

I was familiar with the tone of Gene's statement. There was a reason for him remembering this particular woman, and it was not because she was Rosie's mother. In fact, it seemed that he didn't know the connection, and I made a quick decision not to inform him.

His finger moved one space to the left.

"Geoffrey Case. Not a great return on his tuition fees."

"He died, correct?"

"Killed himself."

This was new information. "Are you sure?"

"Of course I'm sure," said Gene. "Come on, what's this about?"

I ignored the question. "Why did he do it?"

"Probably forgot to take his lithium," said Gene. "He had bipolar disorder. Life of the party on a good day." He looked at me. I assumed he was about to interrogate me as to the reason for my interest in Geoffrey Case and the reunion, and I was thinking frantically to invent a plausible explanation. I was saved by an empty pepper grinder. Gene gave it a twist, then walked away to exchange it. I used a table napkin to swab his wine glass and left before he returned.

CHAPTER
TWENTY-NINE

I cycled to the university on Saturday morning with an unidentifiable, and therefore disconcerting, emotion. Things were settling back into their normal pattern. The day's testing would mark the end of the Father Project. At worst, Rosie might find a person that we had overlooked — another tutor or caterer or perhaps someone who had left the party early — but a single additional test would not take long. And I would have no reason to see Rosie again.

We met at the lab. There were three samples to test: the swab from Isaac Esler's fork, a urine sample on toilet paper from Freyberg's floor, and Gene's table napkin. I had still not told Rosie about the handkerchief from Margaret Case, but was anxious to get a result on Gene's sample. There was a strong possibility that Gene was Rosie's father. I tried not to think about it, but it was consistent with Gene's reaction to the photo, his identification of Rosie's mother and his history of casual sex.

"What's the napkin?" asked Rosie.

I was expecting this question.

"Retest. One of the earlier samples was contaminated."

My improving ability at deception was not enough to fool Rosie. "Bullshit. Who is it? It's Case, isn't it? You got a sample for Geoffrey Case."

It would have been easy to say yes but identifying the sample as Case's would create great confusion if it tested positive. A web of lies.

"I'll tell you if it's the one," I said.

"Tell me now," said Rosie. "It *is* the one."

"How can you know?"

"I just know."

"You have zero evidence. Isaac Esler's story makes him an excellent candidate. He was committed to getting married to someone else right after the party. He admits to being drunk. He was evasive at dinner. He's standing next to your mother in the photo."

This was something we had not discussed before. It was such an obvious thing to have checked. Gene had once given me an exercise to do at conferences: "If you want to know who's sleeping with who, just look at who they sit with at breakfast." Whoever Rosie's mother had been with that night would likely be standing next to her. Unless of course he was required to take the photo.

"My intuition versus your logic. Wanna bet?"

It would have been unfair to take the bet. I had the advantage of the knowledge from the basement encounter. Realistically, I considered Isaac Esler, Gene and Geoffrey Case to be equally likely. I had mulled over Esler's reference to "people involved" and concluded that it was ambiguous. He might have been protecting his friend but he could equally have been hiding behind him. Though, if Esler was not himself the father, he could simply have told me to test his sample. Perhaps his plan was to confuse me, in which case it had succeeded, but only temporarily. Esler's deceptive behaviour had caused me to review an earlier decision. If we reached a point where we had eliminated all other candidates, including Esler, I would test the sample I had collected from Margaret Case.

"Anyway it's definitely not Freyberg," said Rosie, interrupting my thinking.

"Why not?" Freyberg was the least likely, but certainly not impossible.

"Green eyes. I should have thought of it at the time."

She interpreted my expression correctly: disbelief.

"Come on, you're the geneticist. He's got green eyes so he can't be my father. I checked it on the internet."

Amazing. She retains a professor of genetics, an alien of extraordinary abilities, to help find her father, she travels for a week spending almost every minute of the waiting day with him, yet when she wants the answer to a question on genetics she goes to the internet.

"Those models are simplifications."

"Don, my mother had blue eyes. I have brown eyes. My real father had to have brown eyes, right?"

"Wrong," I said. "Highly likely but not certain. The genetics of eye colour are extremely complex. Green is possible. Also blue."

"A medical student — a doctor — would know that, wouldn't she?"

Rosie was obviously referring to her mother. I thought it was probably not the right time to give Rosie a detailed account of the deficiencies in medical education.

I just said, "Highly *unlikely*. Gene used to teach genetics to medical students. That's a typical Gene simplification."

"Fuck Gene," said Rosie. "I am so over Gene. Just test the napkin. It's the one." But she sounded less sure.

"What are you going to do when you find out?"

This question should have been asked earlier. Failure to raise it was another result of lack of planning but, now that I could picture Gene as the father, Rosie's future actions became more relevant to me.

"Funny you should ask," said Rosie. "I said it was about closure. But I think, subconsciously, I had this fantasy that my real father would come riding in and . . . deal with Phil."

"For failing to keep the Disneyland promise? It would surely be difficult to devise a suitable punishment after so much time."

"I said it was a fantasy," she said. "I saw him as some sort of hero. But now I know it's one of three people, and I've met two of them. Isaac Esler: 'We must not revisit the past lightly.' Max Freyberg: 'I consider myself a restorer of self-esteem.' Wankers, both of them. Just weak guys who ran away."

The lack of logic here was astounding. At most, one of them had deserted her.

"Geoffrey Case . . ." I began, thinking Rosie's characterisation would not apply to him, but if Rosie knew about the manner of his death she might interpret it as a means of escaping his responsibilities.

"I know, I know. But if it turns out to be someone else, some middle-aged guy who's pretending to be something he isn't, then time's up, arsehole."

"You're planning to expose him?" I asked, horrified. Suddenly it struck me that I could be involved in causing great pain to someone, very possibly my best friend. To his whole family! Rosie's mother had not wanted Rosie to know. Perhaps this was why. By default, Rosie's mother knew more about human behaviour than I did.

"Correct."

"But you'll be inflicting pain. For no compensatory gain."

"*I'll* feel better."

"Incorrect," I said. "Research shows that revenge adds to the distress of the victim —"

"That's my choice."

There was the possibility that Rosie's father was Geoffrey Case, in which case all three samples would test negative, and it would be too late for Rosie to wreak her revenge. I did not want to rely on that possibility.

I turned off the machine.

"Stop," said Rosie. "I have a right to know."

"Not if it causes suffering."

"What about me?" she said. "Don't you care about me?" She was becoming emotional. I felt very calm. Reason was in control again. My thoughts were straight.

266

"I care about you enormously. So I can't contribute to you doing something immoral."

"Don, if you don't do the test, I'm never going to speak to you again. Ever."

This information was painful to process, but rationally entirely predictable.

"I'd assumed that was inevitable," I said. "The project will be complete, and you've indicated no further interest in the sexual aspect."

"So it's my fault?" said Rosie. "Of course it's my fault. I'm not a fucking non-smoking teetotal chef with a PhD. I'm not *organised*."

"I've deleted the non-drinking requirement." I realised that she was referring to the Wife Project. But what was she saying? That she was evaluating herself according to the criteria of the Wife Project? Which meant —

"You considered me as a partner?"

"Sure," she said. "Except for the fact that you have no idea of social behaviour, your life's ruled by a whiteboard and you're incapable of feeling love — you're perfect."

She walked out, slamming the door behind her.

I turned the machine on. Without Rosie in the room, I could safely test the samples and then decide what to do with them. Then I heard the door open again. I turned around, expecting to see Rosie. Instead it was the Dean.

"Working on your secret project, Professor Tillman?"

I was in serious trouble. In all previous encounters with the Dean, I had been following the rules, or the infraction had been too minor to punish. Using the DNA machine for private purposes was a substantial breach of the Genetics Department regulations. How much did she know? She did not normally work on weekends. Her presence was not an accident.

"Fascinating stuff, according to Simon Lefebvre," said the Dean. "He comes into my office and asks me about a project in my own faculty. One that apparently requires that we collect his DNA. As you do. I gather there was some sort of joke involved. Pardon my lack of humour, but I was at a slight disadvantage — having never heard of the project. Surely, I thought, I would have seen the proposal when it went to the ethics committee."

Up to this point, the Dean had seemed cool and rational. Now she raised her voice.

"I've been trying for two years to get the Medical Faculty to fund a joint research project — and you decide not only to behave grossly unethically but to do it to the man who holds the purse strings. I want a written report. If it doesn't include an ethics approval that I somehow haven't seen yet, we'll be advertising an associate professor position."

The Dean stopped at the door.

"I'm still holding your complaint about Kevin Yu. You might want to think about that. And I'll have your lab key, thank you."

The Father Project was over. Officially.

Gene came into my office the following day as I was completing an EPDS questionnaire.

268

"Are you okay?" he said. This was a timely question.

"I suspect not. I'll tell you in approximately fifteen seconds." I completed the questionnaire, calculated the result, and passed it to Gene. "Sixteen," I told him. "Second-highest score ever."

Gene looked at it. "*Edinburgh Postnatal Depression Scale*. Do I have to point out that you haven't had a baby recently?"

"I don't answer the baby-related questions. It was the only depression instrument Claudia had at home when my sister died. I've continued using it for consistency."

"This is what we call 'getting in touch with our feelings', is it?" said Gene.

I sensed that the question was rhetorical and did not reply.

"Listen," he said, "I think I can fix this thing for you."

"You have news from Rosie?"

"For Chrissakes, Don," said Gene. "I have news from the *Dean*. I don't know what you've been doing, but DNA testing without ethics approval — that's 'career over'."

I knew this. I had decided to phone Amghad, the golf-club boss, and ask him about the cocktail-bar partnership. It seemed like time to do something different. It had been a weekend of rude awakenings. I had arrived home after the interaction with the Dean to find that Eva, my housekeeper, had filled in a copy of the Wife Project questionnaire. On the front, she had written: "Don. Nobody is perfect. Eva." In my state of heightened vulnerability, I had been extremely affected by this. Eva was a good person whose short skirts were perhaps intended to attract a partner and who would have been embarrassed by her relatively low socio-economic status as she answered questions about postgraduate qualifications and appreciation of expensive food. I reflected on all the women who had completed my questionnaire, hoping that they might find a partner. Hoping that partner might be me, even though they did not know much about me and would probably be disappointed if they did.

I had poured myself a glass of Pinot Noir and gone out to the balcony. The city lights reminded me of the lobster dinner with Rosie that, contrary to the predictions of the questionnaire, had been one of the most enjoyable meals of my life. Claudia had told me I was being too picky but Rosie had demonstrated in New York that my assessment of what would make me happy was totally incorrect. I sipped the wine slowly and watched the view change. A window went dark, a traffic light changed from red to green, an ambulance's flashing lights bounced off the buildings. And it dawned on me that I had not designed the questionnaire to find a woman I could accept, but to find someone who might accept me.

Regardless of what decisions I might make as a result of my experiences with Rosie, I would not use the questionnaire again. The Wife Project was over.

Gene had more to say. "No job, no structure, no schedule. You'll fall apart." He looked at the depression questionnaire again. "You're falling apart already.

Listen. I'm going to say that it was a Psych Department project. We'll make up an ethics application, and you can say you thought it had been approved."

Gene was obviously doing his best to be helpful. I smiled for his benefit.

"Does that take a few points off the score?" he said, waving the EPDS questionnaire.

"I suspect not."

There was a silence. Neither of us apparently had anything to say. I expected Gene to leave. But he tried again.

"Help me here, Don. It's Rosie, isn't it?"

"It makes no sense."

"Let me put this simply," said Gene. "You're unhappy — so unhappy that you've lost perspective on your career, your reputation, your holy schedule."

This was true.

"Shit, Don, you broke the rules. Since when do you break rules?"

It was a good question. I respect rules. But in the last ninety-nine days, I had broken many rules, legal, ethical and personal. I knew exactly when it had started. The day Rosie walked into my office and I hacked into Le Gavroche's reservation system so I could go on a date with her.

"All this because of a woman?" said Gene.

"Apparently. It's totally irrational." I felt embarrassed. It was one thing to make a social error, another to admit that rationality had deserted me.

"It's only irrational if you believe in your questionnaire."

"The EPDS is highly —"

"I'm talking about your 'Do you eat kidneys?' questionnaire. I'd say genetics one, questionnaire nil."

"You consider the situation with Rosie to be the result of genetic compatibility?"

"You have such a way with words," Gene said. "If you want to be a bit more romantic about it, I'd say you were in love."

This was an extraordinary statement. It also made absolute sense. I had assumed that romantic love would always be outside my realm of experience. But it perfectly accounted for my current situation. I wanted to be sure.

"This is your professional opinion? As an expert on human attraction?"

Gene nodded.

"Excellent." Gene's insight had transformed my mental state.

"Not sure how that helps," said Gene.

"Rosie identified three faults. Fault number one was the inability to feel love. There are only two left to rectify."

"And they would be?"

"Social protocols and adherence to schedules. Trivial."

CHAPTER
THIRTY

I booked a meeting with Claudia at the usual café to discuss social behaviour. I realised that improving my ability to interact with other humans would require some effort and that my best attempts might not convince Rosie. But the skills would be useful in their own right.

I had, to some extent, become comfortable with being socially odd. At school, I had been the unintentional class clown, and eventually the intentional one. It was time to grow up.

The server approached our table. "You order," said Claudia.

"What would you like?"

"A skinny decaf latte."

This is a ridiculous form of coffee, but I did not point it out. Claudia would surely have received the message from previous occasions and would not want it repeated. It would be annoying to her.

"I'd like a double espresso," I said to the server, "and my friend will have a skinny decaf latte, no sugar, please."

"Well," said Claudia. "Something's changed."

I pointed out that I had been successfully and politely ordering coffee all my life, but Claudia insisted that my mode of interaction had changed in subtle ways.

"I wouldn't have picked New York City as the place to learn to be genteel," she said, "but there you go."

I told her that, on the contrary, people had been extremely friendly, citing my experience with Dave the Baseball Fan, Mary the bipolar-disorder researcher, David Borenstein the Dean of Medicine at Columbia, and the chef and weird guy at Momofuku Ko. I mentioned that we had dined with the Eslers, describing them as friends of Rosie's family. Claudia's conclusion was simple. All this unaccustomed social interaction, plus that with Rosie, had dramatically improved my skills.

"You don't need to try with Gene and me, because you're not out to impress us or make friends with us."

While Claudia was right about the value of practice, I learn better from reading and observation. My next task was to download some educational material.

I decided to begin with romantic films specifically mentioned by Rosie. There were four: *Casablanca, The Bridges of Madison County, When Harry Met Sally* and *An Affair to Remember*. I added *To Kill a Mockingbird* and *The Big Country* for Gregory Peck, whom Rosie had cited as the sexiest man ever.

It took a full week to watch all six, including time for pausing the DVD player and taking notes. The films were incredibly useful, but also highly challenging. The emotional dynamics were so complex! I persevered,

274

drawing on movies recommended by Claudia about male-female relationships with both happy and unhappy outcomes. I watched *Hitch, Gone with the Wind, Bridget Jones's Diary, Annie Hall, Notting Hill, Love Actually* and *Fatal Attraction*.

Claudia also suggested I watch *As Good as It Gets*, "just for fun". Although her advice was to use it as an example of what *not* to do, I was impressed that the Jack Nicholson character handled a jacket problem with more finesse than I had. It was also encouraging that, despite serious social incompetence, a significant difference in age between him and the Helen Hunt character, probable multiple psychiatric disorders and a level of intolerance far more severe than mine, he succeeded in winning the love of the woman in the end. An excellent choice by Claudia.

Slowly I began to make sense of it all. There were certain consistent principles of behaviour in male-female romantic relationships, including the prohibition of infidelity. That rule was in my mind when I met with Claudia again for social practice.

We worked through some scenarios.

"This meal has a fault," I said. The situation was hypothetical. We were only drinking coffee. "That would be too confrontational, correct?"

Claudia agreed. "And don't say fault, or error. That's computer talk."

"But I can say 'I'm sorry, it was an error of judgement, entirely my fault', correct? That use of 'fault' is acceptable?"

"Correct," said Claudia, and then laughed. "I mean yes. Don, this takes years to learn."

I didn't have years. But I am a quick learner and was in human-sponge mode. I demonstrated.

"I'm going to construct an objective statement followed by a request for clarification, and preface it with a platitude: 'Excuse me. I ordered a rare steak. Do you have a different definition of rare?'"

"Good start, but the question's a bit aggressive."

"Not acceptable?"

"In New York maybe. Don't blame the waiter."

I modified the question. "Excuse me. I ordered a rare steak. Could you check that my order was processed correctly?"

Claudia nodded. But she did not look entirely happy. I was paying great attention to expressions of emotion and I had diagnosed hers correctly.

"Don. I'm impressed, but . . . changing to meet someone else's expectations may not be a good idea. You may end up resenting it."

I didn't think this was likely. I was learning some new protocols, that was all.

"If you really love someone," Claudia continued, "you have to be prepared to accept them as they are. Maybe you hope that one day they get a wake-up call and make the changes for their own reasons."

This last statement connected with the fidelity rule that I had in my mind at the beginning of the discussion. I did not need to raise the subject now. I had the answer to my question. Claudia was surely talking about Gene.

★ ★ ★

I organised a run with Gene for the following morning.
I needed to speak to him in private, somewhere he
could not escape. I started my personal lecture as soon
as we were moving. My key point was that infidelity
was totally unacceptable. Any benefits were outweighed
by the risk of total disaster. Gene had been divorced
once already. Eugenie and Carl —

Gene interrupted, breathing heavily. In my effort to
get the message across unambiguously and forcefully, I
had been running faster than normal. Gene is
significantly less fit than I am and my fat-burning
low-heart-rate jogs are major cardiovascular workouts
for him.

"I hear you," said Gene. "What've you been
reading?"

I told him about the movies I had been watching,
and their idealised representation of acceptable and
unacceptable behaviour. If Gene and Claudia had
owned a rabbit, it would have been in serious danger
from a disgruntled lover. Gene disagreed, not about the
rabbit, but about the impact of his behaviour on his
marriage.

"We're psychologists," he said. "We can handle an
open marriage."

I ignored his incorrect categorisation of himself as a
real psychologist, and focused on the critical issue: all
authorities and moral codes consider fidelity critical.
Even theories of evolutionary psychology concede that
if a person discovers that their partner is unfaithful they
will have strong reasons for rejecting them.

"You're talking about men there," said Gene. "Because they can't afford the risk of raising a child who doesn't have their genes. Anyway, I thought you were all about overcoming instinct."

"Correct. The male instinct is to cheat. You need to overcome it."

"Women accept it as long as you don't embarrass them with it. Look at France."

I cited a counter-example from a popular book and film.

"*Bridget Jones's Diary?*" said Gene. "Since when are we expected to behave like characters in chick flicks?" He stopped and doubled over, gasping for breath. It gave me the opportunity to present him with the evidence without interruption. I finished by pointing out that he loved Claudia and that he should therefore be prepared to make all necessary sacrifices.

"I'll think about it when I see *you* changing the habits of a lifetime," he said.

I had thought that eliminating my schedule would be relatively straightforward. I had just spent eight days without it and while I had faced numerous problems they were not related to inefficiency or unstructured time. But I had not factored in the impact of the enormous amount of turmoil in my life. As well as the uncertainty around Rosie, the social-skills project and the fear that my best friends were on the path to domestic disintegration, I was about to lose my job. The schedule of activities felt like the only stable thing in my life.

In the end, I made a compromise that would surely be acceptable to Rosie. Everyone keeps a timetable of their regular commitments, in my case lectures, meetings and martial-arts classes. I would allow myself these. I would put appointments in my diary, *as other people did*, but reduce standardisation. Things could change week by week. Reviewing my decision, I could see that the abandonment of the Standardised Meal System, the aspect of my schedule that provoked the most comment, was the only item requiring immediate attention.

My next market visit was predictably strange. I arrived at the seafood stall and the proprietor turned to pull a lobster from the tank.

"Change of plan," I said. "What's good today?"

"Lobster," he said, in his heavily accented English. "Lobster good every Tuesday for you." He laughed, and waved his hand at his other customers. He was making a joke about me. Rosie had a facial expression that she used when she said, "Don't fuck with me." I tried the expression. It seemed to work by itself.

"I'm joking," he said. "Swordfish is beautiful. Oysters. You eat oysters?"

I ate oysters, though I had never prepared them at home. I ordered them unshucked as quality restaurants promoted their oysters as being freshly shucked.

I arrived home with a selection of food not associated with any particular recipe. The oysters proved challenging. I could not get a knife in to open them without risking injury to my hand through slippage. I could have looked up the technique on the internet, but it would have taken time. This was why I had a schedule based around familiar items. I could remove the meat from a lobster with my eyes closed while my brain worked on a genetics problem. What was wrong with standardisation? Another oyster failed to provide an opening for my knife. I was getting annoyed and about to throw the full dozen in the bin when I had an idea.

I put one in the microwave and heated it for a few seconds. It opened easily. It was warm but delicious. I tried a second, this time adding a squeeze of lemon juice and a grind of pepper. Sensational! I could feel a whole world opening up to me. I hoped the oysters were sustainable, because I wanted to share my new skills with Rosie.

CHAPTER
THIRTY-ONE

My focus on self-improvement meant that I had little time to consider and respond to the Dean's threat of dismissal. I had decided not to take up Gene's offer to construct an alibi; now that the breach of rules was in my conscious mind, it would be a violation of my personal integrity to compound the error.

I succeeded in suppressing thoughts of my professional future, but could not stop the Dean's parting comment about Kevin Yu and my plagiarism complaint from intruding into my conscious mind. After much thought, I concluded that the Dean was not offering me an unethical deal: "Withdraw the complaint and you can keep your job." What she said was bothering me because I had myself broken the rules in pursuing the Father Project. Gene had once told me a religious joke when I questioned the morality of his behaviour.

Jesus addresses the angry mob who are stoning a prostitute: "Let he who is without sin cast the first stone." A stone flies through the air and hits the woman. Jesus turns around and says, "Sometimes you really piss me off, Mother."

I could no longer be equated with the Virgin Mary. I had been corrupted. I was like everyone else. My stone-casting credibility had been significantly compromised.

I summoned Kevin to a meeting in my office. He was from mainland China, and aged approximately twenty-eight (estimated BMI nineteen). I interpreted his expression and demeanour as "nervous".

I had his essay, partly or entirely written by his tutor, in my hand and showed it to him. I asked the obvious question: Why had he not written it himself?

He averted his gaze — which I interpreted as a cultural signal of respect rather than of shiftiness — but instead of answering my question, he started to explain the consequences of his probable expulsion. He had a wife and child in China, and had not yet told them of the problem. He hoped some day to emigrate, or, if not, at least to work in genetics. His unwise behaviour would mean the end of his dreams and those of his wife, who had managed for almost four years without him. He was crying.

In the past, I would have regarded this as sad but irrelevant. A rule had been broken. But now I was also a rule-breaker. I had not broken the rules deliberately, or at least not with any conscious thought. Perhaps Kevin's behaviour had been similarly unconsidered.

I asked Kevin, "What are the principal arguments advanced against the use of genetically modified crops?" The essay had been on the ethical and legal issues raised by advances in genetics. Kevin gave a comprehensive summary. I followed with further questions, which Kevin also answered well. He seemed to have a good knowledge of the topic.

"Why didn't you write this yourself?" I asked.

"I am a scientist. I am not confident writing in English about moral and cultural questions. I wanted to be sure not to fail. I did not think."

I did not know how to respond to Kevin. Acting without thinking was anathema to me, and I did not want to encourage it in future scientists. Nor did I want my own weakness to affect a correct decision regarding Kevin. I would pay for my own error in this regard, as I deserved to. But losing my job would not have the same consequences for me as expulsion would for Kevin. I doubted he would be offered a potentially lucrative partnership in a cocktail bar as an alternative.

I thought for quite a long time. Kevin just sat. He must have realised that I was considering some form of reprieve. But I was incredibly uncomfortable in this position of judgement as I weighed the impact of various decisions. Was this what the Dean had to do every day? For the first time, I felt some respect for her.

I was not confident I could solve the problem in a short time. But I realised that it would be cruel to leave Kevin wondering if his life had been destroyed.

"I understand . . ." I started, and realised that this was not a phrase I was accustomed to using when talking about people. I stopped the sentence and thought for a while longer. "I will create a supplementary task — probably an essay on personal ethics. As an alternative to expulsion."

I interpreted Kevin's expression as ecstatic.

I was conscious that there was more to social skills than knowing how to order coffee and being faithful to your partner. Since my school days, I had selected my clothes without regard to fashion. I started out not caring how I looked, then discovered that people found what I wore amusing. I enjoyed being seen as someone not tied to the norms of society. But now I had no idea how to dress.

I asked Claudia to buy me some suitable clothes. She had proved her expertise with the jeans and shirt, but she insisted on me accompanying her.

"I may not be around forever," she said. After some reflection, I deduced that she was talking not about death, but about something more immediate: marriage failure! I had to find a way to convince Gene of the danger.

The actual shopping took a full morning. We went to several shops, acquiring shoes, trousers, a jacket, a second pair of jeans, more shirts, a belt and even a tie.

I had more shopping to do, but I did not require Claudia's help. A photo was sufficient to specify my requirements. I visited the optometrist, the hairdresser (not my regular barber) and the menswear shop. Everyone was extremely helpful.

My schedule and social skills had now been brought into line with conventional practice, to the best of my ability within the time I had allocated. The Don Project was complete. It was time to commence the Rosie Project.

There was a mirror on the inside of the closet in my office which I had never needed before. Now I used it to review my appearance. I expected I would have only one chance to cut through Rosie's negative view of me and produce an emotional reaction. I wanted her to fall in love with me.

Protocol dictated that I should not wear a hat indoors, but I decided that the PhD students' area could be considered public. On that basis, it would be acceptable. I checked the mirror again. Rosie had been right. In my grey three-piece suit, I could be mistaken for Gregory Peck in *To Kill a Mockingbird*. Atticus Tillman. World's sexiest man.

Rosie was at her desk. So was Stefan, looking unshaven as always. I had my speech prepared.

"Good afternoon, Stefan. Hi, Rosie. Rosie, I'm afraid it's short notice but I was wondering if you'd join me for dinner this evening. There's something I'd like to share with you."

Neither spoke. Rosie looked a little stunned. I looked at her directly. "That's a charming pendant," I said. "I'll pick you up at 7.45." I was shaking as I walked away, but I had given it my best effort. Hitch from *Hitch* would have been pleased with me.

I had two more visits to make before my evening date with Rosie.

I walked straight past Helena. Gene was in his office looking at his computer. On the screen was a photo of an Asian woman who was not conventionally attractive.

I recognised the format — she was a Wife-Project Applicant. Place of Birth — North Korea.

Gene looked at me strangely. My Gregory Peck costume was doubtless unexpected but appropriate for my mission.

"Hi, Gene."

"What's with the 'Hi'? What happened to 'Greetings'?"

I explained that I had eliminated a number of unconventional mannerisms from my vocabulary.

"So Claudia tells me. You didn't think your regular mentor was up to the job?"

I wasn't sure what he meant.

He explained. "Me. You didn't ask me."

This was correct. Feedback from Rosie had prompted me to reassess Gene's social competence, and my recent work with Claudia and the movie exemplars had confirmed my suspicion that his skills applied to a limited domain, and that he was not employing them in the best interests of himself and his family.

"No," I told him. "I wanted advice on socially appropriate behaviour."

"What's that supposed to mean?"

"Obviously, you're similar to me. That's why you're my best friend. Hence this invitation." There had been a great deal of preparation for this day. I gave Gene an envelope. He did not open it but continued the conversation.

"I'm like you? No offence, Don, but your behaviour — your old behaviour — was in a class of its own. If you want my opinion, you hid behind a persona that you thought people found amusing. It's hardly surprising people saw you as a . . . buffoon."

This was exactly my point. But Gene was not making the connection. As his buddy, it was my duty to behave as an adult male and give it to him straight.

I walked over to his map of the world, with a pin for every conquest. I checked it for what I hoped would be the last time. Then I stabbed it with my finger, to create an atmosphere of threat.

"Exactly," I said. "You think people see you as a Casanova. You know what? I don't care what other people think of you, but, if you want to know, they think you're a jerk. And they're right, Gene. You're fifty-six years old with a wife and two kids, though for how much longer I don't know. Time you grew up. I'm telling you that as a friend."

I watched Gene's face. I was getting better at reading emotions, but this was a complex one. Shattered, I think.

I was relieved. The basic male-male tough advice protocol had been effective. It had not been necessary to slug him.

CHAPTER
THIRTY-TWO

I went back to my office and changed from my Gregory Peck costume into my new trousers and jacket. Then I made a phone call. The receptionist was not prepared to make an appointment for a personal matter, so I booked a fitness evaluation with Phil Jarman, Rosie's father in air quotes, for 4.00p.m.

As I got up to leave, the Dean knocked and walked in. She signalled for me to follow her. This was not part of my plan, but today was an appropriate day to close this phase of my professional life.

We went down in the lift and then across the campus to her office, not speaking. It seemed that our conversation needed to take place in a formal setting. I felt uncomfortable, which was a rational response to the almost-certain prospect of being dismissed from a tenured position at a prestigious university for professional misconduct. But I had expected this and my feelings came from a different source. The scenario triggered a memory from my first week at high school, of being sent to the headmaster's office as a result of allegedly inappropriate behaviour. The purported misconduct involved a rigorous questioning of our religious education teacher. In retrospect, I understood that she was a well-meaning person, but she used her position of power over an eleven-year-old to cause me considerable distress.

The headmaster was, in fact, reasonably sympathetic, but warned me that I needed to show "respect". But he was too late: as I walked to his office I had made the decision that it was pointless to try to fit in. I would be the class clown for the next six years.

I have thought about this event often. At the time my decision felt like a rational response based on my assessment of the new environment, but in retrospect I understood that I was driven by anger at the power structure that suppressed my arguments.

Now as I walked to the Dean's office another thought occurred to me. What if my teacher had been a brilliant theologian, equipped with two thousand years of well-articulated Christian thinking? She would have had more compelling arguments than an eleven-year-old. Would I have then been satisfied? I suspect not. As a scientist, with an allegiance to scientific thinking, I would have had a deep-seated feeling that I was being, as Rosie would say, bullshitted. Was that how Faith Healer had felt?

Had the flounder demonstration been an instance of bullying as heinous as the one committed by my religious education teacher, *even though I was right?*

As we entered the Dean's office for what I expected to be the last time, I took notice of her full name on the door, and a minor confusion was resolved. Professor Charlotte Lawrence. I had never thought of her as "Charlie", but presumably Simon Lefebvre did.

We entered her office and sat down. "I see we're in our job interview clothes," she said. "I'm sorry you didn't see fit to grace us with them during your time here."

I did not respond.

"So. No report. No explanation?"

Again, I could not think of anything appropriate to say.

Simon Lefebvre appeared at the door. Obviously this had been planned. The Dean — Charlie — waved him in.

"You can save time by explaining to Simon and me together."

Lefebvre was carrying the documents that I had given him.

At that point, the Dean's personal assistant, Regina, who is not objectified by having the words "The Beautiful" included in her name, entered the room.

"Sorry to bother you, Professor," she said, ambiguously, as we were all professors, for the next few minutes at least, but the context made it clear she was addressing the Dean. "I've got a problem with your booking at Le Gavroche. They seem to have taken you off the VIP list."

The Dean's face registered annoyance but she waved Regina away.

Simon Lefebvre smiled at me. "You could've just sent me this," he said, referring to the documents. "No need for the idiot-savant impression. Which I have to concede was beautifully done. As is the proposal. We'll need to run it by the ethics guys, but it's exactly what we're looking for. Genetics and medicine, topic's current, we'll both get publicity."

I attempted to analyse the Dean's expression. It was beyond my current skill set.

"So congratulations, Charlie," said Simon. "You've got your joint research project. The Medical Research Institute is prepared to put in four mill, which is more than the budget actually specifies, so you're set to go."

I presumed he meant four million dollars.

He pointed to me. "Hang on to this one, Charlie. He's a dark horse. And I need him to be part of the project."

I got my first real return on my investment in improved social skills. I had worked out what was going on. I did not ask a silly question. I did not put the Dean in a position of untenable embarrassment where she might work against her own interests. I just nodded and walked back to my office.

Phil Jarman had blue eyes. I knew this but it was the first thing I noticed. He was in his mid-fifties, about ten centimetres taller than me, powerfully built and extremely fit-looking. We were standing in front of the reception desk at Jarman's Gym. On the wall were newspaper cuttings and photos of a younger Phil playing football. If I had been a medical student without advanced martial-arts skills, I would have thought carefully before having sex with this man's girlfriend. Perhaps this was the simple reason that Phil had never been informed of the identity of Rosie's father.

"Get the prof some gear and get his signature on a waiver form."

The woman behind the counter seemed puzzled.

"It's just an assessment."

"New procedure starts today," said Phil.

"I don't require an assessment," I began, but Phil seemed to have fixed ideas.

"You booked one," he said. "Sixty-five bucks. Let's get you some boxing gloves."

I wondered if he realised that he had called me "prof". Presumably Rosie had been right, and he had seen the dancing picture. I had not bothered to disguise my name. But at least I knew that he knew who I was. Did he know that I knew that he knew who I was? I was getting quite good at social subtleties.

I changed into a singlet and shorts, which smelled freshly laundered, and we put on boxing gloves. I had only done the occasional boxing workout, but I was not afraid of getting hurt. I had good defensive techniques if necessary. I was more interested in talking.

"Let's see you hit me," said Phil.

I threw some gentle punches which Phil blocked.

"Come on," he said. "Try to hurt me."

He asked for it.

"Your stepdaughter is trying to locate her real father because she's dissatisfied with you."

Phil dropped his guard. Very poor form. I could have landed a punch unimpeded if we were in a real bout.

"Stepdaughter?" he said. "That's what she's calling herself? That's why you're here?"

292

He threw a hard punch and I had to use a proper block to avoid being hit. He recognised it and tried a hook. I blocked that too and counterpunched. He avoided it nicely.

"Since it's unlikely she'll succeed, we need to fix the problem with you."

Phil threw a straight hard one at my head. I blocked and stepped away.

"With me?" he said. "With Phil Jarman? Who built his own business from nothing, who bench-presses a hundred and forty-five kilos, who plenty of women still think is a better deal than some doctor or lawyer? Or egghead?"

He threw a combination and I attacked back. I thought there was a high probability that I could take him down, but I needed to continue the conversation.

"It's none of your business but I was on the school council, coached the senior football team —"

"Obviously these achievements were insufficient," I said. "Perhaps Rosie requires something in addition to personal excellence." In a moment of clarity, I realised what that something might be in my own case. Was all my work in self-improvement in vain? Was I going to end up like Phil, trying to win Rosie's love but regarded with contempt?

Fighting and contemplation are not compatible. Phil's punch took me in the solar plexus. I managed to step back and reduce the force, but went down. Phil stood over me, angry.

"Maybe one day she'll know everything. Maybe that'll help, maybe it won't." He shook his head hard, as though he was the one who had taken a punch. "Did I ever call myself her stepfather? Ask her that. I've got no other children, no *wife*. I did all the things — I read to her, got up in the night, took her horseriding. After her mother was gone, I couldn't do a thing right."

I sat up and shouted. I was angry too. "You failed to take her to Disneyland. You lied to her."

I scissored his legs, bringing him down. He didn't fall competently, and hit the floor hard. We struggled and I pinned him. His nose was bleeding badly and there was blood all over my singlet.

"Disneyland!" said Phil. "She was ten!"

"She told everyone at school. It's still a major problem."

He tried to break free, but I managed to hold him, despite the impediment of the boxing gloves.

"You want to know when I told her I'd take her to Disneyland? One time. Once. You know when? At her mother's funeral. I was in a wheelchair, I was in rehab for eight months."

It was a very reasonable explanation. I wished Rosie had provided this background information prior to me holding her stepfather's head on the floor with blood pouring from his nose. I explained to Phil that at my sister's funeral I made an irrational promise to donate to a hospice when the money would have been better applied to research. He seemed to understand.

"I bought her a jewellery box. She'd been on her mother's case forever to buy it. I thought she'd forgotten about Disneyland when I came out of rehab."

"Predicting the impact of actions on other people is difficult."

"Amen to that," said Phil. "Can we get up?"

His nose was still bleeding and was probably broken, so it was a reasonable request. But I was not prepared to let him go yet.

"Not until we solve the problem."

It had been a very full day but the most critical task was still ahead. I examined myself in the mirror. The new glasses, vastly lighter, and the revised hair shape made a bigger difference than the clothes.

I put the important envelope in my jacket pocket and the small box in my trouser pocket. As I phoned for a taxi, I looked at my whiteboard. The schedule, now written in erasable marker, was a sea of red writing — my code for the Rosie Project. I told myself that the changes it had produced were worthwhile, even if tonight I failed to achieve the final objective.

CHAPTER
THIRTY-THREE

The taxi arrived and we made an intermediate stop at the flower shop. I had not been inside this shop — or indeed purchased flowers at all — since I'd stopped visiting Daphne. Daphne for Daphne; obviously the appropriate choice for this evening was roses. The vendor recognised me and I informed her of Daphne's death. After I purchased a dozen long-stemmed red roses, consistent with standard romantic behaviour, she snipped a small quantity of daphne and inserted it in the buttonhole of my jacket. The smell brought back memories of Daphne. I wished she was alive to meet Rosie.

I tried to phone Rosie as the taxi approached her apartment building, but there was no answer. She was not outside when we arrived, and most of the bell buttons did not have names beside them. There was a risk that she had chosen not to accept my invitation.

It was cold and I was shaking. I waited a full ten minutes, then called again. There was still no answer and I was about to instruct the driver to leave when she came running out. I reminded myself that it was I who had changed, not Rosie — I should have expected her to be late. She was wearing the black dress that had stunned me on the night of the Jacket Incident. I gave her the roses. I read her expression as surprised.

Then she looked at me.

"You look different . . . really different . . . again," she said. "What happened?"

"I decided to reform myself." I liked the sound of the word: "re-form". We got in the taxi, Rosie still holding the roses, and travelled the short distance to the restaurant in silence. I was looking for information about her attitude towards me, and thought it best to let her speak first. In fact she didn't say anything until she noticed that the taxi was stopping outside Le Gavroche — the scene of the Jacket Incident.

"Don, is this a joke?"

I paid the driver, exited the taxi and opened Rosie's door. She stepped out but was reluctant to proceed, clutching the roses to her chest with both hands. I put one hand behind her and guided her towards the door, where the maître d' whom we had encountered on our previous visit was standing in his uniform. Jacket Man.

He recognised Rosie instantly, as evidenced by his greeting. "Rosie."

Then he looked at me. "Sir?"

"Good evening." I took the flowers from Rosie and gave them to the maître d'. "We have a reservation in the name of Tillman. Would you be kind enough to look after these?" It was a standard formula but very confidence-boosting. Everyone seemed very comfortable now that we were behaving in a predictable manner. The maître d' checked the reservation list. I took the opportunity to smooth over any remaining difficulties and made a small prepared joke.

"My apologies for the misunderstanding last time. There shouldn't be any difficulties tonight. Unless they overchill the white Burgundy." I smiled.

A male waiter appeared, the maître d' introduced me, briefly complimenting me on my jacket, and we were led into the dining room and to our table. It was all very straightforward.

I ordered a bottle of chablis. Rosie still seemed to be adjusting.

The sommelier appeared with the wine. He was looking around the room, as if for support. I diagnosed nervousness.

"It's at thirteen degrees but if sir would like it less chilled . . . or more chilled . . ."

"That will be fine, thank you."

He poured me a taste and I swirled, sniffed and nodded approval according to the standard protocol. Meanwhile, the waiter who had led us to the table reappeared. He was about forty, BMI approximately twenty-two, quite tall.

"Professor Tillman?" he said. "My name's Nick and I'm the head waiter. If there's anything you need, or anything that's a problem, just ask for me."

"Much appreciated, Nick."

Waiters introducing themselves by name was more in the American tradition. Either this restaurant deliberately chose to do so as a point of difference, or we were being given more personal treatment. I guessed the latter: I was probably marked as a dangerous person. Good. I would need all the support I could get tonight.

Nick handed us menus.

"I'm happy to leave it to the chef," I said. "But no meat, and seafood only if it's sustainable."

Nick smiled. "I'll speak to the chef and see what he can do."

"I realise it's a little tricky, but my friend lives by some quite strict rules," I said.

Rosie gave me a very strange look. My statement was intended to make a small point, and I think it succeeded. She tried her chablis and buttered a bread roll. I remained silent.

Finally she spoke.

"All right, Gregory Peck. What are we doing first? The *My Fair Lady* story or the big revelation?"

This was good. Rosie was prepared to discuss things directly. In fact, directness had always been one of Rosie's positive attributes, though on this occasion she had not identified the most important topic.

"I'm in your hands," I said. Standard polite method for avoiding a choice and empowering the other person.

"Don, stop it. You know who my father is, right? It's Table-Napkin Man, isn't it?"

"Possibly," I said, truthfully. Despite the positive outcome of the meeting with the Dean, I did not have my lab key back. "That isn't what I want to share."

"All right then. Here's the plan. You share your thing; tell me who my father is; tell me what you've done to yourself; we both go home."

I couldn't put a name to her tone of speech and expression, but it was clearly negative. She took another sip of her wine.

"Sorry." She looked a little apologetic. "Go. The sharing thing."

I had grave doubts about the likely efficacy of my next move, but there was no contingency plan. I had sourced my speech from *When Harry Met Sally*. It resonated best with me and with the situation, and had the additional advantage of the link to our happy time in New York. I hoped Rosie's brain would make that connection, ideally subconsciously. I drank the remainder of my wine. Rosie's eyes followed my glass, then she looked up at me.

"Are you okay, Don?"

"I asked you here tonight because when you realise you want to spend the rest of your life with somebody, you want the rest of your life to start as soon as possible."

I studied Rosie's expression carefully. I diagnosed stunned.

"Oh my God," said Rosie, confirming the diagnosis. I followed up while she was still receptive.

"It seems right now that all I've ever done in my life is making my way here to you."

I could see that Rosie could not place the line from *The Bridges of Madison County* that had produced such a powerful emotional reaction on the plane. She looked confused.

"Don, what are you . . . what have you done to yourself?"

300

"I've made some changes."

"Big changes."

"Whatever behavioural modifications you require from me are a trivial price to pay for having you as my partner."

Rosie made a downwards movement with her hand, which I could not interpret. Then she looked around the room and I followed her eyes. Everyone was watching. Nick had stopped partway to our table. I realised that in my intensity I had raised my voice. I didn't care.

"You are the world's most perfect woman. All other women are irrelevant. Permanently. No Botox or implants will be required."

I heard someone clapping. It was a slim woman of about sixty sitting with another woman of approximately the same age.

Rosie took a drink of her wine, then spoke in a very measured way. "Don, I don't know where to start. I don't even know who's asking me — the old Don or Billy Crystal."

"There's no old and new," I said. "It's just behaviour. Social conventions. Glasses and haircut."

"I like you, Don," said Rosie. "Okay? Forget what I said about outing my father. You're probably right. I really *really* like you. I have fun with you. The best times. But, you know I couldn't eat lobster every Tuesday. Right?"

"I've abandoned the Standardised Meal System. I've deleted thirty-eight per cent of my weekly schedule, excluding sleep. I've thrown out my old t-shirts. I've eliminated all of the things you didn't like. Further changes are possible."

"You changed yourself for me?"

"Only my behaviour."

Rosie was silent for a while, obviously processing the new information.

"I need a minute to think," she said. I automatically started the timer on my watch. Suddenly Rosie started laughing. I looked at her, understandably puzzled at this outburst in the middle of a critical life decision.

"The watch," she said. "I say 'I need a minute' and you start timing. Don is not dead."

I waited. I looked at my watch. When there were fifteen seconds left, I assessed that it was likely that she was about to say no. I had nothing to lose. I pulled the small box from my pocket and opened it to reveal the ring I had purchased. I wished I had not learned to read expressions, because I could read Rosie's now and I knew the answer.

"Don," said Rosie. "This isn't what you want me to say. But remember on the plane, when you said you were wired differently?"

I nodded. I knew what the problem was. The fundamental, insurmountable problem of who I was. I had pushed it to the back of my mind since it had surfaced in the fight with Phil. Rosie didn't need to explain. But she did.

"That's inside you. You can't fake — sorry, start again. You can behave perfectly, but if the *feeling's* not there inside . . . God, I feel so unreasonable."

"The answer is no?" I said, some small part of my brain hoping that for once my fallibility in reading social cues would work in my favour.

"Don, you don't feel love, do you?" said Rosie. "You can't really love me."

"Gene diagnosed love." I knew now that he had been wrong. I had watched thirteen romantic movies and felt nothing. That was not strictly true. I had felt suspense, curiosity and amusement. But I had not for one moment felt engaged in the love between the protagonists. I had cried no tears for Meg Ryan or Meryl Streep or Deborah Kerr or Vivien Leigh or Julia Roberts.

I could not lie about so important a matter. "According to your definition, no."

Rosie looked extremely unhappy. The evening had turned into a disaster.

"I thought my behaviour would make you happy, and instead it's made you sad."

"I'm upset because you can't love me. Okay?"

This was worse! She wanted me to love her. And I was incapable.

"Don," she said, "I don't think we should see each other any more."

I got up from the table and walked back to the entrance foyer, out of sight of Rosie and the other diners. Nick was there, talking to the maître d'. He saw me and came over.

"Can I help you with anything?"

"Unfortunately, there has been a disaster."

Nick looked worried, and I elaborated. "A personal disaster. There is no risk to other patrons. Would you prepare the bill, please?"

"We haven't served you anything," said Nick. He looked at me closely for a few moments. "There's no charge, sir. The Chablis is on us." He offered me his hand and I shook it. "I think you gave it your best shot."

I looked up to see Gene and Claudia arriving. They were holding hands. I had not seen them do this for several years.

"Don't tell me we're too late," said Gene, jovially.

I nodded, then looked back into the restaurant. Rosie was walking quickly towards us.

"Don, what are you doing?" she said.

"Leaving. You said we shouldn't see each other again."

"Fuck," she said, then looked at Gene and Claudia. "What are you doing here?"

"We are summoned to a 'Thank you and celebration'," said Gene. "Happy birthday, Don."

He gave me a gift-wrapped package, and put his arm around me in a hug. I recognised that this was probably the final step in the male-male advice protocol, indicating acceptance of the advice without damage to our friendship, and managed not to flinch, but could not process the input any further. My brain was already overloaded.

"It's your birthday?" said Rosie.

"Correct."

"I had to get Helena to look up your birth date," said Gene, "but 'celebration' was a clue."

I normally do not treat birthdays differently from other days, but it had struck me as an appropriate occasion to commence a new direction.

Claudia introduced herself to Rosie, adding, "I'm sorry, it seems we've come at a bad time."

Rosie turned to Gene. "A 'thank you'? Thank *you*? Shit. It wasn't enough to set us up — you had to coach him. You had to turn him into you."

Claudia said, quietly, "Rosie, it wasn't Gene's —"

Gene put a hand on Claudia's shoulder and she stopped.

"No, it wasn't," he said. "Who *asked* him to change? Who said that he'd be *perfect* for her if he was *different?*"

Rosie was now looking very upset. All of my friends (except Dave the Baseball Fan) were fighting. *This was terrible*. I wanted to roll the story back to New York and make better decisions. But it was impossible. Nothing would change the fault in my brain that made me unacceptable.

Gene hadn't stopped. "Do you have any idea what he did for you? Take a look in his office sometime." He was presumably referring to my schedule and the large number of Rosie Project activities.

Rosie walked out of the restaurant.

Gene turned to Claudia. "Sorry I interrupted you."

"Someone had to say it," said Claudia. She looked at Rosie, who was already some distance down the street. "I think I coached the wrong person."

Gene and Claudia offered me a lift home, but I did not want to continue the conversation. I started walking, then accelerated to a jog. It made sense to get home before it rained. It also made sense to exercise hard and put the restaurant behind me as quickly as possible. The new shoes were workable, but the coat and tie were uncomfortable even on a cold night. I pulled off the jacket, the item that had made me temporarily acceptable in a world to which I did not belong, and threw it in a rubbish bin. The tie followed. On an impulse I retrieved the daphne from the jacket and carried it in my hand for the remainder of the journey. There was rain in the air and my face was wet as I reached the safety of my apartment.

CHAPTER
THIRTY-FOUR

We had not finished the wine at the restaurant. I decided to compensate for the resulting alcohol deficit and poured a tumbler of tequila. I turned on the television screen and computer and fast-forwarded *Casablanca* for one last try. I watched as Humphrey Bogart's character used beans as a metaphor for the relative unimportance in the wider world of his relationship with Ingrid Bergman's character, and chose logic and decency ahead of his selfish emotional desires. The quandary and resulting decision made for an engrossing film. But this was not what people cried about. *They were in love and could never be together.* I repeated this statement to myself, trying to force an emotional reaction. I couldn't. I didn't care. I had enough problems of my own.

The doorbell buzzed, and I immediately thought *Rosie*, but when I pushed the CCTV button, it was Claudia's face that appeared.

"Don, are you okay?" she said. "Can we come up?"

"It's too late."

Claudia sounded panicked. "What have you done? Don?"

"It's 10.31," I said. "Too late for visitors."

"Are you okay?" said Claudia, again.

"I'm fine. The experience has been highly useful. New social skills. And final resolution of the Wife Problem. Clear evidence that I'm incompatible with women."

Gene's face appeared on the screen. "Don. Can we come up for a drink?"

"Alcohol would be a bad idea." I still had a half-glass of tequila in my hand. I was telling a polite lie to avoid social contact. I turned off the intercom.

The message light on my home phone was flashing. It was my parents and brother wishing me a happy birthday. I had already spoken to my mother two days earlier when she made her regular Sunday evening call. These past three weeks, I had been attempting to provide some news in return, but had not mentioned Rosie. They were utilising the speaker-phone function, and collectively sang the birthday song — or at least my mother did, strongly encouraging my other two relatives to participate.

"Ring back if you're home before 10.30," my mother said. It was 10.38, but I decided not to be pedantic.

"It's 10.39," said my mother. "I'm surprised you rang back." Clearly she had expected me to be pedantic, which was reasonable given my history, but she sounded pleased.

"Hey," said my brother. "Gary Parkinson's sister saw you on Facebook. Who's the redhead?"

"Just a girl I was dating."

"Pull the other leg," said my brother.

The words had sounded strange to me too, but I had not been joking.

"I'm not seeing her any more."

"I thought you might say that." He laughed.

My mother interrupted. "Stop it, Trevor. Donald, you didn't tell us you were seeing someone. You know you're always welcome —"

"Mum, he was having a lend of you," said my brother.

"I *said*," said my mother, "that *any time* you want to bring *anyone* to meet us, *whoever* she or *he* —"

"Leave him alone, both of you," said my father.

There was a pause, and some conversation in the background. Then my brother said, "Sorry, mate. I was just having a go. I know you think I'm some sort of redneck, but I'm okay with who you are. I'd hate you to get to this age and think I still had a problem with it."

So, to add to a momentous day, I corrected a misconception that my family had held for at least fifteen years and came out to them as straight.

The conversations with Gene, Phil and my family had been surprisingly therapeutic. I did not need to use the Edinburgh Postnatal Depression Scale to know that I was feeling sad, but I was back from the edge of the pit. I would need to do some disciplined thinking in the near future to be certain of remaining safe, but for the moment I did not need to shut down the emotional part of my brain entirely. I wanted a little time to observe how I felt about recent events.

It was cold and the rain was pouring, but my balcony was under shelter. I took a chair and my glass outside, then went back inside, put on the greasy wool jumper that my mother had knitted for a much earlier birthday and collected the tequila bottle.

I was forty years old. My father used to play a song written by John Sebastian. I remember that it was by John Sebastian because Noddy Holder announced prior to singing it, "We're going to do a song by John Sebastian. Are there any John Sebastian fans here?" Apparently there were because there was loud and raucous applause before he started singing.

I decided that tonight I was also a John Sebastian fan and that I wanted to hear the song. This was the first time in my life that I could recall a desire to hear a particular piece of music. I had the technology. Or used to. I went to pull out my mobile phone and realised it had been in the jacket I had discarded. I went inside, booted my laptop, registered for iTunes, and downloaded "Darling Be Home Soon" from *Slade Alive!*, 1972. I added "Satisfaction", thus doubling the size of my popular music collection. I retrieved my earphones from their box and returned to the balcony, poured another tequila and listened to a voice from my childhood singing that it had taken a quarter of his life before he could begin to see himself.

At eighteen, just before I left home to go to university, statistically approaching a quarter of my life, I had listened to these words and been reminded that I had very little understanding of who I was. It had taken me until tonight, approximately halfway, to see myself reasonably clearly. I had Rosie, and the Rosie Project to thank for that. Now it was over, what had I learned?

310

1. I need not be visibly odd. I could engage in the protocols that others followed and move undetected among them. And how could I be sure that other people were not doing the same — playing the game to be accepted but suspecting all the time that they were different?
2. I had skills that others didn't. My memory and ability to focus had given me an advantage in baseball statistics, cocktail-making and genetics. People had valued these skills, not mocked them.
3. I could enjoy friendship and good times. It was my lack of skills, not lack of motivation that had held me back. Now I was competent enough socially to open my life to a wider range of people. I could have more friends. Dave the Baseball Fan could be the first of many.
4. I had told Gene and Claudia that I was incompatible with women. This was an exaggeration. I could enjoy their company, as proven by my joint activities with Rosie and Daphne. Realistically, it was possible that I could have a partnership with a woman.
5. The idea behind the Wife Project was still sound. In many cultures a matchmaker would have routinely done what I did, with less technology, reach and rigour, but the

same assumption — that compatibility was as viable a foundation for marriage as love.

6. I was not wired to feel love. And faking it was not acceptable. Not to me. I had feared that Rosie would not love me. Instead, it was I who could not love Rosie.

7. I had a great deal of valuable knowledge — about genetics, computers, aikido, karate, hardware, chess, wine, cocktails, dancing, sexual positions, social protocols and the probability of a fifty-six-game hitting streak occurring in the history of baseball. I knew so much *shit* and I still couldn't fix myself.

As the shuffle setting on my media player selected the same two songs over and over, I realised that my thinking was also beginning to go in circles and that, despite the tidy formulation, there was some flaw in my logic. I decided it was my unhappiness with the night's outcome breaking through, my wish that it could be different.

I watched the rain falling over the city and poured the last of the tequila.

CHAPTER
THIRTY-FIVE

I was still in the chair when I woke the next morning. It was cold and raining and my laptop battery had exhausted itself. I shook my head to test for a hangover but it seemed that my alcohol-processing enzymes had done their job adequately. So had my brain. I had unconsciously set it a problem to solve and, understanding the importance of the situation, it had overcome the handicap of intoxication to reach a solution.

I began the second half of my life by making coffee. Then I reviewed the very simple logic.

1. I was wired differently. One of the characteristics of my wiring was that I had difficulty empathising. This problem has been well documented in others and is, in fact, one of the defining symptoms of the autism spectrum.

2. A lack of empathy would account for my inability to respond emotionally to the situations of fictional characters in films. This was similar to my inability to respond as others did to the victims of the World Trade

Center terrorist attacks. But I did feel sorry for Frank the fire-fighter guide. And for Daphne; my sister; my parents when my sister died; Carl and Eugenie because of the Gene-Claudia marriage crisis; Gene himself, who wanted to be admired but had achieved the opposite; Claudia, who had agreed to an open marriage but changed her mind and suffered as Gene continued to exploit it; Phil, who had struggled to deal with his wife's infidelity and death and then to win the love of Rosie; Kevin Yu, whose focus on passing the course had blinded him to ethical conduct; the Dean, who had to make difficult decisions under contradictory rules and deal with prejudice about her dress and relationship; Faith Healer, who had to reconcile his strong beliefs with scientific evidence; Margaret Case, whose son had committed suicide and whose mind no longer functioned; and, critically, Rosie, whose childhood and now adulthood had been made unhappy by her mother's death and her father problem and who now wanted me to love her. This was an impressive list, and, though it did not include Rick and Ilsa from *Casablanca*, it was clear evidence that my empathy capability was not entirely absent.

3. An inability (or reduced ability) to empathise is not the same as an inability

to love. Love is a powerful feeling for another person, often defying logic.

4. Rosie had failed numerous criteria on the Wife Project, including the critical smoking question. My feelings for her *could not be explained by logic*. I did not care about Meryl Streep. But I was in love with Rosie.

I had to act quickly, not because I believed the situation with Rosie was likely to change in the immediate future, but because I needed my jacket, which was, I hoped, still in the rubbish bin where I had thrown it. Luckily I was already dressed from the previous evening.

It was still raining when I arrived at the bin, just in time to see it emptied into a garbage truck compactor. I had a contingency plan, but it was going to take time. I turned the bike around to head for home and crossed the road. Slumped in a shop doorway, out of the rain, was a hobo. He was fast asleep, and he was wearing my jacket. I carefully reached into the inside pocket and extracted the envelope and my phone. As I remounted my bike, I saw a couple on the other side of the street watching me. The male started to run towards me, but the woman called him back. She was making a call on her mobile phone.

It was only 7.48a.m. when I arrived at the university. A police car approached from the opposite direction, slowed as it passed me, then signalled a U-turn. It occurred to me that it could have been summoned to deal with my apparent theft from the hobo. I turned quickly down the bicycle path, where I could not be followed by a motor vehicle, and headed towards the Genetics building to find a towel.

As I opened the unlocked door of my office it was obvious that I had had a visitor, and who that visitor had been. The red roses were lying on my desk. So was the Father Project file, which had been removed from its home in the filing cabinet. The list of father-candidate names and sample descriptions was on the desk beside it. Rosie had left a note.

Don, I'm sorry about everything. But I know who Table-Napkin Man is. I've told Dad. I probably shouldn't have but I was very upset. I tried to call you. Sorry again. Rosie.

There was a lot of crossed-out writing between *Sorry again* and *Rosie*. But this was a disaster! I needed to warn Gene.

His diary indicated a breakfast meeting at the University Club. I checked the PhD area, and Stefan was there, but not Rosie. Stefan could see that I was highly agitated, and followed me.

We reached the club, and located Gene at a table with the Dean. But at another table, I saw Rosie. She was with Claudia and seemed very distressed. I realised that she could be sharing the news about Gene, even prior to a DNA ratification. The Father Project was ending in total disaster. But I had come for something else. I was desperate to share my revelation. We could resolve the other problem later.

316

I ran to Rosie's table. I was still wet as a result of forgetting to dry myself. Rosie was obviously surprised to see me. I dispensed with formalities.

"I've made an incredible mistake. I can't believe I've been so stupid. Irrational!" Claudia made signals for me to stop, but I ignored them. "You failed almost every criterion of the Wife Project. Disorganised, mathematically illiterate, ridiculous food requirements. Incredible. I considered sharing my life with a smoker. Permanently!"

Rosie's expression was complex, but appeared to include sadness, anger and surprise. "It didn't take you long to change your mind," she said.

Claudia was frantically waving at me to stop, but I was determined to proceed according to my own plan.

"I haven't changed my mind. That's the point! I want to spend my life with you even though it's totally irrational. And you have short earlobes. Socially and genetically there's no reason for me to be attracted to you. The only logical conclusion is that I must be in love with you."

Claudia got up and pushed me into her chair.

"You don't give up, do you?" said Rosie.

"I'm being annoying?"

"No," said Rosie. "You're being incredibly brave. I have the best fun with you, you're the smartest, funniest person I know, you've done all these things for me. It's everything I want and I've been too scared to grab it because —"

She stopped but I knew what she was thinking. I finished her sentence for her.

"Because I'm weird. Perfectly understandable. I'm familiar with the problem because everyone else seems weird to me."

Rosie laughed.

I tried to explain.

"Crying over fictitious characters, for example."

"Could you live with me crying at movies?" said Rosie.

"Of course," I said. "It's conventional behaviour." I stopped as I realised what she had said.

"You're offering to live with me?"

Rosie smiled.

"You left this on the table," she said, and pulled the ring container from her bag. I realised that Rosie had reversed her decision of the previous night, and was in effect rolling back time to allow my original plan to proceed at an alternative location. I extracted the ring and she held out her finger. I put it on and it fitted. I felt a major sense of relief.

I became aware of applause. It seemed natural. I had been living in the world of romantic comedy and this was the final scene. But it was real. The entire University Club dining room had been watching. I decided to complete the story according to tradition and kissed Rosie. It was even better than the previous occasion.

"You'd better not let me down," said Rosie. "I'm expecting constant craziness."

Phil walked in, his nose in a plaster cast, accompanied by the club manager. She was followed by two police. The manager pointed Gene out to Phil.

318

"Oh shit," said Rosie. Phil walked over to Gene, who stood up. There was a brief conversation and then Phil knocked him to the floor with a single punch to the jaw. The police rushed forward and restrained Phil, who did not resist. Claudia ran up to Gene, who was slowly rising. He appeared not to be seriously injured. I realised that under the traditional rules of romantic behaviour, it was correct for Phil to assault Gene, assuming he had in fact seduced Rosie's mother when she was Phil's girlfriend.

However, it was not certain that Gene was the culprit. On the other hand, numerous men were probably entitled to punch Gene. In this sense, Phil was dispensing romantic justice on their behalf. Gene must have understood, because he appeared to be reassuring the police that everything was okay.

I redirected my attention to Rosie. Now that my previous plan had been reinstated, it was important not to be distracted.

"Item Two on the agenda was your father's identity."

Rosie smiled. "Back on track. Item One: let's get married. Okay, that's sorted. Item Two. This is the Don I've grown to know and love."

The last word stopped me. I could only look at Rosie as I took in the reality of what she had said. I guessed she was doing the same, and it was several seconds before she spoke.

"How many positions in that book can you do?"

"The sex book? All of them."

"Bullshit."

"It was considerably less complex than the cocktail book."

"So let's go home," she said. "To my place. Or your place if you've still got the Atticus Finch outfit." She laughed.

"It's in my office."

"Another time. Don't throw it out."

We got up, but the police, one man and one woman, blocked our path.

"Sir," said the woman (age approximately twenty-eight, BMI twenty-three), "I'm going to have to ask you what's in your pocket."

I had forgotten the envelope! I pulled it out and waved it in front of Rosie.

"Tickets! Tickets to Disneyland. All problems solved!" I fanned out the three tickets, took Rosie's hand and we walked towards Phil to show him.

CHAPTER
THIRTY-SIX

We went to Disneyland — Rosie, Phil and I. It was great fun and appeared to be a success in improving all relationships. Rosie and Phil shared information and I learned a lot about Rosie's life. It was important background for the difficult but essential task of developing a high level of empathy for one person in the world.

Rosie and I were on our way to New York, where being weird is acceptable. That is a simplification of the rationale: in reality what was important for me was to be able to make a new start with my new skills, new approach and new partner, without being held back by others' perceptions of me — perceptions that I had not only deserved but encouraged.

Here in New York, I am working in the Department of Genetics at Columbia University, and Rosie is in the first year of the Doctor of Medicine programme. I am contributing to Simon Lefebvre's research project remotely, as he insisted on it as a condition of providing funding. I consider it a form of moral payback for using the university's equipment for the Father Project.

We have an apartment in Williamsburg, not far from the Eslers, whom we visit regularly. The Cellar

Interrogation is now a story that Isaac and I both tell on social occasions.

We are considering reproducing (or, as I would say in a social encounter, "having children"). In order to prepare for this possibility, Rosie has ceased smoking, and we have reduced our alcohol intake. Fortunately we have numerous other activities to distract us from these addictive behaviours. Rosie and I work in a cocktail bar together three evenings a week. It is exhausting at times, but social and fun, and supplements my academic salary.

We listen to music. I have revised my approach to Bach, and am no longer trying to follow individual notes. It is more successful, but my music tastes seem to have been locked in in my teens. As a result of failing to make my own selections at that time, my preferences are those of my father. I can advance a well-reasoned argument that nothing worth listening to was recorded after 1972. Rosie and I have that argument frequently. I cook, but reserve the meals of the Standardised Meal System for dinner parties.

We are officially married. Although I had performed the romantic ritual with the ring, I did not expect Rosie, as a modern feminist, to want to actually get married. The term "wife" in Wife Project had always meant "female life partner". But she decided that she should have "one relationship in my life that was what it was supposed to be". That included monogamy and permanence. An excellent outcome.

I am able to hug Rosie. This was the issue that caused me the most fear after she agreed to live with me. I generally find body contact unpleasant, but sex is an obvious exception. Sex solved the body contact problem. We are now also able to hug without having sex, which is obviously convenient at times.

Once a week, in order to deal with the demands of living with another person, and to continue to improve my skills in this sphere, I spend an evening in therapy. This is a small joke: my "therapist" is Dave and I provide reciprocal services to him. Dave is also married and, considering that I am supposedly wired differently, our challenges are surprisingly similar. He sometimes brings male friends and colleagues from work, where he is a refrigeration engineer. We are all Yankees fans.

For some time, Rosie did not mention the Father Project. I attributed this to the improved relationship with Phil and the distraction of other activities. But, in the background, I was processing some new information.

At the wedding, Dr Eamonn Hughes, the first person we had tested, asked to speak to me privately.

"There's something you should know," he said. "About Rosie's father."

It seemed entirely plausible that Rosie's mother's closest friend from medical school would know the answer. Perhaps we had only needed to ask. But Eamonn was referring to something else. He pointed to Phil.

"Phil's been a bit of a screw-up with Rosie."

So it wasn't only Rosie who thought Phil was a poor parent.

"You know about the car accident?"

I nodded, although I had no detailed information. Rosie had made it clear that she did not want to discuss it.

"Bernadette was driving because Phil had been drinking."

I had deduced that Phil was in the car.

"Phil got out, with a broken pelvis, and pulled Rosie out." Eamonn paused. He was obviously distressed. "He pulled Rosie out first."

This was truly an awful scenario, but as a geneticist my immediate thought was "of course". Phil's behaviour, in pain and under extreme pressure, would surely have been instinctual. Such life-and-death situations occur regularly in the animal kingdom and Phil's choice was in line with theory and experimental results. While he had presumably revisited that moment many times in his mind, and his later feelings towards Rosie may have been severely affected by it, his actions were consistent with the primitive drive to protect the carrier of his genes.

It was only later that I realised my obvious error. As Rosie was not Phil's biological daughter, such instincts would not have been applicable. I spent some time reflecting on the possible explanations for his behaviour. I did not share my thoughts or the hypothesis I formed.

When I was established at Columbia, I requested permission to use the DNA-testing facilities for a private investigation. They were willing to let me do so. It would not have been a problem if they had refused. I could have sent my remaining samples to a commercial laboratory and paid a few hundred dollars for the tests. This option had been available to Rosie from the beginning of the Father Project. It is now obvious to me that I did not alert Rosie to that option because I was subconsciously interested in a relationship with her even then. Amazing!

I did not tell Rosie about the test. One day I just packed my bag with the samples that I had brought with me to New York.

I started with the paranoid plastic surgeon, Freyberg, who was the least likely candidate in my assessment. A green-eyed father was not impossible, but there was no other evidence making him more probable than any of the previous candidates. His reluctance to send me a blood sample was explained by him being a generally suspicious and unhelpful person. My prediction was correct.

I loaded Esler's specimen, a swab from a fork that had travelled more than halfway around the world and back again. In his darkened basement, I had been certain he was Rosie's father. But afterwards I had come to the conclusion that he could have been protecting a friend or the memory of a friend. I wondered if Esler's decision to become a psychiatrist had been influenced by the suicide of the best man at his wedding, Geoffrey Case.

I tested the sample. Isaac Esler was not Rosie's father.

I picked up Gene's sample. *My* best friend. He was working hard on his marriage. The map was no longer on his wall when I went in to submit my resignation to the Dean. But I had no recollection of seeing a pin in Ireland, Rosie's mother's birthplace. There was no need to test the table napkin. I tossed it in the waste bin.

I had now eliminated every candidate except Geoffrey Case. Isaac Esler had told me that he knew who Rosie's father was and that he was sworn to secrecy. Did Rosie's mother — and Esler — not want Rosie to know that there was a family history of suicide? Or perhaps a genetic predisposition to mental illness? Or that Geoffrey Case had possibly killed himself in the wake of the news that he was Rosie's father and that her mother had decided to remain with Phil? These were all good reasons — good enough that I considered it highly likely that Rosie's mother's one-night encounter had been with Geoffrey Case.

I reached into my bag and pulled out the DNA sample that fate had delivered to me without Rosie's knowledge. I was now almost certain that it would confirm my hypothesis as to her paternity.

I cut a small portion of the cloth, poured over the reagent, and let it sit for a few minutes. As I watched the fabric in the clear solution, and mentally reviewed the Father Project, I became more and more confident in my prediction. I decided that Rosie should join me for this result, regardless of whether I was right or wrong. I texted her. She was on campus and arrived a few minutes later. She immediately realised what I was doing.

I put the processed sample in the machine, and waited while the analysis proceeded. We watched the computer screen together until the result came up.

326

After all the blood-collecting, cheek-swabbing, cocktail-shaking, wall-climbing, glass-collecting, flying, driving, proposal-writing, urine-mopping, cup-stealing, fork-wiping, tissue-retrieving, toothbrush-stealing, hairbrush-cleaning and tear-wiping, we had a match.

Rosie had wanted to know who her biological father was. Her mother had wanted the identity of the man she had sex with, perhaps only once, on an occasion of emotion-driven rule-breaking, to remain a secret forever. I could now fulfil both of their wishes.

I showed her the remains of the blood-stained singlet from Jarman's Gym with the sample square cut out of it. There would be no need to test the handkerchief that had wiped Margaret Case's tears.

Ultimately, the entire father problem was caused by Gene. He almost certainly taught the medical students an oversimplified model of the inheritance of common traits. If Rosie's mother had known that eye colour was not a reliable indicator of paternity, and organised a DNA test to confirm her suspicions, there would have been no Father Project, no Great Cocktail Night, no New York Adventure, no Reform Don Project — and no Rosie Project. Had it not been for this unscheduled series of events, her daughter and I would not have fallen in love. And I would still be eating lobster every Tuesday night.

Incredible.

Acknowledgments

The Rosie Project was written quickly. I poked my head up for just long enough to consult with my writer wife Anne, daughter Dominique and my novel-writing class at RMIT, led by Michelle Aung Thin.

After being adopted by Text Publishing, the manuscript benefited enormously from the attentions of my editor, Alison Arnold, who understood exactly what I was aiming for, and the passionate support of Michael Heyward and his team, in particular Jane Novak, Kirsty Wilson, Chong Weng Ho and Michelle Calligaro. Anne Beilby's efforts in bringing *Rosie* to the attention of international publishers have ensured that Don and Rosie's story will be told in thirty languages.

But the underlying story has a longer pedigree. It began as a screenplay, developed during screenwriting studies at RMIT. Anne, my son Daniel and I workshopped the original plot during a walk in New Zealand. A work-up for the characters was published as *The Klara Project: Phase 1* in *The Envelope Please* in 2007 and I completed the first draft of the screenplay, with a different plot and a nerdy Hungarian Klara instead of Rosie, in 2008, having taken some time to decide that it was a comedy rather than a drama. The story changed significantly over five years, very much for the better, and for that I have to thank the many people who encouraged, criticised and pushed me not to be satisfied with what I had.

The faculty at RMIT taught me the principles of storytelling, as well as offering specific advice on the script. Special mentions are due to Clare Renner, Head of School; Tim Ferguson, comedy legend; David Rapsey and Ian Pringle, seasoned film producers who did not stint on the tough love; and Boris Trbic who gave me an appreciation for the screwball comedy. Cary Grant would have made a perfect Don. Jo Moylan was my writing buddy through a year of the most radical changes. Making short films with the audiovisual students, under the leadership of Rowan Humphrey and Simon Embury, taught me much about what worked and what didn't. As I watched my extraneous dialogue hit the digital equivalent of the cutting-room floor, I learned a lot about writing economically. Kim Krejus of 16th Street Actors Studio organised talented actors for an enlightening reading.

I am fortunate to belong to a talented and hard-working writers' group: Irina Goundortseva, Steve Mitchell, Susannah Petty and May Yeung. *Rosie* was regularly on the agenda, and Irina's enthusiasm for the short story was instrumental in my taking it further. Later, Heidi Winnen was the first person outside my family to suggest that the novel might have potential.

The script benefited from the astute feedback of screenwriting gurus Steve Kaplan and Michael Hauge.

Their involvement was in turn made possible by Marcus West of Inscription and the Australian Writers' Guild who sponsored a prize for romantic comedy writing in 2010. Producers Peter Lee and Ros Walker and director John Paul Fischbach also offered valuable criticism.

The path to publication began when *The Rosie Project* won the Victorian Premier's Literary Award for an unpublished manuscript in 2012, and I acknowledge the Victorian State Government and the Wheeler Centre for sponsoring and administering the award. I also thank the judges, Nick Gadd, Peter Mews, Zoe Dattner and Roderick Poole, for their brave choice.

Many other people have supported *Rosie* and me on the six-year journey from concept to published novel, notably Jon Backhouse, Rebecca Carter, Cameron Clarke, Sara Cullen, Fran Cusworth, Barbara Gliddon, Amanda Golding, Vin Hedger, Kate Hicks, Amy Jasper, Noel Maloney, Brian McKenzie, Steve Melnikoff, Ben Michael, Helen O'Connell, Rebecca Peniston-Bird, April Reeve, John Reeves, Sue and Chris Waddell, Geri and Pete Walsh, and my fellow students at RMIT.

Don's lobster salad is based on a recipe from Teage Ezard's *Contemporary Australian Food*. Perfect for a romantic evening on a balcony with a bottle of Drappier rosé Champagne.

The Interpretation of Cubism

MARK ROSKILL

Philadelphia
The Art Alliance Press
London and Toronto: Associated University Presses

Associated University Presses
440 Forsgate Drive
Cranbury, NJ 08512

Associated University Presses
25 Sicilian Avenue
London WC1A 2QH, England

Associated University Presses
2133 Royal Windsor Drive
Unit 1
Mississauga, Ontario
Canada L5J 1K5

Portions of this book have been previously published as follows: Chapter 5, sec. 3 as "On the 'Intention' and 'Meaning' of Works of Art," *British Journal of Aesthetics* 17, no. 2 (Spring 1977): 99–110; sec. 4 as "On the Artist's Privileged Status," *Philosophy* 54 (Apr. 1979): 187–98; Chapter 6, together with Intermezzo iii and iv, as "On the Recognition and Identification of Paintings," *Critical Inquiry* 4, no. 4 (Summer 1977): 677–707. They are reprinted here by permission of those periodicals.

Library of Congress Cataloging in Publication Data

Roskill, Mark W., 1933–
    The interpretation of cubism.

    Bibliography: p.
    Includes index.
    1. Cubism—France. 2. Cubism—Philosophy.
3. Painting, Modern—20th century—France. I. Title.
ND548.5.C82R67   1984   759.4   83-45957
ISBN 0-87982-508-1

Printed in the United States of America

The Interpretation
of Cubism

To all of my students
in gratitude for what they have contributed.

Contents

Illustrations

The illustrations appear as a group following page 301.

Pablo Picasso, *Nude,* drawing, 1910
Pablo Picasso, *Mademoiselle Léonie,* etching, 1910
Pablo Picasso, *Mademoiselle Léonie in a Chaise Longue,* etching, 1910
Georges Braque, *Still Life with a Violin,* 1910–11
Georges Braque, *Woman Reading,* 1911
Pablo Picasso, *Still Life: Le Torero,* 1911
Juan Gris, *Still Life,* 1911
Fernand Léger, *Landscape,* 1911
Jean Metzinger, *Cubist Composition* (Landscape), 1912
Fernand Léger, *The Roofs of Paris,* 1912
Pablo Picasso, *The Violin,* 1912
Georges Braque, *Still Life with Pipe* (Le Quotidien du Midi), 1912–14
Robert Delaunay, *The Three Windows, The Tower and The Wheel,* 1912–13
Fernand Léger, *Still Life with Colored Cylinders,* 1913–14
Georges Braque, *Woman with a Guitar,* 1913
Georges Braque, *Still Life on a Table* (Gillette), 1913–14
Georges Braque, *Glass, Carafe and Newspapers,* 1914
Juan Gris, *The Marble Console Table,* 1914
Gino Severini, *Portrait of Paul Fort,* 1915
Juan Gris, *Still Life with Poem,* 1915
Juan Gris, *Still Life with a Poem,* drawing, 1916
Juan Gris, *Mme Cézanne,* drawing after Cézanne, 1916
Pablo Picasso, *Guitar Player,* 1916
Georges Braque, *The Musician,* 1917–18
Pablo Picasso, *Harlequin and Woman with a Necklace,* 1917
Juan Gris, *The Strawberry Jam Pot,* 1917
Juan Gris, *The Man from Touraine,* 1918
Pablo Picasso, *The Guitar,* 1918–19
Pablo Picasso, *Guitar,* 1919
Pablo Picasso, *Curtain for* [*the Ballet*] *"La Tricorne,"* 1919
Pablo Picasso, *Two Musicians,* drawing, 1921

Pablo Picasso, *Three Musicians*, 1921
Pablo Picasso, *Three Musicians*, 1921
Juan Gris, *Pierrot and Guitar*, 1922
Georges Braque, *The Mantelpiece*, 1922
Pablo Picasso, *Studio with Plaster Head*, 1925
Camille Pissarro, *Self-portrait*, 1873
Paul Gauguin, *Self-portrait with the Yellow Christ*, 1889
Henry Matisse, *Still Life with Plaster Figure*, 1906
Pablo Picasso, *Portrait of Daniel-Henry Kahnweiler*, 1910

Preface

It will help explain the character of this book to say at the outset that it represents a critical and philosophical study, focusing on particular problems of understanding that Cubism poses. It does this in both a reasoned and a historically oriented way.

Most discussion of the major movements in modern art presents the work and the creation of it according to how it sees and defines itself, and correspondingly asks to be spoken of. I am in sympathy with this as a traditional method of exposition, for forms of art that are difficult and have their own internal history, but it also raises fundamental critical problems. One such problem has to do with the relation between the art itself (its structure, imagery, the processes that it physically embodies) and how it is perceived and understood—if the response is not just one of lack of interest or refusal to go further—in its reception by a larger public. A second problem concerns the relation between the intention governing the works, whether expressed by the artists as such or imputed to them by contemporaries, and the actualities of the work itself. These actualities (of subject matter, mood, temper) are necessarily ruled and affected by many other factors—social, political, cultural and psychological—so that the theory that builds up around the art risks becoming overintellectualized in this way, or superimposing a framework of understanding on the work which does not fit, or at least fits inadequately, with the character of the works themselves.

These problems apply particularly to the Cubism of Picasso, Braque and Gris. Daniel-Henry Kahnweiler said in a 1961 interview that the text by Gleizes and Metzinger, *Du Cubisme,* which is often used as a study text in art history courses today, "absolutely must not be regarded as the bible of Picasso and Braque, for it expresses a completely different point of view, which has no relation to what Picasso and Braque were trying to do." And Picasso, in a published conversation of 1935 with Christian Zervos which addressed itself to the enlarged public for his work, stated that "when we created Cubism, we did not have any intention of creating 'Cubism,' but only of expressing what was in us." Statements such as these, by a critic and aesthetician who had won his way to being the leading spokesman on both analytical and interpretative strategies for the discussion of Cub-

11

ism, and by a painter who could be pregnant and oracular about the nature of modern art when he chose to be, but who had been the leading contributor by any account to making Cubism the single most important development of the early twentieth century, are ones that give pause; for they suggest how controversial and challenging the territory is, over which this book is to move. To judge from teaching the subject in the classroom, furthermore, a contemporary audience introduced to Cubism is still today faced with the problems of why it should be and look that way, and why it does not come across more easily.

This book has, then, a story to tell—in each of its parts—about the relation between our problems of interpretation and those of the past, which has the potential of showing how much more clearly we can understand those problems, than was true of past discussions. Hence the title, which does not posit that there is any one interpretation of Cubism to be arrived at, or any particular method of interpretation to be practised on it, but only that there are problems of interpretative understanding linked to the work, which reach back in time and can be theoretically explored in their own right. This is the basic reason for Part II of the book, devoted to the discussion of two of those theoretical issues in depth. It is also the main link with my earlier book *Van Gogh, Gauguin and the Impressionist Circle* (1970), making this the second in a planned trilogy of books dealing with the theory of modern art (since 1880) and its relevance and application to the art itself.

Another way of describing the book, which illuminates how "interpretation" is thought of, is to say that it is an attempt to spell out—especially in Part I—how one gets from the works themselves to interpretation of them. As I explained with relatively simple and straightforward examples in my book of 1976 *What is Art History?*, the traditional way of doing this has been by imposing a certain formal or iconographic "reading" on the work; but this short-circuits the question—at least for modern painting—of whether the work does or does not "come together" in that way for us. Alternative ways of proceeding that are available today are to consider the underlying premises and assumptions of the interpretative procedures themselves (as in semiotics); or the conditions of patronage and underlying characteristics of critical reception (as in Marxist practice). But since what is true of Cubism in those respects applies equally and across the board to all twentieth century avant-garde European art, I have chosen to work more specifically with the connectives between the art and its interpretation that are to be found in the context of production and early response. These include characteristics of imagery, structure and process that are seen as requiring elucidation; philosophical connectives back and forth; parallels with literature, and also music and theater; and the vocabulary of terms and concepts used. Each of these connectives is explored analytically, as to how it or they apply to the discussion of the works; which provides equivalents to the semiotic and social approaches, in contextualizing what can be said about the work and about the processes of interpretation themselves, while allowing space for the climate of creativity and for the most personal contributions, as is appropriate to the twentieth century avant-garde.

These connectives provide a basis between them for reconstructing how Cubism came to be interpreted in its day. And this in turn explains the phase-by-phase structure of Part I. Four kinds of relationship between art and art theory are discussed there. The weight given to the theory and how it is talked about vary correspondingly from chapter to chapter, as does the role and importance of the theorizing from phase to phase. In the Conclusion, the pre–World War I and post–War climates are contrasted, as they bear on the understanding of Cubism; but the book does not aspire to a reasoned critical account of the relations between artistic personality, cultural and social milieu and the visual and verbal vocabulary that the artist uses, inasmuch as that will be the topic of my third book on the theory of modern art, taking Klee and Kandinsky as its central figures and focusing on the judgmental workings of criticism itself and their contribution to art history.

In my discussion of the paintings, I have stripped away all excessive verbiage in order to concentrate on their essential character, and to make what I say understandable to someone not versed in the specialized vocabulary and techniques of art history. I have done the same with quotations from the theory; I have also given attention to what critics outside France were talking about.

The argument of the book as a whole is that Cubist art, especially that of Picasso and Braque, and the theory of Cubism represent two related but essentially independent manifestations of the same time period and the same ongoing cultural context. Despite the seeming dependence of the theory on the art itself, for both subject matter and rationale, the two intersect only partially and occasionally—even in the case of Juan Gris, the third figure whom I consider in detail and the most articulate as a theorist—and the art in no sense requires the theory to be the way it is. Besides offering some unfolding reasons for those discrepancies between art and theory, the book presents a number of new perspectives on Cubism, and sharpens the argument on key issues. But if a reader beginning on the subject learns to take what has been written about Cubism with due caution, and one experienced in that literature comes to understand how certain emphases or assumptions have bedeviled it unduly—so that there is less interference in both cases with what most needs to be said about the works themselves—I shall feel that I have accomplished my basic purpose.

Since it crisscrosses between different areas of study and concerns itself with questions of method in the ways described, this book has been ten years in the gathering of materials for it and even longer in its conception and the gradual ordering of those materials.Part II was written in 1974–75 on an American Council of Learned Societies Fellowship, and the research for the remainder was set on foot at that time; Part I was completed on a sabbatical leave from my University in the spring of 1982. Grateful acknowledgement is due to those institutions for the help and support provided in making the writing of the book possible and to the faculty of Arts and Sciences of the University of Massachusetts, Amherst for assistance in defraying the cost of photographic permissions.

I would also like to use the occasion to thank friends and colleagues who have helped me by reading parts of the manuscript or responding to specific questions. Meyer Schapiro and the late Robert Goldwater gave time to discussing the larger issues with me; Edward Fry, Donald Gordon, Marianne Martin, Robert Rosenblum and Leo Steinberg have helped me greatly in differing ways from their knowledge of the field, and I have been similarly helped in the area of philosophy and aesthetics by Renford Bambrough, David Carrier, Gareth Matthews and Mary Sirridge. Miriam Levin gave much assistance in the area of French social and intellectual history, and I am also warmly indebted to Martin Green, whose books *The Van Richtofen Sisters* and *Children of the Sun* have powerfully affected, as they came out, how I developed this one. Besides the library of my own university, I owe an ongoing debt for assistance to the Mead Art Library, Amherst College and its librarian Betty-Ann Kelly, and to the library staff of the Fogg Art Museum, Harvard University (especially James Hodgson). I am also indebted to present and former students who provided thoughts and suggestions that I was able to expand upon, including Louise Bloomberg, Larry Homolka, Karen Koehler, Joan M. Lukach, Michel Oren and many others whose contributions I can no longer recover from memory or notes, but who must accept in lieu the dedication that seems to me apposite here; and to my wife Nancy for her help with music and dance.

The book is written without footnotes and with only minimal references in the text itself. The materials that would otherwise occupy footnotes are gathered together separately in the notes and references which indicate in ongoing form the primary and secondary sources used in the discussion. For each of the two parts of the book, a basic bibliographical statement on the critical issues raised and the literature that deals with them has also been supplied. This is not by any means a bibliography on Cubism (there being several readily available) nor a complete listing of the writings consulted; but it updates the existing bibliographies on particular topics (as fully as possible for the subjects of Part II) and offers indications of what is most valuable.

Though often the discussion is of groups or sets of works rather than individual pictures, the illustrations have been chosen to provide a small anthology of representative Cubist works, in chronological sequence, with a few additional illustrations for chapter 6 at the end. Individual works by Picasso, Braque and Gris which are referred to, but not illustrated, are identified in the text by their standard catalogue numbers, appearing in parentheses: the prefix D here indicates the catalogue by Daix and Rosselet for Picasso's Cubist years, 1907–16; M indicates the numbered catalogue volume which now exists for Braque's work of 1907–14, in the series published by the Galerie Maeght; and C the complete catalogue of Gris's work by Cooper (see Bibliography for further details of these publications). Translations are my own throughout; when in doubt, I have checked against those of Edward Fry.

The Interpretation
of Cubism

PART ONE

Cubism and the Rationale of Its Theory: 1909–1925

1   The First Phase, 1909–1912: Hermeticism and the Sense of the Modern

> One whom some were certainly following and some were certainly following him, one whom some were certainly following was one certainly working. One whom some were certainly following was one having something coming out of him something having meaning, and this one was certainly working then.
>
> Gertrude Stein, "Pablo Picasso"

The atmosphere in which Picasso and Braque created Cubism, between 1909 and 1912 was, like the atmosphere surrounding Cézanne's work a generation earlier, one of extraordinary concentration and containedness. They were like mountaineers roped together, in Braque's later phrase about the partnership. Each of them could lead in turn and the other follow, in a sustained interaction; and they shared also a particular directness of feeling for their materials, and the use of them in an ongoing process.

Theoretical and supportive writing about Cubism, in its earliest forms, is also a manifestation of that same time-period. But it was the work of men attuned in a very general sense only to the development, and from where it came; or ones who knew the finished product and the problems of apprehension which is presented, not the steps leading up to it; or ones concerned with laying before the public an accomplished fact.

What took place in the studio in the way of reflection and insight had, in contrast, quite a different tenor to it. Typically in that situation one might pause from one's work to look over what one had done, draw on a pipe or cigarette, size up where things stood and then get back to the job. It was a time of silence, when what was shared was a common commitment, and what was said was, if said at all, either oblique or in the form of a joke. It was a period during which Picasso and Braque showed current work not at all; and none except for a few intimates knew in any continuous sense what they were engaged in doing.

The term "hermetic" has been appositely used for this phase, to denote a sealing off from the larger art world, as was the case with Picasso and Braque, but it has also been misunderstood. The negative implication which the term originally carried was, as in the case of modern poetry, that of a danger to be avoided: the danger exemplified in the Hermetic writings—with their mystical and cryptic content, so appealing to Apollinaire—of a deliberate obscurity, impenetrable except in the way that a private code might be, or at least a veiled and allusive form of communication which it was therefore difficult to unravel. But the term came to denote on the positive side, again in parallel to the case of poetry, that the works in question were spare, abstract and disciplined. And because of the suggestion here of both privacy and self-containedness, a second positive meaning also accrued alongside that one: the term could serve to describe a working process in which, in seclusion and detachment from the world of reality, certain artistic premises and processes are intensively explored. Used that way, the term could apply to artists are different from the Cubists as Bonnard or Turner. But it applies particularly, used in this second way, to the kind of restraints on themselves that Picasso and Braque endorsed in one another, during this early period.

If the characteristics that justify the term hermetic made it expectable that the art produced would call for words, as a bridge across to a potential public, this did not mean that the artists would be the ones to supply them. Very much the opposite in fact, in the case of Picasso and Braque. Picasso's cast of mind and disinclination in this respect are explicitly brought out, with remarkable unanimity, in the accounts published by his intimates as to what he was like at this time. For Jaimé Sabartes, looking back to a still earlier period, of youthful companionship in Spain and subsequently in Paris, this was a young man who, from his mother, had "learned to keep quiet when the occasion warranted." Fernande Olivier, his mistress from about 1904 to 1911, summed him up as a man who "did not allow himself to be penetrated" and was always annoyed when people insisted that he explain himself verbally. André Salmon recalled him as being in the habit of saying, from 1908 on, that "he knew nothing, and desired to know nothing of Cubism"; as Max Jacob remembered it, he never at any time "confided anything as to the invention of Cubism," and in Maurice Raynal's recollection, he consistently avoided theorizing. To Daniel-Henry Kahnweiler, in a moment of impatience, he quoted the notice affixed to the bridge of steamers on the Seine, "It is forbidden to speak to the pilot"; and this use of a ploy that amused him was evidently representative of a recurrent strategy on his part, since an American, Gelett Burgess, who attempted an interview in 1908, found that it was only after much humorous fencing and side-tracking on Picasso's part that he could be induced to say anything serious about his concerns as an artist.

Tone and attitude are essentially the same, in the relatively few first person statements of Picasso's of which there is a reliable report assigning them to this time; with the additional points that the comments are brief and sharp-edged and dismissive or cryptic in their import. Salmon recorded early on that, to a younger man who asked whether he should draw feet round or square, Picasso replied with authority "There are no feet in nature." There is the observation, retailed by Leo Stein from memory, that "a head . . . was a matter of eyes, nose, mouth, which could be distributed in any way you liked— the head remained a head." And there are also three remarks preserved by Kahnweiler. Around 1908 Picasso said to him that "In a Raphael painting, it is not possible to establish the distance from the tip of the nose to the mouth. I should like to paint pictures in which that were possible." Again, he told him in 1908 that "he wished that an engineer could execute the objects represented in his paintings", and about 1909 he made the comment that "If I want to paint a glass, I will inscribe a circle on my canvas to indicate its volume, but it is possible that I should make a square of this circle, since this form is not alone on the canvas." Since Raynal remembered Picasso exclaiming in 1907, to a group that was watching him render a nose in a succession of planes coming out from the face, "But that's just how a nose is," the first of these remarks might refer to the kind of treatment of facial physiognomy that Picasso developed in the last stages of the *Demoiselles d'Avignon* and in the wake of that work. The second remark, paralleled in the recollection of Gomez de la Serna, a Spanish friend and poet who came on visits to the studio at this period, which has Picasso emphasizing in 1907 or 1908 the need to measure a table as the first step towards painting it, could then be taken as relating, in logical sequence, to still life studies of the end of 1908 in which the shaping of objects, such as table legs or a fruit dish, is stressed in the way that it might be in an explanatory drawing made to assist an industrial craftsman in fabricating the object; and the third might refer to still lifes of late 1909 in which the profiles and cross-sectional forms of the objects are laid out, and adjusted in relation to one another, as they might be in a structural blue print. But if so, such comments made in the period leading up to Cubism or during its first beginnings have no recorded equivalents after that.

The interview of the same American, Burgess, with Braque in 1908 was somewhat more productive in that it elicited from the painter the explanatory comment, referring to a major figure painting on view in the studio, that he could not "portray a woman in all her natural loveliness," but instead must create "a new sort of beauty" on the basis of attention to volume, line, mass and weight. He must translate what Nature suggested in the way of emotion into art, in order, in Burgess's transcription, "to expose the Absolute, and not merely the factitious woman." Though Braque is more modest and even self-deprecating here than Picasso in the remarks cited, there is a certain community between the two in attitude and also in the generality of their comments. Both sets of observations carry the implication that more could have been said, but was not; and both have a pointing aspect, in the sense that they designate, or take their impetus from visible features of the work which was on hand to be looked at. Temperament and practical orientation already inclined Picasso and Braque this way, even before they embarked on their joint venture. The same applies to their separate but related involvements of 1908–09 with the art of Cézanne, where a sense of what Cézanne stood for and an attention to differing aspects of his coloring and structure can be taken to have co-existed, without any mediating justification in words; just as a feeling for the vitalism of African sculpture and an adaptation of its contours and rhythms went together in the case of Picasso's interest in primitive art. Such things would have been evident to each in the other's work, in terms of background that they already had and the orientation of their interests.

The early theorists and supporters of Cubism were, in contrast, a very variegated group of people in their backgrounds and positions on the art scene. If a rough diagram were made to bring out where each stood, up to 1912, it would show two distinct wings or sectors, centering on the figures of Apollinaire and Metzinger respectively, with the others grouping themselves around and in relationship to them. The axis of common interest running between these two was based on the fact that both belonged to the so-called "Closerie des Lilas" circle in Montparnasse, associated with the editor and playwright Paul Fort; and more importantly, on the unfolding desire of both to be as inclusive as possible in their coverage of Cubism. But they came to the writing of major texts on the subject by separate routes and with correspondingly different credentials.

The grouping around Metzinger, which included particularly his co-author of 1912, the painter Gleizes and the poet and essayist Roger Allard, had its basic origin in the association that the latter two had formed with the Abbaye de Créteil, a communal settlement founded in a Paris suburb in 1906 under the auspices of the socialist writer and journalist Alexandre Mercereau. Gleizes was a member of the Abbaye, and Allard an associate and a regular visitor during 1907–08, so that the political and social outlook of the community and the interest there in finding artistic forms to express the basic changes affecting the tenor and experience of modern life formed a common bond between them. Metzinger, already a poet as well as a painter, began to publish on the subject of Cubism late in 1910, in which year he also met Gleizes at the home of Mercereau; and while Allard contemporaneously discussed his work and that of Gleizes and Le Fauconnier, Metzinger wrote at this time about the work of Picasso, whom he knew from living near him in Montmartre, and about that of Braque, Le Fauconnier and Delaunay. The latter two belonged equally to the Closerie des Lilas circle, and in that sense to the same sector, and so too at this time did Fernand Léger, whose early theoretical writings will come up for discussion in the next chapter. But when, beginning in 1911, Gleizes and Metzinger became friendly with Jacques Villon and shifted allegiance progressively towards the group which held its meetings at the Villon house at Puteaux, the expanding inclusion of different circles of artists in these gatherings took on more of a comradely character.

The same kind of tie which reaches out to include Allard here as a writer brings in also, at a somewhat greater remove, Olivier-Hourcade, a poet who like Allard contributed to newspapers and reviews, one of which, *Les Marches du Sud-Ouest,* he founded and subsequently edited from his home town of Bordeaux. Allard served in 1911 as a fellow-contributor to this review, and the two of them would subsequently take a stand, along with Gleizes and Metzinger, against pure abstraction. Gleizes himself, with articles on Metzinger and on Le Fauconnier which came out late in 1911, made his first appearance as a writer at a point in time when the book which he co-authored, *Du Cubisme,* was already under discussion between him and Metzinger. This book, collaboratively composed in 1912 and first issued at the end of the year, is unified by the use of an ongoing rhetoric throughout, which was probably suggested by the Futurist manifestoes. But comparison of Metzinger's earlier pieces and of Gleizes's later writings on related topics suggests that the latter's underlying contribution was probably the idea of a French tradition in painting to which Cubism could be linked, together with a stress on principles of color and surface organization, reminiscent in its formal viewpoint of Seurat, Charles Henry and Maurice Denis; whereas Metzinger, who had brought up the term tradition in a short piece of 1911 titled "Cubism and Tradition," in a very general sense only, was more attuned to philosophic thinking and to science alongside this, under the influence of Mercereau, Jules Romains and Henri Bergson.

On the side of Apollinaire, the bonding of writers and artists with one another goes back to the so-called "bande à Picasso" which had formed itself in Montmartre in 1904–05. According to memoirs of the period, the members of the "gang" were united by their common spirit of scepticism and irony; by their anti-sectarian attitude towards groups and factions; and above all by their sense of humor and their cult of eccentricity of personality. What they shared in this way fed naturally into their talk as well as their behavior when together, and promoted a spontaneous, mutually supportive interaction of interests belonging, both in painting and in poetry, to the climate of what may be called "late Symbolism."

Max Jacob was the closest of the group to Picasso between 1905 and 1912, particularly in the quality of playful wit and volatility that they shared and the admiration of both, developing strongly during this time, for rigor and compression of a "hermetic" kind. He had apparently embarked on a career as an art critic before being persuaded by Picasso to concentrate on writing, and he was also a practising artist whose drawings and watercolors show him becoming involved in cubistic experiments in 1909–11. But though he was producing poetry continuously during this time, he did not publish anything between 1904 and 1911, and the one direct link between his writings and the first phase of Cubism lies in the graphic illustrations which Picasso provided for Jacob's poetic novel *Saint Matorel* in 1910, attuning what he did here to the mocking, disquieting quality of fantasy and to the impulsions of spirituality that he clearly responded to in Jacob's personality.

André Salmon, in contrast, who had met Picasso in 1904, was very active during this period as both poet and critic. He served as secretarial manager of the literary journal *Vers et Prose* under Paul Fort's editorship from 1905 to 1912 and Apollinaire, who was a frequent contributor to its pages, wrote an article on Salmon's poetry for it in 1908, which brings out their common inclinations in the Symbolist tradition in its praise for the combination of purity with a cult of exotic spectacle. The fact that Picasso and Braque came to the evening sessions organized by Fort at the Closerie des Lilas from about 1907, brought there by Salmon and Apollinaire, provided—at a time when their works could still be seen on exhibition—a link between the two sectors. Salmon also began writing for the daily press in 1909, and from May 1910 through the spring of 1912 he contributed a regular column to *Paris Journal,* titled "Courrier d'Ateliers," in which he reported on what was happening in the art world, as well as doing separate reviews of major exhibitions. During this time he was increasingly depreciatory of those adherents of Cubism whom he saw as detracting from Picasso's originality by the way in which they took up his speculative innovations and turned them in a more formulaic direction; he was particularly critical of Metzinger's work in this regard, but by 1912 had to admit that Metzinger had come to occupy a position of leadership in the exposition of Cubist principles. His involvement in this phase is summed up in the "Anecdotal History of Cubism" contained in his *La jeune peinture française,* which was written in April 1912 and published that autumn. Concentrating mainly on the *Demoiselles d'Avignon* and its aftermath, it again stresses the primacy of Picasso's contribution, and sees the work of Braque, Metzinger and Delaunay alike as drawing impetus from it.

Guillaume Apollinaire's involvement with Cubism during these years was the strongest of the three in its quality of enthusiasm, but it was also the most disputable and least resolved in its intellectual trappings. There are two diametrically opposed views of Apollinaire's activities as an art critic, but they are not really in conflict with one another. His supporters portray him as mercurial, expansive, intuitive in his feeling for the new in any form that interested him, and deeply concerned to help establish the conditions of freedom in which new forms of creativity could find expression: all qualities which appealed in personal terms to Picasso and his immediate circle, especially in the Bateau Lavoir period. Apollinaire's detractors stress the short-lived, shifting quality of his allegiances, necessarily likely to create hostility and ill-feeling in an art scene like that of the Parisian avant-garde round 1912; and the equally infuriating looseness of his thought, more designed to assert himself and his powers of intuitive discernment than to describe or categorize accurately. Both views are essentially correct. Apollinaire was taken seriously by artists, if not as an interpreter of their work, as a representative and publicist par excellence of avant-gardism in their time. Nor did he simply transpose to painting his own creative aesthetic as an experimental poet; for though the character of his perceptions might reflect this, he voiced his belief more than once that the two activities were fundamentally separate, and that the distinction was one that allowed criticism to concentrate on those qualities of expression that were conducive, in either art, to a liberation of energies.

The basic details of Apollinaire's involvement with Cubism tell their own story, in fact. Having met Picasso some time in 1904, he first wrote about his work the following year, in what is basically a Symbolist perspective; two years later he was responsible for introducing Braque to him, and in November 1908 he wrote the catalogue introduction for Braque's first exhibition, at Kahnweiler's gallery. He began that year to produce criticism in a serious way, and also give public lectures, and he now familiarized himself progressively with the work of younger artists of differing persuasions; but it was not until 1910 that the demands of being a regularly contributing critic, to *L'Intransigeant,* and the sense of having a larger audience to address pushed him towards greater concreteness and clarity of exposition. He first brought in the term "cubism" in a review that fall of the Salon d'Automne exhibition, but unenthusiastically, claiming that the works on display (by Metzinger and Le Fauconnier, though he did not specify this) were flat, weak imitations of ones by Picasso which were not exhibited. The following spring his growing recognition took the form of saying that Cubism, as represented at the Indépendants exhibition, was the most promising development amongst those representing the modern style, a "stark and sober" art that promised to lose its rigidity as it became humanized; his comments on Metzinger, whom he named as the only practitioner there of "Cubism properly speaking," and on Léger were correspondingly qualified, alongside more positive ones on Le Fauconnier, Gleizes and Delaunay. Then in

June of that year, in helping to organize an exhibition in Brussels featuring those same artists, he adopted the term in his catalogue as one that was accepted by them. He moved that fall into a more militant phase of defence, claiming that it fell to him to do this as the sole writer who was familiar with the work and responded to it positively, but also continuing to designate it as a provisional stage on the way to a larger achievement. By early 1912 he had taken up on Futurism; he began to look for a more definitive development that could be seen as emergent from the "researches" of the Cubists, and by the end of the year he had shifted both his terminology and his basic point of view in order to make acknowledgement of Orphism, and especially the "pure painting" of Delaunay.

Apollinaire's book *Les Peintres Cubistes* was cobbled together in the course of 1912, with extensive revisions made to the page-proofs from September to November of that year, in order to take account of those shifts taking place in his thinking and his allegiances. It is an amalgam of differing materials which include the texts of 1905 on Picasso and 1908 on Braque, an essay of 1908 on the "three plastic virtues" which serves as the opening chapter, and sections on individual artists that were reworked and updated in the second half of 1912, including even pieces (on Picasso and on the history of the Indépendant exhibitions) that were being readied at the time of the last revisions for publication elsewhere. The central section (II–VI) in between these adaptations and revisions takes the momentum and declarative force of argument that it has (like the manifestoes of Futurism) from being made up of two longer articles (on "subject in modern painting" and the "new painting") that had been written and published during the period, stretching from the fall of 1911 through the spring of 1912, which saw Apollinaire's strongest involvement with Cubism. The method of assemblage parallels Apollinaire's customary practice as a poet, and the particular kinds of suggestive and personal insight which the text affords would have been even clearer had *Méditations esthétiques* been the main title, as originally intended, rather than an appended subtitle. The book is marked out in this way as being like a "reply," from Apollinaire's side, to the more didactic and formal publication of Gleizes and Metzinger. But, as Maurice Raynal recognized in a sympathetic review, the fact that Apollinaire "does not bother to transcribe the emotions or thoughts of the painter but senses them and transforms them according to his own sensibility" makes here for the "weakness of the poet who writes on art." As compared to the straightforwardly historical account of the "beginnings of Cubism" that he published in October 1912, the "umbrella" tactic adopted in order to give everyone a niche in the account and to maintain the existence and continuity of a larger Cubist "school" entails the arbitrary creation of four different categories or varieties of Cubism—named by him the "scientific," the "physical," the "orphic" and the "instinctive"—and some most uncomfortable inclusions and exclusions. The gossipy, knowing quality which his observations of the art scene had always tended to carry from the beginning insinuates itself politically into the comments on individual artists, and makes itself felt also in a larger way in his willingness to pluck from the current climate of critical opinion and from artists' talk whatever could be given a high-sounding resonance.

For all of the diversification of interest and approach in these early advocates of Cubism, the texts of theirs referred to from the first years have a number of features in common. They are not heavily weighted towards philosophy or philosophizing; rather they rest their central argument on dichotomies, in which the negative aspects, representing what is being denied or rejected, preponderate in the force of the discussion over what is offered or put forward in their place. This feature is most clearly evident in the writings of Raynal, who does not begin to address himself to Cubism until the last months of 1912: his piece of October on the Section d'Or exhibition, for instance, rejects as hopelessly inferior those kinds of painting that are "descriptive, anecdotal, psychological, moral, sentimental, educational or decorative" in order to put forward in their place the "conception of a pure painting . . . derived from a disinterested study of forms." But this way of couching the argument is also apparent in Salmon's remarks, earlier that year, on how Picasso conceived of Negro art as aimed at "the depiction of the real being," rather than "the realization of the idea, usually sentimental, that we have of it" and on his corresponding need to create "outside the laws of academicism and of the anatomic system," and in Olivier-Hourcade's advocacy of the return through cubist practice to "a more subjective vision of nature," as well as in Apollinaire's repeated definition of Cubism, towards the end of the year, as made up of elements taken "not from the reality of vision, but from the reality of conception."

There are also five basic affirmations about the nature of Cubism that are shared between these texts. Contributions to their formulation come predominantly early on from the sector surrounding Metzinger, but by 1912 Salmon and Apollinaire, whose earlier writings tended to be more evocative or anecdotal, have joined in. First, the truth that the Cubist seeks is opposed to the semblance of truth that is offered by the "exterior appearance of objects," the transitory, fugitive and relative character of which in Olivier-Hourcade's formulation (February 1912) can lead only to "banal optical illusion"; or as Gleizes and Metzinger expressed it in their book, in the search for the "essential" one must be ready, "in order to discover one true relationship . . . to sacrifice a thousand surface appearances." The most basic opposition at issue here is to Impressionism, representing a superficial form of realism. Apollinaire in his review of the

Indépendants exhibition of 1910 and particularly in his comments on Matisse had already brought up the notion of a "downfall of Impressionism" on these lines, motivated by the desire for freer expression, and there was a general mindfulness of the force of Cézanne's example here. But it was Jacques Rivière, in an essay of March 1912 that was basically critical of the endeavors of the Cubists, who would formulate most explicitly the rejection of conventional lighting and conventional perspective that was necessary, in order to represent objects "as they really are" rather than "the way we see them."

Secondly, Cubism was related to the new reality revealed by mathematics and by physics; but there were different versions of the way in which that relationship was formulated. In one version advanced and speculative thinking in those fields was taken as feeding directly into what the artists did with spatial perspective, either on the basis of some kind of direct knowledge or through an intermediary—the name of the mathematician Maurice Princet being the one which was first brought up in this connection by Metzinger, in his "Note on Painting" dated September 1910, and much repeated thereafter. Alternatively, the dissemination of the principles of non-Euclidean geometry amongst scientists "naturally," as Apollinaire put it in April–May 1912 and again in his book—adding in that case "one might say by intuition"—led painters "to a preoccupation with those new dimensions of space that are collectively designated . . . by the term *fourth dimension*." Or in still a third version, favored by Salmon in his book of 1912, it was the openness of scientific methods and attitudes that served as a model, an "only guide for seekers" who, in their awareness of the changing character of the world's appearance from one generation to another, were impatient to have viewers experience "all the angles of a prism simultaneously." But the basic claim was the same in all three cases; that if, as Gleizes and Metzinger put it, the Cubist depiction of space needed to be tied, for explanatory purposes, "to a particular geometry," this could be done by reference to the appropriate theorems of "the non-Euclidean scientists."

Thirdly, the way in which Cubist canvases were composed was seen as reflecting the changed conditions of modern experience, as a result of such developments as the coming of the automobile and airplane and their effect on consciousness. According to Olivier-Hourcade (February 1912), what made these canvases interesting was the "materialization of the forces which combine together, of the things and the beings . . . the rendition [in them] of life as it really is." His term for the "strange, disturbing but strictly exact" effect that resulted was *dynamism:* a term taken up by Gleizes and Metzinger when they wrote that "To compose to contrast to design reduces itself to this: to determine by our own activity the dynamism of form." It was a term also used by Apollinaire in his April–May 1912 article on the "new painting," carried over to his book, for the way in which the most vital art forms of any period expressed, in representative fashion, the most basic impulses that were affecting humanity then.

A fourth shared concept is that of "duration." The basic idea here is one that seems to have been first introduced by Léon Werth, in his review of an exhibition of Picasso's work that took place in May 1910. Referring to the "turning form(s)" and "opposition of planes" in certain canvases which appear from his account to have been from 1908 to 1909, he wrote of having his attention drawn to the "thought" to which they were cumulatively equivalent: that is, to the "power and right" of these forms to "transfer onto the plane of a picture the sensations and reflections which we experience with the passage of time." It was, however, Le Fauconnier, in a preface that he wrote ("Das Kunstwerk") for the catalogue of a group exhibition held in Munich that September, who first associated the idea with the technique of faceting. He described how facets could be "so oriented with respect to diverse directional forces" as to present the subject from several points of view. The concept was then given a specifically Bergsonian and therefore metaphysical connotation by Metzinger and Allard at the end of the year: Metzinger in the same article in which he wrote of Princet linked it, in the work of Braque, with the concept of "radiation," and Allard, in his November review of the Salon d'Automne published in Lyons, wrote of there now being born, in Metzinger's work, a "pictorial plenitude" which offered to the viewer's understanding "the essential elements of a synthesis located in duration." Gleizes and Metzinger summed up the broader application of the term in their book two years later, in writing that oil painting, in allowing the expression now of "supposedly inexpressible notions of depth, density and duration," encouraged the artist "to present, according to a complex rhythm, a veritable fusion of objects within a restricted space."

Finally there is the concept of simultaneity, which combines the last two sets of ideas with relativism of viewpoint. The basic claim here, as expressed by Metzinger in his August 1911 article "Cubism and Tradition" and restated in his and Gleizes's book is that movement around the object allows the painter to "seize from it several successive aspects" (or appearances) which, when "fused together into a single image, reconstitute it in time." In Olivier-Hourcade's more practical explication, worded to accompany an illustration of a Gleizes still life, "if Gleizes, and I could say the same of Lhote, had to depict a book presented horizontally, he would also show one face of its cover and one of its sides"—rather than "making a concession to the falsehood of optics and perspective" (in despite of what he knows to be the case) and thereby being "responsible for a deliberate lie." Salmon then provided a more ironic perspective in this matter by suggesting, in relation to Picasso's example, how the "new ideal" deriving from this development had the effect of "dividing the men who were beginning to look at each other . . . 'from all sides at once' "; and it remained for Apollinaire to give the concept a more specific place in relation to the work of Picasso, in his book and related article of March 1913. It was on the basis of what Picasso had now moved on to doing that Apollinaire could set aside the idea of a requirement of a reconstitutive kind laid upon the viewer by the "enumeration of the various elements that compose an object so completely and so acutely." "These elements take on the appearance of the object," he wrote, "not because of the effort of the viewers, who necessarily perceive their simultaneity, but because of their very arrangement on the canvas."

To relate these large theoretical claims about the nature and achievement of Cubism to the paintings themselves raises its own special difficulties, and the relevance that they have to Picasso's and Braque's work of 1910–12 is certainly an extremely moot one. At best it can be said that these formulations of an explanatory framework for Cubism put a construction on how the works are to be read, which is not to be confirmed by part-by-part analysis—and was not meant to be. It is the premises of expansion reaching beyond specifics that are to be conveyed or, by 1912, the consolidated principles underlying what has been arrived at.

The claims of an opposition to Impressionism necessarily apply most directly to the phase—pre-Cubist or early Cubist, whichever one chooses to call it—running from 1907 through 1909. It is then that Cézanne's example came into the ascendant amongst younger artists, in the wake of the major retrospective exhibition at the Salon d'Automne of 1907; and by 1909–10, in contradistinction to the classical and rational qualities singled out by the Fauves, his work was being increasingly seen in terms of geometrizing and simplifying tendencies, which stressed solidity and construction. A sense, deriving from this reading of Cézanne, of closing in upon the object of study so that it is brought strongly up towards the picture plane in the shaping and lighting of its surfaces appears as a major shared feature in both Picasso's and Braque's work of 1908–09 and in the earliest works of Metzinger, Gleizes and Le Fauconnier that stress geometry; and also in Léger's and Delaunay's work of 1909–10. It is also in early 1909 (and only then) that Picasso does a group of paintings, of studio nudes, in which differing projections of the front and back of the body are brought together to imply a combination of aspects and viewpoints. But whereas in Metzinger and Le Fauconnier the licensing of simplification is linked to the process of faceting by the imaginative direction that it takes, in Picasso, even when the figure is transformed into a bather by the seashore (D 239), and even when the lessons of simplification in primitive sculpture continue to apply, the sense of direct observation persists. Correspondingly whereas Gleizes and Metzinger carry their account of "superficial realism" back, in the opening pages of their book, so that it embraces Courbet, the heaviness and weightiness of Picasso's half-length figures in 1909 suggests his acceptance that Courbet's example still had some importance then. This is a point that continues to apply in his case as penetration of the volumes of the figures gives place to interprenetration between figure and background in 1909–10. Braque, who had stated in 1908 that in portraying a woman "in terms of volume, of line, of mass, of weight" he wanted "to expose the Absolute and not merely the factitious woman," and had provided to illustrate his statement a drawing (probably after a lost painting of the time) which shows three versions of a female bather arranged so that back, front and side views are combined, occupies a midway position between the two extremes here.

It is of course true that in Picasso's and Braque's work of 1910–12 different parts of the same object—the rim of a glass or carafe or a cup (in the example used by Hourcade) and its stem or base, the sides of a die—are shown from implied viewpoints that are incompatible with one another; but not in such a fashion to imply a "free mobile perspective" (in Metzinger's words of 1910), which is that of a spectator in motion around the objects. Rather the individual "aspects" or "attributes" (as Picasso and Braque later came to call them) are increasingly stressed, in separation or isolation from one another; and this—as Apollinaire noted by 1913, but as was progressively coming to the fore, in fact, from 1910 to 1911 and on—leads to an increasing freedom of orientation and arrangement in relation to other neighboring shapes and planes, which goes with an increasing ellipsis or suppression in the provision of other "cues" to an integral reading.

The term "dynamism" was not used in reference to Cubism until after the Futurist exhibition which opened in Paris on February 7, 1912, had created awareness of its use there, both in the titles of paintings, where it referred to the representation of movement, and in their earlier manifestoes, where its introduction was owed to their original leading spokesman, the writer F. T. Marinetti. Apollinaire, who was critical in his reviews of that exhibition of the banal, "anti-plastic" character of many of their ideas, noted that their titles "often appear[ed] to have been borrowed from the vocabulary of Unanimism." A related set of terms had been used, in fact, in the Symbolist writings of the poet and dramatist Henri-Martin Barzun and those of the novelist, poet and theorist Jules Romains (later a critic, from 1911), while they were associated with the Abbaye de Créteil. "Dynamism" denoted there, much as in Olivier-Hourcade's use of the term, a concern to probe beneath ephemeral aspects of sensation, to the underlying forces and abstract principles governing contemporary life. The quest for a new subject matter, literary and later artistic, that would reflect this thinking was given direction by the appearance of Henri Bergson's book *Creative Evolution* in 1907. It suggested that—

as new patterns of life evolved—barriers between different physical experiences would be broken down, in favor of a vital rhythmic continuum; and Le Fauconnier in turn generalized the role that pictorial structure could have in this connection, in writing of it in his September 1910 text as a "means of expression in universal terms." By then both the initial and the technical Futurist manifestoes had appeared in Paris in translation, so there may well have been some interchange both ways. Apollinaire, while pointing to the anecdotal character of Futurist subject matter, reflected in the concern for painting "states of mind," felt that their titles contained "clues for a more synthetic kind of painting." The kind of subject matter that was looked to and advocated here as fulfilling Unanimist principles was, by 1912, one that was optimistically celebratory of contemporary life, and that focused especially on the City as an environment constantly in flux, but structured on organic and self-renewing principles. The conception, then, was fundamentally a Symbolist one: it corresponded to the Bergsonian interpretation of Symbolism, advanced by Tancrède de Visan in his 1911 book on contemporary poetry (L'attitude du lyrisme contemporain), as "an attempt by means of central and accumulated images to express and exteriorize. . . . a central lyric intuition."

The terms "duration" and "simultaneity" have a similar history. In Bergson's conception of time as a continuum, rather than a series of separate moments, "duration" was given the role of being a basic regenerative force, incorporating the past into the present and working upon the physical and spatial environment to bring together with one another new forms of life and experience. In a review of Metzinger's work which appeared in November 1911, Gleizes wrote of how he "subject[ed] appearances to the shaping power of mind" and, quoting Metzinger himself, used the term in this context to claim that "to space he would join duration." Paradoxically—since it was of Braque that Metzinger said in 1910 that "whether he paints a face or an apple, the images radiates in duration"—the concept is one that is far less fitting to Braque's and Picasso's 1910–12 paintings, with their flickering quality of brushwork and intermittencies of definition, than it is to Juan Gris's still lifes of 1911; paintings in which the warped and slanted treatment of planes that pulls contours into relation to space, the cold lighting and the isolation of independent objects combine to create a static quality of timelessness.

Simultaneity was a term that Bergson had introduced already in his first book of 1889, Essai sur les données immédiates de la conscience. Used there as the connecting link between space and duration, it might, Bergson wrote, "be defined as the intersection of time and space." In Futurist usage, the term referred to interpenetration of objects with the surrounding space, and by extension, in their February 1912 catalogue, the combination of emotions and memories in the experience of an ambience; for Delaunay, who took up the term in

1912 and applied it to his current paintings, it denoted, in kinship with Chevreul's principle of "simultaneous contrasts," the optical reception of two or more colors on the same surface. The paintings of Gleizes and Metzinger in which the concept is put to work as they understood it are ones from 1911 to 1913, in which, in accordance with their 1912 statement that "a painter can show in the same picture both a Chinese and a Frency city, together with the mountains and oceans, flora and fauna, people with their histories and desires, everything which in exterior reality separates them," the world is accounted for, rather than described, in a combinatory view that evokes contrasting aspects and activities. These include urban and rural scenery in adjacent sectors; static, clearly contoured shapes and ones that have their detail bled away in the manner of Cézanne, by transparency and overlap; and the far brought into direct juxtaposition with the near to hand. The feeling for "adjacency" thereby engendered is somewhat like that of early news cinema, in its choppy rhythms and jumpy scale-changes, and this may not be coincidental. Léger's art of the same time, in contrast, is freed from this "cinematic" quality by virtue of its stiff shapes and the internal interaction of large and small units, which are keyed to a continuous vertical spine or axis running up the center of the painting; and the same is true of Le Fauconnier's *Huntsman* of 1912.

As to the invocations of mathematics and physics, there seems to have been a very lively expectation amongst the early theorists of Cubism—especially around Metzinger and in the Puteaux circle—that some figure would emerge versed in the new findings of mathematics and the speculative sciences, who would be able to specify their application to the explorations of Cubism and its resultant structures. Princet appeared for a time to be fitted to this role, after Salmon had put it about in his newspaper column (May 10, 1910) that he would shortly be bringing out a book on aesthetics, which included some reflections on modern painting. But he was an insurance actuary, and although he was friendly with some of the painters, the catalogue introduction that he wrote for the Delaunay exhibition of February–March 1912 was a disappointment. Bergson was famous and widely read, and by 1911 there were already numerous commentaries on his two books and on his theories. He had included in his 1889 *Essai* a passage of advice to an artist as to how to depict reality, freeing oneself from the spatiality of external objects—one in which he used the term interpenetration in reference to the sensations of space and duration—and when shown reproductions by an interviewer, he expressed an interest in what the Cubists were doing, but was not inclined to go further. Henri Poincaré was also felt to be an exponent of ideas that had a special interest for artists, and the mention by Gleizes and Metzinger of the "recourse to tactile and motor sensations [needed] to establish pictorial space," which comes immediately after their reference to non-Euclidean geometry, draws upon his popularization of that geometry early in the century (*La science et l'hypothèse,* 1902). The use of the Golden Section had its proponents too: Gris, Lhote and Villon. It follows an earlier tradition, revived in the later nineteenth century, of seeing in the geometry of proportions universal principles of order and harmony; but the mathematics used for this purpose, like the "chronophotographs" of Marey which suggested harmonies of serial motion, were relatively simple and straightforward.

The "fourth dimension," loosely understood as it sometimes was from the later nineteenth century on as representing a higher dimension of spiritual life or consciousness, acquired in time almost the status of a myth. As distinct from expository versions of the concept which rested on the viewing of planes from different angles, there also came to be a purely metaphorical interpretation which, in its application to the plastic arts as developed by the American Max Weber (*Camera Work,* July 1910), took it as representing the "grandeur of the universe"; or in Apollinaire's version used, after he read that article, in his April–May 1912 essay "The new painting" and in his book, it was "the immensity of space eternalizing itself in all directions at a given moment." An analogue for the way in which both this concept and non-Euclidean geometry appealed, by seeming to ratify some of the paradoxes of familiar experience, would be in the suggestion of seeing the world differently provided by such popular visual devices as the kaleidoscope, or those constructions or overlays where a shifting of the angle of sight changes the image that one sees. In rendering into visible form the principles of convergence and accommodation of the eye that he derived from Poincaré's text, Metzinger used schematic structures which make fairly obvious and accessible reference (especially in the *Landscape,* Fogg Art Museum, 1912–13?) to devices of that kind.

The diagrams found in textbooks and popular publications also come up as having provided a possible stimulus: not only those on the Fourth Dimension using multiple projections (as in E. Jouffret's *Traité elémentaire,* 1903), but also those illustrating stereo-chemistry and chain-structures of minerals, and the new visual psychology as expounded by William James in his *Principles of Psychology* (French trans. 1909) and by Ernest Mach, whose *La connaissance et l'erreur,* as it was titled in its French translation of 1908, included essays on the philosophy of spatial perception as understood from a physiological and psychological standpoint. Such comparisons are not entirely specious, since they indicate an affinity of a very general kind between the "difficulties" of the new art, understood as a way of discovering what lay "behind" appearances, and the concern of the time to make the underlying principles of new speculation in those areas graspable to a more general audience, as principles of "discovery."

That contemporaries looked for such affinities is not surprising, given the impact of the revolution in physics—and also in the mental sciences—affecting all fields at this time. But there is little likelihood of any specific contribution to the paintings themselves, since the diagrams are all more literal and less imaginative in character; and they entail a projective geometry that is totally alien to Picasso's and Braque's inventiveness.

In its main features of continuity and structure, Picasso's and Braque's Cubism of this time has a very different tenor to it than the theory contemporary with it would imply. From the end of 1909 on, they both narrowed and limited their subject matter, so that it was concentrated almost exclusively on two basic categories of image, the half-length or three-quarter length figure and the still life made up of familiar objects in a table-top arrangement. In this respect they were following the practice of Cézanne in the second half of his career, from the 1880s on, which served as the model for a patient, empirical and at the same time logically unfolding process of exploration. But in contrast to Cézanne's combination of those subjects with landscape motifs and bathers, as well as card players (all represented in the 1907 exhibition, and even better in the stock at Vollard's gallery), the subject matter remained in their case, with a very few exceptions, confined to the world of the studio. The figures are either essentially anonymous or they stand, even in the case of portraits, midway between the traditional provision of a likeness and the use of an associate or friend, who was around and available to pose on that basis, as the model for a basically impersonal process of observation and study. The objects in the still lifes are similarly ones that were around in the studio, as elements of the painter's daily existence, or ones that belong in a parallel sense to the everyday world of the café—its tables and counters, and their basically rather blank surrounds, identified and personalized only by the changing display of advertising labels and announcements: much as the studio environment was identified by hanging frames and stretchers on its walls and a few practical objects or personal possessions. The continuities established in this way not only work presentationally—according to a convention that had been increasingly favored for this purpose from the Romantic period on—against the tendency there might be to read the subject in narrative terms. They tend also to weaken the sense of a clear-cut separation between one version of the theme and the next, and to draw attention, even more than in Cézanne's case, to the kind of focus and empirical regard for particulars to which this choice of subject matter lends itself.

The idea of the series as it had developed at the end of the nineteenth century stands in the background here. The relevance of Monet to the way in which Picasso and Braque chose to work lies not in terms of groups of paintings on the same theme, made to be exhibited and experienced together, in a viewing which amalgamates the successive and the simultaneous into a single overreaching state of consciousness; but in terms of Monet's use (from the *Cathedrals* on) of a given structural armature as a constant from version to version, and the liberty this allowed him to elaborate and improvise in a certain "key," suggested by what was on the canvas and what had previously been done, in combination with the visual data themselves, or stored memory of them. What Monet's pre-1910 canvases of water-lilies and Cézanne's successive renderings of the Mont Sainte-Victoire have in common, consequently—for all the differences of their visual and procedural concerns—is the sense that they give of a continuity in which each treatment leads on to the next and makes possible, through its findings and their implications, what takes place there in the way of further development. The intimation of being able to "go on from here"—from the latest version, from what lies behind that—by extrapolation from what has been done and from what it suggests or makes possible, links one treatment of Picasso's and Braque's to the next in a corresponding way, and thereby puts their figure subjects and their still lifes into parallel with one another.

The processes used are equally ones that draw attention to themselves, even more so than in Cézanne's case. The limited and generally monochromatic choice of colors—mainly grays, ochers and browns—is in a range that is both flexible and attuned (as with Cézanne's later palette) to what had traditionally been the preliminary processes of modeling on the canvas itself, being responsive to very subtle or minor inflections which may accentuate either volume or flatness. The equally flexible touches of paint are often thin or semi-transparent. Arranged in clusters or formations which tend (like the arrangement of pointillistic dots in the later Seurat) to "drift" in a certain direction, they have their major concentration on the main axes of composition and bleed out progressively towards the edges on at least three sides, so that an overall effect of flicker or shimmer is set up. This quality seems to represent a deduction from the water-colors of Cézanne (shown at the Bernheim Jeune gallery in 1907 and again in 1909 and January 1910), arrived at in the spring and summer of 1910—a time when criticism began to pay attention to the delicate "nuances" of Cézanne's "notations" (Michel Puy, July 1910)—and expanded upon the following year. In the commitment which they shared, Picasso appears to be the more mercurial of the two, and the more impulsive in his engagement with the processes of "making" themselves; whereas Braque tended to be more concerned with material artifice, as it contributed to the sense of order and arrangement, and with the ways in which touch could help to convey, as it had traditionally, qualities such as those of light and atmosphere. But by 1911, and especially in the winter of 1911–12, their respective paintings have come to share with one another a physically tenuous and floating character, in which the markings in paint, both in line and in the shape of color globules, are individually accentuated. The general effect is not at all of shiftingness of viewpoint or of different angles of sight combined, but of a shallow space in which different lighter or darker forms and planes are sandwiched, as if between two panes of glass, and of an extreme complexity of transitions and interrelationships between them.

The imagery has by this time come to consist of single figures seated or standing in an immediately adjacent, compressed sector of room-space, and of still life arrangements in which the table top on which the objects rest has been tilted up so far as to become virtually identified with the picture plane, so that in both cases frontality goes with the stilling of action and with closeness of focus; the figures often hold instruments but do not play them or rest their hands together in their lap, and their gazes are directed down or away rather than out. The basic structures created in this way, on either side of a central vertical or horizontal axis—those of an equal-sided triangle, in the case of figures, with its base at the bottom edge of the canvas and its apex just above the top, and of an approximate diamond or lozenge in the case of still lifes—become ones that are held over from one version of a subject to the next; but they also become ones that can accomodate, in contrast to the fluid and evanescent character of the composition as a whole, either capricious and whimsical details or clearly readable ones.

It is Picasso who favors the first and more disruptive of these alternatives, as in his still life which includes a pigeon with its legs sticking up in the air and *petits pois* accompanying it (D 453, early 1912, followed by three more with dead birds), and others which show as the central image what appears to be a stiff glove (D 386), an opened fan (D 412) and scallop-shells on a piano top (D 461); whereas Braque avoids that kind of intrusion in order to include, for his purposes of wit and paradox, elements such as the knob of a table-drawer or the rope of a curtain pull which serve as *aides-mémoires* as to where one is in the painting both spatially and contextually. Both, however, make it a principle in this connection that the "attributes" of an object, which constitute the most familiar hallmarks of its identity in the everyday world and thereby provide a basis for recognizing and naming it there, should be treated as detachable "cues" or clues as to the presence of the object within the painting. The appearance of musical instruments as key elements of the subject matter now corresponds to the fact that they were familiar presences in their studio world (and the café also) which possessed such hallmarks and which lent themselves to a dissociation of the elements traditionally defined by pictorial handling—outline shape and internal modeling, color and texture—in terms of their recognizability. The lettering included now is similarly fragmented and elliptical; besides designating the presence of folded newspapers, periodicals, letters, song sheets and announcements in both studio and café, it is used also to evoke the transitory forms of writings that appear on café walls and windows, or the torn residual fragments of posters, tickets and table cards, or the rubbed lettering and numbers on crates. In both artists, then, there is by 1911 a shift of balance in these ways from what is observed towards what is extrapolated or imagined.

There are only two texts of the period—both of them about Picasso—that in any way bring out these qualities of structure and imagery. The first of them comes from a letter of Max Jacob's, giving the text for a suggested prospectus for the publication in 1911 of his novel *Saint Matorel,* with etchings by Picasso which had been commissioned by Daniel-Henry Kahnweiler as editor. The passage regarding the artist's contribution runs:

> The secret charm of his austere art has impressed amateurs. To return pictorial art, which was losing itself in the pleasantries of Japanese imitation, to the ancient laws of aesthetic grandeur, to subject painting to the rigors of a composition both simple and complex, to rediscover reality only by way of style and rediscover it in truer form, such is the exemplary achievement of this artist.

The second comes from an essay by Josep Junoy, published in Barcelona in 1912, while Picasso's work was being exhibited there at the Galerie Dalmau or not long after. Calling his Cubism "a conceptual art, a spiritual abstraction," it goes on to speak of

> the interesting and reasoned way in which his fantasy unfolds the multiple relationship of planes: flat, irridescent, of indeterminate tonalities, opposing each other with mutual support and determining, through reflexive accumulation, a new center: a new irradiating axis from which one will gradually form the rich and real fantasy of the *total Image.*

The first of these passages, written by Picasso's closest associate of the preceding years, is responsive to the qualities of asceticism and rigor in the work, and to the sense of search and the concern for process that it conveys; the second, perhaps because it is by a Spaniard and the exhibition brought out the debts to the Spanish tradition in the very early works that it included, is extremely sensitive to the characteristics of handling and structure which give the work its imaginative richness. But what neither conveys, except perhaps implicitly, is the effect of *dephysicalization* that marks the Cubism of this time; an effect comparable to the leanness of musical structure, with the merest suggestions of orchestral coloring, that is found in Erik Satie's contemporary piano pieces. In Picasso's *Woman* of the fall of 1910 (Boston Museum, D 367) the background appears to change, on the right hand side, to a view through the studio window to the outside; but, as in the outdoor paintings done at Cadaquès that summer, only a more open quality of space and lighting, coupled with directionally slanted planes that angle back from the main image, suggest this. In his cityscapes of 1911, which have been little written about, familiar landmarks of the view—buildings and bridges, roofs and chimneys—take up their positions and jut their planes forward like intermittent notations of a space in which they alone have a concreteness, that is itself partial and fragmentary; and the point of the Ile de la Cité appears from high up, as if it were somehow like the configuration of a ship seen from above. In Braque's still lifes of 1909–10 (M55–59) the objects in the middle ground are shaped and animated in some cases in such a way as to suggest that there might be a humanoid kind of presence there, made up from their combination together; but by 1911 the figure has become altogether more skeletal in its embodiment, even to the point of its appearing that there were a rift or void where it should be plastically completing itself. In the work of both, female figures especially are desexualized; their arms become like tubes of rolled up paper or cardboard; seemingly displaced curves or arcs become like left over references to the shapes of breasts and shoulders and head and to their physical attractiveness, or like self-repeating echoes of them, especially in the shapes of musical instruments; and what does emerge as clearly readable seems to crystallize out of a larger continuum of impalpability and indeterminancy.

A common background to both the art and the theory lies first of all in the personal situation of the artists. At the end of 1909 Picasso and Braque had entered into a partnership with one another, that became particularly close towards 1912. Braque, after his separation from the Fauves, had suffered rejection at the Salon d'Automne of 1908: when only one work out of the eight that he submitted was accepted, he withdrew it. He participated in a group exhibition with Picasso at the Galerie Notre Dame des Champs at the end of this year, showed at another Paris gallery, Berthe Weill's, in the first two months of 1909 and had two paintings in the Salon des Indépendants that spring; but thereafter his recent work was to be seen in Paris only amongst the holdings of the Galerie Kahnweiler. This was by deliberate choice on his part, so that he avoided the group Salons from then on, in which Cubism established itself in the public eye. Picasso had two exhibitions in 1910 at Paris galleries, but they did not include very much in the way of recent work, and essentially he followed suit from that point on.

It was therefore from 1910 a period of artistic isolation for them both, and it was because of this and the psychological tensions that it was causing in his work that Picasso chose to spend the summer of 1911 at Céret on the Spanish border, where Braque joined him for the second month of his stay and they both worked productively. In September he returned to Paris because of the affair of the statues stolen from the Louvre by Apollinaire's "secretary"—two of which had come into his possession without his knowing their source. The theft of the *Mona Lisa* in August had led to Apollinaire's arrest, so that Picasso now found himself taken in for questioning by the police and feared for his status as a resident foreigner. It was a time of nationalism and xenophobia in Paris, in the wake of the Agadir crisis; Cubism was written about correspondingly as a foreign influence (by the critic Vauxcelles especially), and Picasso, being a Spaniard, was branded as a *métèque:* a "no good foreigner." Undoubtedly this must have intensified his most deep-seated anxieties about the reality of the world in which he moved, including its physical reality or object-hood, and in one who had been seen earlier by an acute observer (Leo Stein, around 1905) as possessing an unfocused aggressiveness to-wards the world, would have enlarged the feeling that everything around was subject to arbitrariness and caprice. His relationship with his mistress Fernande Olivier, which had evidently been the first ma-jor love-relationship in his life that was physically consummated, was simultaneously deteriorating and would come to an end the next year. It was therefore a situation in which the relationship with Braque served as a preservative and steadying factor, providing continuity even as the work of both of them was coming to be represented abroad in what was, from 1910 on, a steadily increasing number of international exhibitions: in London, Amsterdam, Munich, Cologne, Berlin and Dusseldorf (and further afield, in Hungary and Russia). In the late spring of 1912 he went back to Céret, but was driven to leave a month later because of the personal problems (over Fernande) from which he had hoped to get away, and chose instead to spend the summer at Sorgues near Avignon, where Braque would join him for another period of work together.

The town of Céret therefore has a special place in the understand-ing of this phase of Cubism. There is no particular reason to suppose that its topography served as a crucial stimulus (as it would later, in the 1920s, for Soutine): the one outdoor subject that Picasso painted during the 1911 stay there is, like the preceding cityscapes of Paris, a view from a window—echoed in this respect by Braque, in a view of roofs that he did when he came (M 90)—and it suggests a place that had its own range of colors and a pleasant seasonal congeniality to it, rather than any special complexity as a site with which to tangle. Much more consequential as a basis of appeal was its location just over the frontier from Spain. This enabled Picasso, in a period of open access between countries, but also rising national feeling, to have artist and writer friends in his company there who were both

French and Catalan, and to see the two cultures freely mixing, if not artistically, then at least in the languages spoken and the objects of daily life and topics of daily talk. Already in two of the still lifes from his first stay he included the masthead title of a periodical issued in Nîmes that was devoted to bullfighting, *Le Torero* (D 413–414), and he would capitalize further on this aspect of the place in a series of still lifes done during his second stay in which the use of lettering is greatly amplified (D 473–476). Though there would be major personal changes in Picasso's life during the second half of 1912, to be taken up later, it could be said, in situational terms, that it is when he is back "on the frontier" that year—and recognizing his identity in this fashion—that the first phase of Cubism ends. Significantly it will be during his third and final stay at Céret, in the first half of 1913, that his father dies (in May); he goes over the border to Barcelona, very briefly, for the funeral, and this will be the last time that he recognizes his roots and his family ties in such a way for a long while to come.

French science and culture of the time also provide a background to both theory and art, insofar as this was seen, very generally but also on a widespread footing, as a period of inventiveness and of "breakthrough" in those fields. The ideology of the avant-garde adapted to this, to create what may be termed a "rhetoric" of modernism—resembling in this respect (and this one only) the expository language of Futurism. That the way in which Cubism was presented embodied such a tendency is most clearly apparent from the negative comments of a critic, Henri Guilbeaux, who unreservedly saw it that way, writing in June 1911 (*Hommes du Jour,* June 24) of "exclusively linear research, systematization to excess; desire for originality and deification of everything and above all oneself" as being amongst its characteristics. At the same time, contrasting with that rhetoric, there was also a more ironic and self-deprecating way of responding to the same basic feeling in the air. Symptomatically of this alternative, when Picasso and Braque called one another by the names of the Wright brothers, Orville and Wilbur, it was meant as a joke; but it was also a way of representing themselves to one another as pioneers of their own, thoroughly earthbound, endeavor.

Still another background factor to be borne in mind is that the growth of Cubism as a group movement between 1910 and 1912 and corresponding public awareness of its existence created in themselves a need for explanation. The appearance together of Gleizes, Metzinger, Le Fauconnier, Léger and Delaunay in Room 41 of the Salon des Indépendants in the spring of 1911 caused them to be baptized in the public eye with the label of "Cubist." Coming on top of this, the controversy about "pure painting" which developed in 1912 seemed to represent—on the Parisian scene—an extension of the same basic problems of comprehensibility and justification. The Section d'Or exhibition at the Galerie de la Boétie in October of that year, even as it pushed the first phase of publicly identified Cubism a little way back in time, made what was happening on this count more tangible. A month earlier, when Odilon Redon, representing an older generation of artists, voiced his belief in a personal letter that Cubism was "passing away and does not contain . . . what is lasting," he took this as bound up with the fact that "it was born out of discussions and theoretical speculations, instead of coming to life through pure instinct. It was born from too many analyses, in Byzantium." Picasso's and Braque's choice was equally for "instinct" and against "analysis." But the fact that having made that choice they maintained it so firmly and so consistently is indicative of their sensitivity by now to the pressure in the other direction.

The same pattern of competing sub-groups and fashionably distinctive appellations marks out the situation of advanced French poetry by 1911–12—particularly as a result of the disbanding of the Abbaye de Créteil as a community in 1908 and the new affiliations in which its former members and associates redisposed themselves now. Supposedly separate developments here have tended to blur into one another, much as they did in the large group exhibitions of those years; and the theoretical explanations offered were ones that fastened comparably on expressive features of rhythms and formal syntax. There are however two more specific parallels to be drawn between Cubism as it evolved in the hands of Picasso and Braque, in the longer perspective of 1905 to 1912, and what was contemporaneously taking place in literature. One of these parallels has to do with the relationship of imagery and mood to structure, the other is more developmental.

It stands as a natural outcome of the close contact between Picasso, Apollinaire, Jacob and Salmon during the years of association together, and of their common personal interests, that there should be some thematic links between his paintings or drawings and their writings. Alongside dedicatory inscriptions and portraits of the three on Picasso's side, themes of the circus appear in Apollinaire's poems contemporary with the Rose period, and one finds Jacob co-signing a portrait of Paul Fort with Picasso in 1905. Those kinds of direct interchange, however, are limited to the time-span stretching from the Blue and Rose periods through to the completion of the *Demoiselles d'Avignon*. More suggestive of a larger parallelism are the facts that in the first stage of conception of the *Demoiselles* in 1906–07, the figure of the poet who is shown entering the world of sex (book in hand) carried the personal association for Picasso of being a representation of Jacob; and that Salmon, who would subsequently give the painting its present title, was closely enough associated with its process of gestation to be able to report in 1912 on how a "close friend" had dubbed it "the philosophical brothel." The shared and mutually enjoyed sorts of preoccupation that are implied here are, in fact, ones that continue well beyond that point in time, into the period of Cubism itself. The passages that follow bring out the bases of the community here; they have been chosen in each case for their representativeness from a larger body of writing that achieved publication during this time, and as one section only of a larger textual whole:

> C'est le printemps viens-t'en Paquette
> Te promener au bois joli
> Les poules dans la cour caquètent
> L'aube au ciel fait de roses plis
> L'amour chemine à ta conquête
>
> Mars et Venus sont revenus
> Ils s'embrassent à bouches folles
> Devant des sites ingenus
> Où sous les roses qui feuillolent
> De beaux dieux roses dansent nus
>
> Viens ma tendresse est la régente
> De la floraison qui paraît
> La nature est belle et touchante
> Pan sifflote dans la forêt
> Les grenouilles humides chantent.
>> Apollinaire, from *La Chanson du mal-aimé*
>> (written 1902–03, published 1909)

(Spring is here, come along Paquette and take a walk in the pretty woodland. The hens in the courtyard are cackling, dawn in the sky makes rosy folds, Love moves towards your submission. Mars and Venus have come back, they kiss with maddened mouths before unsophisticated settings, where beneath roses in leaf beautiful pink gods dance naked. Come, for my tenderness is in command of the flowering now appearing. Nature is fair and touching, Pan whistles in the forest, the damp frogs sing.)

> Comme les grands oiseaux prisonniers au jardin,
> Dans le port sans amour les steamers se balancent
> Leurs mâts font sur la mer flamber des fers de lances
> Et leurs poumons ouverts marquent l'azur marin
>
> De signes absolus attestant la hantise
> Des îles où les fruits ont les vertus du feu.
> Hélas! le lourd désir que des nains noirs attisent
> N'est rien qu'une fumée épars à travers cieux.
>
> C'est à L'ESTAMINET DE L'ETOILE POLAIRE,
> Tenu par une veuve hilare et sans pudeur,
> Que se vend le bon schnik dont la flamme sait plaire
> A ceux-là dont les gueules de requins rêveurs
>
> S'affinent à mâcher tous les jurons du monde;

L'un qui revient du bagne de Poulo-Condor
Et ne saura jamais ce qu'on nommait la honte,
Écrase dans son poing d'ange ivre une fleur d'or.

André Salmon, "Anvers" (Antwerp)
(from *Le Calumet,* published 1910)

(Like the great birds imprisoned in the garden, in the loveless port the steamers are swaying, their masts make lancepoints blaze over the sea, and their open lungs mark the azure main with pure signs attesting to the hauntingness of the isles where the fruits have the properties of fire. Alas, the heavy desire which the black dwarfs stir up is nothing but a smoketrail scattered across the skies. It is at the TAVERN OF THE POLAR STAR, run by a cheerful widow without shame, that the good *schnik* [inferior spirits] is sold, with a flame that can please those whose jaws of dreaming sharks are getting ready to chew out all the oaths of the world; one who is returning from the penal colony of Poulo-Condor and will never know what used to be called shame crushes with his drunk angel's fist a flower of gold.)

Les dents de Léonie sont moins blanches que la voile de ce
Corsaire, son ventre moins poli que n'était l'Atlantique ce jour-là.

Si doux! Si doux était le vent dans les cordages qu'on aurait
dit un chant de flûte. Si doux, si doux était le chant des matelots
qu'on aurait dit la plainte des vagues.

—Monsieur, dit le capitaine à un passenger, nous avons sorti
toutes les lunettes d'or que l'Allemagne exportait et toutes les
affiches contre la licence des rues!

Il tirait de sa poche une poignée de montures en or.

—Et vous n'avez pas de remords? dit le passenger.

Le capitaine montra le Vierge Marie sculptée à la poupe du
vaisseau corsaire.

Le pavillon bleu couvre le pavillon noir.

Max Jacob, from *Saint Matorel*
(written 1909, published 1911)

(Léonie's teeth are less white than the sail of this corsair, her stomach less smooth than the Atlantic was that day. So soft, so soft was the wind in the ropes that one would have said it was a flute-song. So soft, so soft was the sailors' chant that one would have said that it was the murmur of the waves. "Sir," said the captain to a passenger, "we have taken out all of the golden spectacles that Germany was exporting, and all the posters against licence in the streets." He took out of his pocket a handful of gold frames. "And you have no shame?" said the passenger. The captain pointed out the Virgin Mary sculpted on the stern of the pirate ship. The blue flag covers over the black flag.)

What these three passages have in common rests on their combination of earthiness with fantastication; and also the clarity of overall drift and texture that goes with a complexity of internal syntax. These are qualities that also characterize Picasso's and Braque's Cubism of 1909–11, and especially the treatment of the female figure there; and the illustrations that Picasso agreed to provide for Jacob's *Saint Matorel* bring out their continuing relevance for him at this time. It is a book that was originally dedicated to him, with the accompanying words "For what I know that he knows / for what he knows that I know"; and the four etchings that he produced, in the summer of 1910, function as suggestive parallels to the text, attuned to the rhythm and focus of the four chosen sections to which they correspond, but not directly based on them. The first half of the text, *La Terre,* is devoted to the earthly activities of the little clerk Victor Matorel, who is about to die, and the second chapter, following on one that describes the mystical and spiritual side of his life, introduces his ex-mistress, Mademoiselle Léonie, who represents the temptations of the material world and is wittily characterized through endless conversations of hers, discussing her loves and sexual triumphs in brittle and voluble terms. The first etching correspondingly, of Léonie herself, shows her in brittle line and hatching standing with one leg raised, but gives to her body a curvaceous and strong-set physicality which is close to drawings that Picasso had done from the female nude that spring (in one case carrying a child, and similarly posed from the waist down). In the second half of the book, *Le Ciel,* Matorel, now lying sick, has visions of demons and angels which are satirically presented as in many ways more sensuous and graphic than his life on earth. In its second chapter ("The Dance of the Spirits, All the Spirits"), he is tempted to sleep with his friend Cordier's wife and the illustration that comes here, the third (sometimes called "Mademoiselle Léonie in a Chaise Longue") represents a frontal seated figure of a woman who in this case matches the text's combination of worldliness and farce—at a point where the spirits are trying to spark sexual desires in Matorel—by combining strong tokens of physicality in its lower half with the suggestion up above this of a purer and more ethereal state of being. The correspondence that Picasso achieved in these ways between image and text is, then, an indication of how, long after his work had ceased to have any direct thematic connections with what were called earlier the tenets of "late Symbolism," he was drawn to find visual correlates within the vocabulary of Cubism for the basic oppositions of the carnal and the spiritual, the material and the disembodied: oppositions which became carried over correspondingly down through 1911–12 (as in *Ma Jolie,* D 430) as part of his own Symbolist heritage.

The second parallel is with the course taken by Gertrude Stein's writing over the same time-period, from 1905 to 1912. Of all the comparisons that have been made between Cubism and literature (see Intermezzo ii), this is the only one to offer not just parallels of structure or similarities of approach, but virtual contemporaneity from stage to stage and an analogous line of development—informed by, though not dependent on, the awareness that she and Picasso each had, from ongoing acquaintance throughout this time, of what the other was doing. That this is so is brought out by the following passages, chosen again for their representativeness; but in this case to exemplify, alongside the continuities of interest and structure, the most basic shifts that occur sequentially, in the larger import of what Stein seeks to do with language.

Always now Jeff had to go so much faster than was real with his feeling. Yet always Jeff knew now he had a right, strong feeling. Always now when Jeff was wondering, it was Melanctha he was doubting, in the loving. Now he would often ask her, was she real now to him, in her loving. He would ask her often, feeling something queer about it all inside him, though yet he was never really strong in his doubting, and always Melanctha would answer him, "Yes Jeff, sure, you know it, always," and always Jeff felt a doubt now, in her loving.
Always now Jeff felt in himself, deep loving. Always now he did not know really, if Melanctha was true in her loving.

from "Melanctha," *Three Lives*
(written 1905–06, published 1909)

Mary Maxworthing then had a baby in her, it had happened to her and it was a surprise to everyone who knew her who learned it about her. It was the very last thing any one would have expected to happen to her. One would have thought surely Mary Maxworthing would make a man marry her before such a thing would happen to her. It was a surprise to every one who knew her. But she was always then the same that every one thought her only, as she said, alright there is nothing to say about it, it had happened to her. That was the end of the fact for her, that was not the end of the trouble for her, that was the end of the fact for her. As I was saying Mary had stupid being in her connected in her with the impatient feeling she had in her, with the injured feeling she could have sometime in her. She had no stupid being as a bottom to her, by and by this will be clearer.

from *The Making of Americans*
(written 1906–08, with its final section completed in 1909)

She did not darken the whole place. She did not darken any place. She was not interpretive. She was not removing what had been said. She was not dark. She was not dusting carefully. She was not dusting. She was not laying down anything where she was not putting what she had to put there. She was not busy. She had the return of the day and she had the placing of a row so that they were there where they were and she did go anywhere. She was part of the way when she sat and she sat when she looked through what she would look through when she did what she did and she was part of the way. She was not that influence. She was the one. She did not do that thing. She was not planning. She had the placing of organising practicing penetration. She was not disturbing that. She was not distributing anything. She was not underlying repudiating anything. She was not the present one. She had that deliberation. She was a worker.

from "Jenny, Helen, Hannah, Paul and Peter," 1912

A house or a hill and she wishes oh yes she wishes, she wishes oh yes she wishes, and do not worry further. She has come to say that she has come they do not say undoubtedly they do not say, he does not say, how much older, how does he say, how much older, how does he say, and does he say, and does he say, what does he say, how much older is he does he say, does he say how much older he is and does he say how much older, how much older, does he say.

from *A Village,* Are You Ready Yet Not Yet
(A play in four acts, 1921)

In the first three of these passages Stein moves from describing, from the outside, a particular person's consciousness to evoking descriptively the nature of inner consciousness in general. As this shift takes place, the emphasis comes to fall increasingly on the arrangement itself of words and phrases, as units; so that whereas at the beginning there is still an earthy character to the writing, grounded in particulars, this gives place to an artificial and hermetic quality of elaboration for its own sake. "Melanctha" is about two people concerned with and for one another; in the passage about Mary Maxworthing the outside world becomes secondary and incidental, and in the third excerpt every sentence now begins with the impersonal "she" and these sentences describe only "her" operations and relations, as they bear on "her" inner consciousness, not on outside people. This progression, then, matches up with what was referred to earlier as the "dephysicalization" in Picasso's and Braque's Cubism between 1910 and 1912, as compared to what had gone earlier, and with the patterns of obsessive and improvisatory formal elaboration that determine its structures. The parallel is not really contextual—since Stein was writing and working with language as a transplanted American—but rather one of *intentions,* in the third person usage of that term that isolates a tendency of a larger kind in the work, in order to clarify and exemplify the "thrust" over time underlying it (see chap. 5 for this object-predicated use).

The fourth passage of Stein's, published much later (in 1921) is revealing in another way. It shows why the parallel with Cubism does not continue to apply after 1912. Its sing-song intonation and deliberately childlike simplicity of language indicate that Stein has moved into a form of self-conscious primitivism: not like D. H. Lawrence's "primitivism" as seen in the opening evocation of farm life in *The Rainbow,* written in 1912–15, but rather—as begins to be the case in her *Tender Buttons* of that time (1912–14)—relying purely on the play of words and sounds and the associations that these carry. Picasso and Braque, in keeping with the continuing "lesson" of the primitive for them, as they deduced it from the rhythms and configurations of African sculpture, drew back by contrast from allowing an organically and physically based content of feeling and response to bleed out of their art altogether. "And do not worry further": it was precisely the opposite that they chose in 1912.

When Gertrude Stein much later, in the 1930s, came to put into words what was now a retrospective view of the character and significance of the period she had lived through, and her part in it as a creative artist, there were two basic alternative strategies or modes of linguistic presentation available to her. One was to use pithy and intensely humorous story-telling to bring back the atmosphere of that time: this is what she did in *The Autobiography of Alice B. Toklas* (1933), juggling back and forth between what had actually happened and what now appeared most "real," as in the following sort of anecdote from it which arbitrarily interpolates an incident of 1921 into the account of the pre-War period:

> Braque had approached the expert and told him that he had neglected his obvious duties. The expert had replied that he had done and would do as he pleased and called Braque a norman pig. Braque had hit him. Braque is a big man and the expert is not and Braque tried not to hit hard but nevertheless the expert fell. The police came in and they were taken off to the police station. There they told their story. Braque of course as a hero of the war was treated with all due respect, and when he spoke to the expert using the familiar thou the expert completely lost his temper and his head and was publicly rebuked by the magistrate. Just after it was over Matisse came in and wanted to know what had happened and was happening. Gertrude Stein told him. Matisse said, and it was a Matisse way to say it, Braque a raison, celui-là a volé la France, et on sait bien ce que c'est que voler la France. [Braque is right, that man has robbed France, and everyone knows what it means to rob France.]

The second alternative was to bring together, in line with her view of history and its making, what both the "living" and the "composing" had been like then. What she developed here is essentially a "rhetoric" of creativity, that leaves aside, as it has to, the empirical specificity of the work itself and its creation, as in the following section of her book on Picasso (1938):

> I have said there were three reasons for the making of this cubism.

First, the composition, because the way of living had changed the composition of living had extended and each thing was as important as any other thing. Secondly, the faith in what the eyes were seeing, that is to say the belief in the reality of science, commenced to diminish. To be sure science had discovered many things, she would continue to discover things, but the principle which was the basis of all this was completely understood, the joy of discovery was almost over.

Thirdly, the framing of life, the need that a picture exist in its frame, remain in its frame was over. A picture remaining in its frame was a thing that always had existed and now pictures commenced to want to leave their frames and this also created the necessity for cubism.

The time had come and the man.

But what she did not do—because such a recreation was in principle impossible—was to bring back and reduplicate the character of her experimental writings of that time, as exemplified in her "portrait" of Picasso (1909–12) from which the epigraph to this chapter is taken, the companion ones of the painters that she knew best, and her *G.M.P.* of 1911, which is nominally about Matisse, Picasso and herself, but actually about artists in general.

What the parallel with Gertrude Stein brings out, then, is that Picasso's and Braque's Cubism of 1909–12 is essentially what may be called a "hanging phenomenon": dissociated from whatever else was going on contemporaneously, and following, like her work, a path strictly of its own. For them, this phase of isolation ended in the course of 1912: Picasso's work of 1910–11, long kept to himself and his close associates, was now made known in France in reproduction—two examples (D 346, 415) being illustrated in the periodical *Je Sais Tout* in April, and a further painting, of autumn 1911 (D 429) chosen to appear at the end of the year in the Gleizes and Metzinger book; while he and Braque were both represented in the Sonderbund exhibition of May–September in Cologne, with works that included some more recent canvases, and both would appear also in an October exhibition in Munich (Hans Goeltz Galerie) and in the second Post-Impressionist exhibition at the Grafton Galleries in London in October–December. Prior to that, in contrast, they were cut off from opportunities for exhibition and the work of their partnership was essentially conducted in isolation, without acknowledgement of any relevance in other developments or artistic impulses that were going on around. Nor did they accept the implications of the contemporary theory of Cubism, for their way of working or for the understanding of their creations; but for reasons suggested in Stein's "Portrait of Picasso" as to what it meant to have something which was "coming out" of themselves and being "followed," they were willing to let be.

More recent interpretation of this phase of Cubism, stressing fluctuation and oscillation, or ambiguity and playfulness, or the basic tensions set up between surface and depth, or *passage* as a device of linkage between disparate planes, is truer therefore, to the character of the paintings themselves, than is the traditional interpretation based upon the theory of the time. But both kinds of interpretation, in their ongoing developmental emphasis, tend to disguise the rapidity with which a process of self-generated, willed improvisation—in keeping with the "hanging" character of the phase—set limits upon itself and where it could lead. The idea of Cubism in this phase as a "language" that needs to be learned equally does not take account of the separation of the intellectual and cognitive processes that Picasso's and Braque's work enforces (see Part Two, chap. 6). Viewers may be *told* that a certain object is depicted in one or another case, and presented with supporting evidence—in the form of memoirs saying so, photographs of the time showing the presence of the object in the studio, other paintings in which the same object appears; but to tell them this may still not lead, or even help them, to see (recognize, identify) that this is what is there, in that particular part of the canvas. Indeed, the often heard charge that Cubism is "intellectual" in character during this phase—besides missing out on the many visually exciting and retinally stimulating features that the work evinces—seems to derive from this aspect of the response that is generated, in frustrated attempts at a total "piecing together" of what is shown, when this is in fact not feasible.

The crucial interpretative question, therefore, running between the art and the theory in this phase is a matter on the one hand of the claims made about Cubism, accompanying the attempted elucidation of how it appears, and on the other of the artists' attitude towards the nature of creativity in general, and how in particular they think of their own creativity. The claims put forward concern especially the unlikeness of Cubism to traditional art, and the way in which aspects of it can be related to the scientific and intellectual character of the period. This is particularly clear in the writings of early commentators outside France, seeking to do justice to the endeavor.

An English critic, Frank Rutter, for instance, in a booklet which he published at the end of 1910 under the title *Revolution in Art: An Introduction to the Study of Cézanne, Gauguin, Van Gogh and other Modern Painters,* included some comment on the Salon d'Automne which he had just visited in Paris. Noting that Picasso, whom he called the "chief of post-Matisseism," was not represented, but a "great influence", he wrote of

a new vision of form [which Picasso has more recently evolved], building up his paintings with a series of cubes, grayish to yellow-green in colour, about three inches square as a rule, cubes some square to the spectator, others at angles, and all ingeniously fitted together to express his feelings for form. It is highly logical, but it appears to me very complicated, but I confess for its proper elucidation at the moment *je ne suis pas à la hauteur* [I am not at the right level].

Even before reserving judgment in this fashion, on what are presumably the Horta de Ebro paintings of 1909, Rutter stresses the novelty of the vision and its "logical" character.

A year later, another British writer, John Middleton Murry, who had spent the winter of 1910–11 in Paris at the young age of twenty-one, studied Bergson's *Creative Evolution* while there and made contact with the French artistic scene through a Scottish Fauve artist, J. D. Fergusson, returned to England with plans to introduce a sense of recent French artistic, literary and philosophical developments and reproduced two works of Picasso's in his own periodical *Rhythm* (summer 1911). At the end of the year, asked to comment in *The New Age* (November 30) on a reproduction which had appeared there, supplied by the Kahnweiler gallery, of a spring 1911 still life of Picasso's (D 387), and on a letter of his from Paris which had been quoted there (November 23), relating Picasso's "profoundly intellectual" art to Plato's theory of ideas, he wrote

Picasso has done everything [including works of delicacy and beauty] and yet he has reached a point where none have explained and none, as far as I know, have truly understood. Yet he declares *J'irai jusq'au but* ["I will go to the limit"].

Again, despite the reserving of judgment—Murry stands aside from "praise [that] needs understanding"—the sheer difficulty that the works present, in terms of ideas, and the committed experimentalism are stressed.

Meanwhile, in April of that year, to accompany the retrospective exhibition of 83 of Picasso's works held at Alfred Stieglitz's gallery in New York, the American critic Marius de Zayas had written a pamphlet commenting on Picasso's procedures (published also in *Camera Work,* 1911). He presented him there as a translator or interpreter of nature, rather than a copyist: one who, in painting an object, deals "not only [with] those planes which the eye perceives but also those which, according to him, constitute the individuality of form," and who "represents with the brush the impression he has directly received from nature, synthesized by his fantasy." De Zayas makes frequent reference to contact with Picasso, writing of "his way of thinking" and "his judgment," and Picasso, who had agreed to the exhibition, against his principles of the time, as a favor to the critic apparently approved the piece; but it is clear also from the framework of discussion and the terminology of "essences" and "substances" that de Zayas had been exposed to some of the earliest theorizing, probably through conversation with members of Picasso's circle. What comes from these contacts, most evidently, is his opposing of Cubism to traditional art, in terms of perspective, color and representation, and his allusion also to the "sensations" inspired in Picasso by "physical manifestations" as being of a "geometrical" kind.

The Spanish critic Junoy, in the first part of his 1912 article cited earlier, which appeared in the Barcelona periodical *Arte y artistas,* offers a similar opposition of terms:

> Picasso does not paint the image reflected in his own eyes. He is not interested in representing objects more or less—as he says— *photographically,* but rather in representing the idea of those objects his imagination has formed,

and the German writer Ludwig Coellen, in the chapter on Romanticism in the new painting which he included in his book on contemporary art *(Die neue Malerei)* published in Munich that year, again combines the same key emphases, in writing that Picasso has already assumed his historical place: "he has replaced mechanical spatial perspective with a dynamic principle whereby a mental space is created within the picture."

What is claimed here about Picasso's work could also have been said about Braque's, were he not taken as being secondary in importance. The purpose of these claims is, in fact, to characterize Cubism—as it was then known—as having a certain *identity:* one that reflects the atmosphere and thinking of the period (for the general nature of such a claim, as applied to the art of other periods, (see again chap. 5). As for Picasso's and Braque's attitude towards such claims, they neither affirmed nor denied them categorically. Rather, they allowed them to provide a sustaining mythology, in the atmosphere or "space" surrounding their creativity.

2 The Recapturing of Broken Ties, 1912–1915

> The development of music has not brought about the disappearance of the various genres of literature, nor has the acridity of tobacco supplanted the savor of food.
> Apollinaire, *Les Peintres Cubistes*

In the second phase of Cubism, between 1912 and 1915, Picasso and Braque built back into their work an equivalent to every one of the traditional cues for the reading of a painting that they had broken with or eliminated during the preceding phase. The discontinuities and ellipses, the suppression of color, the flattening, the bleeding out of objects and the detachment of floating planes, all of which had made their paintings of 1910–12 hard to read by traditional criteria in Western art for the representation of three-dimensional elements on a two-dimensional surface, were replaced by the appearance of more integrally recognizable forms, objects and words, and by the reconstitution of a sense of mass and tactile surface. Like Matisse moving away from a loose and schematic expressiveness towards more explicit and compressive structuring in those years, like Kandinsky and Delaunay emphasizing construction so that their radically simplified images with their differing degrees of recognizability might still serve as a bridge of sorts between artist and viewer, they also stressed the connection between the consistencies of color and arrangement that are imaginatively imposed, by purely pictorial means, and the potential understandability of the resultant image as an autonomous, self-contained creation.

The changes that brought this about did not all come into being simultaneously. Picasso and Braque, continuing to work in terms of sets or series of paintings, chose to affirm in this way the ongoing nature of their association together: one in which premises were continuously tested and possibilities were played with for their own sake. But by the second half of 1912, all of the major concerns that would characterize this phase had appeared and begun to take their place within it—the use of brighter, more solid internal coloring, the demarcation and disposition of clearly contoured planes so that they mount up towards the surface in superimposed formations, and an involve-

55

ment with textured surfaces and decorative patterning. While their pace of advancement seems less intense thereafter, and their engagement of spirit more deliberate, all of those features would be taken up in the work of the other leading Cubists, most notably Gris and Léger, by 1913–14, and also some of the same technical means for their realization.

There is in fact a shift in the character of Picasso's and Braque's partnership during this phase: one which has personal factors underlying it. After Braque's marriage in 1912—to a good bourgeois citizen, Marcelle Lapré, about whom little is otherwise said, and after Picasso's establishment that year of a new and very fond love-relationship, with Eva (Marcelle Humbert), and his move to a new studio that autumn, the two were less socially and personally dependent on one another than they had been, and quite simply, they saw one another less frequently. The second of their summer stays together, at Sorgues near Avignon after Picasso had left Céret abruptly, was followed in June 1913 by a visit on the part of Braque and his wife with Picasso and Eva at Céret, but it seems to have been a brief stay only, as they were on their way to Sorgues. They would return there once more in the summer of 1914, but the stay was cut short by Braque's mobilization, and though it was the head-wound that he received at the front the following May and his long convalescence from it that put an end to the association for good, it had fallen into abeyance already by the end of 1913. It was also a period of greater economic stability for both as a result of their ongoing association with Daniel-Henry Kahnweiler, who published prints of Braque's and gave both him and Picasso three-year contracts in November and December, 1912 respectively: a form of recognition that he would award also to Gris that year and to Léger the following one.

As the reputation of Cubism grew outside France, the two continued to appear together in exhibitions abroad: in Berlin at the very end of 1912 (Kunsthaus Lepke), in Moscow, Prague, Munich and Berlin (Neue Galerie) in 1913 and in Bremen early in 1914. The framework of parallelism that had come into being during the first phase, allowing each room to express his own personality, continued correspondingly in force beyond 1913 and up to the outbreak of War, but with the difference that within that framework—in keeping with their greater independence of one another—Picasso was now more affirmative of modernity, Braque of tradition. The dialectic arising out of this generated sharpened forms of responsiveness back and forth between them, and this is particularly evident in their uses of *collage* and *papiers collés*. Picasso's introduction of the first in May 1912 and Braque's of the second in September of that year, whatever the element of rivalry in it, brought in a variety of technical practices which they would share, including the imitation of those applied materials in paint. But their use was also characteristically, as will be brought out later, more metamorphic in Picasso's hands, more associative on the part of Braque.

The very few statements by Picasso and Braque that are recorded from 1912 to 1915 suggest that—at a time when their most recent work was being seen and reproduced more—rarity and brevity of comment on it was a deliberate tactic on their part. Picasso's statements as they have come down are more openly paradoxical in character than in the preceding phase. According to Salmon in his book *La jeune peinture française* which came out in the autumn of 1912, he found "Polynesian or Dahomean images" to be "essentially reasonable." The context for the remark as given by Salmon is the creation of the *Demoiselles d'Avignon* in 1906–07, by which time Picasso was familiar with examples of African tribal sculpture, and he also came to know, then or soon after, Oceanic sculptures as well; but the reference is in this case more general. The term "Dahomey" as used at this time could be a designation of the Gold Coast (next to it), or possibly of the Ivory Coast (further west), and the remark could then be taken as referring to the achievement of a harmony between discrete elements in such sculpture, understood as natural and even instinctive on the part of its creators. This suggests a somewhat later stage of response to the "primitive" than that represented in the last stages of the *Demoiselles;* but what attaches the remark more firmly to the second phase of Cubism is the fact that Apollinaire published in September 1912 an article on primitive art titled "Exoticism and Ethnography," in which he wrote of an iron statue of a war-god in the Trocadéro Museum, which he called "the gem of the Dahomey collection" there, saying that "not one of the elements that compose it resemble any part of the human body. The African artist was obviously a creator." If, as seems inherently most likely, this passage reflects recent conversations with Picasso and Braque and observations of theirs based on their study of that collection, then both it and Picasso's remark would fit with the Cubist understanding in 1912—explored in a series of paper, cardboard and sheet-metal constructions—of how separate, disjunct planes running parallel to the surface could be adjoined to make up an object, and how elements that opened up the hollow interior space of the object could be treated as flap-like or cylindrical projections out from it. The other remark of Picasso's recorded dates from the very beginning of the War: according to Gertrude Stein, when the first camouflage trucks passed outside his studio, showing what a device for concealment was like that they had heard about but not yet seen, Picasso "looked in amazement and then cried out, 'Yes, it is we who made it, that is cubism' "; as if the stratagems of artistic disguise for which he and Braque were responsible were now feeding back into the natural world.

Salmon also records in his later book *La jeune sculpture française,* written in 1914, an occasion on which Braque entered into argument with Picasso about "what can be imitated" in painting: "should one, if one paints a newspaper in the hands of an individual, apply oneself to reproducing the words *PETIT JOURNAL* or reduce the enterprise to actually sticking the newspaper on the canvas?" Since the story goes on to tell of Picasso's use of a metal comb, for the man's beard in his painting known as *The Poet* (D 499), this argument can be assumed to date from the summer or autumn of 1912. The feeling for the natural and intuitive use of one's materials that is reflected here, as in the shared admiration for primitive art referred to, seems also to appear in the form of an aversion to overly abstract or "mathematical" kinds of calculation. It is known from lines and markings in pencil that are still visible on the surface that Braque laid out his strips of *papier collé* in preliminary form at this time and adjusted them in their relationships to one another; and a humorous story that he later told of how some criticisms that he offered of a still life of Gris's led that artist to find that he had made "a mistake in [his] calculations" probably also goes back to this time, since it was in 1913 that Gris worked on a series of drawings embodying mathematically calculated proportions, for which he used a ruler and compasses. They served as the basis for paintings of 1914–15, and there are also unfinished still lifes of these years which show the same principles being used.

More importantly, it was at this time that Braque began to write down in the margins of his drawings the observations on Cubism and art in general that would appear in print four years later under the title "Thoughts and Reflexions on Painting." Since it was the poet Reverdy who noticed these aphorisms and was responsible for bringing them together and organizing them for publication, the order and arrangement into which they were put for that purpose belongs to a later phase of Cubism and will be taken up there. Though the majority of the individual observations are likely to have been composed, in the form in which they have come down, during Braque's extended convalescence of 1915–16, there is also a presumption that some of them go back to before the War and were recopied or sharpened at this time: particularly those which refer to the specific materials of *papier collé* and imitation wood-graining used during this phase, and those which, like the anecdote quoted above, advert against the use of any kind of a formula or mathematical device. The larger argument in which these particular comments are embedded has to do with the kind of "certainty" that *papiers collés* stuck down onto the picture provide, by virtue of their being "simple compositional facts," while at the same time serving as "one of the justifications of a new spatial figuration" (paras. 15–17 in the numbered version of the text). The aim of painting, as a mode of representation which entails "think[ing] in terms of form and color" is, according to a further group of comments, to "constitute [such] pictorial facts." It is, then, in extremely trimmed and gnomic form that Braque begins to formulate at this time his sense of the aesthetic principles guiding his creativity as a Cubist and the materials and techniques that he has helped to introduce.

There are no statements of Gris's from before the War, but there are two public lectures of Fernand Léger's which were published soon after they were given, at the Académie Wassilieff in Paris: one in May 1913, on "The Origins of Painting and its Representational Value," the other, almost exactly a year later, on "Contemporary Achievements in Painting." The style of these lectures is completely personal to Léger; unlike Picasso and Braque in their recorded statements, it is expansive, explanatory and readily understandable. Long sentences are linked in logical order, as in a well organized essay. Key ideas are spelled out and key terms reiterated: most particularly the terms *speed, contrasts, plastic values, volumes* and *colors*. All of these features of the presentation are ones reflecting Léger's workmanlike personality and the heavy, proletarian character of his thought; in the words of Apollinaire reporting on the 1914 talk, he was able in this way to be "very clear and candid," and at the same time "[give] quite a trouncing to all of those methods and schools that, under the guise of novelty, are doing their best to oppose the development of the new painting."

The basic theme of these two lectures was that modern painting, "already at a fairly advanced stage of development," was coming into "possession of all those means which [would] permit the realization of absolutely self-sufficient works" and that "if pictorial expression has changed [this was] because modern life has made this necessary." While no specific mention was anywhere made of Cubism, the date of speaking and context of delivery allowed the inference that it was being referred to. But as if to bring out directly that Léger's own period of greatest involvement with Cubism had ended in 1912, the first part of his 1913 lecture was illustrated in its published form with a drawing of a reclining nude in a landscape titled "study of linear dynamism" and the second part a month later with a gouache labeled "dynamism obtained by the contrast of whites and blacks and linear complementaries" (*Montjoie !*, May 29 and June 14–29). Equally, whereas in that lecture he placed greatest emphasis on the purity of means at the painter's disposal—presenting the impressionists and Cézanne as both occupying a transitional place from this point of view between Manet and contemporary developments—in the 1914 talk, in keeping with the break-up by 1913 of his association with Delaunay, and also with the imminence of the War, he gave considerably greater importance to the precedent that Cézanne represented for the capturing of the "deeper meaning of plastic life," because of "his sensitivity to the contrast of forms." He stressed the need for direct, first hand experience of reality, in the form of the changed environment created by "modern means of locomotion," especially the railroad and automobile, and the accompanying appearance of the wall-poster and "flashing advertising signs." In this way also his tone of address was consistently a declarative one.

In contrast again to the statements of Picasso and Braque, the theory of this time was of a broadly popularizing kind. The contributors in this respect included Apollinaire, who published in the Berlin magazine *Der Sturm* in February 1913 a text on modern painting, based on a lecture of the previous month, in which he called Picasso's Cubism one of the two most significant recent tendencies (the other being Delaunay's Orphism) and spoke also of the practice of *collage;* Charles Lacoste, a late impressionist painter, who contributed to the periodical *Temps présent* in April 1913 an article "On Cubism and Painting"; and Alexandre Mercereau, who had been a co-founder of the Abbaye de Créteil and subsequently a contributor to some of the smaller poetic and literary reviews, especially Henri-Martin Barzun's *Poème et Drame* of 1912 to 1914, and used the acquaintance he gained in this way with the work of Gleizes, Metzinger and Delaunay to include them in a large exhibition of Cubism that he mounted for the Manes Society in Prague in 1914, and for which he wrote the catalogue introduction, thereby playing a key role in the publicizing of Cubism in Eastern Europe.

But the major figure whose writings on Cubism took on the character of popularizations at this time was Maurice Raynal: most particularly in a piece that he contributed to the Parisian magazine *Comoedia Illustré* in December 1913, entitled "What . . . is Cubism?" Raynal had known Picasso and his circle in Montmartre since 1910; he seems to have been particularly close to Braque within that circle, having known him since 1904, and was also friendly with Gris, who painted his portrait and his wife's in 1911–12. Raynal had written the preface for an exhibition of modern painting held at Rouen in June 1912, and also a text on the Section d'Or exhibition of October and a further article on "Conception and Vision" for *Gil Blas* that August; but his role as a publicizer seems really to have begun with an essay on the "definition of a Cubist painting" that he contributed to a Barcelona periodical in December 1912. He was on friendly terms with Apollinaire, but it was in keeping with his own differing orientation as a critic that the regular column that he contributed to the periodical *Les Soirées de Paris* under Apollinaire's editorship—from December 1913, some months after it began to appear, to its very last issue of July–August 1914—was one consisting of film reviews ("Chronique cinématographique"); and that he wrote in his review of *The Cubist Painters* cited earlier (*Montjoie !,* Jan.–Feb. 1914) that "in this sort of a poem on paintings" Apollinaire's "essentially poetic nature excused him from commenting on and explaining painting as such." His effort would be precisely to provide such explanation, in straightforwardly written form.

There are two concepts carried over from the first phase of Cubism that are built upon for explanatory purposes. One of these is *simultaneity*. Though Apollinaire would completely deny in an article of 1914 the application of the term to poetry, he accepted it at this time for painting, in the sense in which the Puteaux group used it, to designate successive disclosures of the character of an object that are brought together on a single unitary surface. In his explanation of January 1913 he wrote that "even in the case of simple Cubism, the artist who wishes to achieve the complete representation of an object—especially of objects with a more than elementary form—[is] obliged . . . to disclose all the facets of the geometric surface" and thus render the image in a way that appears remote from its objective reality. He justified this being so first on the empirical ground that the omission of one of the components that a chair is known to have (seat, back, four legs) because of its being seen from a certain angle necessarily "takes away something essential"; and secondly by appeal to the example of the early Italian "primitives" who had made it a principle in painting a city to show it "as it was in reality, that is to say whole, with its gates, streets and towers." Lacoste similarly wrote of the practical need experienced by the Cubists to "depict an object as one knows it to be . . . from several angles at one time," chosen as the principal ones because they are "capable of yielding a complete representation of the object": so that the result is a "real and simultaneous vision of all its faces," which will be a "synthesis of all its aspects, or rather the complex aspect it has in our mind's awareness of its total form considered from all sides at once." Raynal would seek to endow the principle of working in such a way with a logical justification of its own, using the dichotomy he had set up in his 1912 article between "painting one's conception" and painting the sense-data offered by vision "in obedience to the laws of perspective"; and he would follow Apollinaire in citing the practice of the primitives, but would present that practice—as he had in his August 1912 essay already—as based on consideration of the "dimensions given by the mind or spirit" rather than those given by the eyes, as in the example of discrepancies of relative size in Giotto.

The concept of the Fourth Dimension was also brought in, now in the "imaginative" form in which it had become popularly familiar, through publications such as Gaston de Pawlowski's *Voyage au pays du quatrième dimension* of 1912 (reviewed in *Montjoie !*, April 14, 1913) and the American Claude Bragdon's *A Primer of Higher Space: The Fourth Dimension* of 1913, which included an essay illustrated diagrammatically with the aid of an American mathematician, Philip Henry Winne, to show the projections made by a cube in traversing a plane. The understanding of the concept to mean an imaginative seeing of things "all at once" that would normally be perceived separately is brought out in Proust's description in *Swann's Way*, which first came out in 1913, of the Church of Combray as a building which, in his recollective seeing of it, "occupied, so to speak, four dimensions of space—the name of the fourth being Time"; and it is in this way that Raynal used the term, writing that the law which the Cubists had adopted and amplified of painting objects "as they thought them," instead of "as they saw them" was one that had actually been "codified" under that name. Since the new discoveries of molecular science and the theory underlying them were also being opened up to a larger public at this time and the idea, which Léger took up for his purposes, of the machine itself or *machinisme* as dominating modern life was popular as well, it is no surprise that Mercereau should both refer in his piece to how "an age of dynamism and intense drama, of electricity, motor cars and great factories . . . multiplies our faculties of seeing and alternately contracts and extends the scope of our sensibilities," and claim that "in harmony with the innovations of science today's art seeks to discover ultimate laws more profound than those of yesterday."

The other notable features of the theory of this phase are that philosophy is brought in, not just in the reiteration of the distinction between "conception" and "vision," but in the form of reference to "well known ideas" in its history (in Raynal's phrase), on which Cubist conceptions are based; and that Cubism is defined as an art of intellect, that is rational as well as conceptual in character. The philosophizing is in fact quite light in its contribution, the key text being Raynal's of August 1912 in which he refers both to Berkeleyan idealism on the subject of perception and to Kant's aesthetic of beauty. Kant had already been brought up by Olivier-Hourcade in his piece of February 1912 on "The Tendency of Contemporary Painting," but through the intermediacy of Schopenhauer's account of his service in distinguishing appearance and reality—whereas Raynal opposed Icarus's attempt to fly like the birds to the methodical researches of the scientist, in order to accentuate the call of a search for truth of another, more conceptual kind, and he would go on, in his piece of the next year, to cite what Bossuet had said, about being able to conceive of a geometrical figure that one could not possibly see. In fact, Raynal would claim later that he had introduced philosophy to his Cubist associates by showing them how it anticipated their researches: to their initial embarrassment, perhaps, but in a way that he felt had helped develop their creative instincts, on the evidence of three of Braque's aphorisms which he quoted.

As for the emphasis on intellect, it exactly parallels the position taken at this time in respect to literature by Riciotto Canudo. Canudo was a member of Picasso's Paris circle from early on, who wrote novels, studies of musical expression and film criticism and was a co-founder of the periodical *Montjoie !* in February 1913. The manifesto "L'art cérébriste" which he published in the newspaper *Le Figaro* on

February 9, 1914 and also in *Montjoie !* that month emphasized the *cerebrality* of development in French poetry and music since Baudelaire. Canudo called correspondingly for an end to "sentimental art" in all fields, including painting, in which he looked back to the example of the Post-Impressionists and especially Cézanne. What was needed most for the new age, so that there should be no going back, was "a nobler and purer art which does not touch the heart but stirs the brain, which does not charm but makes us think." In direct contrast, then, to the Unanimist influence in Barzun's periodical *Poème et drame,* which continued to the beginning of 1914 and stressed dramatic effect and polyphonic or typographic experiment, Canudo had no specific techniques or practices to adduce on behalf of a "school," but only a very general aesthetic principle that he spoke for: one that entailed "the transposition of artistic emotion from the sentimental plane to the cerebral plane," so that the use of the intellect served to concretize the individual artistic vision. The tenor of *cerebrism,* then, as a statement for its time, is very much akin to Raynal's affirmation of 1913 that "the Cubists always try to know why they do what they do."

The development of both Léger and Gris during this phase is based on the premise that there is now a set of established means available for the practice of Cubism and its application to differing kinds of subject matter. These established means include most particularly the combination or piecing together of large and small units of form within the same work, and the inclusion of "intellectual" or "conceptual" elements alongside representational ones. In his large canvas *The Smoker* of 1911–12 Leger had shown his absorption of the ideas of Unanimism, as reflected also in the work and theory of Gleizes and Metzinger now, in his coupling of a foreground room or balcony, which includes a table-top still life of domestic objects alongside the main figure, with a landscape vista of fields, roadside trees and small suburban buildings or houses, and in his showing of the action of the body and position of the head as if successive moments were combined. While he had come to know Delaunay earlier, the period of their strongest personal association fell between 1910 and 1913. In keeping with the imagery of Delaunay's *Eiffel Tower* and *Ville* paintings of 1910–11, Léger moved by 1912 to subjects which suggest the interaction of the urban or mechanized world with the more traditional and expansive world of landscape: city roofs are shown with touches of blue sky further back, a railway crossing appears against a background of open and rolling hillside. Solidified balls of smoke become an equivalent to the Delaunay motif of cloud configurations, and as in Delaunay's *Windows* series of 1912–13 large floating arcs are used to suggest the interactions of light and atmosphere with the space at large. The highlighting and curvature given to the smaller forms also causes them to become more metallic in character during the course of the year, as in the *Woman in Blue,* and the combination of this from the end of 1912 with more sharply angled planes—in line with the impact of Futurism—leads on directly to the *Contrast of Forms* series of 1913–14 in which this vocabulary is applied both to landscape and figure subjects and also to experimental compositions of an essentially abstract kind, with a more physically immediate kind of handling and tilting and skewing of the forms, rather than inter-penetration, used to convey the interaction between them.

Like Léger, Gris had begun his entry into Cubism in 1910 with a direct dependance on Cézanne's example. From the beginning he had adopted the pre-Cubist principle, that Cézanne had anticipated and Picasso and Braque had adumbrated in 1908–09, whereby shapes seem to slide directionally across and against a background, while at the same time they are firm and clear-edged in their abutment and interlocking with one another. The stiff quality that results from this in his case—almost as if the shapes were ones cut out of metal—suggests that, in addition to his knowing Picasso's sculpture of 1909, Futurism may have some relevance. Possibly Gris may have seen Severini's work of 1910: in which case his alertness to outside stimuli differentiated him at this time from the self-enclosure of Picasso and Braque. But he avoided anyway the kind of subjects which lent them-selves to penetration in their version of Cubism: bodies with a strongly physical presence, especially female ones, and intricacies of layering or folds, preferring hard, internally sectioned objects with their own "given" color that appeared to resist internal mutation. Derain's still lifes of 1910–11 may initially have been suggestive here in their choice of elements and immobility, but if so Gris moved rapidly, for his paintings of 1912, to his own selection of components: a watch, a sherry bottle and heavy curtain, painted metal struts and even a tuxedo being particularly relevant ones in his work of that year. Both in the still lifes and in the single figure images of 1911–12 ridges are flattened, as though the surface had been bent over or creased to indicate planes and then folded out again; and the drawn contours are ones which evade as far as possible the turning of a volume through space. As if afraid of his own sensuality—as Picasso and Braque were not—Gris found no softening of incident or saving irony in his portrayal of the young and attractive Mme Raynal (C 28, 1912, with preliminary drawing). Like the portraits of his mother and of Picasso (C 13–14), it comes out as a scheme of frozen planes.

By 1912–13, along with the introduction of more piquant colors and their wider use, Gris has taken over from Picasso's and Braque's example the use of *trompe l'oeil* details and collaged elements. But apart from some continuing difference in the choice of materials for this purpose (a piece of mirror, a section of an engraving, actual playing cards), the way in which they are used and incorporated has what may be called a popularizing side to it. The humor of his 1912 *Man in a Café* (C 25) directly recalls, in its focus on such elements of dress as the top hat, shirt cuffs and trouser-ends, the caricatural drawings that Gris had done for *L'Assiette au Beurre* and other French magazines between his arrival in Paris in 1906 and 1910. The lettering of the label on a sherry bottle (1912) or on other bottles of drink thereafter exactly replicates the character of the familiar lettering associated with that product, and the same with his rendition of particular newspaper mastheads and posters. And again segments of prints are used (1913) to suggest that the whole image is hanging on the rear wall of the room in a heavily moulded frame in one case, or in another hangs suspended on a picture wire, painted as coming down from an illusionistic nail (C 38, 42). In still lifes of 1914–15, the very well known and widely read series of mystery novels that had come out in 1911–13 under the title *Fantômas* is even brought in; in keeping with their being about a master criminal who works by illusion and surprise, an actual page from one of the books is juxtaposed with an open drawer with a key in it (with newspaper cuttings also included with detection and disappearance as their theme); while in another instance the emblem of the black mask is reproduced as part of the book cover, with "teeth lines" added below to give it a primitivistic kind of look (C 90, 146).

Since Gris joined the Puteaux group in 1911–12 and attended their discussions—which is what enabled him to participate in the Section d'Or exhibition of October 1912—these leanings on his part towards familiar accessible detail of an intellectually graspable sort can be connected up with the concerns of that group, most particularly Metzinger. Some of the key devices that Gris used in 1912–13 in order to link together larger and smaller units held parallel to the picture surface—namely vertical strips arranged so that the same element overlaps from one strip to the next, but in changed form, or wedge-stripes kaleidoscopically fanning out from one another, as in the Céret landscapes of 1913 (C55–56)—are also found in Metzinger's work of this time. While it may be that the direction of contribution here was from Metzinger to Gris, rather than the other way around as has usually been taken to be the case, problems over the chronology of Metzinger's work made it difficult to be sure. But what is certainly true is that the combination of larger and smaller elements in this sort of way, with solid colors and a generally rectilinear and squared off form of organization, is also found in the work of other members of the group: in Marcoussis by 1912, and to a lesser extent in Gleizes. It may therefore represent more simply a method of composing that was adopted in parallel and in common by those artists. What is more distinctive in Gris's practice towards 1915 is the way in which forms diagrammatically representative of modern life—in the same general sense as Delaunay's and Léger's discs and mechanical forms are in

1911–13—take their places in a domestic context or café setting, in the shape of the foam on a glass of beer, the oilcloth over a table top, the target form at the bottom of a glass, the double bend of a chair-back. In Gris's marvelous command of the use of painting and *collage* alongside one another, especially in 1914–15, these elements are combined with a kind of shading reminiscent of Seurat's early drawings, and a use in some parts of pointillism, so as to provide atmosphere and subtlety of transition across the whole. It was perhaps this fusion of clarity and restraint which, by 1914, made a strong impression on Matisse.

In so far then as one can speak of a general development in Cubism between 1912 and 1914 towards structural integration by means of color, texture and geometric bonding, and towards enhanced clarity of presentation, Picasso and Braque were countering the trend of their own first phase. But it is misleading to suppose that their re-introduction now of what they had previously dispensed with—solid coloring, enclosing contours, consistently textured surfaces—extended to the point of constituting a reversal of direction. It is here that the use of contrasting terms to designate the two phases is most likely to give a false impression; and this is particularly true of the commonest of those pairings, *analytic* and *synthetic*. Those are indeed terms that first came into use in the theory of Cubism at this time: they appear in the texts cited by Raynal (Aug. 1912) and Lacoste. But whether separately or together, they were used now—as will be brought out later—as they had been from the later nineteenth century on, to designate separate stages or processes in the *same* artistic work, thereby emphasizing evolution of a natural and even inevitable kind: as from realism to a greater use of imagination.

Rather than a critical break, there is in fact complete continuity from mid-1911 on in the two major principles which give impetus to Picasso's and Braque's second phase of Cubism: namely the inclusion of lettering and what will be called here the principle of "wandering imagery." Picasso had used formal lettering, as on a book or program, on the scroll of his *Homage to Gertrude Stein* of spring 1909 (D 248), and Braque had included decorative lettering in a still life of his from that year (M53). But the principle from 1911 on governing the use of such lettering—how it appears within the work, either in stencilled or in painted or drawn form, and what it contributes—is that it serves to designate the presence of the object that bears that name or wording on it; and this continues to be so, even though the wording is only partially or incompletely specified, and even though as a result of the play with shapes that takes place it appears not to form part of the object's physical presence or to belong to its surface. In the example of a newspaper masthead, a wall poster or the cover of a piece of sheet music—all favored from 1911 on because the lettering is already highly stylized and ornamental—it can be said that a proc-ess of *excerption* takes place: certain letters and configurations are singled out as a subject of attention in their own right, and because they are so singled out, to represent the presence of the object *as a whole,* which may not be otherwise identifiable, they take on a *suggestive* character.

The principle of "wandering imagery" equally follows on directly from the detachment or displacement of individual "aspects" or "attributes" belonging to an object. By 1911 Picasso and Braque had made it their practice to include amongst the constituent elements that they treated in this way the contour, coloring and texturing of an object and also the most familiar hallmarks of its identity, most nota-bly those belonging to musical instruments such as a violin, accordion or piano. The redeployment of these "aspects" in relation to one another set up an effect of angular or rectilinear refractions and echoes over the picture surface, in which only hints or glimpses ap-peared of how the parts shown might be rationally and consecutively fitted together. By the autumn of 1911 both the incidence of elements treated in this way increased and their material obtrusiveness grew stronger. In what are again the commonest examples, a round table top treated as if from above, so that the differing segments of its curved outline and the tassels or fringe accompanying them are in-completely and discontinuously specified, and a guitar similarly treated in terms of curves surrounding its sound-hole and glimpses of its strings, the elements in question are freed to assume their own relative positions by a process of *condensation,* of an *iconic* kind: that is to say, the presentation in a compressed or distilled form in itself becomes the basis for evoking the character of the object, through the search in the viewer's memory that is set up.

In 1912–13 such "iconic" and "suggestive" qualities to the presenta-tion as a whole are both expanded upon and made more prominent. The greater clarity and completeness of the lettering included means that differing fragments of the word *JOURNAL* or the word *VIN,* drawn in, can designate respectively the presence of a newspaper or a wine bottle, simply by virtue of their appearance either in proximity to an arrangement of table top objects, or on some kind of a bounded and shaped segment of the picture surface, since suggestiveness of placement combines here with the iconic property or quality of the letters themselves. Similarly the texture, coloring or shape associated with a particular object such as a musical instrument or table top can be taken as free to "wander" apart from the other aspects or hall-marks of the object, and take up its position within, or in relation to, a quite different segment of the total imagery. The patterning and tex-ture of wallpaper that forms essentially the background and surround-ing context to a still life arrangement can "come forward" simultaneously within one of the objects; or the properties of coloring and shape associated with wainscoting or a table drawer can be "transferred" into a situation of mutual interchange with other aspects and properties of the central image, so as to set up further evocative resonances there. The "wandering" of the imagery can take place accordingly either spatially—which is to say forward and back in relation to the picture surface; or it can take place laterally, which is to say up, down and across in relation to a ground against which it is read. One sound-hole of a violin hanging vertically down may therefore be differentiated from its twin not only in terms of size and symmetrical inversion, but also in terms of the different size and shape of the rectangular "strip" of color against which it is shown (as in D 573 of early 1913).

The particular contribution made here by the introduction of *collage,* first used by Picasso in May 1912 in the form of pasted-on oil cloth (D 466), and of *papier collés,* brought in by Braque that September (M 146, 150), lies first of all in the fact that the materials used for this purpose were ones that were around in the studio and café world anyway. Newspapers, music sheets and such elements as matchbook covers and wine labels were familiar everyday presences in both of those worlds; colored papers and pieces of wrapping, in strips and in fragments, were used in the studio for all kinds of practical or constructive purposes; and such additional materials as wallpaper and oil cloth imitating wood-graining were bound to fascinate an artist who had had early training, as Braque had, as an interior decorator. But there is also the further point that the use of *collage,* in combination with drawn lines and shading, drew attention to the processes themselves, not just for their flexibility, but for the latitudes that they permitted. For example, the cutting process is such that it can make one element like the missing piece or "negative" of the other, wherever it may be pasted down. Lines and shading, as used against a consistently colored ground (usually white) can deny space and atmosphere, as well as assert their presence intermittently. And the combination of a certain contour or hallmark of an object with a texture and coloring that does not intrinsically belong introduced a severance of "inside" and "outside" which is quite independent of the character of the object. All of these forms of interrelationship set up by the processes that are deployed are, in fact, autonomous in character; a point which extends to the more variegated kinds of stippling and texturing that both Picasso and Braque introduced in the first half of 1914, in the very last stage of their parallelism.

Whereas therefore the first stage of Cubism had confronted the viewer with the ghost of a three-dimensional presence and the skeleton of its positional and directional coordinates, coupled with left-over references to space and atmosphere, the second phase is built around a re-assemblage of components, which asserts the *constructive* nature of the operations used for this purpose: Picasso and

Braque both did actual constructions, working between two and three dimensions and using the same materials and procedures in 1912–13, but Braque's are entirely lost. It also puts emphasis on what may be called the *fetishistic* properties of the resultant image: as is particularly evident in the long series of Heads in collage that Picasso did in the autumn–winter of 1912, and again in the spring of 1913, but also appears more generally in such expedients as his use of cut-out colored engravings of individual apples and a pear to designate a bowl of fruit (D 530), or in Braque's fascination with isolated circular shapes or "buttons," which sometimes seem to represent his own invented connection between one object and another. This is the "primitivistic" side of the endeavor, inasmuch as it reflects, in a very general way, the observation of how in African or Oceanic sculpture individual elements which seem quite unnaturalistic in their depictional properties can be combined together to make up a body as a whole.

Against this background of shared premises and procedures, which enabled Picasso and Braque to work themselves out of the situation that they had worked themselves into, the differences between their practices in the second phase can now be defined more closely. Braque's production of this time is most often treated as if, in the making of his own contributions, he were complementing, but also playing second string to Picasso's inventiveness. But in fact, where the vocabulary and its deployment moves towards the realms of metaphor, this is not the case at all. Braque's work may be the subtler here, but it may equally be seen as the deeper in its qualities of resonance. This is best seen in his uses of both simulated lettering and imported typography.

In 1911–12 Braque's use of lettering in his paintings consists of complete short words or fragments of words, which have to be identified by the viewer either by reference to other objects forming the surrounding context, or by reference to other works in which they occur (see chap. 6). For example, the letters *"Tien/MIDI"* designate the newspaper Le Quo*ti*[di]*en*/Journal du *Midi* (M 148), and there are similar references to music, featuring the names of composers or musical forms. In this respect Braque's practice is like Picasso's, but less mysterious or allusive as to what the words in question are, and without the mixture of the French and Spanish languages side by side that Picasso was intrigued with at Céret in the spring of 1912—on the frontier as he was then between the two countries in his life.

Up to September 1912 Braque used the established techniques of *trompe l'oeil* (like *pochoir* stenciling) such as he had learned as an apprentice painter-decorator: ones in which individual letters are adjusted to one another in size and shape. Then, in line with the new principles of incorporation and assemblage that the introduction of *papiers collés* brings, he used both hand-formed lettering and machine-printed typography. He continued at first to give each its own spatial integrity and sense of adherence to the picture surface, and to harmonize their look by the deployment of the same tones and textures that the lettering has in other sectors of the composition. But he increasingly made the distinction between the two plain, especially when the surfaces carrying the lettering have shadowing painted or drawn upon them, and where the presence of a fold or pleat is implied in the surface in question, without there literally being one. In Picasso—whose use of words and lettering had always been more quixotic and disruptive—the two types of lettering are presented as more inherently interchangeable, especially in the way shadowing is used. The identification of the surface carrying the lettering with the surface of the composition as a whole is also more forced, so that transformational wit and metamorphic manipulation are more aggressively stressed. In Gris, by comparison, the imported lettering is invariably more *literal* in relation to the object to which it belongs, as in *The Marble Console* of 1914 (C 86) where the collaged segment of a book page is one that is headed "DE L'AUTEUR."

There are also more specific ways in which Braque's practice with lettering and cuttings becomes distinctive during this phase. He uses clippings and printed hand-outs that refer to the kinds of entertainment and leisure interest available to a man of his sort, a bourgeois about to be married or just settling into marriage and thereby domesticated. These materials consist specifically of cinema programs, representing the "inclusive" billings offered at the newly opening "Tivoli" at Sorgues in 1913 (M 189, 194) and an announcement for *Le Cyclotour,* an organ of publicity offering information on bicycles and motor-bicycles (M 243). When Picasso uses typography of this sort, such as the cover of the propaganda booklet of February 1912 "Notre Avenir est dans l'Air," with those words lettered on it against a tricolor background, the material itself is more adventurous and so also is his interest in it. There are also the inclusions by Braque of sheet music carrying the names and the musical forms of classical composers: Bach, Mozart and Gluck. The words here are always written or painted in rather than clipped; but the inclusion is comparable in that they represent the kind of classical music that was at the height of its public appeal now, precisely because the publication and widespread distribution of sheets of this sort made it available for home performance and offered adaptations of it for such instruments as mandolin and guitar (Braque himself played the concertina). The inclusion in one case (*The Violin,* 1912, M 121), of a hand bill carrying the name "KUBELICK"—which is to say the Czech violinist and composer Jan Kubelik, born in 1880, who was giving concerts internationally at this time—is to be seen here as Braque's personal and musical reply to Picasso's "KUB," a pun on Cubism that is based on the familiar little bouillon stock-cubes known by the Swiss-German trade name of MAGGI-KUB, which Picasso had placed as the centerpiece of a still life that spring, and would use once more in a similar way in the summer (D 454, 501). But the musical references that Picasso for his part includes take the form, contrastingly, of popular songs which are introduced in the form of actual pages of the music in question (D 506, 513, 518–21, all from autumn 1912); otherwise, in his practice, the painted lines, staves and notes and the wording that may or may not accompany them are simply a general contribution to the musical theme.

Braque's choice of pages from newspapers that were to hand includes advertising announcements and reading material which also tie in with his recently married state; but they go with other materials that are completely everyday or neutral. In his *The Mandolin* of 1914 (M 242, see also M 169), the advertisements that appear on the cut-out piece of newspaper include ones for hygiene in marriage and the treatment of impotence, alongside ones for bicycles, midwives, remedies against maladies and wine. Whether or not fully conscious in the way that it was arrived at, the undertone of a reference here to Braque's marital state is underscored by the central image of the still life; a black circle in the center is interrupted by a long piece of corrugated cardboard which, as in the finger-language familiarly used to denote sexual intercourse, appears to go through it. Another clipping that is used from late 1913 includes comment on jewelry and on the financial situation (M 196). In one 1913 still life (M 193) an advertisement for ladies' fashions and furs, including engraved figures, appears together with one for paper products. In another, of 1914 (M 224), advertisements for soap and for *violette de parme* accompany a news story about a parricide; and, in a third case from that year (M 228), a clipped advertisement for a firm specializing in automobile parts is accompanied on the main segment of a newspaper by a text headed "Obligatory love, the stages of a woman's life"—with *tramer,* to weave a plot, as the last word that occurs above. Finally there is a still life from 1914 (M 231) in which a passage about the troubles of modern love is coupled in the same segment of newspaper with notes on the current scene: on one side these deal with a ball, selling jewelry and travel, and on the other with Bergson's election to the Académie and the preservation of Victor Hugo's teeth.

All of this corresponds to the gentle, restrained, unobtrusive (but not self-effacing) side of Braque, according a place to what is naturally a part of his consciousness at the time. The cuttings used by Picasso are by comparison more startling or eye-catching in the news stories that they contain: one about horse-doping, one about a chauffeur who had killed his wife, a third about letting down a line deep into the sea and a fourth about a lamp that lights in all directions (the last two illustrated with diagrams). Already in an ink drawing of 1907 of a Head closely related to the *Demoiselles* he had included a cutting which features a fragmentary part of a serialized novel and its ornamental frame; and the portions of a romance that similarly figure amongst the clippings that he introduced late in 1912 have a less settled character than in Braque's case, since the particular excerpt used is concerned with the institution of divorce proceedings. There is also his use of clippings from an 1883 issue of *Le Figaro*, concerning the Coronation of Alexander III, and ones that include reports, from November–December 1912, on the war taking place in the Balkans.

There is probably also a reference to Braque's recent marriage in the still life titled *Le Courrier* of 1913–14 (M 226). The folded newspaper masthead here makes the line below *Le Courr* read "ORGAN[E] DE MADA [MES]," "organ of ladies." Placement next to it of a piece of paper with a heart cut out of it introduces a possible assonance of *coeur/courr,* and shows that the organ in question, pertaining to a woman and made into a possible homophone of *organdie* by the *de* adjoined to it is neither external nor sexual as it would be in Picasso's case. He for instance uses *JOU,* from *LE JOURNAL,* to include a possible punning reference to *jouir/jouissance,* denoting sexual pleasure; whereas Braque's use of *NAL* from the same source suggests the role of some intervening shape or an act of placement that obscures or separates off *JOUR,* that is day or daylight. In the same spirit Picasso places the indecent inscription *TROU ICI,* made up of cut out letters, beneath a clipped advertisement for the department store *La Samaritaine,* which includes an engraving of a well turned out female figure, and a card in between advertising the lingerie of another large store, *Au Bon Marché* (D 557, early 1913); and in March 1914, having used *URNAL* from *LE JOURNAL* to suggest "urinal," particularly in the 1913 representation of a student reading the paper (D 621), he now couples *RNAL* from the same source with the cut-off story heading below *IER DE SANTÉ,* suggesting "y est de sans thé" (there is no tea to be had), to set off the image immediately above the newspaper of a bottle inscribed *VIN* (D 662). Other references to bodily functions that appear in his choice of cuttings include a clipping about "La Vie Sportive" used in the winter of 1912, and one about physical education used the following spring (D 530, 600); one annoucing a medical discovery that facilitates circulation, which is echoed as to theme in the circular form cut out of the paper to go with the image of a violin, and another in which a passage about a breath sweetener and references to the nose and teeth are placed against those body parts in the head of a man depicted, while a passage about tuberculosis comes next to his chest (D 524, 534, autumn and winter 1912).

But there is at the same time a deeper side to Braque's practice here. His *Young Woman with a Guitar* of 1913 (M 198) will give an idea of what is in question. It is inscribed *LE REVE* to indicate that the subject has the newspaper *Le Réveil* in her lap, below the guitar that she holds, and also includes sheets of music labelled *SO[N]ATE* and *FANTAISIE* (on separate surfaces) and one with music staffs on it. It is misleading to take *reve* here as a punning verbal equivalent to the girl's state—which is a conceit that Picasso might have used. The girl is to all appearances pensive and withdrawn rather than sleeping. Thus the word *rêve* invokes the state of meditation and quiet repose appropriate to a young woman's presence in the environment of artistic creation, as visitor and model; some of Corot's late representations of women in studio settings, which carry the suggestion of an attendant muse, are shown similarly seated with stringed instruments. Braque's personal likings in music, brought up earlier, are equally referred to in the words *fantasy* and *sonata*.

The choice of lettering also serves by extension to suggest—as in Symbolist theory in general and most especially that of Mallarmé—how a state of concentration and withdrawal on the artist's part is conducive to the distancing and disciplining of immediate experience, in a fashion that makes for the imaginative creation of poetic harmonies, and a corresponding transformation of the elements of given reality. *Rêve* and *réveil* ("awakening", in the actual title of the morning paper) are, in that context, opposed states of creative and responsive being. One is obtained in Braque's presentation from the other—in an act of cutting off that is both verbal and visual in what it does to the masthead: procedurally straightforward as an act, but rich in its implications, which allude to and at the same time exemplify the differing but complementary procedures which are available to the artist. The remaining words also fit in here: *organ[e]* and *so[n]ate*, which are aligned and supply in each case the missing letter that is left out in the other, are associated together through the comparable availability to the general public of newspapers and sheet music; Picasso deals more often, in this domain, with comestibles and goods available for consumption. And it is by dint of *fantaisie*, which signifies in its Mallarméan sense the exercise of both imagination and caprice, that the visual and verbal elements are linked, in this sector of the painting.

Nor is this a unique case, for a similar understanding of the principles of *collage*, that turns inward to the workings and the potentials of the creative process itself, is found in other still lifes of the time. In the one of 1914 (M 243) which contains the announcement of the "Cyclotour," the round shape evoked by cycling and the round shape of the composition may entail a correspondence between the shape of a wheel (or the circuit that the wheel makes) and the table top on which the objects are set; also the letters *ESS[E?]* that appear lower down may be part either of *presse*, indicating the presence of a newspaper, or of *impresse*, which designates the process of stamping out letters, in a form and manner exemplified by the letters themselves. In the 1913 *Le Quotidien* (M 196) the masthead of the newspaper of that name is tailored to show *Le Qu∅* (with the *o* cut in half) and on the next line *Du M* (also half cut through). The pipe, cut from paper, overlaps this area with its end, which is homophonically a *queue:* as if two different sense of "cut," to cut through, and to cut into and across, were being distinguished and individualized here, while in the newspaper cutting to the right—cut through as a page, cut into as a piece of paper—they are combined together. In a related use of the same masthead (1912–14, M 235) [*L*]*e Qu*[*otidien*] / *DU* is rendered in part in an experimental form of lettering, shaded inside and accompanied to the right by a reproduction of the lettering *EAU/DE/VIE,* within an oval, that is to be found on a brandy bottle. The brim of the pipe is made into an oval contiguous to that one and the double ring of the stem end is fitted to the *e* of the masthead, so that its circle rounds out and complements the circle there.

In the 1914 *Still Life with Pipe and Die* (M 234) the newspaper masthead *LE JOURNAL* is cut to show *NAL,* and underneath, to the far left of the clipping, *TATUE* / [*Na*]*poléon* / *destination* appear on successive lines as fragments of a news story about a statue of Napoleon in the process of being moved. The incomplete word *tatue* created in this way corresponds homophonically to the third person of *tatouer,* to tattoo: which is a method of making images permanent. In the *Still Life on a Table* of 1913–14 (M 240), a Gillette razor blade wrapping is pasted in the center so that it stands out in silhouette as a sharp-edged shape, like the blade itself. On the newspaper clipping to the left, *GILLETTE SAFET*[*Y*] appears in the top corner next to the wrapping (with the last letter missing), as part of an advertisement of which the framing border is visible, and the words *CHAU*[*D*] / *DORÉE* / *E*(*?*)*TRENNES*—which introduce warmth and color—form part of another advertisement below it. Under the wrapping appears a table of stock exchange transactions, which is treated as if its leftmost section had been folded over to show the section referred to: which corresponds in this way even if it is not actually the same piece, and has in fact been cut and pasted down flat. That is to say, both the slicing of the advertisements and the use of clippings refer metaphorically, side by side here, to what the razor blade does: as if its presence in the center brought into the work by association the use to which it had been put in the making of the *collage.*

Finally, the 1914 *Glass, Carafe and Newspaper* (M 233) contains a combination of the principles that apply in the last two cases. In the piece of newsprint pasted at the top left, *CAF* presumably, in this context of objects, represents *CAFÉ,* but it is left implied that it could be from another word: particularly since the text beneath, headed *COMUNICA*[*ZIONE*] is in Italian. At the bottom of the composition the newspaper heading announcing the title of a serial appearing in translation and the one to succeed it is overlapped and cut at its two ends, to yield the words "*VIOLON* / *Suivi de L'HOMME AU. . . .*"

The music staffs drawn on the white sheet above take their place between this clipping and a drawn shape to the right, which is to be recognized in this light as the lower half of a violin, turned on its side and tilted away. The wording in the clipping then raises the expectation that a man to play the violin is indeed coming into the work, to complete the imagery that experience and other images of Braque's would lead one to expect, and to link up with what is brought together on the table top. And the central image of the glass *(coupe)* is associated in this connection with the act of cutting *(coupure)* which has produced the overlapping surfaces upon which its existence and that of the accompanying carafe are graphically situated, and the edges against which its volume is defined.

Such verbal associations and their use again recall Mallarmé's practice, and he and Rimbaud were both in fact receiving new attention at the time, in the form of much expanded editions of their writings, scholarly or biographical articles and the first books about them. The way in which Mallarmé's aesthetic aims could be seen as finding fulfilment in the new art was also beginning to be commented upon; and Braque, in what he does in the ways described with the incomplete and the evocative, was in effect playing Mallarmé to Picasso's Rimbaud. The implications that disengage themselves in his deployment of *collage* and *papiers collés* entail an understanding on his part that, as in Mallarmé's use of language and his accompanying poetics, one and the same terminology can designate both the processes used and the objects or entities that are thereby given embodiment. Thus *pli,* a fold, can also designate an envelope, letter or message; *tailler,* to cut to a certain shape, can also mean to deal in the case of cards, which are a frequent image in Braque's work of this time; and the term *collage* itself can signify paper hanging, as in Braque's early training as a house decorator, and *coller* to bewilder or non-plus, as well as to glue or press down onto a surface.

This is very much the kind of double association, mediating between the concrete and the imaginative, that Mallarmé was putting into poetic practice when he began his poem *Salut* of 1893, which he recited at a banquet for his Symbolist friends, with the words, spoken holding a champagne glass

> Rien, cette écume, vierge vers
> A ne désigner que la coupe
> (Nothing, this foam, virgin verse / serving to designate only
> the glass; but *coupe* is also the "cut" or caesura at the end
> of the line)

and ended it with the dedication

> A n'importe ce qui valut
> Le blanc souci de notre toile

(To whatever it is that made / the blank concern of our canvas worthwhile; here *toile* is the white page awaiting poetic endeavor as well as the sail of the ship evoked in the intermediate lines)

It is also what Mallarmé was developing as an aesthetic principle, in more discursive terms, when in his essay *Quant au livre* of 1895 he compared the experience of a newspaper and of a book, particularly from the point of view of *le pliage* (foldings) and characterized the layout of words in a newspaper as "verging on a ritual of typographic composition."

Picasso in contrast, comes out as more like Rimbaud in the anarchic, ribald and sometimes scatological character of what he does at this time. The multiple and competing claims of the imaginative self, as evinced in such a passage of Rimbaud's as

> Je suis un inventeur bien autrement méritant que tous ceux qui m'ont précédé: un musicien même, qui ai trouvé quelque chose comme la clef d'amour.
> (I am an inventor of a very different caliber from those who have preceded me, I am a musician who has found something like the key of love)
> from *Illuminations,* written 1875–78, republ. 1912

are also akin in the two cases. Picasso's practice incorporates into itself the clinical and the prosaic in the same way as Rimbaud's prose-poems do—which had greatly influenced in this respect his friends of the Bateau Lavoir period, Jacob and Salmon, and most of all young Apollinaire, who was also responsive to the revival of interest now. The most crucial conceit to which Rimbaud's example contributes, particularly during 1913, is that the shape of the *collage* as a whole parodies, and can be read as, that of a human figure. This kind of reciprocal punning or confounding of identities on Picasso's part extends particularly to the analogies between the forms and shapes of musical instruments and those of a woman's body. Thus in the *Violin and Fruits* of late 1912 (D 530) there is a head corresponding to the head of the violin, breasts to its curves, and buttocks to the contour of the table top; and the same in the *Guitar* (*El Diluvio,* D 608) of spring 1913, which also generates hands that are holding the instrument.

Both in the interplay between the conceptual and the referential brought about in this way, and in the overriding of expected distinctions between the animate and the inanimate, Picasso's uses of *collage* and cut out newspapers become metamorphically charged. This too is unlike Braque's concerns, and specifically unlike the way in which, as in the musical forms to which he makes explicit reference— *étude, sonate, rondo*—he returns to a basic theme and integrates it into the larger texture of his work. It is the theme of how a spare, ever graceful kind of harmony can be attained out of elements which (as in Mallarmé's latest poetry) are themselves simply lines, shapes and textures appearing on the white of the page. The assumption, then, that the two men shared basic intellectual premises in this phase sees them as making common cause in the continuing use of analogous and overlapping devices—which is true, even down to the more piquant colors and weightier shapes of early 1914, which form a kind of coda to the pre-War achievement; but it is also true that their forms of creative insight become more deeply differentiated.

Common features that reach across between the art and the theory in this phase and form a background to both are first of all, the impetus towards restraint and containedness. The popularizing theory reveals this in its emphasis on the rational and intellectual aspects of Cubism. Implicit here is a contrast both to Futurism, with its advocacy of dynamic thrust and energy as expressed in spiraling and intersecting arcs of movement (particularly in Boccioni's example, known through his manifestoes of 1912–13) and to the theory of "pure painting" from 1912 on, which claimed for painting wider, more cosmically embracing parameters of expression and access to a vocabulary of "sensations" that were communicatively unattached to any specific human presence—as in Stravinsky's *Sacre du printemps,* first performed by the Ballets Russes in Paris in May 1913. Picasso found the fact that the Florentine periodical *Lacerba*—representing the Italian contribution here from 1913 to 1915—should put out a book of poems titled *Almanacco Purgativo* ("Purgative Almanac") funny enough for him to include the advertisement and a clear indication of its source in a still life of his with wine, glass, plate and fork from early 1914 (D 702); and Braque's table top still lifes of musical instruments become like little islands at this time—almost literally so, in the case of one known as *Music* (M 232) which has the look of a contour model seen from above—in the effects of enclosure provided by an inner frame or contour and in their gentle atmospheric consistency.

Most striking of all, however, in this connection is the response of Matisse to Cubism in his work of 1913 to 1915. It is a response that appears initially in very generalized form, and in sculptures of 1913 (*Jeannette* V, last of a series begun in 1910–11, with this version subsequently added in 1913; *The Back II,* from the autumn), rather than in paintings. This is in keeping with an awareness of Cubist developments at large that went back several years already, through the intermediacy of Gertrude Stein, Apollinaire, Maurice Raynal and their direct contacts with the Cubist painters. It is also in keeping with the self-contained nature of the sculptural artefact: its separation as an object of study and contemplation from the surrounding space and atmosphere, and particularly so when, as in these two works, the point of departure was an already existing piece. This favors a concentration on the relationship of one plane or surface to another, at the expense of the defining of texture and substance. In a major painting such as *The Blue Window* (Museum of Modern Art, New York) which comes intermediately in the same period, effects of that sort are much less marked; and what happens in structural terms in the way of compressions and simplifications cannot be separated entirely from Matisse's awareness of Futurism, since the rhythmic curves that balance the vertical struts and alignments here take the form of extended arcs. But it is precisely in the consistent separation or isolation of the individual still life objects from one another and the more coolly contained character of their shapes—most evident of all in the central object which is a sculpture, the cast of an antique head, but picked up presentationally in all of the remaining imagery—that Matisse's treatment suggests his having pondered how structure and flattening were linked to mood in the Cubism of 1912–13 which had reintroduced coloring alongside bonded geometry. This would be his concern also when in the second half of 1914 and on into 1915 (*Pink and Blue Head;* version of the *Goldfish,* from the winter) he would adopt—probably with Gris's example as the main stimulus, since they were together that September at Collioure, but again the relationship is fairly general—a scheme of surface organization, based on angled struts or bars, that allowed him to segment his compositions into large enclosed areas which contrasted in their solidity and restraint or negation of color with ones that were warmer or more painterly in their coloristic properties. It is also in 1913–15 (beginning with the 1913 *Portrait of Mme Matisse*) that generalized references to the stoniness or woodenness of archaic or primitive sculpture enter into his figure subjects, and a response to the distinctive kind of "chiseling" used there for such inner rhythmic features as eyebrows and noses.

While Matisse's structural emphasis in 1913–15 and the restraint of his coloring, as it is used in relation to planes, represent one sort of analogue to the second phase of Cubism, there also appears in his work a gnomic kind of wit, such as is found in Picasso's and Braque's statements as well as their paintings of this phase. This again can be put into a larger context. Matisse's form of visual wit is more acerbic than theirs; when, two years after Gris had done her portrait, he used Germaine Raynal as the model for his *Woman on a High Stool* of 1914 (Museum of Modern Art, New York) he included on the rear studio wall a painting of a vase that he owned, done by his young son Pierre, as if deliberately and unmistakeably to make a point of the similarities of harsh and ungainly shape between it and her. It is, then, an element in this very spare and uningratiating composition that is chosen and handled relationally so as to intensify its suggestiveness. Matisse, working with pared down, suspended forms that contribute order rather than incident to the space that they occupy has in common with Picasso and Braque that he is led to do this sort of thing under the aegis of the renewed interest of the time in the aesthetic concerns of Symbolism and its poetic practices. Like Picasso, he had a background of intense earlier involvement with the themes of Symbolism, which had lasted in his case too down towards 1907–08; the shift, after 1912, was towards a very broadly conceived sense, which Symbolism could both support and exemplify, of how traditional expectations of what art had to offer were amplified, rather than undermined, by new kinds of formal departure and the pursuit of new kinds of "sensation." It is in this context that the passage of Apollinaire's chosen as epigraph to this chapter should equally be understood. Two of the terms in it, "development" and "savor," are ones that Matisse could certainly have used in relation to his own preoccupations of this time. The savor of a wit that functioned associatively could work in tandem with the development of arrangements of an aesthetic kind: ones that declared themselves to be just that, arrangements. And in the increasing role that they gave towards 1915 to *artifice,* made visible as such, Picasso and Braque were following suit here.

So also was Gris. Léger, on the other hand, is a special case. To a large extent this is because of the influence of Unanimism and Futurism upon him, and his association with Delaunay. But it is also to the point that he was distrustful in principle of theory, and of writing in general, in a fashion that is reflected in the tone of his 1913–14 lectures. The *Contrast of Forms* series of paintings, begun in 1912, that he was working on concurrently show him reverting to the traditional subject-categories of Impressionism, with which he had started out (in 1905–08), in order to demonstrate the variety of subjects to which the vocabulary of pictorial "contrast" was applicable, and thereby confirm what he took as a premise in his lectures. The result of this is an interchangeability of art and theory, whereby the work came first and the theory was deduced from it; and a straightforward, direct and unselfconscious simplicity also comes into the verbalization, in order to make that interchangeability manifest. Those qualities also mark out his later accounts of the relationship with Delaunay: whereas Delaunay would affirm (rather bitterly) that Léger "had not understood [and the relationship] was of no profit to him," Léger's claim would be, more simply, that whereas Delaunay insisted on "nuances" of coloring, he was already committed by 1912 to the use of "forthright" color. By 1914, in any case, the break with Delaunay is spelt out in the emphasis of his paintings on dissonance as a vehicle of contrast, the tangible weightiness of the forms and the rougher modelling that accompanies this. Those values in turn would be tied by his experience of the War to the personal touchstones for the quality of art that he developed then: those of accessibility and of contact with the common man, as represented by the French soldiery with whom he served in the trenches from August 1914 on. He would remain true to the view that he presented in the 1913 lecture of *realism* and plastic values as the essence of Cubism; but his development of those qualities during the War and after signalizes the end of his Cubist affiliation.

The second phase of Cubism therefore takes its place, in the hands of Picasso, Braque and Gris, in a larger context in which it opposes itself to forms of outreach based on the response of the modern sensibility to the implications of speed and change; to ambitions of the time to make the play of energized forces in art into a way of effecting a liberation of consciousness; and to the now rampant factionalism of the avant-garde in its international manifestations. Alongside Léger's detachment of himself from Cubism proper, through contrasts and dissonances and his robot-like forms moving through an impersonal environment (as in *The Stairway*, 1913), and De La Fresnaye's and Delaunay's drawing of aviation into their imagery, in order to evoke the pioneer spirit of its first adaptations to commercial and military uses (*Conquest of the Air*, 1913; *Homage to Blériot*, 1914), there were also alternatives impinging on the Parisian scene of a more intuitively or anarchically contentious kind. Kandinsky, who had spent time in Paris in 1906–07 and had exhibited and published his work there in association with some of the Fauves, was favored by the appearance of an English translation of his *On the Spiritual in Art* in 1914; his ideas in that text were familiar by 1912 to the Delaunays, who corresponded with him, and Apollinaire's respect for his seriousness grew in 1913, after protest on the part of the Der Sturm group in Berlin at the harsh treatment given to an exhibition of his at a Hamburg gallery gave a stronger sense of its significance.

More specially representative of such forces was the role of the writer Blaise Cendrars, after his return to Paris in the summer of 1912: not only for the images of travel and aviation which his poems included and their fractious and discordant syntactical effects, or his friendship with the Delaunays and Apollinaire, but for the fact that he became that year the French editor for a Franco-German periodical which had originally come out in Paris in 1910 under the title *Neue Mensche*, then in Vienna and Munich the following year, and now was due to appear as a "revue libre" under the new title *Les Hommes Nouveaux*. In this capacity Cendrars established contact with Otto Gross, the most anarchic and ideologically revolutionary of Freud's followers, inviting him to contribute and offering him free rein to edit the German section of the periodical, if he would come to Paris. Gross, who had been a leading advocator of the advanced social and artistic ideas current in Munich, in the bohemia of Schwabing, was now in Berlin, and in the protest arising from his arrest there by the police in 1913, Cendrars would participate to the extent of writing in the Munich-based periodical *Revolution*—borrowed from its editor for the occasion by Franz Jung, who would become one of the leading organizers of Berlin Dada two years later—that Gross was "one of the most appreciated in France of contemporary German intellectuals."

Knowledge of the differing tendencies that were accommodated under the name of Cubism was also spreading in the reverse direction in those years: to Munich and to Berlin through well publicized exhibitions there, and concurrently to Moscow and Prague. The effect of this was to make Cubism known in the larger sense that had been defined by the Section d'Or exhibition of October 1912; but it was also to make artists in those centers, who had preoccupations of their own to puruse and accommodate, aware of the shifts of allegiance and rival declarations that now muddied the waters of interrelationships with Futurism and Expressionism. It was Picasso's clear-cut separation of himself from the tenets of successive movements that struck Heinrich Thannhauser correspondingly as most worthy of emphasis, when he wrote the catalogue introduction for the first large retrospective exhibition of Picasso's work, held at his Munich gallery in February 1913 and including works in different media from 1901 through 1912. "Picasso," he wrote, "has never expressed his artistic intentions in programs, manifestoes or similar pronouncements. . . . He has stood still in his studio and produced his paintings and smiled at the others, who were meanwhile out on the streets talking their heads off about the necessity of a renewal in painting and the like."

In contradistinction to such dispersive tendencies, the work of Picasso, Braque and Gris in this phase affirms the world, or sphere of consciousness, within which art is created to be a restrictive one, with its own internal properties of organization and order. Particularly in Braque's case, there is a purity that is distilled from this. It is a purity that is most apparent in the motif of the "picture within the picture." The inclusion of a painting or drawing, shown as hanging on the background wall of the room or studio, served in Post-Impressionist and Symbolist art to identity the setting as one within which creation, or thought directed to that end took place; to link up the artist's personality with the objects forming part of his everyday environment; and to tie in the main subject, whether portrait or still life, with this existent image both structurally and associatively. Matisse and Picasso had both on occasion, in their work prior to 1910, adopted such a practice for their own purposes (see chap. 6). But in the first phase of Cubism the picture frames that Picasso and Braque sometimes include as forming part of the studio setting are characteristically empty, or there is no indication of what is inside them; and Matisse in his *Red Studio* of 1911 treated the room setting as marked off from the outdoor world by virtue of its conduciveness to repose and meditation, so that the prior works of his shown hanging there or stacked against the wall participate in the creation of a corresponding atmosphere of distilled tranquillity.

A year later, in contrast, in his *Nasturtiums and the Dance* (two versions, Pushkin Museum, Moscow and Worcester, especially the first) Matisse uses the device in a more precisely suggestive way. Here his 1909–10 painting of *The Dance,* showing primal energies releasing themselves in the outdoor world of nature and warmth, appears on the studio wall behind the still life of flowers. Subtle kinds of interrelationship back and forth between the images make the table top and vase come to seem as if they belonged more to the *Dance* canvas than to the interior itself; the flowers become associated with the landscape in which the dance takes place, and the vase is located absolutely in the middle of the dance, at the point where the tension of the moving circle has snapped and the hands are endeavoring to rejoin. The vase of flowers interposes itself in this way into the circle of driving rhythmic movement, as a point of rest and of return to the indoor contemplative world—as if the primal, unfettered impulses that provide the source and vitality of outdoor subject matter could only be brought indoors in the shape of art, and then must exist in forced conjunction with the embodiments of contained activity. An analogue to this kind of implication within Cubism is to be found in Braque's use in still life contexts of the motif of a drawn bunch of grapes. At its first introduction in *The Fruit Dish* of September 1912 (M 150), the grapes are given their shadowed and modeled existence within a bounded rectangular format, as if a notebook sheet with the fruit drawn on it had been affixed to the surface beneath the strips of *papier collé.* Then in the winter of 1912–13, when Braque re-used the general form of the composition for his *Still Life with Playing Cards* (M 151) he substituted for that earlier bunch of grapes—and for a pipe-smoking head in an intermediate version of the composition (*Man with a Pipe,* M 159)—a now more intrusively present version of the motif. The grapes now seem to take up their own independent position, intermediate between two- and three-dimensional space, standing upright and casting shadow but unattached to anything else. The background against which they are seen is more specifically akin to a picture within the picture, since it gives the effect of framing borders and an internal spatial recess; but the border is also one that serves like a shelf below the grapes, and the accompanying single fruit is now more clearly defined in front of it.

Braque's treatment of the grapes is therefore like a metaphor in itself for the separateness of the restricted world within which art is created and its transformational re-orderings. The same is also true, without the poetic touch, of Gris's 1913 use of engravings referred to earlier: the frame-moulding there is, in its geometric literalness, both a separating and a re-ordering device. And in a group of compositions from the spring of 1914 Picasso used pasted paper and wall paper to create both a mock frame and a ground for the figuration out of the same basic materials (D 683–85). The still life itself at the center thereby becomes isolated and stressed in its artificiality, through a play with shape that has a concentration and self-sufficiency to it that is analogous to Matisse's treatment of the painted vase in his 1914 work that was also discussed earlier, the *Woman on a High Stool.*

Alongside this self-imposed restrictiveness and the recapitulation of its internal logic towards 1914, the second phase of Cubism also ties the readability of the work as a total entity to an understanding on the part of the viewer of its constituent processes. Difficulties and hesitations as to what the images and objects are and how they are used (see Part Two, chap. 6) can only be resolved through knowledge of those processes and an awareness of how they operate. To bring out more fully here the essence of the demand placed on the viewer, apart from what other works of the time may suggest, or the hints of objects present (as in the first phase), comparison can be made with the Imagist poetry of the time, most particularly that of Ezra Pound:

> Green arsenic smeared on an egg-white cloth.
> Crushed strawberries! Come let us feast our eyes
> *L'Art 1910*

The title of this two-line poem probably refers to the first Post-Impressionist exhibition of 1910 in London, and it was first published in June 1914, in the opening issue of the Vorticist periodical *Blast;* but the structure of the poem, which is almost certainly of 1913, brackets it between those two phases in Pound's career and the corresponding alignment of his critical and didactic interests one year earlier and one year later. In the autumn of 1912, that is, Pound had published his volume of poems *Ripostes,* in which he included as an appendix five poems of T. E. Hulme's and his own notes on them. He thereby affiliated himself with the first stage of Imagism, that of 1908–10, which favored, according to his subsequent elucidation of its principles in 1912–13, directness of treatment, severe economy and a rhythmically musical kind of phrasing: all very much on Symbolist lines. By February 1914 he had shifted his interests, as an occasional art critic as well as a poet, towards the premises of abstraction and the declarations of Futurism; and just as the second phase of Picasso's and Braque's Cubism was coming onto exhibition in New York (Gallery 291, December 1914–January 1915), in the wake of the Armory Show, the anthology of poems which Pound edited under the title *Les Imagistes* also appeared there. In the six poems of his own that he included there, Pound favored those that were in the "Chinese" manner: hokku-like in form and imagery. His own corresponding choice of a work of his, to illustrate Imagism and its underlying theory, was the celebrated *In a Station of the Metro,* also of 1913 ("The apparition of those faces in a crowd / Petals on a wet, black bough"): a poem that he claimed to have cut down progressively, until the stark juxtaposition of the human and the natural in two spare lines came to him, and which was printed in the Chicago magazine *Poetry* in April 1913 in a form which indicated the spacing apart of its constituent rhythmic units.

Though Pound and his associates of 1912–14 never defined in any full and accurate sense what exactly Imagism entailed—Pound's own preference being for mystery or elusive vagueness on the subject— the characteristics of the 1913 poem quoted, and particularly those that distinguish it from Symbolist precedent, in fact present very interesting correspondences to what had emerged now in the practice of *collage.* To take up its components individually: *arsenic* in the first line is chemically a green and metallic substance; *egg-white* is traditionally used in the bonding and preparation of pigments; *smeared* is a term for the application of paint that denotes a specific kind of process, and that carries both textural and spatial implications in what results. The elimination of connectives (green *like* arsenic, white *as an* egg) in favor of collocation and evocation means that the connotations of adjective, verb and noun in this line are collapsed into one another. Then in the second line *crushed strawberries* summons up a third color, as well as another action associated with the preparation of colors. The image given embodiment in this way is one to *feast* upon, as with real eggs and strawberries; but only in visual terms—this being modern art, in the form of a still life. And it is again only through awareness of how the condensation and the syntactical coupling operates that the thematic concern of the poem, with the relations between art and visual experience, becomes one that the reader can grasp hold of. It is in fact in the tying of comprehensibility to the way in which a part, or aspect, of a thing can stand in for the whole—as in an ideographic form of presentation, whether verbal or visual—that the parallel to Cubism is finally closest.

The figure of T. E. Hulme on the British literary and artistic scene provides a concluding perspective on this phase of Cubism, much as comments on Picasso from outside France did for the first phase. It also adds a political dimension to the understanding. Hulme came to the discussion of contemporary art and its broad tendencies against the background of a completed career as an Imagist poet, to which Pound had given recognition by republishing his "Complete Poetical Works" in 1912, after they first appeared so labeled in the periodical *The New Age* in January of that year. Two of the five poems in question had first been printed in January 1909, and a "Lecture on Modern Poetry" that Hulme gave at that time draws directly on Franco-Belgian Symbolist theory, most especially the principles concerning *vers libre* that had been set out by Gustave Kahn and Rémy de Gourmont's advocacy of a purification of poetic style. The period from 1909 to 1912 was one in which Hulme, whose background was strong in philosophy, immersed himself in the thought of Bergson. He talked with Bergson at the Bologna Congress of April 1911, and thereafter embarked on a series of articles on his thought and influence that were intended to lead on to an introductory text on his philosophy in general. Though this would never be written, he would give four lectures on the subject in London in 1913, at a time of growing interest in Bergson's ideas in England, paralleling from 1911 on the expansion of popular interest in France; he is also credited with having produced the translation of Bergson's *Introduction à la metaphysique* (1903) which came out in London in 1913. By that time he had become directly involved with aesthetics, so that what did get written was a chapter on Bergson's art theory, for a projected book on modern theories of art. His plan for that book shows also his acquaintance with German aesthetic thought, most particularly the theory of *Einfühlung,* or empathetic response to art on the viewer's part, put forward by Lipps and Volkelt. On a visit to Berlin late in 1912 he had attended the lectures of Wilhelm Worringer and had been to see him to discuss aesthetics. The final and most crucial ingredient of his critical and philosophical thought came to be Worringer's distinction, founded on the theory of empathy, between periods in art in which a naturalistic tendency predominates and ones in which geometric stylization comes to the fore. It may be noted that at this time Alois Riegl's related ideas about the tendency towards ornamental patterning in certain stylistic phases of a culture were being used by Ludwig Coellen, in his text in German on "The Romanticism of the New Painters" (1912), to justify Picasso's "systematic working out of an artistic principle" that "necessarily led to the decorative." To the eclectic compound of his exposition, Hulme further added, in support of Worringer, the German philosopher Wilhelm Dilthey's idea of a prevailing *Weltanschauung,* or interpretative attitude towards life, distinguishing different cultural periods.

It was with this armory of philosophical concepts, and with a basically popularizing bent to his thought, that Hulme began to write about the contemporary London art scene for *The New Age* in 1913. It was a period of strong cultural interchange between France and England, in the fields of both art and poetry. *The New Age* itself, A. R. Orage's "Weekly Review of Politics, Literature and Art" to which Hulme, Pound and a third theorist of Imagism, Frank S. Flint, all contributed, was to be found in Picasso's studio by the winter of 1911–12 (after it reproduced a work of his that November): its presence is signaled by the lettering included in a still life of that time (D 446). Flint, who wrote a regular "French Chronicle" for Harold Monro's periodical *Poetry and Drama* from March 1913 to the end of 1914, would provide an essay on English and American Imagist poetry for *Les Soirées de Paris,* for its very last number of July–August 1914; and *The New Age,* probably under his guidance, would print some of Max Jacob's prose-poems in May 1915. These are representative indications of a larger pattern at work. Meanwhile Futurist art, as known through exhibitions in London, was beginning to have a major impact, in 1912–14, on the early development of Vorticism; and from the time of the second Post-Impressionist exhibition held at the Grafton Gallery in November 1912, some recent Cubist art was available to be seen also, though the coverage was much less strong.

A directly political orientation entered into Hulme's writings about art when, in January–July 1914, in a series of four articles on "Modern Art" for *The New Age,* he took up a position against the current authority of Roger Fry on the British scene and his claims about Cézanne, and simultaneously formulated, as he had already in a public lecture of January on "Modern Art and its Philosophy," the application of Worringer's argument about the "tendency of abstraction" to the current work of the "London Group," particularly Epstein's sculpture *The Rock Drill.* Exactly how much he knew about Cubism is not clear from the terms in which he discusses or refers to it on those occasions. He knew both Apollinaire's book and the one by Gleizes and Metzinger: perhaps in its English edition of 1913, but the illustrations to which he refers were the same in that case as they were in the original French edition, so that neither Picasso nor the two authors were represented there by works later in date than 1911–12. After the Grafton Gallery exhibition of November 1912, work of Picasso's did not appear in a London gallery showing until January 1914, and then only in one or two examples, supplemented with photographs. From the standpoint of the London Group, in any case, this limitation of acquaintance provided Hulme as critic with a vehicle of suggestive and forward-looking contrast. The association with modern machinery and the "hard, structural" character of the forms that he found in Picasso's work could be seen as a more promising tendency than "the more scattered use of abstractions of artists like Kandinsky," whose *On the Spiritual in Art* he had also read, and which he associated with a totally imaginative, "out of the head" way of working. But if this was so, the consolidation of that geometric character—to fit with Bergson's concept of the artist as one who disentangles definite and crystalline shapes from within the continuity of consciousness—remained still in abeyance. Cubism was taken accordingly as still in flux; as offering, in its simplifications and its emphasis on planes, the promise of a more clear-cut structure and cohesion. The need as Hulme explained it was for the simplifications "to be built up into a definite organization," rather than being "accepted" passively, as in the hands of Cézanne, or in the "theories about interpenetration" of Metzinger.

Over this line of thought, as with Léger's 1914 lecture, there hovers the shadow of the impending War, in which Hulme would serve and die. But it is not for his advocacy (and Pound's also) of what are actually Vorticist tendencies on the English art scene that Hulme's writings serve as an appropriate coda to this phase of Cubism, and as a bridge to the post-War scene. The "new constructive geometric art" that he discerned as emergent—in the work of Wyndham Lewis and David Bomberg as well as Epstein's (though with qualifications in both cases reflecting his personal preferences)—simply confirms once more the dispersive nature of the influence that Cubism exerted abroad. What, on the other hand, is illuminating in Hulme's pre-War critical role is the form of relationship that he establishes between responsiveness to the current art scene and the use of art as a take-off point for independent philosophizing, in which the individual creative personality subsumes itself to the collective tendency.

The broad effect of this is to separate the "intention of the work"— roughly, what it can lead to (see Part Two, chap. 5)—from the intention of the artist. Such a separation is possible in principle because on the one hand art is conceived of as being, in a post-Symbolist view of its genesis and workings, an "autonomous" creative activity: one that has no need to draw on intellectual premises or ideologies of the time in order to support and justify its own ordinances. And yet at the same time there is also the recognition, encouraged by German theorizing, that art takes its developmental course over time by virtue of an underlying conformity to larger intellectual trends, which can themselves be hypostatized on the evidence of the work. The "aesthetic" and the "intellectualizing" aspects of how current pictorial manifestations are viewed thereby become detached—as they were not in the first phase of Cubism. In which case, as Hulme expressed it in one of his jottings sketching out the idea of a "new Weltanschauung," "one must recognize thought's essential independence of the imagery that steadies it." The second phase of Cubism, though more straightforwardly structured in its essentials than the first phase had been, was conducive to such a liberation of thought about it from the actual postulates and demands of its imagery.

3 The Post-War Character of Cubism: Clarity, Order and Tradition

> Remember, only, that Cubism is simply a new notation susceptible of improvement . . . with the help of means chosen in the most judicious and the most traditional way.
>
> Maurice Raynal, *Quelques Intentions du Cubisme*

After the outbreak of War interfered with its experimental temper and its ongoing consistency, Cubism was never again the same—either in the public front that it displayed, or in the writings and supports for itself that it solicited. While the War lasted on, the immediate task for those in Paris was simply to pick up the pieces again, or to keep hold on the feasibility and value of doing this in some affirmative way; and from this there devolved, by the end of the War and more self-evidently once it was over, a reorientation as to the capacities and potentials of Cubism. The concentration of the artists fell, in this fashion, on matters of practical affirmation; on maintaining a momentum, or recovering one in the case of Braque; and by 1917–18, on showing the adaptability of Cubism to new ends. Such commentary as there was about Cubism during the War was correspondingly re-constitutive in tenor, in the sense of stressing order, harmony and tradition; while after the War, and particularly in 1919–20, the renewed artistic climate would generate a theory of a more philosophical sort.

The formation of a post-War aesthetic for Cubism, of a more "classical" kind, had accordingly several different strands or contributory ingredients to it. Insofar as the art and the theory were directly interlinked and to be taken together, initially, from 1915 to 1917, the concern for order and arrangement stood to the fore. Braque, as he completed his long convalescence from his 1915 head wound, celebrated his recovery back in Paris early in 1917, and returned to painting that summer. He came into association in this connection with Pierre Reverdy, poet, critic and founder in 1917 of the periodical

88

Nord-Sud which ran through the following year; while Gino Severini, resident in Paris from 1915 on, played a similar role in 1916–17 in relation to the periodical *SIC,* and at the same time organized some of the cooperative, unsectarian exhibitions of the "Lyre et Palette" group. Daniel-Henry Kahnweiler, in exile in Switzerland for the duration of the War and with his gallery holdings of Cubist paintings sequestered by the French government, composed in 1914–15 the opening chapters of his book *Der Weg zum Kubismus* (The Rise of Cubism), which were published in their original form in a Swiss-German periodical in September 1916 (under the adopted French pseudonym of Daniel Henry), and also a long philosophical introduction, on the nature of aesthetics, which was meant to be attached. Picasso meanwhile, after the tragic death of his mistress Eva at the end of 1915, formed new associations, with Jean Cocteau, Erik Satie and the Ballets Russes, which culminated in the May 1917 performance of the ballet *Parade* in Paris. The overtones of this performance and of Apollinaire's new play *Les Mamelles de Tirésias,* put on that June, led to a formal protest in which Gris joined his name to those of Metzinger, the sculptor Lipchitz (another friend by now) and Severini. But the political implications of this "closing of the ranks" became exacerbated only the following summer, when the dealer Léonce Rosenberg, whose Galerie de L'Effort Moderne had taken over Kahnweiler's pre-War role—bringing together under its patronage from mid-1917 on both the major figures of Cubism, Picasso, Braque and Gris, and also their followers or satellites of this time— began to be subject to attacks, on the harmony and taste associated with an "integral" Cubism.

Such attacks became more concentrated the following year, 1919, after Braque's exhibition at the Galerie in March and Gris's in April, with Blaise Cendrars and also André Lhote joining in. Kahnweiler published in Switzerland extracts from his larger aesthetic, in the shape of articles on the relation of form and vision and on the essence of sculpture, and then returned to Paris in February of 1920, reopened his gallery and took over as dealer to Braque, Gris and Picasso. On the basis of what he had already published and could now elucidate, he moved with Rosenberg and Maurice Raynal towards the formulation of a fully-fledged aesthetic for Cubism, that was more philosophically grounded and that began also to have impact on Gris. Picasso had at this point confirmed the neo-classical orientation that he had been developing alongside Cubism from 1915 on and in his production of portraits and figure pieces, by accepting to work on two further ballet productions. In these ways the post-War phase of Cubism entailed adaptations, and new departures arising from them, which had a strongly socio-economic, as well as intellectual, relation to what was happening on the art scene more generally.

That this should be so was in keeping with a larger shift in the framework of cultural values now, and their momentum towards self-renewal. All across Europe, experimentation in the arts took on a less radical flavor or had less of a dynamic verve to it, compared to the pre-War period. This applied not only to the look and feel of what took place in the visual arts—including sculpture and architecture—but also to the tenor of poetry and prose, and to the formal structures of music and dance. From a case such as that of Matisse—from what he did during his seasons in Nice from 1916 on, in contrast to his pre-War work—one might judge this to represent simply a *détente:* a toning down of excitement, or relaxation, that offered the opportunity for refinement. But the terms that were used internationally to convey the thrust of the developments in question, and the feeling for underlying principles that the terms themselves conveyed, show the import to be in fact of a much broader kind. In Holland there was talk by 1917, when Mondrian and van Doesburg joined forces on *De Stijl,* of "reconstruction": of a new "formation" or shaping. Into the pages of *De Stijl* that year was introduced also—by the architect J. J. P. Oud, discussing art and the machine—the term *Sachlichkeit,* with connotations of both practicality and sobriety which were to be taken further in the adoption of the term in Germany. By 1920, Tatlin in post-Revolutionary Russia addressed himself as a Constructivist to the need for a "modern classicism," by which was meant a fixed and clear vocabulary of forms, of a kind associated traditionally with classical values. In Paris at this time, the notion of a "call to order"—a concept already in general use by 1919—could encompass painters as fundamentally disparate in character as Severini, an ex-Futurist, and Derain, an ex-Fauve; while in Italy it could embrace what was written and felt about the example of Giotto and Piero della Francesca.

Similarly, in the field of literature, when Jacques Rivière—discussed in the first chapter as critic of Cubism—was appointed to the post-War editorship of the *Nouvelle Revue Française,* he wrote in the introduction to the first issue (June 1, 1919) "We believe that a direction can be perceived in which the creative instinct of our race, as new and as bold as ever, is engaging itself. . . . We will speak of everything which seems to us to foretell a classical renewal"; and he went on to give his endorsement to the trend which he saw as represented in literature by Valéry, Gide and Cocteau's friend Raymond Radiguet. The cultural implications of this trend were, accordingly, charged with a restorative force that had social and political dimensions to it; the time being seen as one in which the stability, authority and sense of attachment belonging to an inborn tradition needed to be reestablished or reborn. Feelings of that sort went back in turn, in more individualized and protective form, to the period of the War itself—very early in which Rivière had lost his close friend and brother-in-law Alain-Fournier: the younger novelist whom the pre-War editors of the *Nouvelle Revue* had most consistently published.

T. E. Hulme, whose writings of 1911–14 were brought up at the end of the last chapter and who also lost his life in the War, serves as a representative bridge to the post-War period in terms of his influence in England during this phase and the French sources that feed into it. Hulme was wounded at the Front in the spring of 1915, and during the period of his recovery and retraining as an artilleryman, before he returned to the trenches late in 1916, he published a series of articles in *The New Age,* under the heading "War Notes by North Staffs," and another series in *The Cambridge Magazine* in which he opposed himself, on political grounds, to pacifism. Though the main brunt of his argument was directed against Bertrand Russell's position, he devoted one of the "War Notes" (January 13, 1916) to attacking Clive Bell, first as an aesthetician and then secondarily as a pacifist; he also brought out that year a translation of Georges Sorel's 1910 book, *Réflexions sur la violence,* with a critical introduction of his own which had first appeared in *The New Age* the previous October. Hulme argued in these writings, in a more authoritarian tone now that reflects his war experience, the need for "discipline, ethical, heroic or political" if human accomplishments were to have any value. The views of the "pacifist, rationalist and hedonist" belonged in essence, he suggested, to the history of "democratic romanticism" going back to Rousseau; and to this line of thought there opposed itself the "classical," and ultimately pessimistic, view of the nature of man which took the transformation of society, as Sorel did, to be a heroic and regenerative task—not one to be advanced, as in the romantic conception, by dint of humanistic "progress." This basic contrast of points of view, or "temperaments," was one that Hulme had already laid out in a series of articles of 1912 titled "A Tory Philosophy" (*The Commentator,* April–May), with reference to both art and literature— and particularly to the kind of poetry that he advocated and had written himself. Both then and again now, in reiterating that opposition and expanding upon it in a primarily political context, he made reference to the comparable way in which the terms had been used in France, by Charles Maurras and the writers who grouped themselves with him to form the association known as *L'Action française,* and expressed sympathy with their viewpoint.

T. S. Eliot's first acquaintance with Hulme's writings came after he settled in England, in the form of knowledge of the "Poetical Works," as republished through Ezra Pound's agency in 1912. He had met Pound in London by September 1914, and Pound at that point in time would certainly have drawn his attention to these poems, and to his responsibility in connection with them, particularly since he was responding then, in letters and in print, to an earlier admiration of

Hulme's discussed in the last chapter, the poetic rhythms of the Symbolist Rémy de Gourmont, to which he had been introduced in 1912. Eliot also knew Pound's critical writings of 1913–14, on art and literature, as published in *The New Age* and *Blast*. He never apparently met Hulme; but an extension course on recent French literature that he gave at Oxford in September 1916 served as the opportunity for him to make a much fuller use of Hulme's ideas, including the more recent prose-writings. For the segment of the course that he labeled the "reaction against Romanticism," he paved the way with a discussion of Bergson, whose philosophy he had studied in Paris in 1910–11, and used the translation of Bergson's *Introduction to Metaphysics* which had appeared over Hulme's name in 1913, and also the "Notes on Bergson" that Hulme had published in *The New Age* in 1911–12. He brought in the ideas of Maurras, to which he had been introduced at Harvard by Irving Babbitt, and particularly the book titled *L'avenir de l'intelligence* that had come out in Paris in 1911, and which he knew from having kept up with French intellectual writings on this front. He also used Sorel's *Reflections on Violence* as translated by Hulme, together with its preface, and brought in Hulme's personal view of Christian humanism, in order to define the opposing "classicist" attitude or world view.

By 1915–16 Pound had shifted his interest in Rémy de Gourmont towards recognition of his contributions as a critic, and Eliot comparably shifted his concerns from 1917 on towards basic principles of criticism, publishing his own appreciation of De Gourmont's importance here in 1920. By Pound's account, 1916 was also the year in which the two of them got together and decided to counter the dilution of *vers libre* with a "dose" of Théopile Gautier's poetic example, which entailed the use of rhymes and regular strophes, and the quality that Pound called "hardness." The social and cultural preoccupations that had been fueled by Hulme and his French sources then resurfaced with the publication in 1918 of Julien Benda's *Belphégor*. Benda's standpoint had been of interest to Eliot from much earlier on, because of the way in which he used Bergson's philosophy, and the social and artistic values embodied in its popular success, as a point of departure. For Benda, rather than being a philosopher, Bergson was a representative of the Romantic sensibility in purely artistic form; he exemplified in extreme fashion both its cultivation of sensations and emotion at the expense of intellect and its address to non-rational aspects or areas of consciousness.

In a book of 1914, Benda extended the argument so that responsibility for Bergson's success became laid upon the society of the time. And in the 1918 book he took the idea of a "betrayal" of cultural and intellectual values and went much further with it, claiming that in the actual "documents" of pre-War art, evidence was to be found as to how the cult of dynamism and interpenetration and the celebration of movement and fluidity had worked against those clear distinctions, sharp separations and absolute contours which are the mark of "intellectuality." Amongst the social causes brought to account here, which included economic and psychological as well as intellectual factors, the idea of a loss of touch with "classic culture" had a special appeal for Eliot, who was engaged in defining at the time what exactly a sense of "tradition" in the arts was to be taken to entail, and its impress upon modern writers' and artists' awareness ("Tradition and the Individual Talent," 1919, and related essays brought together in *The Sacred Wood*, 1920). He was also in personal touch by the end of the decade with Jacques Rivière, for whom, as the new editor of the *Nouvelle Revue Française*, he developed a strong admiration.

In these ways the development of a post-War aesthetic in England can be traced, which emphasized the "classical" under successive but interacting aspects, and also the French texts which exercised the greatest impact or authority in this connection. The comparable stages of response in Paris to the wartime and post-War situation of French painting and poetry are to be found in the association together of particular artists and writers, and in a more refracted way in the paintings themselves, as they provide evidence of stimulus and response on the part of the writers.

Gino Severini's 1915 *Portrait of Paul Fort* (Centre Pompidou, Paris) is a painting, from the beginning of this phase of transition and reconstitution, which not only records the warm personal attachment between the still young Italian futurist, after he came back to Paris in July 1915, and the French poet and editor of a much older generation, who had become his father-in-law two years earlier; it also marks out, in the selection of texts that are pasted into it and the way they are disposed, how the War experience and the French Symbolist tradition were seen as standing in relation to one another at this point in time. More concretely, it makes a declaration, on behalf of poet and painter equally, of the value of that cultural continuity in relation to the War. One of the elements that it includes for this purpose is a program for the Théâtre d'Art, with a Bonnard drawing forming part of it. The accompanying title "La Geste du Roy" (the King's heroic deed) shows this to be the program for the performance of December 10, 1891, organized by Fort at the very youthful age of nineteen, which began with a fragment of the "Chanson de Geste" and went on to include works by Rémy de Gourmont, Mallarmé and Laforgue and also Maeterlinck's play *L'Aveugle*. This inclusion, then, harks back to the high days of Symbolism in both poetry and drama, as well as recalling the organizing and imaginative role played by the young Fort in that connection. Also included, in two different forms, one white and the other green, is the index for the first year and the first volume of Fort's periodical *Vers et Prose,* along with a page giving the contributors.

The year in question, March 1906 to February 1907, was also the period during which the weekly meetings of the "Closerie des Lilas" circle in Montparnasse, organized by Fort on behalf of the periodical, came to serve as a focus, as described in the first chapter, for all of the major artists and writers who were shortly to participate in the creation of Cubism and its accompanying theory. As far as both poetry and prose were concerned, the discussions were at that time still centered around Symbolism, or fell within its larger orbit. These pages thus mark out the intermediate stage of Fort's involvement, between Symbolism and Cubism. It was a stage that had included Severini himself, since he came to Paris in 1906, was drawn into the Closerie circle, and became friendly in this way with many of its members, including Picasso, Jacob and Apollinaire. Still another inclusion, bringing Fort's contribution down towards the present and into the War period, is a half-page of his bimonthly wartime publication, *Poèmes de France:* specifically the first issue, of December 1, 1914, chosen to show Fort's own poem which appeared there, "La Cathédrale de Reims." This was a poem excoriating the bombardment of the great Cathedral by German troops on September 19, 1914, which was a subject of shock and outrage and which inspired correspondingly in Severini one of his first War subjects, the late 1914 drawing *Flying over Reims* (Metropolitan Museum, New York) showing this symbol of the French heritage, as it now became, from an overhead viewpoint which includes the propellor and wings of an airplane.

At the top right of the portrait, balancing the signature and dedication in "affectionate homage" at the bottom, appears the best known line of Fort's early poetry:

> si tous les gens du monde voulaieint [*sic*] s'donner la main
> (if all the people in the world were to join hands together)

This is the final apostrophe of the poem "La Ronde autour du Monde," which appeared at the front of Fort's first publication of "ballads" that he had composed (*Chansons,* 1895) and had been reprinted in a selected edition just before the War (*Choix de ballades françaises,* 1913). The result of such a joining of hands, it is said there, would be to create a "circle around the world." This was a sentiment entirely in keeping with pacifist and universalist feelings of the early War period; and hence the choice of the line—as well as for reasons of familiarity, and for the way in which the poem represented the charm and affective simplicity attaching to Fort's use of the ballad form. And just as Fort's periodical and his own literary pursuits, bridging the private and public spheres, had combined together the lyrical tradition of French poetry, emphasizing both plasticity and stillness, and the more dynamic qualities of drama, so here Fort appears, warmly characterized as a personality by the inclusion of his snuff-box and pince-nez and in the rendering of his moustache, and is also paid tribute to professionally, in the presence of a medal of cultural honor and of his calling card. That kind of use of associative elements, organized and placed for suggestive effect, is a staple of Post-Impressionist and Symbolist portraiture; here, however, the pieces of actual text put in represent an adoption for his own purposes by Severini of the Cubist technique of *collage,* and correspondingly the treatment of the body and facial features is set up to provide a stabilizing accent of plastic definition, as against the dispersive interplay and pull of those two-dimensional elements.

Shortly thereafter Severini became associated with the wartime periodical *SIC,* which derived its name from the futuristically oriented combination of "*S*ounds, *I*deas, *C*olors, Forms" that was announced in its sub-title, and which began to appear in January 1916 under the editorship of Pierre Albert-Birot. That month Severini held an exhibition of his work at the Galerie Boutet de Monvel in Paris, under the title "First Futurist exhibition of plastic War art and other antecedent works," and Albert-Birot, in an open letter to Severini about this exhibition which he wrote for the second number of *SIC,* praised these paintings for the way in which they represented a "plastic" synthesis of the idea of War; while Severini himself, in an article which also came out that month (*Mercure de France,* February 1) and derived from a lecture that he gave at the exhibition, contrasted "plastic" and "literary" forms of Symbolism with one another in his title, and also wrote of how the artist's transposition of an object onto canvas necessarily involved a "reconstructive" process: one which could both be scientific in its foundations, as architecture was, so that it "spoke" to the viewer on an intellectual basis, and also be in accord with the personal psychology of the artist. Visitors to the exhibition included, among artists who were still on the Paris scene and conspicuously committed to Cubism, Picasso, Gris and Ozenfant; and Severini would become personally linked with the latter two by the second half of the year, and move correspondingly in his paintings towards an emphasis on order and precision which, in keeping with a statement of Albert-Birot's that appeared in *SIC* that autumn, invited comparison with the qualities of a machine.

The most significant younger poet to emerge into prominence during these years, against the same background of Symbolism, was Pierre Reverdy, who had been writing steadily since his arrival in Paris in 1910, when he joined himself to Paul Fort's circle and came to know both the major Cubists and also Severini; but who first began grouping his poems together for publication in 1915–16. Gris did drawings specially for the 1915 edition of his *Poèmes en prose,* and their personal friendship became a close one at this time, remaining as such at least until 1919. In token of this, they began collaborating towards the end of 1915 on a project that was to involve the publication of twenty of Reverdy's poems, belonging to a collection to be titled *Au soleil du plafond,* in combination with gouaches of Gris's that related in each individual case to the imagery of the poem.

The first specific reflections in Gris's work of this association and its relevance to his own endeavors come in November of 1915, in the form of a table-top still life that has a poem signed "Pierre Reverdy" included in it, as if it were a manuscript page pinned to the inner, mulberry colored frame of the work, at the base of the painting as a whole; and another composition of that month, this one in gouache and charcoal, which is dedicated in friendship to the poet's wife Henriette and has a similar text included in it, in *collage* form (C 152, 151a). The first of the poems in question that goes with an imagery of pipe, bottle, glass and playing cards, with a marbled mantel behind, reads:

> Se tiendrait-elle mieux sous ton bras ou sur la table
> Le goulot dépassait d'une poche et l'argent dans ta main,
>   moins longue que la manche
> On avait gonflé le tuyau de verre et aspiré l'air
> Quand celui qu'on attendait entra, les premiers assistants
>   s'attablèrent. . . .
> Et la flamme qui luit dans leur yeux . . . d'où leur vient-elle.

(Would she behave herself better under your arm or on the table / The bottle's neck stuck out of a pocket and the money in your hand, less long than the sleeve / They had inflated the glass tube and breathed in the air / When the person they were waiting for came in, the first of those present took their places at the table . . . And the flame that gleams in their eyes . . . from where does it come?)

while the poem pasted into the drawing, of a coffee grinder, cup and glass on a table, runs:

> Sur la table il y avait quelque grains de poudre ou de
> café. La guerre ou le repos: mais pourquoi tout ensemble?
> L'odeur nous guida le soir plus que nos yeux et le moulin
> bruyait du noir dans nos têtes. Pourquoi les levez-vous en
> remuant les lèvres? Le voisin connaîtra vos pensées.

(On the table, there were several grains of powder or of coffee. Strife or repose: but why all together? The smell guided us in the evening more than our eyes and the mill brayed black in our heads. Why do you raise them up while moving your lips? The neighbor will recognize your thoughts).

How far, beyond the basic imagery, the poem and its visual counterpart might correspond here is less significant than the fact that one and the other offer, in each case, a logical and credible though fictive space which the objects inhabit: one which so defines itself by virtue of the actions which have been performed, or are performed in it (the placement of playing cards or of a pipe that is temporarily put down, the action of turning a coffee grinder or bringing a glass up to one's face). In a third case of the same sort, on the other hand, which most probably dates from April or May 1916 and consists of a still life drawing with an excerpt this time included from the printed text of a poem, the visual-verbal relationship is somewhat different in character. The poem, which is unattributed but must again be one of Reverdy's runs:

> As de pique
> > ce verre
> > > la cendre de la pipe
> Bougie éteinte plantée sur mes amours
> > > > Matin pluvieux
> > > et cet ennui qui pèse
> Le jeu de cartes ou rêve l'avenir

(Ace of clubs/this glass/the ash of the pipe / Extinguished candle set over my loves / Rainy morning/and this boredom which weighs upon / The game of cards, in which the future dreams).

The still life is limited to the same specific elements: ace of clubs, pipe with ash, glass and game of cards. Here, then, the correspondence is one that depends on the quality of mood that is created in each case, by the consonance of the individual objects with one another and with the larger environment. It was that kind of a correspondence that was attempted also in the larger gouache series which Gris on his side never completed—leaving till last, it appears, those poems that had no specific objects in them, presumably because of the difficulty of establishing there an equivalent or parallel consonance.

By the beginning of 1917, Reverdy had begun to edit and put out his own periodical, *Nord-Sud*, which would last through the end of 1918. Besides Severini's one-man exhibition, there had been several opportunities in the course of 1916 for Cubist work to be exhibited at Paris galleries. The idea of an art capital was, in that sense, in the process of reviving, but questions were also raised thereby, as to whether there actually was a community of concerns or a true affiliation of interests, amongst those whose work appeared under the label of "Cubist" in such exhibitions and such contexts. The "Lyre et Palette" group exhibitions, as put together in 1917 by Severini himself, had the aim of being non-partisan. But it was also possible for such exhibitions to stir up wartime and patriotic feelings of protest, as happened when the Salon d'Antin organized by André Salmon in July 1916, under the broad title "Modern Art in France," led to the accusation that such art was *boche* in character—because of its being held at the gallery of the designer Paul Poiret, who was "tainted" by his pre-War participation in a large design exhibition in Munich—and Apollinaire, who had served at his own request in the infantry and been wounded in the head that March, had to take on the task of responding to this charge in print (statement in *Paris-Midi*, December 9, 1916) on behalf of the "Art and Liberty" association established two months earlier.

Reverdy's tactic, in contrast, was to remain detached from that kind of controversy. His own response to the regroupings—in which the dealer Léonce Rosenberg was now beginning to play an increasingly prestigious role—was to see them as a symptom of a more general wartime confusion regarding the character and aesthetic of Cubism, in the ranks of the artists as well as outside. In the article "On Cubism" that he published in the opening issue of *Nord-Sud* in March 1917, he wrote of "a feeling [on all sides] of a need to come together and understand one another better," rather than trying to end the confusion on an individual basis. Reverdy accepted that there had to be "divergencies of taste" among artists, but he also held it to be crucial to distinguish what counted as "serious efforts" from "more or less [artistically] honest fantasies"; and in order for the larger "effort" that Cubism represented to continue, it was also necessary to dismiss as claims to a further evolution what were, in fact, simply backward steps.

Reverdy's conception here of intellectual understanding, as a disciplining and organizing force, exercising control over the promptings of feeling or sensibility—so that a balance of forces was maintained, without dilution or facile compromise—is strongly analogous in principle to the balance between reason and sensibility that Severini advocated, in the preface that he wrote in the winter of 1916–17 for an exhibition of his work held at Stieglitz's Gallery 291 in New York in March 1917, and also to the emphasis that he placed on rationality, as a necessary ally of intuition in creation, in an article of 1917 on "Avant-Garde Painting" (*Mercure de France*, June 1) which was based on a lecture given at the "Lyre et Palette" exhibition of that January, and entitled in its second part "Intelligence and Sensibility." The view of "Intelligence and Creation" that the poet Paul Dermée advanced in the pages of Reverdy's periodical in August–September 1917, in follow-up to an article of his in the opening number of March positing the "death" of Symbolism, is equally akin in the faith that it places in the "constructive" role of the intellect, and in the contention that the aesthetic purpose of a work of art and the means used in it are both to be defined and analyzed by the use of reason. Reverdy is more rigorous in his exclusions and more idealistic in his stress on "extract[ing], in the service of the picture, what is eternal and constant (for example, the round form of a glass, etc.)"—no doubt as a result of his association with Gris. But what is most distinctive in his 1917 text is the distillation of aesthetic principle in a form that excludes individual examples or cases, and the feeling that goes with this for the arrangement of words, phrases and sentences on the page.

In giving over the pages of his periodical to concentrated aesthetic reflection, Reverdy particularly favored economy of expression and aphoristic turns of phrase. So it followed naturally from this preference that he should develop an interest in the course of 1917 in the aesthetic maxims and pithy formulations of artistic principle that Braque had taken to writing down in the margins of his drawings and his notebooks, particularly during his convalescence of 1915–16, and should address himself also to the bringing of them together in print, under the title "Thoughts and Reflections on Painting," in *Nord-Sud* that December. In taking charge of these aspects of ordering and arrangement, Reverdy paid an extraordinary degree of attention in what he did to format, balance and emphases: all in a way designed to fit, both structurally and typographically, with the character of the formulations, and to give them an ongoing quality of definitional refinement and clarification that at the same time respected the self-imposed limitations and consistencies of the aphoristic form itself.

To give a sense of how this works on the page: the masthead title, in large capital letters, is followed by three introductory editorial sentences, which are italicized and arranged in paragraphed form, and which move succinctly from the *interest* of the notes as evidence of a painter's thinking, to the *clarification* that they offer (*clarté*, which denotes limpidity and clearness) to those who are engaged in following the course of contemporary art, and from there to their character as *aesthetic reflections,* which serve as pointers for an art that has been subject to much diversified interpretation. Thereafter, in the text itself, wide spacing is introduced between each distinct sentence or grouping of sentences and internal punctuation and a repetition or balancing of phrases is used to give each statement its own individual stamp, down to the very shortest units of sense and grammar ("New means, new subjects"; "the painter thinks in forms and in colors"; "painting is a mode of representation"; "to work after nature is to improvise"; "nobility comes from contained emotion"). Slightly longer formulations are set in smaller type, and italicization is used for key words or concepts, in the second and third of the three pages. Not until the very end is the author's name provided, and then it appears in a form which is both like the placement of a signature (as at the end of a personal statement) and also, since it is in capitals, like the identifying label attached to a painting.

At the same time the topics that are taken up (originally unnumbered in their sequence) are arranged so that they move from the concept of progress in art (#1–3) to the procedural groundwork for the new art (#4–7)—never identified by the name of Cubism, or even as the "new painting," but simply by the use of the adjective "new" here; and from there to the topic of creation (#8–10), and on to the theory of reality and emotion and to their ultimate expression in work such as Braque has been doing, identified by the "simple facts" of what takes place there (#11–15), with a coda following on the need to discipline emotion (#16–18). The effect therefore is of an elaborated and interlocking web, within which each statement retains its self-sufficiency. Clarification proceeds by accumulation, insofar as there is a drift towards reaffirming, in successive groupings of maxims, the idea of artistic progress, the act of painting, the creative act, and finally *esprit* (intellect) as the source of all three. When, however, the reflections are read back, as assembled, from what is most practically oriented in them to what is most deliberately set at the opposite pole, of absolute, unsupported declaration, one moves from the identification of Cubism by virtue of its characteristic use of *papiers collés* as "simple compositional facts," to the attribution to it of the creation of certainty, in the way it improvises from nature and at the same time respects the reality of nature; and from its being identified successively as a "mode of representation," a "pictorial fact," a "new unity and lyricism," to its being brought into absolute correlation with both creation and *esprit*. It is also true, therefore, that the clarifying process is one that resists any fuller definition than its individual constituent sentences and its key terms provide. The visual and for-malized aspect of the arrangement on the page makes, in these ways, for an analogue to Severini's paintings of mid-1916 to 1917, which give the impression of flat cut-out pieces joined together by an overall geometry that has a rational and constructive stamp to it; and also to Picasso's Cubist paintings of 1916–17 which are compounded of large, strip-like shapes, repeated bright colors and regularized decorative stippling. In both of these cases the effect is comparably of an ar-rangement in which the elements are equalized with one another, in their constitution as very generalized "signs," and lose their indi-vidual and piecemeal character under the control of a larger unity of artifice and design.

Gris's works of the first half of 1916, also with pointillistic stippling, are that way inclined; but in his paintings of late 1916 to 1917, includ-ing figure subjects as well as still lifes, he moves towards a more rigorously translucent and frozen kind of idiom. The sense of self-renewal here on Gris's part turns on the strength and rigor of the image itself; it entailed a distancing in principle of any too intrusive intimations of physical reality. Rather, according to a developing viewpoint of 1916–17 in both painting and poetry, the image was to be given a stopped and condensed quality, so that, in the example of Poussin's art and the way that Cézanne was being seen now as having "recreated" it—which was the double paradigm that Severini used in his March 1917 catalogue preface—it stood as articulate in itself. The terms adopted here, "distancing" and "strength," are to be found associated together in a short piece of Reverdy's, on the poetic image, which appeared in *Nord-Sud* in March 1918. And that carrying through on such principles could lead to the work's possession of a dreamlike quality, without any sense of fantasy, and to analogy, or "resemblance by rapport" in Reverdy's words, between totally distinct things is particularly clear in Gris's paintings of 1917 which have an open window and landscape as their subjects—and that have a purified, and yet at the same time apparitional quality to their geometrization of buildings and trees.

This purification of viewpoint as to the fundamental idiom of Cubism, which was supported by Reverdy in his editorial role—though he resisted, quite justly, the application of the term Cubism to poetry (see Intermezzo ii)—corresponds in time to a closing of the ranks on the part of the Cubists who had been linked together both commercially and in the sharing of wartime exhibitions, in Paris and New York. In the newspaper *Le Pays* there appeared, in June 1917 or soon after, a statement of protest on behalf of "cubist painters and sculptors" which was signed by Gris, Metzinger and Severini, along with Diego Rivera, André Lhote, the sculptor Lipchitz and also Hayden and Kisling. It was directed against "certain literary and theatrical fantasies" that had been mistakenly linked to their work and which, they indicated, needed to be forcibly distinguished from the events of the association "Art et Liberté" and of *SIC*, in which they had actually participated. The repercussions of this statement made it evident that the protest was nominally against the first performance of Apollinaire's play *Les Mamelles de Tirésias* on June 24, with its decors by the Russian-born Serge Férat who had been doing Cubist paintings since 1913, and secondarily against the literary output of the writers Henri-Martin Barzun, Sebastien Voirol and Fernand Divoire; but that it also reached out in its implications to include the première of the ballet *Parade,* which had taken place in Paris slightly earlier, on May 17. Amongst those repercussions was a letter from Apollinaire to Reverdy (of June 28), in which he explained how the success of his play had provoked this protest. He also brought out very clearly how the business dealings of Léonce Rosenberg's Galerie de L'Effort Moderne lay in the background to the attack, for he claimed that Gris had foolishly signed the statement because of the commercial pressures upon him to do so. This, Apollinaire went on to say, had given him the opportunity to separate himself—unlike Gris—from "commercial Cubism," and to affirm for the future that he belonged rather with the "great painters of Cubism."

By the summer of 1918, Cubism—as represented by the different figures that the Galerie de L'Effort Moderne had brought together under its patronage—became subject to more direct attack. The critic Vauxcelles made a point of putting forward Derain as the true representative of a classical direction in painting now—as against the whole-hearted or "integral" kind of Cubism that had geometry and "distancing" from reality as its basis; and to make the split more complete, Léger, whose War experiences had led him in a more socially conscious and implicitly moralizing direction, signed a contract with Rosenberg in July of that year. As for Picasso, his first public exposure of this time in Paris was at the gallery of Paul Guillaume, a dealer whose taste inclined strongly towards Derain; it was an exhibition of pre-Cubist work shared with Matisse, for which Apollinaire provided a double preface, and in fact Apollinaire had written a catalogue statement in October 1916 about Derain, when his work was shown at that gallery, in which he stressed that artist's development towards "sobriety and measure," and the discipline and detachment implicit in his work. Now, contrastingly, he stressed innovation of direction and freedom of experiment on Picasso's part, as he had already, more broadly, in his comments in the program for *Parade* on the Picasso-Massine collaboration there.

The shift here in the valuation of Cubism away from a collectivity of procedures shared between artists, and towards a stress on individuality, as reflected in the choice and deployment by each artist of his personal means, is also expressed in the writings of Reverdy in the course of 1918. In complement to the definition of an artist's aesthetic, in the October number of *Nord-Sud*, as the "complete set of means at his disposal," he contrasted "means" to "procedures" in an article that came out in *SIC* that month, called suggestively "Some Advantages of Being Alone." In a work of art, he now claimed, that is "presentational" rather than "representational" in character, it is "creation through concentration" that serves as the criterion of absolute value. This set of terms can be applied quite directly to Gris's work of 1918, in the sense that the avoidance in them of concrete detail as any kind of an essential for presentational purposes creates an effect of "concentration," such that a more magical and a more expansive quality enters into the disposition of the "signs" now.

The following year, 1919, was the last one of close association between Gris and Reverdy; during it, while Reverdy dedicated to Gris the pamphlet containing his aesthetic credo, *Self-Defence*, Gris provided three drawings of differing subjects—a harlequin with a guitar, a still life and a city view—as illustrations, in pure outline form, for Reverdy's book of poems *La guitare endormie*, and also an author's portrait to go at the front. A one-man exhibition of Braque's work at Léonce Rosenberg's gallery in March led Bissière, in a review, to call it undeniable that Cubism "had brought painting back to its traditional means," inculcating respect once more for the painter's materials and professional command, and had thereby "contributed to saving modern art"; and André Lhote, having just been appointed reviewer for the *Nouvelle Revue Française* by Jacques Rivière, took up the theme of a needed recall to order and tradition in his comments on the exhibition. The point was accepted by Blaise Cendrars in an article of May, titled "Why the 'Cube' is Disintegrating," but he criticized that tradition for its cold rationality, stubborness and solemnity. The Cubists, he claimed, had neglected the "study of depth" and color—elements strongly present in the art of Léger, with whom Cendrars was now closely associated. Their renovation of painting had stayed in this way within the "confines of taste," in not being built on a strong enough sense of reality. And in contradistinction to what Apollinaire had suggested the year before as to the continuing spirit of experiment, he made it the spearhead of his argument that Cubism "[did] not succeed in troubling the young," in that it "no longer offered enough novelty and surprise to provide nourishment for a new generation" (*La Rose Rouge,* May 15).

The Braque exhibition was followed at the same gallery by one of Gris's work and one of Picasso's, and in the London periodical *The Athenaeum,* for which he was now an occasional contributor reporting on the arts, Lhote wrote about the latter exhibition and the responses to it, under the title "Cubism and the Modern Artistic Sensibility" (September 19). Speaking here as one who had participated in the earlier unfolding of Cubism, he went back to its origins and to the way in which Cézanne's "grave and measured voice" and the "recall to classical order" which he represented lay behind the dissection and decomposition of the first phase of Cubism. The "continuous oscillation of all the different planes" and the "kind of space, less real than suggested" that marked out this phase in Picasso's case had led on to a "simplified technique"; and the call for the future was accordingly for the principles in question to be "employed sanely," as he put it, and in a "Totalist" spirit. Lhote's argument shared with Cendrars—and with the work of Derain too—the idea of principles of order and construction deduced *from* reality; so that when Gris in 1919–20 moved towards stressing in his paintings the use of abstract shapes as his point of departure, this amounted procedurally to a contrary way to theirs of assenting to the claims of "intellect" and rationality, as well as a way of affirming—in what the creative imagination is able to do with those shapes—his continuing allegiance to Reverdy's conception of "creative means." It is at this time also that Gris moves towards composing on request his first public statement of a formal sort (April 1920), relating to the nature of his interest in Negro art: generalized, as the statements of Cendrars and Lhote were, but also rationally lucid and succinct.

Within this wartime and post-War pattern of interchanges and allegiances, the interpretation of Cubism itself shifts from the delineation of an aesthetic, in terms that are more suggestive in character than they are analytic, to the provision of arguments that have a more justificatory and philosophically reasoned character to them. For Reverdy in his 1917 essay, in keeping with his larger view of imaginative and creative means in both painting and poetry, Cubism is "an eminently plastic art; but an art of creation, not of reproduction or interpretation." It is a "profound" art, which in the hands of a "few chosen individuals," for whom the means established in the initial stages of Cubism constitute a recognized and established discipline, leads to works that "address themselves directly to the eye and the senses of lovers of painting." This is an aesthetic that—in its coverage of poetry also—has basic affiliations with the view of poetic creation that Max Jacob sketched out in his "Preface of 1916" to *Le cornet à dés,* his book of prose-poems which came out in 1917. Jacob's terms there are characteristically idiosyncratic ones, which define themselves in contrast to Romantic and Symbolist poetic practice; but they include the basic polarities of "situation" as oppposed to "disorder," and "transplantation" as opposed to a "surprise" that is merely charming in its effect. If those terms are taken in parallel to Reverdy's view of how works of art "in detaching themselves from life, find their way back into it," inasmuch as "they have an existence of their own apart from the evocation or reproduction of the things of life," there is a community in both cases with the way in which Apollinaire explains the role and character of Cubism, in discussing in the May 1917 program for *Parade* the nature of Picasso's contribution there: "The costumes and scenery in *Parade* show clearly that its chief aim has been to draw the greatest possible amount of aesthetic emotion from objects. . . . The aim is, above all, to express reality. However, the motif is not reproduced but represented; more precisely, it is not reproduced but rather suggested by means of . . . an integral schematization that aims to reconcile contradictions by deliberately renouncing any attempt to render the immediate appearance of an object." There is also a community with the poem about Picasso's art, "Pablo Picasso," that Apollinaire published in *SIC* that same month: a poem which evokes the mood and experimental temper of that art over time as well as its subjects, with the lines arranged on the page so that the blank spaces in between suggest the character of one of Picasso's paintings.

There is, then, no theory of Cubism at this time in the sense of a full and updated explanation or definition of direction; rather, "reflections" on painting—the term adopted in 1917 for the publication of Braque's maxims—are keyed to a shifting set of aesthetic concerns and emphases. The basic terms of aesthetic approval that go with this are themselves somewhat variable, in the way that they can be applied: in recapitulation of the ones that are most important in reference to Cubism, they include *clarity, discipline, purity* and *plasticity.* By the end of the decade, however, the idea that the philosophy can justify the character of the art, rather than just help to explain it, enters into the theorizing and gives it a greater amplitude. Maurice Raynal and Léonce Rosenberg, along with Kahnweiler who is writing and publishing in Switzerland as he was during the War already, are the key figures in bringing this about.

Raynal's pre-War contribution was discussed in the last chapter and continuity through the War period is provided by an article on Severini that he published in *SIC* in May 1917 and by regular contact with Gris, recorded in letters between them which are few in number because they corresponded only when one or the other was out of Paris. But he becomes more heavily philosophical as a writer on Cubism in 1919, in a pamphlet published under the title "Some Intentions of Cubism" and a related essay "Ideas on Cubism" which appeared in the issue of the Italian periodical *Valori Plastici* (February–March 1919) devoted to the subject. In the pamphlet, which came out of a debate held at Léonce Rosenberg's gallery during Severini's one-man exhibition there, Raynal cites not only Kant and Bossuet, as in 1912–13, but also Plato, Cicero, Montesquieu, Malebranche and Hegel—using in most cases particular statements of the philosophers in order to show the primacy of *esprit,* intellect, over the evidence of the senses. With this there goes an emphasis on the "absolutely pure truth" that a picture affords. The anti-materialistic address here to the transcendence of reality will become progressively more marked in Raynal's writings on art of the 1920s, and so will the didactic stress on the role of forms and their study, and on the "disinterested" values and certainties of tradition: "We will have then," he affirms here, "the research into surface contrasts, study of their reciprocal influences, and finally the examination of the influence of straight lines and curves on their neighbors; but always, in this case, with the goal of discovering their interconnection *(rapports).* Hence these researches too will be based on the example of tradition. The artists will transpose and transform according to the nature of his modern sensibility, but he will always keep the same vital quality of balance *(le même esprit d'équilibre)."*

The dealer Léonce Rosenberg, as manager of the Galerie de L'Effort Moderne and publisher of the pamphlets and writings associated with it, including Raynal's essay, and as controller of Kahnweiler's stock of Cubist paintings in his absence, was in a position to join himself to these new lines of exposition also; and no doubt the attacks there had been on the policies of his gallery over the last two years, as much or more than his purely intellectual gifts and inclinations, encouraged him to do this. Thus for the February–March 1919 issue of *Valori Plastici* devoted to French Cubism, to which Raynal contributed as described, he sent in a letter including seven of Braque's maxims (one previously unpublished) and also arranged for a short statement by Gris and one by Léger to appear (the latter subversively turning out, like Cendrars' article two months later, to be against harmony and good taste). The short text entitled "Cubism and Tradition," based on his own contribution here, which he issued as a pamphlet in 1920, and also used that year as the preface to a large exhibition of his Cubist artists that he organized in Geneva, quotes from Plato's *Philebus* and follows Raynal in using the opposition of *l'esprit,* intellect, to *le sens,* the senses. Its main argument, following on some rather sententious aesthetic phrasing about Art, Beauty and the Absolute, is that the Cubists, following Cézanne, sought "not to reconstitute an aspect of nature but to construct the plastic equivalents of material objects, and the pictorial fact built up in this way becomes an aspect created by the intellect." In creating rather than imitating, they rise above "the sentimentality born of the picturesque appearances of some spectacle in nature" and, in sum, "disengage from its fugitive aspects the constant and absolute and with the aid of these two elements construct a reality equivalent to the one they have in front of them. Then, by means which they draw from their emotion, they give life to the work they have produced." The key terms in this essay, *creation, emotion* and earlier, *elements* and *means* are given an aesthetic weighting such as they had in the theory of the War years; but they are strung together, to give them a more generalized application over time which is appropriate again to the term *tradition,* on a more ambitiously philosophical thread.

As for Kahnweiler, he was in exile in Switzerland and writing and publishing during this period in German; but his philosophical inclinations were known to all of the Cubists of his pre-War gallery, whom he would return to Paris to reclaim early in 1920, and Gris would write to ask him his opinion of Raynal's pamphlet (letter of December 22, 1919). He began what was to become his book *The Rise of Cubism* (*Der Weg zum Kubismus,* first German edition 1920) in 1914–15 and the parts of it that appeared under the title "Der Kubismus" in the Zurich periodical *Die Weissen Blätter* in September 1916, corresponding roughly in content to the first three chapters of the book, dealt with the opening phases of Cubism in the hands of Picasso and Braque and the practical and aesthetic context of its first unfolding. In its use of anecdote and personal recall, this part of the projected book provided a way to sum up and thereby conserve historically the character of the pre-War phase, as André Salmon's 1919 article "The Origins and Intentions of Cubism" (*Demain,* April 26) would also do, and as the section on Cubism did in his *La jeune sculpture française:* a pendant to his 1912 text on painting which had been written in 1914, but did not appear until five years later. But unlike Salmon's more limited and pragmatic purposes, Kahnweiler had had the idea from the beginning of making what he wrote on Cubism form part of a larger text, which dealt with issues of aesthetics in general (in German, *Der Gegenstand der Aesthetik*). He was also working simultaneously, by 1917, on an historical text, on art and the Reformation. This breadth of scope kept the project going into the post-War period, particularly in the form of separate essays on "Form and Vision" and on "The Essence of Sculpture" which were published in 1919, again in the Swiss-German *Die Weissen Blätter* (July) and in the Weimar periodical *Feuer* (November–December). These essays, which stake out Kahnweiler's capacity to combine the conceptual vocabulary of the philosophy of perception, as it descends from Kant's *Critique of Pure Reason,* with aesthetic concerns of a primarily formal kind (like Raynal's), and to compare with one another, much as Worringer had done, but again in a more strictly formal manner, the plastic arts of different cultures, correspond to sections on those subjects included in the fourth and most extended chapter of the book.

Also of concern to Kahnweiler are the cultural affiliations of Cubism: not in the sense of there being tightly drawn national boundaries between differing modern developments—in discussing Futurist art, he accepts Marcel Duchamp's similarity of aim to those of the Italians (chap. 6)—but in the sense of there being a "spirit of the time," or *Weltanschauung,* by which "the appearance of the aesthetic product is conditioned in its particularity" (chap. 3), and also a French pictorial tradition of attention to structure, which included Corot, Cézanne, Seurat and Derain, and in which Cubism takes its place, by virtue of the problems that it sets for itself and how it deals with them (chap. 1). That the affirmation of such a linkage, and being able to make it on the grounds of personal acquaintance loomed as important during the War—not just for reasons of nationalism brought up earlier, but on the more general ground of a felt threat to the cosmopolitanism of pre-War French culture—is apparent in a letter of comment that Guillaume Apollinaire contributed to the *Mercure de France* in 1917 (September 22): Gustave Kahn, the regular art critic of the periodical, had written that July of the Spanish origins of Cubism, and Apollinaire contended in response that it should properly and simply be called a "Latin" school. He cited Salmon and Raynal as art critics who could similarly offer their personal witness here, and Kahnweiler, who had settled in Paris and opened his gallery there in 1907, had similarly participated intimately in that climate before being driven out as a German national by the War. The sense of the tradition here equally revived and continued after the War, and it is a testimony on Kahnweiler's part to his feeling for it, especially in his exile and its aftermath, that from 1915 on he chose to publish all of his writings under the French nom-de-plume Daniel Henry, and that he contributed to the Bern periodical *Neues Leben* in 1917 an article that was contrastingly directed against Expressionism in the visual arts. He also wrote in 1919 about Derain's work, for the Berlin periodical *Das Kunstblatt,* and added a section to *The Rise of Cubism* on Léger (chap. 5).

Much of Kahnweiler's text is taken up with factual and recollective detail: its basic purpose being to "fix the position of Cubism in the history of painting and to demonstrate the motives which guided its founders," the "inner urges" of the artists are extrapolated from those details or reconstructed from his conversations and close acquaintance with them. But apart from an introduction of the term *esprit* which is like Raynal's and Rosenberg's and a use of philosophy which is quite heavy in its citation of Locke on primary and secondary qualities of an object, as well as Kant, there are also two places in which the discussion takes a theoretically bolder turn. The first of these passages concerns the application of the terms "analysis" and "synthesis" to the Cubist treatment of the object. In reference to the paintings done by Picasso at Cadaqués in 1910 and the "great advance" that they represent, Kahnweiler wrote that in contradistinction to an "analytical description," the possibility was opened up in this way of creating a "synthesis of the object," which is defined as signifying in the words of Kant that one is able to "put together the different representations and grasp what is manifold in them in one act of knowledge"; a direct quotation from *The Critique of Pure Reason* (I, #10). These, however, are presented as alternatives to one another, to be so used according to the artist's preference.

The terms "analysis" and "synthesis" which had been introduced in the second phase of Cubism, as briefly indicated in the last chapter, to designate basic methods or procedures available to the artist, had been so used already in the literary theory of the Symbolist period. Alfred Vallette, for instance, in an article of April 1890 in the *Mercure de France* ("Intuitivisme et réalisme") had written of how "the author must be an analyst, but in order to reconstitute the fact after having disengaged it, to make it concrete under the salient and characteristic aspect which answers to the aim of the work"; and Jean Royère in his Symbolist manifesto of 1909 (*La Grande Revue,* August 26) had written of an artistic evolution as "an analysis between two syntheses," defining synthesis as a "more or less considered grouping" and analysis as "the individual differentiation which follows that" so that works "show their period of analysis, but it is in the midst of synthesis that they are elaborated." But invariably in such cases the terms denoted stages in the creation of a work of art that followed upon one another sequentially. This is the way that T. E. Hulme in his January 1914 article on Modern Art used the term "analytical", to be succeeded by a "constructive geometric art," in reference to the example of Cubism as he knew it; and it is also the way in which Raynal continued to use the term in his 1919 pamphlet "Some Intentions of Cubism,"

> When therefore the painter finds himself in the presence of the objects, the first task of his imaginative understanding consists of an analysis of those same objects, which he studies in his sketches or preliminary painted versions (*ébauches*). . . . Finally by a process of synthesis (*un travail synthétique*) which he carries out with the aid of all of his pictorial means, he constitutes a new whole out of all these elements.

It is true that Apollinaire in 1917, within the appreciation quoted earlier from the program for *Parade,* used the terms in such a way as to suggest that the two alternatives could be fused, writing of "an analytical synthesis that embraces all the visible elements of an object," and that when interviewed about the situation of poetry in July of the following year, he denied there to be a relationship with Cubism, on the grounds that whereas Cubist paintings were "works of analysis" (whether simple or complex) in revealing to the eyes of the spectator the volumes and dimensions of the elements from which they were constructed, lyrical poetry in contrast "was more directly beamed towards the intellect, in terms of which it performs more of a function of synthesis." The term "synthetic" was also used by Pierre Albert-Birot in reference to poetry in his periodical *SIC,* to imply that the work was artificially put together and built up, which is basically compatible with the leanings and emphases of Cubist painting at this time. But these variations of usage would not have been known to Kahnweiler when he was completing his text. His own understanding of "synthesis" based on Kant made it—as in Raynal's use of the term—a summative and reconstitutive process. That the procedures that he designated as optional ones should be used in such a way as to give a geometrically regulated and condensed character to the resultant image *as a whole,* rather than to individual elements incorporated into it, was an insight not available to him in 1915 on the basis of his pre-War exposure to Cubism, nor again as a result of circumstance in 1919, when he put in a discussion, in the chapter that he now added on Léger, of the ways in which that artist, prior to 1914, still remained attached to Cubism in his "adherence to the visual experience." Though not prognostically incorrect for the work of Picasso and Braque, and also that of Gris before 1919–20, this feature of Kahnweiler's text would, by the time it appeared in print as a retrospect, be displaced as a contribution to theory and therefore confusing.

The second and much longer passage of theoretical consequence, immediately following that one, has to do with the novelty of Cubism as a "language" and the problem that it poses of seeing what is depicted, for a spectator unfamiliar with this language:

> The assimilation which leads to seeing the represented things objectively . . . always takes place finally, but in order to facilitate it, and impress its urgency upon the spectator, cubist pictures should always be provided with descriptive titles, such as *Bottle and Glass, Playing Cards and Dice* and so on. In this way the condition will arise which H. G. Lewes referred to as "preperception" and memory images connected with the title will then focus much more easily on the stimuli in the painting.

The reference here is to the writings of George Henry (not H. G.) Lewes, and specifically to his *Problems of Life and Mind* (1874–79), with its chapters on "Certitude" and "Is and Appears" which appear to lie behind the larger argument and choice of examples that follow; while "preperception" (introduced in series 3, problem 2, chap. 9) was a term that had come into general philosophical usage in England around that time, as a way of designating the *a priori* knowledge of spatiality that Kant had argued to be a necessary precondition for all sensory experience of forms and objects. Lewes's book played an important role in the later nineteenth century for a more general public in its attempted philosophical reconciliation of the rival claims of rationality and spirituality, and Kahnweiler demonstrates, in the larger consideration of form and vision into which he enters here, a comparable desire to bring together an empirical or scientific understanding of how reality is perceived, and a post-Hegelian view of imaginative creativity. Kahnweiler's bent in this direction—fueled evidently by his readings in art history, which included Wilhelm Worringer's *Abstraktion und Einfühlung (Abstraction and Empathy),* a dissertation of 1906 which came out as a book in 1908, had reached its third edition by 1910, and was followed in 1912 by his *Formprobleme der Gotik*—is apparent in his reference to architecture and the applied arts, as evidencing the basic "longing" of humanity for geometric lines and forms, and to the sculpture and painting of periods which have "turned away from nature" and "give expression to the same longing in the use of 'basic lines.'"

The argument from this direction, in turn, is used to support the contention that Cubism is not to be taken by the viewer as a "Geometric Art." Rather, "in accordance with its role as both constructive and representational art, [it] brings the forms of the physical world [in its actual works] as close as possible to their underlying basic forms," and the "geometrical impression" is therefore unjustified, since "the visual conception desired by the painter by no means resides in the geometric forms, but rather in the representation of the reproduced objects." Again titling of the work is taken as being able to help here, by preventing a misleading form of "sensory illusion" in the viewer. But the onus of averting the wrong "impression" or "illusion" here is laid, basically, upon the Cubist's artist's own premises or attitude concerning the character of the forms that he uses, and on the creative procedures that he brings to bear in this regard:

> The unconscious effort which we have to make with each object of the phsycial world before we can perceive its form is lessened by cubist painting through its demonstration of the relation between these objects and basic forms. Like a skeletal frame these basic forms underlie the impression of the represented object in the final visual result of the painting; they are no longer "seen" but are the basis of the "seen" form.

For the viewer to familiarize himself with the "method of expression" here is for him or her to gain in perception, so that the "geometric impression" will then disappear completely—an argument with philosophical implications to be taken up later. And it is from this that the clarity of presentation and constructive or architectural quality of Cubist painting derive: it "provides the clearest elucidation and foundation of all forms."

A basic way to characterize the Cubism of 1916–18, that puts into context the qualities in the paintings referred to earlier, is to say that in Picasso, Gris and Severini there is an effect of *restraint* and *containment* at work that rests, primarily or most essentially, on the sense of arrangement that is imparted, and that a concern for *stabilization* plays a large part here. Certainly Picasso's paintings of 1916 with large flat areas of pointillistic stippling contrast in this way with the skewed axes and nervously sexualized shapes of his 1915 works, and the quality of shrillness which reflects his emotional response later that year to the sickness and death of his mistress Eva is replaced by a playfulness that is limited to shape alone, as if human implications were being deliberately kept to a minimum or denied. The paintings in question (D 885–93) are quite few in number and generally large in scale; the shapes are overlaid in an axially massed, blueprint-like form which suggests in many places the overlapping profiles of buildings and towers; and while the Ingres-like portrait drawings of 1915–16, with their room settings of mantel, mirror and dado, table and chair feed into the choice of settings in these paintings and their specific legible or recognizable features, the discontinuities of shading and the bleeding out towards the edges in those drawings give place to complete consistency here within each segment.

Comparably Gris introduces in 1915 and makes more explicit in 1916 the combination of transparency with what has aptly been called "fossilized" shading (or "flattened chiaroscuro"): the principle whereby the shadows cast by objects or their internal shading are segmented and flattened so that—with an increasing sharpness and sonorousness to the black itself (from the spring of 1916 on)—they become equalized in their role as two-dimensional planes and overlapping units of shape with the more "positive" elements of subject-matter itself. Fossilized shading will be adopted by Metzinger in 1916 and also by Maria Blanchard, both of whom belonged at this time to the group led by Gris and Severini. In the last months of that year, at Beaulie-sur-Loches, Gris does landscapes again and also exercises himself afresh with figures subjects by doing drawings after black and white reproductions of several paintings of Cézanne's, one after Velasquez's *Don Gaspar de Guzman,* and a drawing and a painting (of September, C 197) after Corot's *Woman with a Mandolin.* Whether or not this step implies some awareness of Picasso's work of 1915–16—especially the 1915 *Still Life in a Landscape* (D 814), which passed to Léonce Rosenberg, and the portrait drawings—in all of the copies extended lines are used together with shading inside the figure to give an enhanced sense of firmness and purification; and Gris deploys the same structural principles, together with the elements of wainscoting and chair and a few selected physical features of an ideographic kind—limited mainly to the head and hands—for his October *Portrait of Josette* (C 203).

Thus whereas Futurism in 1915–16, as represented in Paris by Severini, was combining an adhesion to the basic tenets of Symbolism, as to the workings of allusion, evocation and suggestion, with the adoption of new and striking images (or words), deriving from the War (as in Severini's 1915 subject of the Red Cross Train), Cubism was holding to its basic, pre-War subject matter of figure and still life (with an occasional pure landscape), but was using images which were no longer suggestively evocative and referentially reflexive, as in its pre-War understanding of Symbolism, but rather in the process of becoming "transparent." Severini wrote in his February 1916 article, referring back to his War subjects, of the need to invent "new signs and symbols" to express the concepts of the day, so that art should speak to the viewer both intellectually and ideologically; but by the end of that year he had abandoned the "dynamic" aspects of pre-War Futurist practice, which were associated with the conveying of movement, in favor of still lifes, domestic interiors and landscapes. He affiliated himself with wartime Cubism correspondingly in the flat, lucid and strictly demarcated character of his arrangements now, which could serve in themselves to carry the implication of continuity and stability, as when the subject of a *Seated Woman* (1916) recalled in those respects Italian art of the fifteenth century, or the objects in a still life (1917) were made recognizable in their everyday, familiar character by the inclusion of the word "Pure" on a scroll and of the identifying label "Quaker Oats" on its own reserved rectangle of color.

In 1917–18, on the other hand, as the War dragged on and the insistencies of its presence so close to Paris made the need for distraction of some sort or other impelling, the question of the adaptability of Cubism to other kinds of end came increasingly to the fore. Jean Cocteau, who had begun paying visits to Picasso's studio in December 1915, invited him in the spring of 1916 to collaborate on the production of a ballet, to be performed by the Ballets Russes in Paris; but the discussions on the subject, with Cocteau, the composer Erik Satie and Diaghilev, whom Picasso now met, were mainly devoted for the rest of the year to the form that the ballet should take. Picasso did not start serious work on the production until the beginning of 1917, when he developed his ideas for the costumes and decor, first in Paris and then in Rome for eight weeks, after he joined the company there. The paintings *L'Italienne* (Bürhle Collection, Zurich) and *Harlequin and Woman with a Necklace* (Centre Pompidou, Paris) have a purified quality to their coloring and the use in them of flat colored shapes, including shadowed areas, has much in common with Gris's practice that year, but they combine this with the use of the popular costuming of the Commedia dell'Arte (in the manner of a playing card) and with the placing of full-face and profile side by side in interlocking fashion—a motif that Picasso had first begun to work with consistently in this sort of way during 1915.

In *Parade* itself, which opened in Paris on May 18, the drop curtain painted by Picasso and assistants uses the familiar types of the Commedia and the circus to express, seemingly, his warm sense of affiliation with the company at large—with the motif of the winged Pegasus brought in to make the connection with his artistic inspiration, while for the costumes of the American and French managers with their megaphones, in keeping with Satie's inclusion in the musical score of such modern urban sounds as dynamos, sirens and typewriters, he adapted the technique of his Cubist paintings of 1916–17 and his constructive sculptures in wood or cardboard to bizarre and humorous effect. Ten foot high structures stalked the stage, as if in a satirical mating with the Futurist concern for movement, with the "strips" of the 1916 paintings become skyscrapers, in the case of the American Manager, and the stippled dots their windows. Apollinaire, in his program for the ballet, would christen the adaptation of Massine's choreography to the character of the costumes and scenery with the name of *surréalisme,* and proclaim it as the point of departure "for a whole series of manifestations of the New Spirit *(l'esprit nouveau)* that is making itself felt today and will certainly appeal to our best minds." And though he would not write again on current developments in the visual arts, his lecture of that November titled "The New Spirit and the Poets," which appeared posthumously *(Mercure de France,* December 1, 1918) after he died a year later of the influenza epidemic that followed the Armistice, would proclaim in exactly similar terms the virtues of experimentation, humor and above all surprise in poetry.

The reception of *Parade* at the hands of its invited audience was however a fiasco—with an odor of scandal to it, relating to the current situation of the War and the extreme nearness of the front lines to Paris—and Picasso spent much of the remainder of 1917 away from Paris, following the Ballets Russes on its visits to Madrid and Barcelona. His contributions to the ballet were in effect—as Apollinaire's view of them suggested—too stilted, or too arbitrarily whimsical for that point in time. The same can also be said of Braque's work, after he returned to painting in the summer of 1917 and through the first half of the next year. Flattening and a cut-out quality to the shapes, against a fairly neutral background, combine to give an effect of bas-relief which is cardboard-like in character; and this is true even, or perhaps especially, when the subject is a figurative one (*The Musician,* autumn 1917–summer 1918, Kunstmuseum, Basel). It is against that background that Braque returns now to the artificiality of the *collage* technique itself (*Musical Forms,* Philadelphia Museum), using a greater complexity of process in the preparatory stages of the work than in any pre-War *collage* of his, but with a greater straightforwardness and basic simplicity of result. Picasso, for his part, when he returns in 1918 to Commedia dell'Arte subjects, makes more explicit the reference in the surrounds of the figure— even where the setting remains a room interior, with paneling or dado—to the "worlds" of theater and popular entertainment; he is more stylish in the choice of colors, which give a motley effect; and the general air of the work is more dandyish, in keeping with his enhanced social status now, and his freer movement (like Satie's) in high society. All of this is particularly evident in the *Harlequin with Violin,* shown carrying the song sheet "Si Tu Veux," and the *Harlequin with Guitar* begun in 1914 which was completed at this time also (D 762), with related changes made in the head and upper torso and in the background, which turned a guitar player into a Harlequin with the addition of mask and hat. The schematically depersonalized character of the figure here—all sense of a real physical presence behind the mask and costume being excluded—allows Picasso both to recapitulate the tradition of the Harlequin figure in art, and to comment on it.

Gris, who took up the theme of the Harlequin in a comparably depersonalized fashion at the end of 1917 (C 241), arrives at a treatment of figure subjects analogous to this in his *Miller* of May 1918 and his *Man from Touraine* of that September. While the late 1917 works are busier and are more dependent on superimposed line for their detailing, he now moves to a firmness and clarity of contour that resembles Léger's at the time and is probably the basis for his report of "progress in composition" in a letter of September (to André Level, September 2). The *Miller* (C 263) done from recollection of a neighbor, who did not pose, is devoid of concrete physical details except for those—the blouse and hat, the shape of the building behind—which establish the character of the man as a type. In the *Man from Touraine* Gris works entirely from imagination, to epitomize the identity of such a man, appearing in a café setting with hat, pipe and newspaper, in the most general terms possible. And both paintings reach back to the tradition of rendering the static or seated figure in Corot and Cézanne, embracing its relevance but at the same time giving a special inflection to the way it is understood—as in the copies of Cézanne's *Portrait of Mme Cezánne* from March of this year (C 257, with related drawings)—through the rigidifications and effects of very shallow relief that are introduced.

In 1919 and on into 1920 Gris built his compositions increasingly around extended or repeated rhythms and internal "rhymes" between one markedly geometrized element and another. His working process leads to greater artificiality and impalpability in the look of the result, in the sense of its becoming increasingly apparent that he is laying out the basic armature of the composition in the form of abstract shapes, and then fitting in the recognizable details within that structure, or accommodating them to it. As if to counter that effect, and at the same time justify it in the nature of the imagery, he consistently takes now the stock figures of the Commedia dell'Arte, Harlequin and Pierrot with musical instrument or baton, as the subjects of his figure pieces, using settings that provide containing patterns of chequered tiling or plank on the floor, and a diaphanous quality of lighting, so that the figure seems to take up its pose within a niche or concavity receptively provided for it. Severini also uses at this time—in the last phase of his attachment to the group of artists around Léonce Rosenberg, before he breaks away in 1920—a similarly traditional subject matter, such as gypsy figures playing the guitar, and an underlying scheme of geometrical coordinates, but the predominant use of straight lines and angles and the superimposition of flat planes makes in his case for a distinctly more rigid effect.

Braque also makes specific use during this time of internal "rhyming" between his shapes. The effect of low relief that he gives to his still lifes in 1918—very much as in Picasso's 1914 constructions that used textured oil paint in combination with glued pieces of wood (particularly D 788)—leads on in 1919 to the provision of a darker surround or matrix which, aided by the use of black paint, causes the table top arrangements to tilt and angle back into space, as if the surface in question were moored indeterminately midway between the flat integrity of the picture plane and a full three-dimensional extension. He achieves in this way an enrichment of the basic simplifications at work, and a compensation for what would otherwise seem an overintellectualized quality to the presentation, which corresponds to the restitution of *measure* that Lhote called for in his writings on Cubism of this time.

It is in Picasso's work of 1919–20, however—as he continues to pursue the adaptability of Cubism to other ends—that a shift in the character and identity given to the image is most apparent. The severance and individuation of the elements that introduce some hint or partial analogue of reality is pushed to the point where their relationship to one another becomes quite arbitrary and piecemeal (as on a stage set); at the same time abstract shapes are treated in such a way as to bring out the power that they have in themselves to construct a sense of mass and environment. Thus it is no longer a matter of contradictions or tensions between alternative modes of depiction; rather, differences of "designation" in the two cases are effectively obliterated. This is especially apparent in the *Guitar* of late 1919

(Museum of Modern Art, New York), which can be compared with its predecessor of 1918–19 (Rijksmuseum Kröller-Müller, Otterlo): both include shadowing, sound hole and strings and a simulated peg or pin, treated as if it were holding up a piece of paper. But the sense in which the 1919 work designates a guitar is no longer the sum of the different overlaid components, all of which derive ultimately in some way from the constructive make-up of the instrument itself. Rather, certain ideas or properties that can be conceptually assimilated to the familiar idea and presence of a guitar are brought into conjunction: heraldically compartmented lozenge and harlequin colors, peg (acting like a pin) and strings (like music lines), and also indices of the various uses to which black can be put, to designate vacancy on the one hand and the solidification of shadowing on the other. This creation, furthermore, represents an enlargement and expansion of an idea that had been developed that summer, for the curtain of the current Ballets Russes production, *La Tricorne* (The Three-Cornered Hat), which tested out Picasso's inventive capacity to prolong his association with the company, by providing a suitable décor for a very different type of production: in this case a traditional and simple village tale about a Catalan miller and his wife, to music composed by Falla and with a choreography that incorporated the character of Spanish folk-dancing. For the curtain, Picasso provided a view, as if through a window, of arena and viaduct, with painted drapes drawn back to show this, and fictive wooden panels above, below and either side on which the same basic lozenge forms appeared, here both monumental and decorative at the same time in the emblematic character, and including to the left and right highly abbreviated indications, in a free graphic shorthand, of their musical signification.

Artistic theory and literary theory, then, are looking during this period for "signs," in which the "signified" becomes an immaterial *idea* or *concept*. As Raynal explained it in his 1919 pamphlet, at the point of climax in this development leading away from Symbolist practice:

> To conceive an object is, in fact to aim at knowing it in its essence, at representing it in the mind—that is to say, for this purpose, as purely as possible, as a *sign,* or a *totem* if you like, absolutely freed from all useless details . . . and just as he will capture, on canvas or in marble, not what passes but what endures, so the artist will not situate the object in a particular place, but in space, which is infinite.

Whereas the Symbolist use of the sign was basically referential in character, in the associative and suggestive "play" that was made with the character and identity of the image, in this succeeding development in contrast the sign becomes more idealistic in character, as Raynal's account implies, and also more imaginatively "distanced."

Painting provides "signs" correspondingly—of continuity and stability during the War, of reconstruction and order after it—in the sense of generating images, in the Cubist idiom and in adaptations of it, which are arranged and organized so that they can be so read. Here, in the larger pattern of wartime and post-War developments in the arts, Cubism opposes itself diametrically to the thrust and implications of the Dada movement. Dada was born of the turmoils and upheavals of the War, but in a neutral country, Switzerland, without a strong artistic tradition of its own, and by the time it reached Paris in 1918 it had come to represent, across the frontiers of Western Europe, a spirit of anarchic disruption and a post-War mood of rebellious or devil-may-care playfulness. Cendrars, who returned to Paris in the spring of 1917 and (as well as being associated with Léger) became a strong and reinforcing stimulus by the end of the decade on the emergent poetry of Surrealism, is much closer in fact to the Dada spirit, and even representative of the Parisian version of Dada, than is either Apollinarie or Satie. Their cultural position is more dandyish in contrast, and on the side of élitist taste—which Centrars and Léger both opposed. Apollinaire did not survive the War for long enough to be able to explore the possibilities here, but the emphasis in his program note for *Parade* on "charm" and "the [unsuspected] gracefulness of the modern movements," as well as "surprise" and "experiments" brings out where his inclinations lay. In the case of Erik Satie, providing the music for *Parade* was followed by a deepening involvement with Cocteau and greater freedom of access to the *haute monde* in general; by the composing in 1919 of a "symphonic drama," *Socrate,* based on the dialogues of Plato and put on under the patronage of the Princesse de Polignac, with Picasso, Braque, Gide, Valéry, Claudel and Stravinsky all attending its premiere; and by a collaboration in 1920 with Darius Milhaud on music, "not to be listened to," to be played between the acts of a Max Jacob play. Picasso's career followed a similar line of direction during those years, of cosmopolitanism and dandyism, particularly in his association with the Ballets Russes and its composers, dancers and choreographers, and in his coopting of some viable aspects of the Cubist idiom for its décors.

In its view of the role of experiment and adaptation in the arts, Cubist theory moved in this period to a narrowed, or at least narrowing, view of the kind of public attention and understanding that was possible. For Reverdy in March 1917 "pleasing the public," as aim, means and therefore result became different, was "only a matter of the public becoming educated"; but Raynal's position in his pamphlet two years later was that Cubism "ha[d] never claimed to be an art for everyone." The Cubist painters were correspondingly *for* the group, particularly during the War (with the Lyre et Palette exhibitions and the Galerie de L'Effort Moderne in 1917–18 serving as foci for a sense of togetherness) and against arrant individualism. But they were also for the individual's power of decision and choice within a group situation. This is the essential force of the passage of Raynal's chosen as epigraph for this chapter. The "new notation" developed in the quest for artistic truth, insofar as it was "not exactly comfortable"—with any kind of a larger audience—depended, if there was to be "improvement," on the judgment and the sense of tradition that the individual artist exhibited, in the means that he chose.

The word *judicious* that is used here is one that carries connotations of both cultural discretion and restraint (working in favor of control, stability, *mesure,* as opposed to impulsive spontaneity); and also of knowing and savant perspicacity (working to sift out what is truly valid and productive in the way of experiment from what leads to a dead end). The Cubist artist, in the work of creation that he represents, or should ideally represent, comes to stand in this way for a clarifying and reordering of the complementary claims of intelligence and sensibility; but with a growing implication during this phase that there is a strong component of cultural awareness and critical discernment to his being (as in T. S. Eliot's thinking of the time) in a position to contribute in this way. The fundamental opposition between "Apollonian" and "Dionysian" impulses in artistic creation which had come into discussion before the War—as Nietzsche's contrast of the two in *The Birth of Tragedy* became popularized—and the drawing up of lines between them can be said in this way to have continued in force into the post-War period; but with the difference that the choice is now taken to be a matter of socio-cultural affiliation and leanings on the artist's part, rather than a strictly intellectual one. And it is here that the attribution of a position of "privilege" to the artist, or the artist's claiming of one, in the directions that he sees himself as taking and the goals that he sets himself, becomes a significant consideration, entering into the interpretation given to a development such as Cubism.

The concept of "privilege," or of a "privileged status," introduced in this connection is a philosophical one, which has nothing inherently to do with socio-economic or class-based forms of privilege (though success for a modern artist in these latter respects may well lead to a higher valuation or putting forward of himself here). In a specialized and recent usage having to do with the limits and bases of knowledge and perception in all fields, including the arts, to speak of a person as being in a "privileged position," or in a position of "privileged access," means that the person is in a position to know or be aware of something, that others are not comparably in a position to know or be aware of. So, to claim (as Kahnweiler does) that there is a *unity* to be apprehended in the Cubism of Picasso and Braque, or to write (as Raynal does) of the achievement of *certainty* in Cubist paintings—both of which are culturally and socially loaded terms—is to choose and use those terms with the implication of speaking from a privileged position as to how they apply there. The qualities in question are not just in the beholder's eye. Nor, obviously, is there an objective and generally accessible basis for speaking of their presence, in the sense that representative members of a larger public with access to the paintings would recognize this to be right and say the same themselves. But it then becomes appropriate to ask—as part of the more general issue (explored in chap. 5), of the bases on which the artist's claims to a privileged status may rest—from what sort of a privileged position the attribution of those qualities is made. Most particularly, there is the question of the degree to which, or the respects in which, the artist himself may assume or have ascribed to him a position of authority here, regarding the character of his creations and the way in which they are viewed and read.

One way in which, in the post-War phase of Cubism, the artist tended to assume a privileged position concerns the direction of development of his art, and the application to it of an aesthetic that was in the air at the time. Thus, whereas Braque in one of the maxims of his published in 1917 asserted that the inclusion of *papiers collés* in his drawings had provided him with "a kind of certainty," Raynal would affirm more explicitly and generally two years later that to pursue the conceptual path of Cubist painting meant that "the picture would offer a guarantee of certainty in itself." The idea put forward in this way is of a *consistency* to Cubist art, that is *shown* rather than left to be sensed on the part of the viewer. Gris in his first published statement of early 1919, sent in to the Italian periodical *Valori Plastici* for its special issue on French Cubism, would affirm correspondingly his belief that "we can produce [a poetic effect] with beautiful elements [rather than beautiful models or subjects]; for those of the intellect [*l'esprit*] are certainly the most beautiful." To work with beautiful elements was to build into one's work accordingly the consistencies that could generate a higher or more surpassing kind of beauty; and the work was "poetic" to the degree that the artist inculcated and strove intellectually for that result.

A second respect in which the artist's claim to a position of privilege asserted itself now has to do with the recognition or identification of the elements included in the paintings and the corresponding nature of the viewer's response to them. Here, Kahnweiler introduced a very explicit formulation into his text on Cubism, in his discussion of the way in which, alongside Picasso's "piercing of the closed form" in 1910, Braque had begun the introduction of "undistorted real objects" into the paintings. "When real details are thus introduced," he wrote, "the result is a stimulus which carries with it memory images." In combination with the "scheme of forms," these images "construct the finished object in the mind." Hence, as a result of the apprehended unity of the work, the "desired physical representation" comes into being in the spectator's mind. Kahnweiler went on to support this contention, as to what takes place perceptually, with the assertion that it was not in geometric forms that the "visual conception desired by the painter" resided, "but rather in the representation of the reproduced objects." Through the way in which he did this representing, therefore, the artist could assure that "sensory illusions" were banished or circumvented, and that the viewer was led towards "seeing the represented things objectively."

In actuality, the artist (or his spokesman) has no effective way of disciplining or restraining viewers from seeing "in" the work whatever they might be stimulated into believing that it contains or shows. The workings of imagination and suggestion that lead to that kind of "seeing," both in the way they are prompted and in the kinds of comment that they elicit, are basically separate and distinct from those processes that lead the viewer towards the recognition and identification of particular objects (see Part Two, chap. 6); but the notion of the artist's authority or power to "objectivate" here on the viewer's behalf offers a promise of controlling those forms of response to Cubist art in the viewer that would otherwise risk getting out of hand. Certaintly Gris seems to have thought of himself increasingly during this phase as in a position to exercise that kind of control or authority over the effect of his work on the viewer. In discussing his progress in a letter to Kahnweiler of December 1915 he had juxtaposed the potential for "becoming more concrete and concise" that he found in his work with the feeling on his part that it ought also to have a "sensitive and sensuous side" to it, and regretted that he had not so far to his satisfaction been able to "find room" for the latter. Contrastingly, in August 1919, the year before Kahnweiler's return to Paris, he wrote to him of having replaced a "too brutal and descriptive reality" in the rendering of objects with a treatment that could be considered more "poetic" in its effect. He hoped for the future, as he now put it, to "express very precisely, and by means of pure intellectual elements, an imaginary reality" (letter of August 25)—as if, by the choice of objects that he adopted and the way in which he marshaled them, he could render it unmistakeable to the viewer what kind of "reality" it was. For "how can you control and make sense of your representational liberties," he said in the same letter, opposing himself to abstract painters, "when you have no plastic intentions?"

The appeal to clarity and order came to be vested in this way in a set of aesthetic mandates that the individual stood in a position to enforce and reinforce. And by 1920, tradition itself had come to be thought of increasingly, in both painting and poetry, as exercising a delimiting, and impersonal kind of authority over the unruly and disjunctive impulses of the individual: as in Pound's new poetic thinking and in T. S. Eliot's aesthetic, as with Jacques Rivière and his art critic André Lhote. The French tradition was seen as one of consistency and of adaptability which in a broadly "classical" mould, both intellectually and pictorially, could reconcile together conflicting opposites: most especially in the case of Cubism the rival claims of representation and structure, which were to be taken as having been handed down from the pre-War to the post-War scene. This is the position that Kahnweiler's book *The Rise of Cubism* supported and explained when it came out in 1920: as its opening chapter states, "The nature of the new painting is clearly characterized as representational as well as structural. . . . Representation and structure conflict. Their reconciliation by the new painting and the stages along the road to this goal are the subject of this work." Out of the wartime and post-War climate of Cubism, in sum, to which it belongs in its deepest affinities, the idea of such a reconciliation was now read back into the past, as a crucial motivating principle.

4 Consolidation and Orthodoxy, 1920–1925

> We see, then, the true Cubists continuing their work imperturbably; we see them also continuing their influence on men's minds; while the others are plundering the neighboring orchards, they keep steadily on.
>
> Amedée Ozenfant and Charles-Edouard Jeanneret,
> *La Peinture Moderne*

With the publication of Kahnweiler's book *Der Weg zum Kubismus* (The Rise of Cubism) in 1920, Cubism had begun to develop its own conceptual history. It was a history that had its acknowledged leaders, Picasso and Braque, for whom Kahnweiler began acting as dealer again after he returned to Paris in the spring of 1920. Gris would be added as the third key figure soon after, with the publication by Maurice Raynal of a short monograph illustrating twenty of his paintings, and a long article on his work in 1921 (*L'Esprit Nouveau*, February), though Kahnweiler, who signed a fresh contract with Gris on his return, would not write about him until after his death in 1927.

It was at this point in time also that Cubism was forced to deal with the challenge of an emergent and rival development, that of Purism, and in particular to expand upon the framework of its own conceptual history in order to meet that challenge. One of the founders of Purism, the painter Amédée Ozenfant, had already been somewhat critical of Cubism in the last number of the wartime periodical *L'Elan*, which he edited in 1915–16. In 1918 he joined the architect and designer Charles-Edouard Jeanneret, later to call himself Le Corbusier, to produce a short booklet entitled *Après le Cubisme*, with sections devoted to both architecture and painting. The term Purism was introduced in its pages, but it was not until 1920 that the axioms and aesthetic principles that they formulated in that connection became the basis for the production, by both of them, of paintings that were projected and organized correspondingly. They used the periodical *L'Esprit Nouveau*, founded in November 1920, as their organ of publication and exposition over the next five years, and in 1925 brought together the larger argument that they had presented there into the form of an illustrated book entitled *La Peinture Moderne*.

The basic reason that Purism posed a challenge to Cubism, and most particularly to Juan Gris, was not that it was critical of some of the supposed "insufficiencies" of the Cubist language—since such criticisms were in the air by 1918–19, as described in the last chapter—but that it offered a built-in sense of rivalry, as to where Cubism led. The strong philosophical input that Purism used to support its claims, for the existence of immutable laws governing the achievement of strictness, order and harmony, in art or in architecture, meant that in extending in that light the tendencies of wartime and post-War Cubism towards purification and geometrization, it could profess to be doing so on a more rigorous and controlled basis. Ozenfant and Jeanneret believed, in addition, in the role and example of machinery in modern life, and this is reflected in their paintings from 1920 on not only in the regularized and often modular geometry of their compositions, but also in the choice of everyday familiar and manufactured objects for imagery, and the treatment of them in a way that emphasizes their stereotyped character. While this way of working had its origin in Cubism, and particularly in Gris's work of 1914–16, the effect and temper are very different, pointing in a more solidified and depersonalized direction.

Apart from the claims it laid to a more "universal" kind of language, appropriate to the age of the machine, Purism also affirmed its commitment to a certain line of tradition in the art of the past, and specifically in French art. In contrast to the more general and recuperative idea of tradition brought up in the last chapter, and also the tenor of reconstruction and redirection that is built into such international tendencies, emergent towards 1925, as Surrealism and Constructivism, the line in question was one that included Jean Fouquet from the fifteenth century, Poussin, Ingres and Corot. In other words, individual features and period qualities of style were subsumed completely for definitional purposes to the notion that French painting over the centuries could be seen to embody and show forth, in the forms of organization adopted, clearcut "laws" of pictoral ordering. Those artists of the past were all made the subjects of articles in *L'Esprit Nouveau* and to them was added, from the later nineteenth century, the example of Cézanne, seen now primarily in terms of the geometrizing tendencies of his art; and also increasingly, from 1920 on, the example of Seurat, seen in terms of the modular and harmonic proportions to be discovered in his work. The Cubists were certainly anything but strangers to those particular exemplars in French art of the past, from far back in their careers, and they had during the War and after their own particular interests in, or inclinations towards, each of those earlier masters, as manifested in drawn and painted copies that each made between 1916 and 1925. They were equally in a position to enjoy the progressive reopening of the main galleries of the Louvre after the Armistice, which brought on display in January

1920 the French collection that included the masterpieces of Fouquet, Poussin and Corot, and gave opportunity to appreciate their qualities to the full after the wartime closure. But the tradition that the Purists invoked was more concentrated in its nature and also had a more authoritarian cast to it.

Such a linking of concentration and control with the authority of tradition also makes its appearance in T. S. Eliot's critical writings of the early 1920s. Whether he is considering the development of English poetry since the Renaissance and the "dissociation of sensibility" that can be supposed to have set in during that time, or more generally discussing European literature—as in his introduction of the role of "thought" in Dante and in Shakespeare, seen in relation to the character of their audiences—this is in fact the main theme in the newly social and political orientation of his thinking now; and what is explicit here in his critical pronouncements also applies equally to his own practice as a poet, most notably in *The Waste Land* as it came out in its final, revised form in 1922. It is most particularly in his essay "The Function of Criticism," published in 1923, that he takes up again the implications of his 1919 essay, "Tradition and Individual Talent," which was referred to in the last chapter. Quoting at the beginning one of its key passages, he expands upon it by writing of there being "something outside of the artist to which he owes allegiance . . . a common inheritance and a common cause," which forms the basis for an "unconscious community between the artists of a particular time." And he goes on to introduce the idea of "Classicism" and defines the differences, in his perception, between it and Romanticism by reference to the loss of a true and embracing socio-cultural sense of community in the modern world: the cult of the individual's feelings and sensations, as fostered and exacerbated by Romanticism, means that it stands aesthetically for what is fragmentary, immature (or childlike) and chaotic; whereas Classicism, contrastingly, holds out the promise of compensating for the underlying situation of loss by the offering of works that are complete, adult and orderly. The adoption here of emotional detachment or disinterest as a positive aesthetic value in itself, and the implication that the modern cultural situation necessarily sets those artists who are highly gifted apart from the remainder represent values that are also prominent in Maurice Raynal's writings of the early 1920s, especially those devoted to Picasso.

Unquestionably T. E. Hulme's ideas, as discussed in the last chapter, were once again influential upon T. S. Eliot's outlook now, and especially on the more prescriptive aspect of these writings of his. Eliot continued, as he had already in scattered writings of 1919–1920, to make note of Hulme's poetry as worth more attention than it had received, making reference in the essay of 1923 cited to its particular qualities of diction. But it was in his own periodical *The Criterion*, which he founded and edited from October 1922, that he gave recognition in a renewed way to Hulme as a thinker, immediately upon the appearance in 1924 of *Speculations,* the volume which brought together in collected form Hulme's unpublished essays and other writings in philosophy and aesthetics. Noting its "very great significance," even though it was "unlikely to meet with understanding," in his "Commentary" of April 24 that year, Eliot called Hulme "a forerunner of a new attitude of mind, which should be the twentieth century mind, if the twentieth century is to have a mind of its own"; and he went on to identify him as a "classical, reactionary and revolutionary" figure who represented "the antipodes of the eclectic, tolerant and democratic mind of the end of the last century." He found Hulme's closest affinities as a thinker to lie in France, in the writings of the *Action française* group (Maurras, Lasserre and Sorel), thereby making it plain that he was responding specifically to the text titled "Romanticism and Classicism," included in *Speculations,* which he could not previously have known and in which these writers are referred to.

Hulme had planned towards 1915 a series of pamphlets dealing combatively with the history of Western thought and philosophy, and this was his draft for one of them, directed against Romanticism. The companion essay "Humanism and the Religious Attitude" (which had been published in *The New Age* in December 1915, but in installments and under his initials only) would exercise a comparable influence as a text on Eliot's religious thinking; but that would come later, from about 1929 into the 1930s, as shown in passages that Eliot chose to quote then. In the mid-1920s, in contrast, it was to Hulme's ideal of detached and serene aesthetic contemplation and to his advocacy of a "new classicism," validated by the controls of reason, that Eliot was drawn, on the social and political side of his critical sympathies.

The editor of *Speculations* in 1924 and the author of a short introduction to it was Herbert Read, who also published the "Notes on Language and Style" from amongst Hulme's papers in Eliot's *Criterion* in July 1925. Read was primarily concerned at this time, as a poet and critical theorist, with literature, but he was becoming increasingly drawn to the field of art, and especially modern art, that he would make his own after 1930, and he was led by Hulme's writings to the basic distinction formulated by Wilhelm Worringer and explicated by Hulme in the essay "Modern Art and its Philosophy" (published in *Speculations*) between "two different kinds of art," corresponding to different historical periods and cultures:

> You have [in Hulme's words] first of all the art which is natural to you, Greek art and modern art since the Renaissance. In these arts the lines are soft and vital. You have other arts like Egyptian, Indian and Byzantine where everything tends to be angular, where

curves tend to be hard and geometrical, where the representation of the human body, for example, is often entirely non-vital, and distorted to fit into stiff lines and cubical shapes of various kinds.

The difference was, that while Worringer viewed these contrasting tendencies in a balanced and non-judgmental historical perspective, Hulme in that essay linked the emergent geometrical or abstract tendency which he found in the art of his time with the "break-up" now of the basic "humanism," of world-attitude or *Weltanschauung,* that had prevailed since the Renaissance.

In developing his argument here in "Romanticism and Classicism," Hulme identified Romanticism as representing the last efflorescence of that humanistic attitude, and as having now after a hundred years of ascendancy, by a natural process of exhaustion, run dry. Taking issue especially with Ruskin's notion of the imagination and the corresponding idea of feeling or emotion as an expansive reaching out of the individual towards the infinite—which he associated with Romanticism—he advocated in opposition to this not just a different way of seeing on the artist's part, but an effect of *exactness* based upon *concentration;* as in the example (which he had already used in writing on Bergson's art theory) of selecting, from amongst a variety of pieces of wood with flat curvature—which he calls "architect's curves"—the one that is "exact" for an "object or idea in the mind." T. S. Eliot would, in a preface of 1924 to a book that he never wrote ("Four Elizabethan Dramatists") use very similar phrasing to affirm that "no artist produces great art by a deliberate attempt to express his personality"; rather, this is done by "concentrating upon a task which is a task in the same sense as the making of an efficient engine or the tuning of a jug or a table-leg." Again, Hulme in that essay specifies the "conception of a limit" and a "holding back [or] reservation" as fundamental to his notion of the "classical"; denying the contrast with the romantic as being simply one "between restraint and exuberance," he refers to Nietzsche in order to distinguish as he did between "two kinds of classicism, the static and the dynamic." And towards the end of the essay he brings in Bergsonian "intuition" as the agent and instrument of *synthesis* in the creative process: building upon the powers of analysis of the intellect, but also going beyond them.

Herbert Read, who knew about Bergson's and Sorel's writings by 1916 and also about Futurism and Imagism, became a writer on poetic theory towards the end of the War. He issued the first number of the periodical *Art and Letters* in July 1917, with Frank Rutter the art critic as its editor while he was still in service, met Ezra Pound the following year, and began to publish T. S. Eliot's poetry and criticism in 1918–19 while dissenting on aesthetic grounds from the supporting view of "tradition"; but it was not until 1923–25, the period of his work on Hulme's papers, that—particularly in his contributions to *The Criterion*—he moved to an advocacy of "control," "intellect" and "reason" that was similar to Eliot's own. His adoption from the "Romanticism and Classicism" essay of the terms "dry" and "hard" for poetry led on to his acceptance and use of the basic distinction set out there, and also led him back to the contribution of Worringer himself to its formulation: he would provide an introduction to *Form in Gothic,* the English translation of Worringer that came out in 1927, and would quote extensively there from Hulme's exposition of Worringer's basic polarity in *Abstraction and Empathy* (not translated till much later) between an "organic" or "vital" tendency in art and an "abstract" or "geometric" one. As he devoted himself increasingly, into the 1930s, to the classifying of modern art movements on the basis of aesthetic directions, corresponding to philosophical attitudes, Read would incline on the whole towards "abstract," formalistic tendencies, both historically and in the present, and he stands out in that sense as the truest continuer of Hulme's line of thought in England. But in the essays that he brought together in 1926 as *Reason and Romanticism,* it is also clear that he believed in the ultimate reconcilability of subjectivity of feeling and objectivity in form, through the restraining force of reason; and in the January 1925 essay for *The Criterion* on "Psychoanalysis and the Critic" which he reprinted there, he made the potentiality of reconciliation explicit by taking up Jung's antithesis of introversion and extroversion, in his *Psychological Types*—the 1924 English translation of a text that was of growing moment at this time to the Surrealists, for its fit with their concerns, but which in Jung's own interpretation offered a correspondence to Worringer's basic polarity.

An analogous gravitation at this time towards emphasizing the claims of rationality and exactness is to be found in the development of the Purist aesthetic between 1918 and 1925, and the key terms are often the same. There had been rather little pertaining to Cubism in Amedeé Ozenfant's wartime periodical *L'Elan,* except for some related drawings by Ozenfant and his friends and some experiments in typography which were probably inspired by Apollinaire's *Calligrammes,* but in his "Notes on Cubism" in the final issue (December 1916), while praising Cubism for "cleansing the plastic language," Ozenfant criticized it for being too decorative, using too much pseudo-scientific jargon and being élitist and ivory-towerish. Art should, rather than that, evoke "emotion" and express the "organic laws of nature." Ozenfant's general outlook at this time is reflected in the exhibition that he organized with André Salmon, including artists who also appeared—along with Jacob, Salmon and Riciotto Canudo—in the first numbers of *L'Elan:* Gleizes and Metzinger, Lhote and Severini. But his meeting the following year with Jean-

neret sharpened immediately his leaning, based on a strong understanding of mechanics and a deep knowledge of the history of
science, towards efficiency and practicality. In the "manifesto" of
Purism which they issued together in October 1918, *Après le
Cubisme,* the collaboration was basically one in which each contributed separate chapters: Ozenfant those reflecting his knowledge of
recent painting, particularly Cubism, into which his criticism of its
theory could be incorporated; Jeanneret those involving architecture.
But the interaction was not quite that simple, insofar as Ozenfant's
inclination had been up to then to stress freedom within the necessary
formal constraints and oppose Cubism for being too rigid and rigorous; whereas Jeanneret pushed him, and the manifesto as a whole in
consequence, towards his own beliefs in absolute laws of harmony
and reliance on geometry or numbers, taking responsibility correspondingly for those sections in which the modern factory machine is
introduced, as representing order and clarity. Together, they brand as
"Romantic" accordingly any modernist who does not extract from the
new machine world (such as steamships) what is both permanent and
balanced, and they stress the appropriateness to the new collective
and industrialized society of the processes of "generalization" and of
"synthesis."

In November 1918, to accompany the appearance of the text, the
two of them held a small joint exhibition of their work at the Galerie
Thomas. Although in *Après le Cubisme* they argued in the third chapter for a hierarchy in types of subject matter, with the human figure at
the top, landscape below that, and inorganic forms at the bottom, the
works exhibited concentrated exclusively on still life subjects, with
the human figure entirely missing, and this was again a turn of direction for which Jeanneret was responsible. The effect in these paintings is of simplification and "purity" insofar as the objects are kept
few and as distinct as possible from one another, the lighting is cool
and the colors limited; while an effect of solidity is preserved by the
use of contours that are essentially (as in architectural practice) of a
drawn rather than painted kind.

By 1920–21 Ozenfant and Jeanneret had founded their own periodical, *L'Esprit Nouveau,* which ran through 1925. The formal
insufficiences of Cubism continued to be brought out in the early
issues, but by the third one they were talking of *"le bon Cubisme"*
with its positive qualities of order and construction, and would also
emphasize the contributions of the major figures in regular articles on
the subject. In their most recent paintings, which they exhibited at
the Galerie Druet in February 1921, those of 1920 were marked by an
increasing mechanical and logical emphasis. Typically, as in Jeanneret's *Still Life with a Pile of Plates* of 1920 (Kunstmuseum, Basel)
the table top objects are made to look more like the funnels and
machinery of a ship's deck than like familiar domestic entities; the

sense of scale and simplifications of spatial environment being like those in Leger's work of this time. Their larger justification for such a combination of the representational and abstract is given in an article of Ozenfant's on "Picasso and the Painting of Today" (*L'Esprit Nouveau,* 13, 1921): the fact that, as in Cubism, the "organization of disorganized forms can act directly on our minds through our senses, without involving the sensations associated with the representation of human figures" . . . makes it a suitable medium "for speculative emotions." But, as in Picasso's current combination of Cubism with figurative painting, the possibility of being able to combine the two lies freely open to each individual artist.

Cubism could be regarded in this way, towards 1925, as more of a respected and necessary antecedent; but insofar as Purism entailed a separate "grammar" of its own, the regulation of the laws governing that grammar, and their controlled application became all the more essential tasks. As Ozenfant and Jeanneret put it in an article of late 1925, "Personal Ideas" (*L'Esprit Nouveau,* 27), which appeared as a section of their book:

> Purist composition proceeds from Cubist composition, but in Cubism . . . the object is modified, often in excess, to provide for its organization in the picture; Purism considers it of importance to preserve the structural norms *(normes de constitution)* of the objects. It does not assume the right to transform these beyond a certain limit.

The "orthodoxy" of their didactic position here, as it may be termed, and the lines of inheritance in the French tradition that they trace leading up to it are, in fact, much less anti-Romantic and anti-humanistic than they would appear to be; for their legislative prescriptiveness is accompanied by a still "inspirational" theory of individual creativity, and by a wishful idealism that, like T. S. Eliot's critical position, sets an enclosing "frame" around the work of art, as instrument or agent of consciousness. As Ozenfant and Jeanneret put it in their book of 1925 which concludes this phase, *La Peinture Moderne:* "as each artist seeks to express his personality," the language of Cubism "stays pure with those whose ideal can be expressed by pure means."

The response of Cubism to all this is recorded, in the case of Juan Gris, in the form of conversations that took place between him and Ozenfant in 1920–21, and in the shape of a drawing that he did in Ozenfant's studio on one of those occasions (April 15, 1920), in order to explain how exactly he solidified objects. In this drawing, of a carafe, he stressed the squaring of the shoulders and transformed the convex base and the round hole at the top into two triangles. In one of the conversations later recalled by Ozenfant, Gris claimed correspondingly that the forms in his paintings represented "illusions," rather than actual objects; his pictures, in being made up of such "fictional, imaginary, totally invented" forms, were "pure poems" and not to be judged as if they contained objects. When Ozenfant and Jeanneret's article "Le Purisme" came out in the fourth number of *L'Esprit Nouveau,* early the following year—one issue before the appearance there in February, over Ozenfant's pseudonym "Vauvrecy," of a biographical statement about Gris and a short statement of his own—Gris found Cubism criticized for showing only the "accidental aspects" of objects and for its "fantastic and arbitrary forms," including "triangular bottles" in association with "conic glasses." He replied patiently to Ozenfant in late March that his choice of canvas size and methods of working did in fact allow him compositional flexibility, and that there was still a "substantial" character to the objects that he painted, but he was irked enough to complain to Kahnweiler more succinctly about the content of the piece, saying that he found it "grotesque to talk of a craftsman copying the objects in one of my pictures. More particularly since a picture should not be a plan which can be executed in three dimensions. If Picasso ever started this hare [as he had in a statement of 1908 reported by Kahnweiler, see chap. 1] so much the worse for him!" (letters of March 25 and 30, 1921). Clearly Gris, whose earlier work (especially that of 1914–16) was now making a direct contribution to Ozenfant's and Jeanneret's treatment of the object, was sensitive to being judged the more arbitrary and formulaic for the manner in which, according to the words of his which Ozenfant printed, he made "a bottle—a particular bottle" out of a cylinder. And in his desire to reconcile the claims of "poetry" with a more extended geometry of shape and contour, now that he was working regularly towards the object, rather than away from it, he found himself in competition with an aesthetic that aspired to a more purely functional perfection.

The nature of the Cubist aesthetic in this phase can be characterized more broadly by putting into place side by side how Cézanne's art was seen at the time and the way in which Negro art was viewed. Kahnweiler had introduced the discussion of both into the context of Cubism in his 1920 book; they were the only forms of art other than Cubism referred to there (apart from the additional and critical chapter on Futurism at the close). Both were also the focus of a renewal or broadening of discussion now: Negro art formed the subject of an inquiry conducted by the Parisian periodical *Action,* which was published in April 1920, and in December of that year an exhibition of Cézanne's work—the first held in Paris since 1914, including thirty three oil paintings and some watercolors—opened at the Galerie Bernheim-Jeune.

Cézanne appeared in Kahnweiler's book as the "father of the entire new art," by virtue of his "return to structure"; as his example came to be understood in the pre-Cubist phase, between 1906 and 1908, his concentration on outdoor objects as affected by light allowed " a more penetrating delineation of their forms without, however, destroying their fidelity to nature" (chaps. 2–3). T. E. Hulme in his 1914 lecture on Modern Art, which would be published in 1924, similarly took the "strongly accentuated" and "geometric" character of Cézanne's forms as marking out a "tendency towards abstraction," based on "research into nature," that was to be carried forward in pre-War Cubism. In between those dates of publication, however, Emile Bernard, who had originally published in 1907 Cézanne's famous statement, made in a letter to him of April 1904, about *treating* nature "by means of the sphere, the cylinder and the cone," and had offered a separate commentary of his own explaining the meaning of this to be that nature should be *reduced* to those particular forms (*Mercure de France,* October 1 and 15, 1907), boldly changed the tenor of that interpretation—which Hulme had adopted—by substituting, in an article which he brought out in 1921 (*Mercure de France,* June 1) concerning a conversation of his with Cézanne, the very different idea that "one should begin by studying geometric forms" and by adding the example of the cube.

At about the same time Gino Severini was writing a two-part article on "Cézanne and Cézannism" which came out, somewhat belatedly, in *L'Esprit Nouveau* at the end of 1921 (nos. 11–12 and 13, November–December). In their piece of January there on Purism, Ozenfant and Jeanneret had been critical of Cézanne, referring to him as a confused and troubled being who practised an "obstinate, maniacal search for volume" and was like an orchestra leader trying to make musical sounds on the wrong instrument. Severini, for his part, rejected altogether the "classical tendency" in Cézanne which he and "everyone else" had believed in and which he associated with the two other best-known recorded statements of Cézanne's, the one about "redo[ing] Poussin after nature" and the desire expressed "to become classical again through nature, that is through sensation." As he put it in the section of his 1921 book *Du Cubisme au Classicisme* that dealt with the same subject, "one does not become classical by sensation, but by the mind": the work of art must commence by analysis of *cause* (not *effect*) and construction requires method, not vague general notions. Gris's comment upon this would be (letter to Raynal of January 3, 1922) that Severini had purloined the "deductive" theory and even the example of turning a cylinder into a bottle from his own statement in that periodical. "Empiricism," a term which Severini brought in, was linked with Cubism by Léonce Rosenberg in the title of a pamphlet that he published in 1921, consisting of brief philosophical aphorisms; but for Severini it was associated in Cézanne's late work with the application of instinct to the "realization" of his sensations, rather than constituting a genuinely regulative principle.

"Negro art," as it was then called, was referred to by Kahnweiler in his book first of all as the source of inspiration for Picasso's painted figures of 1908 "resembling Congo sculptures," and again for the relevance to Picasso's and Braque's work of 1913–14 of the way in which "real details," in the form of painted eyes and mouth and raffia hair, were added to Ivory Coast dance masks, to constitute "a tight formal scheme of plastic primeval force." In the article that he published in 1919, "The Essence of Sculpture" (*Feuer,* November–December) Kahnweiler related this practice in negro sculpture—including also the addition of clothing or necklaces—to the "geometric rigor" that the art had attained, in its "degree of deformation" corresponding to the "spiritual life of the era." T. E. Hulme in his 1914 lecture rather similarly explained the "romantic return to barbarous and primitive art" in the early stages of the modern movement in terms of the geometric and structural tendencies that that art had in common with the "archaic" arts of the past (including the early Greek and the Byzantine). In 1915 there appeared the first scholarly publication on African sculpture, the *Negerplastik* of the German poet Carl Einstein, a friend of Kahnweiler's with whom Gris would correspond about his work in 1923; in 1916 the New York critic Marius de Zayas (see chap. 1) made its influence on modern art into the theme of a short book, and the following year in Paris the gallery owner Paul Guillaume brought out a documentary contribution, *Sculptures nègres,* consisting of twenty-four photographs, a text by him and an introductory essay by Apollinaire. When in a corresponding piece for *Les Arts à Paris,* the advertising publication of the gallery ("African and Oceanic Sculptures," July 15, 1918), Apollinaire explained the attractions of this "new field of exploration" and curiosity, he still stressed the outlandishness, "very far removed from our conceptions," of these "fetishes which. . . . are all related to the religious passion"; and he characterized the power of their "plastic form" and its influence on modern artists as relating to the "first principles" of hieratic presentation found in Egyptian and early Greek sculpture—which he thought that they might have influenced!—rather than as matching itself against the "models of classical antiquity." But he also felt that it was "high time . . . to arrive at a rational classification of them."

By the early 1920s "melanomania," as Apollinaire had called it—in a variant of his text for the Guillaume publication (*Mercure de France,* April 1, 1917) which was now reprinted by the periodical *Action* in the special issue on the subject for which it sought current opinions—had become not just a growing, but a rapidly expanding fashion; it was alternatively known in its popularized or cultist forms as "negromania," a term embracing the enthusiasm for negro jazz, which had begun equally around 1917. In an article "Negro Art" which appeared in translation early in 1920, in the English art historical journal *The Burlington Magazine,* André Salmon traced the growth of interest, from the late nineteenth century on, and referred to the exhibition of it held at a Paris gallery the previous year. Illustrating its quality of "naked beauty" with examples from the Guillaume collection and from the British Museum, he referred to the sculptor's "plastic translation" of emotion, preferably at its most intense instant, in the interpretation of the facial features and to the anti-classical orientation that was involved. He also wrote of a "premeditated harmony of the whole" in some examples, and a finding of "purity" here, under the "lesson" of Cézanne. Gris, in his response of that time to the *Action* inquiry, wrote similarly of how negro sculptures provided striking proof of "the possibilities of an anti-idealistic art. Animated by a religious spirit, they are diverse and [yet] precise manifestations of great principles and universal ideas." The shift here is away from stressing the "strange" and "primeval" potency that the sculpture possesses, corresponding to its fetishistic origins of a darkly "savage" kind, and towards an emphasis on those communal or generalizable features which, as in other forms of "translation" into an autotelic sculptural language, can be taken on their own evidence as rational and purposive in character. Part of the explanation for this interpretative shift can be taken to lie, quite simply, in the spread of interest itself. As the number of examples of such sculpture that were known or accessible multiplied, it was natural that shared features underling the manifest variety should be sought, and that those features in turn should bring up issues of race, custom and religion. From Cendrars' *Anthologie nègre,* a gathering of legend, folk tales, poetry, song and dance from all over the world—undertaken in 1920, with the first of three projected volumes coming out in 1921—it is apparent that the very processes of anthologizing and collecting led that way; they put into juxtaposition (like T. S. Eliot's *The Waste Land*) diversified examples of a cultural and social "otherness." But it is also true that to rationalize the structural principles underlying such artefacts was to move the interested public from a mere sense of the work as "alien" to a more focused understanding of it.

Separately and together, these reinterpretations of the period can be seen in relation to the feeling amongst the Cubists now of a loss of community. The immediate causes of that feeling were discernible all across the art scene. Personal ties were no longer efficacious as a form of support, and any sense, even lingering, of there being a common cause that Cubism as a label represented was disastrously hit by the low prices fetched in some cases at the auction sales of Kahnweiler's sequestered holdings in 1921–23. Picasso and Braque had long since gone their own separate ways, with a personal coldness between them since the War. Gris at Céret in the winter of 1921 and on into the spring of 1922 was ridden with intense feelings of isolation (letters to Kahnweiler, especially those of December 11 and February 5); having been hospitalized in 1920 with the illness which would turn into pleurisy, he was increasingly subject to fits of depression and only accepted an invitation from Diaghilev in 1922 to work on a production for the Ballets Russes—after a similar project had fallen through the previous year, with the commission ultimately going to Picasso—because of a wish that he admitted to better his reputation thereby. The exhibition of the Indépendants that opened in February 1920 offered what was probably the last opportunity for an appearance of unity, but both its hanging and the favorable press notices given to Picasso, Braque, Léger and Metzinger were a cause of jealousies and backbiting (letter of Gris, January 31). The attempt by Albert Gleizes in 1919 to revive the Section d'Or in a new version of its pre-War form led to an exhibition at the Galerie de la Boétie in March 1920 which traveled to Holland and Belgium and to Rome, but it was equally unsuccessful as a group effort.

Through the activities and publications of his Galerie de L'Effort Moderne and through group exhibitions that he organized, Léonce Rosenberg made efforts to fill the gap. But he made the mistake of purchasing Purist paintings of Ozenfant's and Jeanneret's from their February 1921 exhibition, and then including them with Cubist work, and a Mondrian of 1921 also, in an exhibition at his own gallery; Gris had already by that time broken off his contractual relation with him as a dealer, only to hear now of an exhibition of his work at the gallery, which was in fact of earlier canvases. Having planned in 1919 a series of monographs on his artists, which would include texts by Raynal on Picasso, Gris and Léger (all of which appeared), by Bissière on Braque and by Severini on himself, Rosenberg withdrew the offer to the latter because of dissatisfaction with the use of traditional perspective in his most recent work. Ozenfant and Jeanneret then expressed interest in the book that Severini had decided to produce himself, *Du Cubisme au Classicisme,* but after a short period of friendly contact the relationship fell off—nominally because of delay in their publishing the article of Severini's on Cézanne referred to. Evidently Severini was attracted to the range of subjects that their periodical covered, including long pieces on the main figures of Cubism, but ended up feeling that their commitment was ultimately a separatist one. Rosenberg did succeed in bringing the major Cubists together in the exhibition that he organized at the Galerie Moos in Geneva in 1920, for which he used his "Cubism and Tradition" as introductory text; but there and again in an exhibition of 1925 the labels used for this purpose ("Young French Painting"; "The Art of Today") had, like the Section d'Or label used for exhibition purposes in those same years, no other merit in their favor than convenience.

It is understandable, therefore, that a regulatory principle that stressed the role of prior mental ordering, and especially geometric ordering, in the art should prove appealing, particularly in counteraction to the incursions of Purism. It allowed Cézanne's treatment of the object to appear as architectonic and solidifying, without being mechanical in character. Similarly structure as a device of linkage and community between disparate idioms, including the abstract and the figurative, provided an avenue of public access to the work, as in Negro sculpture, without its being necessary to posit that the experience of art, in order to bring people together, had to serve as the reflection of some kind of a common faith. The experience needed only to be intellectually rationalizable on its own account, by reference to internal principles of design—rather than in relation to Utopian social or political ideals, as exemplified in the hope of Auguste Herbin, an artist who had drawn on both Cubism and Orphism previously, that his free-standing "concrete objects" in wood and cement of this time might come to serve communistically as an example of the "monument that represents the faith of all, its radiance which represents absolute equality . . . [a truly popular art] which contains all forms of art, all artists and artisans" (from an undated letter, probably of 1920).

Unlike the emergent Surrealism of 1922–25, accordingly, Cubism put emphasis in this phase on command of scale and on the showing forth of the coordinates of structure on the surface. Joan Miro between 1918 and 1922, first in Barcelona through the Cubist works exhibited at the Galerie Dalmau, and then in Paris after he moved there and had his work presented at a gallery showing of 1921 by Maurice Raynal, was exposed to what Ozenfant and Jeanneret in their 1925 book called the tendency of Cubism, from 1916 on, "towards the crystal." He molded his art in those years around a correspondingly crystalline treatment of shapes and planes; and the same is true of André Masson, in the self-imposed apprenticeship that he underwent with Gris towards 1924. But by 1925, the year in which Miro exhibited with the Parisian Surrealists (having joined the group the year before) both of these artists have moved by comparison towards stressing their improvisatory technique, and towards concentrating on minutely pointed intricacies of detail. Unlike the emergent forms of Constructivism, equally, Cubism held to a straightforwardly human content. Represented in Paris in those years was not only the "constructive" production of artists such as Herbin and, by this time, Gleizes, with their commitment to a pure painting of form and color, but also examples of De Stijl, and particularly Mondrian's current work, that were to be seen there or were reproduced in *L'Esprit Nouveau*. But as in Cézanne's example and as in Negro sculpture—and as if to bring together their twin relevancies— the Cubist aesthetic remained committed through the early 1920s to the presentation of hieratically standing figures or frontally seated ones, and to a rendition of domestic objects that, even when they were radically simplified or ornamentally embellished, declared their origin in, and their amenability to, an everyday and straightforwardly practical kind of usage.

In Gris's production of paintings, the period from 1919 to 1921 brings in warmer colors, such as earthy browns and ochers and rather dark and somber blues; a more atmospheric handling of tones; and a geometry of curves which is schematic yet at the same time supple. This geometry is, in fact, like a transposition into painted form of the character that the contours have in the pure outline drawings that Gris did now, both of portrait subjects and of still lifes, with subtle distensions and purifications of the given image in each case.

In the still lifes of 1921 which consist of arrangements of objects in front of open windows, with views of blue water or sky and a band of mountain range in between, concrete space behind the objects is bounded at the rear by a solid plane of color, corresponding to the total rectangle of the canvas. The still life is centrally placed in this space—in fact suspended—to create a box-life effect. Planes angle back from it, and the application of the principles of transparency and translucency, carried over from the second decade, to the relationships of the objects to one another gives the whole set-up a somewhat ghostly quality, as if it stood somewhere halfway between a cardboard and celluloid mock-up and an actual still life. The organization of the geometry here and in the following year in relation to the corners of the format creates an effect that is increasingly canonical, in its trued regularity of curvilinear and rectangular outlining and its interlocking of overlapping shapes.

In the figure paintings of those two years, mainly of Commedia dell'Arte subjects, the effect is more specifically akin to de Chirico's work. Examples of de Chirico's "metaphysical" paintings, as he called them, had been known in Paris in 1912–14 already, through Salon showings of those years in which a few of them appeared; Apollinaire had written about their qualities at that time, and in 1919 Maurice Raynal, who became a commentator on Gris's art in the early 1920s, had contributed a critical notice to a small anthology of illustrations which came out in Rome. Even more concrete as a link is the fact that the first *soirée* of the periodical *Littérature* in January 1920, organized by André Breton, included a display of paintings of de Chirico's alongside ones by Gris and Léger and also sculptures by Lipchitz. It is also interesting that the term *metaphysical* itself, which was adopted by Apollinaire from de Chirico to denote the imaginative and cerebral qualities of this art, was now being used, as in T. S. Eliot's 1921 essay on "The Metaphysical Poets" of the seventeenth century, in reference to the responsive sensibilities of the audience for such work: those able through their possession of a "refined sensibility," as Eliot put it, to appreciate the difficulty and varied "complexity" of such an art, and the "comprehensive" and "allusive" command in it of the language that civilization made available. That usage, in turn, paralleled de Chirico's own premise in his 1919 essay "On Metaphysical Art" that the "overwhelming burden" of civilization is such that an art which seeks to restore "clarity of vision and sensitivity" must necessarily be "enormously complicated . . . in its spiritual values" and the achievement of a gifted few only, if it is to overcome the separating effect of a "mythical awareness" that it will otherwise engender in its audience.

It is possible that Gris could have known this latter essay as well as Apollinaire's comments, since it came out in the same Italian periodical, *Valori Plastici*, as his own first published statement, in the issue following (April–May 1919); but it seems simpler to assume that his temperament, philosophically inclined and increasingly melancholy now, as a result of his illness, found an echo in de Chirico's artistic personality at this time. His Pierrots especially suggest this. The subject of the Harlequin, on its first appearance in his work at the end of 1917 (C 241), had been presented in a way that directly reflected his admiration for Cézanne, as seen in his drawn copies of that time, two of them after one of Cézanne's paintings on this theme. In a succession of paintings of 1919, of Harlequins and one Pierrot (C 302, 307–8, 320), a patchwork effect to the colors and shapes is combined with a semihumorous freezing of movement. The motif of the mask is used to amalgamate two different views of the face—profile, three-quarter or frontal—at an angle to one another, and the setting becomes more explicitly theatrical in character, with stage curtains over the seated figure in one case, and the Harlequin holding a baton in another. Then in 1921–22 a more haunting quality intrudes, conveyed by the choice of color, with a stress on whiteness or paleness, and by a melancholy bleakness of facial expression (C 379, 409–10). What is most akin to de Chirico here is the combination of a cut-out effect in the figure with angled perspectives and the implication, even while the figure as a whole is mannequin-like, of a discomfited or strangely animated kind of response that is imparted by the head and body positions.

Later in 1922 and in 1923 Gris's forms become rounder and his quality of surface more fresco-like. A more awkward and even clumsy quality of contour and an attempt to make the image project more forcefully out towards the eye together make for a woodenness which becomes increasingly like that found in Derain's art of this time. In 1924–25 sculptural clarity and an overall static quality of ordering, parallel to the picture surface, are both pushed further, and as if in direct response to the Purist insistence on a French tradition of classicism going back to the Renaissance, Gris invokes the Fontainebleau frescoes of the sixteenth century as embodying the kind of monumentality to which he aspires, with the example of Pompeii behind that (letters of January and February 1926); but unfortunately the results, as he became progressively weaker and lost manual control, are marked by bathos and vacancy.

Braque's consolidation of his interests during these years was oriented more towards the gentle rhythms of Corot and the sensual richness of Chardin's art. But he combined a "classicism" in those respects with an illogicality, of both spatial and material consistency, in the way in which different components of his still lifes challenge one another in both density and material shaping. For figure subjects, the female *canephorus* or basket-bearer, fleshly in bulk yet depersonalized and sanctioned in its caryatid-like role by classical and Renaissance precedent, plays a similar role to the accompaniment of fruits from 1922 on. The modern side of Braque's practice here, consolidated now in terms of proportions and rhythmic shapes, entails a turning in upon the nature of the medium itself; and what is thereby afforded becomes like a sustained meditation on the tradition of *belle peinture,* its subjects and its effects.

Picasso was the most insistent of the three now that Cubism and a classically reminiscent way of working could be both a challenge and a mutual enhancement to one another. Whereas for Gris in his reply to a questionnaire of the end of 1924 (*Bulletin de la Vie Artistique,* January 1925), it was impossible to conceive of expressing himself "sometimes in the Cubist manner, sometimes in another artistic manner," since Cubism represented an aesthetic, for Picasso in the statement that appeared in the New York magazine *The Arts* in May 1923, there was no such distinction to be made between different "school[s]" or "manners" of painting: "the same principles and the same elements are common to all." How he expedited this in practice is best seen in an extended comparison between his two versions of the *Three Musicians* (Museum of Modern Art, New York and Philadelphia Museum), painted at Fontainebleau in the summer of 1921, and Igor Stravinsky's "Russian dance scenes with songs and music," as he called them, which became the basis for the production of Diaghilev's Ballets Russes, *Les Noces,* that was first put on in Paris in June 1923. The background to both of these works brings out the more openly international character of the European art scene now, and the feeling for its civilizing role that Picasso and Stravinsky shared. It also mirrors the concern that they had in common for direct interaction between the different arts. And finally the comparison encapsulates the major structural differences between their large-scale work of this phase and their pre-War art.

The first idea for a musical score on the theme of the traditional peasant wedding in Russia had come to Stravinsky in 1911–13, during the composition of the *Sacre du Printemps.* He first thought about the project seriously in 1914, and wrote a short score during the War period (1914–17). Then beginning in 1921, the year of the *Three Musicians,* he expanded it into definitive instrumental form. He had by that time provided the music for two productions of the Russian ballet, *Histoire du Soldat* (1918) and *Pulcinella* (1920) for which Picasso, who was by now a close friend and social companion within Diaghilev's circle, did the décor. *Les Noces* was produced, at the Gaiété Lyrique, under the patronage of the Princesse de Polignac—who had sponsored Satie's *Socrate* in 1919 and was an art collector also—with choreography by Branislava Nijinska, and costumes and decor by the Russian artist Goncharova which were neo-classical in spirit and, on the evidence of the surviving drawings, entailed studies of on-stage groupings which were much like Picasso's drawings of 1919 of ballerinas from the company, except that they were more austere.

From the first *Les Noces* was conceived of as a logical successor and pendant to *Le Sacre du Printemps,* concerned similarly with themes of ritual and regeneration. At its initial performance in Paris in May 1913, response to the *Sacre* had ranged all the way from outrage at its pagan subject, set in Russia at some imaginary and timeless moment in pre-civilized history, and at the harshness of its rhythms and patterns of movement, to the feeling expressed by Jacques Rivière six months later in an extended review of that first performance (*Nouvelle Revue Française,* November 1913) that the music and the choreography, by Nijinsky, were perfectly matched to one another. The difficulty and strangeness of the work made this inevitable: for the music, contemporary in its gestation (1910–13) with the first two phases of Cubism and the choreography, which Stravinsky did not like in retrospect, were permeated by a sense of discontinuity and by a convulsive quality that were a direct function of the harmonic tensions and contractions of sound that Stravinsky built into the piece. According to Rivière, who responded more favorably than he did to Cubism at this time, the avoidance of chords that were too representatively evocative of the human voice meant that the music was extremely contained in its effect of remaining "within the space that it originally filled up": "full of bold hiatuses, simplifications and expanded shapes," as he put it, and at the same time "acrobatic" in the sense that it conveyed of the marvelous and the strange. *Les Noces,* by contrast, was to be more like a *divertissement* in its quality of spectacle. It entailed a completely free use of ritualistic elements taken from the village customs of Russia, as established over the centuries for the celebration of marriage. In this way it represented an obverse, of a civilized social kind, to the "barbarity" of the *Sacre,* and an "orthodox" equivalent to its pagan subject. The words of its songs were adapted from Russian folk stories, and its varying rhythmic themes were melodically packed and blended together, so that they embraced both comedy and solemnity.

It is crucial to the imagery of the *Three Musicians* that different musical instruments, and the way they are held and used in performance, are juxtaposed and contrasted with one another: violin, clarinet and accordion in the Philadelphia version, which probably came first, with a female profile imposed on the clarinet to mark out its musical character; guitar and clarinet (or recorder) in the second version, with the music sheet now shifted to the hands of the monk on the right, who is providing vocal accompaniment from it. Picasso had included guitars, violins and clarinets in his paintings in 1911 but they had appeared there singly, either in the hands of figures or in a table top arrangements. This continues to be true, with increasing frequency in the case of the first two instruments, in 1912 and on into 1913; but it is not until early 1913 that they appear paired together within the same composition (D 574–77). Thier basic configurations of shape are now counterpointed against one another, in the same sort of way as simple rhythmic movements were to be contrasted in Stravinsky's conception of the *Sacre;* and the same continues to be true of a further series of still lifes from late in the year (D 622–24, 626–27), where the syncopations are more pronounced and the "hallmarks" of strings, stops, pegs and mouthpiece are arranged along with the lettering of sheet music, newspaper and beer bottle to evoke the popular use of these instruments in the environment of bar and café.

Then in 1915 and 1916 Picasso returned to the theme of the Harlequin (D 844–56) which had not appeared in his art since the pre-Cubist years, and also to the combination of different musical instruments on a table, now in a studio setting (D 818–29), in order to create a play back and forth between the animate and the inanimate, and particularly between the rounded forms of woman and guitar and between the strip-like extension of the clarinet with its protruding reed and the simplified shapes of Harlequin or Pierrot. When he comes back to the pairing of Harlequin and Pierrot in 1918–20, during his period of association with the Diaghilev Ballet, it will be in order to show them frontally, side by side, in a room setting; and in one particular drawing of 1918 he shows them performing together in a room corner. Harlequin here plays the guitar, Pierrot the violin, and the overlapping of their arms and the concerted turn of their bodies and gazes on opposed diagonals suggest the complete reconcilability of their differing "voices" with one another, cutting through time and across national boundaries like the Commedia dell'Arte itself.

In a drawing from 1921, the year of the *Three Musicians,* the two figures equally appear together, in a rapid mapping out of outlines and of light and shade: one of them masked and playing the guitar, identified by his hat as the Harlequin, the other seen from behind, in tights rather than pantaloons, but identified by the ruff and conical hat as Pierrot and shown playing a short pipe or recorder. Though there is only a drawn horizon line and decorative border around, the raked ground plan and the shadows cast on it by overhead lighting clearly point to a stage setting. The sheet is made up of two cut pieces, one for each figure, which have been joined together (with a higher horizon line added in between) and the relative positioning of the two figures, as if moving in towards one another while they play, implies that, unlike the 1918 pair, they are challenging one another with their music. This sense of challenge widens out, in fact, to include certain universal aspects of the Commedia dell'Arte theme: the contrast of youth and greater maturity, and of light and dark values, which corresponds to the technical contrast of contour in one figure and modeling in the other. The poses furthermore appear intensely animated, particularly in the sense that they impart of a jaunty and dandyish accosting of one another: but they seem also stopped in their tracks, as if in a ritualized proceeding between them that typifies their opposed characters.

The related features of the *Three Musicians,* and especially the New York version, are that a box-like space and theatric colors suggest an actual stage setting; that a static, centralized composition is enlivened by witty details of anatomy, pose and expression; and that the figures appear as about to play rather than actually playing. While the basic arrangement of the trio—seated facing out, side by side behind a table—affords a sense of classical harmonization, appropriate to the Commedia dell'Arte with its Italian origins and later French development, it is now the overlapping of shapes and the shared music that carries the sense of challenge: as if the three were independently engaged in improvising from that music, and the everyday atmosphere implied by the still life of pipe and tobacco pouch on the table and the dog underneath it were transformed as a result. The theme becomes in this way one of animation and artificiality contrasted; so that it corresponds to the larger antinomy in Picasso at this period—following on from his work with the Diaghilev Ballet and directly resulting from it—between the claims of dandyism and those of physicality. The different interlocking pieces of the design here seem laminated together, as if they were made out of wood; and yet there is also a specific atmosphere, of a ritualized and consecrative kind. It is here that the analogy with *Les Noces* stands out most clearly. Stravinsky called his work a "sort of scenic ceremony"; but he was also insistent on not identifying any of the characters with the singing voices, so that the latter became effectively depersonalized; and he was pleased at the conception of the choreography "in blocks and masses" which went with an extraordinary bonding of the musical themes throughout. Furthermore, he put the orchestra (four pianos and percussion) on the stage itself at the first performance, so that the songs served as a direct challenge to it: one which was like the challenge of the different musical "voices" in Picasso's case.

Also marked in the *Three Musicians* is a sense of the faces as masks without eyes behind them, or indeed (in the New York version) anything at all; for one seems to look directly in that case through the holes to the background. This tends to make the viewer's recognition of the familiar characters of the Commedia more difficult and more troubling. It also renders the atmosphere more oppressive, as it is in the *Three Women at the Spring,* worked on at the same time. Cendrars had written in his article of 1919 on Cubism (cited in chap. 3), ironically but also evocatively, "Some Cubist paintings remind me of black magic rites; they exhale a strange, unhealthy, disturbing charm; they almost literally cast a spell. They are magic mirrors, sorcerer's tables," and it is as if Picasso were answering that charge with a pair of paintings for which it effectively, but also majestically, held true. It would seem that he found a suggestive lead here—as Gris did also soon after—in the example of De Chirico. It is particularly relevant in this connection that in 1915–16 Picasso had done a series of paintings in which the flattened silhouette of a figure is combined with angulations of perspective and with rigidly geometric shapes and constructions which seems, like De Chirico's images of this sort, as if they were cut out of wood. These paintings include particularly ones in which the breasts of a woman are treated as if they were see-through holes in a mask or an artist's palette (D 860–62, 864, 876) and one in which the upper half of a man with a guitar (D 875) is handled as if it consisted of a narrow vertical picture, in which head and torso were framed, with the face split in two down its center and blank holes for eyes. It was to these ideas, suggesting a kind of mummified presence in the world like that of De Chirico's shadow-figures, that Picasso returned now, and to a corresponding play with proportions and mood.

In the Cubist still lifes of the early 1920s, there is a move towards witty and light-hearted subjects: ones which, like some of Matisse's subjects of the time, are reminiscent of the eighteenth century in this respect. The *Bird Cage* of 1923 (Ganz collection, New York) recapitulates the structural procedures and stark simplifications of the Cubism of 1912–16, in the same ways as still lifes of 1919 and 1921 had done; but with the difference that the sutures between the parts are made more self-consciously evident—like the stitching and seams in a decorative fabric such as a quilt. The *Red Tablecloth* of 1924, with its classical bust on a stand and the *Mandolin and Guitar* done at Juan-les-Pins that summer (Guggenheim Museum, New York) are like the *Open Window at Saint Raphael,* a gouache of 1919, in including a setting of blue sky seen through an open window. This, together with the reflected Mediterranean lighting within the room in the second of those works and the scheme of interrelated curves in both, gives a sense of easiness and relaxation. But in the *Studio with Plaster Head* of 1925, also done at Juan-les-Pins (Museum of Modern Art, New York) the effect is somewhat different, and also like a concession on Picasso's part towards the emergent language of Surrealism. In November of that year, in fact, he would appear in the first group exhibition of Surrealist painting at the Galerie Pierre in Paris, along with de Chirico; and here the stimulus of de Chirico appears relevant once more, this time for the way that artist had related fragments of statuary and inanimate objects to an irrationally constructed "theater" of space, and for his boxed-in references to the worlds of architectural construction and artistic creation, in the classical and Renaissance tradition (as became more marked in his work after 1918).

The dismembered shards or disembodied fragments of the classical tradition occupy the studio setting now: not only the antique philosopher's head on its stand and the broken off arms of an actual statue in plaster-cast, showing its hollow inside, but also the patch of sky with white clouds in it, the segments of classical buildings next to it, including pediments at raked angles, the discontinous mouldings in the upper half and the stacked rectilinear frames below the table which have no spatial or volumetric continuity with one another. The fleur-de-lys pattern and the laurel branch, the book and the scroll together recall the older medieval and Renaissance tradition in French art and poetry. Implicit here is an orthodoxy, of an essentially high-minded kind, as to the way in which elements can hold their place artistically in the modern world: by virtue of the effect of their juxtaposition and arrangement on the viewer's consciousness, rather than through any continuing efficacy that they may have in themselves, or through their subordination to a "machine aesthetic" of manufacture and display, as in Léger's art of this time. The "worlds" of theater (in the form of a toy one made for his son Paul) and of architecture (as in his ballet set of 1920 for Stravinsky's *Pulcinella*) are also alluded to, in the stage-set decoration with its enlarged apple in the city square; so that they appear as rivals to the more solid mode of construction demonstrated in the table top arrangement and to the combination of different views together in the philosopher's head. In this way the set-square that links together picture frames and moulding and the plain rectangular base of the statue that is balanced upon it become finally, with their shadowing that also defines their weight and spatial existence, the consolidated keystones of the composition as a whole. In their very simplicity and functional practicality, they have the capacity to shore up this mixed world of disparate artistic idioms; to recrystallize its separated pieces into a mutually responsive, as well as challenging, relationship to one another.

The theoretical pronouncement of Picasso and Gris from this period can now be put into place. Gris's statements, as they become longer and weightier between 1920 and 1925, are increasingly oriented towards procedural and developmental questions, and in the process certain key terms that he uses become more metaphysically charged: particularly *architecture,* which he interpreted as meaning for painting the homogeneous build-up of colors and containing forms; *unity,* entailing the elaboration and "modification" of all of the elements into a complete coherence; and *particularity* or *concreteness,* which enables the artist to express the "primary idea" or "conception" of an object which is known and common to everyone. As he expanded upon these three concepts in his lecture at the Sorbonne of May 1924, given to a philosophical and scientific audience, their explication enabled him to respond to a statement of Braque's that he quoted—attributing it only to a "painter friend"—to the effect "Nails are not made from nails but from iron" with the counterclaim that nails could in fact be made from the pre-existent idea of a possible nail. It also enabled him, in his concluding statement to the effect that the "sole possibility" in painting was "the expression of certain relationships *(rapports)* between the painter and the world" and that making a painting entailed putting these relationships "into an intimate association between them and the limited surface that contains them," to reply implcitly to Ozenfant's and Jeanneret's definition, in their 1918 book, of technical realization in painting as "nothing more than a rigorous materialization of the concept," which appeared to leave out entirely what Gris called the "imagination" or the *a priori* "idea of painting."

After the short 1919 statement on the role of the intellect (cited in chap. 3) and the one of April 1920 on Negro art, the next statement is the one that appeared over Ozenfant's pen-name "Vauvrecy" in *L'Esprit Nouveau* in February 1921, and in which Gris provides a brief outline of his career up to 1912. He then goes on to an account of his procedure in which he differentiates it, as described earlier, from Cézanne's, saying that whereas Cézanne "turn[ed] a bottle into a cylinder," he did the opposite: he "proceed[ed] from the general to the particular" or "start[ed] from an abstraction in order to arrive at a real fact." It was in this connection that he introduced the term synthesis, associating it with *deduction* and making acknowledgment to Maurice Raynal as having used it for his art. He was referring here to the Kantian opposition of *deduction* to *induction,* which Raynal had adopted in an article on Gris, which actually came out in the same issue of *L'Esprit Nouveau,* and would use again in his book of the next year on Picasso. In a conversation of March 1920 recorded by Kahnweiler Gris had correlated the distinction between "synthetic" and "analytic" Cubism with the way in which he moved—as a matter of principle from now on—from "organizing" his picture to "qualifying" the object in it: by which he meant, according to his 1921 statement, the "arrangement" (or adjustment) that he made when the "color abstractions" with which he started had "turned into objects." The idea of "synthesis" as a culminating deductive process which begins to emerge here and is found in the May 1924 lecture in the comparing of a picture to "true architecture" as a "synthesis," corresponds to Severini's analogous use of the term in an article of late 1924, "Towards an Aesthetic Synthesis" (*Bulletin de L'Effort Moderne,* October–November) in the implication that it carries of a controlling aesthetic judgment, and it may be that here again Severini was the borrower; but it is not until the response to a questionnaire which came out in print at the very beginning of 1925 (*Bulletin de la Vie Artistique,* January 1) that Gris made this connotation clear by specifying that "synthesis" entailed procedurally "the expression of relationships amongst the objects themselves."

By this time Gris's claim to a privileged position (see chap. 3), both in respect to the qualities that his work has reached the stage of displaying, and in regard to the viewer's reading of it, has also become more assured in the ways in which it expresses itself. Whereas the wording of the February 1921 statement runs "[working with] the elements of the intellect, with the imagination, I try to make concrete that which is abstract. . . . I want to arrive at a new qualification," by the time of his correspondence with the German critic Carl Einstein, published as "Notes on my Painting" in the Frankfurt periodical *Das Querschnitt* in the summer of 1923, he has become "his own spectator" in "extract[ing] the object from [the] picture," so that the emergent identity of what is shown becomes set up in this way for the viewer's recognition; if, he says there, he "particularize[s] pictorial relationships to the point of representing objects," it is "to avoid its happening that the viewer of the painting does this on his own and this combination of colored forms suggests to him a reality not foreseen." This position is generalized still further, much as it had been by Kahnweiler, in the 1924 lecture: "The power of suggestion in all painting [being] considerable . . . one must foresee, anticipate and ratify this abstraction, this architecture." And after his retrospective affirmation of January 1925 that the "analysis of yesterday" in Cubism, dependent on "the relationships between the painter's comprehension and the objects" had given place to a way of working that was no longer "purely descriptive," he even reached the point of believing in the last years of his life—according to a statement made to Raynal in 1927, prior to his death that May—than an analytical phase in his art had lasted right up to that time in three distinct stages, and that he was only now arriving at a "new period of expression" which was to be accounted "synthetic."

Picasso's statement of 1923, made to the critic Marius de Zayas who had written about him in 1911 and published in English translation in the New York magazine *The Arts* that May is by comparison more openly declarative and politically charged with respect to the art scene. The artist is credited in it with the power of being able, in Nietzsche's terms, to impose his vision on society: as in the example of Velazquez convincing us of the personality of the people that he painted by "his right of might." And with this there goes an opposition to the conceptualization both of artistic evolution in general and of the creative principles at work in the case of modern art.

The basic objection that Picasso has to talk of evolution, whether it concerns the "great painters of other times" or his own art, is that it makes art seem as if it had its existence in the past, or in the future, rather than concretely in the world of the present. To talk about evolution and transformation in art as if they were "philosophical absolutisms," or laws that had to apply, is to imply that art is necessarily transitory. "Many," correspondingly, "think that Cubism is an art of transition." But insofar as it has "kept itself within the limits and limitations of painting, never pretending to go beyond," it is not to be interpreted as if it were an experiment on the road to something else; and the application to it of theoretical constructs, such as those of mathematics or music, has "been pure literature, not to say nonsense, which has brought bad results," As for his own art, his "several manners" must not be considered, by the same argument, as an evolution at all: "I have never made trials nor experiments. Whenever I had something to say, I have said it in the manner in which I felt it ought to be said."

Picasso's remarks that address themselves to creative method are even more polemically slanted. Having opened with the comment that it is hard for him to understand the importance given to the word "research" in connection with modern painting—since in his opinion to "find" rather than to "search" is what matters—he later maps out, in the space of a few short sentences, some of the ways in which the misdirected or poisoning effect of this idea can be traced in modern art, to constitute "perhaps [its] principal fault." It has "often . . . made the artist lose himself in mental lucubrations," which could be understood at this time as an allusion to the Purists' cult of theorizing. It has also encouraged artists to "attempt to paint the invisible, and therefore the unpaintable," which takes in the practitioners of "pure painting," perhaps especially Kandinsky. And much as Reverdy would claim in his book of the following year on Picasso that he had always striven, from his first beginnings until now, "towards an art of realist conception," in the sense of a "genuinely plastic art, concerned for the reality of objects," so Picasso criticizes the inclination to speak of naturalism "in opposition to modern painting," for the distinction it sets up between Cubism and another, supposedly rival or more traditional "school" of painting, that is in fact quite arbitrary and unreal in terms of creative principles.

In this phase of Cubism, therefore, in the formulations offered by the artist as to its nature and overall contribution, as well as in ongoing practical terms, there is a concern with creative procedures as they may or may not prove relevant to the understanding, and with what may or may not count as an appropriate response on the part of the viewer. The philosophical issues thereby raised, in regard to the artist's intentions and the viewer's perceptions, are now the judgmental ones of *necessity* and *sufficiency* (see Part Two, chap. 5): whether or not, that is, it was necessary to the work as a significant achievement that it should have a particular quality that the artist wished it to have; and whether fulfillment of an intention that the artist had was sufficient to give the work merit.

For Picasso in his 1923 statement, intentions are not sufficient to make the work meritorious; what one does is what counts, and not "what one had the intention of doing." Gris's position on this subject is that he "make[s] no claim to arrive at any determined form of appearance, be it cubist or naturalistic," and so is not being consciously "Cubist" by choice; rather, he thinks of himself as "classical" in technique as the old masters were and the merit of what he does lies there, in the method or technical means "of all times." As he put it in a letter of the end of 1921 (to Kahnweiler, November 27), "the quality of an artist is due to the amount of the past that he carries in him. . . . The more of this inheritance he has, the more quality he has"—quite irrespective of natural gifts or talent, as they bear on either the choice of style or the capacity to realize one's intentions.

As for the question of necessity, Picasso's key assertion here is that "Art is a lie that makes us realize truth. . . . The artist must know the manner whereby to convince others of the truthfulness of his lies": an assertion which parallels Nietzsche's contention in *The Will to Power* that the true artist is possessed of exceptional powers of affirmative vision and discernment, and that his falsification can accordingly give to society a significant understanding of the truth about itself. Picasso may have gained an awareness of Nietzsche's line of thought here through his friendship with André Salmon, who continued to attribute such qualities to him in his writings now, as he had before the War; and Léonce Rosenberg in 1921 had included in his *Cubisme et Empirisme* a passage from Nietzsche on the theme of artists' fear of the eye that can see through their little deceptions and their artifices to their underlying motivations and qualities of thought. But there is also the difference that whereas Nietzsche had used the romantic-classic antithesis in his critical observations on the needs and failings of modern art, Picasso's reinforcing claim is that there is no opposition of concrete and abstract in art: that art, quite simply,

"expresses what nature is not." For Gris in his 1924 lecture—
according to an idea of fundamental period divisions in art which he
appears to have drawn, probably through Kahnweiler, from Worringer—the mode of representation adopted in each age fulfills the desire
of that age to see the spiritual and substantial represented, in accordance with its mental ideas and governing aesthetic: one which, in the
period through which he has lived and worked, has been a developing
one, whether or not it be called "Cubist." For a painting to be truly
responsive to the felt needs of its period, it was necessary accordingly
that the artist should will into being the kind of coherent unity, of
form and expression together, that is impossible in a nonrepresentational or purely imitative work.

How Cubism is thought of here, in relation to the present moment
in culture and its needs or limitations of perception, entails an ideal of
recognition and wider dissemination. The artists' statements themselves were prepared or sent out with a larger diffusion in mind:
Picasso's appeared in English translation in the United States, Gris's
lecture was published in *The Transatlantic Review,* out of Paris, and
then in Germany the following year, while his texts of 1923 and 1925
came out in German, in Frankfurt and Potsdam respectively. Texts of
appreciation on the leading artists equally followed the same pattern:
Raynal's book on Braque appeared in both Rome and Paris in 1923,
Waldemar George's text of 1924 on Picasso came out in English in
Rome, and Gertrude Stein's 1924 article on Gris was written for the
Chicago *Little Review* (winter 1924–25), for its special number on his
work. But apart from those publications, there were also writings on
Cubism in general which treated it as a wideningly available pictorial
language: one which, in the words of Waldemar George in his
foreword to a Berlin exhibition catalogue (*Der Sturm,* January 1921)
which *L'Esprit Nouveau* reprinted a month later, made it possible for
"outstanding personalities [to] express themsleves with the same ease
everywhere."

The larger argument of such texts, as they came out in different
countries between 1920 and 1925, is that Cubism as a whole teaches
one to "see differently" or leads that way—in a particular sense of
that phrase that is applicable to it (see chap. 5), having to do with the
emphases of one's perceptions or their increased refinement. Thus
Gino Severini in his book of 1921 *Du Cubisme au Classicisme,* which
dealt with Cubism only at the end of its "historical introduction,"
found that it constituted "the only interesting tendency from the point
of view of discipline and method," and that it can come to serve in
this way as the basis of a new, rule-governed "classicism." For Rudolf
Bluemner, in his German text *Der Geist des Kubismus und die Künste*
which came out in Berlin that year and actually devoted only three of
its twenty short chapters to Cubism, with almost no artists named and
very few illustrations, the "spirit" of the art, as it may lead to new

perceptual understanding, is what counts. For the painter Andrew Dasburg, writing in the New York periodical *The Arts* in November 1923 on "Cubism—Its Rise and Influence" and using as illustrations five works done by Picasso between 1912 and 1922, its "contagious force" and the idiosyncrasies of its different phases have greatly affected American artists, yet without producing anyone who is to be called "either its disciple or exponent"; for as in Europe, its abstract-constructive ideas, especially in its latest phase, have not "with a few distinguished exceptions" been understood. And for Ozenfant and Jeanneret, in the passage from their book of 1925 used as epigraph to this chapter, it is simply that in "continuing their work imperturbably," the Cubists also continued to exercise "their influence of men's minds." Whether discussed in terms of influence, spirit or spread, then, the effect of such writings was to make Cubism into the most canonical form of twentieth century modernism. The consolidations and the orthodoxies of its final phase, actual and perceived, became the basis in this way for the prolongation of its authority and its influence.

Conclusion
The Nature and Development of Cubism in Ideological Perspective

The interpretation of Cubism evolved (as structuralists and audience theorists would claim) according to the needs, assumptions and expectations of particular groups or audiences. In this it was unlike the art itself, which did not need the existence of criticism or theorizing to keep it going or redirect it in its experimentation, insofar as it established its own autonomous principles as it went along, and was moved by intuitions and promptings which could not be expressed in words. Rather, in a non-parasitic way and in line with what it meant in the early twentieth century for art to be avant-garde, what was written about Cubism addressed the need which the art presented for exposition and justification.

At the same time the interpretation was responsive (as Marxists of today would insist) to the ideological shifts of the culture and society surrounding it, and even drew incentives from that ideology. In this it was like the art, which also changed responsively from phase to phase, but the relationship was one of parallelism, not of identity: a distinction which reflects not only the differences between visual and verbal media, but also the differing ways in which literary forms of expression—including critical writings and the philosophy of art—and pictorial ones are affected by the social and political climate in which they exist.

A review of the main characteristics of Cubism, as they have been convered in this book, can serve to put the pre-War and post-War developments into a larger social and political as well as intellectual context. If the contrast between the two periods carries a larger representativeness and suggestiveness, it does so in the nature of the avant-garde itself and its social, cultural and ideological accoutrements. Cubism is the most significant manifestation of the early twentieth century in this respect, at least as far as the visual arts are concerned. It holds this position by virtue of its duration of development; its mode of address to the audience for "advanced" art; and the range of creative impulses that it involved or sheltered. The rapidity of its impact outside France at the same time provides a control over reading what took place interpretatively with it as a purely national phenomenon.

Cubism comes into being before 1914 against the double background of Post-Impressionism, particularly the example of Cézanne, and Symbolism. It inherited in this way from the later nineteenth century the dialectical conflict between the claims of the material, building its advance upon the authority of science, applied reason and evolutionary progress, and those of the spiritual, with its contrasting stress on intuition or instinct; and between the dictates of privacy and those of accessibility and comprehensibility, which could be seen now on either side of the balance as a function of talent and temperament as well as of class and education.

The qualities of difficulty, reflexiveness and arbitrariness that attend upon Cubism in this period tend to promote the same kind of "subjective" emphases as are found in the writings of Gertrude Stein and the poetry of Ezra Pound: elaboration for its own sake, an obsessive pushing to extremes. But they are accompanied by a concern to see the processes of search and discovery and what they yield in terms of a logical, self-validating continuity. The invocation here of a step-by-step process, of a liberating sort, allies Cubism to a certain degree with the development of Orphism in Paris and of abstract art at this time; but it stands closer to the trajectory of Matisse's pre-War art in its admission of the "decorative" for its own sake, without mysticism as to its role, and in the combination of concrete details of the observed world, and especially the studio environment, with extreme generalization and improvisation, particularly with the human figure and in series.

Cubism spread rapidly abroad and attracted considerable public interest; but it actually had a very small audience that really responded or understood. This division between the small and the larger audience corresponds to the ultimate ideological clash of the public and private spheres of culture at this time. In the public sphere, as the authority of liberalism declined, republican progressivism and belief in the entrepreneurial interests of the different members of society—which included those of artists and dealers— were confronted with the need for keeping order, in the face of the disturbances wrought by anarchism and syndicalism. In the more private and philosophical sphere, of the conceptualization of discovery and material change, a sense of expansion to one's physical existence and awareness—particularly in relation to the experience of space and time—was accompanied by a concern for maintaining controls. The clashes here were pushed, in both cases equally, to an extreme point of tension of the eve of World War I.

The post-War period brought an expansion of the potential audience for the arts, and the sense of a potentially attainable universality of language. But militancy of opinion as to the need for changes in the existing order was accompanied by reactionary or elitist misgivings as to the extent to which access on the part of the rank and file, or crowd, was possible or desirable. Culturally, the alternative to a reconstitution to match the new spirit was that "order" and "tradition" could be tailored and redirected to suit authoritarian constraints.

In the resultant gap between ideal and actuality, the artist was put in the position of using his personality, his style of performance, his interest in the popular media or his cultural predisposition as mediating elements, much as political and social ideologists were doing. Examples of the varying strategies adopted here include, amongst the leading Cubists, Picasso's dandyism, in the tradition of Manet and the later Seurat in its championing of visual wit and piquancy; Braque's cultivation of "good taste," as opposed to the involvement of Léger with advertising images and with cinema; and Gris's flexible and meditative philosophizing.

As to how these strategies situate post-War Cubism ideologically, it may be compared, as of 1925, with the International Style (or Art Deco) as represented in the great Exposition des Arts Décoratifs in Paris that year, and with Expressionism in the post-War meaning of that term, stressing the release of impulsive forces into art and distortions imposed by a vision of social or psychic alienation, as it was now becoming known in France, as well as in Germany in the form of the "New Realism." At the 1925 Exposition the Pavillon de l'Esprit Nouveau, put up and decorated in the face of intense opposition from officialdom by Ozenfant and Jeanneret (now using the name of Le Corbusier), included an abstract painting by Léger, whose work also appeared in another pavilion, and sculptures by Laurens and Lipchitz; in contrast to which Braque moved that year into a house designed for him by the architect Perret, and did the decor for the Diaghilev ballet *Zéphyre et Flore.* As for Expressionism, it was represented in Paris by the paintings of Soutine, made known to those interested from 1922 on through the offices of the dealer Paul Guillaume; to which may be contrasted Picasso's equally violent and personal *The Embrace* (Musée Picasso, Paris), from the summer of 1925.

It then becomes clear in these comparisons that, thematically and in the creative temper that it manifested, Cubism was less responsive than any of those other developments to social and political realities. But to say in this way what Cubism sees "through," or steps aside from, is not to resolve the problem of its accessibility (any more than with T. S. Eliot's poetry). The meaningfulness of its input into later art—as in Masson's works of the later 1920s, or Pollock's of the later 1930s—is quite different from its meaningfulness to a museum audience, which is also exposed to "neo-classical" and "expressionist" tendencies. Cubism, finally, remains suspended between the power that the visual image has to compel, because what it shows "speaks" to basic features of the human condition, or interpersonal aspects of human consciousness—which is the alternative towards which Picasso gravitated in his early work, prior to 1905, and would attempt again in *Guernica;* and its power to create an artificial syntactic construction in which resonances and echoes of other artistic "voices" of the past are pitted against one another—as is characteristic of Braque's post-War development. In European painting after 1925— as in poetry after *The Hollow Men*—the split between these two alternatives, in Surrealism and in Constructivism, becomes more pronounced and more absolute.

Intermezzo
Traditional Approaches
in Art History and the
Problems of Cubism

i. Internal Periodization and the Problem of Style-Change: "Analysis" and "Synthesis" as Applied to Cubism

One traditional art historical approach that has long been applied to Cubism consists of dividing up its development into self-contained stylistic phases. Each of these phases is taken as marking a clear-cut separation from the one before. Each is also seen as working within its span—which is shorter than would customarily be the case in earlier periods (where five to ten year stretches are the norm with individual artists, and anything from a decade up in the case of larger trends or tendencies)—with a consistent set of formal principles, that are progressively brought to realization.

Such an approach to Cubism goes back, in fact, to the 1920s. Within Juan Gris's lifetime, as has been seen in Chapter 4, *analysis* and *synthesis* came to be used as more or less polar terms for characterizing what had taken place within the development of Cubism; and the idea of a significant break within that development, such that what followed and what preceded stood in an antithetical relationship, was also first mooted. The early texts which contributed to the conceptualizations at work here, including some of Gris's own, were reviewed in that chapter. After 1927, and with increased force of argument closer to the present, the use of those same terms and their application to what happened in Cubism has been re-opened. Some writers on the subject seek to clarify, others to expand, and others again to reinterpret the fitting of those terms to the works themselves; but all basically take some account of the address made to these topics within the original theory of Cubism. The different ways in

154

which clarification or accommodation has taken place are to be looked at here.

Before coming to that, however, mention deserves to be made of a text, from the year 1927, which happens to be parenthetically relevent, for reasons arising from the writer's background; reasons which at the same time exclude any mention of Cubism. This is an article on "Mechanics of Form Organization in Painting" by the American painter Thomas Hart Benton, which the magazine *The Arts* brought out in successive installments beginning in November 1926; and the section of particular interest is that of the following January. It deals with the general possibility that spatiality in a painting may be inferred from pictorial flatness, by way of an alternative and mutually enhancing complement to the cubic rendering of forms. Benton had much earlier spent the three years from 1908 to 1911 in France, out of which came short-lived admirations for Cézanne and for Braque; and his first public exhibition in 1916 showed him using synchromist methods of composition and coloring which equally reflect that European experience of his. He then became a convert to regionalism in 1918, but before that commitment became programmatic in subject matter and scope, he embarked in 1920–24, for Albert Barnes, the great Philadelphian collector of French art, on a diagrammatic analysis of the compositional history of Western painting. The *Arts* article represents sections of this project, which was never completed. In the section referred to he indicates how flat areas may serve as a basis for projection, and discusses the method of *superposition,* which he associates with Oriental art: "flat spaces definitely bounded are superimposed in such a manner as to lead the eye back from one plane to another." From the accompanying explanatory diagram, and from the appearance of the features in point in Benton's work of 1919–24, it is evident that his sense of this basic alternative to one-point perspective in pictorial construction goes back to his early experience of European modernism; and that it ratified itself at this later point in a form which, though certainly one would never refer to Benton as a "synthetic Cubist," or indeed a Cubist at all, bears a remarkable analogy to the way in which, in Cubism after 1914, areas which carry the implication of being modeled, in shape, color, and texturing and flat, planar ones are interlocked. A paradox of circumstance, therefore, makes Benton's little-known piece the first explanation, in general artistic terms, of this basic principle of Cubist composition, and one with considerable perception as to its implications.

The general change-over date of 1914 for the development of Cubism offered by Ozenfant and Jeanneret in their 1925 book brought up problems when combined with the division into successive phases adumbrated by Gris in 1925 and 1927. Kahnweiler in a 1929 text on Gris combined the artist's interpretation of 1925 that Cubism had earlier been through a stage of analysis with the application of this to Gris's own development, and suggested correspondingly that a phase in that development which could be called analytic had ended towards 1914. He also affirmed that in the importation of "foreign" collage materials each artist was in effect following his own bent, on which basis the paths taken by Picasso and Braque could be classed as synthetic cubism. The division into phases was also taken up by Carl Einstein in 1929, his suggestion being that a period of "simplistic distortion" was followed by one of "analysis and fragmentation," and finally by one of synthesis, so that in this way the structural characteristics of the two earlier phases became a little more focused.

Alfred Barr in his 1936 text for the exhibition "Cubism and Abstract Art," and his 1939 one on Picasso which was further expanded in 1946, formalized the classification of Cubism into analytical and synthetic phases. He put the change-over at first in 1913, with the qualification of its being decisively accomplished by the end of 1914 at the latest, but then significantly brought the date back to around 1912, calling Cubism after that date comparatively synthetic, insofar as it entailed simpler composition with larger forms and fewer details. He maintained at the same time the interpretation of synthetic Cubism as a matter of surface enrichment on Picasso's and Braque's part, beginning with the interest in textures implied in their introduction of collage materials in 1912, and continuing to a climax in the use of ornamental pointillistic dots in 1914 and the mixing in with the paint of materials such as sand and sawdust. The term "synthetic" itself he explained (1946) as referring to the invented character of the images, as exemplified particularly in the make-up of Picasso's 1913 reliefs, and as being used, for lack of a better term, for a whole phase in Picasso's art culminating in the *Three Musicians* of 1921.

Kahnweiler, returning to the subject in his 1946 book on Gris, in a chapter headed "Papiers Collés and Synthetic Cubism," proposed a relationship between synthetic Cubism and medieval painting, both being conceptual in character. He said that Gris moved this way from 1914 on, citing the *Smoker* of mid-1913 as marking the extreme of analysis. Apollinaire had, he observed, called Cubism "conceptual" in his 1912 book already, and the artists had indeed talked of conceptual painting then; but they were still at that point empiricists in the Renaissance tradition. In a passage following this on the construction of space, he characterized Gris's paintings from 1914 on as being composed like those of Picasso and Braque, in that they entailed a flat and spatially delimiting background against which the forms stood out in low relief: the effect of the superimposition, or layering, being that the objects were read as coming out from that background towards the spectator. What is said here about Picasso and Braque is to be amplified in the light of two passages in *The Rise of Cubism,* written before Kahnweiler came to think of analysis and synthesis as successive stages, one of them attributing to Picasso in 1910 a new method of composition which entailed working frontwards from a clearly defined background so that the spatial positions of objects were plainly indicated, and the other suggesting that Picasso and Braque in 1913–14 were concerned to eliminate the use of color and chiaroscuro by an amalgamation of pictorial and sculptural means. It then becomes clear that Kahnweiler's overall conception of the development of Cubism associates a change of color usage with a change of spatial construction, and ascribes to Picasso a forward-looking awareness of both potentialities as early as 1909–10. Picasso, Braque and Gris are also said to have all three used collage to a new degree, beginning in 1914, and this is taken as a new development arising out of the use of "real details" discussed previously: Braque's *trompe l'oeil* nail of 1910 and the introduction of lettering that year also, followed by the first use in 1912 of collage materials. The range of materials used anti-illusionistically and the new "architecture" has proved itself capable of absorbing such (as in the 1928 text) "foreign bodies."

✗ Herbert Read's formulation of 1948, in the retrospective section of an essay on the art situation of that time, requires to be quoted in full: "Synthetic cubism, while no longer dependent on the real object in the same sense as analytical cubism, returns to the object by a process of concretion: the object emerges from the canvas like the image of a lantern-slide in the process of focusing. But the focus, when precise, reveals, not an illusory image of some familiar object (for example a guitar) but a different order of reality with distinct values, only related to the object by suggestion or association. Poetry emerges from the forms, a species of nostalgia is created, an essence is distilled." Apart from the addition of a comparison of Read's own, that of a lantern-slide coming into focus, which can hardly be taken literally and even as a metaphor appears likely to be misleading (see Intermezzo iv), this is to be recognized, in keeping with the surrounding remarks about Gris, as essentially a rephrasing of Gris's own theory. Rather similarly L. A. Reid in his *Meaning in the Arts* (1969), again using Gris's theory, describes the representation in synthetic Cubism of the "abstract forms or essences of things," which are then particularized on the canvas surface, as analogous to the way in which the Platonic Essences represent reality, or an approximation to that on the artist's part; though he adds that this can in principle only be an analogy.

For Maurice Raynal in his 1950 *History of Modern Painting* the starting point of the synthetic phase of Cubism is to be placed in 1913–14. The same artistic means continued to be used, but with differences now which are described in essentially qualitative terms: a "much larger vision," and generally a greater breadth of composition and freedom of structure, as exemplified in the greater breadth and solidity of planes and the replacement of somber colors with an "unashamed" use of "pure, prismatic" ones. For Chipp in his 1955 thesis, on the other hand, Cubism after 1914 evinces a very different set of general features: flat planes of a geometric or ornamental nature, environments without atmosphere or lighting, texture as applied design, often mechanically repetitive, and a basic loss of weight and volume. These are all certainly technical features, but ones which are hard to isolate in any absolute sense. Christopher Gray in his *Cubist Aesthetic Theories* of 1953 meanwhile adopted an approach to the nature of the change-over which is a conceptual one, in that it rests on philosophical and aesthetic considerations, and on a cross-comparison with the poetry or poetic theory of Apollinaire and Max Jacob.

He dates the transition to synthetic cubism, and to a corresponding phase in the poetry, as beginning already in 1911–12, but suggests that the break was at the same time a gradual one, so that its effects are not fully evident until after 1913–14, and reach their apogee in 1916 with the emergence of Max Jacob, in the preface to his *Cornet à dés* (published 1917) as a spokesman for the new concerns. As to the nature of these concerns, when Gray says that a focus exclusively on the creation of aesthetic objects replaced the earlier "epistemological" focus on the creation of ideas, and presents this as essentially a re-statement of the familiar classical-romantic antithesis, with reference to texts of 1922 by Jacob and Raynal, it becomes clear that he is in fact contrasting the emerging post-War aesthetic, discussed in Chapter 3 above, with its pre-War counterpart; and this aesthetic, insofar as it corresponds to Gray's terms of definition, correlates not with the synthetic cubism of 1911–12 on, but with the more specific phase of 1916–17 on which has been called, on its own terms, "classical." One is therefore a considerable way forward in time here from the 1913 work of Gris's which Soby, in his 1958 catalogue, singled out as exemplifying a shift into synthetic cubism, parallel to that of Picasso and Braque in the same year; the argument here being based directly on Barr's account of the enrichment of color and form, and the corresponding qualities referred to in Gris's case being a new variety of handling, emphasis on tonal and textural change and absorption in modeling.

Clement Greenberg in his 1958 essay on "Collage" has Picasso taking a spurt forward into synthetic Cubism between late 1913 and late 1914. He rests his case for saying this on the valid observation that collage, in Picasso's use of it beginning at this point, declares the canvas surface to be surface so explicitly as, in the dialectic which concerns Greenberg between depth and flatness, to save the latter from "swamping the Cubist picture." Since he declares that in taking this spurt, led up to by the same three landmarks in the development of Cubist vocabulary as Kahnweiler had first used, Braque's 1909–10 nail, the introduction of lettering and then the bringing in of collage, Picasso was outdistancing Braque's contemporary level of achievement, and going beyond the level of what Gris would do until the latter's real successes of 1915–18, his account is essentially a qualitative one. Based, as characteristically with this critic, on his sensibility towards form, it has a corresponding kind of distinction and forcefulness, which is more a matter of individual perceptions cogently formulated than of a fully supported reasoning. But to use the term synthetic for the spurt forward in question, and exclude any other Cubism of the same time-period from deserving the same label, though the implications of this for what follows are made fully understandable in their own terms, seems peremptory. Like Kahnweiler, Greenberg associates the application of the term with a developed use of collage towards 1914; but for Kahnweiler it had simply been a matter of more collage at this point, as compared to paintwork and drawing.

Golding in 1959 encouragingly qualified still further the idea of a complete turnabout in the development of Cubism, by finding already in Picasso's and Braque's paintings of the first half of 1912 signs of what lies ahead: namely, a reawakening interest in color, which is to be consummated by the end of 1913, and "a move towards a clearer, more explicit kind of painting." But though his findings here pin down in date, on both counts, what Barr had previously adumbrated, he was still unwilling to let go of the synthetic-analytic polarity; and this is understandable, given the attention that he accorded, throughout his account, to contemporary theory. Instead, he took the polarity as referring to different procedures for composing a picture, depending on whether the artist began with a concrete object or set of objects, or with abstract forms which were then secondarily treated so that references to reality were brought in. One therefore gets the odd result that, for Golding, Gris is always synthetic, from about 1914 on, insofar as by his own account (1924) he began with abstract architecture, which he then "qualified," in Kahnweiler's phrase, so that the forms came to represent the painting's subject. In Braque's case, evidence left behind of his working procedure suggests that, in most of his 1913 canvases involving collage, he experimentally laid down and shifted around the pieces of paper until he arrived at a definite grouping, which he then recorded, prior to beginning to paint on the canvas. As for Picasso, in 1913 he very often combined, according to this account, synthetic and analytic procedures; the reason being that whereas Braque used collage at this time only in combination with drawing, Picasso used it together with both independent drawing and paintwork.

In Rosenblum's book of a year later, the primary theme presented is the continuity of the dialectic in Cubism between illusion and reality, and he passes over accordingly the issue of present concern, saying only that the idea of a complete about-face in the Cubists' relation to nature does not really hold good; their presumed independence of nature, after 1912, being "more often of degree than of kind." This, like Golding's specifying of the transition in 1912, is well said, and Rosenblum limits himself to characterizing the way in which structure becomes reorganized after 1912. Here he speaks of how collage made possible the radically new principle that pictorial illusion takes place upon an opaque surface, rather than behind a transparent plane; but he means "new" in relation to earlier Cubism. And he also designates the emergence in Cubism after 1912 of "newly enlarged and clarified pictorial elements—line, plane, color, texture."

Discussion since then, to complete the record, has focused primarily on questions of terminology. According to Fry in the introduction to his 1966 anthology, the term *synthetic* is to be taken as equivalent to "synthesized," as in a 1913 text of Charles Lacoste's which he reprints; and correspondingly it is the use of "condensed signs" synthesizing the formal character of the object represented which, as it begins to appear in Picasso's work of 1916, looks forward to later, synthetic cubism, and beyond that to what he suggests should be called the "synthesized, synthetic" Cubism of 1918 on. The contribution here, going back to 1913–14, of a certain type of African Grebo sculpture—one which had been proposed by Kahnweiler in a 1948 essay on "Negro Art and Cubism" and developed further by Golding—is also brought up. Rubin, in his 1972 Picasso catalogue, notes the evident discrepancy between that use of the term, implying an invented and semi-autonomous vocabulary of forms arrived at by a constructive process, and the use, somewhat related to Gauguin's term "synthetism," which implies large, flat and more readable elements as compared to those of the analytic phase. Noting the gradualness of evolution as it occurs on the latter front with no necessary increase of abstraction, he takes the term as more apposite to Picasso's work of 1913–14 in its other sense, inasmuch as while there is a greater legibility to the images, there is also a more schematic, as opposed to illusionistic, mode of representation. Kozloff (1973), criticizing the terminology on similar grounds in his chapter on "Papiers Collés and Collage," takes it that the artists both synthesize and analyze concurrently in their procedures here, and that a "synthetic" approach would seem to imply less particularization and variegation of handling, and more of a generalizing tendency than one finds characteristically in the treatment of objects in 1912–14. Simplicity and complexity, homogeneity and heterogeneity are, he notes, in themselves relative and have different applications here, depending on whether the make-up of the image or its presentation is in question; and if therefore "synthetic" is taken as referring roughly to an increased directness, this is not to be understood as entailing clarification.

Finally, Cooper in his text for the 1972 exhibition "The Cubist Epoch" finds the accepted terms for the phases of Cubism largely meaningless, since they are not capable of being properly defined. He specifically decries subsequently the appropriateness of the alternative term "hermetic" for the analytic phase; and he also notes as part of his general account that Delaunay had later evolved for his own development the alternative terminology of a "constructive" period (from 1912 on) succeeding a "destructive" one (from 1910/11 through 1912). He prefers in that light a historical rather than a stylistic subdivision of Cubism, into early (to mid-1910), high (to the end of 1912) and late (to the outbreak of war), with an aftermath reaching to 1921. On the question of whether there is an overall consistency to the "fundamental change" of the three major artists between the second and third of those phases, he appears to be self-contradictory. For he gives an account of the procedure developed by Picasso and Braque in the winter of 1912–13 and that of Gris beginning in 1914 in essentially parallel terms, and yet he characterizes the latter procedure as significantly different from that of Picasso and Braque and personal to Gris. Even subsequent to his "aftermath," furthermore, comes the phase designated by Greenberg, in several essays of the later 1950s, as arrived at by Picasso and Braque, Gris and Léger in the early 1920s, and as entailing a post-Synthetic "canon" of drawing, coloring and shape, so that it may be styled on this basis, as in Chapter 4 above, "canonical" or "orthodox" Cubism.

The above writings are therefore to be seen, in this review, as varying attempts at solving a problem which basically cannot be solved: there being an indeterminacy in the word synthetic itself, as to whether it is to be understood here as meaning artificial, built up, abstractly contrived or assembled together, and whether its application to Cubism is to be taken as a matter of technique, procedure or structure, or of overriding concept. How exactly it contrasts to the term analytical, which has at least some reference to the way objects are treated, and the time-spans for which the two terms are used depend on whatever constructions are adopted on those fronts. Yet at the same time, by virtue of its most general and philosophical overtones, the term "synthetic" remains a convenient label for a distinct phase of Cubism, and one which is now familiarly established, beyond the point where it is really possible to dispose of it.

ii. Cross-Reference to the Other Arts: Applications of the Term Cubism

Another traditional method for giving Cubism a place in the ongoing cultural history of its time, in larger terms than simply the kinds of material inventiveness that belong to the visual media, is to look for analogies to its development in the other arts contemporary with it, and especially in literature. To do this entails either the notion of a "transfer" from one art form to another, or the idea of some kind of a basic comparability of means and ends in the two cases.

Cubism has been taken in this book, as, by definition, a development in painting. To a lesser extent it represents a parallel development in sculpture, in that Picasso and Gris did a few contemporaneous pieces of sculpture; and Duchamp-Villon, Archipenko, Laurens and Lipchitz developed related sculptural idioms. But the term has also been used at different times, varyingly and indeed conflictingly, for developments in other art forms as well. A review of those applications of the term, some of them very early in date, may begin with the fields of music, drama and the novel, and then move from there to more particular cases.

Music was introduced in this connection by Kahnweiler when, in his 1946 book on Gris, he made cross-reference to Satie and Schoenberg, in terms of polyphony, atonalism and serialism, and to Webern's "laconic" structures. Rosenblum in 1960 then compared Picasso's *Demoiselles* (1906–07) and the music of the second decade in terms of primitivism, citing Bartok's *Allegro barbaro* (1910), Stravinsky's *Sacre du Printemps* (1911–13) and Prokofiev's *Scythian Suite* (1914–16). He further cited Stravinksky's *Petrouchka* (1911) for its polytonality; and for Cubist techniques as applied to the novel, Joyce's *Ulysses* (1914–21) and Virginia Woolf's *Mrs. Dalloway* (1922–25), both being examples of the tension between the "two realities," nature and art, their plots being both about authors who transform real events around them into the art of literature; and a play and an opera, Pirandello's *Six Characters in Search of an Author* (1921) and von Hofmannstahl's and Richard Strauss's *Ariadne auf Naxos* (1912, revised 1916), which both involve a shifting back and forth between dramatic fiction and the realities of dramatic production, this being likened to the concern in the synthetic phase of Cubism with "the examination of aesthetic substance itself." In 1960 also, Wylie Sypher in the last part of his *Rococo to Cubism in Art and Literature,* titled The Cubist Perspective, compared the same Gide novel, re-using for this purpose material in a 1949 article of his; the same Pirandello play; and a Gertrude Stein story (of 1924) for the "cinematic" mode exemplified there. This story, being contemporary with Joyce's *Ulysses* and *The Waste Land* (both published in 1922) thereby brought up both the "stream of consciousness" thread in the modern novel, and also the technique of juxtaposed fragments in modern poetry, as at the end of *The Waste Land,* described now by A. Walton Litz (1972) as containing "literary variations on the effects of collage Cubism," and as in Pound's development from the *Lustra* (1916) on, characterized by Hugh Kenner (1971) as "the longest working out in any art of premises like those of cubism."

The argument leading to all of those varied comparisons is, as with Shattuck's penultimate chapter in his *The Banquet Years* (1958), extremely general in character. Based on a recognition that Cubism is both revolutionary in relation to the past and fundamental for later twentieth century art, it involves the idea that all of the arts of the early twentieth century are linked by the presence of what Shattuck calls "self-reflexiveness": that is, a turning in of the art form upon itself, which is associated in turn with a concern for process, and with hermeticism or hermeneuticism. It is said that the medieval art historian Wilhelm Koehler once, in a lecture on modern art, put up for comparison slides of a piece of Bach's music in manuscript, and a manuscript sheet of Stravinsky's, his point being that the latter was quite evidently more complex, simply in look and arrangement on the page. In an essay on the English novel around 1907, Frank Kermode extends the same basic argument to bring in Conrad's novel *The Secret Agent* (1907) and the importance of Henry James's prefaces; and John A. Richardson in his 1971 book *Modern Art and Scientific Thought,* in the chapter on Cubism and Logic, widens the context again to include early formalist art criticism (Roger Fry, Clive Bell) and Gertrude Stein's "poetry," which may perhaps refer to her *Stanzas in Meditation* (written in the early 1920s, published 1933). One might add also in this connection Ford Madox Ford's novel *The Good Soldier* (1915).

To review now some of the suggestions which have been made from the side of literature, and especially poetry, over the same more recent time-span, Georges Lemaître in his 1941 book *From Cubism to Surrealism in Modern French Literature* compared to Cubist painting the combining of telling, powerful fragments in a jerky and disjointed manner found in Apollinaire, and also discussed Max Jacob, and André Salmon and Pierre Reverdy more briefly, as Cubist poets. Kahnweiler in the 1946 book on Gris already cited wrote similarly of a "Cubist spirit" in literature, uniting Apollinaire, Jacob and Reverdy; and in a 1948 essay on Mallarmé and painting he affirmed that Mallarmé had contributed to the plastic arts, after 1907, the idea of "inventing signs that create reality," thereby presenting Mallarmé as another late nineteenth century father-figure for twentieth century modernism—along with Henry James and Cézanne. Christopher Gray in his 1953 *Cubist Aesthetic Theories* distinguished two different phases of Apollinaire's poetry. The second, which he called Cubist, he dated as beginning in 1914 with the *calligrammes* and continuing to 1918; and Michel Butor in a 1968 essay extended the argument here by writing of the *calligrammes* in terms of the fluidity of connection back and forth created by the suppression of punctuation, which dates from the 1913 publication of *Alcools*. There has however been substantial disagreement, requiring separate review, as to which poems, or which aspects of Apollinaire's poetry and sensibility in general, are to be designated as Cubist.

The same also applies to Gertrude Stein as an imaginative prose writer, there being in her case equally a long and even established tradition of using the term Cubist, but one which again needs to be looked at critically in terms of its progressive elaborations. The nature of that tradition is well summarized by Fry in his anthology of Cubist criticism (1966) when he writes that the parallel with analytic Cubism is "rather striking," in terms of the repetition of a phrase with progressive variations, the treatment of words and phrases as like physical objects, and the sense, behind the opaque surface of the prose, of the circling of an "unapprehended subject." The most notable offering of a new angle on this subject is Katz's comparison, in the "Four Americans in Paris" catalogue of 1970, between Picasso's *Portrait of Gertrude* and his *Demoiselles* and her *Making of Americans:* the new mask-like portrayal in one case, and the psychologically diagrammatic characterizations in the other, being said to represent a "conceptual iconography that itself ultimately becomes the object of the composition." A similar kind of orientation in the case of poetry is reflected also in two recent book-length studies: Bram Dijkstra's *The Hieroglyphics of a New Speech; Cubism, Stieglitz and the Early Poetry of William Carlos Williams* (1969) and Gerald Kamber's *Max Jacob and the Poetics of Cubism* (1971).

Also to be mentioned, for its seminal role over the same time-period, is Joseph Frank's celebrated article "Spatial Form in Modern Literature" (1945, revised 1963). This article uses *The Waste Land* and Pound's Cantos as instances of a "perception in space" of word-groups which have no comprehensible relation to each other when read consecutively in time. To those examples it joins the *A la recherche du temps perdu* (1906–22) of Proust, who in a 1913 newspaper interview spoke of the psychology of space and time, as opposed to plane psychology, reflected in that cycle of novels of his, and Joyce's *Ulysses* (1922); and William Faulkner's novels *The Sound and the Fury* (1929), *Sanctuary* (1931) and *Light in August* (1932) would qualify on the same counts. But the addition of this latter example suggests that, in the previous two cases also, the argument has effectively shifted to the space in which the sensations described are received and interpreted by the narrator: which is to say, to an interest and focus belonging in the tradition of Mallarmé's *Prose pour des Esseintes.* Mallarmé's *Un coup de dés* (first published in 1897) and its twentieth century aftermath, though relevant to the first part of Frank's argument in terms of concern for page arrangement, are not discussed by him except in a brief addition to the 1963 version of the essay.

Still another kind of general suggestion has the fundamental language of Cubist painting reappearing in equivalent forms in other twentieth century media of expression once it had become established, as a result of diffusion and assimilation in the broadest sense. Comparable here to Frank's overarching concept of spatial form is the premise of Elly Jaffé-Freem's 1966 book, *Alain Robbe-Grillet et la peinture cubiste,* to the effect that the French *nouvel roman* can be linked with Cubism, not in terms of any specific connections at all, but rather in terms of three broad traits of organization: absence of depth, "fixation," which is used to mean the arresting of time and space, and ambiguity, which is defined to include transitions, doublings, paradoxes and the enigma of "the true and the false." To these traits can be added in fact, as equally relevant or more so, the Cubist and post-Cubist conception of the *tableau-objet.*

The application of the term Cubism to architecture, and also to film, raises similar problems. In the case of architecture, the link between Le Corbusier's developed work of the later 1920s and the Cubism of the early 1920s is firmly established by the intermediacy of Purism, and particularly through the connection between Juan Gris, Ozenfant and Le Corbusier first as a painter and then as an architect. Less convincing is John Jacobus's suggestion, in his 1966 book *Twentieth Century Architecture,* of an adaptation there of structural characteristics of analytical Cubism as well; for the link here, insofar as it is to be recognized in the shape of a corresponding architectural language of fluctuation and instability, derives from the Cubo-Futurist aesthetic in general: an aesthetic which, as demonstrated by Reyner Banham (1960), runs from the pre-War concepts of dynamism and simultaneity through *l'esprit nouveau* to the periodical of that name. And still less convincing is the association of Frank Lloyd Wright's architecture of 1909–10 with contemporary analytical Cubism: an association seen by the two writers who bring it into view, Siegfried Giedion in his *Space, Time and Architecture* (1941) and Vincent Scully (1960), as a matter of unconscious community of invention, since certainly Wright knew nothing of the relevant paintings. The word "cubist" applied to Wright's developed architecture of that time in itself, in fact, brings up misleading implications; for the blocks, cubes and rectangular emphases that are its hallmarks belong in a tradition going back to the eighteenth century, with further antecedents or parallels in late nineteenth century Europe, and the proper term here, against the background of that tradition, should be "cubic." In the field of film, Standish Lawder (1975) has somewhat similarly applied the term "Cubist" to avant-garde European developments of the 1920s, most especially Léger's *Ballet Mécanique* of 1923–24. With a single possible exception, however, the imagery in that film and the way it is handled relate in a quite obvious sense, such as the film's title would suggest, to Léger's post-War rather than his pre-War painting; and the interrelationships between Cubism as a movement and the films surveyed are a matter of artists with a pre-War affiliation to the scene surrounding Cubism choosing to extend themselves later into the new medium, so that the connection is hardly more substantial than that which allows Francis Carmody (1954) to conceive of a "School of Apollinaire" linked in the creation of "Cubist poetry."

If the focus is now narrowed to applications of the term Cubist to French poetry, the interpretations divide themselves up into four phases corresponding, as it happens, to those of Cubism itself. The term was already being used in periodical writing by 1912, in reference to Marinetti and also Rimbaud, whose work was attracting renewed attention at that time. But it was in 1917, in Frédéric Lefèvre's

similar poems, Reverdy, who was known among the painters for not speaking with them as a poet, found this absurd, and Braque commented that if it was a matter simply of arrangement, he would prefer to speak of "cubist typography." Apollinaire's enthusiasms, furthermore, embraced Orphism, which has its own phases termed by Delaunay "destructive" and "constructive," and from 1912 on Futurism. His own writings foreshadowed Surrealism, in the shape of *Les Mamelles de Tirésias* (claimed to have been written in 1903, produced only in 1917) and extended on towards the end of the War to the *esprit nouveau* aesthetic, which he denied in a 1918 interview bore any relation to Cubism. Jannini therefore (1971) quite properly termed Apollinaire's personal aesthetic, in the period of Cubism, "Cubo-Futurist," a particularly relevant point here being that in 1912, the year of *Zone* and also the *Fenêtres* (published January 1913), the poet himself spoke of new sources that he was finding in prospectuses, catalogues and posters. A similar detaching viewpoint has also been offered by Breunig (1962), who brings out that Apollinaire was ambivalent in his attitude towards Cubism in those same years. So directness of parallelism in the years in question here has a good deal against it, and rather little for it except in a very loose sense of the word parallel.

The period following Gertrude Stein's death in 1946 similarly saw an attempt to consolidate the application of the term "Cubist" to her writings, as one way of vindicating their importance. Here again four phases of interpretation in all can be discerned, correspondingly roughly in date and line of approach. Already in 1914 George Soule, in the first number of *The Little Review,* wrote, in reference to the portraits of *Matisse* and *Mabel Dodge,* of the "Cubist literature" of Gertrude Stein, asking if it had awakened echoes in Chicago, and of the "multiplicity of her planes." A second phase is bracketed on one side by Edmund Wilson's sharp critical discussion in his *Axel's Castle* of 1931, and on the other by Donald Sutherland's 1951 "biography" of the work, with Kahnweiler's pronouncement (1946) that the Cubist spirit outside of France was exemplified in her and the German poet Carl Einstein falling in between. This period saw the first attempts to reconcile the seemingly free use of words in her writings with the sense of an underlying order, pattern and logic which is at the same time communicated; and reference across to Cubist art, because of her known interest in that art as collector and writer, was made in order to suggest similar underlying causes and justifying reasons for simplification and abstraction of an equally concentrated kind.

It then remained for John Malcolm Brinnin, in an overly clever presentation in his book of 1959 *The Third Rose,* to present the art scene of that time and the connections with art in a pieced together fashion which appeared to support the parallel with Cubism altogether more continuously and cohesively, from the inspiration of Cézanne as it may have affected *Three Lives* (1905–06, published 1909) through *The Making of Americans* (1906–11) and *A Long Gay Book* and *G.M.P.* (1909–12), to *Tender Buttons* of 1912–14. Finally, Norman Weinstein's 1970 book *Gertrude Stein and the Literature of the Modern Consciousness* is representative of a more recent inclination to seek a firm contributory place for this writer within the mainstream of literary modernism; the orthodoxy here being in the premise that a play with the shapes and sounds and word-formations of language, in order to convey a continuously present reality, is not only the main thrust of her imaginative writings, but also a theoretically buttressed and conceptually accepted principle of modernism generally, so that a comparison can be made accordingly with the way motion is conveyed in Duchamp's "cubistic" *Nude Descending a Staircase* (1911–12).

The problems raised by these latter interpretations are, again, several. Just as Gertrude Stein's references to the writing of her *Three Lives* under the stimulus of Cézanne's *Portrait of Mme Cézanne* and the "new feeling about composition" which Cézanne's work gave her present that work as more emblematic for her than strictly contributory, so also she referred to Cubist works as having played a similarly emblematic role for her, saying, in asides or informal comments only, that she was doing in writing what Picasso was doing in painting. The claims of Braque and Salmon, in the "Testimony against Gertrude Stein" published in reaction to *The Autobiography of Alice B. Toklas* by the magazine *Transition* in July 1935, to the effect that she understood nothing of what went on around her, or of her period, are false as far as the new disciplines and discoveries of scientific and psychological thought are concerned, but not untrue to the workings of her creative ego, which was always inward oriented and, where it reached out to the consideration of art to which she responded, proceeded primarily from an intuitive and self-defining empathy with the artist's personality, or what she saw as that. The specifics of search and innovation in Cubism were not therefore germane to her, it being the abstracted inventive drive which counted and fueled her own one-sided sense of parallelism.

The standard comparisons made, since Wilson and Sutherland, are between the surface character of her prose, as exemplified in *The Making of Americans,* and the surface character of analytical Cubism; and between the fragmented still-life descriptions of *Tender But-*

tons and the treatment of the object in Synthetic Cubism. But unless one goes back, as Katz did in the essay referred to earlier, to the pre-Cubist moment of Picasso's 1906 *Portrait of Gertrude,* there is no channel of access between Cubism and her writing, or in the reverse direction, to justify any such one-to-one comparison. Both comparisons are, furthermore, misleading on Gertrude Stein's side as to the nature of her work. The sheer range of the individual features which have been brought up in the making and re-making of the first comparison implies as much: flattening of the traditional biographical dimension to characterization, reduction in quest of an underlying reality, an intellectual, geometric and conceptual emphasis, repetitions and incantations, concentration on the "plastic" potentialities of language. Such features add up to an inventory of technical and structural characteristics, without it being possible to specify at what point cumulatively they give the comparison real force; and it seems doubtful that they would be picked out without reference to the theory of Cubism, in which Gertrude Stein herself had no interest.

In the case of *Tender Buttons,* whatever stimulus as to subject-matter came from Cubist still life, according to report, the application to the writing of terms such as collage and construction can only, in their nature, be metaphorical; and the essential severance found here is between the conveying of the character of familiar objects in words and the naming of them, not between the whole object or amalgam of objects and their independent parts or attributes. More crucially, the basic step taken at this time is markedly different, for reasons having to do with primitivism (see Chap. 1), from those contemporaneously taken by Cubism. As to Gertrude Stein in the perspective of modernism, the point commonly emphasized in this connection is her contribution to the early prose style of Hemingway, and also to O'Neill and Sherwood Anderson; but even there the combination of an elemental phrasing and disciplined attention to rhythms takes effect as a matter of technique, as distinct from long-term imaginative reverberations.

It emerges from this review, therefore, that for a cross-comparison between the arts of the kind in question to be both valid and truly effective, three conditions have to be met: first, chronological synchronism, or a close approximation to that; secondly, personal association, or at least knowledge of the related development; and finally, specific analogies of structure, direction or both. The comparisons made in my text, between late Symbolist poetry in the circle around Picasso and certain ongoing veins in Picasso's imagery, and between the development of analytical Cubism and that of Gertrude Stein, satisfy all three of these criteria. In the case of Gertrude Stein, the comparison is in fact illuminating both ways, clarifying the general character of Cubism in this phase, and also the change of direction in Gertrude Stein at the point where the relationship breaks off.

iii Subject Matter and Meaning: Panofsky on Recognition and Identification in Front of Paintings

Iconography has established itself, in the period stretching from the 1920s and 1930s down to the present, as a basic art historical method for dealing with the subject matter of a work of art, and analyzing it in such a way that an overall "meaning" for the image is set up. It does this by correlating the subject matter with existing texts in such a way as to allow for and make possible a progressive "deepening" of interpretation.

The theoretical model owed to Panofsky of what takes place in the analysis of the subject matter of a work of art is best known in the form in which it appears introducing his 1939 *Studies in Iconology;* or from the re-use of that essay in his 1955 collection of papers, *Meaning in the Visual Arts.* There are in fact some modifications introduced in the latter version. More important, however, is the fact that the formulation of the model used here goes back still earlier, to an article of 1932 on the description and interpretation of the content of works of art. That version presents much more significant differences, both in the discussion of the individual elements of the scheme and in the nature of the scheme as a whole. It is therefore best to begin with what is said there, within a Kantian rather than, as later, a neoscholastic framework, and with some advantages of clarity or directness; and to consider against that background the variations of the subsequent versions.

The same example from everyday life being used to establish the scheme throughout, namely the meeting of an acquaintance on the street who greets one by lifting his hat, the particular way in which the apprehension of meaning there is subdivided into successive levels or strata can be followed through in terms of what is included under each. In the 1932 version, the subdivision is into, first, the concrete meaning, of the act of lifting the hat, smiling and nodding the head. "Meaning" would seem intrinsically an odd term to use in this connection, what is recognized being the performance of the act or actions in question. This difficulty is shaded over by the later change to "factual" meaning, which is now described in terms which bring in identification rather than recognition and take it as based on comparison with what is already known from practical experience. Second comes the expressive, or, as it is later called, expressional meaning, which is a matter of the feelings towards the other person reflected in the way the act is performed. The subsequent amplification, that this is identified by means of empathy, on the basis of sensitivity to expression in general, invites the qualifications that, if an implication as to how the person feels is being read into the act, as that account would imply, then the expression of feeling detected and attributed to the person may be in fact illusory, in the sense of being simply not there; and that the feeling may also merely inflect what the man does rather than express itself more generally and openly. In the 1939 version, the factual meaning and the expressive are brought together to constitute, between them, the primary or "natural" meaning. Third in order comes conventional meaning, the act being taken in the light of custom or habit as a sign of courtesy; this becomes later designated as secondary or conventional meaning, in indication of the shift here to a different level, as intelligible rather than sensible, and as a consciously imparted overlay to the action. Yet it is not clear why convention, in the sense of recognized practice, should come in only at this point rather than in the making of the gesture of greeting, which is itself formalized and normally so taken without need for interpretation. Finally, "beyond all these phenomena" (in the 1932 version) there lies the "impression of an internal structure" to which all of those factors that bear on personality and philosophy of life have equally contributed. The gaining of that impression is said to be independent of will or knowledge, and to preserve that independence, when what is in question has become redesignated as intrinsic meaning or content, experience is made the basis of the apprehension, rather than power of penetration or inference. The coordinates of observation and interpretation in this connection are at the same time extended, to include now character or personality, background or origin, present surroundings, and also period and previous history. And content now becomes the unifying principle which underlies and explains what takes place both on the first two levels and also on the third.

As applied to the analysis of works of art, this breakdown yields, in Panofsky's earliest choice of example, the identification of the figure in Grünewald's *Resurrection* as a man, on the basis of practical experience of objects and expressions; as a man suspended in midair, on the basis of the history of style; as Christ ascending to Heaven, on the basis of the history of types, which is to say on the secondary level; and then beyond these lies the ultimate and essential content of the work, put alternatively as the world attitude which it reveals. In the 1939 version, where the example correspondingly used is Van der Weyden's *Three Magi,* primary or natural subject matter at the first level, comprising in its scope both the factual and the expressional, is the basis of pre-iconographic description. At that level, the child in the Van der Weyden is interpreted, in terms of the history of representation, as hovering in midair. At the second level secondary or conventional subject matter supports iconographical analysis in a narrow sense; and at the third intrinsic meaning or content is the basis for iconographical analysis in a deeper sense. The first two levels of analysis are taken as prerequisites for the third, and this carries over to the later, 1955 version. There, however, the modification of the scheme so that the second level of analysis is termed iconography, entailing the articulation of the work into the history of types, themes and concepts, and the third one termed iconology, entailing articulation into the history of cultural symptoms and symbols in general, comes into seemingly irreconcilable relationship with the concluding declaration which has all three approaches fusing into "one organic and indivisible process."

The main difficulty attending Panofsky's scheme, however, is that the processes of recognition, identification and interpretation in question cannot in practice be circumscribed and separated into successive strata in the way that the scheme would imply. The application of this point both to life situations and works of art can be illustrated by what takes place in the case of photographs. At what is for Panofsky the basic or primary level of response, one may on looking at a photograph make such comments as: (1) This is a figure, or a human being—that much being presumably recognized by a very young child who points at a picture or photo and says, wrongly, that it is "Daddy"; (1a) This is a man and not a woman—as that might be said of the picture in Cracow, by Raphael or his school, which is variously called a portrait of the Fornarina or of Raphael himself; (1b) This is George—as a very young child, again, may identify a portrait of himself at a still younger age as his brother, who is now that age.

In the second and third of these cases, one is already dealing with this application of special knowledge. The young child who in (1a) gets it wrong before a painting, may perhaps be helped by having it pointed out to him how hairdo, physiognomy or clothing point the other way. That is something done internally. In (1b), on the other hand, the tendency is to go, in terms of special knowledge, outside of the image itself: to the time the photograph was taken, what is written on the back of it or the association of the setting with a place that one visited in a certain year. But it may also be possible here to arrive at a resolution on an internal basis, as for example by pointing out the qualities of feature which make it definitely not George. The kind of remark which consists of saying "There's George" in front of a tombstone or fresco, when it could not possibly be him, rests on the same dual set of alternative possibilities, both of them entailing special knowledge: for either the situation in question, or the presence of information telling who it really is, may apprise one of its being a joke.

A further range of typical comment, in front of a photo, might be: (2) That's a man skiing; (2a) That's a man three seconds after completing a Telemark; and (2b), with an aerial view, That's the skiing lodge, and the slope with the cable is there. It is not at all necessary, in the case of (2), to have an experience of the history of action photographs of skiing in order to make such an identification. It could be done purely on internal evidence, as in (2b): at first, perhaps, one is not able to read the photo, but then someone starts to explain how to do that, and one can go on from there. Here again the assistance given is a matter of special knowledge, and it is this also that makes possible the step from (2) to (2a); knowledge external in that case to what can be read by going further into the image itself but open to being gained by looking in the right place rather than from experience, as for example by looking up a diagram of the Telemark and seeing that it fitted.

Or again the comment might be: (3) That's David skiing; (3a) That's David skiing at the age of about fifteen; (3b) That's David skiing on Mont Blanc in 1972. These are cases in which an answer could be arrived at by internal scrutiny together, in various proportions and combinations, with external knowledge. There will be no need, in (3a), to have a series of photos for comparison, or mental reference, of David at various ages; the age or rough age of the boy here may well be deducible from internal details. And in (3b) one may recognize internally that it is David, recognize it as a skiing photo, and apply the external knowledge that the only time David went skiing was on Mont Blanc in a given year.

It follows from these considerations, therefore, that learning to read things in photographs, or films, posters or paintings, and learning what to call them go, from childhood up, hand in hand. The capacity to visualize things independently of having them before one obviously has some degree of correspondence to the stage reached on the first of those fronts; but it is also only natural that, as one's ability on that front becomes increasingly firm, there should be a tendency to use external knowledge the more in combination with it—as happens when the imaginative component of what is shown in art, which has not been discussed here, is seen in the light of an historical and conceptual tradition. All through the cases discussed, in any event, it is special knowledge each time that makes it possible to go further.

The main borderline here is, in fact, between those cases where one goes further by dint of reference to the image itself, and those where one does this by virtue of external information or some other person's knowledge. And even this is not a firm and absolute borderline.

The three types of procedure described by Panofsky as being involved in the identification of what one sees in the Grünewald example as a man, as a figure in the air and as Christ correspond to operations which do certainly take place, and may well occur in that sequence. The critique here is not therefore of the levels in his account as such but of their logical interdependence as stated by him, and their boundaries as drawn up by him, both of which aspects raise problems in the ways separately indicated. Panofsky's construction here might, it is true, be taken simply as a pleasantly argumentative piece of exposition prefacing the studies that follow, with a scheme to it that does not ask to be taken too literally. But whether or not the view of philosophy that this implies, as something of a decorative embellishment to the serious business of the art historian, is an over-indulgent one in what it allows, it would certainly seem proper to question the separation of acts or levels in a theoretical model of this sort when they are not separated in practice. And the increasingly hieratical organization of the scheme, as Panofsky developed it, appears as a source of troublesomeness both in itself, and in terms of what happens when its application is turned back to be tested against reality.

Applied to Cubism, the Panofskian model yields an uncertainty as to how to distinguish between superficial appearances in a work of art (particularly with a straightforward or traditional subject) and what might lie behind or beyond them; and between the internal dictates of imagery in a painting and whatever, in the way of motivation and promptings, might be regarded as coming from outside of the work itself. With an art so intricately wrought in terms of choice of elements and the relationships between them, this is a distinct liability.

iv. Representation, Perception and the Reading of a Painting: Gombrich on Cubism

Still another approach in art history, of more recent vintage than iconography but equally buttressed by theoretical principles, entails correlating the way in which a painting, or visual image in general, is read on the one hand with conventions of representation, as they have established themselves and become accepted in successive historical periods, within the Western tradition, and on the other with the psychology of perception on the viewer's part. This approach runs into the general problem of assuming that there is a continuity of principles that extends itself into the modern period, but also finding that there is a breakdown in many ways of the traditions of representation that takes place in the art of this century.

Gombrich's discussion of Cubism in *Art and Illusion* (1960) comes in Part III, *The Beholder's Share,* at the end of the chapter entitled "Ambiguities of the Third Dimension." It deserves special review, because he is the only writer on questions of perception to have given major attention to Cubism, first in a lecture of 1953 on "Psychoanalysis and the History of Art" and then again in *Art and Illusion* and in a 1961 article on "How to Read a Painting." Gombrich's stance in both book and essays is broadly antiphilosophical in the sense, implicit in all his later writings, of seeking in science and scientific psychology a concrete basis of some kind to set against the dangers, real or imagined, of dealing in philosophical terms—whether conceptually or analytically—with the relationship between spectator and work of art. The effects of this attitude on the terms in which the argument is presented, and the way it proceeds, will be the focus here.

The opening statement of the account, giving the essence of Gombrich's interpretation, is that Cubism is "the most radical attempt [in the history of art] to stamp out ambiguity and to enforce one reading of the picture." The key word here, ambiguity, as generally applied to Cubism, serves to conjure up in that connection a complexity of structure that is visually fascinating and at the same time fraught with internal contradictions of a seemingly baffling kind. But while this might seem fully in accord with Gombrich's subsequent talk of contradiction, bafflement and elusiveness, there is an opposition beyond this in what is being said. For while in Rosenblum's account (1960 also), and Greenberg's of two years earlier, ambiguity is seen as willfully enforced, in the analytical phase of Cubism, by the oscillation of planes and a whole series of shifting plays on the relationship between art and reality, in Gombrich's account it is potentially eliminated. It is therefore necessary to consider how exactly the term is being used for this divergence to be possible.

There is a tradition in modern literary criticism according to which ambiguity designates the fact that, in a poem especially, a word or phrase can be taken in more than one way. Insofar as this represents something deliberate and consciously sought—rather than a function of the fact that certain words and combinations of words having more than one possible meaning inherently require a context in order to bring out which of those meanings is in question, and may without adequate context fail to do so—ambiguity is associated with such willed qualities and controlled effects in literature as compression, wit or irony, and paradox. Rosenblum's use of the term clearly belongs in this tradition. There is also a usage in psychoanalytic theory, going back to Freud, and in the theory of symbolism and symbolic communication, whereby an image may, as in a dream, appear to signify and even to be two or more mutually exclusive things at once; and this kind of ambiguity may, upon more complete or deeper interpretation, yield to the understanding of those two different meanings or identities in a way that conjoins and even integrates them with one another. But Gombrich uses the term in a third and, as it may be called, technical sense: one deriving from the field of experimental visual psychology, where a particular kind of configuration such as the celebrated duck-rabbit, which he uses as a key illustration, and others like it in principle, are used to stimulate and to gauge the faculty of visual projection because of their being susceptible to alternative readings which are mutually exclusive.

Gombrich's use of ambiguity, therefore, corresponds to the first dictionary sense, "having two or more possible meanings," rather than the second dictionary sense of "unclear." The connecting link between these two different senses lies in the notion of openness to being taken in more than one way, which may apply in the case of art either to any individual element within the work or to the image as a whole, and comparably in the case of literature either to any particular unit of sense, such as a phrase or line, or to overall elements governing the whole such as story line or mood; and in the element or situation of puzzlement which is thereby generated. The distinction between them rests, philosophically, on whether or not the degree of specificity is sufficient either way for defining or characterizing purposes. An unresolved ambiguity may, in that perspective, be one either so left or so established that there is, or can be taken to be, equal justification for more than one alternative definition or characterization of what is in question; and this covers both of the possibilities presented by the two dictionary senses, since the justification, to be equal, does not have to be equally sufficient. To be talked of as unresolvable, on the other hand, ambiguity has to be of the kind designated by the second dictionary sense rather than the first; for it is necessary for this purpose that, in the case of literature or art, it should result from deliberate omission or other contrivance on the artist's part.

Gombrich uses the term "unresolved" for the ambiguities of Cubism, with the evident implication of sufficient specificity either way, as in the duck-rabbit example; and the illustrations which he brings into the 1961 essay in continuation of what he says about Cubism—

Rorschach blots, Tchelitchew's *Hide and Seek* and the work of Escher—confirm that implication, in offering equal or, as with the geometric mosaics discussed in *Art and Illusion,* almost equal justification for alternative readings. But in interpreting Cubism as directed towards the stamping out of ambiguity, by sheer extent of contradictoriness, he brings in the idea of unresolvable ambiguity as the ultimate form of unresolved ambiguity, higher in degree on the same scale. The linking bridge here, in what he says, is provided by the use of Thiéry's figure, which Gombrich compares with the mosaic patterns and in which he finds the "quintessence" of Cubism. But the features which give that figure its incorrigible instability, to which he refers, and its resulting oscillation show that a special form of unresolved ambiguity is in question, and one in which the ambiguity, rather than being eliminated, is recognized as unresolvable.

A second problem, related through Gombrich's general view of all artistic images as ambiguous, concerns identification and "seeing as" and their respective roles in the reading of works of art. Gombrich begins the preceding chapter, titled "The Image in the Clouds," with a passage from Apollonius of Tyana which juxtaposes without differentiation the seeing of a cloud as a stag or antelope from its shape and the identification of a depicted figure as an Indian from the physiognomic features shown; and the same implication of their being no need for distinction here emerges from statements of his own. He discusses the statement "this picture looks like the castle there" as a comparative one, which is one possibility with this phrasing, and the most likely one in common practice; but it is also possible that an imaginative construction might be being put on the picture, and what it suggested to the viewer might have primacy over the factor of resemblance. The same basic point is philosophically more explicit in the claim, formulated in reference to Maurice Denis's well-known statement about the essential nature of a painting, that it is impossible to "see" simultaneously both plane surface and a battle horse; for the effect of the quotation marks put around "see" here is to merge into one inseparable process the seeing of a painting as plane surface and the identification of a horse in it.

Since to argue from these cases against Gombrich's general overview of the operation of projection is to risk circularity, it is a more tangible measure of the difficulty to consider the application of what is philosophically debatable here to the specific illustrations used. Mantegna in his *Virtue Chasing Vice* is described as "making us see" human faces in the clouds, though in fact the faces are painted in such a way as to be recognizably there in the clouds, and there is no question correspondingly of being led through suggestion to see the clouds as faces. In a poster by Fabian, the image of a factory chimney reading a newspaper is said to remain a chimney but to be also a face; whereas, except for two possible eyes, the way the relevant part of the chimney is treated seems neither to encourage nor to allow that it should be seen as a face. But it is in his later introduction of the Ames chair experiments that Gombrich most clearly implies that a bridge can be made between identifying and seeing as, on the basis of what, under scientific testing conditions, is shown to be the case there.

Insofar as the illusion of seeing a chair in these experiments is comparable to what takes place with the patches of paint that make up a painting, it can be said the effect of Gombrich's general argument about illusion is to represent identification in both of these cases as one kind of "seeing as." One sees the assembly of forms in space as a chair, as a consequence of the effective working of the illusion; and one identifies what one sees as a chair, when asked to say what is there. But, whether or not the relation between those two processes can be a matter of proof—and it is not shown to be that in the book—ordinary discourse distinguishes two relevant senses of seeing as: the seeing of a hill as steep, or steeper than one had thought, which corresponds to the seeing of a shape as a surface configuration or as being in front of another shape; and the seeing of a cloud as a map of Europe. The distinction rests on the dissociative character of the perception in the latter case: the cloud is seen as something other than what it is. The Ames experiments are similarly dissociative in character. This is made clear by the fact that, as Gombrich brings out, the illusion persists on the second viewing. Knowing what one is looking at, one still sees the assembly of wires as forming a chair. So this cannot truly serve as a bridging case. And this point has an obvious carry-over to the discussion of Cubism, where the identifying of a table as such may depend on quite different factors than, in Gombrich's phrase, being made to see the outline of a table.

Finally, at least some comment is called for on Gombrich's attribution of a single purpose or direction to Cubism, irrespective of artist, date or stage of development. Having earlier specified that one learns within the context of one's culture to interpret artistic images as "records and indications of the artist's intention," he then suggests, as already cited, that Cubism is to be taken as directed towards the stamping out of ambiguity; and later, that the "representational clues included" force acceptance of the "flat pattern in all its tensions." Here, as compared to the use in the 1961 essay of a Picasso of 1911 to represent the devices of superimposition and telescoping, the argument is illustrated with two individual Cubist works, a Picasso of 1918 and a Braque of 1928. This choice is appropriate to Gombrich's point about inconsistency and bafflingness insofar as, in both cases, the elements fit or sit together like pieces of a jigsaw puzzle. But the kind of segmentation found here, which consistently denies continuity and connection across contours and dividing lines, is characteristic only of late Cubism (after 1916–17). When it is said, therefore, that the Cubists "discovered" that familiar shapes can be read and interpreted "even across a complete change of color and outline," it seems appropriate to ask when this took place, in terms of specific practice, and whether discovery refers here to anything more than a general territory of interest that the artists are exploring. More generally, if it were, say, the art of the High Renaissance or of Michelangelo that was in question, it seems highly doubtful that a comparable overall intention or "point of it all" could be so easily ascribed to any phase or development. And certainly a unitary consciousness or sense of artistic direction, such as Gombrich's account hypothesizes, is uncharacteristic in principle of developments in modern art, and modern culture in general, that cover any span of time and diversity of inclinations.

In his 1954 essay Gombrich had taken a French academic painting of the *Three Graces,* from about 1900, photographed it through rolled glass, and compared the look that resulted with the general look of post-Cézanne and post-Fauve painting as illustrated by Picasso's *Demoiselles d'Avignon.* How exactly the comparison here is to be taken presents some difficulties. If it were Delaunay's 1912 *City of Paris* that was used, with its Three Graces, rather than the Picasso, the kind of resemblance that Gombrich is positing would seem more strongly, and even specifically, conveyed. There, however, one gets a form of modeling deriving directly from Cézanne, and an interplay of rhythms and planes which construct relationships between figures and environment, rather than making them difficult to grasp. The comparison might alternatively be taken as a metaphorical one, in the way that Herbert Read's comparison of the emergence of objects in a synthetic Cubist painting to a lantern slide coming into focus has to be metaphorical in cast if it is to convey anything about what takes place in front of the work that is not either false to the nature of the viewing process or factually untrue. When Gombrich presents it as matter of attitude or decision on the modern artist's part that he should "apply the wobbly glass," there would certainly seem to be no question of any actual or ascertainable relationship to the way in which Picasso and his contemporaries conceived of what they were doing; but a suggestion on that subject, based on surmise, would still be possible. Such being the case, Gombrich would then be attributing to the Cubists generally a kind of provocative, and not necessarily altogether serious, play with the viewer's responses; and it would be the appearance of the work, rather than anything known about the process leading up to it, that gave rise to this view on his part. There would also be the implication that the recognizability of the images depends solely on the artist's structural treatment of them. The resulting picture of Cubism then bears a striking resemblance to the story, published only later, of Picasso's teasing of Braque on the grounds that there was a squirrel to be seen in one of his pictures, so that Braque felt compelled to revise it. This, though a story about Cubism and in keeping with Picasso's personality, in no way constitutes evidence as to either creation or commitment. Whatever it contributes is tangential to the real issues there, and even irrelevant to them.

PART TWO
Philosophical Perspectives

5 The Artist's Intentions and Some Related Issues

> But of what use is it to say what we do when everybody can see it if he wants to?
>
> Picasso ·

To enter into the theoretical and critical question of the artist's intentions and the difficulties that it poses is to become aware of a number of different issues embedded in it or brought up by it. What links those issues, in the history of the topic and again here, is a concern in principle with the statements that the artist makes, or could make or agree to, about his work, and the relationship of those statements to the art itself. Yet one finds in the development of the discussion to date surprisingly little attention paid either to the kinds of things that artists actually say, or to the terms and language used and their relation to life situations outside of the arts. The topic therefore brings with it the need for a whole range of actual or suitably imaginary examples, taken from both art and literature—since the problem spans both fields, and has indeed been traditionally weighted on the side of literature—with references also to the performing arts, such as theater and music.

The approach to the problem here will be guided by a critical sense of actual practice in the field, with questions and answers chosen to reflect this. The philosophical method adopted takes its methods and tools of inquiry from what is now generally known as linguistic or analytical philosophy. These are methods and tools which were evolved in order to discriminate and diagnose why confusion has occurred in cases of this sort, but they have not so far been applied in this specific area. The aim of the discussion as a whole is not to put an end to the problem's existence by any kind of solution—it being not of that kind—but to redelineate it, so that its elements and facets stand out more clearly, in a stripped down form and a commonsensical light; and at the same time to bring out how certain ideas and assumptions have misdirected the discussion, imposing their own terminology. These tasks of delineation and clarification are substantial ones, with a general application to the theory of modern art, so

185

that they act as supports or further elaborations of what was said in the first half of this book.

Intention in Literary Theory and in Philosophy

To review what has been written about intentions is to find that there has been a division of concerns, reflected in the issues that have been taken up in each subject area. In the literary theory of the last half century, intention has been taken either as a moral issue, of trust in the artist, or else as a procedural question, of ruling or distinguishing what is internal and what is external to the work of art, considered as an entity. The first of these views is raised to the status of a principle in D. H. Lawrence's saying "Never trust the artist, trust the tale," and in the commitment of F. R. Leavis and the *Scrutiny* critics to a cultural diagnosis that would reveal the "deep animating intention" of an author in relation to his society and times. The second viewpoint equally took its inspiration from author-critics seminal, in this dual role, for modern literature: in this case, from the practice and supporting theory of Yeats, Pound and T. S. Eliot, and specifically from their shared concept of the poem as an impersonal and dramatic structure, excluding any possibility of real identification between the speaker and the poet himself. From this descended, by direct inheritance, the regulative insistence of the New Criticism on what is to be accepted as belonging to a poem and what rejected, the corresponding codification of the "intentional fallacy," and an accompanying stress on the poem's organic unity and integrity. The extended influence of these latter principles over half a century and their value in establishing both a needed focus in the reading of a poem and a basic procedure for its analysis should not obscure the fact that they work better for a lyrical poem or a short story than for, say, an epic or a long discursive and philosophical novel. For the study of works of art as a professional and academic discipline, larger contingent issues raised by the internal-external dichotomy and the argued irrelevance of materials outside the work are first, what forms of evidence are acceptable or unacceptable in the interpretation of a work of art, either as a whole or in respect to some element in it; and the relative role or weighting of opinion and fact, what is known and what is surmised, as this affects the general shape of critical discourse. Edmund Wilson's interpretation of *The Turn of the Screw,* a brilliant and highly suggestive construction but one which, in a clearly demonstrable sense, plays false to the story, and certainly to James's own view of it, serves as an illustration here. It demonstrates how a reading of a text may be more subjective than objective, in the sense of having more of the critic and his interests in it than is found warranted by the text itself, with or without available statements of the author as to how this text is to be taken. It also illustrates the other broad issue of principle affecting the disciplines which study both works of art and their authors: namely the respective claims of analysis on the one hand, and biographical, including psychographic, exegesis on the other. This, while related to the first issue, would seem more a matter of proportion, focus or simply preference. And so it would ordinarily remain, with contributors on either side naturally complementing one another, except that evidence from or about the author, as it bears on the discussion of intentions, spreads out to include biographical and contextual materials; and beyond that, but in the same general territory, lies the province of unconscious or unstated intentions. A progressive extension of inquiry away from the text, or what is seen as that, comes in this way to be at issue, and not just the validity or application of what the author says.

On the side of philosophy, in contrast, the discussion of intentions has been primarily concerned with situations or contexts involving action. The emphasis in analytical philosophy has correspondingly fallen on the legal and the behavioral aspects of intention; and specifically on two main issues, that of responsibility and that of causation. The question of responsibility, in law and particularly in criminal law, involves the considerations of excuses, exceptions and mistakes, the concept of diminished responsibility, and the admissibility of evidence in that connection and how it is treated as evidence; and the terms around which discussion of principles revolves are, correspondingly, foresight, prediction, premeditation and deliberation. The question of causation rests on the relationship between mental states and physical actions, or is subsumed under the more general question of interaction between mind and body; and the terms that come in for discussion in this connection are, correspondingly, motives, dispositions, efforts and inclinations: all terms used to describe, or suggest, states of mind "veering towards" actions which then ensue. Beyond those two topics, again, lie larger issues with their relevance to the discussion of works of art. In relation to responsibility, there is the factor of awareness or application on the artist's part, as opposed to spontaneity. To say, in law, that a man "intends the consequences of his actions" is normally taken to mean that he recognizes, or ought to recognize, the consequences of what he does. It could however also carry the implication that a man "means" what he does, and looks forward to its results; and if a motivation of the latter kind were shown to be paramount in a case of forgery, the charge would have a much deeper and different force than it would with the author of a skilful pastiche who allowed it to go onto the market.

Similarly, to talk of causation in the case of a work of art is to bring up the larger issues of the work's historical genesis and of how it came to be the way it is. Such questions might be answered in a relatively determinist fashion, in terms of reasons or factors such as where the author was at the time and why he was there—with the emphasis thereby falling on the immediate circumstances of creation. Or they might be answered with a behaviorist emphasis, in terms of "mental events" which bent, turned, directed or pressured the author in creating the work and doing so in this particular form, such as the stimulus of other writers; or the emphasis might be on those same lines, but on psychological factors such as the desire for a fresh start. Where one stops on any of those fronts, what is considered most crucial, and in particular how far back and how far across the span of consciousness the unfolding of awareness or a gradual preparation is traced would all be matters of varying principles or emphasis. At the same time, to modify the openness of the situation here, certain notions or assumptions concerning the workings of creativity are to be recognized as being likely to mislead, especially if they are applied from a prejudiced or rigidly fixed position.

The asymmetry in the above account between the concerns of literary study and criticism and the very different ones found in the philosophy of law and of causation is quite certainly a striking one. To follow out its implications is to bring up already how a moral weight is characteristically attached to the artist saying something about his work, which is not normally given to the man in the dock; and how the principles which, in the lawcourt, regulate the admission of hearsay, and caution as to the drawing of deductions or presumptions from the evidence, would, if applied in the study of works of art, drastically limit the scope of what took place. But while this may be an unalterable fact about the history of the topic, what is of greater importance in the present context is that in recent times the concept of intention has been, on both sides equally, an expansive one. On the side of philosophy, this expansiveness follows from the use of ordinary language as a guide, and from the consideration of a whole range of situations and concrete examples, in order to see empirically how these situations or speech-acts group themselves. Consideration of the term intention itself, while focusing mainly as described on aspects or examples relating to action, has at the same time left room for varying uses of the term to be recognized. One such use that has been brought out is to indicate that the action is to be judged as a whole; in which case the coherence, order or pattern of the proceedings is likely to be stressed. The variety of ways in which a commitment can be made, in forms which include the use of intentional language, has been opened up; and the fact that intentions can be ascribed as well as described. It has been recognized also that there are cases, especially ones connected with meaning and reference, where intention involves a desire, disposition or inclination, rather than a "plan" to be carried out. And finally the concept has been extended to include the possible factor of audience response, in the form of "uptake." What happens here is to be seen as a recognition of meaning or reference taking place as desired; and such recognition has its obvious application to the reception of works of art.

The conception of intention in critical theory and aesthetics has also widened out, over a somewhat longer time-period, in the sense that, while the definitions of intention offered may be restrictive ones—intention as conscious or unconscious aim; or as design or plan in the author's mind—what is included in the terms of the discussion covers a much wider scope. In evidence of such broadening, the very attempt to keep out of criticism any elements of a biographical sort has led to an alignment of intentions with those elements, as more or less equivalent; and questions of interpretation have been posed also as ones to which intentions are germane, in cases where the relevant evidence takes the form not of anything said by the author, but rather of information about him and his cast of mind. In this way the discussion of intentions has not remained confined to the evaluation of works of art in terms of quality or achievement, or more narrowly yet to the adjudgment of them as successful or unsuccessful. Rather it has shifted across to include the province of interpretation, where historical and psychological factors may well come up alongside, or in possible opposition to, the operation of critical judgment in the most general sense.

Intentional Statements and Statements of Intention

To say what an intention is, or what it is like in form, is in fact quite tricky. That this is so is best brought out by a single example of the term in action. If, after meeting a young couple socially one hears the woman described later as the man's "intended wife," the implications of this could run all the way from a contract having been signed (in some countries) or a proposal made, or about to be made, through the existence of a longstanding agreement, or the sense of an agreement, to an intention not yet stated between the pair or, perhaps not inconceivably, one never put into words at all. At its latter end, furthermore, this spectrum of possibilities omits unconscious intentions, of which the persons are totally unaware; and there may be subconscious intentions working against the overt situation, which are brought to light psychoanlytically on the basis of special evidence, as in the suggestion that a man's mother, rather than his wife, is his "intended victim." Which of those possible alternatives is the one that applies will depend, in fact, on the purpose of the statement, the context in which it is made, and the conventions of the society; and the sense of the phrase will be so understood, rather than from any unitary idea of what an intention is or entails.

The issue of recognizing and identifying intentions in the case of works of art brings up the question of whether it is necessary to separate off a type or category of intentions, to be called "artistic," as distinct from those which figure in real-life situations; and to do this seems neither axiomatically necessary nor justified on the basis of special characteristics that reveal themselves in the language used or the forms of inquiry that are adopted. It might seem in principle that such intentions had to be stated or written about the work, and correspondingly separate from it; but if so, then those cases must be reckoned with where the statement of intentions, rather than being separate from the work, forms part of it textually, or where the intention derives its amenability to being spoken of from consideration of the work itself. And if the impression holds that, outside of the work, intentions are revealed or clarified in a certain type of utterance or declaration, that is certainly sometimes the case; but it is also true that it is extremely difficult to designate what kinds of statement, by or about the artist and relating to his work, do not in some way provide evidence of intention, or a possible contribution to what might count as that.

Given this variety of ways in which the making known of intentions takes place in the case of works of art, a preliminary distinction between intentional statements and statements of intention may be useful. Intentional statements are to be understood, very generally, as any statements of the artist's bearing on the process of creation of the work, or the artist's own conception, characterization or evaluation of it. Intentional data, as they may be called, consist more broadly of any such materials, not necessarily furnished by the artist himself. Thus questions as to what was happening in an artist's life, what mood he was in, what he was thinking of, or what idea led him to take a certain step, would be answerable either by the artist in a form that revealed something of his intentions, or by the provision of information which bore on the intention in some way. Rather than the intention being stated or recorded in such cases, it would, according to the character of the evidence, be inferred, assumed or reconstructed.

Statements of intention, in contrast to the more extensive category of intentional statements, would be ones in which the artist said in the first person that he or she was going to do something; or ones in which, in place of "going to," such a corresponding phrase appeared as "plan to," "mean to," "intend to," and so on down through a range of examples in which the factor of explanation was stressed, as often in the last two cases, and ones where the element of commitment on the speaker's part was weaker, as with "contemplate," "have in mind" or "envisage," to cases where the commitment shaded progressively into the description of facts and feelings, as with such phrases as "I am disposed to" or "trying to," or "I am moving into. . . ." The general heading of statements of commitment, emphasis, policy or direction, under which all of these varying forms of statement can be placed, would also be one that covered in principle promises, threats and disclosures of a design or strategy, in those typical cases where the speaker equally said, or implied, that he or she was going to do something. Notwithstanding the possibility of a common phrasing, these are not so much variations on statements of intention as allied forms of statement, with differences of implication in more specific instances which comparison can bring out.

Very commonly artists make statements affirming or explaining a particular concern or interest of theirs, or pinpointing or denying knowledge of something on their part, in a form which cannot be said to represent, strictly, the stating of an intention. Specific examples, from the visual arts, will bring out more clearly the character of such statements, formal or informal, and suggest some classifications:

> It is exactly the opposite that I am striving for, strength and inwardness. (Nolde)
>
> I want to express my feelings rather than state them. (Jackson Pollock)

These may be considered definitions of purpose, of a broad and general kind. Beyond the presence of a commitment in both cases, they have no analogy with promises, but rather are like avowals.

> On one seascape there is an excessively red signature, because I wanted a red note in the green. (van Gogh, in a letter)

This is again a definition of purpose, but here one that is specific, calling attention to the significance of a particular element. The more particularized statements which do this are, the more they tend to become intentional in character, by virtue of the "pointing," directive aspect which is brought in.

> The bull . . . is brutality and darkness. . . . the horse represents the people. . . . That's the reason I used [for symbolism, allegory] the horse, the bull and so on. (Picasso on *Guernica*)
>
> To me in this painting the landscape and the struggle exist only in the imagination of these praying people as a result of the sermon. That is why there is a contrast between these real people and the struggle in this landscape which is not real and out of proportion. (Gauguin, on his *Vision of the Sermon*)

In both of these cases an explanation, relating to a particular work, is given; in one case the explanation of a motif, in the other of a feature of the work.

> Painting relates to both art and life. . . . I try to act in that gap between the two. (Robert Rauschenberg)

One should not think about Nature when painting. . . . it is personal sensation that matters most. (Paula Modersohn-Becker, in her diary)

Both of these statements may be said to define an area of commitment; in the second case this is done antithetically, by the ruling out or playing down of alternative possibilities. Comparison can be made here both with specific commitments, made in the form of promises—such as a promise to finish work on a ceiling in ten days and make it eye deceiving—and also with statements of policy of a broad nature.

[Asked about the origin of a certain drawing of his] Picasso was explicit. This drawing has no relationship to a 'negro' mask, from the Congo or elsewhere. 'As you can see [he said] it is a pot of flowers with heads. That's how it came out, it's a drawing of a kind I have done by the thousand and the thousand, to see. . . . one of those drawings that one does while waiting at the telephone.'

Here, though the force of the recorded statement is to confirm once more what the artist had unvaryingly maintained, namely that awareness of African sculpture was not yet a directive factor in his work at that time, the statement is in itself an informational one.

It can also happen that the kinds of thing that are said by artists in the above examples may be expressed as statements of intention, or as closely cognate statements of ambition or desire:

I want to give the scene something more serious, more considered, more religious. I want to paint a general and his soldiers readying themselves for battle like true Lacedaimonians. . . . I want neither passionate movement nor passionate expression [except in certain figures]. . . . I want to characterize in this painting that deep, great and religious feeling that love of one's country inspires. As a result I must banish from it all those passions which not only are alien to it, but also would alter the sanctity. . . . I want to try and put aside those movements, those theatrical expressions, to which the moderns have given the name of "expressive painting." . . . I shall show Leonidas and his soldiers calm and promising themselves immortality before the battle. (David on his *Leonidas at Thermopylae,* as reported by Délécluze)

In the *Sheep Which Have Just Been Sheared* I tried to express that kind of bewilderment and confusion which sheep feel when they have just been clipped, and also the curiosity and stupefaction of those who have not yet been sheared when they see such naked creatures come back among them. I tried to make this dwelling-place convey a peaceful and rustic air and to suggest that behind it is the little field where the poplars are planted which give it shade; finally to suggest that all this was begun long enough ago for generations to have lived here. (Millet, in a letter to the critic Thoré)

Declarations in the prospective and retrospective forms which are exemplified here are associated, most often, with artists whose work has, especially at that time, a specifically spiritual aspiration or emphasis, as in these two cases; the point being that such aspirations are more easily put into words, less easily rendered in visual terms, than other aspirations for one's work that might be entertained. The motivation for the statement might correspondingly be doubt on the artist's part that he had really fulfilled the aspiration, and a need for self-justification; or the feeling that it was desirable to provide some explanation.

I would like my pictures to look as if a human being had passed between them, like a snail. . . . (Francis Bacon)

Here the artist records, in the shape of a desire, his quest for a certain visual appearance to his work.

My intent in painting flags is to show that the flag can and should be a subject in the visual arts. (John Castagno, a Philadelphia artist, in a letter to the *New York Times*)

This statement serves as justification of what the artist has chosen to paint. It could be put in the alternative form that his work rests on, or reflects, a belief as to viable subject matter, and is in this respect like declarations of a moral and intellectual attitude or stance. Since only the actual painting of flags, and not any supporting belief, can bear out the claim that the statement makes, its intentional aspect might be taken as gratuitous—except insofar as it may serve, in a negative sense, to rule out other possible intentions that might be attributed to the artist.

Unrepresented in the above range of examples are what may be called prophetic statements, such as van Gogh's reported saying to a sitter of his, "Mme Ginoux, Mme Ginoux, your portrait will be placed in the Louvre in Paris"; statements of the function assigned to a work, at whatever stage in its creation and subsequent existence, such as where it is to go; and statements of decision, indicating what the speaker has made up his mind to do. Prophetic statements may be a kind of promise, but they involve a proffered expectation or hope rather than an expected part in bringing it about. To speak of the function of a work is, strictly, to say what it is for, in the same kind of sense as a combination exists to unlock a particular safe, or a golden key is given to commemorate a directorship. But function here shades off into purpose; to say of a certain work that it was made to commemorate a king's death may be more like saying it was done to shock, or to please a particular patron, than like saying that it was created for a particular room. Statements of decision slide into descriptive or informational statements in the case of works of art just as characteristically as in situations of other kinds, as when a chess-player announces that he is going to castle. They are also relatively rare, and the reason for this would seem to be that, while there may well be statements which embody or reflect the artist's decisions, the decisions themselves are likely to be empirical or intuitive ones: more like those made while driving a car than those made while mounting a campaign. Correspondingly, if decisions are talked about, what is said is likely to be worded not in terms of choice, but rather of preference, inclination or interest.

Contrary to a common supposition, statements of intention do not necessarily either imply or identify an anterior psychological state, The idea that this is invariably the case is one misleadingly suggested by the legal view of intention, with its accompanying framework of mistakes, accidents and infelicities. An intention that is entertained and announced, according to this conception, is seen as failing to take effect in the form of an action because of some intervening interference or slip; as one might say that one meant to castle in a game of chess, indicating that the intention was there but one had moved the pieces wrongly. The concept of excuses in law also works along similar lines, as where mental incapacity is taken as interfering with a person's sense of what it means to do as he did; and evidence may be adduced that a person did not really intend to do what he said that he was going to do, on the supposition that he was making an idle threat or was joking.

The law's treatment of promises is, however, revealing. It can be said that a promise is characteristically the expression of an intention, as in the case of a formal promise to care for someone. But it is possible to go through a contractual formula of promising, such as marriage vows at the altar, without intending to do what the words specify. Legally, the psychological state at back of the promise is irrelevant here, what matters being the form of words used and their being uttered in an appropriate context. The words "I make no promise" serve to place a limit or restraint on the expectation that something will come about, and to promise may be, in other cases, to express a confidence of opinion, as when one promises that an affair is over, or that the letter carrier will come. In these ordinary life situations, the psychological state behind the statement may again be irrelevant, here to the speaker's being in a position to make the statement, and to the convincingness which tone and delivery give to it.

The same considerations are what establish that "I am going to Rome" is a statement of intention rather than an account of where one is going—by supplying, for example, "whether you come or not." To say that one is determined to go to Rome, where the determination is a psychological state, like a conviction or certainty that one will get there, may indeed be equivalent in some circumstances to saying that one fully intends to go there; but it is also possible that two different kinds of announcement should be separately made here, one of the determination and the other of what one proposes to do (this year or never), or is perhaps already starting to do. It might still appear that a psychological state was there, unannounced, in the second of these cases, but it would not have to be. What lies behind "I am going to castle" in chess would be, if anything, knowing how to castle and being in a position to do so and the remark could be accompanied by a simultaneous shifting of the pieces, where the words then became like a self-reminder on those subjects (of the procedure and the conditions for it). If this intention were voiced a move or two ahead, the opponent, fitting the remark to the situation on the board, could respond "I am not going to let you castle," and thereby abort the intention, much as good intentions may be aborted in a pattern of behavior and response. Similarly, "I am not going to put up with this abuse any longer" may be said to put a halt to a pattern of behavior which only now makes itself felt as insufferable; and one may shout "Out!" as a way of communicating that one wants a person to leave, without that intention existing first or independently.

The Object-predicated Use of the Term *Intention*

It is possible, besides talking of the artist's intention, to speak of the intention of a work of art. Through some of the most serious contributions to modern criticism and theory, though the critics did not necessarily formulate the point theoretically in such terms, and may not even have understood it in that way, there is in fact a recognizable distinction to be found between these two usages. Thus one finds T. S. Eliot writing of a "harmonics of poetry" which would interfere with the poem's intention (rather than the poet's); the Marxist critic George Lukacs of the "intention realized in the work [which] need not coincide with the writer's conscious intention," and in art history, for reasons somewhat similar to Lukacs's, the term *Kunstwollen,* introduced by Alois Riegl and usually translated as "artistic intentions," was taken up by Panofsky in a Kantian framework which explicitly distinguishes it from the artist's intentions.

This third person and object-predicated use of the term *intention* has some lexical history and authority to justify it, but the line of descent to the modern critical usage is not entirely clear. One reason for this is that there is no real Latin equivalent for the term *intention,* in law or otherwise; either a noun is used with essentially different connotations in reference to mental states, such as *voluntas, animus, consilium,* or the sense is rendered by a conjunctive phrase indicative of aim or purpose. *Intentio* always carries the implication of application or effort. This carries through to medieval Latin, where it is used

in that sense of an author, and also of a thing, without any appearance
of a distinction in this respect. In the sixteenth century and later,
intention or intent is correspondingly used, of a poetic allegory to be
explicated or a philosophical precept recommended, in a form which
couples it with meaning, purpose or some equivalent word, very
much as in the common phrase "the spirit and intent of the law." In
the nineteenth century the intention of a collective entity, such as a
multitude or a movement, may be spoken of, which has its equivalents already also in late or medieval Latin, but with the difference
that what is in question now may be more a matter of spiritual bent or
sincerity. And where the use of intention in reference to a text, again
either poetic or philosophical, has to do with an underlying scheme of
thought or ideas which is to be unfolded, the medieval Latin use of *sic
intendit* or *hic intendit quod,* in the sense of "the author means by this
. . . "would seem especially relevant. This, indeed, is perhaps the
beginning of that transposition to the third person in the case of art
works, which takes the form "the intention here is. . . ." and other
variations.

The object-predicated or, more generally, object-oriented use of
intention may have established itself in this way as a familiar, and
even representative, feature of critical discussion, but to say this is
not to imply either clarity or consistency. Other examples could be
added in where there is confusion between the two uses, or a sliding
back and forth between them, and others again where a terminology
that includes intention is effectively part of a closed system with no
external or properly logical justification. What is evident, though,
from the passages cited, is that the phrase can be used by a critic of
poetry, as it is by Eliot, in reference to features and resources which
are particular to the medium, such as assonance or irony. It can be
used by the critical theorist, such as Lukacs, of a longer work such as
a novel, and the reference is then to the essential ideological concept
or orientation underlying the work's form, as this is to be seen and
understood in its historical context. Talk of the intention "realized" or
"enacted" in the work is a form of critical stringency which can be
argued and supported in either of those ways. In philosophy of criticism there may also be talk of the intention of a fiction such as a
myth, where the reference is again a contextual one, here to the ideals
and aspirations of the culture which are reflected in the myth and give
it its collective validity; and in art history it becomes possible, in
relation to a movement or development such as Cubism, to speak
both of the artistic intentions of the period, in the manner of Riegl,
and also of the "real" intention of the style that was developed. Analytical philosophy, for its part, recognizes that one can speak of the
intention of an appliance, as for example that it should act as a brake;
and an occasional writer in aesthetics, noting that it is possible to
speak of a work's intention, equates this with what is "going on" in

the work or its "point," as if struggling in this way to bridge the gap between the creative and the created.

There are, then, these precedents in particular disciplines, but the basis in ordinary language usage for speaking of the intention of a work of art is not so easily arrived at. A suitable starting-point here is the analogy of moves in a game, such as chess. One can speak of the intention of a certain move there, where no words are used at the time, and yet the player could be asked by a questioner if the intention of the move had been understood correctly. If the analogy here with the case of a work of art is an incomplete one, this is because art does not normally involve a competitive element, as between chess-players, but rather a cooperative form of relationship on the respondent's part. Significantly, it is certain kinds of "trick" drawing which seem to offer the closest correspondence: those drawings which first succeed in puzzling one as to what they might represent, and then succeed in convincing one that they could represent what the answer to the puzzle is, such as a bear climbing a tree; or those which tempt the respondent into thinking that a pair of lines could not be parallel to one another, when a ruler establishes that they are, or into adding feet when it should be legs that are added. In all of these cases, there is an element of gamesmanship, it being the intention of those drawings to deceive, tempt or mislead: an intention which, like the move in the chess-game, may or may not be seen through, or resisted.

Questions that might be asked about a strange but clearly man-made object or set of objects, and about a building of a certain type, point towards some of the reasons for the shift to the third person referred to earlier. The question "What is it for?" or "What is it there for?" might be asked about an unfamiliar object in circumstances where, if there was a specific function or use that was implied or recognized, it was of only secondary interest to the speaker, and also where consideration of the object as a work of art was unsettled. In the case of buildings, one might say in explaining the character of the Roman atrium that it was not just done that way to catch the rain—which would be the object or purpose of it—but to create a pleasant living atmosphere with an interaction between inside and out. Such a comment could be made of a building irrespective of the architect, who might be either unknown, or a participant in a collective and growing tendency in structures of this kind. These very factors, indeed, might positively encourage the shift to the third person; for ignorance as to who the architect was, or the possibility that there might be more than one, or again a reluctance to ascribe to a single personality what might be the shared tendency of a whole period or school would all be relevant sources of discomfort here.

As some of the phrasing which has now been used would imply, talk of the intention of a work of art can be seen as equivalent to asking, in the Latin, *quo tendit*—with the proviso that Classical and

Renaissance art theory lacked any such conception. Analogies with situations outside of the arts are again helpful: here, ones from law and from history show how the intention is not in this case to be taken as separable from the work itself, as it otherwise tends to be, and how correspondingly the artist's capacity to help here relegates itself to a possibility only, dependent on the sort of thing that he is prepared to say and how what he says is taken.

Whereas the criminal law, as described earlier, characteristically conceives of intention as lying behind a person's act, prior to it and most often separate from it, the civil law does sometimes include in its terminology a different and apposite consideration of intent. In the case of acts of defamation, a published statement may be adjudged to be malicious in intent; and when a law has been introduced but its enforcement has not yet come into effect, action may be taken against it on the grounds that—to the exclusion here of any individual responsibility, including the drafters'—it is discriminatory in intent. Again there is no equivalent to this in Roman law, because the concept there of criminality based upon *mens rea* precluded any possibility of this. The nearest equivalent in Latin generally would be *propositio* or *propositum* used of a thing, such as a person's life; and this is closer to the retrospective and interpretative concept of intention that comes up in the writing of history.

Intention in that conception is depersonalized, in the sense that results or upshots become bound to occur, to the exclusion again of any individual responsibility. Hitler's armies entered Poland in 1939, and this event, comparable as an event to the creation of a certain work of art in a given year, meant war for the British. Or a hunger-fast of Gandhi's, it may be said, meant the beginning of a disturbance of accepted conditions among the factory workers, leading on to organized strikes and so on—and was perhaps so intended by Gandhi. Rather than being taken as having specifically triggered a sequence of events, Gandhi's action is treated here as a symbolic marker. Or it may be suggested and argued, at the time in this case rather than retrospectively, that the hidden or undeclared, or the real intention, of the ordering of a paratroop attack on a prison camp in North Vietnam was to lead up to, or promote or justify, an extension of the war further north. No statement here by the person responsible is needed, and it is possible to say, in the light of unconscious or unadmitted factors, that the attack effectively meant an extension of the war, without the person who ordered it intending this. An intention of this kind, correspondingly, cannot be affected or altered in direction by a change of mind or shift of tack in the way that a stated intention can, but it can be aborted by an intervention of other factors, such as may interfere with execution or fulfilment in that case also.

The concept of *Kunstwollen* or "artistic intentions" in art history is therefore an abstraction from the third-person use of intention, into the dimensions of time and history. It arose from cases where the individual is subsumed within a collective organization such as a workshop; and where, in addition, there is no historical evidence apart from the works as to what the intentions of the persons responsible—whether as commissioner, designer or executant—might have been, and no evidence that those people would have either given or accepted an account in the terms in question. Intentions of this sort would thus be both unrecorded, so far as is known, and unstated in the sense that one speaks of the apparent unstated agreement of a group such as a village; and those points also apply to the extension of the concept on Riegl's part to the group portraiture of seventeenth century Holland.

The third person use of intention, while most familiar to art historians in this latter guise—as when it is said that the intention in a Gothic cathedral is to lift up the soul towards God, or in the Dutch group portrait to express civic pride—may also occur for other and simpler reasons. It can sometimes be an extrapolation from the first person use, as when Gauguin, by way of conveying his approach to symbolism as compared to that of Puvis de Chavannes, wrote that "Gauguin under the title *Purity* would paint a landscape with limpid waters." Sometimes it may be like a use of the editorial "we," rendering the statement akin to one of policy, on the same lines as when a civil law is called discriminatory in intent, or the government representative at a conference table pronounces "This means war." Talk of unconscious intentions would seem characteristically a third-person usage, and possibly the prime source for the tendency to assume in modern criticism that intentions are accessible in a progressive deepening of critical scrutiny. Nevertheless it is a confusing usage, at least according to the legal and behavioral concepts of intention. It would seem stricter in that light to talk of unconscious motivations and inclinations, which impel without plan or deliberation, as feelings and instincts may do also, and of subconscious intentions. In post-Freudian parlance subconscious intentions are ones which come to be recognized later as having been there all the time, in an action and comparably in a work of art. They may suggest a motivation on the artist's part, or show one to have been present implicitly rather than overtly, but they may do so without the artist's cognizance or agreement as well as with it, and without need to ask whether or not the feature that proves revealing here was an intended one. Thus Henry Moore, faced with a psychoanalytical explication of the holes and protrusions in his sculptures, could say that this was something of which he preferred to remain unconscious; and Dylan Thomas' use of the name Llareggub for his Welsh village in *Under Milk Wood,* when identified as representing "Buggerall" spelt backwards, may suggest a latent aggressive urge of a childlike kind, but not that he was unaware of the joke as such. The reason, on this front, why the intentions of the artist and those of the work are not interchangeable is not that exploration of the latter is invariably more probing and comprehensive, by virtue of the tools and evidence which are brought to bear; but rather that the artist's attitude towards explorations of this sort is at least as important as what he is prepared to say.

The process of reconstruction from what the artist gave or left to posterity may also aim towards a kind of blueprint of the work's structure, in the sense that a textbook or the companion volume for a novel offers summaries of this sort; and where the author is dead and the task is to complete what is missing, it may entail a following of notes on the subject which, it could be said, show the intention here. Further reasons why the two kinds of intention are not interchangeable emerge from these contexts. A blueprint reconstructed from the work may not coincide with the author's own sketch-plan, where one survives—though it also may. And to talk of completing a work posthumously according to the author's intentions, or of its being done contrary to them, would suggest fulfilling or going against what was stated in a set of instructions, such as a will, rather than a following of notes and drafts.

How the intention of the work differs from that of the artist stands in particular need of clarification when it is a matter of explanations, motivations of the artist's or references to concerns of his being put forward and discussed. One may give an account of why the work is the way it is and how it came to be that way, as in saying of Goya's Black Paintings that the artist had suffered severe mental stress, that he needed to get the bile out of his system, that he was obsessed with human superstition and violence. One can also discuss in terms of explanations, motivations and concerns what the artist originally had in mind or planned and subsequent changes or shifts in what he did. This is what happens in the case of a discrepancy between the avowed intention, or what a first draft or sketch shows, and the final work. That the work as it is comes in for comparison here may be a source of confusion, but it needs to be recognized that the two kinds of discussion are in fact distinct in procedural character, if not in their materials.

In what could be called the most objective usage of the phrase, the intention of a work of art can be said to represent an aspect of the work's identity. To consider it along with other aspects which include the work's category or genre, its purpose and the context of its creation is to see the work for what it is in itself, and for what it represents in time and history. It is important that in ordinary life situations, comparable statements of such a kind concerning people may be predictive as well as retrospective and explanatory. Just as it is possible for the historian or biographer to say, in interpretation of his subject's personality and career, that this person was too overweening to be able to remain long in office, so it may also be said, in the future tense, that a certain combination in a man of education and background, or of generosity and tactlessness, means that he will be bound to clash with his superiors. The interpretative art historian may move similarly, through knowledge of a certain body of art, to a characterization of what has been called here its identity. The statement that Greek sculpture exemplifies, or urges on the viewer, the dignity of man carries the implication of comparison with the sculpture of other periods, which the artists in question would not have known. It also clarifies and isolates a tendency in the art, so as to make it easier to grasp, in the same sort of way that an author may say that he is writing a preface to clarify the intention of a book, which may or may not be his own. A modern equivalent in art would be Nolde's affirmation, quoted earlier, of a striving in his art for strength and inwardness, as against their opposites, which serves both to clarify and to prescribe a certain line of development on his part.

Two questions already intimated here, which bear on the use of the term *meaning* also, are how there can be an intention without an intender, and how the discussion of intention can, in the case of a work of art, go beyond describing a property of the work. On the first of these points, the intender may as has been seen be plural, or a collective entity; and in a case such as the Gothic cathedral, the intention to lift up the soul to God resists being called anyone's insofar as, like Nazi participation in the Final Solution, it breaks across the conventional boundaries between responsibility and assent. But while human agency is normally and naturally expected of works of art, with the exceptions serving as a kind of fiat to the contrary, it is also possible to debate, in the realm of meaning, whether or not the coherence given to the plot of a play such as *Hamlet* by a certain interpretation is or could be an intended coherence, and at a further remove from the playwright's control, or for that matter the director's, whether or not certain associations that a line might carry would be ones that any audience—not just that of the time—could be intended to grasp. Illuminating here, and also more generally, for the shift of viewpoint that takes place is the distinction between ascribing an intention and describing one.

The process of ascribing an intention entails, in ways that differentiate it from the describing of one, the use of experience, comparison and inference. By those means, furthermore, it is possible to move progressively towards, and then into, the ascribing of an intention to a non-human agency, as in the case of a phenomenon such as hauntings. When this happens, it becomes clear that both an interpretation and a claim are being made. Thus when Hamlet says, concerning the Ghost and before he has met with it, "My father's spirit in arms! All is not well" (1.2.255), he is effectively doing both of those things, in the same line. And what is read into the happening in this way, though it may be based on observed properties such as pattern, and how they are understood, cannot itself be or become a property of the happening. To attribute or ascribe a meaning to something represents an exactly parallel process.

A look at the uses of the word *meaning* supplies a background to how this comes about. As with intending and intention, so also with meaning, there is a tendency for two uses, one of a person, the other of a thing, such as an act or word, to become confused. Analogies with codes and games are helpful here, and especially games which involve both rules and conventions: like the bidding in bridge, where there are both rules as to the circumstances in which a certain bid can be made, and also particular bidding systems. To ask what is meant when a person redoubled in a game of bridge might seem on the one hand like asking what it meant to make that bid, and on the other like asking what the player had meant by it, and a beginner learning the game might indeed be liable to run the two forms of question together. But they are distinctly separable questions, the first like asking the point or object of castling in chess, which would invite a general explanation of the move and its uses; the second like the request to specify how one takes or understands one's partner's last bid, which can be made by the opposing pair in bridge. Inasmuch as the latter question concerns the meaning of the bid in the system being played, it is like asking what a certain symbol means in a code being used; and just as, however private the code, and even where there is a slip or may have been one in the coding, the question is still this, and not what the coder meant that symbol to mean, so also retrospective discussions of a pattern of bidding in a bridge game are not in principle accounts or explanations of what the bids were intended to mean.

In the case of literature and other appropriations or inflections of language to special ends there may be, beyond basic meaning and use such as a standard gesture has, either a further implication carried by conventional words, or a special meaning introduced by the context. But whatever the intricacies of these kinds, and their role as clues to what may be considered the "real" or underlying meaning, the basic distinction holds between the meaning of a word or phrase, and what a person means by something. To ask "What is Proust's meaning there?"—attaching the word meaning in this turn of expression, and perhaps this one only, to a person—is not the same as asking the meaning, either generally or in that specific instance, of the words that Proust wrote. Rather it is a question of the drift or general idea, as in "he got my meaning." One also talks in a related way about the meaning that certain happenings have (or had) for different people, and in retrospect and impersonally, about the meaning of events for history, and of concepts in the history of ideas; and to say in this connection that an event meant nothing to someone, or to contemporaries, is not to imply that it was meaningless. Then there are further kinds of question that can be asked and responded to, as to the meaning of a piece of behavior, on stage for example, or when it was not clear at the time; the meaning of a personal situation as in "what is the meaning of this?"; and the meaning of a person's life, either for him or for the world. In this grouping such notions as coherence and integrity are brought in. Thus the search for and finding of meanings leads variously to the dictionary or the code-book; to appeal to someone with experience or authority; and to the hazarding or affirmation of ontological or teleological significance.

In all of these cases the lines of inquiry tend to be different, and the same is also true in respect to purpose and raison d'être. These two terms, as applied to works of art, show how the very articulation of speculative questions as to why something was done, and why it is the way it is, leads across into the more general realm of meaning. A work of art has no purpose, or is dispossessed of one, insofar as it is conceived and treated as unavailable, in Kantian terms, for any kind of practical use. It is possible to ask a historical question about the purpose for which a painting was made or a poem or play written, but the answer is likely to be one that restricts itself to a classification of the work—as altarpiece, satire, masque—with supporting details. Raison d'être is generally backwards-looking also, as one might speak of parts of the body no longer serving their original raison d'être; and the use of the term of a work of art goes beyond simply the reason that might be given for its being in a certain physical state, as for example that acid was thrown or paint dripped onto a painting. The term reaches out to comprehend a disposition or attitude, such as one that accepts accident in the creation or subsequent history of a painting, or leads to the building of a ruined castle. Purpose and raison d'être may be reconstructed, by these accounts, from internal or external evidence or a combination of the two; but not on the basis of an intention somehow inherent in the work now. And there remains the sense in which a work of art is a construct, made up of invocation to the Queen and addresses to her, drips on raw canvas, tower and gateway juxtaposed: a construct in the sense in which lives or parts of lives, in their actions and interactions, are constructs, and the universe is taken as one in the argument from design.

To ask the meaning of a work of art is, it may be said in this light, to recognize—from whatever point of view—a complexity of feature calling for that term. What one receives in response is, if it is to qualify as a response to this particular question, the attribution of a certain meaning to the work as a whole; and this entails, in recapitulation of what was said earlier about comparable acts in other contexts, the combination of an interpretation and a claim, which may or may not be convincing. Both an account of the work's properties and features, and a statement of its historical significance, however

slanted towards judgment, are likely to fall short of carrying the conviction that is apposite here. For an assent or even partial assent to
the interpretation put forward requires what may be called an act of
faith. The word faith is used here not in the sense of religious faith,
but rather as in such phrases as "in good faith" and "faith in one's
own judgment," where it implies confidence and positive expectations. Understanding comes correspondingly, not necessarily as a
matter of sudden or dawning enlightenment, but in terms of feeling
able to go further with the work, and the effects of this.

The understanding of meaning raises a last question as to how it is
possible to say, in response to a work of literature, that one understands what the words mean, but not what the poem means. This is a
phrasing special to literature, meaning in the visual and performing
arts being generally a matter of subjects and themes, while individual
elements such as figures or musical phrases are talked of in terms of
what they represent or connote. Certainly there is a shift in the sense
in which meaning is used from the first half of this sentence to the
second, where the meaning in question is like that of a piece of
behavior, or a person's life. Further, the failure to understand in the
second half may, like saying that one does not understand someone,
represent one or another of two things: either aversion or lack of
interest, as when a person says that something means nothing to him;
or alternatively and perhaps more probably, that the work in question
has not yet "come together" for the speaker, or not yet fully registered in the way that other works have by the same author. Tone and
context will between them establish which of these alternatives is the
relevant one, by implying in the latter cases that there is an effort of
comprehension on the speaker's part. Assent to the existence of a
meaning is necessary for that effort. A continuous taxing of it could,
at the same time, be part of the work's intention, and even its prime
intention.

The Question of the Artist's Privileged Status

The topic that goes under this name is one more alluded to than
actually studied, both in current philosophy of art and in the theory of
criticism. There is a reason for this, which both clarifies the issue and
suggests how it is to be approached. To suppose that the person
responsible for a work of art has at least something interesting to say
about it is only natural, and even commonplace. But granted this, the
qualifications to be put upon that assumption in individual and particular cases become of much greater interest. The major question
would not then be whether or not, in an absolute sense, the artist is in
a position to talk definitively about his own work, but rather on what

basis or criteria a claim to that effect can be made to rest, and how far it extends in its implications.

A poet may choose to tell his readers what a word or line or set of lines in his poetry means, by providing an appended explication, as Yeats did in a note for the phrase "honey of generation" in his *Among School Children,* or by offering a free and extended kind of paraphrase, as Gerard Manley Hopkins did in a letter for the opening lines of his sonnet on Purcell. But it is possible also to claim that the poem implies a different meaning from the one that the poet indicated, or that both meanings may be entertained as co-existent alternatives, or in cases of the second kind that no paraphrase is really feasible.

The critical question raised here is whether or not intentional statements by the artist about his work possess a special authority, or can claim one, by virtue of the fact that they come from the artist. Put philosophically, this is a matter of whether the artist stands in a privileged position, or more explicitly a position of privileged access, in respect to his creations. As those terms are used in recent philosophy of language and epistemology, being in a privileged position means having a special claim to knowledge or awareness of something; and privileged statements are ones which have a particular authority or status reflecting the speaker's privileged position. Whether or not a statement is privileged is tested in terms of the grounds for the knowledge or awareness in question; and in particular by considering the challenges to which it is or might be susceptible.

If the intentional statements of the artist's that came up for consideration here were limited to ones that supplied background to the work's evolution, or ones that dealt with concrete and specific aspects of the creative process, there would scarcely be problems on this score. An artist may place on record, in a form that carries documentary authority such as a journal, both the date at which he began a certain work, and also his state of feelings at the time. He may record at the time, or equally in retrospect, the general aim underlying his engagement in the project, as for example the winning of a certain prize, or the directions in which his progress on the project was shifted and turned by changes made along the way. In default of specific evidence which would indicate deception or self-deception, or unless and until he is proved untrustworthy, for such due cause as self-contradiction or general unreliability of memory, the artist is taken to be in a position to know and tell, on these subjects, what is or was the case. He might indeed have misrepresented a feature of what he did or felt, for the purpose of self-aggrandizement, but the discrepancy can in that case only be one that emerges later, and unless his statements should appear so unaccountable as to imply complete mental confusion, he is, so to say, given the benefit of the doubt until then. Challenges which are then made would argue either that he was not in a position to know what he claims to know, or that there was evidence in the work itself suggesting him to be mistaken in his belief or feeling about it. But those are challenges to which any statement of a comparable kind may be liable, irrespective of the immediacy or the extent of the speaker's involvement with what he is speaking about. The degree of certainty or conviction with which the statement is made also makes no difference here, since an artist might fully believe that he had never been affected by the example of a predecessor, or say with absolute firmness that a certain drawing was a forgery rather than his own, and yet be persuaded otherwise by evidence that could be put before him.

Then there are those moves and decisions made by the artist in the course of working, which concern what may be called practical or technical aspects of the work's creation, and which may be formulated in intentional terms: the choice of a gesture to recall the Apollo Belvedere, or of a red so that it would not fade; the placing of a work in a series, now perhaps destroyed; the painting of a watch-fob in a portrait so that it will stand out particularly. The last of these examples especially may seem to involve an academic kind of thinking on the artist's part; but there are analogies in the case of artists who work directly on the canvas in an empirical fashion, as Titian and Cézanne did, without any prefiguration of what is to be done in preliminary drawings, and yet at the same time keep the whole in mind as they work. Artists may equally picture what they do not as a matter of knowledge or thought of any conceptual kind, but simply, in Puvis de Chavannes' words, as "getting on with the job." Just because of his having such a working method or attitude, the artist may be less likely to offer any accompanying or subsequent explanation in words; but he may nevertheless do so, if for example asked by someone who happens to be present at the time, or someone to whom he is showing the work for comment.

Insofar as the concern here is with a particular aspect of what the artist does in the course of creation, or with the reason for a particular thing being done at a certain point or stage along the way, rather than with the creative performance or finished product as a whole, the artist's privileged status seems again assured. He is privileged in the sense of being able to answer questions as to why he wanted a note of red in a certain place, or why he made a red so red, in the same sort of way as a person putting in a nail, asked why he is doing it that way, is in a position to reply in terms that should satisfy the questioner. The assumption here is that the driving in of a nail at a certain angle, or to a certain depth, is intentional; and in the same way the existence of a pun in a work of literature, as for example in a choice of name by Dickens, may be taken as being undoubtedly intended.

So long as the scope of the discussion is limited in the way defined here, the introduction of the term *meaning* makes no effective difference. When Hopkins wrote to Bridges, in explication of his "Sonnet on Purcell," "By moonmarks I mean . . . ," and said that "The sonnet . . . means this. . . . In particular, the first lines mean . . . ," he was indicating how certain words or phrases in the poem were to be taken, and giving along with this an outline of the general sense or drift of the poem as a whole; technical aspects here take the form of unusual word-formations and the like, and practical aspects considered include, for example, the relationship of continuity between the octet and the sextet. An account of this kind can be challenged, and in the case of Yeats's explication of "honey of generation" such a challenge has been made, but it brings with it at the very least a certain discomfort. It seems that, in order to make it convincing that Yeats was in fact wrong in what he said on the subject, it is necessary to show both that the alternative interpretation which is being put forward works better at that point in the poem, and also that there is some good reason, such as Yeats's immersion at the time in occult philosophy, to explain why confusion and consequent misleadingness should have entered into his own understanding of the phrase. Similarly in the case of puns, to show that there is a humorous reference in the choice or creation of a character's name, where the author denies this, requires both the presence of other comparable puns in the writings, and also an explanation for the author's refusal of admission or failure of recognition.

Also to be considered, as possible subjects for statements of an intentional kind, are what are sometimes called "secondary" features of a work of art: as for example titles and dedications, epigraphs or notes, frame and varnishing in the case of a painting, and in the case of a poem the layout used in publication and the exact way in which it is printed. These are all features which, very generally, concern the presentation of a work of art; but that term is not helpful for deciding on what grounds here privileged status can be attributed to the artist whose work it is. It brings up too many problems reflecting different connotations that the term has from one art form to another, particularly as to what is integral to the work and what is not, and about the varying roles played by the artist or by others in specifying or deciding what is to be the case here. If it is said that in Gerard Manley Hopkins' *Spring and Fall* the word "will" in the line "And yet you will weep and know why" was accented by the poet in order to make a certain sense clear, or clearer than it would otherwise be; or that a painting has been titled wrongly, as a Braque still life of 1911 was long labeled "The Battleship," or hung in a fashion or a context that the artist would not have endorsed; or that the notes to *The Waste Land* represent a kind of intellectual ballast, as T. S. Eliot implied was the case in a statement as to why he had put them in, there are two points such findings have in common. First, these are all matters on which the artist is taken to have a legitimate say. And secondly there is the overtone or implication of an obligation of a moral kind, taking the form either of scrupulousness or of courtesy towards the artist. Evidence as to intention in these matters may in fact appear and be honored at any point in later time, as the discovery of a signature may cause a drawing to be differently mounted. And the sense of obligation does not exclude certain liberties. Hopkins's accent may be said to reinforce both possible meanings of the line quoted; it may be said that a painting could go either way up, when this seems possible in principle and there is no clear indication to the contrary; and T. S. Eliot's specification that the notes to *The Waste Land* were originally to have been simply references for the quotations may be taken as implying that those particular notes are more integral to the character and substance of the poem than the remainder. But these are liberties of interpretation, not ones which go against the known or surmised intention.

The limits of the artist's privileged position, as it has been delineated so far, are indicated by certain marginal cases, in which the argument could go either way. One such case concerns the unfinished. It becomes explicit in this connection that the artist at a certain point releases the work from his care. Where the work, in the example of a painting, is one released with unpainted areas in it, or elements not brought to the degree of finish of the remainder, the artist may say that he intentionally left the painting unfinished in those respects, and would be speaking here from a privileged position on the subject; or the point might be surmised in those same terms. But it might also be that there was a more overall criterion of the unfinished to be considered, based on the increased tendency of the artist late in life to leave off work on a canvas at a relatively early stage. If so, there would be no necessary reason to call a work unfinished because the artist had expressed dissatisfaction with it and continued to work on it. In the shift here from specific features to the work as a whole, the first kind of incompleteness gives place to a second kind, with an accompanying change of viewpoint.

Again, there is the sort of case represented by a statement of Franz Kline's:

> I think there is a kind of loneliness in a lot of [my paintings], which I don't think about as the fact that I'm lonely and therefore I paint lonely pictures.

While the second half of this disclaims any autobiographical explanation, it might be taken that the artist was talking here about an inclination in his work which, from acquaintance with its appearance there and a sense of its significance, he chose to call by the name of loneliness; as a portraitist might speak of a phase in his work as his "Goya" period, or of being "drawn to red," or as a writer might call a group of stories of his "excursions into fantasy." The basis for calling such a statement a privileged one would then be intimate familiarity on the artist's part with the way in which the inclination showed itself in the works' creation; and "Jewishness" or "vehemence" might be talked of in a similar way. But Kline's qualifying of his commentary with "I think" and "a kind of" suggests his own sense of being on a borderline here, beyond which the loneliness would be a quality of mood in the paintings, such as Munch's bridge subjects could more obviously be said to have, and one that was open to being talked about either by the artist in an unprivileged sense or by any other person responsive to its presence. The labeling of a period in an artist's work would certainly be more likely, in common practice, to have a basis of this latter kind.

These examples bring out how the temptation makes itself felt to extend and generalize the artist's privileged position from specific features and aspects of the work to all of its aspects, or to apply to the work as a whole. They also show that the attribution of privileged access in the terms described does not rest either on the artist's responsibility for the work, or on his perception of it. An assumption to this effect might be encouraged by the terminology of "knowing at firsthand" and "perceiving directly," with its appearance of giving a conceptual footing for distinguishing the artist's position of awareness, observation and comment in relation to his work from anyone else's. But whatever those terms, left over from earlier philosophy of perception, may be taken to mean, they do not validly account for those ordinary life situations in which it is a familiarity or a circumstance that puts one in a position to know something as another person does not. One may know that it is a tree, at dusk, from familiarity with the terrain, or that a person is mortally ill from the arrival of a priest as one is leaving; and similarly with the artist's being in a position to know that he is drawn to red, or that his model has shortened her dress.

There remains to be considered those intentional statements of the artist's which are like statements of a desire or need in oneself, that one is motivated to fulfill. But since such statements are concerned with feelings, which are the subject of self-knowledge or self-awareness on the speaker's part, it is necessary, before coming to why it should be that the artist is not in a privileged position here, to review what may be relevantly said about self-knowledge, and also those ways in which intentions and feelings may be known, other than through a statement on the subject of the person in question.

Discussion, in analytical philosophy, of self-knowledge has centered mainly around the question of whether it is possible, or makes sense, to say "I know that I am in pain." The broader issue here, of whether it is possible to know one's own mind or feelings in the same sense that one speaks of knowing what another person has in mind or feels, has met, since Wittgenstein focused it in that particular form, with three distinct kinds of response. The first of these has been to say that "knowing one's pain" is a grammatical barbarism; in ordinary language usage one has a certain feeling, such as anger, and one knows, or comes to recognize, or is brought to agree, that that is what one is feeling. According to the second view, the point that "I know that I am in pain" represents an odd or unusual thing to say is taken to hold, and a reason for this is sought either in their being a lack of point to saying such a thing, because of its obviousness; or in the limited sort of context in which it might be said, as perhaps in response to a very unusual type of question, which cast doubt in some way on whether one really, or actually, was in pain. Finally, and most constructively for present purposes, it has been suggested that the argument deriving from the case of pain should be limited by the making of a distinction between discovery, for which it holds, and knowledge, for which it does not. This distinction would carry the implication that while other people may cause or help one to discover one's feelings, they are not thereby put in a position of knowing one's mind, or body, in the way that one speaks of knowing it oneself.

Complex as the workings of self-knowledge undoubtedly are, the last of these approaches brings up several further points germane to the types of artistic statement to be considered. To begin with a term which has already been introduced: alongside knowledge that one has of one's limits, potentials, preferences and so on, there belongs also, in respect to feelings and emotions, the operation of self-awareness. "Knowing" in the sense of being conscious of something and "being aware" are most often used in a virtually interchangeable way, with the distinctions, such as they are, being established by tone and context. But in respect to feelings or states of feeling—which are not the same as emotions, though sometimes overlapping with them, or sensations either—awareness is used in a way that differentiates it from consciousness. Special or particular perceptions are implied, which an artist may or may not have; and whereas self-consciousness designates an exaggeration, beyond the ordinary or the natural, self-awareness serves as the basis for the discovery or recognition of what one's feelings are. Also, when it is a question in philosophy of whether one can know or be aware of one's feelings, in the sense of having supporting evidence for them, the examples most discussed—pain, anger, and comparably joy, fatigue, or fear—are not necessarily representative ones. For the idea of discovery or recognition, though possible—if for example one came out of a daze, which would entail recovering consciousness—is odd in those cases. More revealing would be desires, like a desire for independence; feelings on a certain subject, such as his success, her behavior or kingship; and feelings for something, such as rhythm, texture or revolutionary action. Self-awareness in these cases, as something gained or developed, carries with it the possibility of mistakenness. And what is true here for ordinary life situations carries across to the arts.

As to how feelings are established or verified without the availability of any first person statement on the subject, the processes of discovery and recognition bring up exactly the same possibilities here as with the discovery of a person's intentions or the recognition of one's physical condition. To take a range of examples illustrating this, one discovers that an enemy is intent on poisoning one from the sediment in the soup; and that a man has no intention of behaving decently, or of being faithful to his wife, from his general attitude or from his behavior over a period of time. Correspondingly, one discovers that one's leg is broken from finding that one cannot walk, which would be an indication to this effect; or from the pain and where it is located, which is to say by inference; or from the X rays showing this, which would represent a confirming proof. In the case of feelings, that a person is angry or ill-disposed towards one may equally be indicated by his expression, inferred from his refusal to discuss something, or confirmed by his subsequent conduct; and one may come to recognize the state of his feelings in any or all of these ways, without his saying anything as to how he feels, and indeed without his having said anything at all. Those procedures are also available in the case of one's own feelings, with the difference only that here one discovers that one is really angry—the extent or degree of one's feeling—from the impulse that one has to run out of the room; or that one is in fact agitated, rather than calm as self-deception had led one to think, from the headaches that one gets.

What a person means by something that he says or does is likely to entail feelings on his part, in a way that is recognized in such phrases as "meaning well," "saying it with meaning," "giving the words their full meaning" and "saying it and meaning it"; and in a work of art meaning, in the broad sense referred to earlier of what it all adds up to, is at the very least associated with feelings. Meaning of this sort is correspondingly open to being discovered and verified by the same procedures once more. How this works in practice, as distinct from the establishment of what something means, such as a word or line in a poem, is shown by the following literary examples.

What "dark satanic mills" means (in Blake's *Jerusalem*), and what Blake meant by the phrase, or more clumsily but also more strictly, what he meant it to mean, are not really different questions in terms of the kinds of answer they would imply. For though the first version invites a historical and lexicological consideration of what the word *mills* would have conveyed at that time, and the second recognizes the possibility that Blake might have used the word in a personal symbolic sense, those two approaches are both geared to establishing what connotations the phrase carries in the context in which it appears, and meet or clash on that common ground. But if what is being talked of is a line or couplet, such as Keats's "Beauty is truth, truth beauty . . . ," rather than a word or phrase, then it would seem that the meaning, in the sense of the force and resonance of feeling that the lines have, can ultimately be determined only by analysis of the poem itself; and that what Keats meant by beauty and truth leads off into the quite different territory of Keats's concept of beauty, which might have some relevance, but might also not fit with the use of the terms in this particular case.

As, in the expansion from a line or section to the work as a whole, meaning becomes something to be cumulatively grasped, "What did he mean here?" may well be replaced by some such introductory question as "What is the poet doing in this poem?" which avoids the implication of one answer being called for; and the impersonal version, "What it means," is likely to suggest an exploration to be embarked on, in which particular passages in the work will serve as indications or supports. On either count, a pattern or pull of feelings in the work will be part of what comes to be recognized. What is intimated here, or brought to notice by the method adopted, could be a subtlety and richness of implication which the author could claim had not come home to him until someone else pointed it out, as Melville effectively claimed for his *Moby Dick* after receiving the Hawthornes' interpretation of the whole. Or it could be a tenor of feeling which the author denied was present, as T. S. Eliot denied at different times that, from his point of view, *The Waste Land* expressed "the disillusionment of a generation" or represented a "criticism of the contemporary world." The legitimacy of the inference from the work is not thereby impugned, any more than by the author's silence. For either such remarks send one back to the work, and may be so intended—which would seem to be the force of such pronouncements as "The meaning is in the poem," if they are not self-evident. Or it could be said that the correspondence normally assumed between what people mean and what they think they mean is here suspended.

To turn now to intentional statements which express a desire or need felt by the speaker, examples of this would be an artist saying that he wants to be gay and whimsical, or that he is seeking more independence—rather than that one corner of a painting needs more red. A belief or surmise that one's work is moving along satisfactorily, or becoming more lyrical, would be projective in the same way. And insofar as the raison d'être for such statements is to offer a kind of purchase that can give focus and direction to the work, one can set with them statements of intention such as "I mean to get away from my teacher's influence," "I intend to make the painting now on my easel into an allegory of faith" and "I plan to make my paintings more like sculptures than before."

That such statements do not qualify as privileged ones follows from what has been said on two counts, one practical and the other logical. The practical point is that the feelings in question, whether in the present tense or retrospectively, are designated as motivations or impulses at work at the time, not ones discovered or recognized through self-awareness. That the direction in which one's endeavors were pointed gradually dawned on one would call for a different phrasing. The more obvious logical point is that, far from the work itself as a subject of intimate acquaintance being the basis for the artist's awareness here, it may serve to challenge that awareness. This would be what happens when the artist is apprised of a change of character in the work by what takes place in the creative process; and an outside person may also draw on the work, or on general experience of the artist's endeavors, to do the same.

The point made here represents a clarification of what is generally taken for granted about comparable statements in ordinary discourse. But that being so, the question arises as to why there should be a particular temptation or pressure, in the case of art, to regard such statements as privileged ones. At least four different ideas or assumptions suggest themselves as having a possible effect of this kind. There is a tendency to attribute to the artist in principle, first, a special knowledge of what he wants and a particular directedness arising from that; secondly, a capacity to make statements of a kind that, as with a religious leader or seer, can have an absolute value attributed to them irrespective of context; third, a special degree of self-awareness as to his feelings and inclinations, and a capacity to voice them correspondingly; and fourthly, a responsibility for whatever takes place in the course of the creative process.

While each of these things may be true of some artists, and it may also be true that artists are psychologically inclined in these ways, assumptions on such subjects go to work undiscriminatingly. As a result, the first of these tendencies may lead to unprivileged statements being treated as if they were statements that gave information, and the third to their being treated as if they were statements about feelings and inclinations, like "I know that he is upset" or "I realize that I am impatient," rather than statements of feeling. The second tendency may lead to such statements being considered in an inappropriately naked sense, and the fourth to their being treated as if they had a guaranteeing force such as promises and affirmations of knowledge have, where the speaker states what can be expected in a ritual or contractual sense. In any of these ways the statements may be invested with an undue authority.

It is also true that there is a general expectation of sureness rather than vagueness in the artist, and of lack of hesitancy in speaking. As with Napoleon's statement, "I know men, and I tell you that Jesus Christ was not a man," a deference may be prompted by the sheer presence of those qualities. Or it may be that statements which are basically avowals of what the speaker likes, or cares about, are assimilated to explanations and clarifications of the character of the work, on the assumption that, when a person does something creative, whatever he might have to say on the subject is likely to have an elucidative value. But here one is back with a notion of value which, if broadly enough defined to include all manner of possible contributions, becomes commonplace and not likely in practical terms to have any objection made to it.

The Evaluation of Intentions and Their Critical Use

It may be valuable to consider an artist's statements as forming part of a dialogue with a real or imagined interlocutor, or as if this were the case. There are then several possible reasons for a breakdown of communication to occur, or for the communication to be ineffective. It is not simply that the speaker may, consciously or unconsciously, be practising a deception or misrepresenting what was in fact the case. There are other possibilities too, having to do with the form of what is said or the context in which it is said. Useful here, for understanding how those factors prove relevant, is the concept of "defeasibility" that has been developed in ethics and jurisprudence. According to this concept, certain kinds of statement—as for instance, promises—count as such unless something defeats them, rendering them thereby void or negating their force. Examples of potentially defeasible statements would be, accordingly, the giving of a command where one has no authority to do this, and a promise made to do something when it is too late in time for it to be possible to do it.

These cases show how, apart from the condition of good faith required to make such statements effective, there is also what can be called a circumstantial condition which may invalidate them; and how the speaker's degree of responsibility in such cases is assessed according to conventions, which establish what for instance is a serious promise and what is not. To bring out the application of defeasibility, so understood, to artists' statements bearing on their work, one might point particularly to the notices placed at the start of novels, with their implied authorial quotation marks around the assurance or directive that they comprise, and their invitation to acceptance by the reader specifically as he sees fit: as for example the personally worded disclaimer in Evelyn Waugh's *Brideshead Revisited*, "I am not I; thou art not he or she; they are not they," or the "notice" which prefaces *Huckleberry Finn*, "Persons attempting to find a motive in this narrative will be prosecuted. . . ."

With intentional statements of the artist's, there certainly are—as with anything that the artist says—clearcut grounds on which a statement may be faulted, so that its value is put objectively into question. Falsehood or falsity of recollection may be in question, and it may be possible to prove this, as with Kirchner's claim to the priority of his own development over the other members of the Brücke group, and his contention that he discovered New Guinea carvings and responded to them in his work at a much earlier date than the true one. Or it may be a matter of reconstructing the psychological and contextual factors at work in the artist's personality and cast of thought which could cause him, in the commonest sort of case, to rationalize retrospectively the way in which his work had developed. Context also enters into the assessment of an artist's originality of thought and verbal expression, or conversely his dependence on others. For in such an extreme case as Gorky's appropriation of whole sections from the letters of Gaudier-Brzeska for use in his own, the question arises of whether, once this was known, the words used could in any sense be regarded as Gorky's; much as a threatening statement overheard will appear in a different light, if found to represent a line that is being read from a play. The idea of responsibility on the speaker's part, as with promising, comes into play here; and in more normal cases, dependence on the source is balanced against personalization on the artist's part, and the relevance of the statement to the work of the artist's which is in question will be limited or circumscribed in this light. Since, however, the purpose of an intentional statement is most often to clarify and offer guidance in some way, it is more relevant to consider cases where content and form together are involved in the pattern of intercommunication, and its effectiveness. There would be then, in this scheme of things, the question or implied question, how it is posed, on what topic and in what context; there would be the way the question is taken, or the assumptions of the speaker who responds to its character and form; and finally what both questions and answer, jointly or in association together, manage to convey.

Questions which start things off on the wrong foot, where intentions are concerned, are those belonging to types which may be termed the sardonic and the over-respectful. On the one hand the artist may be asked what he or she is trying to do, or some such question with the implication of its not being easy to grasp what it is that he is attempting; and on the other he may be approached with a question phrased in terms of what he was thinking of, or had in mind, when he did what he did. Both types of question in fact posit, one way round or the other, a gap to be filled between what is thought and what is done; and both use a language appropriate to a situation or an action, rather than to the product of an act of creation.

In response to these approaches, in turn, certain familiar strategies are available to the artist, which may be called the laconic, the apologetic and the defensive. The laconic type of response is illustrated by the reply that the playwright Friedrich Dürrenmatt is reported to have made, when asked by an interviewer about his attitude to the Swiss problem: Switzerland was no problem, merely a pleasant place in which to work; and the apologetic by John Constable's rejoinder, when Blake praised a sheet in a sketchbook of his with the words "This is not drawing but *inspiration*": "I never knew it before, I meant it for drawing." The laconic answer is of a non-constructive kind, which cuts off that line of questioning; and it may well reflect a more general attitude, to the effect that the qualities which make a writer interesting as a writer do not necessarily spill over into his thinking about matters of common concern to the world that he lives in. The apologetic response is explanatory in a limiting sense only; a framework is proffered within which to see the relevant aspect of the artist's work, but a less exalted framework than the questioner had supposed.

The defensive mode of response is one that is illustrated both in Max Beckmann's staunch insistence that his symbolism was open to being read in any way that a person could find of reading it, and also, in a different way, in Juan Gris's claim that his fellow artist Ozenfant had no right to see objects in his paintings. Here the stating or restating of a given principle, or perhaps tone or the making of an excuse, conveys the impression that any such question about the work would receive the same kind of answer. Unwilling to be pinned down and showing this, the artist is at the same time not to be saddled with the literal implications of what he enjoins; so that there is an impression likely to be given that he could be more positive if he wished to be, and might indeed be so with a different questioner.

On the assumption that the initial approach has been a sympathetic and interested one, the artist's response in the form of an intentional statement is likely either to be corrective in a mild and encouraging sense, or explanatory of the conventions within which the work is to be seen; and the questioner's gain from here on of a sense of understanding will consist either of a recognition of the point of what the artist is doing that he did not have before, or of a recognition of the basis for his prior misapprehension on the subject, which again leads to his forming a different picture, or at least makes him open to that. But it is also possible, and even familiar in modern art, that in continuing exchanges of question and answer, the artist should slip into a pattern of obfuscation or mystification of some kind. He may respond in a fashion that seems simultaneously both to affirm and to deny the point that is being asked about, as Franz Kline did when questioned as to whether or not his black-and-white paintings looked like bridges; or he may play possum with his questioner so that the thrust of the questions is blunted and the answers are not truly answers, as T. S. Eliot did in a recorded conversation about a production of his *Sweeney Agonistes* and the acceptability to him of its carrying a different meaning from the one that he took the play to have.

Whatever the artist's exact intentions might have been, they are in such cases either skated over or held back. Not from dishonesty in the normal sense, for it is one of the special characteristics of the field of art, as opposed to ordinary life situations, that it seems positively to invite or promote mystification and confusion of such kinds; or at the very least there is a tension between confession and concealment, between the offering of connectives between artist and work and the withholding of them. And apart from the various kinds of role-playing that the artist may find acceptable or have thrust onto him in this context, such as the roles of teacher or sage, there is one more alternative strategy available to him, that of silence about his work. Beyond the refusal to make statements, this option, as exercised by authors such as B. Traven and J. D. Salinger, has entailed the withholding of biographical and personal information about themselves. The point, psychological reasons apart, being presumably to restrict or discourage speculation as to how the work might relate to the author's life and character, it remains to be said that, whether funded by information or not, there is likely to be a natural curiosity on that subject anyhow; and the result here may simply be that the mystery and the concealment on the author's part come to be treated as substitutes in themselves for the missing intentional data.

Attention needs finally to be directed to how intentional data are actually used in criticism. The questions that arise here are not simply a matter of cautions to be borne in mind, as to the possibility of lies, mistakes, self-deception or role-playing on the artist's part, but concern also the ways in which such data may validly serve as critical instruments. The criteria of their usability are, from this standpoint, what they may offer in respect to the issues raised or implied by the work, how much is said, in what spirit and so on.

If the standard division of criticism into description, interpretation and evaluation is called into service here, there is no evident problem on the first of these scores. In default of evidence to the contrary, the artist is assumed to have relevant factual information to provide; and his giving of it may direct attention to features of the work that merit descriptive recognition or emphasis. With respect to interpretation, the major points arising from what was said earlier would seem to be that one defers to the artist's authority in regard to limited and practical aspects of the work, less so as one moves towards the larger aspects; and that intentional statements, when the artist chooses to make them, may serve to pass on to others the kind of guidance and clarification which they can also provide for the speaker, or have provided for him. They are to be taken in this sense, rather than as binding on the maker or as contributions to knowledge, with the corollaries that the sort of help they can give may depend on one's own situation and stance in respect to the work, and the art generally;

and that interpretations can be supported, from outside the work, in other ways than this one. Evaluation is then left over, and here two interrelated matters of principle call for attention; one having to do with the measurability of the artist's success in the light of his intentions, the other with criteria for judgment which rest on there being other factors to consider than the work as it is.

On the first of these points, there is a tendency to assume in criticism that if the artist has made known his intentions in respect to a particular work, it is then possible to judge from it whether or not he succeeded, or to what extent. As to why such an assumption should exercise an appeal, possible reasons would be that an intentional statement appears somehow contractual, on the order of the way in which, in the case of a bet, the end result does or does not correspond to what the maker of the bet contended would occur; and the application of a deceptive model or picture deriving from the performing arts, where it is particularly likely to appear that there is a plan or design, in the sense of a broad outline, governing the whole performance, and successive steps which are taken in fulfilment of that design. In any case, scrutiny of a range of cases in which intentions are declared shows how the assumption can mislead. It works for cases such as the announced intention to use a six-foot canvas, or to put a straight line between the red and blue color areas, since whether or not the artist did what he said that he was going to do can be verified in such cases, much as a passport can be consulted to see if a person actually went to France, as he said that he would, or marriage records can be looked up to find out if a person did in fact fulfil his promise to marry someone. But the "general resolves" set down by Gatsby in Scott Fitzgerald's novel include both "No more smoking and chewing" and "Be better to parents," and it would hardly be possible to check if the second of those resolves was carried out, in the same sense as is possible with the first.

What applies there to a projected improvement of conduct applies also in ordinary life situations to a continuously held intention, like that of making a person happy through all the years of one's marriage to them, or to the attempted communication of an intention by prearranged means, as in the use of a signal to indicate that one is ready to leave a party. Whatever claims might be made, in the first of those examples, that all of the relevant things had been done appropriately, it could still be judged that there was some general obstruction of character or circumstance all through. And if in the second example the message failed to get across, the reason for this might be adjudged to be not that the agreed use of the sign had not been made, but that the sign proved misleading in that particular context, or there was a distraction at the time, or perhaps it was not taken seriously.

The addition of a second clause to the judgment, of a qualifying or contrasting kind, may well occur in such cases, and be expected.

Correspondingly, where an artist had stated that he intended to make his paintings more poetic, it might be possible to say that he had succeeded in bringing this about, but with the provisos that the quality in point could not necessarily be designated as present or absent in any particular canvas, and that there might be other factors affecting whether or not the quality was recognizable as being there. The lack of a firm resolution here, arising from such factors as the generality of the intention and the length of time over which assessment might occur, helps to explain why there should be a tendency to shift to the object-predicated use of intention in such cases. If a wife, whose husband's intention of making her happy was unmistakable, judged him to have failed to do so, but then at the end of her life changed her mind on the subject, it might be said that she had misjudged what was intended, or what exactly the intention entailed. And similarly a critical appraisal based on access to what was intended need not imply any too hard-and-fast a criterion of what would be needed to justify speaking of the intention as accomplished.

The claim that factors external to the work of art cannot be the basis for assessing its quality or the extent of its artistic success would appear to state a point that is generally true in principle for the process of evaluation. It could even be said to represent a truism, what is there in the work being there as the proffered basis for judging it—though a truism that may be of value in directing attention to the work, or deeper into it. But it is not clear from the claim, so expressed, how intentions are to be regarded accordingly. If what was done with a work of art was being judged as appropriate or inappropriate to it, as in the case of music of Bach's played on a piano instead of a harpsichord, or a Toulouse-Lautrec poster reproduced to advertise a new and different product, the appropriateness of the tone in one case and the satire in the other might be appraised in terms of the original intention, which here appears to coincide completely with what the artist intended; and yet the judgment could be made exclusively on the basis of the two versions.

There are, furthermore, certain kinds of case in the arts, special but not exceptional, where intentions are naturally or normally taken into account in evaluation. Examples would be cases involving classification in terms of genre or physical character, as when a mawkish novel is singled out as a splendid parody of a romance, or a seascape which is judged to be the freest of the entire eighteenth century is in fact a fragment from the background of a larger whole; cases of performance and rendition, where for instance a famous singer in old age makes a controlled substitution of other notes, rather than giving an imperfect rendition; cases of a work left unfinished due to outside circumstances on record, where one can refer to a sketch-plan; and cases where the conditions of execution proved unfavorable, as with Leonardo's *Last Supper* or Eisenstein's Mexico film.

The claim under consideration, if taken as covering intentions, would appear to be factually incorrect in terms of what happens in such cases.

If the claim is phrased differently, to the effect that what is intended but not accomplished cannot serve as a basis for judgment, then it is apposite to make a distinction between what may be called "unrealized" intentions, where the person did not realize what he or she set out to realize, but there are nevertheless clear and acceptable indications of what the intention was; and unfulfilled intentions, where there is evidence indicating what a person would have gone on to do, had his or her progress not stopped at the point where it did. While unrealized intentions may be a source of dispute when it comes to judgment, with one party claiming for instance that a singer's failure to reach a very high note was a magnificent failure, and another that she failed, and that is all there is to it, unfulfilled intentions are characteristically taken into account in a positive sense, as in the last two of the examples given, or the case of a writer whose actual production as extremely small, but who left notes for more ambitious projects which he was never able to carry out.

To turn now to the actual use of intentional statements in evaluation, two examples, notably different in character, will serve to bring out the kinds of thing that happen here:

> I have two new drawings now, one of a man reading his Bible and the other of a man saying grace before his dinner, which is on the table. . . . My intention in these two . . . is one and the same. Namely, to express the peculiar sentiment of Christmas and New Year. Both in Holland and England, this is always more or less religious. (van Gogh, letter of December 1882)

> The primary objectives [of *Façade,* 1922] were to exalt the speaking voice to the level of the instruments supporting it, to obtain an absolute balance between the volume of the music and the volume of the sound of the words—neither music nor words were being treated or taken as a separate entity—and thus to be able to reach for once that unattainable land—wherein parallel sound and sense, which here never meet, can be seen, even from this distance, to merge and run in one broad line on the horizon. Another chief aim equally difficult was the elimination of the personality of the reciter, and also—though this is of lesser consequence—of the musicians, and the abolition, as a result, of the constricting self-consciousness engendered by it [the musicians were seated behind a painted curtain, the speaker used a sengerphone built into the center of the curtain]. . . . [*Façade*] was, in short, the discovery of an abstract method of presenting poetry to an audience. (Osbert Sitwell, 1948)

Van Gogh, in the statement of his selected, does not describe a specific symbolism, such as could be written about just before the work was begun, or while it was in progress. Rather he voices an aspiration, for a certain kind of mood or sentiment, such as any artist might wish to evoke. It would therefore be inappropriate to the kind of statement this is to take the intention as given and ask from that standpoint whether or not the work evinces the quality in point. It is possible that van Gogh was reading into his own work at this stage of his career, and the drawing could be taken simply as a piece of naturalistic recording. The critical question would then be one of necessity: whether or not it was necessary to the work as a significant achievement that it should have the quality of mood that van Gogh wished it to exhibit.

In the second example, along with the descriptive elements indicating what was done, and the interpretative ones, which have the general aim of saving the work from being judged according to traditional conventions which an audience might expect and look for, a retrospective claim is being made that involves an ideal or set of ideals, and various means or techniques for their realization. The facts as to what the Sitwells did are not in dispute; what may be are the ideals in question, their justification and the execution of the work that embodies them. The critical issue is therefore, here, one of sufficiency and feasibility: whether fulfillment of the intention is sufficient to give the work significance or merit, and whether, in regard to the first part of the statement, it was possible in principle to bring off the fusion described. Judgment will correspondingly entail placing the ambitions of the work in the general tradition of synesthetic theory and experiment, assessing how the synesthetic elements are put together in this particular case, and judging in addition a particular performance. Contextual factors are therefore brought into the judging in this case also, and the same with the example brought up earlier of the notes to *The Waste Land*. Judgment of how effectively they contribute to the poem in its final printed form, and whether they need to be taken into account at all, entails—irrespective finally of T. S. Eliot's statement on the subject, and the relevance it has to interpreting the character of the notes—questions of precedent, the context of the poem's appearance, and the kind of poem it is.

In adopting such critical procedures, one is not, it should be noted, saying of the artist that in his intentional statements he spoke unthinkingly, or did not know what he was saying; or that he was in error in his theory, or mistaken in the conception that he had of his work, or under an illusion on the subject. It is not a matter of laying claim to a facility which the artist himself lacks, but of having a way available of dealing with such statements, which brings out certain qualifying or limiting aspects of their relevance to the work, their coherence, appropriateness as a type of statement, distinctiveness within the history of the type, and so on. To assess and evaluate in this light is not to establish any "wrongness" on the part of the artist in what he contributes. The word *wrong,* if it finds its way in here, does so inappropriately; for what is done with the artist's words is a matter of methodology, based for example on the grouping of statements by type and form, and not of truth versus falsehood.

The preceding remarks are based on what actual practice and the terms that go with it would imply; they are not prescriptive in character, nor has there been a central argument. But if a conclusion of a summarizing kind seems called for, it would be that in the evaluation of works of art intentions are sometimes relevant, seldom decisive, often irrelevant. Intentional statements, where they exist, are ignored at one's risk; but their application is likely always to be a matter of judgment. A binding theoretical principle holds out the promise of reducing the element of troublesomeness here, so that arguments for such a principle are likely to have an inherent and recurring appeal. But it is also of the nature of critical theorizing that sharpness and persuasiveness in such a case are attained to at the cost of at least partially misrepresenting the empirical facts, and the methods of the discipline.

Critics may and will disagree on the abstract principle, but they have the intentional statements of the writer or artist in mind as they do their work, or at least in the back of their minds. Once having acknowledged the existence of this material, they deem it relevant or inappropriate to their particular undertaking in differing ways; but whatever their method or bias, they adopt in so doing an approach into which its use comes anyway.

6 On the Recognition and Identification of Objects in Paintings

It's all the same to me whether a form represents a different thing to different people or many things at the same time. And then I occasionally introduce forms which have no literal meaning whatsoever.

Braque

There are certain ways in which the spectator's response to a work of art is liable to interference or a potentially deflecting kind of persuasion. What one is told is there in the work, or relevant to it, may play such a role; and so may what one supposes to be there, as opposed to what actually is. Since similar problems apply in the perception of the real world, including the people and the actions in it, to say this is not yet to say that there is, or should be, a pure and untrammeled kind of perception that one aims at, or learns to use in front of works of art; that being already a form of critical theorizing which places some kind of limits or ideal construction on what is permissible in the form of a response. But to stop short of such a step is also to leave open the question of whether there are in fact two distinct realms in which perception and related cognitive processes occur, one artistic, the other non-artistic. For present purposes, rather than any larger presupposition being entertained here, it is assumed simply that, differences of situation and context notwithstanding, there is no type of statement concerning the perception of a work of art which does not have a parallel or equivalent in the perception of the real world. Such is the philosophical basis for the line of inquiry to be followed here.

In the case of modern art, the question of the artist's authority in regard to what he has done, and the kinds of possible evidence that may substantiate what is said or observed about a work, are intrinsically likely to take on an increased importance because of the absence or reduction of recognizable imagery. The topic of recognition and identification places itself, from this point of view, alongside the issue generally known as that of the artist's intentions. But while the latter has been the subject of continuous and sustained debate, both as it applies to literature and in a more broadly philosophical sense, the issue to be taken up here has scarcely been written about at all. Narrowed so as to deal only with paintings, it may indeed have the look of being widely different in substance. But the two topics are in fact joined, or at least linked in the broad sense indicated, raising as they do questions pertaining to knowledge and how it is come by, and detaching themselves on that basis into a series of comparable sub-issues.

On the Workings of Imagination and Suggestion

The use of imagination and response to suggestion clearly play an important part in the reading of works of art. But the way in which this happens forms, generally speaking, a self-contained subject of inquiry, which is germane for present purposes only insofar as lines of separation need to be drawn. In the drawing of those lines, a key consideration that needs to be recognized is that not all identification or recognition, of whatever kind, involves interpretation as a necessary part of it.

The notion that this should be so takes its force from the longstanding premise, in the philosophy of perception, that there is a sense-datum provided by the object of perception and also, separately or following that, what the perceiver does with it. But though description of what is seen does indeed in some instances shade into interpretation, no such generalized assumption as to what takes place in the process of perception can be made to rest on those cases. In the most often debated examples in philosophy, of the stick half submerged in the water and looking as if it were bent, and the round penny which appears elliptical from a certain angle and viewpoint, the stick is recognized or identified as being a straight one, not actually bent by the water but appearing to be, and the penny as being really round, with again an appended statement of why it should look as if it were not. What is seen may in these examples be interpreted, in the sense of an explanation being given; but this is not to say that the stick as one sees it is being interpreted as a bent version, or image, of a straight stick. In the case of a map of the world, it is one thing, where the map is modern, to find or recognize America from its shape; it is quite another, where the map is old or one with a strange projection, to interpret a shape, which is perhaps unrecognizable, as America. And though the recognition of an acquaintance by recall might suggest a memory image which is held in the mind and is conjured up for consultation and comparison, the extreme case of matching in which cups patterned in varying ways are drawn from a box and juxtaposed in turn to the one for which a pair is being sought, is one in which, revealingly, the pattern is recognized each time as being or not being the same one; there is no interpretation to that effect, and certainly no imagination is involved in the sense of a mental picture to which reference is made.

From this group of examples, therefore, interpretation appears as a varyingly inductive or deductive process, but as one probably detached from the perception itself, which may quite possibly be imaginative in character. Recognition and identification, on the other hand, do not necessarily entail a picture or image held in the mind, which is used in a step or process separate from the perception. The concept of "seeing as," which needs to be taken up also for present purposes, has been much discussed in the philosophy of perception. As distinct from the general question of whether all seeing is to be regarded as in some sense seeing as, reasons for the use of the phrase in ordinary life situations could include an uncontrollable propensity or repeated tendency that one finds in oneself, as for example the inclination to see a certain face as a laughing one, however hard one tries otherwise, or seeing in a series of dreams a person as alive whom one knew or discovered to be dead. The phrase may be used for an interpretation (and one reflecting knowledge and experience) or recognition of a firm kind, as in the case of a doctor pronouncing on symptoms of cholera; but usually it is so used in a context where there is room for difference and where politeness may be important, much as with the shift to the subjunctive in French, or where there is an element of mystery or puzzlement, as on a panel show where there is a mystery object to be identified.

In front of works of art, there are cases where the use of imagination on the spectator's part is encouraged, allowed or assumed. The language used shows, in the sense that certain distinctive phrases are employed, where this is the case. "I see this as . . ." designates in this context the making of an imaginative construction, as when a sequence of clouds is seen as the different countries of Europe. The phrase commonly entails the noting of some, but only some, suggestive similarities or resemblances between two dissociated things, as when a mark on a wall or a cloud is seen as a camel, in terms of shape alone. One may also speak of seeing something "in" the work, as for example a certain configuration or color; and what it is that a person sees here may very well tell more about the person than about the work. Lastly, the phrase "It looks like so and so to me" may be used, and here both tone and context will be relevant, in addition to the importance of the attached "to me."

With the substitution of "sounds" for "looks" and "hear" for "see," and with exceptions made for special cases of so-called program music and the evocations of sounds such as bird-song, all of these types of statement have their equivalents in the case of music. What happens there is indicative in that, while the circumstances and conditions under which music is listened to may encourage fantasy and the giving of free rein to whatever images come into the mind, comments of the kind that are being considered are likely to bear at least some relationship either to what happens in the music at a particular point, or to the kind of formal structure the music has. Correspondingly, the typical functions of this kind of language in front of works of art, perhaps most especially for the novice in the field, would be to convey, in a metaphorical or relatively poetic sense, how a particular element strikes one, as when one speaks of seeing a "dark tunnel" in a piece of sculpture; or alternately as a way of describing the arrangement of forms, as when one says that one is beginning to be able to see the work as organized into a triangle. It may also be that, by an extension of the same language, a move towards interpretation takes place: as when the sound of the bugle at a certain point in a piece of music is taken as the morning bugle-call of the village, or, on the analogy of a grouping of tea-leaves being seen as a portent, a painting is seen as lonely in character.

There is, however, a possible troublesomeness in the fact that statements and comments of the kind in question here may sometimes be cast in the barer form "I see . . ." Again the analogy of music is helpful. To say while listening to a piece of music that one hears bird-song may be a true statement, if one is listening to the *Pastoral* Symphony; or it may be an interpretative one, on the same general lines as in the case of the bugle-call. But just as flippancy, gratuitousness of comment or self-projection on the speaker's part may be involved in the statement that "it sounds like bird-song" or "it looks like falling rain to me," so also there is a first person use of "seeing as" or "seeing" which stresses subjectivity. To illustrate this, one may take the third-person use which allows one to say, of a Surrealist double image, that one can see it, simultaneously here, both as a fruit dish and as a face; and compare that use with the first-person use in "I like to see this as . . . ," or some such remark as "I see a wood-nymph when you enter the room," which is essentially a matter of self-indulgence, in a familiar, recognized pleasure in one case and a flight of fancy in the other.

Easy as it may be, on such grounds, to be dismissive of a person's saying, in front of a painting, that he sees dark shadows or a piece of coal on the end of a stick, consideration of purpose rather than psychology brings up the fact that statements of the form "I see . . ." are commonly used with works of art either to express an extreme broadness or generality of response or to show lack of further interest. Such statements are not then to be taken as either mindless or absurd. In a context of appreciation they may appear as misleadingly promising more in the way of perception than they really have to offer, but in informal discussion the qualification to be made is more of their not being to the point, in the sense that either there will be no way of locating more exactly within the work what the comment refers to, or there will really be nothing more to be elicited from the speaker. So understood, these are in either event a special kind of statement.

It emerges, therefore, that when a person talks about works of art in terms that involve the exercise of imagination, he is not thereby loosening his hold on accuracy or firmness of recognition and identification, any more than a person about to die who sees his whole life flash before him. The idea of an opposition between hitting the mark in what is said and just narrowly missing it is misplaced here. Comments on what something in a painting is may be phrased speculatively or cautiously, for whatever reasons, but to speak of what one sees something as in a painting is not normally a loose or less specific version of such phrasing. What one sees as a left arm or as part of the background may in fact be that, as with the puddle that looks like gasoline rather than water; but the phrasing most often distinguishes the two types of statement from one another, as do also their differing criteria of supportability.

How the Identity of an Object May Be Unclear

In determining for what reasons the identity of an object may be unclear in a painting that one is dealing with directly, one can properly exclude two types of consideration as irrelevant for present purposes. There are those cases in which special circumstances or conditions may affect one's ability to see or read a painting. Impairments to one's vision that fall under this rubric would include such factors as the fall or amount of light, obstacles in the way, distance, drunkenness or dazzle; impairments to the work would consist especially of physical damage to it, such as a blackened segment. The phrasing most typically used for such cases is that the object "appears to be" a knife or a clockface: it appears to be that in a raking light, from here, or under interfering circumstances which are then detailed or referred to. Also to be left out of account are cases in which a special knowledge or experience that could be brought to bear is lacking or not available: one may not know what a certain object, such as a viola-da-gamba, is like, or what the X rays of the painting reveal.

With these exclusions, four kinds of reason are then left. First there will be the liability of the object itself to misreading. It may for example be similar in appearance to something else, as a whole or in one or another respect; and the unfamiliarity of the object could well be a contributing factor here, it being quite often the case that assimilation to a more familiar object may occur. Second, there would be the lack of an assisting context, consisting for example of other related objects or an indicative placing of more complete or more detailed renderings of the same object. The effect of hanging a painting upside down or otherwise wrongly may qualify for inclusion under this heading, as as special case, insofar as correction here causes the elements to fall into place contextually, as perhaps with the growth of roses out from a sketchy green background. And thirdly there will be factors in the structure of the painting which naturally have or tend to have such a consequence: as for example overlap, atmospheric dissolution, simplification or change of color.

The fourth and final kind of reason, which calls for consideration on its own, may be designated as deliberate ambiguity on the artist's part. "Ambiguity" is used here in the second dictionary sense, of being unclear and therefore susceptible to alternative interpretations, as opposed to the sense of having more than one meaning. It may be unclear, for example, whether a particular figure is of a boy or a girl; it may be taken either way, or indeed as an androgyne, the degree of specification on the artist's part being insufficient to resolve the matter one way rather than the other. "Deliberate" is used here in contradistinction to accidental; as for instance, in dealing with a typed or printed version of a poem one might have doubts as to whether a particular misspelling, or an unusual word order, was or was not deliberate. The inclusion of this adjective here lays stress on the ambiguity being an intrinsic part of the artist's style or conception. In that regard, the kind of "naive" ambiguity that is found in the art of children, or in so-called primitive art—where what is shown may be simply wrong, in terms for example of how the head joins onto the neck, or the specification insufficient for the purpose in question, as for instance to identify a man as dead—is still deliberate in the sense that recognizable conventions are adopted, as in early Greek vase-painting.

The four factors which have now been reviewed group themselves in a sequence, or spectrum, which goes by gradual shift from the nature of the object to the artist's treatment of it. It is against the latter end of the spectrum that comments of a derisive or indignant kind align themselves, asking where something is in a painting or claiming rhetorically a failure to make out anything. When, correspondingly, a hostile critic makes a similarly directed remark such as asking, in a well-known instance, how Monet's "innumerable black tongue lickings" could represent figures on a boulevard, it is doubtful if either change of viewing distance or further consideration of the nature of the subject would make any effective difference to the tenor and tone of what is said.

On the Resolution of Difficulties and Hesitations

Difficulties and hesitations experienced in front of a work of art, for the reasons now given, as to what an object is, may be resolved in a number of different ways which bring out more generally the bases and criteria for doing this. The object or objects themselves may serve this purpose, as for example the actual instruments kept by the artist in his studio. So may other works by the artist, which show the same object or include a similar treatment of it. In both of these cases special knowledge to which one may have access is at issue. Then there are the available records of the creative process leading up to the work: drawings, studies, photographs or pattern-books that the artist knew or consulted, or possibly the paint on the studio floor. There is the title given by the artist to be considered as something attached to the work. And lastly there is the possibility of the spectator's presence during the creative process and his viewing of it.

Excluded here is the righting of the way the work is framed or hung, since, except in the special kind of case already considered, what is eliminated here represents, or is akin to, an impediment to the spectator's viewing; especially in the case of a frame, which may, for example, have overlapped and therefore obstructed part of the work. It is then clear that, with the objects themselves and other works of the artist's, one is dealing with factors which are definitely external to the work of art, as a self-contained entity; and the same would arguably be true of the records of the creative process. In the remaining two cases, whether one regards the title given by the artist, and the process of execution, as external or internal is itself a critical or aesthetic judgment, as to where limits should be put on the traditionally maintained autonomy of the work of art. That autonomy has been variously conceived of as entailing the work's separation from functional interaction with the real world, as when a spoon is placed in a museum case; or the separation of the work from a context affecting it physically, as when it is taken off the paint-marked studio wall and placed in a frame for display; or again in terms of the work's independence of the process which produced it, including preliminary versions and related works. In further extension of the argument, cases might also be cited in modern art, such as Klee's titling or Duchamp's ready-mades, where the tendency has been to take a positive, inclusive attitude here.

While the concern in these remarks has been with objects in paintings, it is fairly self-evident that the same points and criteria apply to the recognition of people in paintings, and in photographs also. Notions of a "primary" basis of recognition enabling one to say that a figure is a man, before the sophistication of special knowledge as to who he is comes in, cannot be justified empirically, because though what happens may quite well and commonly proceed in such a way, the criteria of resolution are thereby ranked into an ascending order of what they contribute conceptually, instead of being recognized as coequal possibilities.

The Question of Authority in Resolving Difficulties

In terms of the way arguments are settled and doubts are resolved or remain unresolvable, the objects in works of art are not in a unique and special category as compared to objects in real life. The non-predictivity of statements about works of art—which means that, in a case of doubt or dispute as to what something is, there can be no recourse to an action, like the opening up of a box or a fish, in order to settle the matter—makes no actual difference here. The reading of shapes into clouds represents one instance only, but a particularly clear one, of an everyday activity which is analogously divorced from the possibility of action; and a final agreement that one is dealing with a cross between two objects, or two breeds of animal, is as possible an outcome in real life as it is in front of a painting. The situation, in the latter case, of not being able to know or settle such a point as the color of a man's eyes is, if it is to be differentiated from a comparable situation in historical research or necrology, paralleled there in every respect except one: the choice of the artist as to what is relevant.

Knowledge and experience are indeed relevant to resolving difficulties in front of works of art, but the particular manner in which this happens needs stricter specification. For present purposes, special knowledge and experience, as for example of what X rays reveal or of the artist's interests, have previously been excluded. As distinct from their contribution, commonly phrased in terms of "it seems to be" or "must be," there is the knowledge or experience to be considered which is gained on the way to making an identification, as part of the process, or used to verify, support or confirm an identification. In illustration of what this means, one may go through a catalogue of paintings looking for a certain object, such as a particular kind of jug or rug, for the purpose of possibly identifying the same object elsewhere, as against using for that purpose knowledge that one already has about jugs or rugs of the time. Or one may think that it could be a rug and proceed on the same basis, thereby ascertaining that it is one.

The authority of the artist enters in here through his being a supplier or potential supplier of evidence. In normal circumstances evidence of such a kind, if available as in the form of memoirs, is likely to be found acceptable; or at the least there will be a feeling of obligation to take it into account. The tendency to assume, beyond questions of credibility, that the artist has authority as creator of the work is predicated, in present terms, on the fact that he gives the work its title, at least most often; that he owns or chooses the objects depicted in it; and that he does the painting including all that leads up to it. However, that authority does not constitute, as an attitude of over-esteem may lead one to suppose, a source of extraspecial certainty in the perceiver as to what he sees, or indeed certainty at all. In the first place, the artist is not the only person who by virtue of experience or of explanatory and analytical powers in front of the work itself can or may help out here. A work of art is not unique here amongst objects of perception, or indeed different in this respect, as indicated previously, from any other artefact. And secondly knowledge, whether the artist's or anyone else's, is not to be understood or defined as the acme on an ascending scale of presumption and certainty; nor as the necessary inspiration or fount of certainty, for though it may be that in the case of the third-person usage "It is certain that . . . ," the same does not at all necessarily apply to first-person statements in the form "I am certain . . . ," which record a personal conviction.

If the artist says that an object in his work which has some of the defining characteristics of a mandolin is in fact a guitar, it might be demonstrable that he knew nothing whatever about musical instruments, but it is conceivable even then, and more likely in general, that his identification would win out, since reasons for the disputed feature being that way might plausibly exist and be given. To show the practical application of the points just made, however, it is more instructive to take up actual cases of what happens, in the move towards identification and recognition, and delineate in so doing some possible sources of confusion.

Examples of a convincingness of evidence, deriving from elsewhere than from the artist himself and tied to a consideration of what the work itself shows, would be, first, Gauguin's *Self-portrait* of 1889 with the crucified Christ to the left of it. Asked what one sees to the left here, and with no information to go by outside of the work itself, one would, beyond identifying Christ and a landscape, be most likely to say that this is probably a painting, or that one takes it to be that; for though planes and edges provide no clearcut evidence to this effect, consistency of handling and the implausibility of the Christ appearing in front of an exterior landscape view would suggest this. And it is in fact, as one can discover or be shown from a volume of plates, an earlier work of Gauguin's, the *Yellow Christ,* only partially shown, in reverse, and somewhat altered, but with enough of a correspondence for it to be recognizably that painting.

Here special knowledge of Gauguin's earlier work leads to or supports the recognition that this is a painting shown hanging on the wall behind the sitter. Gauguin himself did not, so far as is known or recorded, say anything or offer any enlightenment on the subject. In the case of Pissarro's *Self-portrait* of 1873, which similarly has paintings on the rear wall, even the possibility of considering the evidence as deriving from the artist, because he did the work in question, is effectively eliminated. Asked what he sees to the rear here, a person is likely to say unframed paintings of landscapes, or what seem to be that. The expert can go beyond this and affirm that these are landscapes of Pissarro's own. Here, not only is there no guidance of Pissarro's to this effect; the canvases in question do not survive for comparison, and conceivably never existed. Yet the expert can still make his identification with confidence. Subject matter and handling, the framing and hanging of the works, and also the existence of a tradition of self-portraiture showing the artist in his studio with objects of his creation around him, may be presented as the expert's basis. Yet these are only pointers; the confidence comes from their joint and interlocking contribution in a reading of the work as a whole.

If the identification in those cases is called a certain one, it is probably because of physical characteristics, shown or implied, and correspondences which rule out potential alternatives. But the distinction between knowledge and certainty, as it applies to recognition and identification, is more decisively illustrated by what one is told is there in the left background of Picasso's 1910 portrait of *Daniel-Henry Kahnweiler,* and what one can make out visually in that part of the painting. It was put on record, from recollection, by Picasso that the object which appears alongside the sitter here was a New Caledonian sculpture. This information is of course valuable as documentary evidence of Picasso's interest in primitive sculpture at the time; and given that there is a 1908 photograph showing such a sculpture on his studio wall, it helps to corroborate factually what can be deduced structurally from many of his paintings and drawings of 1907–09. But if one turns back to the portrait armed with that information, it seems doubtful, given the fragmented character of every image and part of an image, that one would say that one now saw clearly that it was a primitive sculpture, or that it undoubtedly was one. Rather the likely comment would be that one could see that it might be such a sculpture, or that it might indeed be the particular sculpture shown in the studio photograph. Since before the information was given, or without it, the comment could be offered that it might be, or could very well be, a piece of sculpture there in the background, the difference in phrasing resulting from the acquisition of special knowledge is not a matter of increased certainty, even if it might appear from the narrowing down that one was being more definite. Another possibility also would be to say that the object in question was, "we are told," a New Caledonian sculpture, where the qualifying phrase is both symptom and expression of a reservation that the visual indications impose. While this may seem like a version of the familiar conflict between visual evidence and factual authority, in which either one may prevail, the case is really one entailing the separation of intellectual and cognitive processes.

The last of these examples leads into the question of authority in the domain of abstraction, and here again the terminology itself may be a source of confusion. Talk about abstraction from nature, signifying simplification, the elimination of detail, intensification of color, stylization of contour and so on, conceives of what is done as a creative process personal to the artist, thereby suggesting his authoritative knowledge or understanding of the extent to which the resulting object or image will be recognizable inasmuch as he has control over the factors leading to that result. And indeed, asked to explicate what something is in a painting of his, the artist may emphasize his abstraction from the object, rather than its representation, saying that this derives from a bottle, or is not really an apple any longer, or is only a hint of a door; or there may be evidence, in studies or the work itself, that recognizable imagery has been, in a systematic way, painted over or painted out. But the degree of abstraction and the process involved constitute only one possible reason for the identity of an object to be unclear; and more important, abstraction is not the antithesis of representation, where both are intended, the distinction being normally an aspect of the total structure—or to put it in terms of degree, in inverse proportion to recognizability. A certain amount of abstraction, and some manipulation generally of the objects' character, might indeed facilitate recognition. Correspondingly, when an artist such as Kandinsky or Mondrian represents a work of his as being a nonrepresentational painting, and the historian or critic says retrospectively that it is in fact a landscape with towers or a seascape of ocean and pier, the disagreement between them would either be an evaluative not an interpretative one or else more apparent than real.

The workings of the subconscious, which may come into what the artist offers in the way of imagery, represent a whole extra dimension of inquiry bearing only peripherally on the present topic. When questioned from this point of view, the artist may generally say, with authority, that what is being talked of, such as the sexual connotation of a shape, is not something of which he was aware. The argument may then shift to the level or domain of the subconscious, which tends to have its own rules and principles of evidence and corroboration. In that area of discussion one tends to say, not that a certain object, in a dream or a painting, looks like a phallus, or that it is a phallus, but rather, in a special kind of language, that this is a phallic form, or one that has phallic significance. In the Freudian scheme of things, the artist when psychoanalyzed should be able to say that, though he was not aware of it till now, the phallic character or sexual nature of the object was there all the time, like an overtone to a word which is now brought out and retroactively recognized.

The Move towards Recognition and Identification

The circumstances can now be considered in which one moves to a recognition or clear identification in front of a painting, saying for example "I see now that it is a bottle" or "Now I can see what it is." With all such questions as faulty vision and its correction left aside, where a new pair of glasses might remove the difficulty in the same sense as an obstacle in the way is eliminated, what is in question here is a process: namely the way in which enlightenment comes to the spectator as to what an object is. On that basis a distinction can be made between mental states or conditions which may lead to an object being misidentified or not recognized at all—such as fixation on something else, overimagination or a contempt for the whole process of looking, these being like predispositions—and psychological factors—such as closeness of attention or the existence of a prior framework of assumption—which may play a mediating role in the process under consideration, and will come into an account of it correspondingly.

The focus being, then, the kind of experience or intermediate step which leads or enables one to see, recognize or identify something in a painting as one could not do before, there appear to be essentially three different kinds of possibility. On the basis of special evidence, whether it comes from the artist or someone else, one is likely to say, as in the Picasso example, "Now I can see that it might be a sculpture." To say here "Now I can see that it is that" would seem misleadingly to imply that whatever basis one's previous reading rested on was relinquished; and certainly there are cases which argue strongly against that being so. In both a Matisse still life of 1906 and one by Picasso of 1907 or 1908, what had appeared plausibly enough to be a mirror included in the background has turned out to be a painting of the artist's; and yet the factors, such as quality of surface handling, framing and placement, which led in each case to this being taken for a mirror do not thereby disappear or cease to apply, but rather an adjustment to the claims of the evidence is made, as a result of which the painting within the painting can be seen and characterized as indeed so treated that it might seem to be a mirror, or suggest one.

On the basis of other of the artist's works that are compared, or on the basis of presence during the creative process, one would on the other hand be likely to use the phrase, conveying a move towards recognition and enlightenment, "Now I can see that it is . . ." In the case, for example of Picasso's 1911 painting *The Accordionist* (D 424), the view of the one-time owner, based on the artist's recording on the painting's back of the place where it was done, Céret, was that it was a landscape; and such a view could be corrected by the comparison of other works of the period and the pointing out of comparably recognizable elements in them in the same or similar places, so that it was seen that this was in fact a figure painting, with the head at the top and the arms of the chair lower down. These or comparable elements might also be pointed out or noticed by a person present as they emerged or came into view during the painting of the work.

On the basis of looking at the title or an inscription on the back of the work for help, and then looking back at the picture, both of the above wordings seem possible. If it were a photograph that one were looking at, with a caption identifying who was in it, it might be that not having seen or not having identified Mary before, one looked for her in the photograph and found her. Or one might say of a certain figure that it must be Mary, although it did not look like her, from some identifying element such as the scarf she had on; or see that it might be Mary, with back turned perhaps, when there was special evidence or no doubting that Mary was there at the time. In none of these cases would one be inclined or tempted to say "Now I can see Mary"; nor can it be said that one sees the figure in question differently.

But there is also the possibility of a process like that of seeing, or being invited or led to see, a spot or stain on the wall as, for example, a face. According to a story told by Picasso many years later, he once teased and worried Braque by saying of a Cubist still life of tobacco, pipe and cards that Braque was working on that he saw a squirrel in it; and he indeed persuaded Braque into a long and arduous fight to remove what he saw, which he described as an almost impossible struggle because the squirrel kept coming back. Though exaggerated response is the source of the humor here, a totally or potentially misleading title attached to a work and a statement about a painting of the kind that the story illustrates might function similarly for the spectator. Rather than providing a clue of a more or less authoritative indication as to what is there, or where to look for what, as "Dead Bird" or "Bowl of Peaches" would typically be taken to do if there was any doubt on the subject, such a title or comment stimulates a particular kind of looking. It might be called looking with emphasis, or with more refinement, to bring out its character; with the understanding that there is nothing mechanical to it, or in the way of an impediment disposed of, as can be said to be the case where magnification is used on a photographic image of insufficient size, or a print is given clearer resolution, or a film image brought into focus. It could also be said that one looked under the direction of title or statement, as in looking for the figure in a pattern. And as with the stained area of the wall and like Braque when he too saw the squirrel, one ends up seeing that area of the painting, or the whole work, differently.

There remains the question of what, more exactly, "seeing differently" means here, as applied to a painting, part of one, or something included in one. For comparison there would be first seeing a configuration differently, as in the duck-rabbit example, or figure drawings of the kind that give a humorous change of image when turned upside down; the point in common here between these being, it might be said, that they can be read a different way round. Then there is the sense in which one says that one sees a person differently, as a result perhaps of finding out that he has been married twice and has five children. Whether such a remark is made of a person in the flesh, or as it could equally be of a portrait or a photograph, seeing of what is to be called an interpretative kind is in any event entailed. That this is so is brought out by such cases as seeing the moon differently, namely as spherical, now that the astronauts have landed on it; seeing from the caption to a photograph that a certain area or group has to contain an additional figure, namely Mary; and seeing analogously, in a complicated and confusing grouping within a painting, that a certain hand has to be the Virgin's left one. Lastly, there is seeing differently in the sense of seeing or noticing, as a matter of freshness or surprise, what one did not notice before: the face in the bush in a painting of Gauguin's, or that there are black geese flying to the left in a print of Escher's as well as white ones flying to the right. Omitted here is the case of seeing a speck turn into an aeroplane, as it comes closer, since this is a matter of changed conditions that gradually allow one to see more, or in more detail, whereas the face, if unmistakeable once seen, was there to be seen all the time.

If, in the examples brought up earlier of the Gauguin *Self-portrait* and the Matisse *Still Life,* one spoke of seeing the relevant area of the background differently as a result of being told that it consisted of a painting, it might be said that the elements had re-grouped themselves, or had grouped themselves in a way that one was not aware of before. But it would be the interpretation put on their relationships to one another and their surrounds, or the corrective to one's prior assumption or interpretation—not to one's seeing—which here brought this about, perhaps gradually and not without struggle or resistance. The knowledge that it was a painting could be described as inclining one's perception a certain way, towards a reading particularly in terms of plane rather than depth, and one that brought with it certain further implications; or as giving an extra kind of dimension to one's seeing, as when one sees a face as more unhappy than one had previously taken it to be. By either account this would be a case of the second kind, into which belief may be said to come as support to the change, the word being used as in "I believe you" and in the phrase "suspension of disbelief."

The stain on the wall, on the other hand, would probably be most like the first kind of case, with some features of the third. Just as, told that there is a duck, one may still only see the rabbit, deference to authority will not cause one to see differently here; and it may simply be a matter of narrowing one's visual search, in the sense of focusing it in one place rather than another. If, with a painting, what one had previously described as a "sort of maze" becomes clearly a still life, the process may well be something like what takes place with the stain. One may look at the title, as indicated, or may simply be told to "look again." The total image stays the same, as with the duck-rabbit configuration and as the stain remains a stain. One's way of reading what is there changes, in the sense of acquiring a refinement or emphasis that it did not previously have; but only in that sense.

Afterword
On Making Sense of the Modern

The differing sections of this book can be brought together to suggest, at the close, why art history as traditionally practised does not work for Cubism.

It may simply be that it mimics the criticism and interpretation of the period itself, and in so doing reproduces the problems, of connection with the art itself, that were discussed in Part One. But there is also the question of whether its underlying principles really work here: those of style analysis and iconography.

Certainly one can speak of Picasso's style of 1908–09, or of a post-War stylistic drift shared by him and Braque; and also of an iconography that refers to, or reflects, the creative situation and psychology of the artists. But on the first of these counts the situation is more complex than in earlier periods, in terms of the rate of change entailed, and its internally reflexive features. And on the second count, the paintings are obviously not at all easy to read, as paintings had traditionally been in subject and the scope of their imagery.

It is here that intentions, on the artists' part, and the recognition and identification of what takes place in the paintings come in as theoretical issues in themselves, which formed the subject of Part Two. For it is in the nature and character of Cubism that a consistent intention cannot be attributed to the work (or to the artists) and also that elements found in the work can only be identified and explained through an intermediate or preparatory kind of "experience," that is not supplied by the visual image itself. Since this last is not true of Impressionism and Post-Impressionism (nor of Picasso's and Braque's work up to 1908), we can speak of a specifically twentieth century kind of difficulty.

So it is not just, in the twentieth century, that notions of a freedom to improvise and abstract, in the processes of making a picture, and of a liberation from "textuality," in the sense of an explanatory text of some kind underlying the work, put a block in the way of traditional approaches. The terms on which "intention" (on the part of the artist) and recognition and identification (on the part of the viewer) both operate are profoundly altered now. And this in turn foreshadows a situation, of exploration on the one hand and comprehensibility on the other, that becomes centrally characteristic of modern art after 1910—even when the presentation is relatively realistic, or informed by a linkage with literature.

The role of a critical art history, in defining and evaluating what occurred, also alters correspondingly, and this can only be talked about by considering the weight and thrust (rather than the internal politics) of criticism itself. This will become especially true of modern art, in fact, from the point in time at which this book ends.

Notes and References

Chapter 1. The First Phase, 1909–1912

Hermeticism: the application of the term "hermetic" to Cubism has been criticized by Douglas Cooper, *The Cubist Epoch,* (London: Phaidon, 1970), p. 50, on the grounds that its dictionary meaning is either "impenetrable" or "airtight." This is to take no account of the connotations of the term in the case of *poésie hermétique,* or for Italian poetry, *ermetismo.* There being no treatment known to me, in book or dictionary form, of critical usage here, I rely for this purpose on the review (anon.) of Silvio Romat, *L'Ermetismo* in *Times Literary Supplement* (August 18, 1972), p. 967, and on the helpful comment of H. S. Hughes, *The Sea Change: The Migration of Social Thought 1930–1965* (New York, 1975), p. 6, that it denotes "the cultivation of an intensely private aesthetic sphere." Early cases of the use of the term in this sense for Cubism, if not the earliest, are those of Raynal in his 1923 introdn. to the Gris exhbn. at the Galerie Simon, Paris (communicated to me by Edward Fry): "L'on accuse l'oeuvre de Gris d'hermétisme, mais c'est qu'on n'a jamais pris la peine de démêler les intentions de sa pure science lyrique," and of Ozenfant and Jeanneret, *La Peinture Moderne* (1925), cited by Golding, p. 114. These form an interesting pair in that the first, while negative, indicates the nature of the turn away from that implication, and the second parallels closely the positive use for poetry. Earlier applications of the term to Cubism (cited by Gamwell, *Cubist Criticism,* [1980], p. 27) are in Gleizes, "A propos du Salon d'Automne." *Les Bandeaux d'Or,* (Nov. 1911) and Henri Guilbeaux, *Hommes du Jour* 11 (Nov. 1911); but there it is used in the Symbolist sense, to mean simply "riddling" or "obscure."

Reports of Picasso's disinclination to theorize: Jaimé Sabartes, *Picasso* (Milan, 1937), trans. as *Picasso: An Intimate Portrait* (New York, 1948), pp. 11–12; Fernande Olivier, *Picasso et ses amis* (Paris, 1933), pp. 181, 189; André Salmon, *Souvenirs sans fin,* 2 vols. (Paris, 1956), 2:308, and cf. also his article "Pablo Picasso," *Paris Journal* (Sept. 11, 1911) (Fry #14) with its report of how Picasso would "deny being the father of Cubism"; Max Jacob, "Souvenirs sur Picasso," *Cahiers d'Art* 2 (1927): 202; Maurice Raynal, *Picasso* (Paris, 1922), p. 27; Kahnweiler, *Juan Gris* (1946, Eng. ed., 1968), p. 179 and *Mes galeries et mes peintres* (Paris, 1961), Eng. trans., *My Galleries and Painters* (London, 1971), p. 43; Gelett Burgess, "The Wild Men of Paris," *Architectural Record* (New York) 27 (May 1910): 407–8 (Fry, "Cubism 1907–1908: An Early Eyewitness Account," *Art Bulletin* 48 [Mar. 1966]: 70–73).

Reported statements of Picasso's: Salmon, *Paris Journal* (Sept. 11, 1911) (Fry #14); Leo Stein, *Appreciation, Painting, Poetry and Prose* (New York, 1947), p. 177; Kahnweiler, *Der Weg zum Kubismus* (written 1914–1919, German ed., Munich, 1920), Eng. trans., *The Rise of Cubism* (New York, 1949), p. 8; "Un inédit de Juan Gris" (1956), repr. in his *Confessions esthétiques* (Paris, 1963), pp. 211–12, and cf. also *My Galleries,* p. 57 and Roland Penrose, *Picasso: His Life and Work* (New York, 1958), p. 160. Raynal's report is trans. in his *History of Modern Painting,* vol. 3, *From Picasso to Surrealism* (Geneva, 1950), p. 56. For the suggestion that the statement about measuring is based on Picasso's admiration for the work of Rousseau, whose practice of measuring noses for portraits would be remembered from around this time (as by Apollinaire, *Les Soirées de Paris* [Jan. 15, 1914], special number dedicated to Rousseau, commenting on his *Portrait of Apollinaire and his Muse* from 1909), see George H. Hamilton, *Painting and Sculpture in Europe 1880–1940* (Harmondsworth, Middsx., 1967), pp. 145 and 372 n.75; but this seems far-fetched. For Gomez de la Serna's recollection, see his *Picasso,* (Turin, 1965), first publ. in Spain as "Completa y veridica historia de Picasso y el Cubismo," *Revista del Occidente* (Madrid) Jul.–Aug. 1929): 30–31. He gives factual information about the contents of Picasso's studio, but he did not write anything down about Cubism till much later, and his writings on the subject are very freely elaborated: thus the other statement that he attributes to Picasso at this time, "I paint objects as I think them, not as I see them" is more dubiously authentic, at least for this date. The related works of Picasso's cited in connection with his statements are Daix 38, 41 and 32 (see also D 28 and 5); D 210 (as winter 1908, rather than spring 1909) and also Zervox, 6, 1076, dated 1908 (Rubin, *Picasso in the Museum of Modern Art* [1972], p. 201, fig. 37, and cf. also the drawing reprod. at p. 54); D 316–17 and also D 309–10, the watercolors D 306–7 and the drawings Zervos 6. 1095, 1097, 1104, 1106–9 and D 321.

Reported statements of Braque's: the phrase quoted in the opening para. is from Dora Vallier's interview, "Braque, la peinture et nous," *Cahiers d'Art* 1 (1954): 14. The interview of Burgess *(Architectural Record* [1910]: 405; Fry #6) is one of a group reported on together. It is dated by Fry to autumn–winter 1908, but internal evidence suggests that it may date from earlier, after the Salon des Indépendants in March.

Early theorists of Cubism—texts cited and secondary sources: Roger Allard, "Au Salon d'Automne de Paris," *L'Art Libre* (Lyons, Nov. 1910): 442 (Fry #10). See also "Sur quelque peintres," *Les Marches du Sud-Ouest* (June 1911): 57–64 (Fry #11) on the importance of Cézanne's example. Gleizes illustrated a volume of poems by him (publ. 1911).

Albert Gleizes, "Art et ses représentants: Jean Metzinger," *La Revue Indépendante* 4 (Sept. 1911): 161–72 (Gamwell, p. 161 n.75); "Le Fauconnier et son oeuvre", ibid. (Oct. 1911); "A propos du Salon d'Automne," *Les Bandeaux d'Or* (Nov. 1911). See also his response to the inquiry "Le Cubisme devant les artistes," *Les Annales Politiques et Littéraires* (Dec. 1, 1912) (cited by Ellen Oppler, *Fauvism Re-examined,* Columbia Ph.D. dissertation, [publ. New York: Garland Press, 1976], pp. 229–30); "Le Cubisme et la Tradition," *Montjoie !* 1 (Feb. 10, 1913): 6; 2 (Feb. 23): 2–3; "Opinion," ibid. 11–12 (Nov.–Dec. 1913): 11.

Jean Metzinger, "Note sur la peinture," *Pan* (Paris) 3, no. 10 (Oct.–Nov. 1910): 649–52 (Fry #9); "Cubisme et Tradition," *Paris Journal* (Aug. 16 and Sept. 15, 1911) (Fry #13). See also his interview of 1908, Burgess (1910), pp. 413–14. (Fry, 1966, p. 72).

The book by Gleizes and Metzinger, *Du Cubisme* (Paris: Eugène Figuière, 1912, with date of printing given as Dec. 27; Eng. ed., London, 1913) appeared originally with 24 illustrations, including 5 works each by Gleizes, Metzinger, and Léger and one each by Cézanne, Picasso, Derain and Gris; other illustrations were added later (including one by Braque). Refs. are to the Eng. trans. by Robert Herbert, *Modern Artists on Art* (Englewood Cliffs, N.J., 1964), pp. 1–9; (repr. in excerpts, Fry #23): pp. 3–5 (sec. 1), p. 8 (sec. 2), p. 13 (sec. 3), p. 17 (sec. 4).

Olivier-Hourcade, "La tendance de la peinture contemporaine," *Revue de France et des Pays Français* (Paris) 1 (Feb. 1912): 35–41 (Fry #16; in a fuller version, P. Cabanne, *L'epopée du cubisme* [Paris, 1963], pp. 206); "Discussion" (reply to Vauxcelles), *Paris Journal* (Oct. 23, 1912), Golding, pp. 26–27.

Guillaume Apollinaire: Apollinaire's complete reviews and incidental writings on art are to be found collected in *Chroniques d'art* 1902–11, ed. L. C. Breunig (Paris, 1960); also incl. as vol. 4 of *Oeuvres complètes* (Paris, 1966) and in *Anecdotiques* (first ed., 1936, with many cuts; rev. ed., Paris, 1955: a series publ. in *Mercure de France,* 1911 on, under the pseudonym "Montade"). The articles publ. earlier in *Il y a* (1925) are included in the first of these. The trans. of *Chroniques,* by S. Suleiman, *Apollinaire on Art, Essays and Reviews 1902–1918* (London and New York, 1972), includes additional material and some excisions; it is used for convenient reference below. The standard edition of *Les Peintres Cubistes—Meditations esthétiques* (Paris: Figuière, 1913; Eng. trans., ed. R. Motherwell, New York, 1944, rev. ed. 1949) is now that of L. C. Breunig and J.-Cl. Chevalier (Paris, 1965), with much background and supporting material (hereafter: Breunig).

Texts cited: "Les jeunes: Picasso Peintre," *La Plume* (May 15, 1905) *Apollinaire on Art,* pp. 14–16; "Les trois vertus plastiques," preface to *Catalogue de la IIIe. exposition du Cercle de l'art moderne* (Le Havre, June 1908), pp. 47–49; preface to catalogue of *Exposition Braque,* Galerie Kahnweiler (Nov. 9–28, 1908), pp. 50–52, reused with variants as "Georges Braque," *Revue indépendante* 3 (Aug. 1911); "Le Salon d'Automne," *Poésie* (autumn 1910): 113–14; "Les Indépendants," *L'Intransigeant* (Apr. 20, 1911): 149–54; 150–52 are on Rousseau and Room 41; preface to *Catalogue de la 8e. Salon annuel du Cercle d'art, "Les indépendants,"* Musée Moderne (Brussels, Jun. 10–Jul. 3, 1911), pp. 172–73); "Le Salon d'Automne," *L'Intransigeant* (Sept. 30–Oct. 14, 1911): 182–84 on the Cubists; "Du sujet dans la peinture moderne," *Les Soirées de Paris* (Feb. 1, 1912): 197–98; "Les peintres italiens futuristes," *L'Intransigeant* (Feb. 7, 1912): 199–200 and also "Nouvels d'art: les futuristes," *Le Petit Bleu* (Feb. 9): 200–201; "La peinture nouvelle; notes sur l'art," *Les Soirées de Paris* (Apr.–May 1912): 222–25; review of Salon d'Automne, *L'Intransigeant* (Sept. 30–Oct. 3, 1912): 249, on new work by the Cubists; "Le Cubisme," *L'Intermédiaire des chercheurs et des curieux* (Oct. 10, 1912): 256–58, successor to a piece on Futurism there; "Art et curiosité: les commencements du Cubisme," *Le Temps* (Oct. 14, 1912): 259–61; "Note: Realité, peinture pure," *Les Soirées de Paris* (Dec. 1912), variant publ. in *Der Sturm* (Dec. 1912): 262–65; "Picasso," *Montjoie !* (Mar. 14, 1913): 279–81; review of Salon des Indépendants, *Montjoie !* (Mar. 18, 1913): 286, opening section used for book. For his view of the relationship of art to literature, see "Henri Matisse" (interview), *La Phalange* (Dec. 15, 1907): 36–37 refer and "Le critique des poètes," *Paris Journal* (May 5, 1914): 373–75. All of the different places in which his art writings appeared during this time are represented here.

André Salmon, early criticism of Cubism in *Paris Journal:* "Le Salon d'Automne" (Sept. 30, 1910), with C. Morice; "Picasso" (Dec. 22, 1910); "Le 26e. Salon des Indépendants" (Apr. 20, 1911); "Albert Gleizes" (Sept. 14, 1911); "Jean Metzinger" (Oct. 3, 1911); "Georges Braque" (Oct. 13, 1911); "Le Salon des Indépendants" (Mar. 19, 1912), Gamwell, pp. 24–25 and 168 n.18. Salmon's book *La jeune peinture française* (Paris, 1912) contains his "Anecdotal history of Cubism" (Fry #18). On science, see pp. 49–50 there and also his *La jeune sculpture française* (written 1914, publ. Paris, 1919), pp. 10–11. Apollinaire's article on his poetry, *Vers et Prose* (Jul.–Aug. 1908), is repr. in Apollinaire, *Oeuvres complètes,* vol. 3, pp. 822–23.

Max Jacob: on his relationship with Picasso, see L. C. Breunig, "Max Jacob et Picasso," *Mercure de France,* 331 (Dec. 1, 1957): 581–97; H. Henry, "Max Jacob et Picasso; jalons chronologiques pour un amitié," *Europe* (Apr.–May, 1970): 199–204, and also Theodore Reff, "Picasso's Three Musicians: Maskers, Artists and Friends," *Art in America* 68, no. 10 (Dec. 1980): 124–42. For his art work (four examples of which belong to the Musée d'Art Moderne, Céret), see now Marcelin Pleynet, Christian Parisot and Jeanine Warnod, *Max Jacob—Dessins* (Paris, 1970).

Maurice Raynal: "L'exposition de la Section d'Or," *La Section d'Or* (Paris, Oct. 9, 1912): 2–5 (Fry #21).

Jacques Rivière, "Sur les tendances actuelles de la peinture," *Revue d'Europe et d'Amérique* (Paris, Mar. 1, 1912): 384–406 (Fry #17).

Léon Werth, "Exposition Picasso," *La Phalange* (Jun. 1910): 728–30 (Fry #8, but omitting the sentence quoted).

Henri Le Fauconnier, "Das Kunstwerk," preface to catalogue of *Neue Kunst-vereinigung* exhbn. (Munich, 1912); see Ann H. Murray, "Henri La Fauconnier's 'Das Kunstwerk': An Early Statement of Cubist Theory and its Understanding in Germany," *Arts* 56, no. 4 (Dec. 1981): 125–33.

On the Abbaye de Créteil and its artists and writers, see Christopher Green, *Léger and the Avant-Garde* (New Haven and London, 1976), chap. 1 and Virginia Spate, *Orphism, The Evolution of Non-Figurative Painting in Paris 1910–1914* (Oxford, 1979), chap. 1. Also Daniel Robbins, "From Symbolism to Cubism: the Abbaye of Créteil," *College Art Journal* 23, no. 2 (Winter 1963–64): 111–16; M.-L. Bidal, *Les écrivains de l'Abbaye* (Paris, 1938).

On the "bande à Picasso," see M. Jacob, "Souvenirs sur Picasso," *Cahiers d'Art* 6 (1927): 202; Fernande Olivier, *Picasso et ses amis* (Paris, 1933), pp. 27–28; A. Salmon, "Testimony against Gertrude Stein," *Transition* no. 23, suppl. (The Hague, Feb. 1935): 14–15. (McCully, *A Picasso Anthology* [1981], pp. 48–49, 54–55, 63.) Also M. Décaudin, *La crise des valeurs symbolistes* (Paris, 1960), p. 266; Jean-Paul Crespelle, *La vie quotidienne à Montmartre au temps de Picasso 1900–1910* (Paris, 1978), chap. 4.

On Apollinaire as art critic: for representative opinions of the artists, see Francis Steegmuller, *Apollinaire, Poet among the Painters* (London, 1963), pp. 141 (Braque), 142–43 (Picasso, citing Cooper); Robert Delaunay, *Du cubisme à l'art abstrait* (Paris, 1957), pp. 67, 169 (written ca. 1939–40) and for the view of Kahnweiler, *Juan Gris* (1946, 1968 ed.), p. 178 and "Reverdy et l'art plastique," in *Pierre Reverdy 1889–1960* (Paris: Mercure de France, 1962), p. 171. Also E. L. T. Mesens, introdn. to exhbn. cat. *The Cubist Spirit in its Time,* London Gallery (London, 1947), pp. 10–15; Jeanine Moulin, "Apollinaire critique d'art," *Le flâneur des deux rives,* no. 2 (Jun. 1954), pp. 12–14; Roger Shattuck, *The Banquet Years: The Origins of the Avant-Garde in France, 1885 to World War I* (1958; rev. ed., New York, 1968), pp. 254–55; M. Le Bot, "Guillaume Apollinaire, critique d'art" (review of *Chroniques d'art,* ed. Breunig), *Europe* 40 (Feb.–Mar. 1962): 254–56; John Golding, "Guillaume Apollinaire and the Art of the Twentieth Century," *Baltimore Museum of Art News* 26, no. 4–27.1 (Summer–Autumn 1963); Fry, *Cubism* (1966), pp. 46–47; Charles Tournadre, ed., *Les critiques de notre temps et Apollinaire* (Paris, 1971); H. B. Chipp, "Robert Delaunay and the New Color and Form," in exhbn. cat. *Color and Form* (San Diego, Oakland, Calif., and Seattle, Wash., Nov. 1971–May 1972), p. 34; Pierre Daix, "Critiques et témoins de la peinture moderne" (on recent exhbns.), *Gazette des Beaux Arts,* 6e. sér., 80 (Jan. 1975): 40–42; and more recently Spate, *Orphism,* pp. 60–61 and Harry E. Buckley, *Guillaume Apollinaire as Art Critic* (rev. of 1969 thesis, Ann Arbor, Mich. 1981). On the politics of his relations with Cubism, as reflected in *Les Peintres Cubistes,* see L. C. Breunig, "Apollinaire et le Cubisme," *Revue des lettres modernes* 69–70 (Spring 1962): 8–24; E. Grabska, *Apollinaire y teoretycy Cubizmu w latach, 1908–1918* (Warsaw, 1966) (review by M. Rieser, *Journal of Aesthetics and Art Criticism* 26, no. 1 [Fall 1967]: 143–44, summarizing its content); Scott Bates, *Guillaume Apollinaire* (New York, 1967), pp. 115ff. (for treatment of individual artists in the book); and most recently *Cahiers du Musée National d'Art Moderne* (Paris, no. 6, 1981), special issue on Apollinaire, including an essay on this subject. Maurice Raynal's review appeared in *Montjoie !,* 1–2 (Jan.–Feb. 1914) (*Les Peintres Cubistes* [1965 ed.], pp. 136–37). A gossipy, knowing character is apparent already in the jottings Apollinaire made in his catalogue on a visit to the Indépendants in 1906: see Michel Décaudin, "Apollinaire et les peintres 1906 d'après quelque notes inédits," *Gazette des Beaux Arts,* 6e. sér., 75 (Feb. 1970): pp. 117–22, and also his "Le changement de front chez Apollinaire," *Revue des sciences humaines* (Paris, Nov.–Dec. 1956): 255–60.

Common aspects of early theory: Leo Steinberg, in his review of Rosenblum, *Harper's Magazine,* 223 (Dec. 1961): 57ff. noted the same five aspects, but phrased their content somewhat differently.

Criticism of Cézanne, 1909–10: see Henri Ghéon, "A propos des Indépendants," *Nouvelle Revue Française* (May 1909): 389–90 (Breunig p. 151) and Michel Puy, "Le dernier état de la peinture," *Mercure de France* 86 (Jul. 16, 1910): 245 for emphasis on the qualities referred to (solidity and volume; constructive qualities and nuance). For the contrasting valuation of Cézanne by the Fauves, see Oppler, *Fauvism Re-examined* (1976), chap. 6 and John Elderfield, *The Wild Beasts: Fauvism and its Affinities,* exhbn. cat., Museum of Modern Art (New York, 1976), pp. 117–21.

The relationship of Metzinger's and Delaunay's work to the example of Picasso and Braque is discussed in Angelica Z. Rudenstine, *The Guggenheim Museum Collection, Paintings 1880–1945,* 2 vols. (New York, 1976), 2:79–80 and in Spate, 1979, chaps. 1–2 (both supporting Golding and Cooper on this subject); for a contrasting argument, of direct derivation from Cézanne's example, see André Dubois, "Cubisme et cubismes" and Bernard Dorival, "Robert Delaunay et le Cubisme," in Université de Saint-Etienne, Travaux IV, *Le Cubisme* (1973), pp. 77–91, 98–102.

The Braque drawing of *Three Nudes,* given to Burgess and reproduced by him (Fry p. 54), of which the artist said that it was "necessary to draw three figures in order to portray every physical aspect of a woman," may be a study for, or perhaps after, a lost painting of earlier that year in which he was involved in such an endeavor. See, however, W. Rubin, "Cézannisme and the beginnings of Cubism," in exhbn. cat. *Cézanne, The Late Work,* Museum of Modern Art (New York, 1977–78), pp. 170–71 for the suggestion that the "sketch for a painting entitled *Woman*" shown at the Salon des Indépendants refers to the *Standing Nude* in an intermediate state of Feb.–Mar. 1908.

On Futurism in Paris and Unanimism, see Marianne W. Martin, "Futurism, Unanimism and Apollinaire," *Art Journal* 28, no. 3 (Spring 1969): 258–68; F. Cachin Nora, "Le Futurisme à Paris," in exhbn. cat. *Le Futurisme 1909–1916,* Musée National d'Art Moderne (Paris, Sept.–Nov. 1973), pp. 21–30, and for paintings of 1910–12 reflecting the ideas of Unanimism, *Albert Gleizes 1889–1953, A Retrospective Exhibition,* Guggenheim Museum (New York, 1964), cat. by Daniel Robbins, and John Elderfield, "The Garden and the City: Allegorical Painting and Early Modernism," *Bulletin of Museum of Fine Arts, Houston* 7, no. 1, (Summer 1979): part 2, 14–22. The Tancrède de Visan book was reviewed by T. E. Hulme, *The New Age* 9 (Aug. 24, 1911): 400ff., from which the quotation is taken.

On simultanism: see especially P. Bergman, *"Modernolatria" et "Simultaneita," recherches sur deux tendances dans l'avant-garde littéraire en Italie et en France à la veille de la première guerre mondiale* (Uppsala, 1962), C. Green, "Léger and L'Esprit Nouveau 1912–1928," in exhbn. cat. *Léger and Purist Paris,* Tate Gallery (London, Nov. 1970–Jan. 1971), pp. 29–31 and *Léger and the Avant-Garde* (1976), p. 74; Spate, *Orphism* (1979), pp. 19–22, 77–81.

On the Golden Section, see William A. Camfield, "Juan Gris and the Golden Section," *Art Bulletin* 47, (Mar. 1965): 128–34 and also the preface to exhbn. cat. *Albert Gleizes and the Section d'Or,* Leonard Hutton Galleries (New York, 1964) and the exhbn. cat. *Jacques Villon,* ed. Daniel Robbins, Fogg Art Museum, Harvard University (Cambridge, 1976), pp. 49–50, cat. no. 28.

On Cubism and science, see for the general connections Raynal, *History of Modern Painting,* vol. 3 (1950), p. 47; John Malcolm Brinnin, *The Third Rose, Gertrude Stein and her World* (Boston and Toronto, 1959), pp. 138–39; Carlo L. Ragghianti,

"Revisioni sul Cubismo," *Critica d'Arte* 46 (Jul. 1961): 1–6, repr. in his *Mondrian e l'arte del XX secolo* (Milan, 1962); John A. Richardson, *Modern Art and Scientific Thought* (Urbana, Ill.: University of Illinois Press, 1971), chap. 5, "Cubism and Logic"; and Eunice Lipton, *Picasso Criticism 1901–1939* (New York: Garland Press, 1976), p. 101.

Manolo claimed to remember that Picasso was familiar with both the "fourth dimension" and Poincaré's writings; Joseph Pla, *Vida de Manolo contada por el mismo* (Madrid, 1930), p. 161 (McCully p. 69). For Princet, see A. Salmon, "Courrier des ateliers," *Paris Journal* (May 10, 1910), Gamwell, p. 163 n.86 and for later refs., Gris, letter to Raynal (Feb. 1919), *Letters* ed. D. Cooper (London, 1956), no. 82 (referring to an article in the post-war *Carnet de la Semaine*, for which Vaux-celles wrote after the War); André Warnod, *Les berceaux de la jeune peinture* (Paris, 1925), p. 87. Princet's famous and legendary reported question to the Cubists was first publ. by André Lhote, *L'Amour de l'Art* 9 (1933): 216. Cf. also the critical comments of Kahnweiler, *Juan Gris* (1968 ed.), p. 109 and Fry (1966), p. 60. On Bergson's influence, see Maurice Verne, "Un jour de pluie chez M. Bergson," *L'Intransigeant* (Nov. 22, 1911); A. Salmon, "Bergson et les Cubistes," *Paris Journal* (Nov. 28–30, 1911) Gamwell, pp. 32 and 161 nn. 76–77; and the comments of Fry, p. 67 and also Timothy Mitchell, "Bergson, Le Bon and Hermetic Cubism," *Journal of Aesthetics and Art Criticism* 36, no. 2 (Winter 1977): 175–84.

The "metaphorical" interpretation of the Fourth Dimension was especially made available by Charles Howard Hinton: see his *A New Era of Thought* (London, 1888) and *The Fourth Dimension* (London, 1904) (discussed by Robert C. Williams, *Artists in Revolution: Portraits of the Russian Avant-Garde 1905–23* [Bloomington, Ind.: Indiana University Press, 1977], chap. 5 and by Tom Gibbons, "Cubism and 'The Fourth Dimension' in the Context of the Later Nineteenth Century and Early Twentieth Century Revival of Occult Ideas," *Journal of Warburg and Courtauld Institutes* 44 [1981]: 130–47). Apollinaire's knowledge of Max Weber's "The Fourth Dimension from a Plastic Point of View," *Camera Work* 31 (Jul. 1910): 25–26 (repr. in *Camera Work, A Critical Anthology,* ed. Jonathan Green [New York,1973], pp. 202–3) is documented by Willard Bohn, "La quatrième dimension chez Apollinaire," *Revue des lettres modernes;* Guillaume Apollinaire 14, ed. M. Décaudin (Paris, 1978), pp. 93–104, and "In Pursuit of the Fourth Dimension: Guillaume Apollinaire and Max Weber," *Arts* 54, no. 10 (Jun. 1980): 166–69. On Apollinaire's use of the term, see also Breunig, pp. 103–5 and *Apollinaire on Art,* p. xxiv. The larger issue surrounding the use of the concept in relation to Cubism (taken up by Meyer Schapiro in lectures) is excellently discussed by Linda D. Henderson, "A New Facet of Cubism: 'The Fourth Dimension' and 'Non-Euclidean Geometry' Re-interpreted," *Art Quarterly* 34, no. 4 (Winter 1971): 411–48; based on her Ph.D. diss. "The Artist, 'The Fourth Dimension' and Non-Euclidean Geometry, 1900–1930, A Romance of Many Dimensions" (Yale University, 1975), where she gives greater importance to Princet. Poincaré's appeal to artists was mentioned by Gino Severini, "La peinture d'avant-garde," *Mercure de France* 121, no. 455 (Jun. 1, 1971): 416–17. The use of his 1902 text by Gleizes and Metzinger was identified by Henderson, and she also reproduced one of the diagrams in E. Jouffret, *Traité elémentaire* (1903), discussed further by Lucy Adelman and Michael Compton, "Mathematics in Early Abstract Art," in *Towards a New Art: Essays on the Background to Abstract Art 1910–20,* Tate Gallery (London, 1980), pp. 64–71. Ernest Mach's publications (esp. *Erkenntnis und Irrtum, Skizzen zur Psychologie der Forschung* [Leipzig, 1905]) and those of William James were drawn to my attention by the work of Marianne Teuber, as now presented in her lengthy essay in the exhbn. cat. *Kubismus, Künstler-Themen-Werke 1907–1920,* Kunsthalle (Cologne, May–Jul. 1982), pp. 9–58, arguing for the specific stimulus of James's diagrams; see in addition Anne C. Hanson, "The Human Eye: A Dimension of Cubism," in *Art the Ape of Nature, Essays in Honor of H. W. Janson,* ed. Mosche Barasch and Lucy F. Sandler (New York, 1981), pp. 739–48.

For earlier attempts to relate Cubism to contemporary mathematics and science, see Paul M. Laporte, "The 'Space-Time' Concept in the Work of Picasso," *Magazine of Art* 41, no. 1 (Jan. 1948): 25–26; "Cubism and Science," *Journal of Aesthetics and Art Criticism* 7, no. 3 (Mar. 1949): 243ff.; "Cubism and Relativity," *Art Journal* 25, no. 3 (Spring 1966): 246–48, and also John A. Richardson, "Cubism and the Fourth Dimension," *Diogenes* 65 (Spring 1969): 99–107 (denying the connection); Wolfgang Paalen, *Form and Sense, Problems of Contemporary Art,* vol. 1 (New York, 1945), chap. 3, pp. 23ff. (comparing crystal structures, on which point see Ragghianti's generally cogent critical remarks). For Cubism and photography, see Aaron Scharf, *Art and Photography* (Harmondsworth, Middsx., 1974 ed.), pp. 268–72 and "Marey and Chronophotography," *Artforum* 15, no. 1 (Sept. 1976): 62–70.

Picasso's and Braque's Cubism, 1910–1912: Maz Kozloff, *Cubism/Futurism* (New York, 1970), p. 37 (continuity); Werner Spies, *Sculpture by Picasso* (New York, 1971) (also in German ed.), p. 55 (status of portraits); F. Will-Levaillant, "La lettre dans la peinture cubiste," Université de Saint-Etienne, Travaux IV, *Le Cubisme* (1973), p. 45 and Spate, *Orphism* (1979), p. 342 (idea of series); Jonathan Silver, "Giacometti, Frontality and Cubism," *Artforum,* 13, no. 6 (Summer 1974): 42 and Andrew Forge, "On Giacometti," *Artforum* 13, no. 7 (Sept. 1974): 40 (aspects of brushwork and coloring echoed in Giacometti); Golding (1959, 1968 ed.), p. 21 (citing Uhde, 1928), Rosenblum (1960), pp. 37–38 and André Chastel "Braque et Picasso 1912, la solitude et l'échange," in *Pour Daniel-Henry Kahnweiler,* ed. Werner Spies (New York, 1965), pp. 80–87, repr. in his *Fables, Formes, Figures,* 2 vols. (Paris, 1978), 2:425–33 (on differences of personality between the two affirmed in the works themselves); T. Reff, review of Rosenblum, *Art Bulletin* 44 (Dec. 1962): 365–68; John Elderfield, "The Language of Post-Abstract Art," *Artforum* 9, no. 6 (Feb. 1971): 46–48; Werner Spies, "La guitare anthropomorphe," *Revue de l'Art* 12 (1971): 89–92; Michel Benamou, *Wallace Stevens and the Symbolist Imagination* (Princeton, N.J.: Princeton University Press, 1972), chap. 4 "Apollinaire," pp. 103, 105; V. Spate, review of Golding, *Burlington Magazine* 116 (Mar. 1974): 163 (structure, processes, imagery).

Texts on Cubism cited: Max Jacob, suggested prospectus for *Saint Matorel* (from undated letter to Kahnweiler, *Correspondance,* ed François Garnier, 2 vols. (Paris, 1953), 1:53. Josep Junoy, "L'Art d'en Picasso," *Arte y artistas* (Barcelona, 1912), repr. in *Vell i Nou* (Barcelona) 3, no. 46 (Jun. 1, 1917): 452–55 (McCully p. 89); Henri Guilbeaux, "La vie et les arts," *Hommes du Jour* (Jun. 24, 1911) (Breunig p. 159); Odilon Redon, letter to Gabriel Frizeau (Sept. 1912), "Quelques lettres de Odilon Redon," *La Vie* (Dec. 1916): 381 (trans. in Richard Hobbs, *Odilon Redon* [Boston, 1977], p. 133).

Other aspects of the art:
Cityscapes of Picasso's: see D 339 (Sacré-Coeur, winter 1909–10) and D 400 (La Pointe de la Cité, as spring 1911), 401 (Pont-Neuf), 443 (Avenue Frochot from studio, autumn), 444 (Rue d'Orchampt, winter). In my reading D 374–76 (labeled as still lifes, from winter–spring of 1910–11) may be views of rooftops. The suggestion about Braque's still lifes I owe to Alvin Martin, who discusses "metamorphic metaphor" in Cubism, including these examples, in his essay "Georges Braque et les origines du language du cubisme synthétique" publ. in exhbn. cat. *Georges Braque, Les Papiers Collés,* Centre Pompidou (Paris, Jun.–Sept. 1982), pp. 43–56.
For exhibitions in which Picasso and Braque participated, see Fry (1966), pp. 103–4; Daix's listing for Picasso (specifying dates of works included, where known) and for both together, and also Cézanne, Donald E. Gordon, *Modern Art Exhibitions 1900–1916,* selected catalogue documentation (Munich, 1974).
On the affair of the stolen statues, see Penrose, *Picasso,* pp. 166–68. For Picasso's psychology, see Leo Stein, *Appreciation* (1947), p. 96; Gertrude Stein, in *G.M.P.*

(1910) and *Picasso* (1938), cited by Leon Katz, "Matisse, Picasso and Gertrude Stein," in *Four Americans in Paris, The Collection of Gertrude Stein and her Family*, exhbn. cat., Museum of Modern Art (New York, 1970), pp. 55–59; and for a further hypothesis, Rosalind Krauss, "Cubism in Los Angeles," *Artforum* 9, no. 6 (Feb. 1971): 32–38. For the character of the relationship with Fernande Olivier as evidenced in the watercolor *Meditation* of late 1904, see Leo Steinberg, "Sleep Walkers," *Life* 65, no. 26 (Dec. 27, 1968), and W. Rubin, *Picasso in the Collection of the Museum of Modern Art* (1972), p. 20.

Céret: on the chronology of the stays there, see Pierre Daix, "Les trois séjours 'cubistes' de Picasso à Céret (1911–1912–1913)," in exhbn. cat. *Picasso et la Paix*, Musée d'Art Moderne (Céret, Summer 1973), n.p., and the corresponding chronology in Daix (1979). For the landscapes done at Céret, see D 419, discussed by Rudenstine, *Guggenheim Museum Collection* (1976), 2:602 and Rosenblum (1960), pp. 60–62, pl. 31 (citing critically, p. 313, the role given to Céret by Victor Crastre, *La naisssance du Cubisme (Céret 1910)* [Geneva, 1948]).

On Picasso's and Braque's admiration for the Wright brothers: it is noteworthy in this connection that Louis Vauxcelles's review of Braque's Nov. 1908 exhibition appeared in *Gil Blas* above an announcement, headed "La Conquête de l'Air," of Wilbur Wright's gaining of a prize for height at Le Mans (see the reproduction that appears in *Braque, Le Cubisme fin 1907–1914* [Paris, 1982], p. 12). Picasso's habit of addressing Braque as "Wilbur" may have evolved directly from this.

On the 1910–12 exhibitions making Cubism known to the public, see Golding (1959), chap. 1; Green, *Léger and the Avant-Garde* (1976), chap. 1. On the literature of the time, see Cyrena N. Pondrom, *The Road from Paris: French Influence on English Poetry 1900–1920* (Cambridge, 1974), p. 63.

On the *Demoiselles*, see Leo Steinberg, "The Philosophical Brothel," *Art News* 71, nos. 5–6 (Sept. 1972): 20–29; (Oct. 1972): 38–47. On the *Saint Matorel* illustrations: a student, Ann Giese, in a 1962 undergraduate thesis provided valuable points here about the relationship of images to text; Gerard Bertrand, *L'Illustration de la poésie-l'époque du cubisme* (Paris, 1971), pp. 89–101, claims them to be "almost totally independent of the text." For Jacob's interests as a writer, see also S. I. Lockerbie, "Realism and Fantasy in the Work of Max Jacob," in *Order and Adventure in Post-Romantic French Poetry, Essays presented to C. A. Hackett*, ed. E. M. Beaumont, J. M. Cocking, and J. Cruickshank (Oxford, 1973). The *Nude* drawings of Spring 1910 referred to are discussed by Ann Edgerton, "Picasso's 'Nude Woman' of 1910," *Burlington Magazine* 122 (Jul. 1980): 499–502, as forming part of a group showing a mother and child; but see Douglas Cooper's letter, ibid., 123 (Mar. 1981): 164–65, with arguments as to dating which leave only her figs. 51, 53–54 (Zervos, 2.1, 204–5, and 2.2, 723) as being acceptable from this time.

Gertrude Stein's writing: on her sense of the relationship with Cubism ca. 1912, see Richard Bridgmann, *Gertrude Stein in Pieces* (Oxford, 1970), p. 120 and for the motives underlying her later retrospective texts, cf. Earl Fendleman, "Gertrude Stein among the Cubists," *Journal of Modern Literature* 2 (Nov. 1972): 481–90; Neil Schmitz, "Portrait, Patriarch, Mythos: The Revenge of Gertrude Stein," *Salmagundi* 49 (Winter 1978): 69–91, and also Frederick Hoffman, *The Twenties* (London and New York, 1965 ed.), pp. 158, 211–22.

More recent interpretations of Cubism cited: see Judkins (1948), Rosenblum (1960), Greenberg (repr. 1961); Rubin (1972), p. 70. For a contemporary version of the continuing traditional view, see Cooper, *The Cubist Epoch* (1970). The differences between the two are very clearly brought out in Kenworth Moffett's review, *Art Bulletin* 66 (June 1974): 305–7. For the problem posed for the viewer by the character of Cubism, cf. Gombrich's view of Cubism as discussed in Intermezzo iv and Podro, *The Listener* (Aug. 20, 1970).

Commentaries on Picasso from outside France: a copy of Rutter's booklet, publ. by the Art News Press, London, is in the Victoria and Albert Museum Library; John Middleton Murry, "The Art of Pablo Picasso" (reply to Huntly Carter, "The Plato-Picasso Idea," *The New Age* [Nov. 23, 1911]: 88), *The New Age* (Nov. 30, 1911): 115. (McCully, pp. 81–84; for biographical information about Murry at this time, see F. A. Lea, *Life of John Middleton Murry* [London, 1959], pp. 18–25); Marius de Zayas, "Pablo Picasso," *Camera Work* 34–35 (Apr.–Jul. 1911): 65–67 (repr. in *Picasso in Perspective,* ed. Gert Schiff, [Englewood Cliffs, N.J., 1976], pp. 47–49; Picasso's approval, made known in a letter of De Zayas to Stieglitz, has been noted by William I. Homer); Junoy, "L'Art d'en Picasso" trans. McCully, (1981, p. 88); Ludwig Coellen, "Die Romantik der neuen Malerei," *Die neue Malerei* (Munich, 1912), pp. 61–71 (based on the Cologne Sonderbund exhbn.; McCully p. 97).

Chapter 2. The Recapturing of Broken Ties, 1912–1915

Picasso's and Braque's relationship, 1912–14: for the stays at Céret, see Pierre Daix, "Les trois séjours 'cubistes' de Picasso à Céret (1911–1912–1913)," in exhbn. cat. *Picasso et la Paix,* Musée d'Art Moderne (Céret, Summer 1973), n.p., and the corresponding chronology in Daix (1979); for Braque's 1913 visit there, see exhbn. cat. *Picasso,* Musée des Arts Decoratifs (Paris, 1955), p. 25 (info. from Kahnweiler), confirmed by a letter from Jacob visiting at Céret to Apollinaire, saying that Braque and his wife are expected to visit in June, en route to Sorgues (*Pablo Picasso, A Retrospective,* Museum of Modern Art [New York, May–Sept. 1980], chronology, p. 153). Picasso's contract with Kahnweiler is reproduced in full in Daniel-Henry Kahnweiler (with François Crémieux), *Mes galeries et mes peintres* (Paris, 1961), Eng. trans., *My Galleries and Painters* (London, 1971), pp. 154–55, and in facsimile, Daix (1979), p. 359; for Braque's contract, see now the info. given in exhbn. cat., *Georges Braque, Les Papiers Collés,* Centre Pompidou (Paris, Jun.–Sept. 1982), pp. 41, 180. For the exhibitions in which the two participated abroad, see the listings of Daix (1979) and Donald E. Gordon, *Modern Art Exhibitions, 1900–1916: selected catalogue documentation,* 2 vols. (Munich, 1974). The revised dates for the introduction of *collage* and *papiers collés* (supplied to Douglas Cooper by the artists) are given by Rosenblum (1960), 68–69 and have been accepted into the literature since.

Reported statements of Picasso's and Braque's: A. Salmon, *La jeune peinture française* (Paris, 1912), p. 42 (Fry, #18, p. 82). Apollinaire's article "Exotisme et ethnographie," *Paris Journal* (Sept. 1912), appears in English in *Apollinaire on Art,* ed. L. C. Breunig, trans. S. Suleiman (New York, 1972), pp. 243–46, as an addition, discovered by Pascal Pia, which is not in the French 1960 edn.; John Golding drew attention to the passage in question in his review of this publication, *Burlington Magazine* 120 (Sept. 1973): 616–17. On the knowledge of African sculpture amongst the painters from ca. 1905–07 on, see Fry (1966), pp. 47–48 and also J. B. Donne, "African Art and Paris Studios, 1905–20," in *Art in Society, Studies in Style, Culture and Aesthetics,* ed. Michael Greenhaigh and Vincent Megaw (New York, 1978), pp. 105–20, which reviews carefully what exactly was available in the way of examples. For the comparison of Picasso's 1912 constructions with African sculpture, see D.-H. Kahnweiler, "Negro Art and Cubism," *Horizon* (London) 18 (1948): 418, proposing the direct influence of a Wobé mask that Picasso owned (shown in a 1917 photograph of his studio) and the more qualified discussion of the connection by William Rubin, in exhbn. cat. *Picasso in the Museum of Modern Art* (New York, 1972), p. 74. See also pp. 207–8 there for the dating of Picasso's constructions, especially the sheet-metal *Guitar* (D 471), which was placed by Picasso in spring

1912, but has also been dated to the fall (see esp. Fry's review of Daix, *Art Journal* 41, no. 1 [Spring 1981]: 91ff.), and for Braque's lost ones of the summer of 1912, Cooper, *The Cubist Epoch* (1970), p. 58, and Alvin Martin, in exhbn. cat. *Georges Braque, Les Papiers Collés* (1982), p. 39 (reproducing a photograph of one of them); also Werner Spies, *Picasso, Das plastische Werk* (Stuttgart, 1971), trans. as *Sculptures by Picasso* (London and New York, 1971), chap. 2. Gertrude Stein, *Picasso* (London, 1983), p. 11 (on camouflage). A. Salmon, *Le jeune sculpture française* (Paris, 1919), p. 13 (trans. Golding, [1968 ed.], p. 104, and see p. 119 there for Braque's practice with *papiers collés*). Braque's story about Gris appears in the interview recorded by John Richardson, "Voice of the Artist-2. The Power of Mystery," *The Observer* (London) (Dec. 1, 1957); for Gris's so-called mathematical drawings, see Golding (1968), pp. 130–31; contrary to their supposed destruction, they survive for study in the form also of a set formerly belonging to the Knoedler Gallery, New York.

Braque, "Pensées et réflexions sur la peinture," *Nord-Sud* 10 (Dec. 1917): 3–5 (Fry #36); I have used the translation in M. Raynal, *Modern French Painters* (New York, 1928), pp. 50–55. For Reverdy's responsibility for publishing the aphorisms, see Jean Leymarie, "Evocation de Reverdy, auprès de Braque et de Picasso," in *Pierre Reverdy, 1889–1960, Mercure de France* 344, no. 1181 (Jan. 1, 1962) (special number on Reverdy): 301.

Léger, "Les origines de la peinture et sa valeur representative," *Montjoie !*, no. 8 (May 29, 1913): 7; nos. 9–10 (June 14–29): 9–10 (Fry #27); "Les réalisations picturales actuelles," *Les Soirées de Paris* (June 15, 1914): 349–54 (Fry #32). I have used the complete English version in Fernand Léger, *Functions of Painting*, trans. Alexandra Anderson, ed. E. Fry (London and New York, 1965), pp. 3–19. For Apollinaire's report on the 1914 lecture (*Paris Journal*, May 14), see *Apollinaire on Art*, trans. Suleiman, pp. 382–83, and cf. also, for Léger's personality, Virginia Spate, *Orphism* (Oxford, 1979), pp. 272ff.; the drawings that accompanied the publication of the 1913 lecture are repr. there, figs. 199–200.

Theorists of second phase: Apollinaire, "Die Moderne Malerei" (trans. Jean-Jacques), *Der Sturm* (Berlin) (Feb. 1913): 272; English trans. in *Apollinaire on Art*, pp. 267–71 (Fry #24); Charles Lacoste, "Sur le 'cubisme' et la peinture," *Temps Présent* (Paris) (April 2, 1913): 332–40 (Fry #26); Alexandre Mercereau, Introdn. to cat. of 45th exhbn. of Manes Society (Prague, Feb.–Mar. 1914) (Fry #31); Maurice Raynal, preface to exhbn. cat. *Salon de Juin: troisième exposition de la Société normande de peinture moderne* (Rouen, Jun.–Jul. 1912), pp. 9–11; "Conception et vision," *Gil Blas* (Aug. 29, 1912); "L'Exposition de la Section d'Or," *La Section d'Or* (Paris) (Oct. 9, 1912): 2–5 (Fry #20–22); "Essai d'une définition de la peinture cubiste." *Correo de la letras y de las artes* (Barcelona) (Dec. 1912); "Qu'est-ce que . . . le 'Cubisme'?," *Comoedia illustré* (Dec. 20, 1913) (Fry #29). For his review of Apollinaire's *Les Peintres Cubistes*, see the edn. of L. C. Breunig and J.-Cl. Chevalier (Paris, 1965), pp. 136–37. Roland Penrose, *Picasso, His Lfe and Work*, pp. 80, 134, states that Raynal met Picasso as a struggling young poet, as early as 1902, and he is referred to as having met Braque in 1904 already (see Henry Hope, in exhbn. cat. *Georges Braque*, Museum of Modern Art, [New York, 1948], pp. 16, 38); a passage in his *Anthologie de la peinture en France de 1906 à nos jours* (Paris, 1927), p. 90 suggests the development of a particular closeness between him and Braque, probably cemented by 1910 through the "Vers et Prose" evenings, and confirmed in the dedication to him of a still life drawing of Braque's from 1912 (Kunsthalle, Karlsruhe, repr. in exhbn. cat. *Kubismus, Künstler-Themen-Werke 1907–1920*, Kunsthalle (Cologne, May–Jul. 1982), no. 17.

Simultaneity: for Apollinaire's attack on the use of the term for poetry, see his "Simultanisme—librettisme," *Les Soirées de Paris*, no. 25 (Jun. 15, 1914): 320–25, and contrast also his statement on Picasso's portrait of him, accepting it, *Paris Midi* (May 29, 1913) and *Apollinaire on Art*, p. 268.

The Fourth Dimension: on Bragdon's text, see Robert C. Williams, *Artists in Revolution: Portraits of the Russian Avant Garde, 1905–23* (Bloomington, Ind.: Indiana University Press, 1973), pp. 108–10 and Linda D. Henderson, "Italian Futurism and the Fourth Dimension," *Art Journal* 41, no. 4 (Winter 1981): 318–19. The passage of Proust's cited is from *Du côté de chez Swann,* trans. C. K. Scott-Moncrieff (London, 1941), p. 80. On molecular science, see George Matisse, "La théorie moléculaire et la science contemporaine," *Mercure de France* (Jun. 1, 1913): 520–25, and for "machinism," Emile Magne, "Le machinisme dans la littérature contemporaine," ibid. (Jan. 16, 1910): 202–7 (including contemporary attitudes towards the automobile).

For Riciotto Canudo, see his manifesto repr. in Bonner Mitchell, ed., *Les manifestes littéraires de la Belle Epoque, 1886–1914: anthologie critique* (Paris, 1966), pp. 173–76, and Raymond Warnier, "Riciotto Canudo (1874–1923) dans l'entourage de Guillaume Apollinaire," *Studi Francesi* 14 (1961): 244–59. Further discussion of him is to be found in *Atti del Congresso Internazionale del Centenario della Nascità di Riciotto Canudo,* ed. Giovanni Dotoli (Faisano, 1978), with essays by L. Semerari on his role in the arts of the time and by O. Blumenkranz-Onimus and others on the review *Montjoie !*

On Léger's development from 1912 to 1915, cf. Christopher Green, *Léger and the Avant-Garde* (New Haven and London, 1976), chaps. 2–3, and Spate, *Orphism* (1979), pp. 229–74. On his relations with Delaunay, see Delaunay's later (1933) statements in *Du cubisme à l'art abstrait,* ed. P. Francastel (Paris, 1957), pp. 73, 76, and Léger's view of the matter, as reported by Dora Vallier, "La vie fait l'oeuvre de Fernand Léger," *Cahiers d'Art* 2 (1954): 149 and André Verdet, *Fernand Léger* (Geneva, 1955), p. 72. Cf. also the critical remarks of Michel Hoog, "Le Cubisme et la couleur," André Dubois, "Cubisme et cubismes," and Bernard Dorival, "Robert Delaunay et le Cubisme," in Université de Saint-Etienne, Travaux IV, *Le Cubisme* (1973), pp. 41–44, 77–102.

On Gris's development: for his early humorous drawings, see D.-H. Kahnweiler, *Juan Gris, His Life and Work* (1946), trans. Douglas Cooper (New York, 1968), p. 11 and the larger selection repr. in Juan Antonio Gaya Nuno, *Juan Gris* (Barcelona, 1974, Amer. edn., Boston, 1975). For the Fantômas imagery, see E. A. Carmean Jr., "Juan Gris' Fantômas," *Arts* 51, no. 5 (Jan. 1977): pp. 116–17. For the links between Gris's and Metzinger's works in 1912–13, see Angelica Z. Rudenstine, *The Guggenheim Museum Collection, Paintings 1880–1945,* 2 vols. (New York, 1976), 2:510–14 (on chronology) and the similar view that the direction of influence now was from Metzinger to Gris in Cooper, *The Cubist Epoch* (1970), p. 77. Cooper argues the same also in the case of Marcoussis (p. 132), for whose work of 1912 see Jean Lanfrancais, *Marcoussis, sa vie, son oeuvre* (Paris, 1961), esp. the etched portraits of Apollinaire, nos. G.30–32. See also the opinion of Jean Leymarie, in exhbn. cat. *Juan Gris* (Paris: Orangerie, 1977), p. 11 that Gris influenced Metzinger, Marcoussis and Gleizes both practically and theoretically at the time of the Oct. 1912 Section d'Or exhibition. Works that could favor a reverse argument include especially Marcoussis's *Still Life with Matches* dated 1912 (now Princeton University Art Museum); Villon's drawing *Renée* dated 1911 (Metropolitan Museum, New York, Lehmann colln.) with Marcoussis-like planes; and Metzinger's *Portrait of Gleizes,* 1912 (Museum of Rhode Island School of Design) with palette and his *Man with the Pipe* from ca. 1912 (Carnegie Institute, Pittsburgh, gift of G. David Thompson) with a café setting and the hat in three positions. On Gris's work of 1913–14, cf. M. Kozloff, *Cubism/ Futurism* (New York, 1973), p. 75. For the relation to Matisse's work of 1914–15, see Cooper (1970), p. 207 n., Leymarie (1977), p. 14 and also Lisa Lyons, "Matisse: Work, 1914–1917," *Arts* 49, no. 7 (May 1975): 74–75.

Picasso's and Braque's work, 1912–14: on the general character of the phase, see

Jean Laude, "Vue d'ensemble: le Cubisme," *Critique,* no. 201 (Feb. 1964): 187, and for the chronology Pierre Daix, "Des bouleversements chronologiques dans la révolution des papiers collés (1912–1914)," *Gazette des Beaux Arts* 83 (Oct. 1973) (Picasso issue): 217–27, with findings incorporated into the 1979 catalogue.

On the use of lettering, see Françoise Will-Levaillant, "La lettre dans la peinture cubiste," Université de Saint-Etienne, Travaux IV, *Le Cubisme* (1973, colloquium given 1971), pp. 45–61; Robert Rosenblum, "The Typography of Cubism," in *Picasso, An Evaluation: 1900 to the Present,* ed. R. Penrose and J. Golding (London, 1972); Amer. edn., *Picasso in Retrospect* (New York, 1973), pp. 45–75 (with rather few examples from Braque's work); also S. Marcus, "The typographical element in Cubism, 1911–1915: its formal and semantic implications," *Visible Language* (U.S.A.) 6, no. 4 (Autumn 1972): 321–40, repr. in *Artforum* 17, no. 5 (May 1973): 24–27, 104. Daix in his 1979 catalogue entries gives identifications for almost every one of the cases in which Picasso uses lettering in this phase (including some which Will-Levaillant had called "indecipherable"). Interpretations of Braque's use of lettering and his viewpoint here that differ explicitly from mine are given by Douglas Cooper and Alvin Martin, in their essays in exhbn. cat. *Georges Braque, Les Papiers Collés,* Centre Pompidou (Paris, Jun.–Sept. 1982), pp. 7–11, 43–56, also publ. in English for the Nat. Gall., (Washington, D.C.) version of the exhbn., (Oct. 1982–Jan. 1983); and by William Agee in his review of the latter exhbn., "Looking at Braque," *The New Criterion* 1, no. 6 (Feb. 1981): 53–54.

On the treatment of the object in this phase, see Ellen Johnson, "On the Role of the Object in Analytic Cubism," *Allen Memorial Art Museum Bulletin* 13, no. 1 (1955): 11–25, repr. in her *Modern Art and the Object, A Century of Changing Attitudes* (London and New York, 1976), as chap. 4, "The Painting Freed," pp. 97–109 (analyzing a still life of late 1911, D 440); Charles M. Rosenberg, "Cubist Object Treatment: A Perceptual Analysis," *Arforum* 9, no. 8 (Apr. 1974): 30–36 (using a *gestalt* approach); and also critical remarks of Rosalind Krauss concerning the writings of Daix, "Re-presenting Picasso," *Art in America* 68, no. 10 (Dec. 1980): 91–96 and "In the Name of Picasso," *October* 16 (Spring 1981): 13–20. On Picasso's choice of musical instruments and anthropomorphic treatment of them, see Werner Spies, "La guitare anthropomorphe," *Revue de l'Art* 12 (1971): 89–92 and *Sculpture by Picasso* (New York, 1971), pp. 46–48, and Johannes Langner, "Figur und Saiteninstrument bei Picasso," *Pantheon* 40, no. 2 (Apr.–Jun. 1982): 98–113, with Eng. summary.

For the newspaper cuttings used by Picasso, see Zervos 26.259 and 6.936 (drawings of 1906–07 which include newspaper); R. Rosenblum, "Picasso and the Coronation of Alexander III," *Burlington Magazine* 103 (Oct. 1971): 604–6; W. Rubin, *Picasso in the Collection of the Museum of Modern Art* (New York, 1972), p. 79 (on D 534); Daix, 1979, nos. 523–24, 532, 535, 549–50 (cuttings dealing with the war in the Balkans, Nov.–Dec. 1912); Gary Tinterow, exhbn. cat. *Master Drawings by Picasso,* Fogg Art Museum (1981), no. 40, p. 112 (info. from Lewis Kachur on D 536 and 525); also D 526 (chauffeur), 528 (line into sea), 538 (horse doping), 543 (electric lamp, and also a story about a tramp turning himself in for a murder), and 568 (including a gramophone advertisement, with the shapes of the engraving relating to those of the glass above—as happens also in D 546).

Braque's *Young Woman with Guitar* and Corot: the Isaac Camondo legacy of 1908, which entered the Louvre in 1911, included a variant of the painting *L'Atelier de Corot,* now in the National Gallery, Washington; see Musée National du Louvre, *Peintures, École francaise, XIXe siècle,* 4 vols. (Paris, 1958), 1:435, and on the imagery of this painting Anthony F. Janson, "Corot: Tradition and the Muse," *Art Quarterly* 1, no. 4 (August 1978): 314.

Mallarmé's poem *Salut* was first pub. in 1895; cf. also his *Toast* (Feb. 1895), which also puns on *coupe.* "Le livre, instrument spirituel," included in *Quant au livre,* first appeared in July 1895. On the possible contribution of Mallarméan ideas to this phase of Cubism, suggested in very general form by D. H. Kahnweiler, "Mallarmé et la peinture," *Les Lettres* 3, nos. 9–11 (1948): 63–68, repr. in trans. in M. Raymond, *From Baudelaire to Surrealism* (New York, 1950), pp. 357–63, and by André Chastel, "Le jeu et le sacre dans l'art moderne," *Critique* 96–97 (May–Jun. 1955), repr. in his *Fables, Formes, Figures,* 2 vols. (Paris, 1978), see Ronald Johnson, "Picasso's Musical and Mallarméan Compositions," *Arts* 57, no. 7 (Mar. 1977): 122–27 (suggesting the relevance of *Un coup de dés,* republ. 1914, particularly to Picasso's sculpture); Christopher Green, "Cubism and the Possibility of Abstract Art," in *Towards a New Art: Essays on the Background to Abstract Art 1910–1920,* Tate Gallery (London, 1980), p. 158 (claiming influence on Picasso and Braque ca. 1912). Spate, *Orphism* (1979), pp. 12, 60, documents Mallarmé's influence now on the Orphist painters, and see also Gamwell, *Cubist Criticism* (1980), p. 146 n. 16, citing Roger Allard's observation of the relationship to the new art, "Le Salon d'Automne," *Les Écrits Francais* (Dec. 5, 1913), p. 14 and also Severini's and Ozenfant's 1916 view that a visual equivalent to Mallarmé's language had now come into being. Severini, "Symbolisme plastique et symbolisme littéraire," *Mercure de France* (Feb. 1, 1916): 467–69; Ozenfant, "Notes sur le Cubisme," *L'Elan* (Dec. 1, 1916). The *Mercure de France* and the *Nouvelle Revue Française* which were also running articles on contemporary art in 1912–13 were leading forces in the development of interest in both Mallarmé and Rimbaud: the *Mercure* publishing the 1912 edn. of Rimbaud's *Oeuvres, vers et prose,* ed. by Paterne Berrichon, which included the *Illuminations,* and also Berrichon's 1912 book *Jean Arthur Rimbaud le poète, poèmes, lettres et documents inédits;* and the *NRF* bringing out the 1913 complete edn. of Mallarmé's *Poésies* and also Albert Thibaudet's book of 1912 *La póesie de Stephane Mallarmé.* The dispute between Berrichon and Georges Izambard about Rimbaud ran in both periodicals in 1911–12, the *NRF* published Rimbaud's famous *Lettre d'un voyant* for the first time there in Oct. 1912 and the *Mercure* also ran several articles on Mallarmé. See further C. A. Haskell, "Rimbaud and Apollinaire," *French Studies* 19, no. 3 (Jul. 1961): 266–71 (suggesting 1913 as the key year of his influence on Apollinaire; M. Jacob, "Souvenirs sur Picasso," *Cahiers d'Art* 6, [1927]: 302, trans. in M. McCully, *A Picasso Anthology* [London, 1981], pp. 54–55, recorded the earlier admiration of the group around Picasso for Rimbaud); S. Bernard, "Le 'Coup de dés' de Mallarmé replacé dans la perspective historique," *Revue d'histoire littéraire de la France* 2 (Apr.–June 1951): 181ff. (on the importance of Thibaudet's book at this time).

On the periodical *Lacerba* as an organ of Futurism, see N. Blumenkranz-Onimus, "'Lacerba' ou le nouvel ordre de désordre," in *L'Année 1913: les formes esthétiques de l'oeuvre d'art à la veille de la première guerre mondiale, travaux et documents inédits,* ed. L. Brion-Guerry, 3 vols. (Paris, 1971), 2:1123–30. This volume also contains essays, pp. 1097–1116, on the periodicals *Montjoie !* and *Les Soirées de Paris.*

On the relationship of Matisse's art to Cubism, 1913–15, see especially John Elderfield, in exhbn. cat. *Matisse in the Collection of the Museum of Modern Art* (New York, 1978), pp. 68–69 (*Jeannette V*), 76 (*The Back* II), 92 (*Woman on a High Stool*), 100 (*Goldfish*), 105–6. Other discussions of the relationship include: Dora Vallier, "Matisse revu, Matisse à revoir," *Nouvelle Revue Française* 18, no. 211 (Jul. 1, 1970): 54–64 (56–58 refer); John Jacobus, *Henri Matisse* (New York, [1972]), pp. 32–36; Frank Trapp, "Form and Symbol in the Art of Matisse," *Arts* 49, no. 9 (May 1975): 56–58 (citing a statement that Matisse had made to him on the subject in 1950); and John Golding, "Matisse and Cubism" (W. A. Cargill Memorial Lecture in Fine Art, University of Glasgow, 1978), esp. p. 16. Relevant works of Picasso's that Matisse would have seen in Gertrude Stein's collection by 1913 would include D 509 and 515 (both from the autumn of 1912).

On Kandinsky's stay in Paris, see Jonathan Fineberg, "*Les tendances nouvelles* and Kandinsky," *Art History* 2, no. 2 (Jun. 1979): 221–46. *Über das Geistige in der Kunst* first appeared in Jan. 1912 (Munich, R. Piper) with three further editions later that year. A copy was sent to Delaunay, who had it translated and subsequently

corresponded with Kandinsky: see here *Du cubisme à l'art abstrait* (1957), pp. 178–
80. Apollinaire, who could read German, probably came to know the text then (see
Spate, *Orphism*, p. 29) and cf. his references to Kandinsky's work, *Paris Journal*
(Mar. 25, 1912) (*Improvisations*, at Salon des Indépendants, seen as reflecting Matisse's influence), "Modern Painting," *Der Sturm* (Feb. 1913) and the further comment
pub. there March 1913 (*Apollinaire on Art*, pp. 214, 270, 277). The English translation
of 1914, titled *The Art of Spiritual Harmony*, was by M. T. H. Sadler (later Michael
Sadleir), son of Sir Michael Sadler who collected works of Kandinsky's.

On Blaise Cendrars, see Spate, *Orphism*, pp. 38–39 and Jean Claude Lovey, *Situation de Blaise Cendrars* (Neuchâtel, 1965); and for the contact with Otto Gross,
Martin Green, *The Von Richtofen Sisters: The Triumphant and Tragic Modes of Love*
(New York, 1974), p. 67 and Jay Bochner, *Blaise Cendrars: Discovery and Recreation* (Toronto, 1978), p. 41.

Heinrich Thannhauser's text, for *Ausstellung Pablo Picasso,* Moderne Galerie
(Munich, Feb. 1913), pp. 1–2, is trans. in McCully, *A Picasso Anthology* (1981), p. 98.
For the exhibitions of Cubism abroad referred to, see Fry pp. 184–85 (summarizing
the artists included).

On the "picture within the picture" in Post-Impressionist and Symbolist art, see
M. Roskill, *Van Gogh, Gauguin and the Impressionist Circle* (London and Greenwich, Conn., 1970), pp. 53–55; and for Matisse, Elderfield, *Matisse in the Collection
of the Museum of Modern Art*, pp. 89, 94 *(Red Studio, Woman on a High Stool)* and
M. Roskill, "Looking Across to Literary Criticism" (contribution to a symposium),
Arts 45 (Jun. 1971): 63 *(Nasturtiums and the Dance)*. Braque's *Fruit Dish* is discussed in related terms by C. Greenberg, "Collage" (1958), *Art and Culture* (Boston,
1961), p. 76.

On Ezra Pound and Imagism, see *Literary Essays of Ezra Pound,* ed. T. S. Eliot
(New York, 1954), pp. 4, 162 (memoirs of 1918 and 1934) and also Richard Cork,
Vorticism and Absract Art in the First Machine Age, 2 vols. (Berkeley and Los
Angeles, 1976), 1:23–25, and Timothy Materer, *Vortex: Pound, Eliot and Lewis*
(Ithaca, N.Y., 1979). For Pound's art criticism of 1914–15, see the articles repr. in
Ezra Pound and the Visual Arts. ed. Harriet Zinnes (New York, 1980), esp. pp. 179–
84. His essays on Vorticism of Sept. 1914 and Jan. 1915 show his awareness of the
writings of Apollinaire and of Kandinsky's *On the Spiritual* in its 1914 translation.

T. E. Hulme's writings, published and unpublished in his lifetime, are collected in
Speculations, Essays on Humanism and the Philosophy of Art, ed. Herbert Read
(London, 1924); *Further Speculations,* ed. Sam Hynes (Lincoln, Nebrasks, 1962).
See also Alun E. Jones, *The Life and Opinions of T. E. Hulme* (London, 1960).

On the "Lecture on Modern Poetry" and its sources, see Cyrena N. Pondrom,
"Hulme's 'A Lecture on Modern Poetry' and the Birth of Imagism," *Papers on
Language and Literature* 5 (1969): 465–70 (arguing for Jan. 1909 as its date) and also
David Martin Heaton, "Two French Philosophical Sources of T. E. Hulme's Imagism,"
Ph.D. diss. (University of Michigan, 1969) (use of De Gourmont's *Le Problème du
Style* and "Du style ou de l'écriture"). On his involvement with the ideas of Bergson
(whom he apparently first met in 1907; the effect of the 1911 Congress is discussed by
Jones, chap. 6) see esp. "Notes on Bergson, I–V," *The New Age* (Oct. 19, 26; Nov. 23,
30, 1911 and Feb. 22, 1912), repr. in *Further Speculations,* pp. 28–63; "The Philosophy of Intensive Manifolds" (ed. from 1913 lecture notes), *Speculations,* pp. 173–214;
and "Bergson's Theory of Art," *Speculations,* pp. 143–69, from book of which the
plan is given in Appdx. B there, pp. 261–64. On Hulme's turn to aesthetics: he refers
to the meeting with Worringer in "Modern Art II: A Preface Note and Neo-Realism,"
The New Age 14 (Feb. 12, 1914): 467–69 *(Further Speculations,* p. 120). See further
A. R. Jones, "T. E. Hulme, Wilhelm Worringer and the Urge to Abstraction," *British
Journal of Aesthetics* 1 (1960): 1–7; Hynes, introdn. to *Further Speculations,* p. 22,
on a precis of Volkelt amongst Hulme's unpub. papers; J. Kanerbeck, Jr., "T. E.

Hulme and German Philosophy: Dilthey and Scheler," *Comparative Literature* 21, no. 3 (Summer 1969): 193–212. Coellen's passage on Picasso, for comparison, is trans. in *A Picasso Anthology,* ed. McCully, p. 97.

On *The New Age,* see Wallace Martin, *"The New Age": A Chapter in English Cultural History* (Manchester, 1967) (where Hulme's 1909 use of Gustave Kahn was established, p. 157). On F. S. Flint, see Cyrena N. Pondrom, *The Road from Paris: French Influence on English Poetry 1900–1920* (Cambridge, 1974), introdn. (noting his special role in relation to the French poetry scene now which is also brought out by Alan Young, *Dada and After: Extremist Modernism and English Literature* (Manchester, 1981), chaps. 2–3); also pp. 14, 23, 34 for Futurism in London. The main Futurist exhibitions were: Futurist Painters, Sackville Gallery (Mar. 1912), Severini's one-man exhbn. (Apr. 1913), and the Post-Impressionist and Futurist exhbn. at the Doré Gallery (Jan. 1914), which included one Picasso painting and three photos. The second Grafton Gallery exhbn., at the Alpine Club Gallery in Jan. 1914, also included one Picasso painting (information from Daix, 1979).

Hulme's articles on "Modern Art" ("I, The Grafton Group," *The New Age* [Jan. 15]; "III, The London Group" [Mar. 26]; "IV, Mr. David Bomberg's Show" [July 9]) are in *Further Speculations,* pp. 113–44; see pp. 114–15 for his attack on Roger Fry and also pp. 117, 129 (referring to Fry's own paintings). His lecture "Modern Art and its Philosophy" (Quest Society, Jan. 22, 1914) is in *Speculations,* pp. 75–109; see p. 104 on Fry and pp. 94, 103 for his knowledge of Gleizes' and Metzinger's *Du Cubisme* (Eng. trans., London, 1913). For references to Picasso and Kandinsky, see *Speculations,* p. 104; *Further Speculations,* pp. 127, 130–31. For Bergson's view of the process of artistic creation in the case of an innovator, see *Speculations,* p. 149. On Cubism, see *Speculations,* p. 94 (referring to "analytical" cubism) and *Further Speculations,* p. 124. On the "new geometric art" see *Speculations,* p. 103 and *Further Speculations,* pp. 113–14; and cf. also William Wees, *Vorticism and the English Avant Garde* (Toronto, 1972), pp. 58, 78–86, 129, 153–54; Cork, pp. 138–44 and chap. 8. For Hulme's attack with the tool of *Einfühlung* on the theory that the contemplation of "form for its own sake" produces "a specific aesthetic emotion"—a view associated with Roger Fry's thinking, and probably also with Clive Bell's *Art,* which appeared in 1914—see "Modern Art, IV," *Further Speculations,* p. 139, and for the quotation from his "Sketch for a New Weltanschauung" (notes assembled under the title "Cinders"), *Speculations,* p. 234.

Chapter 3. The Post-War Character of Cubism

On the post-War artistic scene in general, see the discussions of Henry Geldzahler, "World War I and the First Crisis in Vanguard Art," *Art News* 61, no. 8 (Dec. 1962): 48–51, 63–74; Massimo Carra, "La crisi dell' avanguardie e il ritorno all' ordine," in *Al di fuori delle avanguardie: il ritorno al classicismo negli anni 1920–40,* part. 1, *L'Arte Moderna,* vol. 25 (Milan, 1972), pp. 1–40; Stephen Bann, introdn. to *The Tradition of Constructivism,* ed. Bann (London and New York, 1974), p. 30; John Willett, *Art and Politics in the Weimar Period: The New Sobriety 1917–1933* (London and New York, 1978), chaps. 4, 7 (including discussion of the French scene).

For T. E. Hulme's wartime writings, see *Speculations,* ed. Herbert Read (London, 1924), pp. 249–61 (introdn. to Sorel); *Further Speculations,* ed. Sam Hynes (Lincoln, Neb., 1962), pp. 170–205 (*Cambridge Magazine* articles, with Bertrand Russell's replies). The specific passages quoted are from "Humanism and the Religious Attitude," originally publ. as "A Notebook by T. E. H.," *The New Age* (Dec. 2, 9, 16 and 23, 1915), and from the introdn. to Sorel, *Speculations,* pp. 250, 254. For "A Tory Philosophy" (signed Thomas Gratton) in its original 1912 appearance), see Alun R. Jones, *The Life and Opinions of Thomas Ernest Hulme* (London, 1960), pp. 187–201.

On Sorel's philosophy as it relates to Bergson, see I. L. Horowitz, *Radicalism and the Revolt against Reason, The Social Theories of Georges Sorel* (London, 1961), chap. 2, part 3.

For T. S. Eliot's knowledge of Hulme's writings, see esp. Ronald Schuchard, "Eliot and Hulme in 1916. Towards a Revaluation of Eliot's Critical and Spiritual Development," *Proceedings of Modern Language Association* 88 (1973): 1083–94 (correcting and expanding on earlier accounts). For his relation with Pound at this time and the attention of both to Rémy de Gourmont, see esp. Pound's memoir "Harold Monro," *The Criterion* (Jul. 1932): 590 and K. L. Goodwin, *The Influence of Ezra Pound* (Oxford, 1966), chap. 6 (with refs. to the publications of both on De Gourmont, 1914–20). On Benda's influence and his critique of Bergson, see Robert Niess, *Julien Benda* (Ann Arbor, Mich., 1956), chap. 5. For Eliot's responsiveness to Benda's and Maurras's writings and to Rivière, see Ants Oras, *The Critical Ideas of T. S. Eliot* (Tartu, 1932), part 3 and Herbert Howarth, *Notes on Some Figures behind T. S. Eliot* (Boston, 1964), chap. 6, and for his earlier interest in Bergson, see also Piers Gray, *T. S. Eliot's Intellectual and Poetic Development, 1909–1922* (Brighton, Eng.: Harvester Press, 1982), chaps. 2–3.

Statements of artists, poets and critics relating to Cubism:
Gino Severini, "Symbolisme plastique, symbolisme littéraire," *Mercure de France* (Feb. 1, 1916): 466–76; preface to cat. of exhbn. at Gallery 291, (New York City, Mar. 6–17, 1917), repr. in *Critica d'Arte* 17, no. 3 (May–Jun. 1970): 50–53; "Considérations sur l'esthétique picturale moderne" (lecture of Jan 1917), repr. in its entirety, ibid.: 57–73; "La peinture d'avant-garde" (using extracts from the lecture), *Mercure de France* (Jun. 1, 1917): 451–68.
Pierre Albert-Birot, (no titles). *SIC,* no. 2 (Feb. 1916): 5; nos. 8–10 (Aug.–Oct. 1916): 10.
Pierre Reverdy, "Sur le cubisme," *Nord-Sud* (Mar. 15, 1917): 5–7 (Fry #35), and see also, for his developing argument for poetry, "Essai d'esthétique littéraire," ibid. (Jun.–Jul. 1917); "L'image," *Nord-Sud* (Mar. 1918): 3; "Arts" (reply to Vauxcelles) and also "Note" (on aesthetics), *Nord-Sud* (Oct. 1918); "Certain avantages d'être seul," *SIC,* no. 32 (Oct. 15, 1918) (Fry #37); "Le Cubisme, poésie plastique," *L'Art* (Feb. 1919); *Self-Defence* (Paris, 1919). All of the articles in question are repr. in *Pierre Reverdy, Oeuvres complètes: Nord-Sud, Self-Defence et autres écrits sur l'art et Nord-Sud (1917–1926),* ed. E.-A. Hubert (Paris, 1975) (with information about the interchanges with Gris, p. 343). On *Nord-Sud* and Cubism see further Robert W. Greene, *The Poetic Theory of Pierre Reverdy* (Cambridge and Berkeley, 1967), chaps. 1–2; R. L. Admussen, "*Nord-Sud* and Cubist Poetry," *Journal of Aesthetics and Art Criticism* 27, no. 1 (Fall 1968): 21–25; Etienne-Alain Hubert, "Pierre Reverdy et le cubisme en mars 1917," *Revue de l'Art* 43 (1979): 59–66; Christopher Green, "Purity, Poetry and the Painting of Juan Gris," *Art History* 5, no. 2 (Jun. 1982): 180–204.
On Max Jacob's preface of 1916 to his *Le cornet à dés* (Paris, 1917; the passage quoted is on p. 16), see Gerald Kamber, *Max Jacob and the Poetics of Cubism* (Baltimore and London, 1971), pp. 81–82.
Paul Dermée, "Quand le Symbolisme fut mort . . ." and "Intelligence et création," *Nord-Sud* (Mar. and Aug.–Sept. 1917).
Georges Braque, "Pensées et réflexions sur la peinture," *Nord-Sud* (Dec. 1917): 3–5 (Fry #36); "Pensées," *Valori Plastici* (Rome) (Feb. 1919) (letter from L. Rosenberg to editor, quoting six of the same maxims and adding one more). Laurence Homolka as a graduate student kindly provided me with a photostat of the original publication and made some valuable comments on its character. For Reverdy's role in the arrangement, see Jean Leymarie, "Evocation de Reverdy, auprès de Braque et de Picasso," in *Pierre Reverdy 1889–1960, Mercure de France* 344, no. 1181 (1962)

(special no. on Reverdy): 301, and for notebooks with some of the maxims included (probably in recopied form), see *Cahier de Georges Braque, 1917–1947* (Paris, 1948); rev. version, *Le Jour et la Nuit, Cahiers 1917–1952* (Paris, 1952).

Statement in *Le Pays,* of uncertain date; repr. in an anon. (undated) article of late 1917, "La querelle cubiste . . . ou le cubisme expliqué" (Bibl. Doucet, Paris, Vauxcelles papers; publ. in *Album Apollinaire* (Paris, 1971), pp. 259–61). For Apollinaire's comments on the subject to Reverdy, see *Pierre Reverdy 1889–1960* (1962), pp. 10–13 (letters of Jun. 28 and 29, 1917).

Apollinaire, introdn. to album-catalogue of Exposition André Derain, Galerie Paul Guillaume (Oct. 15–21, 1916); statement, on art and the War, in *Paris-Midi* (Dec. 9, 1916) (not in *Chroniques d'Art,* 1960); "Pablo Picasso" (poem), *SIC* (May 1917); statement in program for *Parade,* Théâtre du Chatelet (Paris, May 18, 1917); letter to *Mercure de France* (on origins of Cubism) (Oct. 16, 1917); preface to cat. of *Exposition Matisse-Picasso,* Galerie Paul Guillaume (Jan.–Feb. 1918): *Apollinaire on Art; Essays and Reviews,* 1902–1918, ed. L. C. Breunig, trans. S. Suleiman (London and New York, 1972), pp. 446–55, 458. His posthumously publ. lecture "L'esprit nouveau et les poètes," *Mercure de France* (Dec. 1, 1918): 385–96, is discussed further by Francis Carmody, "L'esthétique de l'esprit nouveau," *Le flâneur des deux rives* 2, nos. 7–8 (Sept.–Dec. 1955): 11–20 and by P. A. Jannini, *Le avanguardie letterarie nelle idee critice di Guillaume Apollinaire* (Rome, 1971), esp. p. 108, where the interview given by Apollinaire in Jul. 1918 is cited (as trans. from the Spanish and ed. by E.-A. Hubert, *Apollinaire VII, Revue des Lettres Modernes* 183–.88 [1969]: 185).

Roger Bissière, review of Braque exhbn., Galerie de l'Effort Moderne (Mar. 1919), *Opinion* (Paris) (Mar. 29 and Apr. 26, 1919).

André Lhote, "Une exposition Braque," *Nouvelle Revue Française* (Jun. 1, 1919); "Cubism and the Modern Artistic Sensibility," *The Athenaeum* (London) (Sept. 19, 1919): 919–20. See also his article "Le Cubisme au Grand Palais," *Nouvelle Revue Française* (Mar. 1920), dividing the "pure" from the "emotional" Cubists, and the corresponding article "The Two Cubisms," *The Athenaeum* (Apr. 23 and 30, 1920): 547–48, 579.

Blaise Cendrars, "Pourquoi le 'cube' s'effrite?" *La Rose Rouge* (May 15, 1919): 33–34 (Fry #40)—with follow-up articles publ. there on Picasso, Braque and Léger. On Cendrars' position at this time, see Monique Chefdor, *Blaise Cendrars* (Boston, 1980), esp. pp. 46, 62.

Maurice Raynal, "Gino Severini," *SIC* (May 15 and 31, 1917); *Quelques intentions du Cubisme,* pamphlet (Paris, 1919) (Fry #39, incomplete); "Idee sul Cubismo," *Valori Plastici* (Feb.–Mar. 1919). For the ongoing character of Raynal's writings on Cubism, especially on Picasso, in the early 1920s, see Eunice Lipton, *Picasso Criticism 1901–1939* (New York: Garland Press, 1976), p. 165.

Léonce Rosenberg, "Cubisme et Tradition," *Valori Plastici* (Feb.–Mar. 1919), p. 2 (Fry #38, misleadingly labeled), and *Cubisme et Tradition,* pamphlet, (Paris, 1920).

André Salmon, "Les origines et intentions du cubisme," *Demain* (Apr. 26, 1919): 485–89.

Daniel-Henry Kahnweiler (pseud. Daniel Henry), "Der Kubismus," *Die Weissen Blätter* (Zurich and Leipzig, Sept. 1916): 209–22; "Wider den Expressionismus in den bildenden Künsten," *Neues Leben* (Bern), (1917): 354–61; "Vom Sehen und vom Bilden," *Die Weissen Blätter* (Jul. 1919): 315–22; "Das Wesen der Bildhauerei," *Feuer* (Weimar) (Nov.–Dec. 1919): 145–56 (both trans. into French in his *Confessions esthétiques* [Paris, 1963], pp. 84–102); *Der Weg zum Kubismus* (Munich: Delphin, 1920); later eds. 1928, with chap. added on Gris, and 1958. I have used the English trans. *The Rise of Cubism* (New York, 1949) (Documents of Modern Art, ed. R. Motherwell; Fry #41 gives a short extract only), except for the passage from Kant, which is given as it appears in *The Critique of Pure Reason,* ed. N. Kemp Smith (London, 1929), p. 110. For the coming into being of the text, see Kahnweiler's 1958 preface to the German ed. of that year, publ. in French in *Confessions esthétiques* (1963), pp. 9–11. The extant sections from the planned discussion of aesthetics in general, and also those on the Reformation, have been publ. in German as *Der Gegenstand der Asthetik,* introd. Wilhelm Weber (Munich, 1971). The term "pre-perception" was evidently not invented by G. H. Lewes, since the *Oxford English Dictionary* gives refs. indicating that it came into use in British philosophical discussion of Berkeley and Kant during the 1870s.

Juan Gris's contribution to the number of *Valori Plastici* on Cubism (Feb.–Mar. 1919), p. 2, is trans. in D.-H. Kahnweiler, *Juan Gris, His Life and Work* (New York, 1968), p. 192. The letters of his quoted appear (in English trans.) in *Letters of Juan Gris.* ed. D.-H. Kahnweiler, trans. D. Cooper (London, 1956), as nos. 40, 71, 80.

For the more general development of art and theory during this period, the most valuable recent contributions are those of André Fermigier, introdn. to *Jean Cocteau, entre Picasso et Radiguet* (collected writings, Paris, 1967), pp. 24–29; Christopher Green, "Léger and L'Esprit Nouveau," in exhbn. cat. *Léger and Purist Paris,* Tate Gallery (London, Nov. 1970–Jan. 1971), pp. 29–48 and *Léger and the Avant-Garde* (New Haven and London, 1976), chap. 4; Malcolm Gee, "The Avant-Garde, Order and the Art Market 1916–23," *Art History* 2, no. 1, (1979): 95–106. See also, for post-War British perspectives on classicism in French literature, Cyrena N. Pondrom, *The Road from Paris: French Influence on English Poetry* 1900–1920 (Cambridge, 1974), pp. 308–11; the essays of Jean Laude, Denis Milhau and Pierre Daix (on Picasso's portraits), in Université de Saint-Etienne, Travaux VIII, *Le retour à l'ordre dans les arts plastiques et l'architecture, 1919–1925* (1975), pp. 9–44, 83–142; and Kenneth Silver, "Esprit de Corps: The Great War and French Art, 1914–1925" (Yale Univ. Ph.D. diss., 1981), chap. 3. For "signs" in the Cubism of this time, see Fry, *Cubism* (1966), pp. 33–34; however, he puts forward in his later explication of this term, pp. 38–39, the idea of a parallel in 1913–14 already with "eidetic reduction" in Husserl's phenomenology. Lynn Gamwell, *Cubist Criticism* (Ann Arbor, Mich., 1980), chap. 6, briefly indicates the theoretical linkage between Raynal, Rosenberg and Kahnweiler towards the end of this phase and gives some attention (pp. 95–100) to how the analytic/synthetic distinction is now used.

On the work of individual artists during this phase:

Joan M. Lukach, "Severini's 1917 Exhibition at Stieglitz's Gallery '291'," *Burlington Magazine* 113 (Apr. 1971): 196–207 and "Severini's Writings and Paintings 1916–1917 and his Exhibition in New York City," *Critica d'Arte* 20 (Nov.–Dec. 1974): 59–80 discusses both the paintings of War subjects and the subsequent shift. Cf. also, for the relation back to Symbolism, Angelica Z. Rudenstine, *The Guggenheim Museum Collection, Paintings 1880–1945,* 2 vols. (New York, 1976), cat. nos. 230–31. For the Théâtre d'Art performance recorded in the *Portrait of Paul Fort,* see Paul Fort, *Mes mémoires, toute la vie d'un poète, 1872–1943* (Paris, 1944), p. 34; the *première idée* for this portrait, clearly identifiable as such from the related *collage* materials included (the title page of Fort's *Choix de ballades françaises* [Paris: Figuière, 1913] and a card inscribed "Vers et Prose") is reproduced in Gina Franchini's booklet on the artist (Rome 1968), and one or the other version was included in the artist's 1916 exhbn. His *Gypsy playing the Mandolin* of 1919 (Boschi colln., Milan) is ill. in his *Du cubisme au classicisme ed altri scritti,* ed. P. Pacini (Florence, 1972), p. 121.

Christopher Green, "Synthesis and the 'Synthetic Process' in the Painting of Juan Gris 1915–1919," *Art History* 5, no. 1 (Mar. 1982): 86–105 offers a very careful analysis of the evidence and arrives at findings very similar to mine, esp. as regards the relationship to Reverdy. See also Douglas Cooper, *Juan Gris, catalogue raisonné,* 2 vols. (Paris, 1977), introdn., p. 21. For "fossilized shading"—a term introduced for Gris by Clement Greenberg, "Collage" (1958), *Art and Culture* (Boston, 1961), p. 82—as adopted by Blanchard and Metzinger, see the works of both in the Winston colln. (exh. Guggenheim Museum, New York, 1973–74) and Metzinger's *Nature morte au sucrier* of 1917 (ill. *Burlington Magazine* 118 [Dec. 1973], pl. 115). For Gris's copies of 1916, see the exhbn. cat. *Juan Gris* (Baden-Baden, 1974), nos. 2.19–24.

Picasso's *L'Italienne,* dated "Rome 1917," is ill. and discussed in exhbn. cat. *Picasso,* Arts Council of Great Britain (1960), no. 85. For differing interpretations of *Parade* and his contributions to it, see Marianne W. Martin, "The Ballet *Parade:* A Dialogue between Cubism and Futurism," *Art Quarterly* 1, no. 2 (Spring 1978): 85–111; Georgiana M. M. Colville, *Vers un language des arts autour des années vingt* (Paris, 1977), pp. 96–107; Richard S. Axsom, *'Parade': Cubism as Theater* (New York: Garland Press, 1979). The basic components are set out in *Jean Cocteau, entre Picasso et Radiguet,* ed. Fermigier (1969), pp. 15–19, 64–66, and see also Douglas Cooper, *Picasso: Theatre* (London and New York, 1968) for ills. of Picasso's décors here and for La Tricorne (the sketch ref. to in the latter case is ill. in exhbn. cat. *Pablo Picasso, A Retrospective,* Museum of Modern Art [New York, 1980], p. 213). For the 1919 *Guitar,* Zervos 2.2.570 (also ill. there and dated Autumn, rather than early 1919), see William Rubin, *Picasso in the Collection of the Museum of Modern Art* (New York, 1972), pp. 104–5. For another adaptation of Cubism to humorous and theatrical ends contemporary with this, see G. Galatti, "Picasso's *The Lovers* of 1919," *Arts* 56, no. 5 (Feb. 1982): 76–82.

Braque's 1918 *collage, Musical Forms,* is discussed in detail by E. A. Carmean Jr. in exhbn. cat. *Georges Braque, Les Papiers Collés,* Centre Pompidou (Paris, Jun.–Sept. 1982), pp. 57ff. For the exact dating of the *Musician* and the use of black underpainting from 1918 on, see D. Cooper in exhbn. cat. *G. Braque,* Arts Council of Great Britain (1956), nos. 45, 50.

For Picasso's post-War career, see Roland Penrose, *Picasso, His Life and Work* (London, 1958), chaps. 7–8, and for Satie's over the same time period, see *The Writings of Erik Satie,* ed. and trans. Nigel Wilkins (London, 1980), which includes his 1916 lecture "In Praise of Critics." Nietzsche's *The Birth of Tragedy* had first appeared in French in 1901 (*L'origine de la tragédie, ou Hellénisme et pessimisme,* trans. Jean Marnold and Jacques Morland) and had been through several subsequent editions; Apollinaire in his Apr. 1912 essay on the "New Painting" (*Apollinaire on Art* [1972], p. 223), included in *Les Peintres Cubistes* (sec. 3), had linked the Nietzschean contrast of the "cerebral" and the "sensual" with a fragment of dialogue between Dionysos and Ariadne from *The Twilight of the Gods.* For Ezra Pound's poetic thinking in 1919, see the suggestive essay by Donald Davie, "Ezra Pound's Hugh Selwyn Mauberley," in *The Modern Age,* ed. Boris Ford (Baltimore, Md.: Pelican Guide to English Literature, vol. 7, 1961), pp. 315–29.

Chapter 4. Consolidation and Orthodoxy, 1920–1925

On the challenge of Purism in general, see Françoise Will-Levaillant, "Norme et forme à travers l'Esprit Nouveau," in *Le retour à l'ordre dans les arts plastiques et l'architecture, 1919–1925* (Université de Saint-Etienne, Travaux VIII, 1975), pp. 241–265; Christopher Green, *Léger and the Avant Garde* (New Haven and London, 1976), chap. 7, and Kenneth F. Silver, "Purism: "Straightening up after the Great War," *Artforum* 15, no. 7 (Mar. 1977): 56–63.

Copies by the Cubists after the old masters of French art: Gris had done drawings after several compositions of Cézanne's in 1916, including the *Portrait of Mme Cézanne* of which he went on to do a painted copy in 1918 (C 257, March) and a drawing and a painting (C 197, March) after Corot's *Woman with a Mandolin;* Braque would pick up on a much earlier admiration of his for Corot's figures of women playing musical instruments (p. 73) in a "souvenir" that he did of that same Corot in 1922–23 (Centre Pompidou, Paris); and Picasso, who had done a drawing in 1917 after the female figure in Ingres's *Tu Marcellus Eris* and also a copy in 1917–18 of Le Nain's seventeenth century peasant subject of *The Happy Family* would do a drawing after Corot's *Italian Peasant Woman* in 1920 (Zervos 29.306; 3.96, along with drawing 30.14, identified as to correct source in exhbn. cat. *Pablo Picasso, A Retrospective,* Museum of Modern Art [New York, 1980], correction to p. 208; and 4.8). In addition to Le Nain and Corot, Jean Cocteau who had shared in the experience of the reopened Louvre also cited the example of Poussin and Chardin (*Picasso* [Paris, 1923], pp. 10–11; Fry #44).

Writings of Maurice Raynal cited: *Juan Gris* (Paris, 1920) (repr. in *Bulletin de l'Effort Moderne* 16 [Jun. 1925]); "Juan Gris," *L'Esprit Nouveau,* no. 5 (Feb. 1921); *Picasso* (Paris, 1922); *G. Braque* (Rome and Paris, 1923); "Picasso," *Art d'aujourd'hui* (Spring 1924); "Pablo Picasso," *Bulletin de l'Effort Moderne* Dec. 1924–Feb. 1925); also *Fernand Léger, vingt tableaux* (Paris, 1920), with texts subsequently pub. in *L'Esprit Nouveau,* no. 4 (1921) and *Bulletin de L'Effort Moderne* (Oct. Nov. 1925).

For T. E. Hulme's renewed influence on T. S. Eliot now, see J. R. Daniells, "T. S. Eliot and his Relation to T. E. Hulme," *Univ. of Toronto Quarterly* 2, no. 3 (1933): 380–96; John D. Margolis, *T. S. Eliot's Intellectual Development, 1922–1939* (London and Chicago, 1972), chap. 2; and also Kristian Smidt, *Poetry and Belief in the Work of T. S. Eliot* (rev. ed., London, 1961), pp. 230–31. The passages quoted or referred to in Eliot's "The Function of Criticism" (1923) and "Four Elizabethan Dramatists" (1924) are to be found in his *Selected Essays* (London, 1932), pp. 23, 32, 114, and see pp. 247–50 there for "The Metaphysical Poets" (1921) cited later. Hulme's essays "Humanism and the Religious Attitude," "Modern Art and its Philosophy" and "Romanticism and Classicism" appeared in *Speculations* (London, 1924), pp. 1–140, the specific passages quoted or referred to coming at pp. 82, 119–20, 128–29, 132–33 and see also p. 160; "Bergson's Theory of Art," publ. in *The New Age* (Mar. 20 and Apr. 6, 13, 1922); "Notes on Language and Style," first publ. in *The Criterion* (Jul. 1925): 485–97, is repr. in *Further Speculations,* ed. S. Hynes (Lincoln, Neb., 1962), pp. 77–100. On Herbert Read, see Worth T. Harder, *A Certain Order: The Development of Herbert Read's Theory of Poetry* (The Hague and Paris, 1971), esp. pp. 35–36, 43, 94–95, and also David Thistlewood, "Herbert Read's Aesthetic Theorizing 1914–1952: An Interpretation of *The Philosophy of Modern Art,*" *Art History* 2, no. 3 (Sept. 1979): pp. 339–54. There is a strong tradition of critical comment on the Classicism-Romanticism antithesis as formulated and bequeathed by Hulme, the most notable contributions to it for present purposes being Murray Krieger, "The Ambiguous Anti-Romanticism of T. E. Hulme," *ELH* 20 (Dec. 1953): 300–314, re-used in his *The New Apologists for Poetry* (Minneapolis, 1956), chaps. 1–2; Kathleen Nott, *The Emperor's New Clothes* (London, 1953), chap. 3; Frank Kermode, *Romantic Image* (London, 1957), chap. 7; and C. K. Stead, *The New Poetic* (London, 1964), pp. 99, 132, 184–85.

Texts on Purism referred to: A. Ozenfant, "Notes sur le cubisme," *L'Elan* (Dec. 1, 1916) (partially cited in Lynn Gamwell, *Cubist Criticism* [Ann Arbor, Mich. 1980], pp. 186–87 nn. 6–8), and "Picasso et la peinture d'aujourd'hui" (under name 'Vauvrecy'), *L'Esprit Nouveau,* no. 13 (1921), trans. in *A Picasso Anthology,* ed. M. McCully, (London, 1981), pp. 146–47; Ozenfant and Jeanneret, *Après le Cubisme* (Paris, 1918); "Le Purisme," *L'Esprit Nouveau,* no. 4 (Feb. 1921), trans. in *Modern Artists on Art,* ed. R. Herbert (Englewood Cliffs, N.J., 1964), pp. 58–73; "Idées personelles," *L'Esprit Nouveau,* no. 27 (1925); *La Peinture Moderne* (Paris, 1925) (Fry #47, one section only). Their respective contributions are discussed by Paul V.

Turner, "The Education of Le Corbusier: A Study of the Development of Le Corbusier's Thought," 1900–1930 (Harvard University Ph.D. diss., 1971), chap. 5, and also by Roberto Gabetti and Carlo Olmi, *Le Corbusier et L'Esprit Nouveau* (Turin, 1975). A facsimile reprint of the entire periodical was issued by Da Capo (New York, 1968).

Gris's reported discussions with Ozenfant and his explanatory drawing are found in Ozenfant's *Memoires 1886–1962* (Paris, 1968), pp. 131–33; his responses to the 1921 article in *Letters of Juan Gris 1913–1927*, ed. D.-H. Kahnweiler, trans. D. Cooper (London, 1956), nos. 124–25.

Texts on Cézanne cited: T. E. Hulme, "Modern Art and its Philosophy," *Speculations* (1924), pp. 100–102; Emile Bernard, "Souvenirs sur Paul Cézanne et notes inédites," *Mercure de France* (Oct. 1 and 15, 1907), and "Une conversation avec Cézanne," ibid. (Jun. 1, 1921) (with corresponding texts in the reprinted book versions, *Souvenirs sur Cézanne* [Paris, 1921 and 1926])—a change pointed out by George H. Hamilton, *Painting and Sculpture in Europe, 1880–1940* (Harmondsworth, Middsx. and Baltimore, Md., 1967), p. 361 n.33, and see also the sense of Cézanne's words as discussed by Theodore Reff, "Cézanne on Solids and Space," *Artforum* 21, no. 2 (Oct. 1977): 34–37; Gino Severini, "Cézanne et Cézannisme," *L'Esprit Nouveau*, nos. 11, 12 and 13 (1921), commented upon by Gris, *Letters*, no. 154 (Jan. 3, 1922), and *Du Cubisme au Classicisme* (Paris, 1921), chap. 1. For the statements of Cézanne's cited by Severini and their influence, see T. Reff, "Cézanne and Poussin," *Journal of Warburg and Courtauld Institutes* 23 (1960): 150–74.

Texts on Negro art cited: Daniel-Henry Kahnweiler, *Der Weg zum Kubismus* (1914–19) (Munich, 1920), trans. as *The Rise of Cubism* (New York, 1949), pp. 8, 16 and "Das Wesen der Bildhauerei," *Feuer* (Weimar), 1, nos. 2–3 (Dec. 1919), trans. into French as "L'Essence de la sculpture" in his *Confessions esthétiques* (Paris, 1963), p. 98; Hulme, *Speculations*, pp. 98–99; Apollinaire, "Melanophile ou melanomanie," *Mercure de France* (Apr. 1, 1917), used as introdn., "A propos de l'art des noirs," in *Sculptures nègres* (Paris, 1917), and repr. as "Opinion sur l'art nègre," *Action* (Paris) 3 (Apr. 1920); "Sculptures d'Afrique et d'Océanie" (under name "Louis Troeme"), *Les Arts à Paris* (Jul. 15, 1918) (*Apollinaire on Art, Essays and Reviews 1902–1918*, trans. S. Suleiman [New York, 1972], pp. 470–71); André Salmon, "Negro Art" (trans. by D. Brinton), *Burlington Magazine* 36 (Apr. 1920): 164–72; Gris, "Opinion sur l'art nègre," *Action* (Apr. 1920): 24, repr. in D.-H. Kahnweiler, *Juan Gris, sa vie, son oeuvre, ses écrits* (Paris, 1946), p. 276, trans. as *Juan Gris, His Life and Work* (New York, 1968 ed.), p. 192.

Comments of Gris on the art scene: *Letters* nos. 90, 92 (exhbn. of Indépendants, Jan. 1920); 116 (Feb. 26, 1921) (asking about the Rosenberg exhbn.); 128, 129 (Apr. 1921, on invitation from Diaghilev) and also the later comments on the experience of working for him, in 184–87 (Nov.–Dec. 1923) and 193–95 (Jan. 1924); 150–51, 159, 161 (Dec. 1921–Feb. 1922), on his isolation. On the publication history of Severini's *Du Cubisme au Classicisme,* see the edn. of Piero Pacini (Florence, 1972), p. 127. Besides Bissière's *Georges Braque* (Paris, 1920), also publ. in *Bulletin de L'Effort Moderne,* (Mar. 1920), the texts of Raynal's listed earlier and his own *Cubisme et Tradition* (Paris, 1920; German trans. in *Jahrbuch der jungen Kunst,* Leipzig, Jul. 1921) and *Cubisme et empirisme* (Paris, 1921), Rosenberg's *L'Effort Moderne* publications included a reprint of Raynal's 1919 pamphlet, *Quelques intentions du Cubisme* (Fry #39) in *Bulletin de L'Effort Moderne* (Jan.–Mar. 1924) and an inquiry "Ou va la peinture moderne?" with responses by Léger, Metzinger and Gleizes, ibid. (Feb. and May 1924). For the group exhibitions referred to, see Fry (1966), pp. 185–86 and Waldemar George's "Une exposition de groupe (Galerie de L'Effort Moderne)," *L'Esprit Nouveau,* no. 9 (1921).

The statement of Herbin's cited (from an undated letter) is publ. and trans. in exhbn. cat. *The Planar Dimension, Europe. 1912–1932*, Guggenheim Museum (New York, 1979), no. 49. Miro's 1921 exhbn. in Paris was at the Galerie La Licorne. For De Stijl in Paris in these years, see C. Green, in exhbn. cat. *Léger and Purist Paris*, Tate Gallery (London, Nov. 1970–Jan. 1971), pp. 53–57, 72–75.

For Gris's development in this period, see Douglas Cooper, *Juan Gris, catalogue raisonné*, 2 vols. (Paris, 1977), introdn., pp. 21–22 (offering critical remarks on the problem of quality and the factors underlying it). The term "canonical" for the geometry of later Cubism is to be found in Clement Greenberg's writings on the subject from the later 1940s and 1950s; *Art and Culture*, (Boston, 1961), pp. 89, 195, 211–12. The stimulus of the sixteenth-century Fontainebleau Mannerists on Gris in 1923–25, along with Pompeian frescoes, even before its mention in Letters 212–13 of Jan.–Feb. 1926, is implied by Kahnweiler, *Juan Gris* (1968 ed.), p. 152 and seems evident in the monumentality of the figures and pale, lemony colors: as already in the *Seated Harlequin* of early 1923 (C 418).
The possible contribution of De Chirico's art was brought up by William Rubin, first of all in terms of an affinity found in it with Synthetic Cubism (*Dada, Surrealism and Their Heritage*, exhbn. cat., Museum of Modern Art [New York, 1968], p. 80) and subsequently in terms of specific contributions to Picasso's imagery in the 1925 *Still Life with Plaster Head* (*Picasso in the Collection of the Museum of Modern Art* [New York, 1972], pp. 120–22 and 222 nn. 6–7, noting the imagery of tools and scaffolding in De Chirico and referring to Picasso's contact with André Breton now as a likely intermediate link) and earlier, in the facial features of the 1915 *Man with a Pipe*, D 842. ("De Chirico and Modernism," in exhbn. cat. *De Chirico*, Museum of Modern Art [New York, 1982], pp. 68–69, comparing the head in *The Child's Brain* of 1914); but, both for the mid-War period and for the early 1920s, the stimulus asks to be considered in much broader terms, so that it applies to Gris also. On the larger context of response to De Chirico's art in Paris, see Marianne W. Martin, "Reflections on De Chirico and *Arte Metafisica*," *Art Bulletin* 60, no. 2 (Jun. 1978): 342–53, and Willard Bohn, "Metaphysics and Meaning: Apollinaire's Criticism of Giorgio de Chirico," *Arts* 55, no. 7 (Mar. 1981): pp. 109–13. De Chirico's essay " 'Sull' arte metafisica" (*Valori Plastici* 1, nos. 4–5 [Apr.–May 1919]) is trans. in *Theories of Modern Art*, ed. H. B. Chipp (Berkeley and Los Angeles, 1968), pp. 448–53, and for the context of its original appearance, see Joan M. Lukach, "De Chirico and Italian Art Theory, 1915–1920," in exhbn. cat. *De Chirico*, pp. 35–54. A student, Karen Koehler, brought out the points of parallel with T. S. Eliot's 1921 essay; for the term "metaphysical" itself (in English) and Eliot's play with it, see Stephen Orgel, "Affecting the Metaphysics," in *Twentieth Century Literature in Retrospect*, ed. Reuben A. Brower, Harvard English Studies, 2 (Cambridge, Mass., 1971), pp. 225–46.
Theodore Reff, "Picasso's *Three Musicians:* Maskers, Artists and Friends," *Art in America* 65, no. 10 (Dec. 1980): 124–42, recapitulates previous interpretations and documents the development of the Harlequin theme (arguing that the Philadelphia version came first), before putting forward an interpretation based on Picasso's personal life and friendships. The 1918 drawing referred to is Zervos 3.135; that of 1921 is to my knowledge unpublished. Cendrars' statement on sorcery quoted is from "Pourquoi le 'cube' s'effrite?" *La Rose Rouge* (May 15, 1919) (Fry #40). The remaining paintings of Picasso's discussed are Zervos 5.84, 220 and 364, 445 (all reprod. in color in *Pablo Picasso, A Retrospective*, 1980). See also, on his work of 1925, F. Will-Levaillant, *"La Danse* de Picasso et le Surréalisme en 1925," *L'information d'histoire d'art* 5 (1966): 210–14.
On Stravinsky's *Les Noces* and its evolution, basic information is provided by the composer himself, in his *Chronicle of My Life* (London, 1936), repr. as *An Autobiography* (New York, 1962), chap. 7, from which the quotations are taken, and by Eric Walter White and Jeremy Noble, in vol. 18, *New Grove Dictionary of Music and*

Musicians (London, 1980), pp. 240–65 (repr. one of the Goncharova costume designs; which may be compared to such Picasso drawings of 1919 as Zervos 3.343 and 29.43, repr. in *Pablo Picasso, A Retrospective* [1981], pp. 218–19). On the music and choreography of the *Sacre du Printemps* and responses to it, see the *Autobiography*, chap. 3 (Stravinsky disowned the statement about it which appeared in *Montjoie !* [Mar. 29, 1913] as based on an interview with him, but was in fact written entirely by Riciotto Canudo), and Jacques Rivière, "Le Sacre du Printemps," *Nouvelle Revue Française* 10 (1913): 706–30. It was in fact revived, together with *Parade,* for the 1920–21 season of the Diaghilev Ballet in Paris (Théâtre des Champs Elysées, first performance Dec. 15, 1920) with new, simplified choreography by Massine and a single backdrop (Roerich's original design for Part 2). Stravinsky's own comments on this interpretation are to be found in an article in *Comoedia illustré* (Dec. 11, 1920). The production was brought to London in the summer of 1921, for three performances before being taken off; interestingly it was seen during that time by T. S. Eliot, who wrote a commentary ("London Letter," *The Dial* [Oct. 1921]) comparing its music to the mechanical and industrial sounds of modern life.

Léger's statement on the "machine aesthetic" (*Bulletin de L'Effort Moderne* [Jan.–Feb. 1924] and *Propos d'artistes* [Paris, 1925]) appear in trans. in exhbn. cat. *Léger and Purist Paris* (1970–71), pp. 90–92 (Part 1 only) and in *Functions of Painting,* ed. E. Fry (New York, 1973), pp. 52–70.

Gris's statements of 1921 on were originally published as follows: *L'Esprit Nouveau,* no. 5 (Feb. 1921) (over the name 'Vauvrecy'; Fry #43); "Notes sur ma peinture," *Der Querschnitt* (Frankfurt) 1, no. 2 (Summer 1923); "On the Possibilities of Painting" (lecture at Sorbonne, May 15, 1924), trans. from French in *Transatlantic Review* (Jun.–Jul. 1924); "Réponse à l'enquête: 'Chez les cubistes,'" *Bulletin de la Vie Artistique* (Jan. 1, 1925) (Fry #46), re-used with some additions in German trans., *Europa Almanach* (Potsdam, 1925), pp. 34–35. All of his statements are printed together in French in Kahnweiler, *Juan Gris* (1946), pp. 276–92 and in trans., by D. Cooper, in its English version (1968), pp. 191–204. For the term "synthetic," see in addition the conversation of Mar. 13, 1920 reported by Kahnweiler (1968), p. 144, and the statement about his development, reported by M. Raynal in his *Anthologie de la peinture en France de 1906 à nos jours* (Paris, 1927), p. 172, which appears along with the other ones; and also G. Severini, "Vers une synthèse esthétique," *Bulletin de L'Effort Moderne* (Oct.–Nov. 1924), together with the related article by Marcel Bauginet, "Vers une synthèse esthétique et social," ibid. (Apr. 1925), with its specific comment "beyond analysis lies synthesis" (p. 11). For "deduction" as opposed to "induction," see Raynal, *Pablo Picasso* (1922), pp. 19–20 and also comment in Gris's letter 154 of Jan. 3 that year to him on Waldemar George's mistaken use here (referring to an article in *Cahiers idéalistes,* Dec. 4, 1921, already mentioned in 153). Gris's comments about color and design in the 1924 lecture may derive either directly from Charles Blanc's *Grammaire des arts du dessin* (Paris, 1867) or through the intermediacy of the Section d'Or artists that he had known. For his view of abstract art somewhat earlier, see his letter to Kahnweiler of Aug. 25, 1919, no. 130; and for the passage on quality cited, no. 149.

Picasso's statement of 1923 appeared under the title "Picasso Speaks" in *The Arts* (New York) (May 1923), pp. 315–26; it was based on an interview in Spanish and Picasso approved the English translation. It is conveniently reprinted in Alfred H. Barr Jr., *Picasso, Fifty Years of his Art* (New York: Museum of Modern Art, 1946), pp. 270–71 and in Fry, #45. Reverdy's statement cited is from his *Pablo Picasso* (Paris, 1924), p. 5. The Nietzschean overtones of Picasso's words were pointed out by J. M. Nash, "The Nature of Cubism: A Study of Conflicting Explanations," *Art History* 3, no. 4 (Dec. 1980): 435–47, and he refers to the picture of Picasso's Nietzschean genius given in Salmon's pen portrait, *Paris-Journal* (Sept. 21. 1911) (Fry #14); see further in this connection Salmon's *L'Art vivant* (Paris, 1920), pp. 119–20;

"Picasso," *L'Esprit Nouveau*, no. 1 (1920): 59–81 (*A Picasso Anthology*, ed. McCully [1981], pp. 138ff.), and also his *Propos d'atelier* (Paris, 1922). The passage quoted from Nietzsche in Léonce Rosenberg's *Cubisme et empirisme* (1921), p. 3, is "The Dreaded Eye," *The Dawn of Day* #223. The relevant passages about art in *The Will to Power* are #808–24.

Texts on Cubism referred to at close: Waldemar George, "Vorwort zur 93 Sturmaustellung," *Der Sturm* (Berlin) (Jan. 1921) (Fry #42); Gino Severini, *Du Cubisme au Classicisme* (Paris: Povolozky, 1921), chap. 1; Rudolf Bluemner, *Der Geist des Kubismus und die Künste* (Berlin: Der Sturm, 1921), foreword and chaps. 2, 6, 17; Andrew Dasburg, "Cubism—Its Rise and Influence," *The Arts*, no. 4 (Nov. 1923): 279–84 (partially repr., as from 1928, in *Picasso in Perspective*, ed. G. Schiff [Englewood Cliffs, N.J., 1976], pp. 61–62); Ozenfant and Jeanneret, *Le Peinture Moderne* (Paris: Editions G. Crès, Collection de l'Esprit Nouveau, 1925), p. 137 (Fry #47).

Conclusion

There is no basic study of the early twentieth century in France and Western Europe that focuses on the interrelation between cultural, social and political developments. For the period before 1914, I have been helped by the lines of thought pursued by John Berger in the title essay of his book *The Moment of Cubism* (London, 1969) and by George Dangerfield in his classic 1935 study *The Strange Death of Liberal England, 1900–1914* (New York, 1961); and for the contrast of the pre-War and post-War periods, by Eric Cahn's essay "Revolution, Conservation and Reconstruction in Paris, 1905–25," in *Modernism 1890–1930*, ed. M. Bradbury and J. Macfarlane (Baltimore, Md., Pelican Guide to English Literature, 1976), pp. 162–71, and Robert Wohl's *The Generation of 1914* (Cambridge, Mass., 1979), esp. chap. 2. Amongst the many different studies of T. S. Eliot's poetry, I would cite particularly for its value as a sensitive and penetrating cultural reading, Richard Drain's " 'The Waste Land': The Prison and the Key," in *'The Waste Land' in Different Voices*, ed. A. D. Moody (London, 1974), pp. 29–45.

Intermezzo. Traditional Approaches

i. Internal Periodization

T. H. Benton, "Mechanics of Form Organization in Painting" (Part 3), *The Arts* (New York) 11 (Jan. 1927): 43–44. Cf. D.-H. Kahnweiler, *The Rise of Cubism* (New York, 1949 ed.), p. 15, and for an explanation of the same principle as it relates to Cubism, with a similar diagram, John A. Richardson, *Modern Art and Scientific Thought* (Urbana, Ill., 1971), pp. 114–15, pls. 38–39. On Benton's relevant background, see M. Baigell, "Thomas Hart Benton in the 1920s," *Art Journal* 29 (1970): 422ff. and *Thomas Hart Benton* (New York, 1973), pp. 26ff.; also Gail Levin's entries in exhbn. cats. *Synchromism and American Color Abstraction*, Whitney Museum (New York, 1978), and *Synchromist Paintings by Thomas Hart Benton, 1915–1920*, Salander O'Reilly Galleries (New York, Dec. 1981–Jan. 1982). Benton's relevant diagrams are repr. in my contribution "Jackson Pollock, Thomas Hart Benton and Cubism: A Note," *Arts* 53, no. 7 (Mar. 1979) (special Pollock issue), p. 144.

D.-H. Kahnweiler, *Juan Gris* (Junge Kunst, no. 55, Leipzig, 1929); French trans. in his *Confessions esthétiques* (Paris, 1963), pp. 42–51 (pp. 43–45 refer). Carl Einstein, "Notes sur le Cubisme," *Documents* (Paris, 1929): 146ff. A. H. Barr, *Cubism and Abstract Art*, exhbn. cat., Museum of Modern Art (New York, 1936), pp. 31ff., 77–78, 82; *Picasso, Forty Years of His Art*, exhbn. cat., Museum of Modern Art (New

York, 1939), pp. 73ff., 80, 82, rev. version, *Picasso, Fifty Years of His Art* (1946), pp. 66, 77, 82ff. Kahnweiler, *Juan Gris, sa vie, son oeuvre, ses écrits* (Paris, 1946), trans. D. Cooper as *Juan Gris, His Life and Work* (New York, 1947), chap. 6, pp. 85–86 (1968 ed., pp. ‹21ff.); and cf. *The Rise of Cubism* (1949 ed), pp. 11, 15.

H. Read, "The Situation of Art in Europe at the End of the Second World War" (1948), in *The Philosophy of Modern Art* (New York, 1955 ed.), p. 42; L. A. Reid, *Meaning in the Arts* (London, 1969), p. 117; M. Raynal, in *The History of Modern Painting,* vol. 3, *From Picasso to Surrealism,* trans. from French by D. Cooper, (Geneva, 1950), p. 50; H. B. Chipp, "Cubism, 1907–14" (Columbia Univ. Ph.D. diss., 1955), p. 150; C.Gray, *Cubist Aesthetic Theories* (Baltimore, Md., 1953), chaps. 7–9, esp. pp. 113, 127ff., 150; J. T. Soby, *Juan Gris,* exhbn. cat., Museum of Modern Art (New York, 1958), p. 22; C.Greenberg, "The Pasted-Paper Revolution," *Art News* 67 (Sept. 1958): 46ff., 60–61 repr. as "Collage" (with date of 1959) in his *Art and Culture* (Boston, 1961), pp. 70ff., and see pp. 89, 195, 211–13 there for his idea of a later "canon" of Cubism; J. Golding, *Cubism, A History and an Analysis, 1907–1914* (London, 1959), chap. 3, pp. 112ff., 119, 124 (somewhat altered in wording in rev. ed., 1968). R. Rosenblum, *Cubism and Twentieth Century Art* (New York, 1966 ed.), chap. 3, pp. 71–72. E. Fry, *Cubism* (London, 1966), pp. 33 and #26; also Kahnweiler, "L'Art nègre et le cubisme," *Présence Africaine* 3 (1948): 367ff., Eng. trans. in *Horizon* (London) (Dec. 1948): 412ff. and Golding, pp. 123–24. W. Rubin, *Picasso in the Collection of the Museum of Modern Art,* exhbn. cat. (New York, 1972), pp. 84, 86; M. Kozloff, *Cubism/Futurism* (New York, 1973), chap. 5, pp. 59–60; D. Cooper, *The Cubist Epoch* (London, 1970), introdn., pp. 13ff. and 50, 79ff. (referring to Delaunay's writings of 1919–20 on, as publ. in *Du cubisme à l'art abstrait,* ed. P. Francastel [Paris, 1957]), pp. 118, 204. See also L. Gamwell, *Cubist Criticism* (Ann Arbor, Mich., 1980), pp. 105–7, calling in her conclusion for a reevaluation of the problem of correlating these terms with periods; C. Green, "Synthesis and the 'Synthetic Process' in the Painting of Juan Gris 1915–19," *Art History* 5, no. 1 (Mar. 1982): 87–88, commenting on the double meaning of the term and basically following Golding in his usage, but suggesting subsequently that Gris probably did not work in a "significantly synthetic way" before 1917.

Intermezzo. Traditional Approaches

ii. Cross-Reference to the Other Arts

Dates given in the text here are those of first publication or performance, except where hyphened ones are used to give the period of creation.

D.-H. Kahnweiler, *Juan Gris, sa vie, son oeuvre, ses écrits* (1946; Eng. trans., 1968), pp. 173–74; R. Rosenblum, *Cubism and Twentieth Century Art* (1960), pp. 10, 28–29, 58, 71; W. Sypher, "Gide's Cubist Novel:*Les Faux-Monnayeurs,*" *Kenyon Review* 11, no. 2 (1949): 291–309 and *Rococo to Cubism in Art and Literature* (New York, 1960), part 4; A. Walton Litz, "*The Waste Land* Fifty Years After," in *Eliot in his time,* ed. Litz (Princeton, N.J.: Princeton University Press, 1972), p. 8, and see also J. Dixon Hunt, "Broken Images: T. S. Eliot and Modern Poetry," in *The Waste Land in Different Voices,* ed. A. D. Moody (London, 1974), parts 4–5, esp. p. 182; H. Kenner, *The Pound Era* (Berkeley, Calif., 1971), p. 142 and see also J. Prinz Pecurin, "Resurgent Icons: Pound's First Pisan Canto and the Visual Arts," *Journal of Modern Literature* 9, no. 2 (May 1982): 159–74; R. Shattuck, *The Banquet Years* (New York, 1968), chap. 11, "The Art of Stillness"; Koehler lecture, reported to me by the late Frederick Deknatel; F. Kermode, "The English Novel ca. 1907" in *Twentieth Century Literature in Retrospect,* ed. R. Brouwer, Harvard English Studies, 2

(Cambridge, Mass., 1971), pp. 45–64; John A. Richardson, *Modern Art and Scientific Thought* (Urbana, Ill., 1971), chap. 5.

    G. Lemaître, *From Cubism to Surrealism in Modern French Literature* (Cambridge, Mass., 1941), chap. 3; Kahnweiler, *Juan Gris* (1968 ed.), pp. 178ff. and "Mallarmé et la peinture," *Les Lettres* 3, nos. 9–11 (1948): 63–68, repr. in his *Confessions Esthétiques* (Paris, 1963), pp. 214ff., trans. as appdx. to M. Raymond, *From Baudelaire to Surrealism* (New York, 1950), pp. 351–53; C. Gray, *Cubist Aesthetic Theories* (Baltimore, Md., 1953), chap. 5; M. Butor, "Monument de rien pour Apollinaire," *Nouvelle Revue Française* 147 (Mar. 1, 1965): 503ff., repr. in his *Répertoires,* vol. 3 (Paris, 1968), pp. 269ff., trans. as "Apollinaire," *Inventory* (1969): 185ff.; E. Fry, *Cubism* (1966), p. 56 (comment on Gertrude Stein's "Picasso," 1909); L. Katz, "Matisse, Picasso and Gertrude Stein," in exhbn. cat. *Four Americans in Paris,* Museum of Modern Art (New York, 1970), pp. 59–62.

    J. Frank, "Spatial Form in Modern Literature," *Sewanee Review* 53 (1945): 221ff., 433ff., 643ff., expanded in his *The Widening Gyre, Crisis and Mastery in Modern Literature* (New Brunswick, N.J., 1963), chap. 1. See also G. Giovannini, "Method in the Study of Literature in its Relation to the Other Fine Arts," *Journal of Aesthetics and Art Criticism* 8 (1950): 185–95 (reply to Frank); Frank, "Spatial Form: An Answer to Critics," *Critical Inquiry* 4, no. 2 (Winter 1977): 231–52, and *Spatial Form in Narrative,* ed. Jeffrey R. Smitten and Ann Daghistany, foreword by Frank (Ithaca, N.Y., 1981). Applications of the term Cubist to prose-writers on these lines include in addition Philip Adams, "Ernest Hemingway and the Painters' Cubist Style in the *The Sun Also Rises* and *A Farewell to Arms,*" Ph.D. diss. (Ohio University, 1971) and Claude Dangelman, "Proust as a Cubist," *Art History* 2, no. 3 (Sept. 1979): 355–63, and cf. Edward Foye, "Braque's (Real) Art in the 'Still Life with Violin and Pitcher,'" *Artforum* 16, no. 2 (Oct. 1977): 56–58 (bringing in Virginia Woolf) and Archie K. Loss, "Joyce's Use of Collage in 'Aeolus,'" *Journal of Modern Literature* 9, no. 2 (May 1982): 175–82 (comparing Gris and also Severini). The most general argument for this kind of analogy is now that of Wendy Steiner, *The Colors of Rhetoric: Problems in the Relation between Modern Literature and Painting* (Chicago, 1982), which includes a "historiography" with respect to Cubism (chap. 3).

    J. Jacobus, *Twentieth Century Architecture, The Middle Years 1940–65* (New York, 1966), pp. 15, 22; R. Banham, *Theory and Design in the Machine Age* (London and New York, 1960), chap. 15, "Architecture and the Cubist Tradition"; S. Giedion, *Space, Time and Architecture* (1938–39 lectures) (Cambridge Mass., 1941, rev. ed., 1949), pp. 346, 367–82; V. Scully, *Frank Lloyd Wright* (New York, 1960), p. 23. A seminar paper on Wright written for me by J. Garcia Bryce (1963) was helpful on this subject, and see also H. Sting, *Der Kubismus und sein Einwerkung auf die Wegbereiter der modernen Architektur* (dissertation, Aaachen, 1975), and for another way in which the term has been applied in this field, Ivan Margolius, *Cubism in Architecture and the Applied Arts, Bohemia and France, 1910–14* (Newton Abbot and London, 1979) (with a chapter on Raymond Duchamp-Villon's "Maison Cubiste" for 1912 Salon d'Automne). S. Lawder, *The Cubist Cinema* (New York, 1975). The impact of Cubism on photography has not be considered, since it belongs to developments in the U.S.A. rather than Europe; but see on this subject the exhbn. cat. *Cubism and American Photography 1910–30,* text by John Pulz and Catherine B. Scallen, Clark Art Institute (Williamstown and George Eastman House, Rochester, N.Y. and elsewhere, Oct. 1981–Oct. 1982). F. Carmody, Ph.D. diss. (University of California, 1954), cited in Fry's bibl., and cf. also his "L'esthétique de l'esprit nouveau," *Le flâneur des deux rives* 2, nos. 7–8 (Sept.–Dec. 1955): 11ff. (dating Cubism in literature 1912–1919).

    Review of Marinetti in *Fantasio* (Paris, 1912), p. 541 and G. Polti, "Romantisme et Symbolisme ou d'un Cubisme littéraire," *Horizons* 1 (Feb. 15, 1912): 21–22; F. Lefèvre, *La jeune poésie française* (Paris, 1917), pp. 189ff.; A. Malraux, "Des origines de la poésie cubiste" *La Connaissance* 1 (Jan. 1920): 38ff., partially repr. in

Pierre Reverdy (1889–1960), Mercure de France (special no., Jan. 1962): 27; Picasso, report of F. Fels, *Propos d'artistes* (Paris, 1925), p. 145; Reverdy interview, *Figaro littéraire* (May 5, 1956): 4, and J. Cassou, "Reverdy poète cubiste" in *Hommage à Pierre Reverdy*, ed. L. Decaune (*Entretiens* 20 [Nov. 1961], Rodez, 1961), pp. 63ff. Guimey's book (Geneva, 1972) includes chapters on Apollinaire, Reverdy and Jacob, focusing on works of theirs first published in 1917–18, and one on Gide's *Les Faux-Monnayeurs*, first mentioned by him in 1919. See also V. D. Barooshian, *Russian Cubo-Futurism 1910–1930, A Study in Avant-Gardism* (The Hague and Paris, 1974) with rather little in it on Cubism, apart from general references to its application to poetry.

The poetry of the Chilean Vicente Huidobro, as well as that of Reverdy, has been taken up more recently in this connection by George Yudice, "Cubist Aesthetics in Painting and Poetry," *Semiotica* 36, nos. 1–2 (1981): 106–33 (using an "intertextual" approach); and see also the discussion of those two poets, particularly in terms of their personal relations with Gris, in Christopher Green, "Purity, Poetry and the Paintings of Juan Gris," *Art History* 5, no. 2 (Jun. 1982): 180–204, sequel to the article cited in the notes to chap. 3 above.

Apollinaire:

Textes inédits, ed. J. Moulin (Geneva, 1952), pp. 126–27; L. C. Breunig, *Guillaume Apollinaire* (New York, 1960), pp. 34–35. For Apollinaire's relationship with Picasso, see Breunig, "Apollinaire as an Early Apologist for Picasso," *Harvard Library Bulletin* 7, no. 3 (1953): 365ff. and R. Reise Hubert, "Apollinaire et Picasso," *Cahiers du Sud* 53, no. 386 (Jan.–Mar. 1966): 22ff. The April 1905 article (replying, in *La revue immoraliste,* to Charles Morice's cat. preface for Picasso's Feb.–Mar. exhbn. at the Galerie Serrurier) is in *Chroniques d'Art* (1960), trans. in *Apollinaire on Art* (1972), pp. 13–14. For Braque's and Reverdy's comments, see F. Steegmuller, *Apollinaire, Poet among the Painters* (London, 1963), pp. 150–51. On Apollinaire's shifting aesthetic, refs. are to P. A. Jannini, *Le avanguardie letterarie nell' idea critica di Guillaume Apollinaire* (Rome, 1971), pp. 103ff. and Breunig, "Apollinaire et le Cubisme," *Revue des Lettres Modernes* 69–70 (Spring 1962): 8–24. See also P. Bergman, *"Modernolatria" et "Simultaneità"* (Uppsala, 1962), pp. 365–68, 383–84, and P. W. Schwarz, *Cubism* (London and New York, 1971), chap. 4. The 1918 interview, ed. and trans. from Spanish by E. A. Hubert, is in *Apollinaire VII, Revue des Lettres Modernes* 183–88, (1968): 185, and the 1912 statement (in a lecture of Sept. 13) was reported by André Billy, *Les Soirées de Paris* (Oct. 1, 1912).

Gertrude Stein:

G. Soule, "New York Letter," *The Little Review* (Chicago) (Mar. 1914): 43–44. E. Wilson, *Axel's Castle* (New York, 1948), end of chap. 1 and chap. 7, pp. 5, 242; Kahnweiler, *Juan Gris* (1968 ed.), pp. 184–85; D. Sutherland, *Gertrude Stein, A Biography of Her Work* (New Haven, 1951), pp. 54–55, 58–59, 71, 77, 85–86, 91, 113, and cf. also E. Sprigge, *Gertrude Stein and Her World* (New York, 1957), p. 70; B. Reid, *Art by Subtraction: A Dissenting Opinion of Gertrude Stein* (Norman, Okla., 1958), p. 163. J. M. Brinnin, *The Third Rose, Gertrude Stein and Her World* (Boston and Toronto, 1959), pp. 62, 72, 126–27, 129ff., 134–35, 138ff., 142ff., 157, 159, 163, and cf. also M. J. Hoffmann, *The Development of Abstractionism in the Writings of Gertrude Stein* (Philadelphia, Pa., 1965), pp. 26–27, 162, 169–70, 176. N. Weinstein, *Gertrude Stein and the Literature of Modern Consciousness* (New York, 1970), esp. pp. 21–22. See further R. Bridgman,*Gertrude Stein in Pieces* (Oxford, 1970), pp. 117, 222, 228 (relations with avant-garde); V. Thomson, "A Very Difficult Author," *New York Review of Books* 16, no. 6 (Apr. 8, 1971): 3ff. and subsequent correspondence (Jun. 3): 41 and (Jul. 1): 40 (on explaining the relationship to Cubism); L. T. Fitz, "Gertrude Stein and Picasso: The Language of Surfaces," *American Literature* 45 (May 1973): 223–37; M. Gaddon Rose, "Gertrude Stein and the Cubist Narrative,"

Modern Fiction Studies 22 (1976–77): 543–55; W. Steiner, *Exact Resemblance to Exact Resemblance, The Literary Portraiture of Gertrude Stein* (New Haven, Conn. and London, 1978), chap. 4, "Literary Cubism: The Limits of an Analogy"; M. Perloff, "Poetry as Word-System: The Art of Gertrude Stein," *American Poetry Review* 8 (1979): 33–43; and M. DeKoven, "Gertrude Stein and Modern Painting: Beyond Literary Criticism," *Contemporary Literature* 22 (1981): 81–95. The statement quoted (1946) about Cézanne is from R. B. Haas, "Gertrude Stein Talking, A Transatlantic Interview," part 1, *Uclan Review* (Summer 1962), pp. 8–9 (Katz [1970], p. 52); those of Braque and Salmon are in "Testimony against Gertrude Stein," suppl. to *Transition* 33 (Jul. 1935): 15, 17.

Intermezzo. Traditional Approaches

iii. Subject Matter and Meaning

Panofsky's treatments of the subject: "Zum Problem des Beschreibung und Inhaltsdeutung von Werken der bildenden Kunst," *Logos* 31, no. 2 (1932): 103ff., trans. into Italian as "Sul problema della descrizione e dell' interpretazione del contenuto di opere d'arte figurative," in *La prospettiva come forma simbolica e altri scritti*, ed. G. D. Neri (Milan, 1961), pp. 215ff.; *Studies in Iconology: Humanistic Themes in the Art of the Renaissance* (Oxford, 1939), "Introductory," pp. 3ff.; *Meaning in the Visual Arts* (New York, 1955), chap. 1, "Iconography and Iconology: An Introduction to the Study of Renaissance Art," #1.

The change discussed between the 1939 and 1955 versions is one pointed out by J. Margolis, *The Language of Art and Art Criticism* (Detroit, 1965), pp. 79–80. On Panofsky's theoretical scheme, see also Renate Heidt, *Erwin Panofsky—Kunsttheorie und Einzelwerk* (Cologne and Vienna, 1977), and the critique of the texts considered here from a structuralist viewpoint by Christine Hasenmuller, "Panofsky, Iconography and Semiotics," *Journal of Aesthetics and Art Criticism* 36, no. 3 (Spring 1978): 289–301.

Intermezzo. Traditional Approaches

iv. Representation, Perception and Reading

Gombrich on Cubism: *Art and Illusion, A Study in the Psychology of Pictorial Representation* (Mellon Lectures in Fine Arts, 1956) (New York, 1960), pp. 281–85; "Psychoanalysis and the History of Art" (1953), *International Journal of Psycho-Analysis* 35 (1954): 401ff., repr. in *Meditations on a Hobby Horse* (London, 1971), pp. 40–42; "How to Read a Painting," *Saturday Evening Post* (Jul. 29, 1961): 20–21, repr. in *Meditations*, p. 152.

Though there have been some critical reviews of *Art and Illusion* as a whole (e.g., that of Nelson Goodman, *Journal of Philosophy* 57 [1960]: 595ff.), the only discussion known to me which looks critically at the treatment of Cubism is that of E. Bedford, "Seeing Paintings," *Proceedings of Aristotelian Society,* suppl. 40 (1966): 59–61.

Further refs. in *Art and Illusion:* pp. 253 (stance towards philosophy), 238 (ambiguity, as illustrated by the duck-rabbit, p. 5 and fig. 2), 182 (Apollonius of Tyana), 260 (picture and castle), 279 (on Maurice Denis's statement), 190 and fig. 158 (Mantegna), 235 and fig. 194 (Fabian poster), 248–49 and fig. 213 (Ames experiments), 232 (artist's intention). See also pp. 105 and fig. 75 (Rorschach blot), 244 and fig. 210 (Escher).

Ambiguity in analytical Cubism: see Rosenblum, *Cubism and Twentieth Century Art* (New York, 1960), pp. 57–58, 66; C. Greenberg, "Collage" (1958), in his *Art and Culture* (Boston, 1961), pp. 73–74.

Ambiguity in literature: see F. C. Prescott, *The Poetic Mind* (New York, 1922), chap. 11, "The Imagination" (using Freud's *Interpretation of Dreams* and theory of wit), p. 175; W. Empson, *Seven Types of Ambiguity* (London, 1930), also using Freud. Empson's third type corresponds to the first dictionary sense, while his fifth and sixth are related between them to the second dictionary sense, Empson's concern is frequently, however, with what may be called additional nuances rather than ambiguity; see here his preface to the second, revised ed., where he gives as criterion for the use of the term the fact that someone might be puzzled as to what was meant; A. Harrison, "Poetic Ambiguity," *Analysis* 23 (1962): 54ff. For practical instances of its use, see further the analyses by Randall Jarrell, "Texts from Housman," *Kenyon Review* 1 (1939): 260ff. (associating ambiguity with compression, irony, paradox); R. Shattuck, *The Banquet Years* (rev. ed., New York, 1968), pp. 36, 243–44 (using the term in the two different senses in question).

Ambiguity in psychoanalytic theory and theory of symbolism: see especially E. Kris and A. Kaplan, "Aesthetic Ambiguity," *Philosophical and Phenomenological Research* 8 (1948): 415ff., repr. in *Psychoanalytic Explorations in Art,* ed. Kris (New York, 1952), Part 4, "Problems of Literary Criticism" (an attempted revision of Empson for this purpose).

Ambiguity as applying to language generally: see, e.g., A. Kaplan, "An Experimental Study of Ambiguity and Context," *Mechanical Translation* 2 (1955): 39ff. Cf. also here M. Beardsley, "Textural Meaning and Authorial Meaning," *Genre* 1 (1968): 169ff., repr. in his *The Possibility of Criticism* (Detroit, 1970), as chap. 1, "The Authority of the Text." In the light of the distinction made there (p. 30, replying to E. D. Hirsch, Jr.) between the indefinite (or unspecific) and the indeterminate, the claim in structural linguistics and semantics that all syntactical phrases are inherently ambiguous would be better phrased in terms of indeterminacy—resulting either from lack of assisting context, or from being like a coded message without a base. Gombrich's general claim that all images are inherently ambiguous (*Art and Illusion,* p. 249) is of a corresponding kind.

For the technical sense of ambiguity in visual psychology referred to, see R. L. Gregory, *The Intelligent Eye* (London, 1970), pp. 37ff. ("ambiguous figures" in general, going back to those devised in the 19th century by Necker, Schroder, Mach and Rubin); E. G. Boring, "A New Ambiguous Figure," *American Journal of Psychology* 42 (1930): 444–45 (a figure yielding two different readings, in the same way the duck-rabbit does); K. Koffka, *Principles of Gestalt Psychology* (New York, 1935), pp. 183ff. (adopting the term, which has no exact German equivalent); G. H. Fisher, "Measuring Ambiguity," *American Journal of Psychology* 80 (1967): 541ff., and "Who Overlooks the Fat Woman [by Beardsley]?" *British Journal of Aesthetics* 8 (1968): 394ff. The ambiguity of the duck-rabbit is indexed in *Art and Illusion* as deliberate (p. 5) and also as hidden, meaning evidently that it cannot be seen as such (p. 238, see also pp. 259, 263).

The two dictionary senses given are from *Webster's New World Dictionary.*

For Delaunay's *City of Paris,* see J. Golding, *Cubism* (London, 1959), pl. 69B. Herbert Read on Synthetic Cubism: "The Situation of Art in Europe at the End of the Second World War" (1948), in his *The Philosophy of Modern Art* (New York, 1955), p. 42. Picasso's teasing of Braque: see the story as reported by Françoise Gilot, *Life with Picasso* (New York, 1964), p. 69. Sir Ernst, in correspondence, confirmed its appropriateness to his interpretation of Cubism.

Chapter 5. The Artist's Intentions and Some Related Issues

Intention in Literary Theory and in Philosophy

Lawrence: the phrase quoted is from "The Spirit of Place," in *Studies in Classic American Literature* (London, 1923), p. 3, and is to be understood in the context of that essay.

Leavis: the phrase "deep animating intention" is found in *The Common Pursuit* (London, 1952), p. 224. On the question of sincerity in a work of art, see also the approach of Lionel Trilling, *Sincerity and Authenticity* (Cambridge, Mass., 1972), pp. 10–11.

Yeats, Pound, Eliot: for a definition of their role here, cf. Donald Davie, *Thomas Hardy and British Poetry* (Oxford, 1972), p. 136. The relevant early texts of Eliot's are "Tradition and the Individual Talent" (1919) (doctrine of impersonality, emphasis on the poem rather than the poet: *Selected Essays* [1932], p. 22) and "The Function of Criticism" (1923) (work of art as autotelic, ibid., p. 19). On their contribution and that of the New Criticism, cf. the remarks of F. Kermode, *Romantic Image* (London, 1964 ed.), pp. 154–56, and those of M. Bradbury, "The State of Criticism Today," introdn. to *Literary Criticism,* Stratford-upon-Avon Studies 13 (1970): part 1.

Edmund Wilson on *The Turn of the Screw:* "The Ambiguity of Henry James," *Hound and Horn* 7 (1934): 385–406, repr. in his *The Triple Thinkers* (New York, 1938), pp. 122–64. For the ongoing discussion of this interpretation, which has generated a very extensive literature, see G. Willen ed., *A Casebook of Henry James's The Turn of the Screw* (New York, 1960) (reprinting key contributions), the summarizing evaluation of D. Krook, *The Ordeal of Consciousness in Henry James* (Cambridge, 1962) (her 1974 essay, listed in the bibl., relates this case history specifically to the present topic), and the more recent book-length study of E. A. Sheppard, *Henry James and The Turn of the Screw* (Oxford, 1975).

Expansive conception of intention in recent times: for philosophy, see L. Wittgenstein, *Zettel* (1945–48) (Oxford, 1967), #23, 45, 48, 235, 532 and *Philosophical Investigations* (Oxford, 1953), part 1, #591, part 2, p. 214 (varying uses of term); J. L. Austin, "Three Ways of Spilling Ink" (1958), *Philosophical Review* 75 (1966): 437–39 ("bracketing" sense of the term) and also J. Passmore, "Intentions," *Proceedings of Aristotelian Society,* suppl. 29 (1955): 131ff., A. I. Melden, *Free Action* (New York, 1961), pp. 101–2 and M. Bratman, "Intention and Means-End Reasoning," *Philosophical Review* 90, no. 2 (April 1981): 252–65 (implications of coherence, order and pattern); Austin, *How to Do Things with Words* (1955) (Cambridge, Mass., 1962), chap. 12 (ways of making a commitment) and B. Aune, "Intention," *Encyclopedia of Philosophy,* vol. 4 (New York, 1967), pp. 198ff. (the ascribing of intentions); S. Hampshire and H. L. A. Hart, "Decision, Intention and Certainty," *Mind* 67 (1958): 5–6 (recognition of uses involving meaning and reference); P. F. Strawson, "Intention and Convention in Speech Acts," *Philosophical Review* 73 (1964): 450 and J. R. Searle, *Speech Acts* (Cambridge, 1969), chap. 2, #6 ("uptake"). For critical theory see esp. W. K. Wimsatt and M. Beardsley, "The Intentional Fallacy" (1946), repr. in Wimsatt, *The Verbal Icon* (Lexington, 1954), as chap. 1, #4 and F. Cioffi, "Intention and Interpretation in Criticism," *Proceedings of Aristotelian Society* 64 (1963–64): 85ff.—in contrast to the restrictive definitions cited: I. A. Richards, *Practical Criticism* (London, 1929), part. 3, chap. 1, #4 and Wimsatt and Beardsley, #1.

Intentional Statements and Statements of Intention

Cf. for the latter J. L. Austin, *How to Do Things with Words,* pp. 150–51, 156–57, where what he calls "commissives" are discussed and a longer list of verbs is given.

Examples of first-person statements by artists:

Nolde (to a critic who said his work should be milder to sell): Emil Nolde, *Jahre der Kämpfe* (2d vol. of autobiography, 1902–14) (Berlin, 1934), p. 44.

Pollock: from his narration for the film of Hans Namuth, "Jackson Pollock" (1951), repr. in B. Robertson, *Jackson Pollock* (New York, 1961), p. 194.

van Gogh: letter 524 to his brother, Aug. 1888, *Complete Letters of Vincent van Gogh* (New York, 1958), 3 : 17.

Reported statement on van Gogh's portrait of Mme Ginoux (*L'Arlésienne,* De La Faille no. 488), G. Coquiot, *Vincent van Gogh* (Paris, 1923), pp. 187–88.

Picasso on *Guernica:* interview with Jerome Seckler (1945), publ. as "Picasso Explains," *New Masses* (Mar. 13, 1945), and repr. in A. Barr, *Picasso, Fifty Years of His Art* (New York, 1946), p. 268.

On a drawing of Picasso's: P. Daix, "Il n'y a pas d'art nègre dans les 'Demoiselles d'Avignon'", *Gazette des Beaux Arts,* 6 sér. 76 (1970): 258–59. The drawing in question is Zervos, 6. 962, from ca. 1907. For Picasso's previous denials see Zervos, 2. 1, text for pl. 11 and Daix, p. 247 n. 3.

Rauschenberg: statement printed in exhbn. cat. *Sixteen Americans,* Museum of Modern Art (New York, 1959), p. 58.

Modersohn-Becker: diary entry for Oct. 1, 1902, in *Briefe und Tagebuchblätter von Paula Modersohn-Becker,* ed. S. D. Gallwitz (Linz, 1920), p. 177.

David: E. J. Délécluze, *Louis David, son école et son temps* (Paris, 1855), pp. 225–26. "Expressive painting" is, in the French, "peinture d'expression."

Millet: leter of Feb. 18, 1862, in É. Moreau-Nélaton, *Millet raconté par lui-même,* 2 vols. (Paris, 1921), 2 : 106–7.

Bacon: statement printed in exhbn. cat. *The New Decade: 22 European Painters and Sculptors,* Museum of Modern Art (New York, 1955), p. 63.

Castagno: *New York Times* (Jan. 3, 1971), "Art Mailbag," sec. 2, p. 21.

On the idea of a psychological state behind intentions: J. F. M. Hunter, "How do you mean?" *University of Toronto Quarterly* 38, no. 1 (1968), repr. in rev. form in his *Essays after Wittgenstein* (Toronto, 1973), pp. 9–10, 14, makes a similar critical point about the idea that saying something has to be preceeded by meaning to say it; and see also D. Gustafson, "Passivity and Activity in Intentional Actions," *Mind* 90 (Jan. 1981): 52, agreeing that one cannot speak of such an antecedent, separable state.

The Object-predicated Use of the Term Intention

T. S. Eliot: "Rudyard Kipling" (1941), *On Poetry and Poets* (London, 1957), p. 251.

G. Lukacs: "Die weltanschaulichen Grundlagen des Avantgardismus" (1955), publ. under 1956 title "Die Gegenwartsbedeutung des kritischen Realismus" in *Werke,* (1971), 4:469, and in English as "The Ideology of Modernism," in *Realism in Our Time,* trans. J. and N. Mander (New York, 1964), p. 19. The German uses *Intention* for the work, *bewussten Absicht* for the author as contrasting terms; and it is interesting that *Intention* represents a relatively recent alternative to *Absicht* or *Vorhaben* in the German language, not listed in older dictionaries and only in some recent ones.

E. Panofsky, "Der Begriff des Kunstwollens," *Zeitschrift fur Aesthetik und allegemeine Kunstwissenschaft* 14 (1920): 320ff.; trans. K. J. Northcott and J. Snyder as "The Concept of Artistic Volition," *Critical Inquiry* 8, no. 1 (Autumn 1981): 17–37; and cf. the later essay "The History of Art as a Humanistic Discipline" (1940), repr. as Introdn. to *Meaning in the Visual Arts* (New York, 1955), #3.

Lexical background to this usage: for lack of a Latin equivalent, see A. Berger, *Encyclopedic Dictionary of Roman Law* (Philadelphia, 1953), pp. 362, 408, 770–71, and the use of such phrases in lieu as *in mente habebat, eo animo ut* or *quid velit* (I am grateful to E. J. Kenney for help on this subject). For the connotations of *intentio* and *intendere,* see standard Latin dictionaries and also, for medieval Latin, Conradus

Hirsaugienis (ca. 1070–1150), *Dialogus super auctores,* where the *intentio* of the author is distinguished from the *finalis causa,* or divine intention.

For the 16th–19th century usages referred to, see Spenser's letter to Sir Walter Raleigh of Jan. 23, 1589 prefacing *The Faerie Queene:* "the general intention and meaning [of the allegory]" and also "the whole intention of the conceit" (*Works of Edmund Spenser,* ed. E. Greenlaw et al. [Oxford, 1932], 1:167, 170); and the references in the *Oxford English Dictionary* under *Intent* 6 (Chatham, 1754; Kinglake, 1863, corresponding to *intentio plebium* in medieval Latin) and *Intention* 6 (Reid, 1773; Morley, 1878). Cf. also the entries there for the now obsolete *Intendment* 4, used of the law in the same manner as *Intent* 5b, and 5, used (1703) on exactly the same lines as *sic intendit.* My knowledge of the latter medieval usage I owe to Mary Sirridge.

For representative examples of confusion or ambivalence between the two uses of intention, see H. Gardner, *The Business of Criticism* (Oxford, 1959), pp. 74–75, and Davie, *Thomas Hardy and British Poetry* (1972), p. 110; and for the kind of free construction that can be put on the terms, W. Elton, *A Glossary of the New Criticism* (Chicago, [1948], s.v. *intention;* M. Benamou, *Wallace Stevens and the Symbolist Imagination* (Princeton, N.J., 1972), p. xviii.

For "realized" and "enacted" intention, see Leavis, *The Common Pursuit* (1952), p. 224 and Krook (1974). For the intention of a myth, see S. Cavell, "Music Discomposed," appended reply to Beardsley and Margolis, in *Art, Mind and Religion,* ed. W. Capetan and D. D. Merrill (Pittsburgh, 1967), p. 130, repr. as "A Matter of Meaning It" in his *Must We Mean What We Say?* (New York, 1969), p. 236 (one of several uses of intention which are disposed through this essay but not coordinated); for "artistic intentions" and the "real intention" of a style in art history, see J. Golding, *Cubism, A History and Analysis* (pref. to 1968 ed.), p. 7. For the intention of an appliance, see Wittgenstein, *Zettel,* #48; for the intention of a work of art as its "point," C. Downes, "Perfection as an Aesthetic Predicate," in *Art and Philosophy, A Symposium,* ed. S. Hook (New York, 1966), p. 37. The analogy of a move in chess I owe to Searle, *Speech Acts* (1969), p. 43; the suggestion of an equivalent to the Latin *quo tendit* to Sydney Freedberg. For the Latin *propositio* used of a life, see Cicero, *Tusc. Disp.* 3.18.39: hujus vitae propositio et cogitatio. The parallels of the editorial "we" and "this means war" were suggested by Gareth Matthews.

Gauguin on his approach to symbolism: letter to Charles Morice (July 1901), *Lettres de Gauguin à sa femme et ses amis,* ed. M. Malingue (Paris, 1946), no. 174, pp. 300–301.

Henry Moore on psychoanalytic readings of his sculptures: see his reaction to Erich Neumann's book, *The Archetypal World of Henry Moore* (London, 1959), as described in a 1962 interview, repr. in *Henry Moore on Sculpture,* ed. P. James (rev. and expanded ed., New York, 1971), p. 52; and cf. David Sylvester's comment, based on consultation with the artist, that the sexual connotations of the *Two-Piece Reclining Figures* (1959 on) were "not intended," *Henry Moore* (London and New York, 1968), p. 93.

For the case of *Under Milk Wood,* see D. Holbrook, *Llareggub Revisited, Dylan Thomas and the State of Modern Poetry* (Cambridge, 1962), p. 181 and chaps. 8–9 generally.

On the "identity" of a work of art or person: Wisdom comparably writes of showing a work of art "for what it is" and seeing a person "for what he is" in "Things and Persons" (1948), repr. in his *Philosophy and Psychoanalysis* (Oxford, 1969 ed.), pp. 223, 225.

Ascribing an intention to a non-human agency: cf. here the example used by Wisdom, "Gods," in *Philosophy and Psychoanalysis* (1969 ed.), pp. 154–55, of a patch of ground on which plants spring up in an arrangement suggesting a garden, even though there has been no evident sign of any human gardener coming there.

On the uses of the word *meaning,* cf. the related clarifications offered by Austin, "The Meaning of a Word," in *Philosophical Papers* (Oxford, 1961), pp. 23ff., and Wisdom, "The Meaning of the Questions of Life," in *Paradox and Discovery* (New York, 1965), pp. 38–42.

For Kant's conception of works of art as objects of a contemplation "free of utility," see his *Critique of Aesthetic Judgment,* trans. J. C. Meredith (Oxford, 1911), #15, p. 69.

Assent to an interpretation: there are related statements of Wittgenstein's about a kind of conviction which resembles the "faith" that is talked of here (e.g., *On Certainty* [Oxford, 1969], #72ff.), and about what "understanding" something is like (see esp. *Philosophical Investigations* #151ff., 321ff.).

The Question of the Artist's Privileged Status

Examples from literature:

Yeats: see J. Wain, "W. B. Yeats: Among School Children," in *Interpretations,* ed. Wain (London, 1955), pp. 197–99.

Hopkins, "Sonnet on Henry Purcell" (April 1879), *The Letters of Gerard Manley Hopkins to Robert Bridges,* ed. C. C. Abbott (London, 1935), no. 97, (Jan. 4, 1883), pp. 170–71. Cf. letter 60, May 26, 1879, for "moonmarks," and also 98, 99. P. L. Mariani, *A Commentary on the Complete Poems of Gerard Manley Hopkins* (Ithaca, N.Y., 1970), pp. 135–40, brings all the passages together.

"Spring and Fall, to a Young Child" (1880), l.7: I. A. Richards, *Practical Criticism,* poem 6 (1964 ed.), p. 83; W. Empson, *Seven Types of Ambiguity* (New York, 1955 ed.), p. 168 thinks the accent actually intensifies the ambiguity here.

Dickens: Q. D. Leavis, "Bleak House: A Chancery World," in F. R. and Q. D. Leavis, *Dickens the Novelist* (New York, 1970), chap. 3, p. 163.

T. S. Eliot on the notes to *The Waste Land:* "The Frontiers of Criticism" (1956), in *On Poetry and Poets,* pp. 109–10; and see A. Walton Litz, "The Waste Land Fifty Years After," in *Eliot in his Time,* ed. Litz (Princeton, N.J., 1972), pp. 9–10.

On the way critics had interpreted the poem: the statements of Eliot's referred to are in "Thoughts after Lambeth" (1931), in *Selected Essays,* (1932), p. 314; and in *The Waste Land by T. S. Eliot, a facsimile of the original draft,* ed. V. Eliot (London, 1971), p. 1 (report of an undated statement to Theodore Spencer).

Blake: see F. W. Bateson, *English Poetry, A Critical Introduction* (London, 1950), p. 8; *Essays in Criticism* 2 (1952): 105ff. (exchanges between Wain, Robson and Bateson) and 455–56 (Bayley); also 3 (1953): 116ff. (Empson). P. Hobsbaum, *A Theory of Communication* (London, 1970), pp. 210–11, reviews these interpretations and suggest that they are all in fact, in general terms, compatible with one another.

Keats: see J. Middleton Murry, *Studies in Keats* (Oxford, 1930), chap. 5 (rev. and enlarged as *Keats* [New York, 1955], chap. 7), and F. R. Leavis' critical rejoinder, "Keats," *Scrutiny* 4, (1935–36): 376ff., repr. in his *Revaluation* (New York, 1947 ed.), pp. 241ff. (pp. 253–57 refer). For the punctuation of the last two lines of the Ode, and the sense in which they should be taken as a unit, see A. Whitley, "The Message of the Grecian Urn," *Keats-Shelley Memorial Bulletin* 5 (1953): 1–3; E. Wasserman, *The Finer Tone: Keats's Major Poems* (Baltimore, Md., 1953), pp. 58ff. These four discussions are conveniently reprinted together in H. T. Lyon, *Keats's Well-Read Urn: An Introduction to Literary Method* (New York, 1958), as texts nos. 37, 45, 76–77. E. C. Pettet, *On the Poetry of Keats,* (Cambridge, 1957), Appdx. 6, reviews some of these interpretations, and see the correspondence in the *Times Literary Supplement* (Feb.–Apr. 1964): 112, 132, 153, 238, 317, as to whom the Urn addresses. Also more recently I. Jack, *Keats and the Mirror of Art* (Oxford, 1967), chap. 13 and pp. 287–89 n. 42; and M. Mincoff, "Beauty is Truth—Once More," *Modern Language Review* 65 (1970): 267ff.

Melville: letter to Sophia Hawthorne, Jan. 8, 1852, in *The Letters of Herman Melville*, ed. M. R. Davis and W. H. Gilman (New Haven, 1960), p. 146.

Examples from art:

Puvis de Chavannes, reported remark: M. Vachon, *Puvis de Chavannes* (Paris, 1896), p. 58.

Braque, still life mistitled "The Battleship": see exhbn. cat. *G. Braque*, Tate Gallery (London, Sept.–Nov. 1956), no. 20, *Still Life with Dice, Pipe and Glasses*, Eichholz colln.

Kline: interview with David Sylvester (1960), *Living Arts* 1, no. 1 (Spring 1963), p. 10.

For the concept of privileged access in philosophy, see the convenient review by W. Alston, "Varieties of Privileged Access," *American Philosophical Quarterly* 8, no. 3 (1971): 223ff. It includes remarks (p. 232) on how the terms *immediate* knowledge and *direct* knowledge or perception—used by Ayer, Moore, Price, Malcolm and others—are really inappropriate ones.

For the challenges to which a statement of alleged knowledge is liable, see Austin, "Other Minds" (1946), *Philosophical Papers* (1961), pp. 44ff.

"Practical" intentions are discussed by T. M. Gang, *Essays in Criticism* 7 (1957): 175ff., but the examples he gives represent the purpose or raison d'être of a poem (its being written to a lady), and then by extension its tone and the theory behind it; he omits intentions that an artist might describe while working.

The moral obligation that is felt to treat a work of art according to its author's preferences is discussed by S. Gendin, *Journal of Aesthetics and Art Criticism* 23 (1963–64): 193ff.; but his account of the sense of obligation is too broad, especially for the performing arts.

On "I know that I am in pain," see Wittgenstein, *Philosophical Investigations*, Part 1, pp. 89ff., and esp. #246, 408; also *Zettel* (1945–48), #536, 589, and *On Certainty* (1949–51), #41, 389. On anticipations of these remarks in Wittgenstein's earlier thinking, see his *Philosophische Bemerkungen* (1929–30), ed. R. Rhees (Oxford, 1964), Part 6, #57–66; G. E. Moore, "Wittgenstein's Lectures in 1930–33," *Mind* 64 (1955), Part 3, #D, pp. 10–16 (repr. in *Wittgenstein and the Problem of Other Minds*, ed. H. Monck [New York, 1967], pp. 119ff); and the discussion by A. Kenney, *Wittgenstein* (Cambridge, Mass., 1973), chaps. 7, 10. Cf. also the paper of Wisdom, (who attended Wittgenstein's lectures in 1934–37), "Other Minds," *Proceedings of Aristotelian Society* suppl. 20 (1946): 122ff., repr. in his *Other Minds* (Oxford, 1953), pp. 192ff., with summary 218–19; and his "Other Minds, VII," *Mind* 52 (1943): 193ff., repr. in the same book, pp. 118ff. The examples of pain and anger are both used there (pp. 158, 218).

Wittgenstein also has a parallel remark about thinking in Part 2 of the *Philosophical Investigations* (xi, p. 222). For dissatisfaction with the argument about pain and the responses to it cited, see Austin, "Other Minds" (reply to Wisdom's 1946 paper), *Philosophical Papers* (1961): 65, 78; Searle, *Speech Acts* (1969), p. 141, J. W. Cook, "Wittgenstein on Privacy," *Philosophical Review* 74 (1965): 285, and Allston (1971), pp. 223ff.; A. R. White, "Mentioning the Unmentionable" (1967) in *Symposium on J. L. Austin*, ed. K. T. Fann (London, 1969), p. 224.

On "the meaning is in the poem," cf. S. Cavell, "Aesthetic Problems in Modern Philosophy" (1962–66), in *Must We Mean What We Say?* (1969), pp. 74ff., where however the poem's meaning is equated with what a paraphrase would convey. On what a person "really means," cf. Erik Erikson, *Young Man Luther* (New York, 1962 ed.), chap. 6, "The Meaning of Meaning It," esp. p. 210.

The Evaluation of Intentions and Their Critical Use

On suspected cases of witting or unwitting deception and the procedures for dealing with them, cf. Austin, "Other Minds," pp. 80–81. The concept of "defeasibility" has been adopted from H. L. A. Hart, "The Ascription of Rights and Duties," *Proceedings of Aristotelian Society* 49 (1948–49): 171ff.

For psychological and contextual factors affecting the value of what the artist says, cf. R. Arnheim, *Picasso's Guernica* (Berkeley, Calif., 1962), p. 13. For Kirchner's claims (Diary, unpub., March 6, 1923, pp. 136ff.; *Chronik K. G. Brücke* [1913], and *Die Arbeit E. L. Kirchners,* catalogue of Bern exhibition [1954–55], p. 8) see D. Gordon, *Ernst Ludwig Kirchner* (Cambridge, Mass., 1968), pp. 21, 28, 456 n.43, and 458 n.93. For retrospective rationalization on the part of artists, cf. M. Roskill, *Van Gogh, Gauguin and the Impressionist Circle* (London, 1970), pp. 204–6. For Gorky's use of Gaudier-Brzeska's letters (E. Schwabacher, *Arshile Gorky* [New York, 1947], letters of 1941, pp. 85–86 and 109–10, based in fact on H. S. Ede, *Savage Messiah* [London, 1931], pp. 148, 164, 187–89 and 197–98), see N. D. Vaccaro, "Gorky's Debt to Gaudier-Brzeska," *Art Journal* 23, no. 1 (1963): 33–34.

Dürrenmatt: remark reported in an anon. review, *Times Literary Supplement* (Oct. 27, 1972): 1285. Constable, reply to Blake: C. R. Leslie, *Memoirs of the Life of John Constable,* ed. J. Mayne (London, 1951), p. 280. Beckmann: see P. T. Rathbone, "Max Beckmann, in America: A Personal Reminiscence," in P. Selz, *Max Beckmann,* exhbn. cat., Museum of Modern Art (New York, 1964), p. 128. Gris, injunction to Ozenfant, *Mémoires 1886–1902* (Paris, 1968), p. 132 (report of a remembered conversation, or more likely the gist of several parallel discussions). Kline: see 1960 interview cited earlier, p. 7. T. S. Eliot (to whom the phrase "playing possum" is particularly appropriate), on Rupert Doone's production of *Sweeney Agonistes:* see the dialogue with him recorded from memory by Nevill Coghill, in *T. S. Eliot, A Symposium,* ed. R. March and Tabimuttu (London, 1948), pp. 85–86. The identity of "B. Traven," author of *The Death Ship* and *Treasure of Sierra Madre,* is known only at second hand or by guesswork: see Michael Baumann, *B. Traven: An Introduction* (Albuquerque, N.M., 1976). For Salinger's attitude, see the front page story reporting on it, *New York Times* (Sun. Nov. 3, 1974): 1, 69.

For the argument of needing to know what the artist intended in order to measure his success (put forward as if it were commonsense), see Richards, *Practical Criticism* (1964 ed.), p. 182.

Gatsby's resolves: see F. Scott Fitzgerald, *The Great Gatsby* (Harmondsworth, Middsx., 1950), p. 180.

For unrealized and unfulfilled intentions, see Wimsatt and Beardsley's 1944 formulation on the twin topics taken up in this section ("Intention," *Dictionary of World Literature* [New York, 1944], pp. 326ff., cited by T. Redpath, "The Meaning of a Poem," in *Collected Papers on Aesthetics,* ed. W. Barrett [Oxford, 1965], p. 146). Their modified and more familiar 1946 formulation (*The Verbal Icon* [1970 ed.], p. 4) stated now as applying to judgment and specifically to the judgment of success and failure, seems unexceptionable insofar as it reduces itself to: whether the work as we have it succeeds or fails can only be judged in terms of what we have. For the possibility of an unfulfilled potential being evident in the work itself, cf. G. E. Yoos, "A Work of Art as a Standard of Itself," *Journal of Aesthetics and Art Criticism* 26 (1967): 81ff. I am grateful to Mary Sirridge for showing me a paper of hers which answers Beardsley's 1958 formulation (*Aesthetics: Problems in the Philosophy of Criticism,* part 1, chap. 1) with similar counter-examples and a presentation of the position opposed there which reduces it to a virtual caricature of relativism.

Van Gogh: letter 253 to his brother, *Complete Letters*, 1:513.
Osbert Sitwell: from his *Laughter in the Next Room* (London, 1948), pp. 207–8.
On the notes to *The Waste Land*, cf. here Cioffi, in *Collected Papers on Aesthetics*, ed. Barrett (1965), p. 171 (for the concept of their efficacy).

Chapter 6. On the Recognition and Identification of Objects in Paintings

Braque's statement used as epigraph is from his interview with John Richardson, *The Observer* (London) (Dec. 1, 1957).

Perception of art and of the real world: the use of the term "aesthetic" in front of vision, perception, object, appearance and so on begs a large question here; less so when it is used to differentiate situations and contexts, though there too there may be a temptation to posit conditions or circumstances that are special in the sense of otherwise unparalleled.

On the Workings of Imagination and Suggestion

On the stick in the water and the coin which "looks elliptical," cf. J. L. Austin, *Sense and Sensibilia* (Oxford, 1962), pp. 26, 30 (criticizing Ayer).

On "seeing as": the extensive literature on the general question referred to, of whether all seeing is to be regarded as "seeing as," has centered on talk of alternative "aspects" that are perceived, and has basically to do, as in Gestalt psychology, with the formal organization of perception. It has also been generally supposed that the use of "seeing as" must reflect an additional or special reason for making a claim in that form as to what one is seeing.

On the "dissociative" implication of "seeing as," cf. E. M. Wolgast's discussion of "It was [just] as if I were seeing . . . ," "Perceiving and Impressions," *Philosophical Review* 67 (1958): 229, 236. The example used of the Surrealist double image is Dali's *Apparition of a Face and Fruit Dish on a Beach* (1938); cf. his *Anthropomorphic Cabinet* (1936) (both woman's body and drawers), ill. in A. Reynolds Morse, *Salvador Dali* (Greenwich, Conn., 1965), cat. nos. 72, 90. An excellent example of the "flight of fancy" type of case is provided by G. Matthews, "Mental Copies," *Philosophical Review* 78 (1969): 59–61: seeing the White House decked in gold trim, as a decorator might use this phrasing—to indicate the way he visualized it, as distinct for example from what one might dream, or see from looking into the future.

On responses to music, the basic text for later discussion has remained Edouard Hanslick's *Von musikalische-schönen* (Leipzig, 1854), together with his own later reconsiderations on the subject; 7th ed., 1885, trans. G. Cohen, as *The Beautiful in Music* (London, 1891), ed. and introd. M. Weitz (Indianapolis, Ind., 1957). See also the valuable as well as sympathetic characterization of different ways of listening to Beethoven's Fifth Symphony in E. M. Forster's novel *Howards End* (1910), chap. 5, where the kind of imaginative construction which Hanslick opposed is portrayed in a way which brings out its relation to the music's development.

For the example of gasoline looking like water, cf. Austin, *Sense and Sensibilia*, pp. 39–40, 43.

How the Identity of an Object May Be Unclear

For "appears to be" being typically used to refer to special circumstances, as distinct from "looks" and "seems," see Austin, *Sense and Sensibilia*, pp. 36–37.

Roses: this example draws on what actually took place with the orientation of a Cézanne watercolor of that subject, given to the Fogg Art Museum.

Ambiguity: *Webster's New World Dictionary* gives as definitions for *ambiguous*

(1) having two or more possible meanings (2) not clear, uncertain or vague. Gombrich's use of the term and its special sense for literature are discussed in Intermezzo iv.

Derisive and indignant remarks: there especially come to mind here reports—they are only that—of people's behavior at the time in front of Manet's paintings, and of the public looking for whiskers in the case of Franz Marc's *Mandrill.* For Louis Leroy's quoted comment on Monet's *Boulevard des Capucines,* when it was shown in the First Impressionist Exhibition of 1874 ("L'exposition des impressionistes," *Charivari* [Apr. 25, 1874]), see J. Rewald, *The History of Impressionism* (New York, 1961 ed.), p. 320.

On the Resolution of Difficulties and Hesitations

Autonomy of the work of art: the arguments on this subject go back at least to Kant. See esp. his *Critique of Aesthetic Judgment* (1790), ed. J. C. Meredith (Oxford, 1911), Bk. 2, #43. Further consideration of the third type of definition is to be found in David J. Gordon, "The Story of a Critical Idea," *Partisian Review* 47, no. 1 (1980): 93–108; and see also for poetry B. Herrnstein Smith, "Literature as Performance, Fiction and Art" (review of Nelson Goodman, *Languages of Art*), *Journal of Philosophy,* 47 (1970): 553–63, repr. in her *On the Margins of Discourse, The Relation of Literature to Language* (Chicago, 1978), as chap. 3, pp. 10–11.

"Primary" basis of recognition: Panofsky's full schematic framework on this subject, most familiar from the Introdn. to his 1939 *Studies in Iconology,* or the somewhat revised version in his 1955 *Meaning in the Visual Arts,* is separately reviewed in Intermezzo iii.

The Question of Authority in Resolving Difficulties

"Non-predictivity" of statements about works of art: this again goes back to Kant's *Critique of Aesthetic Judgment,* esp. Bk. I, #10 ("purposiveness without purpose" in works of art).

On knowledge as against certainty, see Austin, "Other Minds" (1946), *Philosophical Papers* (Oxford, 1961), p. 67, and Wittgenstein, *On Certainty* (Oxford, 1969), esp. #56, 243, 245, 308, 357, and for first and third person declarations of certainty distinguished, #194, 272, 386.

Examples from painting:

Gauguin's *Self-portrait with Yellow Christ* and Pissarro's *Self-portrait:* M. Roskill, *Van Gogh, Gauguin and the Impressionist Circle* (London, 1970), pls. 31, 38 and pp. 48, 54. For color reprodns., see Roskill, pl. 6, and G. Bazin, *Impressionist Paintings in the Louvre* (London, 1958), facing p. 32.

Picasso, *Portrait of Kahnweiler:* J. Richardson, introdn. to *Picasso, An American Tribute,* exhbn. cat. (New York, Apr.–May 1962), n. p. (citing Picasso); E. Fry, "Cubism, 1907–1908; An Early Eyewitness Account," *Art Bulletin* 48 (1966), pp. 72–73 (comparative photo of sculpture owned by Picasso), and cf. his *Cubism* (1966), pp. 21–22, and ills. 29, 54, with a color reprodn. of the portrait, pl. 3.

Recognizable images painted out: this is known to be true of the work of Kupka ca. 1910. For Kandinsky and Mondrian as discussed, see most recently R. C. Washton Long, "Kandinsky and Abstraction: The Role of the Hidden Image," *Artforum* 10, no. 10 (Jun. 1972): 42ff.; R. P. Welsh, "The Subject Matter of Abstraction, The Birth of De Stijl, Part I, Piet Mondrian," *Artforum* 11, no. 8 (Apr. 1973): 50–53.

On Freud and sexual symbolism, see now J. Spector, *The Aesthetics of Freud* (New York, 1972), pp. 95–97.

The Move towards Recognition and Identification

Examples from art:

Matisse, *Still Life:* see E. G. Carlson, "Still Life with Statuette by Henri Matisse," *Yale University Art Gallery Bulletin* 31, no. 2 (spring 1967): 4–13 and the earlier characterization by Barr of the background which he quotes, *Matisse, His Art and his Public* (New York, 1951), p. 93.

Picasso, *Still Life with a Skull* (D 172): R. Rosenblum, *Cubism and Twentieth Century Art* (New York, 1960), pl. 2 (color) and p. 26, calling it a mirror. It is in fact a version of the *Standing Nude* now in the Boston Museum of Fine Arts (D 116): I owe this point from many years back now to the late Frederick Deknatel, who dated the painting to early 1908 and suggested a possible need to emend the date of the *Still Life* accordingly. See now his posthumously publ. article "Picasso's 'Standing Figure,'" *Bulletin of Museum of Fine Arts, Boston* 76 (1978): 60 n. 11 and the acceptance of both points by Daix in his 1979 cat. Rosenblum in his latest edition (1977) had meanwhile accepted the suggestion of Fry—bridging the two alternatives—that the Boston painting is shown reflected in a mirror; but the shape of the breasts is distinctly different, as well as the colors; and it could equally be a lost version, unreversed, of the leftmost figure in D 123.

Picasso, *The Accordionist,* summer 1911 (Céret): see Barr, *Picasso, Fifty Years of His Art* (New York, 1946), p. 74.

Story of the squirrel in Braque's painting: see Françoise Gilot and Carlton Lake, *Life with Picasso* (New York, 1964), p. 68.

Face in the bush in a painting of Gauguin's: see my *Van Gogh, Gauguin and the Impressionist Circle* (1970), pl. 128 and p. 147.

M. C. Escher, *Day and Night,* woodcut (1938): *The World of M. C. Escher* (New York, 1971), pl. 102, and see also pl. 101, *Study of the Regular Division of the Plane with Birds,* drawing and watercolor (1938), used for woodcut.

Duck-rabbit: originally from the humorous journal *Die Fliegende Blätter,* then publ. in Joseph Jastrow, *Fact and Fable in Psychology* (Boston, 1900), p. 295, fig. 19, from which Wittgenstein took it: *Philosophical Investigations* (Oxford, 1953), Part. 2, xi. Popularized further through its use by Gombrich as an example of ambiguity (*Art and Illusion* [1960], pp. 5, 238), it has been repeatedly used since in the philosophy of perception—and psychology also—in a way that, conveniently established though it may be for reference purposes, invests it with an exaggerated representativeness and power of illumination. The discussion in Wittgenstein's *Philosophical Investigations,* where it is coupled with the example of the schematically drawn face, is in fact less clear on the relevant issues than the prior discussion in his *Brown Book* of 1934–35 (see *Preliminary Studies for the "Philosophical Investigations" generally known as the Blue and Brown Books* [Oxford, 1960], part 2, #16) where only the face was used; yet the face has not been taken up, only the duck-rabbit, and it has been used at the expense of cases, such as the surrealist double image cited earlier, where the alternative readings are not mutually exclusive ones.

The example of seeing the moon as spherical I owe to Mary Sirridge. The speck-plane example is taken from J. M. Hinton, "Perception and Identification," *Philosophical Review* 76 (1967): 421ff. On "seeing differently" and changing a person's way of seeing, see Wittgenstein, *Zettel* (Oxford, 1967), #195 and 461, and on interpretation here, #208, 212 (clearer again on these topics than the *Philosophical Investigations*).

Bibliography

Part I

There are three basic studies of Cubism in existence, all of them written in English:

John Golding, *Cubism, A History and an Analysis, 1907–1914* (London, 1959; rev. ed., 1968).

Robert Rosenblum, *Cubism and Twentieth Century Art* (New York and London, 1960; rev. eds., 1966 and 1977).

Edward Fry, *Cubism* (London and New York, 1966); also in French.

My study could not have been prepared without the information they contain; at the same time they represent very different approaches to the subject. Golding's work consists of a systematic formal and procedural analysis of the early years (to 1914 only), along with extensive quotations from early writings and reviews. It also pays considerable attention to the secondary strands and offshoots of Cubism in those years, with a separate chapter on them. Rosenblum's book uses a representative selection of plates as the basis for enlarging upon the character of Cubism. It introduces parallels to the other arts, especially literature and music, and extends in its later chapters to developments in other countries and the part played by Cubism there. Fry's publication is a carefully compiled anthology of theoretical and historical texts, many of them inaccessible, with valuable notes on each. Its introduction is, as the book's title implies, about the development of Cubism rather than the development of its theory. It includes new photographic comparisons, digests of the known factual details and some brief comparisons with philosophy of the time.

The most complete reference work on Cubism since then is Douglas Cooper's catalogue for the exhibition held at the Los Angeles County Museum and Metropolitan Museum, New York: *The Cubist Epoch* (New York and London, 1970), with its full set of color illustrations and representation of different media and countries. Its text is notable for the way in which it recapitulates and sums up an older tradition of interpretation, with broad categorizations of tendency to it and many value judgments; see on this point the penetrating review by Kenworth W. Moffett, *Art Bulletin* 56, no. 2, (June 1974): 305–7. Books since then on Cubism in general include Paul Waldo Schwarz, *Cubism* (London and New York, 1971) (with an interesting section on Apollinaire); Max Kozloff, *Cubism/Futurism* (New York, 1973) (bringing together some of his essays on Cubism); and Many and Dietrich Gerhardus, *Kubismus und Futurismus* (Freiburg and The Netherlands, 1977), translated as *Cubism and Futurism: The Evolution of the Self-Sufficient Picture* (Oxford and New York, 1979).

Full bibliographies are to be found in Rosenblum, in the form of an annotated essay with supplements of 1966 and 1976; in Golding, revised and updated for the 1968 edition; and in Fry. I have not recapitulated in what follows what is to be found there, since those books already made the material available in three different forms which are complementary for reference purposes: by author (Golding), by topic (Rosenblum) and by date of appearance (Fry). Rather I have listed items of interest and concern for my purposes on an *ad hoc* basis. It is appropriate, however, to add or emphasize some more recent publications, especially ones that date from 1976–82, and some critical articles or reviews which I have found helpful and which do not appear in those cases.

As far as the interpretation of Cubism is concerned, Rosenblum's book may be said to have inaugurated, by virtue of its general approach and terms of reference, the need for a fresh rethinking, and also for a critical explanation of what was to be done with the theory. Rosenblum's form of presentation and his focus on the works themselves entailed a bypassing of the latter issue, but it was brought up specifically in the review by Leo Steinberg, *Harper's Magazine* 223 (Dec. 1961): 57ff. At the same time his interpretation—anticipated in important respects by Winthrop Judkins in his article "Towards a Reinterpretation of Cubism," *Art Bulletin* 30 (Dec. 1948): 270–78 (deriving from his 1954 Harvard University Ph.D. dissertation, "Fluctuant Representation in Synthetic Cubism: Picasso, Braque, Gris 1910–1920," which was subsequently published by New York: Garland Press, 1976), and by Clement Greenberg in his article "The Pasted-Paper Revolution," *Art News* 57 (September 1958): 46–49, repr. as the chapter titled "Collage" in his *Art and Culture* (Boston, 1961)—clearly opposed itself to the older tradition of interpretation referred to above, which descended mainly from Daniel-Henry Kahnweiler's writings, and is also found in Fry. The problems posed by the theory in this connection have been specifically brought up since by a few writers: particularly Michael Podro, "Cubism and Its Worried Interpreters," *The Listener* (London) 84, no. 2160, (Aug. 20, 1970): 238–40, and J. M. Nash, "The Nature of Cubism: A Study of Conflicting Explanations," *Art History* 3, no. 4 (December 1980): 435–47, and see also David Summers, "Cubism as a Comic Style," *Massachusetts Review* 22, no. 4 (Winter 1981): 641–59 and Dennis Farr, "Quintessential Cubism: A New Look" (review), *Apollo* 107 (June 1983): 585–86 which include comment on this subject. The character and development of the theory, which had formed the subject of an earlier and necessarily very tentative study by Christopher Gray, *Cubist Aesthetic Theories* (Baltimore, Md., 1953) has been taken up, since Fry's contribution of many additional texts, by Lynn Gamwell, *Cubist Criticism* (Ann Arbor, Mich., 1980 [her 1977 Ph.D. dissertation]), which adds some additional writings by Salmon, but covers the issues lightly and is marred by inaccuracies of transcription and translation. Additional writings on Picasso from the time are made available in *Picasso in Perspective,* edited by Gert Schiff (Englewood Cliffs, N.J., 1976) and in *A Picasso Anthology: Documents, Criticism, Reminiscences,* edited by Marilyn McCully (London, 1981). There is also Eunice Lipton's *Picasso Criticism 1901–1939: The Making of an Artist-Hero* (1975 Ph.D. dissertation) (New York: Garland Press, 1976), which has value for the critical observations that it introduces. Specifically philosophical discussions of the nature of Cubism are to be found in Jan M. Broekman, "Zur Philosophie des Kubismus," in *Proceedings of 5th International Congress of Aesthetics* (Amsterdam, 1964), edited by J. Aler (The Hague and Paris, 1968), pp. 923–26, seeing neo-Kantian thought as the basis for a development linking all of the arts; and Lorenz Dittman, "Die Willensform in Kubismus," in *Argo, Festschrift für Kurt Badt* (Cologne, 1970), pp. 407–17, a phenomenological interpretation, of the kind represented earlier by Guy Habasque, *Le Cubisme,* (Paris, 1959) influential on Fry and interestingly reviewed by Jean Laude, "Du cubisme à l'art abstrait," *Critique* 156 (May 1960): 426–57; and in Jaakko Hintikka, "Concept as Vision: On the Problem of Representation in Modern Art and Modern Philosophy," in his *The Intention of Intentionality and Other New Models for Modality* (Dordrecht, 1975), combining phenomenology with semantics; discussed further by Meirlys Lewis, "Hintikka on Cubism," *British Journal of Aesthetics* 20, no. 1 (Winter 1980): 44–53. Questions concerning the available methodologies for the study of Cubism and the relevance of the theory are also brought up in the "Actes du premier colloque de l'histoire d'art contemporain" (Musée d'Art et d'Industrie: Saint-Etienne, Nov. 1971), published as *Travaux IV, Le Cubisme* (Université de Saint-Etienne, 1973), and in the second corresponding colloquium, "Le retour à l'ordre dans les arts plastiques et l'architecture 1919–1925" (1974, published as *Travaux VIII,* 1975); particular essays in those two publications are cited individually in my references. In general, however, the time is certainly ripe for a fuller study here.

The most important exhibitions of Cubism since the 1970 one are, for present purposes, *Les Cubistes,* Galerie des Beaux Arts, Bordeaux, and Musée d'Art Moderne, Paris (May–Nov., 1973), with prefaces by G. Martin-Méry, J. Lassaigne and J. Cassou; *Zeichnungen und Collagen des Kubismus: Picasso, Braque, Gris,* Kunsthalle (Bielefeld, March–April 1979), prepared by Ulrich Weismer and Klaus Kowalski, with essays by various hands (in German) and listing of the literature of the preceding years; *Kubismus: Künstler-Themen-Werke, 1907–1920,* Kunsthalle (Cologne, May–July 1982), with essays by seven different authors on varying topics appended to it; and *The Essential Cubism 1907–1920: Braque, Picasso and Their Friends,* Tate Gallery (London, April–July 1983), catalogue by Douglas Cooper and Gary Tinterow. Additional materials of some relevance are also to be found in the catalogues *The Cubist Print,* National Gallery, Washington, D.C.—University Art Museum, Santa Barbara, Calif.—Toledo Museum (October 1981–June 1982), with texts by Burr Walken and Donna Stein, and *Hommage à Picasso: Kubismus und Musik,* Museum Bochum (October–November 1981), with an introductory essay by Patrick-Gilles Persin.

Monographic studies, exhibition catalogues and articles dealing with individual artists that have appeared recently include, for Picasso, the fundamental publication of Pierre Daix and Joan Rosselet, *Le cubisme de Picasso, catalogue raisonné de l'oeuvre peint 1907–1916* (Neuchatel, 1979); translated as *Picasso, The Cubist Years 1907–1916, A Catalogue Raisonné of the Paintings and Related Works* (London and New York, 1979), displacing, with its detailed entries and new chronology in many instances, the earlier catalogue volumes of Christian Zervos for those years, except for drawings: see, for general comments and for possible corrections needed, the reviews by John Richardson, *New York Review of Books* 27, no. 12 (July 17, 1980): 16–24, and of Edward Fry, *Art Journal* 41, no. 1 (Spring 1981): 91–97. The most important exhibition catalogues since 1970 are *Picasso in the Collection of the Museum of Modern Art* (New York, 1972), with detailed entries by William Rubin; and *Pablo Picasso, A Retrospective,* Museum of Modern Art (New York, 1980) with complete reproductions and a full chronology, by Jane Fluegel. See further *Picasso, catalogue de l'oeuvre gravé et lithographié,* 2 vols., vol. 1, 1904–61, edited by Georges Bloch (Bern, 1960).

For Braque, the *Catalogue de l'oeuvre de Georges Braque* issued by the Galerie Maeght, Paris, includes vol. 7 (1962), covering 1924–27 and vol. 6 (1973) covering 1916–1923, which have no numeration for reference purposes, and inadequate comments as to dating; to these has now been added *Braque, Le Cubisme fin 1907–1914* (1982), with numbered entries and revised dates, prepared by Nicole Worms de Romilly and Jean Laude, with an introduction by the latter. Useful also for reference, though incomplete, is Marco Valsecchi, *L'opera completa di Braque, della scomposizione cubista al recupero dell' oggetto, 1908–1929* (Milan, 1971). The exhibition catalogue *Georges Braque, Les Papiers Collés,* Centre Pompidou (Paris, June–September 1982) includes revisions of chronology, documentation and interpretative essays; the latter appear also, in English, in the version of the exhibition, *Braque, The Papiers Collés,* shown at the National Gallery, Washington, D.C. October 1982–January 1983, with catalogue entries by Isabelle Mounod-Fontane and E. A. Carmean, Jr.

For Gris, there is the publication of Juan Antonio Gaya Nuno, *Juan Gris* (in Spanish) (Barcelona, 1974), translated by K. Lyons (Boston, 1975). It includes a full bibliography of writings on Gris, with brief passages quoted from them, and is useful for the biographical details added and for the early humorous drawings reproduced: see the review of the American edition by Douglas Cooper, *Art Bulletin* 58, no. 4 (December 1976): 638. In other respects, since its representation of the works is incomplete and there are some evident misdatings of drawings, it is displaced by Douglas Cooper, *Juan Gris, catalogue raisonné,* compiled with aid of Margaret Potter, 2 vols. (Paris, 1977), which becomes the standard reference source. The revised edition of Daniel-Henry Kahnweiler's *Juan Gris, His Life and Work* (New York, 1968), which is still readable, includes a bibliography by Bernard Karpel, through 1967. For interpretation of the work, see also the exhibition catalogue *Juan Gris,* Kunsthalle (Baden-Baden, July–September 1974) with entries by Cooper and H. A. Peters and essays by various hands, the corresponding catalogue of the exhibition at the Orangerie des Tuileries (Paris: March–July 1974) with preface by Jean Leymarie and, most recently, the one published for the Juan Gris retrospective (National Gallery, Washington, D.C.—University Art Museum, Berkeley, Calif.—Guggenheim Museum, New York: October 1983–July 1984) with catalogue by Mark Rosenthal (attempting, not very successfully, to revendicate the late work). Relevant articles include those of Ernest Strauss, "Uber Juan Gris 'Technique Picturale,'" in *Festschrift für Werner Gross* (Munich, 1968), pp. 335–39—a formal analysis of space relations; see also his "Uber Juan Gris als Zeichner," *Pantheon* 33 (October–December 1975): 334ff.; D. Cooper, "The Temperament of Juan Gris," *Metropolitan Museum Bulletin* 29 (April 1971): 356–62; Werner Spies, "Juan Gris" (from *Frankfurter Allgemeine Zeitung,* 1974), in his *Das Auge an Tatort* (Munich, 1979), translated as *Focus on Art* (New York, 1982), pp. 59–63; and Luis Figueroli-Ferretti, "Juan Gris y el Cubismo hoy," *Goya* 136 (May–June 1977): 355–59 (reviewing the life and work).

Studies of other related tendencies and of the art scene contemporary with Cubism that have been used most directly include: Christopher Green, *Léger and the Avant-Garde* (New Haven and London, 1976) and Virginia Spate, *Orphism, The evolution of non-figurative painting in Paris, 1910–1914* (Oxford, 1979). In addition there is the earlier publication of Pierre Cabanne, *L'épopée du cubisme* (Paris, 1963); and for sculpture the exhibition catalogue by Margit Rowell, *The Planar Dimension, Europe 1912–1932,* Guggenheim Museum (New York, 1979 [Part 1 including artists inspired by French Cubism]).

All other books, catalogues and articles—including basic reference sources for the original texts cited—are given in the notes and references for each chapter. These notes and references are intended, section by section, to provide sources of information on points of detail; to review the most significant contributions in each area of discussion; and to serve as supports for my own formulations and arguments.

I have endeavored to make the references complete through the year 1982, with some additions for 1983.

Part II

I. Background in Linguistic Philosophy

Basic texts used or referred to:

Ludwig Wittgenstein, *Philosophical Investigations,* edited by G. H. von Wright and G. E. M. Anscombe, translated by Anscombe (Oxford, 1953; 3d ed., New York, 1968).

———, *Preliminary Studies for the Philosophical Investigations, generally known as the Blue and Brown Books* (Oxford, 1958).

———, *Lectures and Conversations on Aesthetics, Psychology and Religious Belief,* edited by C. Barrett (Oxford, 1966).

———, *Zettel,* edited by G. E. M. Anscombe and G. H. von Wright, translated by Anscombe (Oxford, 1967).

———, *On Certainty,* edited by G. E. M. Anscombe and G. H. von Wright, translated by D. Paul and Anscombe (Oxford, 1969).

———, *Culture and Value,* edited by G. H. von Wright, translated by P. Winch (Oxford, 1980).

See also David Pole, *The Later Philosophy of Wittgenstein,* London, 1958; critique by S. Cavell, "The Availability of Wittgenstein's Later Philosophy," *Philosophical Review* 71 (1962): 67ff.

For a general introduction to Wittgenstein's philosophy, see George Pitcher, *The Philosophy of Wittgenstein* (Englewood Cliffs, N.J., 1964); also David Pears, *Ludwig Wittgenstein,* Modern Masters series (New York, 1970).

For bibliographies on the subject, see the selected ones in Pitcher, 1964; in *Wittgenstein, The Philosophical Investigations,* edited by Pitcher (New York, 1966); and the fuller ones available in *Ludwig Wittgenstein, The Man and his Philosophy,* edited by D. Pears (New York, 1967; rev. ed. Atlantic Highlands, N.J., 1978), and in K. T. Fann, *Wittgenstein's Conception of Philosophy* (Oxford, 1969). Also Fann, "A Wittgenstein Bibliography," *International Philosophical Quarterly* 7 (1967): 317ff. For more recent additions, another bibliography to consult is that of Robert J. Fogelin, *Wittgenstein,* London and Boston, 1976.

J. L. Austin, *Philosophical Papers,* edited by J. O. Urmson and G. J. Warnock (Oxford, 1961; 2d ed., 1970 (esp. chap. 3, "Other Minds," 1946).

————, *Sense and Sensibilia,* reconstructed from Ms. notes by G. J. Warnock (Oxford, 1962 [esp. chap. 4]).

————, *How to Do Things with Words* (William James lectures at Harvard, 1955) (Cambridge, Mass., 1962; 3d ed., 1977 [esp. Lecture XII]).

See also *Symposium on J. L. Austin,* edited by K. T. Fann (London, 1969 [collected papers, including ones by Cavell and J. Bennett; also bibliography]), and K. Graham, *J. L. Austin, A Critique of Ordinary Language Philosophy* (Hassocks, Sussex, 1977), chaps. 5, 7–8.

Other leading texts representing this type of philosophy (in order of date):

Gilbert Ryle, *The Concept of Mind* (London, 1949).

Essays on Logic and Language, edited by A. G. N. Flew (London and New York, 1951), collected papers.

John Wisdom, *Other Minds* (Oxford, 1952); also his *Philosophy and Psycho-Analysis* (Oxford, 1953), collected papers. See further *Wisdom: Twelve Essays,* edited by R. Bambrough (Oxford, 1974).

Stuart Hampshire, *Thought and Action* (London, 1959).

Stanley Cavell, *Must We Mean What We Say?* (New York, 1969), essays on Wittgenstein, Austin and title essay; review by M. Mothersill, *Journal of Philosophy* 72 (1975): 27–48.

John R. Searle, *Speech Acts* (Cambridge, 1969), and also his *Expression and Meaning: Studies in the Theory of Speech Acts* (Cambridge, 1979), collected papers.

John F. M. Hunter, *Essays after Wittgenstein* (Toronto, 1973), and also his *Intending* (Halifax, Nova Scotia, 1978); review by I. M. Thalberg, *Canadian Journal of Philosophy* 11, no. 3 (September 1981): 545–53.

II. Applications of Linguistic Philosophy to Aesthetics and Criticism

The following texts and anthologies single themselves out for the unfolding sense that they offer of issues and principles here:

Aesthetics and Language, edited by W. Elton (Oxford, 1954), collected papers.

William Righter, *Logic and Criticism* (London, 1963).

Collected Papers on Aesthetics, edited by C. Barrett (Oxford, 1965) includes papers by Cioffi, Sibley, Redpath.

Wittgenstein, *Lectures . . . on Aesthetics* (1966), see above; given 1938.

John Casey, *The Language of Criticism* (London, 1966).

F. E. Sparshott, *The Concept of Criticism* (Oxford, 1967).

Aesthetics, edited by H. Osborne, Oxford Readings in Philosophy series (Oxford, 1972), includes G. E. Moore's notes on Wittgenstein's lectures on aesthetics, 1930–33; Savile on intention.

M. H. Abrams, "What's the Role of Theorizing about the Arts?" (response to M. Weitz, esp. his *Hamlet and the Philosophy of Literary Criticism* [Chicago and London, 1964]), in *In Search of Literary Theory,* edited by M. W. Bloomfield (Ithaca, N.Y. and London, 1972), pp. 3–54.

On Literary Intention: Critical Essays, edited by D. Newton-De Molina (Edinburgh, 1976), reprints some of the basic texts on this subject which are listed individually below.

John Reichert, *Making Sense of Literature* (Chicago, 1977).

Perceiving Artworks, edited by J. A. Fisher (Philadelphia, 1980), essays specially written for this volume, which give a sense of current issues in the philosophy and psychology of perception.

III. The Question of the Artist's Intention

The bibliography that follows aims at being as complete a listing as possible of writings on this subject or directly relevant to it; hence its length and the range of authors included. Items of particular importance in the discussion are starred. Three basic headings are used to group the materials; entries appear chronologically, through 1982–83.

A. Studies from a philosophical standpoint (focusing mainly on the legal and behavioral aspects of intention):

Karl Aschenbrenner, "Intention and Understanding," in *Meaning and Interpretation,* University of California Publications in Philosophy series, (Berkeley, Calif., 1950), pp. 229–70.

John Passmore, "Intentions," *Proceedings of Aristotelian Society* suppl. 29 (1955, Problems in Psychotherapy and Jurisprudence): 131–46. Contribution to a symposium, with response by P. L. Heath, 147–64.

G. E. M. Anscombe, *Intentions* (Oxford, 1957); review by R. Chisholm, *Philosophical Review* 68 (1959): 110–15. See also *Intention and Intentionality, Essays in Honour of G. E. M. Anscombe,* edited by C. Diamond and J. Teichman (Ithaca, N.Y., 1979).

*S. Hampshire and H. L. A. Hart, "Decisions, Intention and Certainty," *Mind* 67 (1958): 1–12. See also Hampshire, *Thought and Action* (London, 1959), chap. 2, "Intention and Action," esp. pp. 134–45.

A. I. Melden, *Free Action* (New York, 1961), chap. 9, pp. 83–104.

Keith S. Donnellan, "Knowing What I Am Doing," *Journal of Philosophy* 60 (1963): 401–9.

Donald Davidson, "Actions, Reasons and Causes," *Journal of Philosophy* 60 (1963): 685–700; reprinted in *The Philosophy of Action,* edited by A. R. White (Oxford, 1968), pp. 79–94.

B. N. Fleming, "On Intention," *Philosophical Review* 73 (1964): 301–20.

P. F. Strawson, "Intention and Convention in Speech Acts," *Philosophical Review* 73 (1964): 439–60.

John J. Jenkins, "Motive and Intention," *Philosophical Quarterly* 15 (1965): 155–64.

T. F. Daveney, "Intentions and Causes," *Analysis* 27, no. 1 (October 1966): 23–28.

Bruce Aune, "Intention," *Encyclopedia of Philosophy,* vol. 4 (New York, 1967), pp. 198–201.

Warren Shibles, *Wittgenstein, Language and Philosophy* (Dubuque, Iowa, 1969), pp. 63–81.

*H. P. Grice, "Utterer's Meaning and Intentions," *Philosophical Review* 78 (1969): 147–77, See also his earlier article, "Meaning," ibid. 64 (1957): 377–88, revised here with responses to criticisms of it.

Christopher Olsen, "Knowledge of One's Own Intentional Actions," *Philosophical Quarterly* 19 (1969): 324–36.

O. H. Green, "Intentions and Speech Acts," *Analysis* 29, no. 3 (January 1969): 109–12.

Jack W. Meiland,*The Nature of Intention* (London, 1970). Deals with the general philosophical conception; bibliography of articles on this subject.

Max Black, "Meaning and Intention: An Examination of Grice's View," *New Literary History* 4, no. 2 (Winter 1973): 257–79, reprinted in his *Caveats and Critiques* (Ithaca, N.Y., 1975) as chap. 4.

Robert Audi, "Intentions," *Journal of Philosophy* 70 (1973): 387–402.

D. F. Gustafson, "Expressions of Intentions," *Mind* 83 (July 1974): 321–40, and "The Range of Intentions," *Inquiry* 18 (Spring 1975): 83–95. See also R. A. Siegler, "Unconscious Intentions," *Inquiry* 10 (Fall 1967): 251–67, and Gustafson, "Momentary Intentions," *Mind* 77 (January 1968): 1–13; the reply to both of R. K. Shope, "Freud on Conscious and Unconscious Intentions," *Inquiry* 13 (1970): 149–59, and that of C. H. Whiteley, "Mr. Gustafson on Doubting One's Own Intentions," *Mind* 80 (January 1971): 108; and in the same subject area D. W. Hamlyn, "Unconscious Intentions," *Philosophy* 46 (January 1971): 12–22.

Roger Scruton, "Self-Knowledge and Intentions," *Proceedings of Aristotelian Society* 77 (1976–77): 87–106.

Edmund L. Wright, "Words and Intentions," *Philosophy* 52 (January 1977): 45–62.

Monroe Beardsley, "Intending," in *Values and Morals, Essays in Honor of William Frankena, Charles Stevenson and Richard Brandt,* edited by A. Goldmann and J. Kim (Dordrecht, 1978).

John F. M. Hunter, *Intending* (1978, see above), esp. part. 2, #9 and part. 3.

Donald Davidson, "Intending," in *Philosophy of History and Action,* edited by Y. Yovel (Boston: Kluwer, 1978), reprinted in his *Essays on Actions and Events* (Oxford, 1980), pp. 83–102.

Lawrence H. Davis, *Theory of Action,* Englewood Cliffs, New Jersey, 1979, ch. 4, "Intentions."

John R. Searle, "What is an Intentional State?," *Mind* 88 (January 1979): 74–92, and "The Intentionality of Intention and Action," *Inquiry* 22, no. 3 (Summer 1979): 253–80; see also his 1979 book, listed above.

E. J. Lowe, "An Analysis of Intentionality," *Philosophical Quarterly* 30 (October 1980): 294–300.

D. F. Pears, "Intentions as Judgments," in *Philosophical Subjects: Essays presented to P. F. Strawson,* edited by Zaak van Straaten (Oxford, 1980), pp. 222–37.

D. F. Gustafson, "Passivity and Activity in Intentional Actions," *Mind* 90 (January 1981): 41–60.

Michael Bratman, "Intention and Means-End Reasoning," *Philosophical Review* 90, no. 2 (April 1981): 252–65.

Alisdair MacIntyre, *After Virtue* (Notre Dame, Ind., 1981), pp. 192–94.

For the legal concept of intention, see further:

H. L. A. Hart, "The Ascription of Rights and Duties," *Proccedings of Aristotelian Society* 49 (1948–49): 171–94, reprinted as "The Ascription of Responsibilities and Rights," in *Essays in Logic and Language,* edited by Flew (Oxford, 1951), pp. 145ff. (for concept of defeasibility).

———, "Acts of Will and Legal Responsibility," in *Freedom and The Will,* edited by D. Pears (London, 1965), pp. 38–47 (for legal concept of volition); and see also his *Causation in the Law* (with A. M. Honoré) (Oxford, 1959); and *Punishment and Responsibility, Essays in the Philosophy of Law* (Oxford, 1968).

J. L. Austin, "Three Ways of Spilling Ink" (lecture on responsibility, 1958, edited and reconstructed by L. W. Forguson), *Philosophical Review* 75 (1966): 427–40.

Anthony J. P. Kenny, "Intention and Purpose," *Journal of Philosophy* 63 (1966): 642–51 (contribution to a symposium with comments by B. Aune and E. Bedford, 652–56), revised version in *Essays in Legal Philosophy,* edited by R. S. Summers (Oxford, 1968), pp. 146–63. See also his *Action, Will and Emotion* (Oxford, 1963), chap. 4, "Motives."

Anthony Duff, "Intention, Responsibility and Double Effect," *Philosophical Quarterly* 32 (January 1982): 1–16. See also the earlier discussions of this subject by F. Will, "Intention, Error and Responsibility," *Journal of Philosophy* 61 (1964): 171–79, and by P. S. Ardal, "Motives, Intentions and Responsibility," *Philosophical Quarterly* 15 (1965): 146–54; and R. Chisholm, "The Structure of Intentions," *Journal of Philosophy* 67 (1970): 633–47.

B. From the literary side:

J. E. Spingarn, "The Growth of a Literary Myth," *The Freeman* 7 (May 2, 1923): 181–83, reprinted in his *Creative Criticism and Other Essays* (New York, 1931), pp. 167–68.

*D. H. Lawrence, *Studies in Classic American Literature* (London, 1923), I, "The Spirit of Place," p. 3.

I. A. Richards, *Practical Criticism* (London, 1929), part 3, chap. 1, #4 and Appdx. A, #2.

T. S. Eliot, *The Use of Poetry and the Use of Criticism* (Cambridge, Mass., 1933), pp. 21–22, and see also his "The Frontiers of Criticism" (1956), *On Poetry and Poets* (London, 1957), esp. pp. 110–11.

C. S. Lewis (with E. M. Tillyard), *The Personal Heresy* (London, 1939), p. 5.

René Wellek, "The Mode of Existence of a Literary Work of Art," *Southern Review* 7 (Spring 1942): 742–43, revised version included in A. Warren and R. Wellek, *Theory of Literature* (New York, 1949).

*W. K. Wimsatt, "Intention," *Dictionary of World Literature,* edited by J. T. Shipley (New York, 1944), pp. 326–29, rev. ed., 1953, pp. 229ff.

*———, "The Intentional Fallacy" (with M. Beardsley), *Sewanee Review* 54 (Summer 1946): 468–88, reprinted in Wimsatt, *The Verbal Icon* (Lexington, Ky., 1954) as chap. 1.

Robert Penn Warren, "The Poem of Pure Imagination: An Experiment in Reading," in *The Rime of the Ancient Mariner by Samuel Taylor Coleridge* (New York, 1946), chap. 7, pp. 61ff.

*F. R. Leavis, "Henry James and the Function of Criticism," *Scrutiny* 15, no. 2 (Spring 1948): 98–99 (reviewing Quentin Anderson on James); reprinted in his *The Common Pursuit* (London, 1952), pp. 223–24.

W. Elton, *A Glossary of the New Criticism* (Chicago, 1948), s.v. "Intention" (citing John Crowe Ransom, *The New Criticism* [Norfolk, Conn., 1943], on "total intention," a term also used by Cleanth Brooks and R. Penn Warren, in *Understanding Poetry* [New York, 1938]).

*R. Jack Smith, "Intention in an Organic Theory of Poetry," *Sewanee Review* 56 (1948): 625–33.

R. W. Stillman, "A Note on Intentions," *College English* 10 (1948–49): 40–41, see also his *The Critic's Notebook* (Minneapolis, Minn. and Oxford, 1950), part. 8, "The Problem of Intentions" (anthology of writings on topic).

Leslie A. Fiedler, "Archetype and Signature; A Study of the Relationship between Biography and Poetry," *Sewanee Review* 60 (1952): 252–73.

William Empson, "Still the Strange Necessity," *Sewanee Review* 63 (1955): 474–77 (review of Wimsatt, *The Verbal Icon*).

Graham Hough, *An Essay in Criticism* (London, 1966), chap. 10, "Intention and Personality." See also his essay "An Eighth Type of Ambiguity," in *William Empson, The Man and his Work,* edited by R. Gill (London and Boston, 1974), pp. 76–97.

E. D. Hirsch, Jr., *Validity in Interpretation* (New Haven, Conn., 1967), chap. 1, "In Defense of the Author."

Monroe Beardsley, "Textual Meaning and Authorial Meaning," *Genre* 1 (1968): 169–81, revised as "The Authority of the Text" in his *The Possibility of Criticism* (Detroit, 1970), chap. 1.

W. K. Wimsatt, "Genesis: A Fallacy Revisited," in *The Disciplines of Criticism, Essays in Literary Theory, Interpretation and History,* edited by P. Demetz, T. Greene and L. Nelson, Jr. (New Haven, Conn., 1968), pp. 193–225.

Morse Peckham, "The Intentional ? Fallacy," *New Orleans Review* 1 (Winter 1969): 116–64, reprinted in his *The Triumph of Romanticism* (Columbia, S.C., 1970) as chap. 22, pp. 421–44.

George Watson, *The Study of Literature* (London and New York, 1969), chap. 4, "The Literary Past."

Paul De Man, "Form and Intent in the American New Criticism," in his *Blindness and Insight* (New York, 1971), pp. 20–35.

Allen Rodway, *The Truths of Fiction* (New York, 1971), chap. 6, "Fictions and Fallacies."

Paul Ricoeur, "The Model of the Text: Meaningful Action Considered as a Text," *Social Research* 38 (1971): 529–62.

Svetlana and Paul Alpers, "*Ut Pictura Noesis?* Criticism in Literary Studies and Art History," *New Literary History* 3, no. 3 (Spring 1972): 454–56, reprinted in *New Directions in Literary History,* edited by Ralph Cohen (Baltimore, Md., 1974), pp. 199–200.

Paul Ramsey, "A Question of Judgment: Wimsatt on Intent," *Essays in Criticism* 22, no. 4 (October 1972): 408–16.

Edward Larrissy, "The Intentional Fallacy," *Essays in Criticism* 23 (1973): 212–15 (reply to Ramsey); see also the letter from W. Empson, "The Intentional Fallacy Again," ibid., 435.

A. J. Ellis, "Intention and Interpretation in Literature," *British Journal of Aesthetics* 14 (Autumn, 1974): 315–25.

Dorothea Krook, "Intention and Intentions: The Problem of Intention and Henry James's 'The Turn of the Screw,'" in *The Theory of the Novel, New Essays,* edited by J. Halperin (Oxford, 1974), pp. 353–72.

Alistair Fowler, "The Selection of Literary Constructs," *New Literary History* 7, no. 1 (Autumn 1975): 39–55, and "Intention Floreat," in *On Literary Intention,* edited by D. Newton-De Molina (Edinburgh, 1976), pp. 242–55.

Michael O. Wheeler, "Biography, Literary Influence and Allusion as Aspects of Source Studies," *British Journal of Aesthetics* 17, no. 2 (Spring, 1977): 149–60.

John Reichert, *Making Sense of Literature* (Chicago, 1977), chap. 3.

*Barbara Herrnstein Smith, *On the Margins of Discourse: The Relation of Literature to Language* (Chicago, 1978), chap. 6, "The Ethics of Interpretation."

Susan R. Horton, *Interpreting Interpreting: Interpreting Dickens's Dombey* (Baltimore, Md., 1979), pp. 103–4 and chap. 8, "Dickens's Intentions and the Interpreter's Conclusions."

K. K. Ruthven, *Critical Assumptions* (Cambridge, 1979), chap. 9, "Intended Meanings."

David J. Gordon, "The Story of a Critical Idea," *Partisan Review* 47, no. 1 (1980): 93–108, on the "autonomy" of a work of art.

William E. Cain, "Author and Authority in Interpretation," *Georgia Review* 34, no. 3 (Fall 1980): 619–38.

Susan L. Feagin, "Motives and Literary Criticism," *Philosophical Studies* 38 (November 1980): 403–18.

Geoffrey Strickland, *Structuralism or Criticism? Thoughts on How We Read* (Cambridge, 1981), chap. 3.

C. In-between studies, representing aesthetics or critical theory in general:
A. K. Coomaraswami, "Intention," *American Bookman* 1 (1944): 41–48, critique of Wimsatt, 1944.

Christian Gauss, *The Aesthetic Theories of French Artists, 1855 to the Present* (Baltimore, Md., 1949), pp. 5–6.

A. Kaplan and E. Kris, "Esthetic Ambiguity," *Philosophy and Phenomenological Research* 8, no. 3 (March 1948): 415–35 (431ff. refer).

F. W. Bateson, "Intention and Blake's *Jerusalem*," *Essays in Criticism* 2 (1952): 105–14, discussion with J. Wain and W. Robson.

F. W. Leakey, "Intention in Metaphor," *Essays in Criticism* 4 (1954): 191–98.

Isabel Hungerland, "The Concept of Intention in Art Criticism," *Journal of Philosophy* 52 (1955): 733–42.

H. D. Aiken, "The Aesthetic Relevance of the Artist's Intentions," *Journal of Philosophy* 52 (1955): 742–53.

George Lukacs, "Die Weltanschaulichen Grundlagen des Avantgardismus" (1955), translated by J. and N. Mander as "The Ideology of Modernism" in *Realism in Our Time* (New York, 1964), p. 19.

T. M. Gang, "Intention," *Essays in Criticism* 7 (1957): 175–86.

Theodore Redpath, "Some Problems of Modern Aesthetics," in *British Philosophy at Mid Century,* edited by C. A. Mace (London, 1957), pp. 361–75; expanded as "The Meaning of a Poem," in *Collected Papers on Aesthetics,* edited by C. Barrett (Oxford, 1965), pp. 145–59.

Monroe Beardsley, *Aesthetics: Problems in the Philosophy of Criticism* (New York, 1958), part 1, chap. 1 and part 10, chap. 24.

H. S. Eveling, "Composition and Criticism," *Proceedings of Aristotelian Society* 59 (1958–59): 213–32; reprinted in *Aesthetics and the Philosophy of Criticism,* edited by M. Levich (New York, 1963), pp. 396–414.

R. Kuhns, "Criticism and the Problem of Intention," *Journal of Philosophy* 57 (1960): 5–23.

Pierre Boulez, *Penser la musique aujourd'hui* (Paris, 1963), p. 13.

*Frank Cioffi, "Intention and Interpretation in Criticism," *Proceedings of*

Aristotelian Society 64 (1963–64): 85–106; reprinted in *Collected Papers on Aesthetics,* edited by C. Barrett (Oxford, 1965), pp. 161–83.

*Sidney Gendin, "The Artist's Intentions," *Journal of Aesthetics and Art Criticism* 23, no. 2 (Winter 1964): 193–96.

Huw Morris-Jones, "The Relevance of the Artist's Intentions," *British Journal of Aesthetics* 4, no. 2 (April 1964): 138–45.

John Kemp, "The Work of Art and the Artist's Intentions," *British Journal of Aesthetics* 4, no. 2 (April 1964): 146–54.

William H. Capitan, "The Artist's Intention," *Revue Internationale de Philosophie* 18 (1964): 323–34, response to Beardsley, 1958.

C. Payzant, "Intention and the Achievement of the Artist," *Dialogue* (Canadian Philosophical Review) 3, no. 2 (September 1964): 153–59.

Joseph Margolis, *The Language of Art and Art Criticism* (Detroit, 1965), chap. 7, "The Intention of the Artist"; revised version in his collected essays, *Art and Philosophy,* (Atlantic Highlands, N.J., 1980), chap. 8.

Emilio Roma III, "The Scope of the Intentional Fallacy," *The Monist* 50 (1966): 250–66.

Stanley Cavell, "Music Discomposed," in *Art, Mind and Religion,* edited by W. Capitan and D. D. Merrill (Pittsburgh, Pa., 1967), pp. 129–31; reprinted in his *Must We Mean What We Say?* (New York, 1969), pp. 235–37.

George E. Yoos, "A Work of Art as a Standard of Itself," *Journal of Aesthetics and Art Criticism* 26, no. 1 (Fall 1967): 81–89.

Robert Goldwater, "Problems of Criticism, I: Varieties of Critical Experience," *Artforum* 6, no. 1 (September 1967): 40–41.

George Dickie, "Meaning and Intention," *Genre* 1 (1968): 182–89.

A. D. Nuttall, "Did Mersault Mean to Kill the Arab? The Intentional Fallacy," *Critical Quarterly* 10 (1968): 95–106.

F. W. Bateson, "A. E. Housman: The Poetry of Emphasis," in *A. E. Housman, A Collection of Critical Essays,* edited by C. Ricks, (Englewood Cliffs, N.J., 1968), reprinted in his *Essays in Critical Dissent* (London, 1972), part 2, "The Necessity of Contexts," chap. 9, pp. 110–16; see also chap. 7, p. 88.

*Anthony Savile, "The Place of Intention in the Concept of Art," *Proceedings of Aristotelian Society* 69 (1968–69): 101–24; reprinted in *Aesthetics,* edited by H. Osborne (Oxford, 1972), pp. 158–76. See also his "Historicity and the Hermeneutic Circle," *New Literary History* 10, no. 1 (Autumn 1978): 49–70.

R. B. Patankar, *Aesthetics and Literary Criticism* (Bombay, 1969), chap. 7, "Intentional Fallacy—A Comment," pp. 104–22.

Marcia Eaton, "Art, Artifacts and Intentions," *American Philosophical Quarterly* 6, no. 2 (April 1969): 165–69.

Kendall Walton, "Categories of Art," *Philosophical Review* 79 (July 1970): 334–67. See also the response by D. C. Nathan, "Categories and Intentions," *Journal of Aesthetics and Art Criticism* 31, no. 4 (1973): 539–41, with rejoinder by Walton, ibid. 32 (1973): 267–68.

Rosemarie Meier, " 'The Intentional Fallacy' and the Logic of Literary Criticism," *College English* 32, no. 2 (November 1970): 135–45; reply by M. Hancher, ibid. 33, no. 3 (December 1971): 343–45.

Peter D. Juhl, "Intention and Literary Interpretation," *Deutsche Vierteljahrschaft für Literaturwissenschaft und Geistesgeschichte* 45 (1971): 1–23. See also his "The Appeal to the Text: What Are We Appealing To?" *Journal of Aesthetics and Art Criticism* 36, no. 3 (Spring 1978): 277–87, and his *Interpretation: An Essay in the Philosophy of Literary Criticism* (Princeton, N.J., 1980), chaps. 2–4 and 6.

Michael Hancher, "Three Kinds of Intention," *Modern Language Notes* 87, no. 7 (1972): 827–51.

Quentin Skinner, "Motives, Intention and the Interpretation of Texts," *New Literary History* 3, no. 2 (Winter 1972): 393–408. See also his "Hermeneutics and the Role of History," ibid. 7, no. 1 (Autumn 1975): 209–32.

A. J. Close, "Don Quixote and the Intentional Fallacy," *British Journal of Aesthetics* 12, no. 1 (Winter 1972): 19–39.

James Collins, "Interpretation, The Interweave of Problems," *New Literary History* 4, no. 2 (1973): 389–403 (394–97 refer).

Stein H. Olsen, "Authorial Intentions," *British Journal of Aesthetics* 13, no. 3 (Summer 1973): 219–31. See also his "Interpretation and Intention," ibid. 17, no. 3 (Summer 1977): 210–18.

Colin Syas, "Personal Qualities and the Intentional Fallacy," in *Philosophy and the Arts,* Royal Institute of Philosophy Lectures, vol. 6 (London and New York, 1973).

Berel Lang, "The Intentional Fallacy Revisited," *British Journal of Aesthetics* 14, no. 4 (Autumn 1974): 306–14.

John M. Ellis, *The Theory of Literary Criticism: A Logical Analysis* Berkeley, Calif., 1974), chap. 5, "The Relevant Context of a Literary Text."

*Richard Harland, "Intention and Critical Judgment," *Essays in Criticism* 25 (April 1975): 215–25.

Ina Loewenberg, "Intentions: The Speaker and the Artist," *British Journal of Aesthetics* 15, no. 1 (Winter 1975): 40–59.

Berel Lang, *Art and Inquiry* (Detroit, 1975), part 1, chap. 5, "Intentionality and the Ontology of Art."

Goran Hermeren, "Intention and Interpretation in Literary Criticism," *New Literary History* 12, no. 1 (Autumn 1975): 57–82.

David Cozens Hoy, *The Critical Circle: Literature, History and Philosophical Hermeneutics* (Berkeley, Calif., 1978), part 1, "Validity and the Author's Intention," critique of Hirsch.

Mary Sirridge, "Artistic Intention and Critical Perogative," *British Journal of Aesthetics* 18, no. 2 (Spring 1978): 137–54.

H. Gene Blocker, *Philosophy of Art* (New York, 1979), chap. 5, part 4, "Intentions," pp. 246–61, summarizing developments.

Richard Wollheim, *The Sheep and the Ceremony* (Leslie Stephen lecture) (Cambridge, 1979), pp. 12–13.

William E. Tolhurst, "On What A Text Is and How It Means," *British Journal of Aesthetics* 19, no. 1 (Winter 1979): 3–14.

Lincoln Rothschild, "Aesthetics and the Artist's 'Intention,'" *Journal of Aesthetics and Art Criticism* 38, no. 2 (Winter 1979): 190–92.

Surash Raval, "Intention and Contemporary Literary Theory," *Journal of Aesthetics and Art Criticism* 38, no. 3 (Spring 1980): 261–77; reprinted in his *Metacriticism* (Athens, Ga., 1981), as chap. 3.

Carol Donnell-Kotrozo, "The Intentional Fallacy: An Applied Reappraisal," *British Journal of Aesthetics* 20, no. 4 (Autumn 1980): 356–65.

Lincoln A. Baxter, "Recent Music: The Intentional Fallacy Revisited," *Journal of Aesthetics and Art Criticism* 39, no. 1 (Fall 1980): 77–79.

Jack W. Meiland, "The Meanings of a Text," *British Journal of Aesthetics* 21, no. 3 (Summer 1981): 195–203.

Alexander Nehamas, "The Postulated Author: Critical Monism as a Regulative Ideal," *Critical Inquiry* 8, no. 1 (Autumn 1981): 133–49 (144–45 refer).

Steven Knapp and Walter B. Michaels, "Against Theory," *Critical Inquiry* 8, no. 4 (Summer 1982): 723–42.

Stephen Davies, "The Aesthetic Relevance of Authors' and Artists' Intentions," *Journal of Aesthetics and Art Criticism* 41, no. 1 (Fall 1982): 65–76.

Susan L. Feagin, "Interpreting Art Intentionalistically," *British Journal of Aesthetics* 22, no. 1 (Winter 1982): 65–77.

Daniel O. Nathan, "Irony and the Artist's Intention," *British Journal of Aesthetics* 22, no. 3 (Summer 1982): 245–56.

Colin Lyas, "Anything Goes: The Intentional Fallacy Revisited," *British Journal of Aesthetics* 23, no. 4 (Autumn 1983): 291–305.

IV. Perception and Identification of Objects in Paintings

The following philosophical studies deal relevantly with perception and identification in general:

J. L. Austin, *Sense and Sensibilia* (Oxford, 1962), chap. 4.

L. Wittgenstein, "Notes for Lectures on 'Private Experience' and 'Sense Data'" (1934–36), edited by R. Rhees, *Philosophical Review* 77 (1968): 275–320; and many passages in his later texts dealing with knowledge, certainty and perception.

See in addition:

Elizabeth H. Wolgast, "Perceiving and Impressions," *Philosophical Review* 67 (1958): 226–36.

A. R. White, "The Alleged Ambiguity of 'See,'" *Analysis* 24 (1963): 1–5.

J. M. Hinton, "Perception and Identification," *Philosophical Review* 76 (1967): 421–35.

Gareth B. Matthews, "Mental Copies," *Philosophical Review* 78 (1969): 53–73.

D. M. Johnson, "Looks," *American Philosophical Quarterly* 18, no. 3 (July 1981): 249–54.

John Heil, "Seeing is Believing," *American Philosophical Quarterly* 19, no. 3 (July 1982): 229–40.

Gareth Evans, *The Varieties of Reference,* edited by John McDowell (Oxford, 1982), chap. 8, "Recognition-Based Identification."

Studies relating the same issues to the perception of *art* are—in direct contrast to the extensive literature on intention reviewed above—quite few and far between. Those that do exist include, most notably:

Arnold Isenberg, "Perception, Meaning and the Subject-Matter of Art," *Journal of Philosophy* 41 (1944): 561–75, reprinted in his *Aesthetics and the Theory of Criticism* (Chicago and London, 1973), pp. 36–52.

Errol Bedford, "Seeing Paintings," *Proceedings of Aristotelian Society* suppl. 40 (1966): 47–62, with response by R. M. Meager, 63–84.

Hide Ishiguro, "Imagination," *Proceedings of Aristotelian Society* suppl. 41 (1967): 37–56, response to I. Dilman. See also on this subject P. F. Strawson, "Imagination and Perception," in *Experience and Theory,* edited by L. Foster and J. W. Swanson (Amherst, Mass., 1970), reprinted in his *Freedom and Resentment* (London, 1974), pp. 45–65; Roger Scruton, *Art and the Imagination* (London, 1974), chap. 8, "The Imagination, II"; Mary Warnock, *Imagination* (London, 1976), part 4, "The Nature of the Mental Image," and more relevantly for present purposes, the elucidations of Wittgenstein's comments on the subject offered by J. F. M. Hunter, "Imagining," in his *Essays after Wittgenstein* (Toronto, 1973), pp. 43–66, and Noel Fleming, "Seeing the Soul," *Philosophy* 53 (January 1978): 33–50.

Richard Wollheim, "Seeing-as, Seeing-in and Pictorial Representation," suppl. essay in his *Art and Its Objects* (1968; rev. ed., Cambridge, 1980), pp. 205–26, with updated bibliography, pp. 244–46.

For the views of Panofsky and Gombrich on the subject, see the references for Intermezzo iii and iv in which those views are discussed separately.

Photo Credits

Paul Gauguin, *Self-portrait with the Yellow Christ,* photo courtesy of Bulloz, Paris.

Camille Pissarro, *Self-portrait,* photo courtesy of Réunion des Musées Nationaux.

The following photographs are reproduced by permission. © by A.D.A.G.P., Paris, 1984:

Georges Braque, *Glass, Carafe and Newspapers,* photo courtesy of owner.

Georges Braque, *The Mantlepiece,* photo courtesy of owner.

Georges Braque, *The Musician,* photo courtesy of Kunstmuseum, Basel.

Georges Braque, *Still Life on a Table* (Gillette), photo courtesy of Fogg Museum Archives.

Georges Braque, *Still Life with a Violin,* photo courtesy of the Musée National d'Art Moderne.

Georges Braque, *Still Life with Pipe* (Le Quotidien du Midi), photo courtesy of E. V. Thaw & Co., Inc.

Georges Braque, *Woman Reading,* photo courtesy of owner.

Georges Braque, *Woman with a Guitar,* photo courtesy of the Musée National d'Art Moderne.

Robert Delaunay, *The Three Windows, The Tower and The Wheel,* photo courtesy of owner.

Jean Metzinger, *Cubist Composition* (landscape), photo courtesy of Fogg Art Musuem.

Gino Severini, *Portrait of Paul Fort,* photo courtesy of the Musée National d'Art Moderne.

The following photographs are reproduced by permission, © S.P.A.D.E.M., Paris/V.A.G.A., New York, 1984:

Juan Gris, *Mme Cézanne,* photo courtesy of Galerie Louise Leiris.

Juan Gris, *The Man from Touraine,* photo courtesy of the Musée National d'Art Moderne.

Juan Gris, *The Marble Console Table,* photo courtesy of the Musée National d'Art Moderne.

Juan Gris, *Pierrot and Guitar,* photo courtesy of owner.

Juan Gris, *Still Life,* photo courtesy of The Museum of Modern Art.

Juan Gris, *Still Life with Poem,* 1915, photo courtesy of the Norton Simon Inc. Foundation.

Juan Gris, *Still Life with a Poem,* 1916, photo courtesy of Fogg Museum Archives.

Juan Gris, *The Strawberry Jam Pot,* photo courtesy of Kunstmuseum, Basel.

Fernand Léger, *Landscape,* photo courtesy of Kunsthistorisches Museum, Vienna.

Fernand Léger, *The Roofs of Paris,* photo courtesy of Fogg Museum Archives.

Fernand Léger, *Still Life with Colored Cylinders,* photo courtesy of Galerie Beyeler.

Henri Matisse, *Still Life with Plaster Figure,* photo courtesy of Yale University Art Gallery.

Pablo Picasso, *Curtain for [the ballet] "La Tricorne,"* photo courtesy of Réunion des Musées Nationaux.

Pablo Picasso, *The Guitar,* 1918–19, photo courtesy of Rijksmuseum Kröller-Müller.

Pablo Picasso, *Guitar,* 1919, photo courtesy of The Museum of Modern Art.

Pablo Picasso, *Guitar Player,* photo courtesy of Moderna Museet, Stockholm.

Pablo Picasso, *Harlequin and Woman with a Necklace,* photo courtesy of the Musée National d'Art Moderne.

Pablo Picasso, *Mademoiselle Léonie,* photo courtesy of The Museum of Modern Art.

Pablo Picasso, *Mademoiselle Léonie in a Chaise Longue,* photo courtesy of The Museum of Modern Art.

Pablo Picasso, *Nude,* photo courtesy of Fogg Museum Archives.

Pablo Picasso, *Portrait of Daniel Henry Kahnweiler,* photo courtesy of The Art Institute of Chicago.

Pablo Picasso, *Still Life: Le Torero,* photo courtesy of E. V. Thaw & Co., Inc.

Pablo Picasso, *Studio with Plaster Head,* photo courtesy of The Museum of Modern Art.

Pablo Picasso, *Three Musicians,* 1921 oil, 80″ × 74″, photo courtesy of the Philadelphia Museum of Art.

Pablo Picasso, *Three Musicians,* 1921 oil, 79″ × 87¾″, photo courtesy of The Museum of Modern Art.

Pablo Picasso, *Two Musicians,* photo courtesy of Fogg Museum Archives.

Pablo Picasso, *The Violin,* photo courtesy of the Philadelphia Museum of Art.

Index

Works of art are individually indexed only where they are cited by title in the text; otherwise they are indexed by date, or a date-bracket within which they fall. An asterisk at the end of the entry for a particular work indicates that there is a plate of it included in the book.

Illustrations

Pablo Picasso, *Nude*, 1910. Ink and watercolor, 29⅛″ × 18⅜″. Private collection.

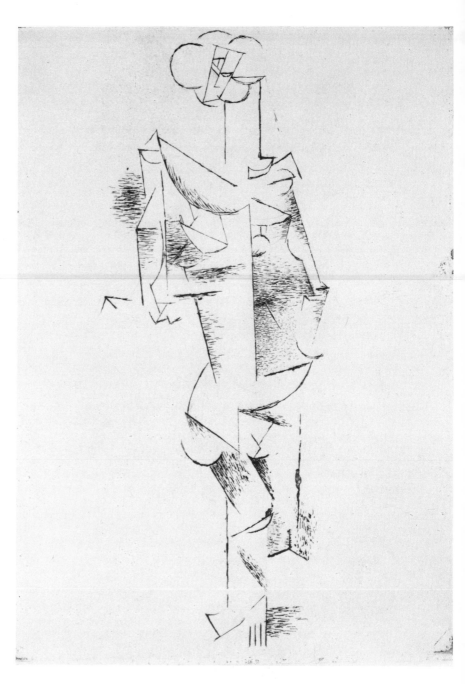

Pablo Picasso, *Mademoiselle Léonie,* 1910. Etching on copper, 7⅞″ × 5¹⁄₁₆″. Plate I in Max Jacob's *Saint Matorel* (Paris, 1911). Collection of The Museum of Modern Art, New York, Purchase Fund.

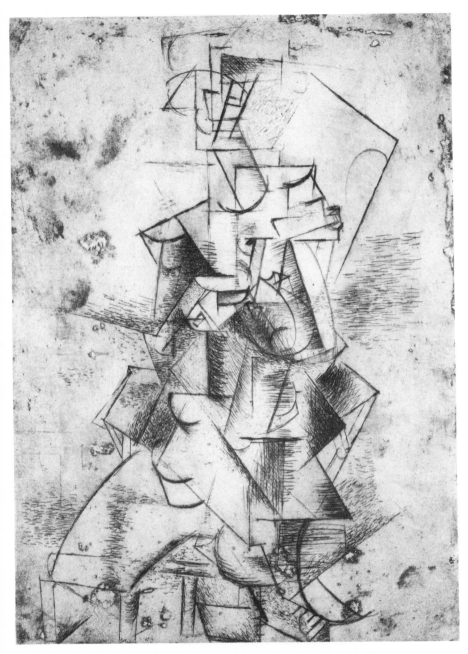

Pablo Picasso, *Mademoiselle Léonie in a Chaise Longue,* 1910. Etching on copper, 7¹³⁄₁₆″ × 5⁹⁄₁₆″. Plate III in Max Jacob's *Saint Matorel* (Paris, 1911). Collection of The Museum of Modern Art, New York, Purchase Fund.

Georges Braque, *Still Life with a Violin*, 1910–11. Oil on canvas, 51⅛″ × 35½″. Musée National d'Art Moderne, Centre Georges Pompidou, Paris.

Georges Braque, *Woman Reading,* 1911. Oil on canvas, 50¾″ × 31⅞″. Private collection, Switzerland.

Pablo Picasso, *Still Life: Le Torero,* 1911. Oil on canvas, 18¼″ × 15¹⁄₁₆″. Private collection, New York.

Juan Gris, *Still Life,* 1911. Oil on canvas, 23½″ × 19¾″. Collection of The Museum of Modern Art, New York, acquired through the Lillie P. Bliss Bequest.

Fernand Léger, *Landscape,* 1911. Oil on canvas, 36¼″ × 28¾″. Kunsthistorisches Museum, Vienna.

Jean Metzinger, *Cubist Composition* (Landscape), 1912. Oil on canvas, 20¼″ × 27″. Fogg Art Museum, Harvard University, Cambridge, Mass., gift of Mr. and Mrs. Joseph Hazen.

Fernand Léger, *The Roofs of Paris,* 1912. Oil on canvas, 29″ × 19¾″. Musée National Fernand Léger, Biot.

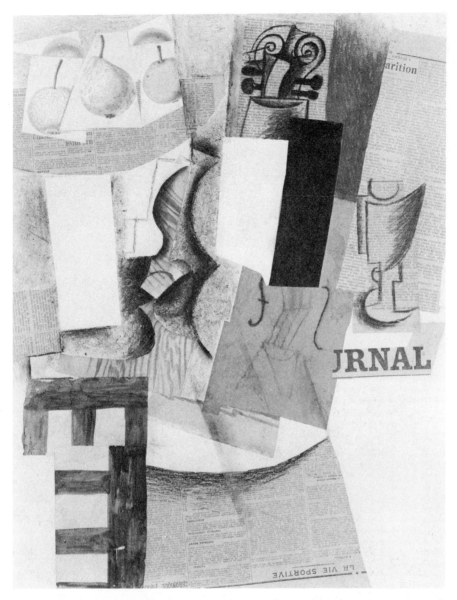

Pablo Picasso, *The Violin* [*Violin and Fruits*], 1912. Colored papers, newspaper and charcoal, 25½″ × 19½″. Philadelphia Museum of Art, The A. E. Gallatin Collection.

Georges Braque, *Still Life with Pipe* (Le Quotidien du Midi), 1912–14. Oil on canvas, 13⅛″ × 16⅜″. Private collection, Switzerland.

Robert Delaunay, *The Three Windows, The Tower and The Wheel*, 1912–13. Oil on canvas, 51″ × 77″. Collection of Mr. and Mrs. William A. M. Burden, New York.

Fernand Léger, *Still Life with Colored Cylinders*, 1913–14. Oil on canvas, 31¾″ × 25½″. Galerie Beyeler, Basel.

Georges Braque, *Woman with a Guitar,* 1913. Oil and charcoal on canvas, 51¼″ × 29″. Musée National d'Art Moderne, Centre Georges Pompidou, Paris.

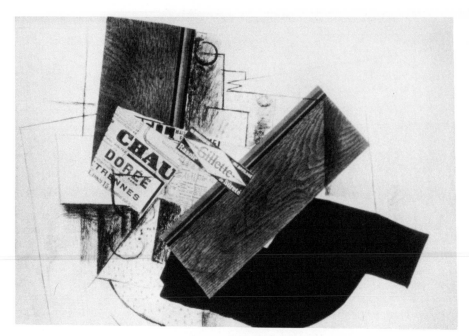

Georges Braque, *Still Life on a Table* (Gillette), 1913–14. Pasted papers, gouache and charcoal, 18″ × 24½″. Private collection, Paris.

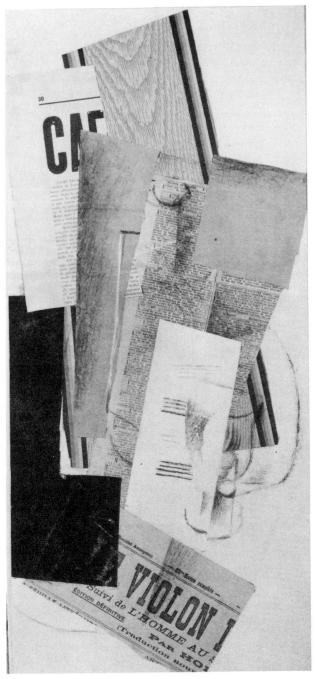

Georges Braque, *Glass, Carafe and Newspaper,* 1914. Pasted papers, chalk and charcoal on cardboard, 24⅝″ × 11¼″. Private collection, Switzerland.

Juan Gris, *The Marble Console Table,* 1914. Oil, paper and glass on canvas, 24″ × 19½″. Collection of Mrs. Thomas J. Hardman, Tulsa, Oklahoma.

Gino Severini, *Portrait of Paul Fort,* 1915. Oil, charcoal, pasted papers and other materials, 24¾″ × 19¾″. Musée National d'Art Moderne, Centre Georges Pompidou, Paris.

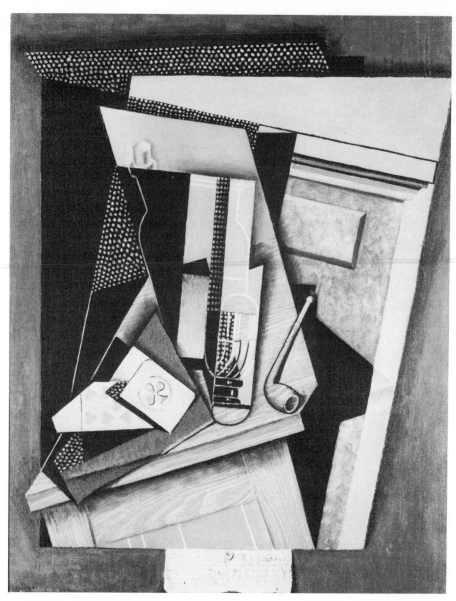

Juan Gris, *Still Life with Poem,* 1915. Oil on canvas, 31¾″ × 25½″. Collection of Norton Simon Inc. Foundation, Los Angeles, California.

Juan Gris, *Still Life with a Poem*, 1916. Charcoal and pasted paper, dimensions and present whereabouts unknown.

Juan Gris, *Mme Cézanne,* drawing after Cézanne, 1916. Charcoal, 6¾″ × 6″.
Galerie Louise Leiris, Paris.

Pablo Picasso, *Guitar Player,* 1916. Oil mixed with sand on canvas, 39½″ × 29½″.
Moderna Museet, Stockholm.

Georges Braque, *The Musician*, 1917–18. Oil on canvas, 86¾″ × 44⅜″. Kunstmuseum, Basel.

Pablo Picasso, *Harlequin and Woman with a Necklace,* 1917. Oil on canvas, 78¾″ × 78¾″. Musée National d'Art Moderne, Centre Georges Pompidou, Paris, bequest of the Baroness Napoléon Gorgaud.

Juan Gris, *The Strawberry Jam Pot,* 1917. Oil on canvas, 28″ × 19¾″. Kunstmuseum, Basel.

Juan Gris, *The Man from Touraine,* 1918. Oil on wood, 30¼″ × 19¾″. Musée National d'Art Moderne, Centre Georges Pompidou, Paris.

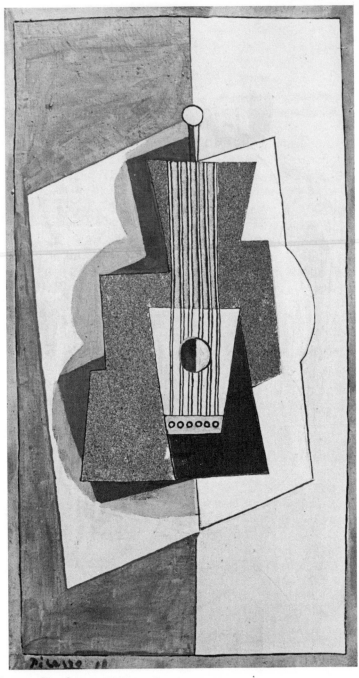

Pablo Picasso, *The Guitar*, 1918–19. Oil mixed with sand on canvas, 31¾″ × 17½″.
Rijksmuseum Kröller-Müller, Otterlo.

Pablo Picasso, *Guitar,* 1919. Oil, charcoal and pinned paper on canvas, 85″ × 31″.
Collection of The Museum of Modern Art, New York, gift of A. Conger Goodyear.

Pablo Picasso, *Curtain for [the ballet]* *"La Tricorne,"* 1919. Gouache on paper, 7¾" × 10½". Musée Picasso, Paris.

Pablo Picasso, *Two Musicians*, 1921. Pen and ink, dimensions and present where-abouts unknown.

Pablo Picasso, *Three Musicians,* 1921. Oil on canvas, 80″ × 74″. Philadelphia Museum of Art, The A. E. Gallatin Collection.

Pablo Picasso, *Three Musicians,* 1921. Oil on canvas, 79″ × 87¾″. Collection of The Museum of Modern Art, New York, Mrs. Simon Guggenheim Fund.

Juan Gris, *Pierrot and Guitar,* 1922. Oil on canvas, 40″ × 21¾″. Collection of Haakon Onstad, Lausanne.

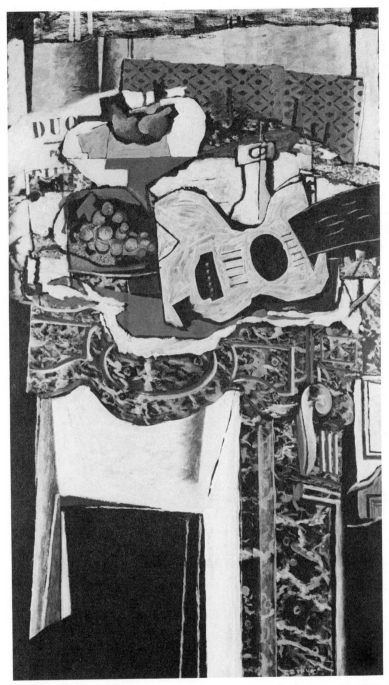

Georges Braque, *The Mantelpiece,* 1922. Oil on canvas, 51⅜″ × 29⅜″. Private collection.

Pablo Picasso, *Studio with Plaster Head,* 1925. Oil on canvas, 38⅝″ × 51⅝″. Collection of The Museum of Modern Art, New York, Purchase Fund.

Camille Pissarro, *Self-portrait,* 1873. Oil on canvas, 21½″ × 18″. Musée du Louvre, Paris, Jeu de Paume.

Paul Gauguin, *Self-portrait with the Yellow Christ,* 1889. Oil on canvas, 15″ × 18⅛″. Private collection, Paris.

Henri Matisse, *Still Life with Plaster Figure,* 1906. Oil on canvas, 22¼″ × 17¼″. Yale University Art Gallery, bequest of Kate L. Brewster.

Pablo Picasso, *Portrait of Daniel-Henry Kahnweiler,* 1910. Oil on canvas, 39½″ × 28⅝″. The Art Institute of Chicago, gift of Gilbert W. Chapman.